CROSSTALK

CONNIE WILLIS

This edition first published in Great Britain in 2017
by Gollancz

First published in Great Britain in 2016
by Gollancz
an imprint of the Orion Publishing Group Ltd
Carmelite House, 50 Victoria Embankment
London EC4Y 0DZ

An Hachette UK Company

1 3 5 7 9 10 8 6 4 2

A CIP catalogue record for this book
is available from the British Library.

ISBN 978 1 473 20094 4

Printed in Great Britain by Clays Ltd, St Ives plc

www.orionbooks.co.uk
www.gollancz.co.uk

To the inimitable—and irreplaceable—Mary Stewart

"In Ireland the inevitable never happens,
and the unexpected constantly occurs."
—JOHN PENTLAND MAHAFFY

*

"In every crowd are certain persons who seem just like the rest,
yet they bear amazing messages."
—ANTOINE DE ST. EXUPÉRY, *Night Flight*

*

"Listen up."
—*Ghost Town*

Acknowledgments

Many, many, many thanks to everyone who helped me with this book, but most especially to:

my daughter Cordelia, who gave me invaluable help with the plot,

my friend Melinda Snodgrass, who gave me endless encouragement and moral support,

and the people at my reading at Cosine, who came up with the title.

CROSSTALK

crosstalk ('krostok) *noun*

1. a disturbance in a communication device's (radio, telephone, etc.) transmission caused by a second device's transmission, resulting in crossover, intermingling, and confusion; the presence of unwanted signals and/or interference due to accidental coupling

2. incidental, off-topic conversation during a meeting

3. witty, fast-paced repartee; banter

One

"Let me not to the marriage of true minds admit impediments."
—WILLIAM SHAKESPEARE, "Sonnet 116"

BY THE TIME BRIDDEY PULLED INTO THE PARKING GARAGE AT COMMSPAN, there were forty-two text messages on her phone. The first one was from Suki Parker—of course—and the next four were from Jill Quincy, all saying some variant of "Dying to hear what happened." Suki's said, "Heard rumor Trent Worth took you to Iridium!???"

Of course you did, Briddey thought. Suki was Commspan's very own Gossip Girl. And that meant by now the whole company knew it. It was a good thing Commspan didn't have a no-fraternization policy— she and Trent could never have kept their romance secret. But she'd hoped to keep them from finding out about last night at least until she could tell her family. *If they don't know already.*

She scanned through her other texts. There were five from her sister Kathleen, eight from her sister Mary Clare, and nine from Aunt Oona reminding her of the Daughters of Ireland Gaelic poetry reading Saturday night.

I should never have given her a smartphone, Briddey thought. It had never occurred to her that her great-aunt would figure out how to use it—she couldn't even set her DVR. Or her clocks. But Briddey had reckoned without Aunt Oona's desire to pester her constantly about the Daughters of Ireland. She'd gotten Maeve to teach her, and she now sent Briddey texts about it twenty times a day.

Briddey quickly read through the rest of their messages, but none of them began, "OMG! You can't be seriously thinking of doing this!"

Good. That meant she still had time to decide what she was going to say to them—though not much, given the speed of communication these days.

She scrolled quickly through the rest of her messages to see if there was one from Trent. There was. It said simply, "Love you. Call me ASAP." She very much wanted to, but the longer she was out here in the garage, the more likely Jill—or worse, Suki—was to drive in and begin interrogating her, and she'd come to work early precisely to avoid that. Talking to Trent would just have to wait till she got safely to her office.

She got out of her car and walked quickly toward the main door, checking the other cars to see who else was here. She didn't see Trent's Porsche. She didn't see Suki's car either, or her assistant, Charla's, which was good, but Jill's Prius was there, parked next to C.B. Schwartz's ancient Honda.

His car was always here—Briddey suspected he lived in his lab, sleeping on the sagging couch that looked like he'd retrieved it from a curb somewhere. But Jill usually arrived late, and Briddey wouldn't put it past her to come early expressly to pump Briddey. She was probably lying in wait for her in the lobby. *I'll have to go in the side entrance,* Briddey thought, changing course, *and hope nobody sees me on the way there.*

Nobody did, and there was no one in the elevator or up on four. *Good,* Briddey thought, hurrying down the hall. With Charla not in yet, she could go straight into her office, barricade the door, and come up with some way to break this to her family before they began bombarding her with calls saying, "Why didn't you answer any of my texts? What's wrong?"

Especially Aunt Oona, who always immediately leaped to the conclusion that something terrible had happened to her and began calling around to all the hospitals. *And this time she'll be convinced she was justified in her premonition,* Briddey thought as she turned down the hall to her office.

"Briddey!" Jill Quincy called from the end of the hall.

So close, Briddey thought, trying to decide whether she could make it to her office before Jill reached her, but Jill was already running toward her, calling, "*There* you are! I've been texting you all morning! I didn't see you come in."

She skidded to a stop next to Briddey. "I was down in the lobby," she said breathlessly, "but I must have missed you. I heard you and Trent Worth went to dinner at Iridium last night. So what happened?"

I can't tell you, Briddey thought. *Not till I've told my family.* But she couldn't refuse to talk either, or *that* would be all over the building within seconds. "Come here," she said, and pulled Jill into the copy room so passersby wouldn't hear them.

"Well?" Jill said the moment Briddey'd shut the door. "He proposed, didn't he? Oh, my God, I knew it! You are *so* lucky! Do you know how many women would *kill* to be engaged to Trent Worth? And you managed to snag him! After only six weeks!"

"I didn't 'snag' him," Briddey said, "and he didn't propose." But Jill wasn't listening.

"Let me see your ring!" she cried. "I'll bet it's gorgeous!" She grabbed for Briddey's hand and then, as its ringlessness registered, asked, "Where is it?"

"We're not engaged," Briddey said.

"What do you mean, you're not engaged? Then why did he take you to a place like Iridium? On a Thursday? Oh, my God! He asked you to get an EED, didn't he? That's even *better* than getting engaged!" She hugged Briddey. "I am *so* happy for you! I can't wait to tell everybody!" She started for the door.

"No, don't!" Briddey said, grabbing her arm. "Please!"

"Why not?" Jill asked, her eyes narrowing suspiciously. "Don't tell me you turned him down!"

"No, of course not," Briddey said. "It's just—"

"Just *what*? He's the most eligible guy at Commspan! *And* he must love you or he wouldn't have asked you to get an EED! And you obviously love him or you wouldn't have said yes. So what's the problem?"

She gave Briddey a searching look. "I know what it is. You're disappointed he didn't ask you to have it *and* propose, aren't you?"

And now that would be all over Commspan, too. "No, not at all,"

Briddey said. "He said he wants to wait to get engaged till after we have the EED, so I'll be able to sense how much he loves me when he asks me."

"Oh, my God, that's the most romantic thing I've ever heard! I can't believe it! He's gorgeous, he's willing to commit, *and* he's romantic! Do you *know* how rare that is? All the guys I date are either commitment-phobes or liars—or both. You are so lucky! It's that hair of yours. Guys go wild for red hair. Maybe I should dye mine red." She frowned. "You still haven't told me why you don't want me to tell anyone."

"It's my family. I'm not sure how to break this to them."

"You don't think they'll be happy? But he's so perfect! He's got a great job and a great car, and the losers your sister Kathleen dates . . . Or is it the EED? Everyone says it's totally safe."

"It is," Briddey said. "But they're kind of—"

"Overprotective?"

No, meddlesome and interfering. "Yes, so don't say anything till I've told them, okay?"

"Only if you tell me all the gory details! I want to know when you're having it done and—"

Briddey's phone rang. It was Trent's ring tone, but that didn't mean it was him. The last time she'd been with the family, Maeve had done something to her phone so that half the time it said it was him when it wasn't, and Briddey hadn't been able to fix it.

But at least it was a way out of the conversation. "Sorry," Briddey said to Jill. "I just need to see who this is." She glanced at the screen. "Look, I need to take this." She opened the copy room door and started out into the hall. "Promise me—"

"My lips are sealed," Jill said. "But you have to promise to tell me *everything.*"

"I will." Briddey turned away so Jill couldn't see her declining the call, then put the phone up to her ear, said, "Hello?" and walked briskly down the hall till she was out of sight.

She stuck the phone back in her pocket. And was instantly sorry when she saw Phillip from Logistics bearing down on her. "I heard via the grapevine that you and Trent Worth are going to get an EED," he said.

How is that possible? Briddey thought. *I only left Jill ten seconds ago.*

"Wow! Just like Tom Brady!" Phillip was saying. "Congratulations! That's great! But I hope you're not going to do it till after your boy Trent comes up with a better idea for the new phone than just more memory and an unbreakable screen. The rumor is Apple's coming out with something that'll blow every other smartphone out of the water, and Trent can't afford to be laid up in the hospital—"

"The EED's not major surgery," Briddey began, but Phillip wasn't listening either.

"If we don't watch out, Commspan could be the next Nokia," he said, and launched into a history of smartphone-company failures. "A small company like us can't compete unless we come up with something revolutionary, a whole new concept, and we need to come up with it fast, or—"

Come on, Aunt Oona, Briddey thought. *You usually call me every five minutes. Where are you when I need you?*

Briddey's phone rang. *Thank you,* she breathed. "I have to take this in my office," she said. "I'll see you at the meeting at eleven," and walked off.

But it wasn't Aunt Oona who'd saved her. It was Mary Clare, and the instant after Briddey sent the call to her voicemail, she got a text from Maeve. "I'm fine," it read. "Pay no attention to my mother."

Which meant they still didn't know, thank goodness, though she felt sorry for Maeve. What was it this time? Videogames? Bulimia? Cyberbullying? Mary Clare was constantly in hysterics over her, even though Maeve was a perfectly normal nine-year-old girl.

In fact, she's the only *normal member of my family,* Briddey thought.

Mary Clare certainly wasn't normal. She obsessed constantly about Maeve's homework, her grades, whether she'd get into an Ivy League college, her friends, her eating habits (Mary Clare was convinced she was anorexic), and the fact that she didn't read enough, even though (or possibly because) Mary Clare was constantly forcing *Little Women* and *Alice in Wonderland* on her.

Last week Mary Clare had been convinced Maeve was sending too many texts, and the week before that that she was eating too much sugared cereal (which didn't exactly square with the anorexia). Today it was probably nude selfies. Or the hantavirus.

For Maeve's sake, Briddey should really call Mary Clare and try to calm her down, but *not* till she'd worked out what she was going to say about the EED. And she didn't have much time. Half of Commspan probably knew by now, and one of them would be bound to mention it to Aunt Oona the next time she "popped in" with Maeve to show her how Maeve looked in her new step-dancing costume and try to convince her to go to some boring Daughters of Ireland thing . . .

Oh, my God, and there was Suki, Grapevine Girl herself, emerging from the Human Resources office. Briddey cast decorum to the winds and sprinted for the safety of her office. She yanked the door open and flung herself inside—and practically into her assistant's arms.

"I thought you'd never get here," Charla said, steadying her. "You've got a million messages, and I want to hear all about last night! You are *so* lucky to be getting an EED!"

Faster than a speeding bullet, Briddey thought. *If Commspan wants a revolutionary form of communication, they should design a phone based on our grapevine.*

"I didn't see your car in the garage," Briddey said.

"Nate gave me a ride to work. I wish I could talk him into having an EED done. It would be great to *know* whether he loves me or not. You are so lucky you won't have to worry about that anymore. I mean, I spend all my time trying to figure out when he tells me he does, is that for real or does he just want to hook up? I mean, last night, he—"

"You said I had messages. Who are they from?"

"Your sister Mary Clare mostly, and your aunt and your other sister. I put them all on your computer. I thought you told them not to phone you at work."

"I did," Briddey said. *But they didn't listen. As usual.*

"Did you talk to them?" she asked aloud, dreading Charla's answer, but Charla shook her head.

Thank goodness for that. "If they call again," Briddey said, "do not, repeat, do *not* say anything to them about the EED. I haven't had the chance to tell them yet, and I want to be the one to break the news."

"They'll be so excited!"

Wanna bet? "Who are the other messages from?" she asked.

"Trent Worth called and said to call him as soon as you got in, and so did Trish Mendez and Rahul Deshnev's assistant. And Art Sampson needs you to look over his memo on improving interdepartmental communication right away and tell him if you have any suggestions to add. It's on your computer. So when he asked you, were you thrilled?"

"Yes," Briddey said. "If anyone else comes in or calls, tell them I can't talk to them till after the meeting." She went into her office, shut the door, and called Trent. He didn't answer.

She texted and messaged him telling him to call her, tried Rahul Deshnev's assistant with the same result, then called Trish Mendez. "Is it true that you and Trent Worth are going to have an EED?" Trish said.

"Yes," Briddey said, thinking, *I don't think interdepartmental communication needs any improving.*

"That's wonderful!" Trish said. "When are you having it done?"

"I don't know. Trent wants to have Dr. Verrick do it, and—"

"Dr. Verrick? Oh, my God! He did Brad and Angelina's, didn't he?"

"Yes, so he has a really long waiting list, and I don't know when we'll even be able to get in to see him, let alone schedule the EED."

"He did Caitlyn Jenner's, too, didn't he?" Trish said. "And Kim Kardashian's, though that one didn't work because she fell in love with somebody else, I can't remember his name. He was in the last Avengers movie."

This was going to take all day. Briddey held her phone close to the desk and rapped twice on the desktop with her fist. "Come in," she called, and put the phone up to her ear. "Listen, my appointment's here. Can I call you back?"

She hung up and, with a feeling of "out of the frying pan, into the fire," checked the twenty-two messages from her family—correction, thirty-one—to make sure they still didn't know, starting with Mary Clare's in case she'd decided Maeve was possessed by demons and had scheduled an exorcism or something.

She hadn't. She'd read an article online about the negative influence that gender roles in movies had on girls, and wanted to know whether Briddey thought she should block Maeve from watching them online.

Good luck with that, Briddey thought, and checked Kathleen's, which were all, "Need to talk to you about Chad," her latest in a long line of odious boyfriends. Aunt Oona's messages—except for three

"Where are you, mavourneen?" inquiries—were all reminders that Sean O'Reilly was planning to read "The Passing of the Gael" at the Daughters of Ireland meeting, and the whole family was going.

That is, if they're not at my apartment trying to talk me out of having the EED, which she was sure they'd do as soon as they found out. They didn't like Trent, as they'd all made perfectly clear when she'd gone to dinner at Aunt Oona's last Saturday.

Mary Clare thought he spent too much time on his smartphone (and not enough listening to her fret about Maeve), Kathleen thought he was too rich and good-looking to still be single and therefore had to be hiding something, and even Maeve, who usually sided with Briddey in family debates, had made a face and said, "His hair's too combed. I like guys with messy hair."

Aunt Oona had, of course, rejected him on the grounds that he wasn't from Ireland, even though she herself had never set foot on "the Auld Sod" in her life. Not that you'd know it to look at her. Or hear her. She talked in a brogue straight out of *Angela's Ashes*—or an old Bing Crosby movie—and twisted her graying red hair into a straggling bun, wore baggy tweed skirts and Aran Isles sweaters summer and winter, and put a shawl over her head when she went to her incessant Daughters of Ireland meetings. "No one in Ireland has dressed like that in the last hundred years," Briddey wanted to shout at her. "And you're not *Irish*! The closest you've ever been to a peat fire was watching *The Quiet American* on TCM!"

But it wouldn't have done any good. Aunt Oona would simply have clutched her rosary beads to her ample chest, called upon Saint Patrick and Briddey's sainted mother to forgive Briddey's blasphemous words, and redoubled her efforts to fix her up with a "foine Irish lad." Like Sean O'Reilly, who was forty, balding, and still lived with his mother—also a Daughter of Ireland.

I don't want Sean O'Reilly or any of Aunt Oona's other aging "lads," Briddey thought. *Or any of Kathleen's ne'er-do-wells. That's why I'm dating Trent. And why I'm going to have the EED with him, no matter what you say.*

She tried to call him again, but he was apparently still on his phone. And now his message box was full. She emailed him.

Mistake. When she clicked SEND, nineteen new emails popped up on her screen, all but three of them headed, "OMG EED! Congrats!"

The three that weren't were from Aunt Oona: "It's checking your phone you need to be. There's something wrong with it" and, "Is it an accident you've had?" And from Maeve: "You have to talk to Mom. She won't let me watch *The Twelve Dancing Princesses* or any of the *Frozen* movies. Or *Tangled,* which is like my favorite movie next to *Zombie Hordes!*"

Thank goodness Mary Clare doesn't know Maeve's watching zombie movies, or she'd really have apoplexy, Briddey thought, and her phone rang.

"Where are you?" Trent said. "I've been trying to—"

"Hello!" she said eagerly. "You have no idea how glad I am to hear the sound of your voice. Last night was so wonderful."

"I know," he said. "You have no idea how happy you've made me."

"And how happy we're going to be when we—"

"Yeah, about that. I'm afraid I've got some bad news. I talked to Dr. Verrick's office, and his nurse said they're not going to be able to get us in till late summer."

"Well, we knew he had a waiting list—"

"His nurse said we were lucky to get in *that* soon, that some patients have to wait up to a year."

"It's all right," she said. "I can wait—"

"Well, *I* can't! This screws up *everything!*" he exploded. "I'm sorry, I didn't mean to shout at you, sweetheart. It's just that I want us to be connected *now* so I can—so you can know what I'm feeling—"

"Which I'm guessing is frustration," Briddey said.

"*Yes!* I'm trying to see if there isn't some way to get us in by May, and in the meantime, we need to fill out the preliminary paperwork—sorry, I've got to take this," he said. "Hold on." His voice cut off for a minute and then came back. "Where was I?"

"Filling out the preliminary paperwork."

"Right. His nurse will be sending a medical history and some questionnaires, and you need to fill them out and get them back as soon as possible so that if he *can* get us in earlier, we're ready. And meanwhile, I've got to figure out what I'm going to do if Schwartz doesn't come through."

"C.B. Schwartz?"

"Yes. He's supposed to have some ideas for the new phone that I can present at today's meeting, but I've been emailing him for the last two days with no response, and he isn't answering his phone either. I don't know what's wrong with him. Half the time when you're talking to him, he doesn't even hear you. It's like he's off in another world. Hamilton thinks he's a genius, the next Steve Jobs or something, but *I* think he's mentally unstable."

"He's not unstable," Briddey said. "He's just a little eccentric. And he *is* really smart."

"The Unabomber was smart, too," Trent said. "Let's hope he's not homicidal, and that he's enough of a genius to come up with some ideas to tide us over till the one I'm working on is ready, or we're dead. We've got to have something ready by the time Apple rolls out the new iPhone, and now that—"

His voice cut off, and Briddey thought he must have another call, but a few seconds later he said, "Sorry, I didn't mean to unload on you like that."

"That's okay. I understand. You've got a lot riding on this."

He laughed harshly. "You have no idea just how—" His voice cut off again.

"Trent?" Briddey said. "Are you there? What happened?"

"Bad connection," he said. "What I was trying to say is, I want everything—the phone, the EED, everything—to be perfect for us, and I can't stand the idea of having to wait to be together, really together. I love you so much."

"I love y—"

"Look, I've got another call coming in. I'll see you at the meeting. And till then, check your email. I sent you something."

He had, a virtual bouquet of golden rosebuds, which opened into lush yellow roses and then morphed into butterflies.

How sweet! Briddey thought, watching them flutter around the screen to the tune of "I Will Always Love You."

The butterflies morphed again, into letters forming the words "Now that you've said yes, our troubles are over!"

Except for me telling my family, Briddey thought. *Which I have got to figure out how to do* now, *before they come over to see why I haven't answered their messages.*

There was a knock on the door. *Oh, my God, it's them,* Briddey thought, but it couldn't be. They never knocked. They just walked in.

Which meant this must be Charla. "Come in," Briddey said, and Charla opened the door and leaned in, looking bemused.

"Art Sampson and Suki Parker want you to call them as soon as possible," she said, "and you got a message from C.B. Schwartz."

Let's hope it's his ideas for the new phone. "Did you put it on my computer?" Briddey asked.

"No, I mean a *message.*" Charla held out a folded piece of paper as if it were a poisonous snake. "He wrote it by hand and everything. I mean, who does that anymore?"

"He's a genius," Briddey said absently, reading the note.

"Really? Are you sure? He never answers his emails."

The note read, "I need to talk to you. C.B. Schwartz." If this was something about his ideas for the phone not being ready, she'd better talk to him before the meeting, so she could warn Trent.

She asked Charla for the number of his lab and called him, but there was no answer, and it didn't let her leave a message. "Get me his cellphone number," she said to Charla.

"It won't do any good," Charla said. "There's no coverage down in that sub-basement where he has his lab."

"What about our voice-texting function?"

"It doesn't work down there."

That was ridiculous; it was designed specifically for areas with poor reception. "Give me the number anyway, in case he's not in his lab."

"He's *always* in his lab."

"Well, then I'll text him," Briddey said, and Charla reluctantly gave her the number.

"I doubt if it'll do any good," Charla said. "He refuses to carry his phone with him. Suki says he never even turns it on." She frowned. "You're not going to make me take a message down there, are you? The sub-basement's *freezing,* and there's nobody down there but him. And he creeps me out, the way he lurks down there and never talks to anybody. Like that guy who lives in the dungeon in that movie, the Hunchback of Notre Dame."

"You mean the Phantom of the Opera," Briddey said. "The Hunchback of Notre Dame lived in a bell tower, not a dungeon. And C.B. doesn't have a hump."

"No, but he still creeps me out. *I* think he's crazy."

"He's not crazy."

Charla didn't look convinced. "He wears a *wristwatch*," she said. "Nobody does that anymore either. And he dresses like a homeless person."

Briddey didn't have an answer for that. He did. Even by Commspan's casual, Silicon Valley–style dress code of flannel shirts, jeans, and running shoes, C.B. looked terrible, as if he'd grabbed his clothes randomly off a thrift-store rack, and they always looked like they'd been slept in. Which they probably had.

"Suki says he doesn't believe in answering emails or going to inter-departmental meetings," Charla said, "and those earbuds he wears aren't connected to anything. I've even seen him talking to himself. What if he's a serial killer and he's storing the bodies in his lab? Nobody would ever know, it's so cold down there."

Don't be ridiculous, Briddey thought. *This is Commspan. They'd know within nanoseconds.* "Well, serial killer or not, I need to talk to him, and I don't want to go all the way down to his lab. Keep trying to get in touch with him," she said, and went back into her office to text C.B.

In the five minutes she'd been gone, she'd accumulated nine more "Congrats!" emails and twelve more voice messages, including one from Darrell in IT telling her he thought having an EED was "Totally phenomenal!" and one from Rahul Deshnev's assistant wanting her to call ASAP. Briddey did, hoping it meant the meeting had been post-poned, but when she got on the line, Rahul Deshnev's assistant said, "I'm so glad you're getting an EED! Greg and I just had one, and it's even better than they advertise. Now our relationship is totally open and honest. We don't have any secrets from each other, and we *never* fight. And the sex is amazing! Greg—"

"Sorry, but my nine forty-five just got here," Briddey said, and hung up, thinking, *Maybe going down to see C.B. would be a good idea.* Staying here, she wasn't going to get a moment's peace, and the fact that there was no reception in the sub-basement meant she wouldn't be able to get calls *or* texts there. And since Charla thought C.B. was some sort of horror-movie monster, she was unlikely to venture down there after her to deliver a message.

Best of all, since C.B. didn't carry a phone and never checked his email, he wouldn't know anything about the EED, and she wouldn't have to engage in another time-consuming conversation about it. She could find out what he wanted and then go into one of the storerooms and figure out exactly what to tell her family without fear of being interrupted.

She started out the door, nearly colliding with Charla, who said, "Suki Parker called again. And your Aunt Oona. She said she needs to talk to you about the poetry reading. And your sister Mary Clare is on line one."

"Tell them all I'm in a meeting," Briddey said. "I'm going down to C.B. Schwartz's lab."

"But how will I get in touch with you?"

You won't, Briddey thought. "I'll be back by ten thirty," she said.

"Okay," Charla said doubtfully. "Do you really think you should go down there by yourself?"

"If he tries to kill me, I'll hit him with an icicle," Briddey said, and to make sure Charla didn't follow her, she added, "I've been thinking about what you said, and you're right. He does look a little like the Hunchback of Notre Dame. Or the guy in those *Saw* movies."

"I *know.* You're sure you'll be all right?"

Absolutely. If I can just get down there without being waylaid by anyone else. She opened the office door and looked cautiously out, convinced Suki would be lying in wait, but for once the "luck of the Irish" Aunt Oona constantly invoked was with her. There was no one in the corridor *or* the elevators, and she made it safely down to the sub-basement without any more encounters.

The elevator opened onto cement emptiness and the sharp, cold smell of a walk-in freezer. No wonder no one came down here. It was absolutely glacial. Ice crystals had formed on the metal door of C.B.'s lab, which had a printed sign on it saying DANGER—NO ADMITTANCE— EXPERIMENT IN PROGRESS and a handwritten one that said, KEEP OUT— THIS MEANS YOU. And when she looked through the door's glass-and-wire mesh window into the lab, C.B. was wearing a pea coat, a wool muffler, and fingerless gloves. And cargo shorts and flip-flops. He was hunched over a lab table, doing something with a circuit board and a soldering iron.

Briddey was glad Charla wasn't here because he looked appalling even for him. He had a two-day stubble, and his hair was even messier than usual. *Maeve would probably like* him, Briddey thought.

He looked like he'd spent all night here again. *Which is good,* she thought, knocking on the metal door. *He won't have overheard anyone talking about the EED on his way down here this morning.* Though he wouldn't necessarily have heard it even so, since he was wearing the earbuds Charla had mentioned.

He didn't look up. She knocked again, and when that didn't have any effect, she opened the door, went in, walked over to where he was working, and waved both hands in front of him. "C.B.? Hello? Are you in there?"

He looked up, saw her, and yanked the earbuds out. "What did you say?"

"I'm sorry to bother you when you're working," she said, smiling. "But you said you wanted to talk to me?"

"Yeah," he said. "You're not seriously thinking of getting an EED, are you?"

Two

"If everybody minded their own business," the Duchess said
in a hoarse growl, "the world would go round a deal
faster than it does."
— Lewis Carroll, *Alice in Wonderland*

"Wh-what ... how?" Briddey said, stammering in her surprise.
"Who told you I was getting an EED?"

"You're kidding, right?" C.B. said, putting down the soldering iron.
"It's all over Commspan. And if you want my opinion, I think you've
lost your mind. Don't you already have enough information bombarding you, what with emails and texting and Twitter and Snapchat and
Instagram? And now you're going to have brain surgery so you can
hear *more*?"

"The EED's not brain surgery. It's a minor enhancement procedure—"

"Where they drill a hole in your head so all your sense can leak
out. Only you don't need to have that done because it's obvious yours
already has! Do you have any idea how dangerous an IED is?"

"EED," she corrected him. "An IED is a kind of bomb."

"Yes, well, wait till it blows up in your face," he said. "What if the scalpel slips and the doctor cuts the wrong nerve? You could end up paralyzed. Or a vegeta—"

"It's a completely safe procedure. Dr. Verrick's performed hundreds of EEDs without anything bad happening."

"To *him*. He's making a pile of money convincing couples they'll be able to read each other's minds. Just because some quack in an Armani suit and Italian loafers tells you he can—"

"Dr. Verrick happens to be a well-respected surgeon with an international reputation in neurological enhancement. And you're not able to read each other's minds. The EED increases your ability to connect emotionally with your partner."

"Connect *emotionally*? What ever happened to kissing? What ever happened to *hooking up*?"

"I am not going to discuss this with you," Briddey said stiffly. "It's none of your business."

"Yes, it is. You're the only person I can talk to around here, and if you're a vegetable—"

"Shouldn't you be working on your proposals for the new phone? The interdepartmental meeting's in an hour—"

"I *am* working on it."

"Oh, is that it?" she asked, pointing at the circuit board he'd been soldering.

"Nope," he said. "That's the control panel for my space heater." He pointed toward a large metal box with a bunch of wires hanging out of the back. "As you can see from the Antarctic atmosphere in here, it's on the fritz again. I've been trying to fix it, but no luck. Speaking of which, do you need a jacket?" He went over to the couch, which had clothes and blankets heaped in the middle of it, and began rummaging through them.

"No, I'm fine," she said, though actually she was starting to shiver.

She looked around at the lab. The walls were covered with pinned-up schematics and lists, assorted KEEP OUT signs, a movie poster for *Scanners Live in Vain,* and a pinup of some 1940s movie star. The lab tables were as cluttered as the walls, piled with laptops, hard drives, and disemboweled smartphones. A pink plastic radio with an old-fashioned tuning dial stood on an even more ancient television set, and the floor was a maze of snaking wires and power cords. She didn't see any bodies, but then again, there was no telling what was in all those file cabinets.

C.B. held up a faded and filthy khaki army jacket. "How about this?"

"No, thank you," she said. "So, about the phone. Are your proposals going to be ready by the meeting, because if they're not, you need to tell Trent—"

"Forget Trent. Do you *know* how many people die on the operating table during brain surgery every year?"

"I told you, it's *not* brain surgery. It's a minor en—"

"Fine. Do you know how many people die from"—he made air quotes with his fingers—"'minor enhancements'? Haven't you ever seen those pictures on TMZ where the starlet's nose has slid halfway down her face, under the headline COSMETIC SURGERY GONE WRONG?"

"An EED is *not* cosmetic surgery."

"Then why has everyone in Hollywood had one? Or you could get a secondary infection like staph or flesh-eating bacteria. Hospitals are breeding grounds for those things. They're horrible places— bedpans, catheters, gowns that open in the back. I avoid them like the plague, and you should, too."

"I—"

"Or they could give you too much anesthetic. Or, even worse, your surgery could go great and work exactly like it's supposed to, because telepathy's a terrible idea—"

"It's not telepathy—" she attempted to interject, but he went right on.

"You don't *want* to know. Trust me. Especially what guys think. It's like a cesspool in there. I mean, it's even worse than the stuff they say on the internet, and you know how bad *that* is."

"We are supposed to be talking about whether your proposals are ready—"

"I *am*," he said. "Commspan promises the same thing—more communication. But that isn't what people want. They've got way too much already—laptops, smartphones, tablets, social media. They've got connectivity coming out their ears. There's such a thing as being *too* connected, you know, especially when it comes to relationships. Relationships need less communication, not more."

"That's nonsense."

"Wanna bet? Then why does every sentence beginning 'We need to talk' end in disaster? Our whole evolutionary history has been about trying to stop information from getting communicated—camouflage, protective coloration, that ink that squids squirt, encrypted passwords, corporate secrets, lying. Especially lying. If people really wanted to communicate, they'd tell the truth, but they don't."

"That's not true," she said and then remembered texting her family that she was in a meeting and telling Rahul Deshnev's assistant her nine forty-five appointment was there.

"They lie constantly," C.B. was saying, "on Facebook, on eHarmony, in person. 'Yes, the report's done. I'm just putting the finishing touches on it.' 'No, I don't think that dress makes you look fat.' 'Of course I want to go.' 'Of course' is a dead giveaway that you're lying. 'Of course I didn't sleep with her.' 'Of course I like your family.' 'Of course you can trust me.'"

"C.B.—"

"And you know who people lie to the most? Themselves. They're absolute masters of self-deception. So even if you have this IED and can hear Trent's thoughts, what good will it do?"

"You can't hear other people's—" she said, frustrated. "I *told* you, the EED doesn't make you telepathic! All it does is enhance your ability to sense your partner's feelings."

"Which are even less reliable than thoughts! People have all kinds of crazy feelings—revenge, jealousy, hatred, rage. Haven't you ever felt like murdering someone?"

Yes, Briddey thought. *I feel like it right now.*

"But your having murderous feelings doesn't make you a murderer. And having nice ones doesn't make you a saint. I'll bet even Hitler had warm, fuzzy feelings when he thought about his dog, and if you happened to pick up his emotions right then, you'd think, *What a nice guy!* Plus, people have no idea what they feel. They convince themselves they're in love when they're not, they—"

"I did not come down here to hear your theories on love," she said. "Or Hitler. I came down here because I *assumed* you wanted to tell me something about your proposals for the new phone."

"That's what I've been *talking* about, my proposals for the phone.

What people really need is less communication, not more." He walked over to the pinup of the 1940s movie star. "Isn't that so, Hedy?"

Trent's right, Briddey thought. *He is mentally unstable.*

"Hedy Lamarr," C.B. said, tapping the photo with his knuckle. "Big Hollywood star during World War Two. She spent her spare time between making movies trying to come up with a frequency-hopping device to hide our radio signals from the Germans so they couldn't find our torpedoes."

He walked back over to the lab table. "She succeeded, too. Patented the device and everything. Unfortunately, they hadn't invented the technology for it to work yet. She had to wait fifty years, and then they used her device to design the cellphone—unfortunately. But she had the right idea."

"Which was?"

"Trying to hide messages, not transmit them. If you *really* want to have a good relationship with your boyfriend, you should be having an *anti*-EED, not—"

"We are *not* discussing the EED," Briddey said. "Do you or do you not have something to show me?"

"I do." He dashed over to his laptop and began typing. A screen full of code came up. "Let's say there's someone you don't want to talk to, or you really need to work on something and don't want to be interrupted."

Like this morning, Briddey thought involuntarily.

"You used to be able to say you couldn't get to the phone in time or didn't get their message," C.B. said, "but thanks to advances in communications technology, those excuses won't work anymore. So this phone warns you in advance when your ex-boyfriend or your boss is calling—"

Or my family, she thought.

"—and gives you a variety of options. You can block the call and have it show up as 'Call cannot be completed'—I call that the Deadzone function—or you can have it cut off two sentences in. Or if you really hate the person, you can use the Blackball function and automatically reroute the call to the Department of Motor Vehicles—or Commspan's call menu. 'Press one if you wish to speak with someone who has no idea what's going on. Press two if you want to stand here all day trying to figure out which button to push.'"

He clicked to another screen. "And *this* feature—I call it the SOS app—lets you surreptitiously touch the side of your phone so it'll ring and you can say you have an incoming call you have to take."

I wish I'd had that this morning when I was talking to Jill Quincy, Briddey thought. *And Phillip.*

"I call it the Sanctuary phone," C.B. said. "Me being the Hunchback of Notre Dame and all."

Briddey blushed. "How did you know about—?"

"See what I mean? There's such a thing as too much communication." He tapped the computer screen. "So what do you think? Of the phone, I mean, not whether I'm the Hunchback of Notre Dame."

I think it's a wonderful idea, she thought, imagining how much easier it would make her relations with her family. But it wasn't what Commspan needed. "Trent wants a phone that will enhance communication, not inhibit it."

"That's exactly what I'm afraid of," he muttered, and bent over the circuit board again.

"So you don't have anything like that?"

"No, I've got just the thing. An app that translates what you say into what people want to hear. I text you, 'You're an idiot to be having brain surgery for any reason, let alone for some infantile notion that it'll bring you true love,' and the phone sends it as, 'Wow! Trent asked you to get an EED! How romantic!' I call it the Hook, Line, and Sinker app."

"That's *it.* This conversation is over," Briddey said, and headed for the door. "If you have any other proposals—any *serious* proposals—they need to be in to Trent before the meeting. If you don't, you need to tell him before that. The meeting's at eleven. You've got an hour."

"No, I don't," he called after her as she slammed the door. "It's already ten twenty."

Oh, no, it was only forty minutes till the meeting, and she wouldn't get another chance all day to work out what to tell her family. And when she got home, they'd be camped outside her apartment building waiting for her. Or inside her apartment.

I need to get my locks changed, she thought. *And decide once and for all how to break it to them.* And in spite of C.B.'s being down here, this was still the best place to do that. She went back down the hallway, past the elevator to the next hallway over, and began trying doors to find a storage room she could use.

After half a dozen tries she found one that wasn't locked, but it was crammed so full of boxes, she could hardly get the door open. But she didn't need room. She needed privacy, and—

"*There* you are!" Kathleen said. "I've been looking for you everywhere."

"Kathleen!" Briddey said, backing guiltily against the door. "What are you doing here?"

"We got worried. You weren't answering any of our messages, and Aunt Oona called me and said she'd had a premonition that something bad had happened, so I came over to find out what was going on."

"I didn't know you'd called," Briddey lied. "I've been down here all morning, and there's no reception on this level. How did you know where I was?"

"Charla told me. She said you'd come down here to talk to the Hunchback of Notre Dame, who I assume is the disheveled guy over that way," Kathleen said, pointing back toward C.B.'s lab, "though I'd call him the Abominable Snowman, it's so cold down here. He gave me these to give you to give to Trent, by the way." She handed Briddey a memory stick and a folded note. "Do you know if he's dating anyone?"

"*C.B.?*" Briddey said, unfolding the note. "You're kidding, right?" The note said:

Sorry about the whole calling you an idiot thing. Here's a different proposal for the meeting. Don't worry, your boyfriend will love it. It's a communication addict's dream. Signed, C.B. P.S. I'm *not* sorry about what I said about the EED. It's a *terrible* idea. Promise me you won't do it without thinking about it first. P.P.S. Ask yourself, WWHLD?

WWHLD? She didn't have time to worry about what that might stand for. She needed to get Kathleen out of here before she talked to anyone. *If I take her up to first and straight out to the parking garage,* she thought, *we might get lucky and not see anyone.*

"I'm serious," Kathleen was saying. "I thought he was kind of cute, or he would be if he'd comb his hair."

Briddey led Kathleen briskly toward the elevator. "I thought you were dating Chad."

"I am, but I don't know . . ." She sighed. "That's why I called you this morning. We had a fight last night."

Surprise, surprise. Of all the losers Kathleen had gone out with, Chad had to be the worst. But the priority now wasn't to do an intervention, it was to get Kathleen out of here, so Briddey kept walking.

"I caught him sexting some girl," Kathleen said. "On *my* phone. And when I called him on it, he got mad and roared off and left me, and I didn't realize till he was gone that my phone was still in his car."

They reached the elevator. Briddey pushed UP.

"So there I am in the middle of the night, trying to find a phone so I can call somebody to give me a ride." The elevator arrived and they got in. "Did you know there aren't any payphones *anywhere* anymore?"

Briddey pushed the button for FIRST, and the elevator started up. "So what did you do?"

"I finally found one outside a 7-Eleven," Kathleen said, "but then I didn't have any change, so I had to walk home, and the whole way I kept thinking, *I need to break up with him.*"

"Yes," Briddey said. "You do."

"I know. But the thing is, he really loves me."

C.B. was right. People were masters of self-deception. The elevator pinged, the door opened, and, blessedly, there was no one there. "Have you talked to Mary Clare about this?" Briddey asked, leading Kathleen firmly toward the parking garage.

"I tried, but she was too worried about Maeve to really listen."

"What's wrong with Maeve?"

"Nothing, but Mary Clare thinks she's been spending too much time online. She's afraid she's addicted or something."

They reached the door. "Listen," Briddey said, "I'd love to stay and talk, but I've got a meeting in half an hour, and I've got to review this proposal of C.B.'s first. So tell everybody I'm fine and I'll call them— and you—after work." She opened the door for Kathleen. "Bye."

"Wait," Kathleen said. "I need to ask you something. Why didn't you tell us you'd decided to have an EED?"

What? "I . . . it only happened last night," Briddey stammered, "and then this morning I had to meet with C.B."

"And you haven't had time *all* morning to send a simple text," Kathleen said sarcastically, "or an email. Or return our calls."

"I couldn't. I told you, there's no reception down there. I haven't had a chance to tell anyone."

"Except apparently the Hunchback guy—what's his name again?"

Benedict Arnold, Briddey thought bitterly. "His name's C.B.," she said. "C.B. Schwartz. I suppose he's who told you about the EED. Or was it Charla?"

"Neither. Maeve told me."

"Maeve?" Briddey said. "How did she find out?"

"From Facebook or Twitter or something."

She does *spend too much time online,* Briddey thought. "Maeve didn't tell Aunt Oona, did she?"

"I don't know. I suppose. She posted it on her Facebook page."

"But Aunt Oona's not on Facebook."

"Yes, she is. Maeve set up an account for her."

Oh, no, Briddey thought despairingly. *Then they all know.* "What did Aunt Oona say?"

"About what you'd expect. 'By the holy blood of Saint Patrick and all the saints of Ireland, what's that lass gone and done now?'"

"I haven't gone and done anything," Briddey said. "Trent asked me last night to have an EED done."

"And you said yes? After only going out with him for six *weeks*?"

"You got engaged to Alex Mancuso after two dates, as I recall."

"Yes, and that was a mistake."

A mistake was putting it mildly. He'd had a wife. And three felony convictions.

Kathleen said, "I just don't want you to make the same mistake I did. You can't possibly know Trent well enough to make a commitment like—"

"But that's why we're having it done. To get to know each other better. The EED—"

"Save it," Kathleen said. "You can tell me at supper. Aunt Oona's having the whole family over for Irish stew and crubeens."

And a session of the Irish Inquisition, Briddey thought. "I can't. Trent—"

"Is in meetings till ten tonight," Kathleen said. "Aunt Oona already called his secretary, so you can't get out of it by claiming he's taking you to dinner. Supper's at six."

She left, only to return a moment later to say plaintively, "I really should break up with Chad, shouldn't I?"

"Yes," Briddey said.

"You're right. See you at Aunt Oona's. And may Saint Patrick protect ye on your journey, mavourneen," Kathleen said gaily, and left.

It was ten fifty, and Briddey needed to check C.B.'s memory stick before the meeting to make sure it didn't have his Sanctuary phone proposal or some other crazy anti-communication thing on it. She started for her office, only to be waylaid by Lorraine from Marketing, who wanted to tell her how wonderful she thought it was that she and Trent were getting the EED. "How did you manage to talk him into it?" she asked.

"I didn't. It was Trent's idea."

"You're kidding! How? Most guys won't even admit they *have* feelings, let alone let anyone else see them. Gina—you know, Rahul Deshnev's assistant?—had to practically blackmail Greg into getting theirs. She said it was worth it, though, that she's never been happier or more relaxed."

That's because she doesn't have to be somewhere right now, Briddey thought, and said, "I'm late for a meeting—"

"I'm going to it, too," Lorraine said, steering her down toward the conference room. "Gina was afraid it might not work. She thought Greg might be cheating on her, and to tell you the truth, so did I. Suki told me—"

Briddey pulled back. "I just remembered, I need to run by my office and tell my assistant something."

"You don't have time. We're already late," Lorraine said, taking her arm. "So, anyway, we were wrong. Greg wasn't involved with someone else, because they connected, and she says things have never been more perfect. No more misunderstandings or misread cues or secrets. Oh, look, everyone's here already."

They were, and the first order of business was C.B.'s proposal, so Briddey didn't have a chance to look at it before she gave it to Trent. Fortunately, it wasn't C.B.'s Sanctuary phone—or his Hook, Line, and Sinker app. It was a design for one called TalkPlus, which made it possible to carry on two phone conversations simultaneously. "No more having to put someone on hold or tell them you'll call them back, and no more saying, 'Sorry, I have to take this call,' or 'I'm afraid I can't talk right now.' With TalkPlus, you'll be able to communicate with everyone all the time."

Very funny, C.B., Briddey thought, but everyone else loved the concept, including Trent, who texted her from across the table, "This is just what we need. Thanks for getting it out of him. Have you filled out Dr V forms yet?"

She texted him back, "I'll do it right after the meeting," and he responded, "Better not wait. Meeting could take awhile."

He was right. They immediately began making suggestions for how to adapt TalkPlus to make more than two conversations possible. The discussion lasted nearly two hours, resulting in them having lunch sent in and Briddey's being able to fill out Dr. Verrick's first questionnaire, even though it asked everything from her medical history to her food preferences, hair and eye color, and hobbies.

She finished the form and refocused on the meeting to find Art Sampson saying, "I like the TalkPlus, but will it be enough to compete with this phone of Apple's? I mean, we're a small company. If the new iPhone is the paradigm shift everybody says it is, being able to talk to multiple people at once isn't going to be enough," and the meeting deteriorated into crosstalk as they speculated about what was on Apple's new phone and discussed possible ways of finding out.

Just send Suki over, Briddey thought, and was about to text Trent that when he texted her, "Hamilton wants to see me. I'll call you after. Love you. Don't forget forms.," and left her to listen to the speculations, which threatened to go on forever.

C.B. has the right idea refusing to go to meetings, she thought. She pulled up the second questionnaire, even though she doubted getting it in quickly would have any effect. When she looked up Dr. Verrick online, his client list included not only Hollywood celebrities but sports figures, royalty—he'd reportedly done Prince William and Kate's—and the CEOs of a dozen Fortune 500 companies. She and Trent were lucky to have gotten on the waiting list at all, and Dr. Verrick wasn't likely to bump David Beckham or the Sultan of Brunei for them. Just in case, though, she started through the questionnaire, which turned out to be a full battery of tests designed to measure emotional sensitivity, empathy, and couple compatibility.

I'll never be able to finish this today, Briddey thought, but by the time everyone at the meeting had finished discussing the likelihood that Apple was only bluffing and whether Apple was spying on them, how unethical that would be, and who they could get to spy on Apple, Briddey'd finished the tests, sent them off to Dr. Verrick's office, and started in on her email, ignoring the flood of messages from her family.

There were two from C.B., one headed, "What Would Hedy Lamarr Do?"

So that's what "WWHLD?" stands for, she thought. *Of course.*

His email was linked to a long article about Hedy Lamarr's accomplishments regarding frequency hopping, and his second one to a news story titled, "Iowa Man Dies from Hangnail Surgery Complications."

When the meeting finally got out at four, she was surrounded with well-wishers telling her what a great catch Trent was and wanting to know how they'd been able to get on Dr. Verrick's waiting list. "We couldn't even get on the waiting list for the waiting list," Lara from Accounting told her wistfully, and Beth from Quality Control enthused, "The EED's the best thing ever invented!"

Could you tell that to my family and C.B., please? Briddey thought as she went back to her office, wondering what excuse she could give to get out of going to supper. A last-minute report due? A co-worker with a broken arm who she had to take to the emergency room? An outbreak of hantavirus?

Whatever she told them, she needed to do it soon. It was already four thirty, and she wouldn't put it past Aunt Oona to send Kathleen to Commspan after work to make sure she didn't back out.

Charla was standing at the door to her office. "These just came for you," she said, pointing to a bouquet of pale pink camellias. "From Trent Worth." She handed Briddey the card. "Longing for you," it read, "and longing for the day when I won't have to tell you that because you'll already know. Trent."

"You are *so* lucky," Charla said. "Nate never sends me—"

"Any messages?" Briddey interrupted.

"No, but your family—"

"Call them back and tell them something's come up," Briddey said, walking past her, "I don't care what, an emergency meeting or some-thing, and I'm not going to be able to make it to supper," and opened the door.

On the whole clan. They were all there, including Aunt Oona in her tweed skirt and cardigan, her knitting in her lap. Mary Clare and Kathleen stood on either side of her, and Maeve sat cross-legged on the floor in the corner. *Please, please don't let them have heard what I just said,* Briddey thought.

"An emergency meetin', is it?" Aunt Oona asked, her brogue even thicker than usual.

"I'll get some more chairs," Briddey said, and went out to Charla's desk.

"I told them you were really busy—" Charla began.

But they didn't listen, Briddey thought. *I know. I have the same problem.* "It's all right, Charla," she said aloud.

"Do you want me to go get them some coffee or something?" Charla asked.

"No," Briddey said, debating whether to tell her to come in in five minutes and remind her that she had to be somewhere. But she doubted it would work, and she had to get this over with sometime. Preferably without Charla listening at the door. So Briddey told her she could go home early and went back into her office to face the music.

"'Twas a feelin' I had that your work would keep you from coming to supper," Aunt Oona said the moment she shut the door on Charla, "so we thought we'd best be coming here to talk to you about this LED thing."

"EED," Maeve corrected her from her corner. "LEDs are those little light thingies. EED stands for—"

"And how should I be knowin' *what* it stands for when herself can't be bothered to even tell her own kin that she's after having it done? And with an Englishman!"

"What Trent and I are *doing,*" Briddey said, "is having a simple medical procedure so that we can sense each other's feelings and com-municate better as a couple."

"Saints preserve us!" Aunt Oona said, crossing herself. "Communi-catin', is it? And since when did an Irishman need an operation for that? Or is talkin' too good for an Englishman?"

"No, of course not. The EED doesn't replace other forms of communication, it *enhances* them." Briddey launched into an explanation of how the EED created a neural pathway that made the partners more receptive to each other's feelings, but Aunt Oona wasn't having any of it.

She folded her cardiganed arms across her ample bosom and muttered, "It's unnatural, that's what it is."

"It's also positively medieval," Mary Clare said. "Agreeing to be lobotomized just to please a man! What kind of message are you sending to your niece?"

Apparently none, Briddey thought, looking at Maeve, who was messing with her smartphone, oblivious to the conversation. "It's not a lobotomy," she said, "and I'm not doing it for Trent. It benefits both of us." But Mary Clare wasn't listening.

"It's bad enough that Maeve's constantly exposed to a popular culture full of weak, helpless females," she declared, "but when it's her own aunt! I spend all my time trying to protect Maeve from things that squelch her intelligence and independence—"

"She means the Disney princesses," Maeve said disgustedly, looking up from her phone. "Aunt Briddey, she won't let me watch *Tangled,* just because Flynn comes to rescue Rapunzel! But sometimes people *need* to be rescued—"

"You see?" Mary Clare said to Briddey. "She's already bought into the notion that a girl should just sit and wait for a man to rescue her, that she's incapable of rescuing herself."

"Because sometimes you *can't!*" Maeve said. "Like when you're tied up. Or turned into ice. And guys can need rescuing, too, like when the witch in *Tangled* kills—"

"Hush now, childeen," Aunt Oona said, patting Maeve's arm. "'Tis not the moment for fairy stories. We've life-and-death matters to—"

"It's *not* a life-and-death matter," Briddey said. "The EED is perfectly safe—"

"Oh, and I suppose *he* told you that. And when did ever a word of truth come out of an Englishman's mouth, I'd like to know. Lyin' brutes they are—"

"Trent is *not* a lying brute. Or an Englishman. His family's been in America for generations."

"As has ours. And are you sayin' that *we're* not Irish?" Aunt Oona said, bridling. "And what'll you be doin' next, child? Changin' your name from Flannigan and dyin' your red locks brown? By the holy blood of Saint Patrick, to think that I'd live to see the day when the child of my own sainted niece would foreswear her heritage! 'Tis Irish you are, lass. 'Tis in your blood, and no good denyin' it. Just as it's no good denyin' he's an Englishman at heart—and a wicked, cruel, lyin' heart it is. Blackguards and seducers, the lot of them. If you'd find yourself a good Irish lad—"

"It doesn't matter who Trent's descended from," Kathleen said. "It's the person that counts."

Thank you, Briddey thought.

"And he's really hot," Kathleen went on. "Plus, I love his car. *I'd* go out with him." Which wasn't exactly an endorsement given Kathleen's track record with men.

Mary Clare immediately pointed that out and added, "I just don't understand the attraction to a man who insists on brain surgery as some kind of prenuptial. What *is* it you see in him, Briddey?"

Well, for one thing, she thought angrily, *he's an only child, and his family never barges in without asking. Or blathers on about a country they've never been to. They believe people should mind their own business. And for another, his apartment has electronic locks and a doorman, and after we get engaged, I'll be able to move in with him and finally have a little privacy. You won't be able to come bursting in every time you feel like it and tell me what to do.*

But she couldn't say that—Aunt Oona would have a stroke. And she obviously couldn't tell them part of the reason she was in love with Trent was that he *wasn't* Irish.

He was the exact opposite of the scruffy, ragtag, irresponsible louts Kathleen dated and the past-their-prime, family-ridden "lads" Aunt Oona tried to set her up with—and the exact opposite of the jerks she'd gone out with before. He was neat and well dressed and gainfully employed, and he paid her compliments, took her nice places, sent her flowers. And didn't sext other people.

Is it so wrong to want a boyfriend who doesn't leave you stranded at a convenience store in the middle of the night? she thought. *And a life where people call before they come over and don't constantly show up, uninvited, at your office?*

But she couldn't tell them that either—and even if she tried, no one would hear her. Mary Clare was busy ordering Maeve to turn off her smartphone, Kathleen was saying, "Trent reminds me of someone, but I can't think who," and Aunt Oona was relating a premonition she'd had about Briddey having the EED.

You're always having premonitions, Briddey thought, annoyed, *and they're just as authentic as that brogue of yours.* As far as Briddey could see, Aunt Oona's psychic ability, which she called "the Sight" and claimed ran in the family, was limited to predicting that Kathleen's boyfriends were "chancers and cheats," which was a safe bet, and that the phone was about to ring. "Mary Clare's goin' to call," she'd announce dramatically. " 'Tis a feeling I have in my bones. It's worried about Maeve she is."

Since Mary Clare was *always* worried about Maeve and called Aunt Oona at least twenty times a day to discuss her fears, this was hardly a feat requiring psychic powers. And the rest of the time her premonitions and "sensings" and feelings of impending doom were dead wrong. Including now. " 'Tis a bad feelin' I have about your having this DED, mavourneen," she said.

"*E*ED," Maeve corrected her without looking up from her phone. " 'DED' is when you're so happy it kills you. Can we *go* now? I'm really hungry."

"Of course you are, childeen," Aunt Oona said. " 'Tis well past time for tea," and she suggested they go down to the cafeteria for a "wee bit of nourishment," which would mean continuing their debate in full earshot of half of Commspan. And Briddey could imagine what Suki and the grapevine would do with that, so she agreed to go to supper.

"And what about your emergency meetin'?" Aunt Oona asked.

"I'll cancel it," Briddey said grimly and, in a last, desperate bid for escape, suggested she meet them there.

It didn't work. Aunt Oona insisted on riding with her, blathering the entire way about the virtues of that fine Irish lad Sean O'Reilly and saying, apparently without irony, what a pity it was that Mary Clare meddled so much in Maeve's affairs. "Why can't she just leave the poor childeen alone? Maeve doesn't get a moment's peace."

And once they arrived, they rehashed all their previous arguments against the EED over dinner, along with some new additions: that

Trent had some sinister ulterior motive for wanting her to have the EED done, that it might very well be a mortal sin in the eyes of the Church, and that no self-respecting Irishman would ever do it—

"That's not true," Briddey said. "Enya had it done with her fiancé. And Daniel Day-Lewis—"

"And if Enya and Daniel Day-Lewis told you to jump off a bridge into the river Shannon, you'd be doin' that, too, would ye?" Aunt Oona said.

"I think she should," Maeve said.

"Jump off a bridge?" Kathleen asked.

"Maeve, I've talked to you about the dangers of peer pressure—" Mary Clare began.

Maeve ignored them. "If Aunt Briddey has the EED, she'll find out what he's like inside," she said. "Like in *Frozen*, there's this prince and Anna thinks he's really nice and in love with her and everything, but he isn't, he just wants her kingdom. And he tries to *kill* her."

"Which is another reason I don't want you watching Disney movies," Mary Clare said. "They're entirely too violent!"

"They're *not* violent!" Maeve said violently. "What I *meant* was, sometimes people are different on the inside from how they are on the outside, and if Aunt Briddey has the EED, she'll find out what he's really like and won't like him anymore, and she'll find a different boyfriend—one who's nice."

"She can do all that without goin' under the knife," Aunt Oona said, and started in on the dangers of "operations" as experienced by various Daughters of Ireland. "Sean O'Reilly's cousin went in for an operation on her bad leg, and they cut off the wrong one!"

I should have asked C.B. to put that SOS function on my phone, Briddey thought. *I could really use it right now.*

Her phone rang. "I'm sorry to bother you," Charla said, "but C.B. Schwartz just called me here at home and asked if you got the ideas for the phone he sent you this morning?"

Thank you, C.B., Briddey thought. "Yes," she said. "No, that's okay. I'll be right there."

"You don't have to go in to Commspan," Charla said, bewildered. "He just wanted to make sure you got them."

"I understand. Right away," Briddey said, and hung up. "Sorry, I've got to go," she told the family, putting on her coat. "There's a problem at work I've got to go check on."

They insisted on going out to the car with her. "When is Trent making you do this EED thing?" Mary Clare asked.

"Late summer," Maeve said.

"How did you know that?" Briddey asked her.

"It was on Facebook."

"Late summer," Aunt Oona said musingly. "Good, then it's a good bit of time you'll be havin' to think it over . . ."

For you to try to talk me out of it, you mean, Briddey thought, and drove away musing, *After I'm married to Trent, I'll never have to suffer through one of those supper interrogations again. I'll move in with Trent and instruct the doorman to keep you and the rest of the world out and finally get some peace and quiet.*

As soon as she was out of sight, she pulled over to call Charla and explain her behavior. The family hadn't wasted any time. There was already a text on her phone from Aunt Oona telling her about a Daughter of Ireland's nephew who'd died from an operation on her varicose veins, and one from Kathleen, saying, "I just realized who Trent reminds me of—Kurt."

Kurt was a previous boyfriend of Kathleen's who'd pledged undying love and then made off with Kathleen's credit cards. Briddey deleted both texts and tried to call Charla but got kicked to her message box. *I'll call her when I get home,* she thought, and as soon as she reached her apartment, she took out her phone to try again.

It immediately rang. *I'll bet Charla checked her call log,* Briddey thought, and answered it even though it was Trent's ringtone.

Mistake. It was Mary Clare. "We just got home, and now Maeve's locked herself in her room," she said.

If you were my mother, I'd lock myself in my room, too, Briddey thought.

"She put a sign on her door that says, KEEP OUT. THIS MEANS YOU, MOM. I MEAN IT."

That sounds like the sign on C.B.'s lab door, Briddey thought. "Well, at least she's asserting herself, and you don't have to worry about her having 'squelched girl syndrome,'" she said.

Mary Clare ignored that. "What am I going to do? She could be doing drugs in there. Or watching snuff videos."

"Her favorite movie is *Tangled*. She's not watching snuff videos."

"You don't know that. She's so precocious, and she's been spending nearly all her after-school time on her phone or her laptop. And I read an article that said her generation's computer skills are so advanced over their parents' that it's impossible to understand them, let alone control them. Do you know how to install a nanny cam?"

"No," Briddey said firmly. "I've got to go. Trent's on the other line." She hung up. Her phone immediately rang again. *If this is Aunt Oona . . .* she thought.

But it was Trent. "I've got great news," he said. "I just talked to Dr. Verrick, and the EEDs he was scheduled to do in Paris got canceled, which means he can move us up."

"To May?" Briddey said, thinking, *That's still two months away. That means at least three billion phone calls and emails and texts, and who knows how many interrogations by the Irish Inquisition. I'll never make it.*

"No," Trent said. "The cancellation caused some shifting around in his schedule, and he can fit us in next Wednesday!"

Three

"Live in fragments no longer. Only connect . . ."
—E.M. FORSTER, *Howard's End*

KEEPING THE SURGERY DATE SECRET FOR EVEN A FEW DAYS TURNED OUT to be a huge challenge, especially after Dr. Verrick's office sent a pre-admission form to Briddey's office email address, and Charla saw it. She immediately asked Briddey if the date of the EED had been moved up.

Briddey managed to convince her it hadn't, and that the hospital *had* to do things months in advance to allow time for the insurance company to process the claims, but it was a close call, and Briddey still hadn't thought of a way to ask Management for the time off that wouldn't alert the grapevine, especially since the EED required an overnight stay. With the Apple rollout looming, and everyone trying frantically to come up with a new design to compete with it, nobody was getting any time off, let alone the better part of two days. But when she texted Trent her concern, he told her not to worry, that he'd take care of it.

He did, and, miraculously, without word getting out so no one waylaid her in the halls to ask her how they'd managed to get in so quickly. But that still left the matter of getting to the hospital to have her pre-op bloodwork done without being seen by somebody from

Commspan—*and with my luck,* she thought, *it'll be Suki*—and of keeping her family from finding out. But here Maeve came to her rescue. Her rebellion over not being able to watch *Tangled* had apparently spilled over to school, and she got sent to detention for reading the latest Secret Haven book in class.

"I hate adults," she texted Briddey. "They don't let you do *anything.*" And when Briddey suggested mildly that she still should have put her book away when the teacher told her to, Maeve replied, "Like I told Mom, I didn't *hear* her."

She had apparently also told Mary Clare the reason she hadn't heard her was that "I was thinking about other stuff"—an explanation that brought on a flurry of anxious conferences with Maeve's teacher, the school counselor, a child psychologist, and a hearing specialist.

Briddey was able to use the excuse of a family therapy session as the reason for her car's being at the hospital when she went for her blood-work, and the family's preoccupation with Maeve gave her the time she needed to pack her overnight bag and stow it safely in the trunk of her car, write out instructions for Charla, whom she'd told she was going to an afternoon meeting downtown on Wednesday and a morning conference Thursday, and answer the emails that couldn't wait.

Kathleen had sent her an ad for a "Spiritual Connection" seminar taught by a psychic named Lyzandra of Sedona with a note reading, "If you go to this, you won't *have* to have surgery to read Trent's thoughts," and Aunt Oona had emailed her about the Daughters of Ireland's upcoming outing to see Riverdance ("Sean O'Reilly's going!"). And C.B., who supposedly didn't believe in emails, had sent her twelve: four news items about minor outpatient procedures that had resulted in death, seven about side effects from EEDs, and a news item about a man who'd shot his wife when they failed to connect.

Wednesday morning, Briddey emailed her family, telling them she'd be in meetings for the next two days—"Do *not* call hospitals if I don't answer my phone, Aunt Oona!"—and then activated the automatic "Bridget Flannigan will be out of the office until . . ." message and turned off her phone, trying not to think of how many lies she was telling.

But only till tomorrow afternoon. As soon as she got home from the hospital, she'd tell them a last-minute opportunity to have the surgery had come up, and there hadn't been time to tell anybody. By then they'd be able to see how harmless it was and how happy she and Trent were, and they wouldn't have a leg to stand on. If she could just get safely out of the building.

She'd planned to drive her car over to Trent's apartment at eleven, leave it there, and go to the hospital with him, but he called her as she got to work to tell her his meeting with Graham Hamilton was running late and he'd have to meet her there. "But don't we have to have it done together?" she asked.

"It's not welding, sweetheart," Trent said. "Dr. Verrick has to do one of us first, then the other. Yours is at one and mine's at two. I'll be there in plenty of time. And then we'll be connected, and our worries will be over. Everything will be perfect."

He was right, and going to the hospital separately was probably better than going together. If they left Commspan at the same time, people might put two and two together. But the change in plans meant she had to think of something else to do with her car. Taking a taxi was out. She couldn't leave her car here overnight without eagle-eyed Suki noticing it, and if she drove home and took a taxi from there and one of the family dropped in and saw it after she'd told them she was in meetings here at Commspan . . .

But she couldn't park it at the hospital either. With her luck, Mary Clare would show up to see some specialist for Maeve and spot it. She'd have to park it someplace out of the way and then take a taxi to the hospital.

So she needed to leave now. Which meant another lie. If she could think of one. A parking ticket? No, Charla would want to know when and where she'd gotten it. Jury duty? A dentist's appointment?

She shut off her phone and went out to Charla's desk. "Is Suki here today?" she asked.

"No."

Excellent. That meant her chances of getting away without anyone finding out had just increased exponentially. Unless she was at the hospital. "Suki's not out sick, is she?" she asked.

"No," Charla said. "She's got jury duty."

Which I nearly used as my excuse, Briddey thought. *Thank goodness after tomorrow I can stop lying, because I'm no good at it.*

"Did you need her for something?" Charla asked.

"No, it can wait. I need you to go up to Records and ask Jill Quincy to help you find everything we've got on the patents for Apple's last three iPhones," Briddey said, and as soon as Charla'd left, she put the instructions she'd written out for Charla on her desk, checked the corridor to make sure it was empty, and walked quickly to the elevator, debating whether she should take the stairs instead, just to be on the safe side.

But Charla and Jill were up in Records, Suki was safely sequestered in a courtroom, and C.B. never came aboveground.

Except today of all days—and, worst of all, she was already inside the elevator and had pushed P when he suddenly appeared in its doorway, looking thrown together and slightly out of breath. "Oh, good," he said. "I'm glad I caught you."

"If it's about your idea for the TalkPlus phone," she said, "everybody loved it."

"Of course they did," he said disgustedly. "It's not about that. There's something else I need to talk to you about. It's important."

"I'm afraid I don't have time right now," Briddey said, hitting the CLOSE DOOR button. "I have a meeting downtown in ten minutes."

"That's okay. I'll ride down with you," he said, squeezing in between the shutting doors. "Did you read those emails I sent you about the IED?"

"Yes, and now that I know that the EED's side effects include sciatica, short-term memory loss, plantar's warts, peptic ulcers, jogger's knee, and getting kicked off *The Bachelorette*, I've decided I definitely want it done. I've always wanted to be thrown off a reality game show."

"I was afraid of that. But there's also a chance it could cause UIC, you know."

And if you think I'm going to ask you what "UIC" stands for, you're delusional.

He must have reached the same conclusion because he said, "You know, unintended consequences."

"What unintended consequences?"

"Who knows? That's the thing with unintended consequences. You have no way of knowing what they might be till they happen, and then it's too late. Look at Prohibition. And DDT. They seemed like terrific ideas, and look what ended up happening—Al Capone and a slew of dead robins. Or look at Twitter. Who'd have thought it would give rise to ISIS and #InsufferablyCuteCats? Look at all those Irish immigrants who thought it would be a great idea to take the *Titanic* to America. If they'd considered what might happen—"

"So you're saying that if I have the EED, I'll be hit by an iceberg?"

"You might. There's no telling what'll happen. What if, when they shave your head in pre-op, your hair grows back in white instead of red?"

"They don't shave your head. They go in at the back of your neck."

"So does a guillotine. Or what if they drill the hole in the wrong spot and you end up unable to communicate at all? Or in a coma, and the doctor harvests your organs and sells them on the black market?"

"He is not going to harvest my organs. Look, I appreciate all this concern, but I know what I'm doing."

"She said as she boarded the *Titanic*. Okay, let's say you do, and the surgery goes great, and you find out everything about each other, but you don't like it. Communication's not everything, you know. I can guarantee you that getting to know Hitler's innermost thoughts wouldn't make you like him any better. The same could turn out to be true for your boyfriend."

"It won't be," Briddey said, looking longingly up at the floor numbers above the elevator door, willing P to blink on.

"Or what if the EED doesn't work? Don't the two of you have to be emotionally bonded to connect? What if you're not? And what the hell is 'emotional bonding,' anyway? It sounds like something out of *Fifty Shades of Grey*. Why can't they just say you have to be in love with each other?"

She was going to be stuck on this elevator with him forever.

"What if he's 'emotionally bonded' to somebody else?" C.B. went on. "Like his secretary?"

"Ethel Godwin is at least sixty," she said.

"Yeah, well, I can think of more mismatched couples than that who've found true love, but fine. What if he's in love with Jan in Payroll? Or Suki? Never mind, bad example. If he was in love with Suki, everybody on the planet would know about it. What if he's in love with Lorraine in Marketing? Or Art Sampson?"

"He's not in love with Art—"

"Or what if the two of you only *think* you're emotionally bonded? I mean, people think stuff that isn't true all the time. Hitler probably thought he was a really nice guy—"

"What *is* it with you and Hitler?" Briddey exploded.

"Sorry. Side effect of spending a lot of time online. Internet conversations always involve Hitler. My *point* is, even if the EED works, it won't necessarily solve all your problems, and in the meantime, it could create a whole bunch of new ones."

"Thank you, I'll take that into consideration," she said. "Now, what was it you wanted to talk to me about?"

"Talk to you about?" he said blankly.

"Yes." She looked up at the floor numbers again. "You said you needed to talk to me about something urgent. Or was Hitler's deluded opinion of himself it?"

"No," C.B. said as the P above the door lit up. Finally. "I thought of some more ideas for the Sanctuary phone. Like a photo function where if people send you photos of their babies and their insufferably cute cats, they automatically disappear into the ether."

Like I wish you'd do right now, Briddey thought, stepping forward to be ready the second the door opened. If it ever did.

"I also had an idea for a hanging-up app," he said, and the doors slid apart.

"We'll discuss it next week. Call Charla and make an appointment," Briddey said, and shot through the doors and into the garage.

"I'll walk you to your car," C.B. said, catching up to her. "You know how in the good old days when you were mad at somebody, you could shout, 'Good*bye!*' and bang down the receiver, and it not only felt good, but it got your message across perfectly?"

I should have parked closer, Briddey thought, accelerating her pace.

"And you know how now all you can do is click an icon, which isn't nearly as emotionally satisfying? I've come up with an app that makes a really loud slamming-down-the-receiver noise."

She reached her car, glad she'd put her overnight bag in the trunk and not the back seat.

"I haven't worked out all the kinks yet," C.B. said. "I want to make sure there aren't any side effects I might not have thought of."

Very funny.

"And speaking of hanging up, that's another disadvantage of telepathy. There wouldn't be *any* way to hang up on the other person."

"For the last time, the EED doesn't make you telepathic!"

"You don't know that. That's the thing with unintended consequen—"

"Look," she said, opening the car door. "As much as I'd like to stay and explain the EED to you *again,* I really have to go. I have a meeting downtown—"

"You're lying."

She looked up at him, horrified. Somehow Suki had found out where she was going, even though she was sitting in a courtroom miles away. And if she'd told C.B., she'd told everyone. Including Facebook. And the Irish Inquisition would be peeling into the parking garage any moment. "H-how—?" she stammered.

"I can see it in your face, and the way you practically ran out here to your car. You can't wait to get rid of me."

True, she thought, relieved. "Look, I appreciate your input—"

"No, you don't. You think I'm sticking my nose in where it doesn't belong," he said. "But when you see somebody heading straight for the edge of a cliff, you can't just stand there and do nothing."

"I am not heading—"

"That's what *you* think."

"Why? Because I'll end up like a patient in *Coma*? Or get jogger's knee? Give me one good reason I shouldn't have the EED. And not one involving black-market organs or lobotomies. A *believable* reason."

"Yeah," he muttered. "That's the problem." He looked at her seriously. "Listen, Briddey, being connected isn't all it's cracked up to be. You think you want to know what other people are thinking—"

"Briddey!" Charla called, hurrying across the garage toward them, waving a piece of paper.

Oh, no, Briddey thought. *If that's a message from Trent, and he mentions the hospital . . .*

She moved to intercept her, but Charla was already at the car, saying breathlessly, "I'm glad I caught you. Your sister Mary Clare called. She said you need to contact her right away. It's an emergency."

It's always an emergency, Briddey thought. "Did she say what the emergency was?"

"No," Charla said. She looked at C.B. "I'm sorry. I didn't mean to interrupt."

"C.B. was just leaving," Briddey said. She looked at him meaningfully. "Weren't you?"

He smacked the top of the car door with the flat of his hand. "Yeah," he said. He stuck the earbuds back in his ears and walked off, his hands in his pockets.

Charla leaned in toward Briddey and whispered, "Was he bothering you?"

Yes, Briddey thought. She shook her head. "No."

"Oh. When I heard you two shouting, I was afraid he was sexually harassing you or something."

"No. We were discussing an idea for the new phone."

"Oh." Charla looked doubtfully after him. "He's so weird. His hair—"

"Tell my sister I'll call her as soon as I can," Briddey said, and got into the car.

She shut the door, started the car, waved, backed out of the parking space, and drove off, feeling like she'd barely escaped disaster. And there was still the call to Mary Clare to get through.

She *had* to call her, in case it was a real emergency and not just Mary Clare's latest obsession regarding Maeve. But what if it *was* an emergency and they had to postpone the EED? There wouldn't be another opening for months. *And I can't take much more of everyone trying to talk me out of it,* she thought. On the other hand, if Aunt Oona had had a heart attack . . .

Briddey fretted about it the whole way to the Marriott and while she parked the car, finally deciding to turn on her phone and call Mary Clare from an inner corner of the parking garage in hopes that the coverage would be spotty.

It wasn't. Mary Clare's voice came through clear as a bell: "Oh, thank goodness you called. I don't know what to do. Maeve's teacher just told me the book Maeve was reading in class wasn't a Secret Haven book, it was *The Darkvoice Chronicles!* Why would she be reading that?"

"All the third-grade girls are reading it," Briddey said. "Like *Apocalypse Girl*. Or *The Hunger Games*. And I thought you said she was spending too much time online and that you wanted her reading—"

"But not *this* book! Do you know what it's about? A schizophrenic teenager who hears voices. And Maeve said she didn't hear her teacher talking to her. What if it was because the voices in *her* head drowned her teacher out?"

Oh, for heaven's sake, Briddey thought. "Maeve is not hearing voices—"

"You don't know that," Mary Clare interrupted. "I read this thing on the internet that said the symptoms of schizophrenia can manifest as early as age seven, and in *The Darkvoice Chronicles,* the heroine hears this voice that tells her to kill her mother—"

"Yes, and in *The Hunger Games* the heroine hunts people with a bow and arrow. Maeve isn't doing that either."

"Then why won't she tell me what she was thinking about? There's something going on. I know it. Listen, could you pick her up after school tomorrow and take her shopping and get her to tell you—?"

"No," Briddey said. "I'm in meetings the next two days. I could do it sometime next week—"

"Next week may be too late. The onset of mental illness can be really rapid, and if it's not diagnosed immediately—"

"Maeve is *not* mentally ill. Or deaf or anorexic or planning to cut off her hair and sell it to get money so her father can come home."

"Cut off her *hair*?" Mary Clare cried. "Why would she—?"

"It's in *Little Women,*" Briddey said. "Which you insisted that Maeve read, as I recall. They're only books, Mary Clare. And you should be grateful she's reading instead of spray-painting graffiti on her school or setting fires or being recruited by terrorists on the internet."

"Terrorists?"

"She's not being recruited by terrorists," Briddey said. "I only said that to show you how ridiculous you're being. Maeve is *fine*. Look, I really have to go."

"Wait," Mary Clare said. "You're not still planning to have that EED done, are you? Because I read this thing on the internet that said they don't last, and you have to have them redone every three months—"

"Tell me later. What?" Briddey said, as if speaking to somebody else. "Yes. Right away. Sorry, Mary Clare. Gotta go." She hung up.

Her phone promptly pinged. She checked to make sure the text wasn't from Trent—it wasn't; it was from Kathleen—and then shut off her phone, got her overnight bag out of the trunk, took the elevator up to the Marriott's lobby, and caught a taxi to the hospital, directing the driver to let her off at the side entrance so there was less chance of someone seeing her.

She might as well have walked in the front door. Once inside, she was told she had to go to Patient Admissions, which was right in the middle of the lobby. She filled out the admission forms as quickly as she could and then waited impatiently as they scanned her insurance card, looking anxiously around.

An aide finally came for her, calling her name out loudly, and Briddey hurried after her, eager to be out of sight. The aide took her upstairs and into an examining room where a large, cheerful nurse fastened a plastic ID bracelet on her. "My, what beautiful red hair you have!" she said admiringly. "The EED is a very routine procedure, and you're in excellent hands with Dr. Verrick, so there's no need to be nervous."

Are you kidding? Briddey thought. *This is the first time today I haven't been.*

"You were very lucky to get him as your surgeon," the nurse went on. "He's very much in demand." She handed Briddey a hospital gown and left her to change into it.

Briddey did and then turned on her phone to see if Trent had texted her. He had. So had Kathleen, with the names of three more psychics, and C.B., with links to articles about the unintended consequences of fen-phen, thalidomide, and the Industrial Revolution, and a picture of Marie Antoinette being led to the guillotine.

Maeve had texted her, too, in all caps, "WHAT DID YOU TELL MOM?," the words almost quivering with outrage, which could only mean Mary Clare had latched on to the terrorist thing with both hands.

I am so sorry, Maeve, Briddey thought, and read Trent's text. It read, "On my way. See you after surgery."

She was about to text him back when the nurse reappeared, plucked the phone from her hands, and said, "We'll put this and your clothes and purse in a locker for you."

The nurse took her vitals and gave her a waiver to sign, which released Dr. Verrick and the hospital from all responsibility if the EED failed to work and/or the connection proved to be only temporary, and an informed consent form listing all the possible side effects of the surgery: coronary thrombosis, hemorrhaging, seizures, paralysis, loss of life.

But not a word about becoming a vegetable. Or about having her organs harvested. *There, you see, C.B.?* she thought, signing the forms. *It's perfectly safe.*

"Now let's get you on the gurney," the nurse said. She helped Briddey onto it, covered her with a white blanket, clipped an oximeter onto her finger, inserted an IV line in the back of her other hand, and hooked up a bag of saline.

"Do you know if Trent's here yet?" Briddey asked her.

"I'll go check," she said, and went out, only to return a moment later with a distinguished-looking man. "This is Dr. Verrick, who'll be doing your surgery," she told Briddey, and to him: "This is Ms. Flannigan."

Thank goodness C.B. isn't here. Or Maeve, Briddey thought. Because his expensive suit and gold Rolex watch fit C.B.'s picture of Celebrity Plastic Surgeon perfectly, and his hair, with a touch of gray at the temples, was even more neatly combed than Trent's.

But his manner was warm and reassuring, and he seemed genuinely pleased she and Trent were having the EED done. "I can guarantee it will add a whole new dimension to your relationship," he told her. He took her through the procedure, telling her just what was going to happen and explaining how the EED worked. "I'm going to do yours first, and then Mr. Worth's. Do you have any questions, Ms. Flannigan?"

"Yes. How long will it take?"

"The procedure takes approximately an hour, but most of that time is spent in imaging. The surgery itself—"

"No, I meant how long after the surgery before Trent and I will be able to sense each other's feelings? Before we'll know whether it worked?"

"There's no need to worry about *that*," he said. "You and Mr. Worth scored exceptionally high on the compatibility and empathetic-intelligence tests. I'll see you in the operating room." He smiled down at her, pleased. "Excellent," he said, patted the gurney, and left before she could ask him again.

She asked the nurse instead.

"It generally takes twenty-four hours after the surgery for patients to establish contact," the nurse said.

Which meant she'd have to go on lying for two more days. "Does it ever happen sooner than that?" she asked hopefully.

"No, the edema—the swelling—has to go down and the anesthetic has to leave your system first. But Dr. Verrick considers you an excellent candidate for the EED, so don't worry."

But that was easier said than done, especially when the nurse produced an electric razor. "You're not going to shave my head, are you?" Briddey asked, remembering what C.B. had said about her hair growing back white.

"Those beautiful red curls? Oh, my, no. Just a tiny patch at the back of your neck."

To make it easier for the guillotine, Briddey thought, and must have said it out loud because the nurse said, "The anesthesiologist's going to give you a mild sedative to relax you."

But it didn't relax her in the least. All she could think about was those links C.B. had sent her about people dying during surgery, especially when the anesthesiologist asked her, "Have you ever had an allergic reaction to an anesthetic?"

She intended to tell him no, but the sedative must have kicked in by then because she asked him instead if they were going to put her in a coma and harvest her organs.

"Definitely not," he said, laughing.

"When can I see Trent?" she asked, but she didn't hear the answer because she'd fallen asleep right there on the gurney. And she clearly wasn't supposed to yet because they immediately tried to wake her up, patting the hand that didn't have the IV on it and saying, "Bridget? Bridget?"

"I'm sorry," she said blurrily. "I must have dozed off—"

"You're coming out of the anesthesia," the voice said, and it was a different nurse. "How are you feeling?"

"What time is it?" Briddey asked.

"A little past three. How are you feeling? Any nausea?"

"No."

"Headache?"

"No."

There were a lot of other questions, and Briddey must have answered them correctly because the nurse said, as Briddey closed her eyes again, "You're doing really well. You're going to stay here in the recovery room a little bit longer just to make sure everything's okay." And when she opened her eyes again, she was in a hospital room with two beds and a window, and the nurse who came in to check her IV said it was five o'clock.

So I must have already had the EED, she thought groggily, even though she had no memory of being taken into the operating room and the back of her head didn't hurt. They'd said it was a minor procedure, but she should feel something, shouldn't she? She tried to feel if there was a bandage back there, but she couldn't. The IV on the back of her hand restricted its movement. But at least her hand moved, which meant she hadn't ended up paralyzed. *You were wrong, C.B.,* she thought sleepily. *The surgery went fine, and in a little while Trent and I—*

She stopped, holding her breath. She'd heard something.

Trent? she called, and then remembered that they weren't supposed to be able to connect till at least twenty-four hours after the surgery.

I must have heard the patient in the other bed, she thought, but when she raised her head slightly so she could see over the nightstand, the other bed was empty, a stack of linens piled neatly at its foot.

The sound must have come from the corridor, then, but she knew it hadn't. It had been in here, and very close. It *had* to have been Trent. *Are you there?* she called, and waited, holding her breath.

Yes, she heard.

But I can't have, she thought. The EED didn't make you able to hear your partner's thoughts. It only made you able to sense his feelings.

I did hear him, she told herself stubbornly, but before she could analyze why she was so sure it had been a voice, she was hit with an explosion of emotion: delight and worry and relief all mingled together. Emotions that hadn't come from her, that definitely belonged to someone else.

It is Trent, she thought. Dr. Verrick had said they'd scored exceptionally high in compatibility, so maybe that had allowed them to connect sooner than twenty-four hours after the surgery. *Trent?* she called.

The burst of emotion abruptly stopped.

But I was communicating with him! she thought jubilantly, and felt a massive rush of relief. She hadn't realized how much she'd let C.B.'s warnings that something would go wrong get to her. *I heard you,* she called happily to him. *Can you hear me?*

There was no response. *Of course not,* she thought. *I need to be sending him emotions, not words.* She closed her eyes and tried to transmit recognition and love and happiness.

Still nothing, and before she could try again, a nurse came in to take her vitals and ask the same litany of questions that the recovery room nurse had asked. "Any dizziness or nausea?"

"No."

The nurse wrapped a blood-pressure cuff around her arm. "Any confusion?"

"No. Are you sure . . . ?" Briddey began, but the nurse had already put the stethoscope in her ears.

She had to wait till after the nurse had helped her into her robe and walked her to the bathroom—an ordeal during which Briddey realized that she was dizzy after all—and helped her back into bed before she could ask, "Are you sure it takes twenty-four hours for the EED to work?"

"Yes," the nurse said, and told Briddey the same things the other nurse had told her about the edema and the anesthesia. "You've only been out of surgery for a few hours. Nothing's going to happen till at least tomorrow."

"But I thought I felt—"

"You were probably dreaming. The anesthetic can cause all sorts of strange dreams. I know you're eager to make contact with Mr. Worth, but you need to give your body a chance to recover first, and the best way to do that is to rest. Here's your call button." She showed Briddey where it was clipped to her pillow. "If you need anything, call."

I did, Briddey thought, *and Trent answered me. I felt it. I need to speak to him and find out if he felt it, too. I need to find out his room number.* But the nurse had already gone. Briddey fumbled for the call button. Before she could push it, though, the nurse returned with a huge bouquet of roses.

She showed Briddey the card from Trent. It read, "In just one more day we'll be inseparable!"

It may not take that long, Briddey thought, and asked the nurse, who was setting the roses in the window, "Which room is Mr. Worth in?"

"I'll check," she said, and came back a moment later to say, "He's still in recovery."

Of course. Briddey'd forgotten that he'd had his EED done after hers. "I need to talk to him," she said.

"He's not out of the anesthesia yet. You can talk to him later. Right now you need to rest," the nurse said firmly, and shut the overhead light off.

He must have come out of the anesthesia for a few minutes and then drifted off again, Briddey told herself, *and that's why he didn't answer the second time.*

She was feeling a little drowsy herself, as if she might doze off at any moment. *The nurse was right,* she thought. *I do still have a lot of anesthetic in . . .* and was asleep before she could complete the thought.

When she woke up again, it was to darkness. *What time is it?* she wondered, groping for her phone, and then remembered that she didn't have it—she was in the hospital. The darkness—and her mind feeling much clearer—told her she'd been asleep for hours, and that was confirmed by the late-night hush in the corridor outside. There were no footsteps, no nurses' voices, no intercom announcements. The entire floor was asleep.

But something had woken her. As before, she had the distinct feeling that she'd heard a voice. Trent would definitely be out of the anesthesia by now. Had he reached out to her? *Trent?* she called.

No response, and after a minute she heard a buzzer from somewhere down the hall and footsteps going toward it. Had she heard an actual sound—a door shutting or a patient calling for the nurse—and was that what had awakened her? And was it a sound like that, plus her imagination and the after-effects of the anesthestic, that had caused the first one, too?

But it had felt so real—and so different from what she'd imagined

Trent would be feeling. She'd expected delight that they'd connected but not relief. Trent had been completely confident about the EED. And there'd been other feelings in that explosion of emotion—surprise and uncertainty and amusement. And some other feeling, which had been suppressed so quickly she hadn't had time to identify it. But she was sure about the uncertainty and the surprise. *Were you secretly afraid it wouldn't work, like I was?* she called.

No answer.

She waited a long minute, listening in the darkness, and then called, *Are you there? Can you hear me?*

Yes.

I knew I heard him, she thought. And realized who the voice sounded like. *But it can't be him! And this can't be happening. The EED doesn't make you telepathic—*

Apparently it does, he said, and this time there was no question at all who the voice belonged to. She clapped her hand to her mouth, horrified.

I told you it could have unintended consequences, C.B. said.

Four

"I can call spirits from the vasty deep."
"Why, so can I, and so can any man;/But will they come
when you do call for them?"
—WILLIAM SHAKESPEARE, *Henry IV, Part I*

PLEASE TELL ME I'M DREAMING, BRIDDEY THOUGHT, BUT SHE KNEW SHE
wasn't. She could feel the sharp pull of the IV needle in the hand that
she'd clapped over her mouth, could hear the beep of the IV monitor
next to her bed.

And C.B.'s voice answering her, saying, *I'm afraid not, unless I'm
asleep, too. Which I'm not. Nope, I hate to tell you this, but we're really talking.*

"But how *can* we be?" Briddey said aloud.

That's what I want to know, C.B. said. *You ignored my warning, didn't
you? I guess it's a good thing I didn't warn you not to jump off a bridge, or
you'd have ignored that, too. You went ahead in spite of everything I said, and
had the IED—*

"It's *not* an IED!"

*Yeah, well, that's a matter of opinion. Where are you talking to me from?
The hospital?*

"Yes," she said. "Where are you?"

My lab. At Commspan, he said, and if that was true, then he was miles away. Which meant they were talking telepathically. Which was impossible.

Apparently not, C.B. said. *I told you having it was a terrible idea, that there could be UICs, but you didn't listen, and now here you are, connected to me instead of Trent.*

"I am *not* connected to you!"

Then what would you call this?

"I don't *know!* Dr. Verrick must have gotten a wire crossed when he—"

Brains don't have wires.

"A synapse, then, or a circuit or something."

It doesn't work like that, C.B. said.

"How do *you* know? You're not a brain surgeon. Dr. Verrick could have spliced the wrong synapses together, so that when I called to Trent, I got connected to you instead."

So I'm what—a wrong number? And speaking of Trent, where is he? And how come he didn't answer if you were calling him?

"I don't *know!*" she wailed. "Oh, how could this have happened?"

I warned you there could be unintended consequences.

"But not telepathy," she insisted. "It's not even a real thing!"

Yeah, well, about that, Briddey. There's something I need to tell you. His voice was so close it felt like he was standing at the end of the bed.

He is, she thought, suddenly convinced of it. He wasn't at Commspan. He'd sneaked in while she was asleep and was hiding somewhere here in her room, and this was all his warped idea of a practical joke.

Hiding? he said. *What are you talking about? Where?*

Under the bed, she thought. *Or behind the curtains.* But when she turned on the light above her bed, she saw that the curtains only reached to the bottom of the window, and the long dividing drape between the two beds was pushed all the way back against the wall, too narrow to conceal anyone.

He could still be down behind the other bed, or in the bathroom or the closet, she thought, though if he was, why had his voice sounded like it had been right next to her?

Exactly, C.B. said.

"You're throwing your voice," she said accusingly. "Like a ventrilo-quist."

He laughed. *A ventriloquist? You're kidding, right?*

"No," she said, and sat up. She swung her legs over the side to go look, but the sudden movement made the room lurch. She lay back down. "You'd better come out now," she said, fumbling for the call button clipped to her pillow, "or I'm calling the nurse."

I wouldn't do that if I were you. It's three o'clock in the morning, which means she's not going to be happy that you're awake, and she's going to be really unhappy when you tell her you're hearing voices. In the second place, she'll call Dr. Whatzisname, and he'll—

"What? Come in here and throw you out? Good," Briddey said, and pushed the call button. "I'd like to see that."

So would I, C.B. said, *especially since I'm all the way across town.*

"Well, if that's true, which I don't believe for one second, then he'll realize something's gone wrong, and he'll go back in and fix it."

Maybe. Or maybe he'll have you moved to the psych ward. And either way, he'll tell Trent.

Oh, my God, Trent. She hadn't thought how this would sound to him. She fumbled for the call button to see if she could turn it back off, but she was too late. The nurse was already there, and she *did* look annoyed. And was going to look even more put out if Briddey told her she didn't want anything, so she said, "I'm sorry I buzzed you. I had a nightmare. There was a man in my room. With a knife. In the bath-room," and thought, *What am I going to do if she doesn't go look?*

But she did, opening the bathroom door wide and switching on the light so Briddey could see inside, and then doing the same thing to the closet, which held only the hospital robe Briddey'd worn to the bathroom earlier. "See? Nobody there."

The nurse came back over to the bed. "Just a bad dream." She picked up Briddey's chart and began entering something. "Confusion's common after surgery. It's the anesthetic. It frequently causes strange dreams. Or you may have seen a nurse's aide or an orderly coming in. Do you need me to help you to the bathroom?"

Not now that I know he's not in there, Briddey thought, wondering if there was something she could drop so the nurse would have to look under the bed, but there was nothing within reach. "No, I'm fine," she said.

"Try to get some sleep," the nurse said, and switched off the light.

"Would you mind leaving that on?" Briddey asked, putting a quiver in her voice. "Or—could you check the rest of the room before you leave? Please? I know it was just a dream, but I'd sleep so much better if you would."

And if I'm asleep, I won't be pushing my call button and bothering you, she added silently, and the nurse must have come to the same conclusion because she turned the light back on and checked under both beds and in the far corner.

"See?" she said, coming back over to Briddey's bed. "Nothing there. Good night." She switched off the light again and went out, pulling the door almost all the way shut behind her.

"Thank you," Briddey called after her and then lay there, trying to make sense of what had happened. C.B. wasn't in her room. Was the nurse right? Had his voice been part of an anesthetic-induced dream?

That must be it, she thought, because C.B. hadn't spoken to her since the moment the nurse came into the room.

Nice theory, but no, C.B. said, and his voice was as clear and close as ever. *And what kind of nurse tells you to go to sleep when there could be a serial killer on the loose in the hospital? I wouldn't trust anything she says.*

How is he doing *this?* Briddey wondered, despairing.

He bugged my room, she thought. He had a mike and speakers hidden in here somewhere.

Bugged your room? C.B. said. *Are you crazy?*

No. It made perfect sense. That was why he hadn't said anything while the nurse was in the room, because the nurse would have heard him. And with a bug, he could hear if she was alone or not. Briddey sat up, switched the light on again, and began looking around the room for a concealed bug.

Briddey, I did not bug your room.

"Liar." It explained everything. How he'd known what the nurse was saying and—

I didn't hear what she was saying, he interrupted. *I heard you thinking about what she was saying. When you have a conversation, you not only think about what you're saying but what you're hearing. And when am I supposed to have done all this? I didn't even know you were having the surgery till a few minutes ago.*

"I don't know," she said, "but you did." He could have hidden the bug and the mike anywhere, on the lining of the curtains, on the windowsill, in the roses Trent had sent. She squinted at them, searching for telltale wires.

But there wouldn't necessarily *be* wires. C.B. could have rigged up some sort of wireless thing. He was a computer genius—

Thanks. I didn't think you'd noticed, he said dryly, and his voice wasn't coming from over by the window. It was right in her ear.

It's in my pillow, she thought, sitting up to feel for an unnatural lump. Nothing. She pulled off the pillowcase, shook it, and then felt down behind the head of the mattress.

It wasn't there. But it could be anywhere—and tiny. It could be on the wall panel above her bed. Or attached to the water jug or the chart or the Kleenex box, or—

I didn't bug your throw-up pan, C.B. said. *I—*

He abruptly stopped talking. *So I can't use his voice to find the bug,* Briddey thought, picking up the throw-up basin.

It wasn't there or on the water jug. And if it was on the wall panel, she'd never find it; it was covered with buttons and switches and inputs, any one of which could be a mike. The only way to prove he was bugging the room was to get out of it and go somewhere the mike didn't reach. She wished she'd asked the nurse which room they'd taken Trent to after recovery. She could go tell him what had happened, and he could find the mike. And have C.B. fired.

But she didn't know which room Trent was in, and buzzing the nurse again was a bad idea. So she'd have to settle for going down the hall far enough that she was out of range. She sat up, put her legs over the side, and sat there a moment to see whether the room was going to veer sideways again. When it didn't, she got carefully out of bed, using the IV-stand to steady herself.

Oh, no, what was she going to do about her IV? The stand had wheels. She could take it with her, but if that was where C.B. had concealed the mike, leaving her room wouldn't accomplish anything.

She'd have to pull out her IV. But what if the monitor beeped when she did and alerted the nurses? *I'll wait till after I get my robe and slippers on,* she thought, and walked over to the closet, pulling the IV-stand with her.

The thin cotton robe was there but not the slippers. *They must be under the bed,* she thought, checking the robe's neckband and ties for a bug and then struggling into it. She managed to get one arm through and the robe up over her shoulders, but the other arm would have to wait till she'd pulled out the IV. She worked her way back to the bed, trailing the robe awkwardly behind her, and bent over to try to see her slippers.

If she hadn't been hanging on to the IV-stand for support, she'd have passed out. As it was, the room banked sharply and then wavered, and she had to cling to the IV-pole till the wobbling stopped and then grope for the edge of the bed.

She sat down and took a steadying breath. There was no point in trying for her slippers again, because even if she did find them, she'd never be able to bend over for long enough to get them on. But she only had to go far enough down the hall to be out of reach of C.B.'s speakers.

I can do without slippers for that far, she thought, and tackled the problem of the IV-stand. She couldn't see an on/off switch, but there *was* a button near the top. She hit it gingerly, braced for the machine to begin beeping.

It didn't. The motor stopped, and the green light went off. *Good,* she thought, and ripped the surgical tape off the back of her hand to look at the place where the IV needle had been pushed under the skin.

This is crazy, some rational part of her brain told her. *You just had surgery. Yanking out your IV and wandering off could be dangerous.*

But that's exactly what C.B.'s counting on, she thought, *that I'm stuck where his sound system is,* and pulled the needle out.

It stung less than she'd expected, but it bled copiously. She pressed the surgical tape back in place to stop it, put her arm into the robe's sleeve, switched the light off so a nurse wouldn't come in to see why she was awake, and felt her way cautiously over to the door, hoping she wouldn't crash into something.

She didn't, but it took her forever to reach the door, and when she opened it, the sudden light from the hall dazzled her. She put her hand up to shield her eyes from the glare and looked cautiously out into the hall. No nurses or orderlies were in sight, and most of the doors were shut or nearly so, with no light showing from inside. She'd been right about it being the middle of the night.

She listened a moment and then started down the corridor, grateful for the railing along the wall. The corridor made a turn just after the next room. If she could just get past that . . .

She wished she had her slippers. The tile floor was freezing. And the back of her head, where they must have gone in for the surgery, felt strange. Not painful. *Not yet,* Briddey thought, and tried to go faster.

"Nurse Rossi," a voice said out of nowhere, and Briddey looked wildly around before realizing the voice had come from the intercom. "Please report to the nurses' station."

Briddey stopped, listening for responding footsteps, but she didn't hear any. Nurse Rossi must be in some other corridor. Briddey started along the hallway again. She hadn't expected walking just a few steps could take so much energy. And take so long. By the time she reached the turn, she felt as though she'd run a marathon.

It's okay, she thought, looking carefully around it. *You only have to go a little bit farther.* Just past the next room on the right was a waiting room with chairs and a sofa. If she could make it there, she could sit down.

But that meant crossing the hall. She wished she'd brought the IV-stand along to hang on to. She tottered across, grabbing onto the wall for support, and saw to her horror that the back of her hand was completely covered in blood.

The bandage hadn't held. She dabbed at the blood with the tail of her robe and then gave up. *You can stop the bleeding when you get to the waiting room,* she told herself. *Right now you've got to—*

Get to the waiting room? C.B.'s voice cut in. *Where are you? Why are you out of bed?*

Oh, God, she thought, looking up at the ceiling tiles. He'd bugged the corridor, too.

What are you doing in the corridor? he demanded, and his voice was just as loud and clear as it had been in the room. *You just had surgery—*

Go away! she said, looking desperately around. If he'd bugged the corridor, he'd have bugged the waiting room, too. *I'll have to go down to the lobby,* she thought.

Lobby? C.B. was shouting at her. *What the hell do you think you're doing?*

Going somewhere you haven't managed to bug, she said, stumbling past the waiting room door toward the rooms beyond it.

I told you, I didn't bug anything. Briddey, listen to me. You need to go back to your room—

And your bugs and speakers and microphones? No, thank you. There had to be an elevator around here somewhere that she could take down to the lobby.

Briddey, you've got no business running around the hospital in your condition. Jesus, if I'd known you'd react like this, I'd never have . . . You need to tell me where you are!

Why? So you can come bug that, too? she said, walking faster, determined to get out of range. But that made her dizzier, and the feeling at the back of her head went from tightness to pain.

A light blinked on above the door just ahead. That meant the patient inside had pressed the call button, and a nurse would be coming to answer it. She had to get out of here. But to where? She still couldn't see any sign of an elevator.

"Nurse!" a woman's voice called from the room, and Briddey heard footsteps coming from the direction she was headed.

I have to hide, she thought desperately, and hurried past the room the patient had called from toward the next one, trying to ignore the dizziness and C.B.'s voice in her ear, saying insistently, *Tell me where you are. Please.*

If she could just reach that next room, she could hide inside it till the nurse passed.

"Nurse!" the woman called again, and the intercom barked, "Dr. Black, please report to the nurses' station." The approaching footsteps speeded up to a run, and Briddey lurched over to the room's door.

It wasn't a patient room. A sign on the door read AUTHORIZED PERSONNEL ONLY, which meant it was probably a nurses' lounge. Or a storage closet. But she had to take that chance. She opened the door.

It was a stairway, leading down. Briddey slipped inside, pulled the heavy door almost closed, and then stood there keeping it from closing all the way, afraid the noise of its shutting would attract the approaching nurse's attention.

The nurse shot past the door and along the hall until she was out of sight. Briddey stood there a minute longer to make sure the nurse was out of earshot, listening to the voice on the intercom repeat, "Paging Dr. Black," and then let go of the door.

It closed, cutting off the sound of the intercom in mid-word, and she was glad she'd waited because the door made a loud clank as it shut. *Good,* Briddey thought. *That means I'll be able to hear anyone coming in. And I can take these stairs down to the lobby.*

She started down the stairs. It was even chillier in the stairwell than it had been in the corridor, and the cement steps were like ice to her bare feet. She had to grip the freezing-cold metal railing to keep from falling, and she was getting dizzier by the moment. There was no way she could make it all the way down to the lobby.

But you don't have to, she thought. Since the sound of the intercom had cut off as the door closed, the speakers C.B. had hidden in the hallway wouldn't reach down here. She tottered down the last few steps to the landing, and eased herself to sitting on the second step above it.

Mistake. Her thin hospital robe provided her no insulation from the cold of the cement, and she instantly began to shiver. *This had better work,* she thought.

She opened her mouth to call to him and then closed it firmly and shut her eyes. *C.B.?* she thought at him. *Can you hear me?*

No answer.

I knew it, she thought. *You are going to be so sorry you did this. I'm going to tell Trent, and he's going to—*

Briddey? C.B. said in her ear. *Thank God! Where are you? Are you all right?*

No, she thought. *No!*

I'm on my way to the hospital, he said. *I'll be there as soon as I can.*

Five

"Well, if I called the wrong number,
why did you answer the phone?"
—JAMES THURBER, *The Thurber Carnival*

WHERE ARE YOU? C.B. ASKED, HIS VOICE IMPOSSIBLY CLEAR, IMPOSSIBLY close. *Are you still in the hall?*

Briddey pressed her fingers hard against her ears to shut him out, knowing with a sick certainty that it wouldn't work.

Tell me, he begged. *Did you go down to the lobby?*

She buried her head in her hands and sat there in the icy stairwell thinking, *It's true. C.B.'s really inside my head. But how can he be? There's no such thing as—*

We'll worry about that later, C.B. said. *Right now you need to tell me where you are so I can get you back to your room.*

And she must have thought, *I can't make it back,* because he said, *That's okay. Don't cry. Just stay there. I'll take care of it.*

"I'm *not* crying," she said indignantly, but that was a lie. Tears were running down her cheeks. She swiped at them with the back of her hand.

Everything'll be okay, C.B. said. *I promise.*

How can it be? she thought. *I'm connected to C.B. Schwartz,* and started crying all over again.

The door above her banged open, and an orderly shouted, "Yes, she's here!" followed by a horde of medical personnel shouting orders and saying, "How the hell did she get all the way down here? Don't you people ever check on your patients?" and "My God, we'll be toast if Verrick finds out!"

Dr. Verrick! Oh, no, if he told Trent—

They bombarded her with questions—"Did you fall?" "Are you sure?" "Did you hit your head?"—and knelt beside her to check the back of her head and her bandages.

"You're positive you didn't stumble and hit your head?" one of the interns asked her, touching her cheek. His fingers came away smeared with blood.

That's from my wiping away the tears, she thought, and looked down at her hospital gown. It was bloody, too. "I didn't fall," she said. "That blood's from where I pulled out my IV." She showed them the back of her hand.

The intern took hold of it. "And why did you do that?"

"I don't know. I . . . ," she said, trying to think of a plausible reason, but he didn't really seem to expect one. He was already listening to her heart and ordering the nurse to start a new IV.

She did, swabbing the blood off the back of Briddey's hand, which only made it look worse. The skin was badly bruised. By the time the nurse had examined it, decided she needed to put the IV in the other hand, and gotten it started, Briddey was completely frozen, and her teeth were chattering.

"Go get her a blanket," the intern told a very young-looking nurse's aide. "And something for her feet." He turned back to Briddey. "Look right here," he said, pointing at a spot in the center of his forehead, and shone a light in each of her eyes in turn. "Do you know where you are?"

"Yes," she said. "In a stairway in the hospital."

"Do you remember how you got here?"

Yes, she thought, *I was trying to get away from the bug C.B. put in my room,* and waited for C.B. to protest.

But he didn't. And he hadn't come racing down the stairs, in spite of his saying he was on his way. He hadn't found her; the orderly had, and that could have been because her nurse had come in to check her IV and seen she was missing. In which case C.B.'s talking to her in the stairwell could still have been part of an anesthetic-induced dream.

Or something worse. What if during the surgery Dr. Verrick had cut a nerve he wasn't supposed to, and C.B.'s voice was the result of hemorrhaging or injured neurons or something? He'd tried to warn her about complications, but she hadn't listened, and now here she was with brain damage.

The intern was looking at her worriedly.

"Yes, I remember how I got here," she said, and knew instantly that she'd made a mistake. It meant she'd yanked out her IV and come down here on purpose, and his next question would be "Where were you going?"

"I mean, I remember getting out of bed . . . ," she said, "and then . . ." She frowned as if trying to recall. "I guess I must have gotten turned around looking for the bathroom and thought this was the door to my room . . ."

But the intern didn't look satisfied with her answer. "What was in the lobby?" he asked. "When your boyfriend called, he said you'd called him and mentioned something about the lobby, and he was afraid you might try to go down there."

The nurse nodded. "He said he was afraid you might have tried to take the stairs."

It isn't the anesthesia or brain damage, Briddey thought. *It's real. And so is telepathy.*

She supposed she should be relieved she wasn't brain-damaged or hemorrhaging, but this was even more of a nightmare. And if she let this line of questioning go on, her nurse was going to remember that she didn't have her phone and couldn't have called anyone. And that her boyfriend was here in the hospital, recovering from an EED, too, and phoneless, and then it *really* would be a nightmare.

"It's a good thing he told us to check the stairs," the nurse was saying, "because hardly anyone uses them. Why did you—?"

"I don't know," Briddey said, reaching unsteadily for the intern's arm. "Oh, dear, I guess I *am* feeling a little dizzy."

It did the trick. The intern stopped asking questions and started giving orders, and they got her up the stairs, into a wheelchair, and back to her room in record time. The floor nurse and the nurse's aide helped her into a clean hospital gown and then into bed.

She was still shivering. "I'm so cold," she murmured as the nurse smoothed the covers over her.

"No wonder," the nurse said. "It was like a freezer in that stairway." She hung the new IV bag on the stand. "As soon as we finish here, I'll get you another blanket."

"You're lucky your boyfriend called," the nurse's aide said. "You could have been down there for ages. We didn't even know you weren't in your room."

The nurse glared at her. "Go get a blanket," she said sternly.

The aide scuttled out. As soon as she was gone, Briddey said, "You don't have to tell Dr. Verrick about this, do you? I was dopey from the anesthetic, and I got confused—"

"That's what your boyfriend said when he called," the aide said, reappearing in the doorway, sans blanket. "He was *so* upset. He said if we didn't find you immediately, he was going to tear the hospital apart."

"I thought I told you to go get a blanket," the nurse said.

"I don't know where they are."

"They're in—never mind, I'll show you in a minute." She reached for Briddey's chart.

If she looks at it, she'll see I had an EED and realize my boyfriend must have had one, too. "Could you get me that blanket now?" Briddey asked plaintively. "I'm so *cold.*"

"Right away," the nurse said. "Now, your call button's right there." She clipped it to the sheet by Briddey's hand. "Call if you need *anything.* You promise you won't run off again while I'm gone?"

There's nowhere to go, Briddey thought hopelessly. *Wherever I go, he'll be there, inside my head.* "I'll stay put," she said. "I promise."

"Good," the nurse said, and went out, but seconds later a student nurse came in, ostensibly to refill Briddey's water jug but obviously to check on her, and a minute later a different intern came in to ask her the same questions the first intern had, followed by an orderly with a mop.

But no nurse's aide with a blanket, and her teeth were starting to chatter again. "Could I get a blanket?" she asked the orderly.

"I'll tell your nurse to bring you one," he promised and went out.

I thought they'd never leave, C.B. said. *Are you okay?*

"Yes, no thanks to you," she said, and then glanced anxiously at the door. If someone came in and caught her talking to herself, they'd definitely call Dr. Verrick. *Go away,* she said silently. *You've caused enough trouble.*

Look, Briddey, I'm really sorry. If I'd known my talking to you would spook you into taking off, I'd never have—

Gotten an EED?

What? C.B. said blankly.

It's the only explanation. When did you have it done? Right after you found out Trent and I were going to do it?

What? Why the hell would I have an EED? I was the one who tried to talk you out of it, remember?

That could have been a trick to throw me off. So I wouldn't realize you were getting one, too.

Oh, right, he said sarcastically. *I thought, Having a hole drilled in your head so you can exchange warm fuzzies is a great idea! I think I'll get one, too.*

"No," she said, speaking aloud in her anger. "To keep me from—"

The student nurse who'd filled her water jug popped her head in the door. "Did you need something?" she asked.

She must have been stationed outside my door the whole time to stop me from bolting again, Briddey thought.

Which is an excellent idea, C.B. said, *since you clearly can't be trusted to take care of yourself.*

And there went the last shred of hope that it was a bug, because the student nurse gave no sign that she'd heard C.B. at all. She was looking at Briddey with concern. "Are you all right?"

No, Briddey thought. "Yes," she said. "I was trying to find my call button. Can you find out what happened to the extra blanket they were supposed to bring me?"

"Oh, sure," the student nurse said, and disappeared.

Nice save, C.B. said the moment she was gone, *but from now on you probably shouldn't talk to me out loud.*

I don't intend to talk to you at all, she said. *I can't believe you did that.*

Let me get this straight, he said. *You think I found out about you and Trent having the EED and decided to steal a march on him? How exactly am*

I supposed to have done that when Dr. Whatzisname's got a waiting list as long as my arm? And when? I saw you this morning at Commspan.

You could have raced over here and paid some patient to let you go first, or . . . A·horrible thought struck her. What if he'd told the doctor *he* was Trent? That would explain why she couldn't hear Trent, because he'd never had the EED at all, and C.B. was talking to her not from Commspan but from right here in the—

Are you kidding? C.B. said. *Hospitals are really big on making sure they're operating on the right body part, let alone the right person. Or do you think I stole his ID, too, and tied him up in my lab, all so I could have a surgery I told you was a terrible idea? And, anyway, aren't you forgetting something? Doesn't a couple have to be emotionally bonded for the EED to work?*

If you're trying to say we're emotionally bonded—

I'm saying, according to what you told me about the EED, it wouldn't have done any good for me to get one unless—

Shh, she said. *She's coming back with my blanket.*

She can't hear me, remember? Or you. Unless you forget and start talking out loud again.

It wasn't the student nurse. It was the resident on duty, accompanied by yet another nurse. "I understand you took a little hike tonight," the resident said jovially, looking at her chart. "Any ill effects?"

Yes, C.B. said. *A huge persecution complex.*

Shut up. "No," she said to the resident.

"No more dizziness?" the resident asked, and took her through the litany of questions again. "Double vision? Headache?"

Making ridiculous accusations? C.B. said.

Go away.

The resident and the nurse were looking at her curiously. *Oh, God,* she thought. *Did I say that out loud?*

No, C.B. said.

Then they must have asked her a question. Which she hadn't heard because C.B. was talking to her. "Sorry, what?" she asked the resident.

"I said, have you experienced any unusual sensations? Tingling? Numbness?"

"No." Numbness would mean they were worried about pressure on a nerve. Could the edema they'd talked about be pressing on something and causing the problem? Or could it be pushing two pathways together? Adjoining electronic circuits often crossed over each other, causing interference with the signal, so that you got a different channel or radio station than the one you were tuned into. Maybe the brain's circuits operated the same way, and C.B.'s voice was some kind of resulting crosstalk.

"What about blurred vision?" the resident was asking.

"No."

He scrolled through her chart, checked her bandage, and then said, "All right, try to get some sleep. And no more moonlight strolls. If you need the bathroom, use your call button." He started out of the room.

The nurse, who up till now had stood there silently, asked, "Is there anything I can get you?"

"Yes," Briddey said. "A blanket. I'm freezing."

Uh-oh, C.B. said. *I don't think you should have said that.*

He was right. The nurse and the resident exchanged worried looks, and the resident came back over to the bed. "Have you been having chills?" he asked sharply.

"No. It was just cold in the stairway, and I—"

They didn't buy it. The resident insisted on listening to her lungs, and it was obvious from his questions that he thought she'd contracted pneumonia. Briddey had to convince him that she didn't need her lungs X-rayed, wasn't having difficulty breathing, had no intention of even getting out of bed again, let alone wandering off barefoot, and there was *no* reason to report any of this to Dr. Verrick.

Finally, after listening to her lungs one more time, the resident departed, and the nurse said, "I'll tell your nurse to bring you a blanket," and left, too.

Briddey expected C.B. to immediately start up again, but he didn't. The nurse didn't bring the blanket either. After ten minutes Briddey decided they'd forgotten, and in spite of the uproar it would cause if they caught her out of bed, she was about to go fetch her robe from the closet when she heard the nurse coming. Thank heavens. Much longer, and she *would* have contracted pneumonia.

Only it wasn't the nurse. It was C.B. She recognized the shaggy outline of his hair in the light from the corridor. "What are you doing here?" she said. "Go away."

"I can't," he whispered, shutting the door. "There's an orderly out there mopping the corridor. He nearly caught me as it was. You wouldn't want him to tell Trent he saw a strange man coming out of your room in the middle of the night, would you?"

She sat up. "Why—?"

"Shh," C.B. said, putting a finger to his lips. "He's right outside." He tiptoed over to the door and listened for a minute. "Okay, he's moved down toward the nurses' station." He pulled the door shut and came over to the foot of the bed.

Briddey switched on the light. He looked even scruffier and more thrown together than he had at Commspan, his dark hair a tangled mess. His T-shirt and sweat pants were badly wrinkled, as if he'd snatched them from that pile on the sofa in his lab, and the hood of his jacket was half caught inside the neck. "Why are you here?" she whispered.

"I wanted to make sure you were okay," he said. "Sorry it took me so long. When I got here, they'd already brought you back to your room and there were a bunch of people around, so I waited till they'd left, and then I had trouble sneaking past the nurses' station. *Are* you okay?"

"I'm fine," she whispered, frowning. He was talking to her. Out loud. Her heart lifted. It had been a dream after all.

Afraid not, C.B. said. *And no, I'm not a ventriloquist.* He pointed at her water jug. *If you want proof, I can drink a glass of water and talk at the same time. No, wait, ventriloquists can do that, so it wouldn't prove anything, would it?*

"No," she said, but it did because he was just standing there, looking worriedly at her and not saying a word, and she could hear him perfectly.

Here, he said, and sat down on the bed beside her.

She shrank away from him. "What do you think you're—?"

Shh. The orderly, remember? He turned his head away and pulled his hair up away from his neck. *No shaved patch, no stitches, no scar.*

"Show me the other side."

It can't be on the other side. The area of the brain the EED—

"Show me."

Fine, he said, and turned his head, lifting his hair on the other side. There wasn't a shaved patch there either.

He stood up. *Now do you believe me? I didn't have a rush-job EED, I didn't bug your room, and I didn't drop a two-way radio into your brain while Dr. Whatzisname wasn't looking. I was just sitting in my lab, minding my own business, when you started talking to me.*

"I wasn't talking to you. I was talking to Trent."

Well, you should have been more specific. All I heard—

"And stop doing that. It's creepy. Talk out loud."

"Fine," he said in a low voice after glancing toward the corridor. "All I heard was you asking, 'Are you there?' and I was, so I answered you."

"But you weren't *supposed* to be there. And what are you doing here now? I thought you said you hated hospitals."

"I do," he said, "and you're Exhibit A of why. They lose track of patients, they try to freeze them to death." He looked around. "Jesus, this room's even colder than my lab."

"The nurse who was just in here is bringing me a blanket."

"Wanna bet? She was the hot little brunette, right?" Briddey didn't dignify that with an answer. "She went off duty fifteen minutes ago. And the rest of the staff have spent the last twenty minutes having a confab at the nurses' station, trying to decide whether to call Dr. Whatzisname—"

"Dr. *Verrick*."

"—about your little escapade."

"What did they decide?"

"I don't know. They were still at it when I came in here, but it seemed to be split fifty-fifty between waiting till morning and not telling him at all."

Please let it be the latter, she thought. But if they were all at the nurses' station, she'd never get her blanket. And she must have accidentally voiced that thought because C.B. immediately took off his jacket and draped it over her shoulders. "Here," he said. "Better?"

"Yes." She reached to pull it around her.

"Jesus, what's that?" he said, staring at her hand. "It's all bruised." He grabbed it up. "I thought you told me you were okay."

"I *am* okay," she said, snatching her hand back. "It's nothing."

"That happened when you pulled out your IV, didn't it?"

"No," she said. "The nurse had trouble getting it started. She had to make several tries."

"Lying doesn't work when you're telepathic," he said. "I can read your mind, remember? Look, Briddey, I'm really sorry. I didn't mean to scare you, and certainly not so badly that you'd do something like this. I mean, I know suddenly finding yourself able to talk mind-to-mind with somebody's kind of a surprise—"

"A *surprise*?" she said, her voice rising. "A *sur*—"

"Shh. They'll hear you."

"I *want* them to hear me. I want them to call Dr. Verrick and tell him something went wrong so he can—"

"What? Drill another hole in your head?"

"No, *fix* this. Uncross our circuits and get rid of the crosstalk—"

"This isn't crosstalk," C.B. said. "It doesn't work like that. Although . . . ," he said. He frowned.

"So you're admitting it *could* be crosstalk," she said. "And if it is, Dr. Verrick can uncross the circuits or unsplice the synapse and hook it to the right one or something." She reached for the call button.

"No, don't do that," he said.

"Why not?"

"Because, as you told me yourself, people don't believe telepathy exists, and even if it did, the EED doesn't *make* people telepathic. So let's say you tell him you're hearing my voice in your head. Either he's going to transfer you to the psych ward or he's going to say, 'But for a connection like that to happen, there's got to be emotional bondage—'"

"Bonding!"

"Whatever. He's going to say, 'If you're hearing Mr. Schwartz, then that must mean you two are—'"

"He will not," she said. "I'll explain what happened—"

"Which is what? You called your boyfriend and somebody else answered? Forget Verrick. How's that explanation going to fly with Trent?"

C.B. was right. If she told Trent she'd connected to someone else— and C.B., of all people—

"Thank you very much," C.B. said.

You weren't supposed to hear that.

"I know. Which is why telepathy's a terrible idea."

"I just meant—"

"I know exactly what you meant. I can read your mind, remember? It's okay. I am well aware of what a comedown I am from the rising young executive and his Porsche. Still, it could have been worse. Think of all the sleazeballs and perverts and people who think they've been abducted by aliens out there. You could've ended up being connected to one of them. Or to a knife-wielding serial killer like the one you lied to the nurse about. Or a religious nut who believes the world's going to end next Tuesday."

The world's already ended, she thought.

"Not even close," he muttered.

"What's *that* supposed to mean?"

"Nothing. You were saying?"

"You were right. I can't tell Trent," she said. "Not until I've figured out what's causing this and how to remedy it. And you can't tell him either. Or anybody else at Commspan."

"I won't. I don't particularly want anybody finding out about this either. Half of Commspan already thinks I'm psycho. I don't want to give them any more ammunition." He looked down at her. "You haven't told anybody else about this, have you? Your nurse? Or the people who brought you back to your room?"

"No—"

"Good. Don't. And I think I'd better go before somebody sees me." He started toward the door and then came back over to the bed. "My jacket," he reminded her, taking it from around her shoulders. "You don't want Trent asking you where you got it."

"You're right," she said, even though she'd just begun to warm up. "Thank you for—" But he was already gone.

C.B.? she called silently, but he didn't answer.

At least I don't have to worry about him telling Trent, she thought, hugging her arms to herself. He wanted to keep this a secret as much as she did. There'd been genuine relief in his voice when she'd said she hadn't told anyone.

Why? she wondered. In spite of what he'd said, she couldn't imagine him caring whether people thought he was crazy. And he hardly seemed the type to have a girlfriend . . .

Footsteps were coming down the corridor. She hastily turned off the light, lay down, closed her eyes, made her breathing shallow and even so they'd think she was asleep, and waited for the nurse or the aide or whoever it was to turn on the light.

They didn't. They came into the room and straight over to the bed. "Turn back your covers," C.B. whispered, and reached to uncover her himself.

"What do you think you're *doing*?" she whispered furiously, grabbing for the covers and pulling them protectively up to her neck. "I don't know what you're thinking, but—"

"I'm *thinking* I brought you a blanket," he said. "And I'm *thinking* I heated it up in the microwave, so it needs to be next to your body."

"Oh," she said. She pulled the tail of her hospital gown down to cover her legs and then pushed back the covers, and he spread the blanket over her.

It was wonderfully warm. She stopped shivering the second it touched her. "*Thank* you," she said.

"You're welcome," he said, pulling the rest of the covers over her. "In spite of the fact that you thought I was trying to attack you."

"I didn't—"

"Yes, you did. I can read your mind, remember?"

"How can I forget?" she said bitterly. "Do you think there's a chance this . . . ?"

She stopped. He was looking toward the door, his head angled to one side as if he'd heard something. "Is someone coming?" she whispered.

"No, but I'd better go before they do. Listen, we'll talk about this in the morning and figure out what to do," he whispered, and after another quick look in both directions, slid out the door. *In the meantime, you get some sleep,* he said. *And no more running around.*

I won't, she thought drowsily, snuggling into the warmth of the blanket. *I plan to stay under here forever.* And *It really was nice of him to get it for me. He's not so bad.*

Exactly what I've been trying to tell you, C.B. said out of nowhere. *Like I said before, you could have done a lot worse. You could've connected with somebody who didn't know where the blankets were.*

Or where the microwave was, she thought, burrowing deeper into the blanket's warmth. *Now go away. You said for me to get some sleep, but how can I with you yammering at me?*

You're right, he said. *Good night. See—I mean, hear—you in the morning.*

Oh, I hope not, Briddey thought, and then worried he'd heard that, too. But he didn't answer, and she thought she detected a difference in the silence, as if he'd gone away.

If only she could make him go away for good. And what was she going to do if she couldn't? If she told Trent, he'd think she was in love with C.B. But if she lied and said she wasn't picking up anything, Trent would think the EED hadn't worked.

Though Trent wouldn't be expecting them to connect till twenty-four hours after the EED, so at least she had a little time to figure something out. But twenty-four hours from when? The time her surgery—or Trent's—ended? Or the time they came out of the anesthesia? Her surgery had been scheduled for one, and Dr. Verrick had said it took an hour, so two o'clock tomorrow afternoon was the earliest the twenty-four-hour mark could be.

Which means you've got till then to think of something to tell Trent and till rounds tomorrow morning to decide whether to tell Dr. Verrick. Because it was obvious the nurses had decided not to wake the doctor up and get him out of bed at this hour, or he would have been here already.

And maybe by morning this will all be fixed, she thought. *The edema will have gone down, and C.B.'s voice will have disappeared.* And even if that didn't happen, the blanket was wonderfully warm, and things were bound to seem less hopeless in the light of day. *If I can just get some sleep and C.B. doesn't interrupt me again,* she thought drowsily, and heard footsteps.

They were coming straight toward her room. *Go away, C.B.,* she said, but it wasn't him.

It was Dr. Verrick. "Hello, Ms. Flannigan," he said. "Now, suppose you tell me what's been going on."

Six

"It is always the best policy to speak the truth, unless, of course,
you are an exceptionally good liar."
—Jerome K. Jerome, *The Idlers' Club*

"Dr. Verrick!" Briddey said, scrambling up to a sitting position and then remembering she was supposed to move the bed up instead, which was good. She had nearly blurted out, "What are you doing here?" Finding the controls and maneuvering the bed up to the proper angle gave her time to change it to "I didn't think you'd still be here so late."

He looked at her sharply and then smiled. "Not late. Early. I have a pair of EEDs scheduled for six. A surgeon's day begins at the crack of dawn, you know."

But it's not the crack of dawn. It's the middle of the night. Or was it? She wished she had her phone so she could see what time it was. It was impossible to tell from Dr. Verrick's appearance. He looked as impeccable as he had yesterday.

"How are you feeling?" he asked.

That's a difficult question, she thought. If he didn't know about her running off she should just say, "Fine." But if he did, she needed to give him some kind of explanation—

No, you don't, C.B. said. *Rule Number Two of Lying is "Never say any more than you absolutely have to."*

Shut up. "I still feel sort of drowsy," she said to the doctor. "And . . . um . . ."

Dr. Verrick leaned forward expectantly.

"Drugged," she said carefully. "A little disoriented."

"That's to be expected," Dr. Verrick said. "It's a common after-effect of the anesthetic." He picked up the laptop to look at her chart. Which very probably contained a notation on her having run off.

"Have you seen Trent yet?" she asked to divert him from it. "How's he doing?"

Dr. Verrick gave her an even sharper look, and she felt a jolt of apprehension. What if something had happened to Trent? That would explain why he hadn't answered when she'd called to him—and what Dr. Verrick was doing here in the middle of the night. Everything C.B. had said to her about brain damage and ending up a vegetable came flooding back to her. "Is Trent all right?" she asked anxiously.

"Yes, of course," Dr. Verrick said, and the surprise in his voice sounded reassuringly genuine. "I saw him just after he came out of the recovery room, and he was doing very well. Now let's see how *you're* doing." He pulled a stethoscope out of his coat pocket, listened to her heart and lungs, took her pulse, and then had her lean forward. "Any discomfort?" he said, pressing lightly all around the incision.

She shook her head.

"Good," he said. "It looks fine. There's a little edema, but that's normal. Any dizziness?"

"No."

"Nausea?" he asked, taking her through the by-now-familiar litany. "Numbness? Tingling?"

She answered no to all of them.

"Nurse Jordan reported you experienced some confusion when you got out of bed to use the bathroom."

I knew it. They told him.

"She said you went wandering off down the hall," Dr. Verrick said. "What happened exactly?"

That depends on what my nurse said. Had she told him about her pulling out her IV and being found in the stairway or just that she'd wandered off? *C.B.'s wrong that being able to read minds is a terrible idea. Right now it would really be helpful.*

"I don't remember exactly." She frowned as if trying to reconstruct her actions. "I remember getting out of bed . . . and somehow I ended up out in the hall . . ."

"Where were you going?" Dr. Verrick asked. "Were you trying to get to Mr. Worth?"

Why didn't I think of that? Briddey wondered. It would have made the perfect excuse. She'd been worried about Trent and, in her drugged state, tried to go find his room. She wondered if she could still get away with it.

No, C.B. said inside her head. *Don't try it. The First Rule of Lying is to stick to one story.*

Go away, she said.

I'm just trying to help. Not being able to keep their stories straight is what always trips liars up. They tell one person one thing, and another something else—

Shh, she said, but he was right. She'd already told them she'd gotten lost looking for the bathroom. And Dr. Verrick was looking at her curiously. "No," she said. "When I realized I was in the corridor, I tried to get back to my room, but I must have gotten turned around somehow and was going the wrong way."

"And that's what you were trying to do when you went down the stairs—find your way back to your room?"

"Yes. I know it isn't logical. It was like a dream, where what you're doing makes sense at the time, but it doesn't really." Which accounted for her having been in the stairway, but what if they'd told him about the hospital's getting a phone call telling them where she was and saying she was trying to get down to the lobby? How was she supposed to explain that?

You don't, C.B. said. *You plead ignorance. But I doubt if the nurses told him. It would make them look too incompetent.*

Let's hope you're right.

Dr. Verrick was frowning at her again. "The stairway's a considerable distance from your room for merely getting turned around," he said. "Are you certain you weren't running away from something?"

"Running away?" she echoed, hoping Dr. Verrick wouldn't suddenly decide to listen to her heart, which was going a mile a minute.

"Yes." Dr. Verrick looked at her chart. "You told one of the nurses you thought a man with a knife was hiding in your room."

"Oh, that," she said, trying to keep the relief out of her voice. "I had a dream, that's all. I was still pretty groggy."

Dr. Verrick didn't look convinced. "A patient's initial experience of contact with the partner's emotions can be a shock, and the first reaction is often to flee."

Or to accuse him of bugging their room, C.B. said. *Or of being a ventriloquist.*

Briddey ignored him. "Initial contact?" she asked Dr. Verrick. "I thought it took at least twenty-four hours after the surgery for the first contact to occur."

"It actually takes longer than that—twenty-four hours after the patient comes out of the anesthesia."

Oh, good, Briddey thought. *Then I have till three o'clock tomorrow afternoon to connect with Trent.*

"But before that occurs, there can be fleeting, fragmentary contact, and the time for that varies considerably, dependent upon the patient's sensitivity and the intensity of the emotional attachment. I've had patients experience momentary contact as early as twelve hours after surgery, which is what might have happened to you." He checked the chart. "Yes, you reported the man with the knife just after the twelve-hour mark." Which still didn't account for her having heard C.B. right after she came out of the anesthetic.

Not necessarily, C.B. said. *You heard the man. It depends on the intensity of the emotional attachment.*

Shut up.

"Those initial, sporadic contacts may be felt by only one of the partners," Dr. Verrick was saying, "and they can take a variety of forms—a momentary awareness of your partner's presence or a feeling of being touched or a sense of happiness. Or more negative sensations. Fear or a prickling of the spine or a sense of being intruded on. Could you have been experiencing something like that?"

Absolutely, Briddey thought.

But the things Dr. Verrick was saying made her think that maybe she should tell him after all. He'd clearly had patients describe experiencing all sorts of unusual sensations after the EED, so hearing a voice wouldn't be that much of a stretch. And if she told him, he might be able to tell her what had caused the misconnection and fix it.

And tell Trent, C.B. said.

No, he won't, she said. *He can't. He's a doctor. Physician-patient confidentiality means he can't tell anyone else what we've talked about.*

But it won't stop him from asking Trent a bunch of questions, which are bound to raise his suspicions. And even if they don't, how do you plan to explain to Trent your having a second surgery?

He was right. Trent would demand to know what was going on.

"I'd like you to tell me exactly what you experienced," Dr. Verrick was saying. "What did this man look like?"

"He was big and hulking," Briddey said. "With a bushy beard and a tattoo of a rattlesnake on his arm."

Good girl, C.B. said.

"And messy hair."

Dr. Verrick looked up alertly. "Was it someone you recognized?"

Now look what you've done, Briddey said. *He's suspicious.*

And whose fault is that?

Yours. Shut up, or he's going to figure out that I'm talking to someone.

Have it your way, C.B. said. *'Bye.*

Dr. Verrick was looking expectantly at her. "You *did* recognize him, didn't you?"

"Recognize him? No ..." She bit her lip and frowned. "Wait. Now that I think about it, there was a man with wild hair like that in a movie I saw last week. He was a stalker who ..." She gasped. "Oh, my gosh, I just realized that must be where the dream came from, that movie. Even the knife was the same."

"That does sound to me like a post-surgical dream rather than an instance of contact," Dr. Verrick said.

Thank goodness.

"And you haven't experienced any of the other sensations I've described? A presence, an alien emotion, a feeling of invasion?"

"No, none of those."

And she must have sounded convincing, because he nodded and said, "Everything else looks good. I want to run a couple of tests, just to make sure, but you should be able to go home today. And in the meantime, I want you to work on establishing a connection to your partner."

I'd like nothing better. "How do I do that?"

"By visualizing him and reaching out to him emotionally. The EED has created the potential for a neural pathway for the feelings between you, but you'll need to make it. You do that by speaking to him. Say: 'Are you there? I love you!' And call his name to direct your emotion to him."

Why didn't you tell me that before? If I'd known I was supposed to call his name, none of this would have happened. "You said a pathway. You mean like a path through a forest?" she asked, imagining a faint woodland trail that became clearer and easier to follow each time you traveled it.

"No," Dr. Verrick said. "It's more of a feedback loop. Each signal you send will be reinforced by the one he sends back to you, exponentially strengthening the connection with each circuit till it becomes permanent and exclusive."

Which means I had no business talking to C.B. like I did, Briddey thought.

"Keep sending whether you receive a response or not," Dr. Verrick instructed. "They're often too faint to detect at first." He shut the laptop. "Do you have any questions?"

Yes, she thought. *But I can't ask you any of them.* "No," she said.

"If you think of anything, or if you experience something which you think might be contact but you're not certain, feel free to call me. Here's my number," he said, and handed her a card. "I'll put a rush on those tests so we can get you home."

He left, and she leaned back against the pillow, exhausted. *Thank goodness that's over,* she thought, and he came back in.

Her heart began to pound, but he'd only returned to tell her he'd scheduled the tests and that she was to use her call button if she needed to get out of bed. "And I want you to rest," he said. "Your body needs time and assistance to heal. The best thing you can do is get lots of sleep."

No, the best thing I can do is establish a feedback loop between me and Trent, she thought. *And stop reinforcing the one I have with C.B.* She needed to connect to Trent and send signals along that pathway till it was stronger than the one she had to C.B., and her connection to him withered away.

It doesn't work like that, C.B. said.

How do you know? she retorted, and then remembered she shouldn't be reinforcing their connection and said it aloud.

Because Verrick was wrong about the whole "time to establish neural pathways" and "initial contact being fragmentary and sporadic" thing, C.B. said. *You and I've been able to talk perfectly since the minute we made contact, and it wasn't any twenty-four hours after surgery. So why would he be right about this?*

"Because he's an expert. He's done hundreds of EEDs, and he knows a lot more about brain function than you."

Yeah, well, that's a matter of opinion. In the first place, neural activity—

"I don't care. I'm not talking to you," she said, wishing there was a way to hang up on him.

See, I told you, telepathy's a terrible idea.

"Go. Away." She turned determinedly onto her side. *Trent, I love you,* she said into her pillow. *Are you there? Come in, Trent.*

It doesn't work like that either. You're not fighter pilots: Night Fighter, calling Red Baron. Come in, Red Baron, he mimicked. *Zeroes at twelve o'clock. Roger that, over and—*

"Out," she said. "I mean it."

I was just kidding. Listen, Briddey—

"No. Go away and don't talk to me again."

Fine. But before I do, you need to know—

"No. There's nothing you can tell me that I'd be remotely interested in hearing."

She snatched up her pillow, wishing she could throw it at him, and pressed it tightly to her ears. *Trent!* she called. *I need to make contact with you. Now! Where are you?* And, in spite of C.B.'s having mocked her: *Calling Trent. Come in, Trent. Over.*

Nothing, not even a flicker, and certainly not a sense of happiness, unaccountable or otherwise.

It hasn't been twenty-four hours yet, she told herself, and sat up to look at the panel behind her bed, hoping there was a clock on it somewhere, but there wasn't. She wished she'd asked Dr. Verrick if she could have her phone back so she'd know what time it was—and so she could text Trent and ask if he'd felt anything.

She debated asking the nurse for it, but in spite of Dr. Verrick's claim that he'd been here for his morning surgeries, the floor still had that middle-of-the-night feel, and after what had happened earlier, she didn't want to draw any more attention to herself. *You could ask C.B. what time it is,* she mused. *He's got a wristwatch.*

But you aren't supposed to be talking to him, she thought. *You'll just have to wait till the nurse comes in.* And in the meantime focus on forging her pathway. *Trent, can you hear me? I love you,* she called over and over, listening intently for any sign of contact.

She didn't hear anything—not Trent's voice or anyone else's, not even an announcement over the intercom—for what seemed like hours. And then she must've dozed off again, because the floor was suddenly full of noise—voices, wheels, the clatter of equipment and trays, and a heavenly smell of coffee. Which meant it was breakfast time, and someone was bound to be in soon.

But no one appeared. Not even C.B. *Maybe his voice* was *a side effect of the edema,* she thought, gingerly feeling the bandage at the back of her neck to see if the swelling had gone down. Or maybe all of her calling to Trent had corrected the problem. In which case she needed to do it some more while she waited for someone to bring her breakfast.

No one did. What felt like hours went by before anyone came in, and then it wasn't a nurse, it was a lab technician there to draw blood. "Is this one of the tests Dr. Verrick ordered?" Briddey asked him.

"Yes," he said, checking her ID bracelet against the order.

"Do you know what other tests I'm supposed to have?"

"No. You'll have to ask your nurse."

"Oh. Can you tell me what time it is?"

He twisted his latex-gloved wrist around to look at his watch. "Seven-oh-eight."

Good. She still had eight hours to connect with Trent before he started wondering what was wrong. If she could make contact with him before then . . .

"Small poke," the tech said, and stuck her finger.

Or if Trent could make contact with her. Dr. Verrick had said the initial contact might be one-way.

Maybe Trent's already connected with me, she thought. If he had, he'd have texted her. She needed her phone. "Would it be possible for me to have my phone?" she asked the lab tech.

"I'll check," he said.

"And can you find out if I'm supposed to get breakfast? I haven't had anything to eat since my surgery yesterday."

"I'll check on that, too," the tech said, stripping off his gloves and throwing them away. He started to wheel the cart out and then stopped. "You're not going to take off while I'm gone, are you?"

Which meant the hospital had as efficient a grapevine as Commspan, and everyone on this floor already knew about last night. *I hope that doesn't mean Trent does.*

"No, of course I'm not going to," she said.

"I'll be right back," the tech said.

He wasn't, but he'd apparently relayed her request to the on-duty nurse, who came in and said, "We'll get your phone for you. Is there anything else you need?"

"Yes," Briddey said. "I had a question. I understand the EED connection sometimes doesn't last—"

"That won't happen to you," the nurse reassured her. "You haven't even—"

"I know, but if it did wear off, how long would that take?"

"I've only ever heard of it happening once, and that was after four months."

Which was not soon enough to help.

"And that wasn't a patient of Dr. Verrick's," the nurse said. "Don't worry. That won't happen to you. And yes, you can have breakfast, but not until after your tests."

Then I hope they do them soon, she thought. *I'm starving.*

But no one entered her room for what seemed like another hour, and then it was only an orderly to mop the bathroom.

That's another reason I hate hospitals, C.B. said. *When you need them, they don't come, but when you just want to be left alone, they're all over you, jabbing you with needles, sucking your blood, waking you up to give you sleeping pills—*

"Go away," Briddey said. "I'm trying to connect to Trent."

So I take it that means you haven't? Your "Night Fighter calling Red Baron" routine didn't work?

"Not yet," she said stiffly, "but it will. If you'll stop talking to me."

Don't you even want to hear what I found out about this telepathy thing? I've been up all night doing research.

"What did you find out?"

That you were right, there's no such thing as telepathy. At least according to Wikipedia, which as we know is always accurate. It said there's no scientific proof that direct mind-to-mind communication exists.

When will I ever learn? Briddey wondered. "Go away."

There's such a thing as hearing voices, however, C.B. went on, *and that can be caused by temporal-lobe damage, brain tumors, sleep deprivation, hallucinogenic drugs, tinnitus, or insanity. And speaking of insanity, they did a study where they had people with no history of mental illness tell doctors they were hearing voices—no other symptoms—and they were all immediately diagnosed as schizophrenic and hospitalized. Which is no surprise, considering the main cause of auditory hallucinations—Wikipedia's name for it, not mine—is schizophrenia.*

But this isn't a hallucination.

That's what all the schizophrenics say. Including Joan of Arc, who several modern psychiatrists have decided after the fact had schizophrenia.

"But don't schizophrenics hear horrible voices, telling them to harm themselves and kill people?"

Usually, though Joan didn't. Her voice told her to save France, and she seemed to have been on quite friendly terms with it.

"But that's different," Briddey said. "She thought she was talking to God."

Nope, an angel, C.B. said. *Not God.*

"My *point* is, her voices weren't real."

Joan thought they were. She talked about them quite matter-of-factly, and her guards testified that they heard her having perfectly sane-sounding conversations in her cell, speaking and answering exactly if someone was there. Which didn't stop the psychiatrists from declaring her nuts. So it's a good thing you didn't say anything to Verrick last night. And I wouldn't say anything to Trent either. An institutionalized girlfriend wouldn't help his chances of moving up in the company.

"Go away," she said. "And do not talk to me again."

I'm just trying to help. I'd hate—

Luckily, at that point an orderly came in with a wheelchair to take her down to X-Ray, or she'd have lost her temper completely, and for the next hour she was busy having X-rays taken of her lungs and then her skull. They obviously hadn't believed her when she told them she hadn't hit her head on the stairs and were worried about her mental state, so it was good she hadn't told Dr. Verrick about hearing C.B.'s voice, much as she hated to admit that C.B. was right. But that didn't mean he was trying to help. Or that he hadn't made up his so-called research.

I need to get out of here so I can do some research of my own, she thought, waiting impatiently to be discharged. But she had to wait for the X-rays to be read and then for a technician to do an EEG and for someone else to read that. "And Dr. Verrick wants to do a CT scan," her nurse said.

"Of my *brain*?" Briddey said, unable to keep the panic out of her voice.

"It's a routine procedure," the nurse began, but Briddey didn't hear the explanation. She was thinking, *They'll find out about the telepathy. I've got to get out of here!*

"C.B.!" she whispered the moment the nurse left. "They're going to do a CT scan."

I know, he said, his voice maddeningly calm. *Don't worry. It can't see what you're thinking. It only shows hematomas and tumors and things like that, abnormalities—*

"And you don't consider telepathy an abnormality?"

Not the kind a CT scan can see. To look at brain function, they'd need to do an fCAT or a cortical MRI. All this'll show them is the brain itself and whether you've got intracranial bleeding or a blood clot or something. There's no way they can find out about the telepathy.

"You're positive it won't show our neural pathway?" she asked, and heard Trent say clearly, "What *about* our neural pathway?"

Oh, thank heavens! Briddey thought. *We've connected!*

Nope, wrong again, C.B. said, and she looked over at the door. Trent was standing there, looking quizzical—and not at all like someone who'd just had surgery. He was wearing khakis and an ironed shirt, and his blond hair was neatly combed. Even the bandage at the nape of his neck was neat. "Trent!" she said, putting a hand up to her own bed-rumpled hair.

"Am I interrupting something?" he asked, coming in. He looked curiously around at the other, unoccupied bed, at the empty bathroom. "Who were you talking to?"

"Nobody," she said, trying to straighten her hospital gown. "I was just . . ." How long had he been standing there? If he'd heard her say "You're positive it won't show our neural pathway?" what could she say to explain that?

Nothing, C.B. said. *I told you, explanations—*

Go away, she hissed. "I was just thinking out loud," she said to Trent. "About our—"

"Hold that thought," Trent said, putting his phone to his ear. "Hello? . . . Who is this?" He held it out to look at the screen. "Hello?"

"Who was it?" Briddey asked.

"I don't know," he said, replacing the phone in his shirt pocket. "You were going to—" His phone rang again. "Sorry. Yes, Ethel. What is it? When does he want to meet?" A listening pause. "Yes, ten will work. I'll be back by then. Thanks."

He hung up. "That was my secretary. Hamilton wants to meet with me again." He came back over to the bed. "Sorry for all the interruptions. You were about to tell me why you were talking to an empty room."

"I wasn't. I was—"

What are you doing? C.B. shouted in her head. *Don't—*

Go away, she said, and to Trent: "I was talking to you. Dr. Verrick said calling to you out loud would help establish our neural pathway."

"And is it?" Trent asked eagerly. "Helping? Have you felt anything?"

"No."

His shoulders slumped in disappointment. "You're sure?" he asked. "I was hoping one of us would have felt *something* by now."

"Dr. Verrick said it takes at least twenty-four—"

"I *know,*" he said impatiently, "but I need—" He stopped, looking chagrined. "I'm sorry. It's just that connecting means so much to me."

"To me, too," Briddey said. *You have no idea* how *much.*

"And Dr. Verrick's nurse said she thought we might connect sooner than the average couple because we got such high scores on the battery of tests. She said Dr. Verrick expected us to have a deeper, more intimate level of communication than most couples experience." He frowned, seeming to notice Briddey's hospital gown for the first time. "Why aren't you dressed? Don't tell me they haven't discharged you yet. I'll go see what the holdup is."

"No," Briddey said, reaching to stop him. The last thing she needed was for him to find out about last night from the nurses. "They have some more tests they want to run before they send me home."

"Why?" Trent said, instantly alarmed. "Did something happen with your EED? Some kind of complication?"

That's one word for it, C.B. said.

Go *away.* "No," she said to Trent. "Everything's fine. I love the roses you sent. They're absolutely beautiful."

But Trent refused to be distracted. "If everything's fine, why do they need to run tests? And what kind of tests?"

If she told him a CT scan, he'd really think something was wrong, and she couldn't think of any benign-sounding tests. "I don't know," she said.

Bad idea, C.B. said.

"You don't *know*?" Trent said, pulling out his phone. "I'm calling Dr. Verrick."

Told you, C.B. said.

"No. You can't call him," Briddey said, and then for the life of her couldn't think of any reason why.

He's going to be in surgery all morning, C.B. prompted.

"He told me he was going to be in surgery all morning," Briddey parroted.

And he said the tests were just routine.

"And he said the tests were purely routine for someone who's had an EED."

No, no, no. *I told you not to say any more than you have to.*

"They didn't run any tests on me," Trent said. He looked sharply at Briddey. "Is there something you're not telling me?"

Yes, she thought, and it must have shown in her face because he said, "What is it, sweetheart? You can tell me."

I wouldn't bet on it, C.B. said. *Remember that guy who shot his wife, and that was just for failing to connect, not connecting to somebody else. And that's if he doesn't think you're crazy. Remember that hearing-voices study.*

"There's nothing I'm not telling you," Briddey said firmly. "Everything's fine, Trent. Dr. Verrick said so when he was in."

"Then why is he running tests?"

He's just being extra cautious.

"He's just being extra cautious," she said. "That's why he's so sought-after as a surgeon, because he's so conscientious."

"You're right," Trent conceded. "All the same, I think I'd better stay here with you while you have them."

No! Briddey thought. "No, you . . . this could take all morning," she stammered. "You know how hospitals are. Things take forever. What about your meeting?"

Trent already had his phone out and was swiping through screens. "You're more important than any meeting," he said without looking up. "And if something's gone wrong, there's no point in even *having* a—" He stopped himself, then went on more calmly. "I mean, I'd be so worried about whether you were all right, there'd be no way I could make a decent presentation."

"I *am* all right. Everything's *fine*," she said, racking her brain for a reason that would convince him to go. "There's no need for you to stay. And if you cancel the meeting, Hamilton—"

"Might think something's gone wrong," he said musingly, and then seemed to come to himself. "With the project, I mean. You're right. We don't want him to think that. I'd better meet with him. You're sure you'll be all right here by yourself?"

I'm not *by myself,* she thought. *More's the pity.* "Yes," she said. "I'm fine. Go."

"Okay," Trent said. "I'll be back as soon as the meeting's over and drive you home." He started out. "If you're ready to go before then, just text me."

"I will. Oh, wait, I can't. I don't have my phone. I asked for it back, but—"

"I'll check on it on my way out," he said. "Text me when you find out what tests they're planning to do. And call me the *moment* you feel any glimmering of a connection, even if I'm in my meeting."

"I will," she promised, "but *my* nurse said the swelling from the surgery has to go down, and the anesthetic—"

"I know, I know, and it takes at least twenty-four hours, but I have a feeling we're going to connect very soon." He stopped at the door. "You're absolutely sure you're okay with my leaving?"

"Yes. Now go. You'll be late for your meeting." The tech would be here any minute to take her for the CT scan, and if Trent found out she was having that . . .

"You promise you'll text me the moment—?" he began, and his phone rang again. "I've got to take this," he said, and started down the hall, saying, "Worth here. What did you find out?"

"Don't forget my phone," Briddey called after him, but he was already gone.

I don't think he heard you, C.B. said.

Will you go away?

Roger that, Night Fighter. Over and out, he said, and either he went away or at least shut up for the moment, though she was afraid he was still there. And right about Trent's not hearing her.

But a few minutes later an aide came in bearing her phone and a bouquet of violets. The attached card had two figures clinking champagne glasses on it and read, "Here's to our connecting—the proof our love is real!"

Oh, don't say that, Briddey thought, wincing, and unlocked her phone.

She already had two texts from Trent—"Have you had tests?" and "Any connection yet?"—and fifty-one from her family.

She texted Trent, "Thank you for the beautiful violets!" and started through Kathleen's messages. Half of them said, "Need to talk to you about Chad! Urgent!" and the other half were articles about EEDs gone wrong, including a TMZ exposé about a *Match Made in Heaven* star whose EED with a Denver Bronco had failed, which quoted her as saying, "I should have known the moment we didn't connect that he was cheating on me. EEDs don't lie."

I was right not to say anything to Trent, Briddey thought, and googled "CT scan."

C.B. had been telling the truth; it only took a picture of the soft tissue of the brain, not of the brain's activity. And when she was taken down to have it done a few minutes later, the technician said basically the same thing. "Everything looks normal," he told Briddey.

Thank goodness, she thought. *Now I can get out of here.*

But when she got back to her room, the nurse said Dr. Verrick needed to go over her test results before she could be discharged. "Then can I have breakfast?" Briddey asked.

"I'll check," the nurse said, and Briddey moved her bed up to sitting position and resumed calling to Trent. But even though she listened intently for an emotion he might be sending or some sense of his presence, she didn't hear anything.

Though she didn't hear C.B. either, which meant her efforts must be having some effect in weakening their feedback loop—or, if she was lucky, eliminating it altogether.

Now all I have to do is establish a new one to Trent, she thought, and redoubled her efforts, but she still didn't get anything. Except hungrier. Where was her breakfast?

She asked the nurse who came in to check her IV and the aide who came in to make her bed, but it was clear the same thing had happened to her breakfast as to that blanket last night. She tried calling to Trent some more—to no avail—and then unlocked her phone and went through the rest of her family's messages. Mistake. Mary Clare had decided that Maeve was definitely talking to terrorists online. "It explains everything. She spends all her time in her room, and she changed the password on her phone. When I ask her what she's doing, she refuses to tell me."

I don't blame her. Every time she does, you go off the deep end. Poor Maeve, Briddey thought, feeling guilty for having inflicted this on her niece, though the idea of terrorists had at least kept Mary Clare's attention off her during these critical two days. And it was obvious from the changed password that Maeve could take care of herself.

But it still wasn't fair to her. *I'll talk to Mary Clare about it as soon as I'm successfully connected to Trent. And out of here.*

But it began to look as though that would never happen. Ten o'clock and then ten thirty came and went without either breakfast or Dr. Verrick's okay. It was nearly eleven before a brand-new nurse appeared to say, "You can go home. We're processing your paperwork. Is your fiancé coming to pick you up?"

"Oh, we're not engaged yet," Briddey started to say and then decided it didn't matter. What mattered was getting out of here and then connecting with Trent.

"Yes," she said instead. "Should I call him now?"

The nurse nodded. "Tell him it'll take about half an hour to get you ready."

Briddey phoned Trent. She got kicked to his voicemail; he was probably still in his meeting. She texted, "Call me," and then tried calling to him mentally, saying, *They're ready to discharge me. Can you come?*

There was no answer to either message, and it was a good thing because the half hour stretched to forty-five minutes and then an hour. Lunch was served, which she didn't get either, and at twelve fifteen a student nurse poked her head in, inquiring, "Did you ask for an extra blanket?"

Yes, she thought. *Last night.* "No," she said. "I'm supposed to go home. Can you find out what's happening?"

"I'll check," the student nurse said. "Be back in a minute."

She wasn't back, and after ten minutes Briddey phoned Trent again. Still no answer. She texted, "Call me," and when he didn't, called his office.

His secretary answered. "Hi, Ethel, this is Briddey Flannigan," Briddey said. "Is Trent still in his meeting?" and when Ethel said yes, "I need you to get a message to him. I think he must have accidentally turned off his phone."

"He doesn't have his phone with him," Ethel said.

"What do you mean? He *always* has his phone."

"It's a secure meeting. No laptops or smartphones allowed."

"Then can you take a message in to him?" Briddey asked.

"I'm afraid not. That's not allowed either."

Management must really be worried about leaks where the new phone was concerned.

"Is there anything *I* can do for you?" Ethel was asking.

Send someone to pick me up, Briddey thought, but if Ethel did, all of Commspan would know about it. She debated asking Ethel to come herself. She didn't spread rumors. In fact, she was the *only* one at Commspan who didn't, and she'd do anything to help Trent. But if someone saw her leaving in the middle of the day, they were bound to wonder where she was going, especially given the secrecy surrounding Trent's meeting. Which meant it was bound to get back to Suki.

"No, that's okay. Just have him call me when he gets out of his meeting," Briddey said, and ended the call.

The nurse came in with Briddey's clothes and a sheaf of papers for her to sign. "Did you reach your fiancé?" she asked.

"Yes, but he's been detained. It's not a problem. I'll just drive myself."

The nurse shook her head. "No driving for twenty-four hours. Dr. Verrick's orders."

But Trent was allowed to drive, Briddey thought. "I'll call a taxi, then."

"You don't have anyone else who could give you a ride?"

If I say no, does that mean you won't let me go? Briddey wondered. "I could call my sister," she said. She could tell her Kathleen was on her way and she was meeting her downstairs, and then call a taxi from the lobby.

"Tell her she can pull up to the main door and call the desk," the nurse said, "and we'll take you down to her."

"I don't really need—"

"Hospital rules. We have to take you down to the lobby in a wheelchair."

So there went that plan. Who could she have come get her? Obviously not anyone from Commspan. And not Kathleen or Mary Clare or Aunt Oona. Or the Daughters of Ireland. *It's too bad Maeve's not old enough to drive,* she thought, racking her brain to think of someone she could call. *Trent, this would be a really good time to get out of your meeting and talk to your secretary.*

The phone rang. *Thank heavens.* She snatched it up.

"Why haven't you been answering your phone?" Kathleen demanded. "I've been calling you since yesterday."

"I've been in conferences."

"All *night*?" Kathleen said, and thankfully didn't wait for an answer. "I needed to talk to you. I took your advice and broke up with Chad, and now Aunt Oona's trying to fix *me* up with Sean O'Reilly. What am I going to do? It never *occurred* to me that—"

"Listen, Kathleen," Briddey cut in, "I need you to do me a big favor. I—"

"Here we are," the nurse said, reappearing with a wheelchair. "All ready to go?"

"Hang on a sec, Kathleen," Briddey said, pressing the phone to her chest so her sister couldn't hear her. "I'm still trying to find someone to take me home."

The nurse looked confused. "Didn't your fiancé call you? He's here."

Oh, thank heavens, Briddey thought.

"I told him to bring his car around and meet us at the front door. Are you ready?"

"Yes." She put the phone to her ear. "Kathleen, listen, I have to go. Meeting."

"Wait," Kathleen said. "What favor did you want me to do?"

"I'll tell you later. 'Bye." Briddey shut her phone off before Kathleen could ask any more questions and grabbed her bag and coat.

The nurse helped her into the wheelchair, lowered the metal footrests, then put Briddey's post-op instructions, her throw-up basin, her box of Kleenex, and the bouquet of violets in her lap. She told an orderly to follow her with Trent's roses and the water jug and wheeled Briddey down the corridor and onto the elevator, giving her orders all the way: "Rest this afternoon and this evening. No strenuous activity for forty-eight hours, no bending, no lifting"—the elevator pinged and the door opened onto the lobby—"and no stress. Don't worry about connecting with your fiancé. The amount of time it takes can vary considerably, especially if you're under stress or fatigued. If that's the case, it may delay contact."

Or not, Briddey thought, thinking about Trent's fortuitously timed arrival. When the nurse said he'd called, she'd assumed he'd gotten out of his meeting and Ethel Godwin had told him she'd phoned, but what if he'd heard her call out to him instead?

When they arrived in the lobby, the nurse wheeled her through the glass doors and outside. "Here we are," she said.

Trent's car wasn't there yet. "He must still be—" Briddey began, and stopped, looking at the battered Honda parked in the drive. *That looks like—*

C.B. got out of it. *My lady,* he said, *your chariot awaits.*

Seven

"Will he always come when you call him?"
she asked almost in a whisper.
"Aye, that he will."
—FRANCES HODGSON BURNETT, *The Secret Garden*

WHAT ARE YOU DOING HERE, C.B.? BRIDDEY DEMANDED, CLUTCHING THE arms of the wheelchair.

He looked a little more presentable than he had last night, but not much. He'd shaved, but he was wearing a London Underground baseball cap, and neither his faded brown T-shirt nor the striped shirt over it was tucked in. The laces dangled untied from his work boots.

I'm saving your bacon, he said, ambling over. "Is she all set?" he asked the nurse.

No, Briddey said, and would have glared up at him if it hadn't been for the nurse standing right there. *I thought you avoided hospitals.*

I do. So let's get out of here. "Do I need to bring the car closer?" he asked the nurse.

"*No,*" Briddey said, and the nurse must have mistaken her vehemence for affirmation that yes, she could walk to the car, because she put the wheelchair brake on and knelt to flip up the footrests so Briddey could stand.

Briddey glowered at C.B. as the nurse dealt with the apparatus. *I am not ready to go,* she said. *And you still haven't told me what you're doing here.*

You called and said you needed a ride.

I wasn't calling you. I was calling Trent.

Yeah, well, apparently he didn't hear you this time either. And there's no telling how long it'll be before he gets out of that meeting and sees your text. C.B. reached for the tote bag in her lap. *I figured I was better than nothing. Unless you want to call your sister. Or Suki. I'm sure she'd be delighted to come get you—as soon as she posts it on her blog. And sends out a few tweets.*

He was right.

Plus, the nurse here thinks I'm your fiancé, C.B. said, nodding toward the nurse, who'd finished with the footrests and was straightening up.

You told her you were my fiancé? Briddey said.

No, she just assumed it. So how are you going to explain that you don't want to go home with me? Especially after your odd behavior last night? They might decide they'd better keep you for observation.

The nurse was looking at them curiously. "Are you feeling all right?" she asked Briddey.

"Yes," Briddey said brightly. "I just can't get up with all this stuff in my lap."

"Sorry, sugar," C.B. said, taking her tote bag and the violets and then the throw-up pan and Trent's roses and stowing them all in the back seat. He came back over and put his arm around her to help her out of the chair. "Ready, sweetheart?"

I am not your sweetheart, she said, and would have loved to shake off his arm, but the nurse was standing right there.

This is like being kidnapped, she thought. *You want desperately to call for help, but you can't because there's a gun stuck in your side.*

May I remind you that you put the gun there yourself? C.B. said, helping her to the car. *You were the one who wanted to have the EED. Now, look like you can't wait to go home with me, so she'll let you leave. You want to go, don't you?*

Yes. She needed to get to Commspan so she could connect with Trent.

Well, then, I'd suggest you act happy.

"I'm so glad I'm going home," she said, and beamed at the nurse. "Thank you for everything."

Atta girl, C.B. said, opening the door to his Honda.

His car was as messy as his hair. There were papers and fast-food sacks strewn all over the seats and the floor. "Sorry, I didn't have time to clean it out," he said, hastily scooping them up and dumping them in the back seat.

He bundled Briddey into the front seat, shut the door, and got in himself. He put the car in gear and pulled out of the driveway and toward the exit. *And I resent being called a kidnapper,* he said as he waited for an opening in the traffic. *I'm just trying to help out here.*

"Good," she said, getting her keys out of her bag. "Then take me to the Marriott. My car's parked there. It's just a few blocks from here. Turn left."

Sorry, C.B. said. *No can do. The nurse said you aren't supposed to drive for twenty-four hours.*

"No, she didn't," Briddey lied, and remembered he could read her mind. "Anyway, you know how overly protective doctors are. You can see I'm perfectly all right—"

What I can see, he said, *or rather, hear, is that there's already been one unintended consequence of your surgery. Who knows what other UICs you might develop? Blackouts? Seizures? Your head might suddenly fall off in the middle of Union Boulevard. I couldn't be responsible for something like that.*

"Fine," she said, thinking, *I'll let him drive me to Commspan, and then I'll call a taxi and go pick up my car,* and then was afraid he might have heard that, too.

But he must not have, because he said, *Great. Let's go,* and leaned forward, watching for a chance to turn onto the street.

"No, wait," Briddey said. "First, you have to promise to talk out loud to me."

Why? Because you think our talking like this is "reinforcing our neural pathway"? That isn't how it works.

"How do you know?"

I went on the internet and did some more research.

What did you—? she began eagerly and then caught herself and asked aloud, "What did you find out?"

I'll tell you on the way.

"No. We're not going anywhere," she said, unbuckling her seat-belt and reaching into the back seat for her tote bag. "Stop the car.

Either we talk out loud, or I'm getting out right here and phoning a taxi."

You really think a taxi driver's going to pick up somebody standing on the curb wearing a hospital ID bracelet and carrying a throw-up pan?

"Then I'll walk."

"Okay, okay. We'll talk out loud. Now can we go?"

"Yes," she said, and settled back into her seat.

He roared out of the drive onto the street and flicked on the turn signal. "Where are you going?" Briddey demanded. "This isn't the way to Commspan."

"We're not going to Commspan."

Oh, my God, he is kidnapping me, she thought.

"Oh, for . . . I am *not* kidnapping you," he said. "I am taking you home. Doctor's orders. When I told them I was there to pick you up, the nurse told me you were supposed to go straight home and rest. You just had brain surgery, remember?"

"But I told my assistant I'd be back by noon."

"So tell her your meeting's running long," C.B. said.

But the longer she was away from Commspan, the more questions it would raise, and—

"So tell your assistant you're back, and you're on your way down to my lab, that I've got a new app to show you and you'll probably be down there for the rest of the day."

"But what if someone calls to check up on me?"

"They can't. There's no coverage, remember?"

"Is that what you do?" she asked. "Tell people you're in your lab and then take the day off?"

"Only when I have to go give somebody a secret ride home from the hospital," he said, and grinned at her.

But I need to connect with Trent, she thought.

"Then you definitely need to go home," he said, "because if you're at work, you won't have a minute to yourself. Let's see, you've been gone since ten A.M. yesterday. That's—what?—nineteen thousand emails to answer? Not to mention memos. And phone messages. Besides, do you really want somebody to see us come in together and tell Suki?"

"Suki's not there. She has jury duty."

"Nope, she's back. The defendant jumped bail."

"I live on South Sherman," she said. "You take Union Boulevard and then Linden. Turn left here."

"I know. I can read your mind, remember?" he said, and promptly turned right.

"I said left!"

"I know. I'm taking you to McDonald's. Or did they finally bring you breakfast?"

"No," she said, and realized just how hungry she was. "You really *can* read my mind. Thank you."

"You're welcome," he said, pulling into the drive-thru. He stopped the car and reared back in his seat so she could lean across him and order a Big Mac and fries.

"You don't realize how lucky you are that you hooked up with me," he said, pulling up to the second window. "You could've—"

"Connected with a *real* kidnapper," she said. "Yes, I know."

"Right. Or with one of those people who make a face and say, 'Do you know what's actually *in* a Big Mac?' Or with someone without a car. Then how would you have gotten home? Speaking of which, you need to text Trent and tell him not to come get you. You don't want him showing up at the hospital."

And finding out she'd already left with someone else who'd said he was her fiancé. She hastily got her phone out, hit Trent's number, and then stopped. Who should she say had come and gotten her? She had to name someone.

"No, you don't," C.B. said. "You're forgetting Rule Number Two. Don't say any more than you have to. Just say 'You don't need to come get me after all.'"

"But what if he asks—?"

"He won't," C.B. assured her. "He'll assume you drove yourself home. He doesn't know the nurse said you weren't supposed to drive."

"Your order, sir," the boy at the window said.

C.B. paid, and the boy handed him the sack. Briddey reached for it.

"Not until you send the text," C.B. said. "He could get out of that meeting any minute."

He was right. She stared at her phone, trying to think what to say. "I found someone to take me home?" No, that would invite him to ask who . . .

"Oh, for—I'll do it," C.B. said, snatching the phone from her and handing her the McDonald's sack. "Eat."

"What are you typing?"

"'No need to come to hospital. Transportation situation taken care of.' What's Charla's number under?"

She told him.

"'I'm back,'" he recited as he typed. "'Meeting with C.B. Schwartz about new app. Move all afternoon appointments to tomorrow morning.'" He hit SEND and then turned off her phone and handed it to her. "There. Now eat."

Briddey dug eagerly into the sack as he pulled out of McDonald's and headed toward her apartment. "You were going to tell me what you found out when you went online?"

"Well, for one thing, I found out there's a lot of junk on the internet."

"I'm serious."

"So am I. You wouldn't believe the crazy stuff on there—people claiming they can hear the voices of Napoleon and John Lennon."

"And Hitler, I suppose," Briddey said.

C.B. shot her a delighted smile. "You're right. They also claim they can hear their pets. And their plants. And bring about world peace by all thinking 'Give peace a chance' at the same moment. Between them and the lunatics who think they're communicating with Martians or the spirit of Ramtha, it's no wonder telepathy's got a bad name."

"So you didn't find any evidence of people actually experiencing telepathy?"

"I didn't say that. Some incidents seemed to be authentic . . ."

"And?" Briddey prompted.

"And unfortunately, most of those support Dr. Verrick's bonding theory. Almost every verifiable incident involved people with an obvious emotional connection. Parents, spouses, children, lovers."

He recounted the instances as he drove. In the middle of the night on April 6, 1862, Patience Lovelace had heard her betrothed calling her name, and a month later had received a letter from his commanding officer telling her he'd been shot at that exact time at the Battle of Shiloh and died a few minutes later. In 1897, Tobias Marshall, while traveling on a train, had heard his wife say clearly, "I need you," and two days later he got a cable saying that she'd gone into labor six weeks early.

"They're nearly all like that," C.B. said, glancing at her. "A mother who hears her son call out to her that it's dark and wet, and it turns out he's fallen down a well. A man who hears the girl he's in love with say, 'Alas, we shall not meet again,' and finds out she's died suddenly. A son who hears his mother call out his name as she's dying half a continent away."

Briddey had heard dozens of stories like that. Aunt Oona had said her great-great-grandmother had heard a lad she knew cry out, "It's done for, I am," as he died at the Battle of Ballynahinch.

"And there was an emotional bond between them, wasn't there?"

"Yes," Briddey admitted grudgingly. "But you said *almost* every instance. That must mean you found some instances where the people *weren't* emotionally bonded."

"Yeah, but those—" He broke off to ask, "Where do I turn?"

"Jackson," she said. "Those what? *Did* you find instances where the people were strangers?"

"Yeah. A bunch of random people claimed they'd heard someone cry out for help at the same time the *Titanic* went down. Ditto the *Lusitania* and the *Empress of Ireland.*"

"Well, there you are, then," Briddey said. "Our connecting must be one of those."

"I don't think so. Most of those people didn't report the cries for help till after news of the disaster hit the papers, and several turned out to be professional psychics with, shall we say, ulterior motives. Speaking of which, did you know there was a psychic on board the *Titanic*? Though obviously not a very good one, or he wouldn't have been there in the first place."

"But there *were* some shipwreck incidents that were authentic?" Briddey persisted.

C.B. was peering through the windshield at the street ahead. "Where do I turn?" he asked. "Is it this light?"

I thought you could read my mind, she thought. "No, the light after next. You turn left."

Briddey waited for him to go on talking, but he didn't, and after they'd gone a block, she asked, "So what were they, these authentic shipwreck incidents?"

He still didn't answer.

"C.B.?"

"Huh? What? Sorry, I was thinking about something I need to do after I get you home. What did you say?"

"I asked you what the authentic *Titanic* incidents were."

"Incident, not incidents. And it wasn't ... this is where I turn, right?"

"Yes," she said, and he promptly turned right. "No, not right. *Left*." She pointed. "My apartment's *that* way."

"Sorry," he said. "I'll go to the next street and then come back."

She shook her head. "It's one-way the wrong way. Pull into a driveway and turn around."

"I can't," he said, glancing in the rearview mirror. "There's somebody coming."

He drove two blocks, came back, and finally turned onto her street. "How far down is your apartment?" he asked.

"It's the second one from the—oh, no!"

"What is it?"

"My sister Kathleen. She's just going into my building. Quick!" she said, sliding down in the seat. "Go! She'll recognize you. Hurry!"

"Okay, okay." He drove back to Linden and turned onto it. Briddey sat up and looked back.

"This isn't a spy movie," C.B. said. "She's not going to chase you. Besides, she didn't see you. She didn't even turn around when we went by. Where am I supposed to be going, by the way?"

"I don't know. Somewhere we can wait till she gives up and goes home."

"How about my apartment?"

"I am *not* going to your apartment," she said. "Just go over a couple of blocks and park."

"Parking. Even better," he said, turning down the next side street and pulling up next to a vacant lot. "Now what?"

"Do you have a pocketknife?" Briddey asked, reaching into the back for her tote bag.

"No. And what for? I told you, she's not following us, and even if she was, you'd hardly need a knife to defend yourself."

"I *need* it to cut off my hospital ID bracelet," Briddey said, rummaging through her bag.

"Why? If we're going to wait here till she leaves—"

"But someone else could come while I'm going into my apartment." She rummaged some more. "And the bracelet's a dead giveaway that I've been in the hospital."

"So is that bruise on the back of your hand from where you pulled out your IV," C.B. said. "What are you going to do about that? Wear gloves?"

"Maybe," she said, and continued to look for the scissors.

He watched her dig awhile without success and then said, "By the way, how long do we need to sit here? Not that I mind. We've got a great view"—he gestured toward the weed-filled lot—"romantic music . . ." He reached forward, switched on the radio, and began turning the old-fashioned tuning knob, moving the dial's needle through static and snippets of country-and-western music and right-wing talk and rap. "I could sit here all day. But how long does it take to knock on a door and figure out you're not there?"

"You don't know my family," Briddey said. "They all have keys, and no respect for privacy. Kind of like you. Kathleen will go inside and check every room to make sure I'm not there, and then try to call me. And when she can't get me, she'll call Charla and ask her if *she* knows where I am. She'll be there half an hour at least. If she doesn't just decide to sit down and wait till I get home."

And meanwhile time was ticking by—time she needed for building a neural pathway if she was going to connect with Trent before the twenty-four-hour mark. She wished she could hear Kathleen's voice the way she could C.B.'s. Then she'd know what Kathleen was doing and whether it was safe to go home.

"You're kidding, right?" C.B. said in disbelief. "You really want to hear your sister's thoughts?" He shook his head. "People always think being telepathic would be like some cute romantic comedy where you could find out secrets and use them to get what you want. Or find out what your enemies are up to. But you know what it would actually be like?"

"What?" Briddey said, since he was going to tell her anyway. She didn't have any way to stop him.

"Exactly," C.B. said triumphantly. "People always assume they'd be able to turn it on and off like a faucet and only hear the stuff they want to. But it—"

"Doesn't work like that."

"Exactly. You wouldn't necessarily be able to pick and choose who you heard. You might not get your sister. You might just as easily get—"

"I know. A kidnapper or someone who hates McDonald's."

"Or one of those crazies schizophrenics hear, the kind who tell you to kill people. And you wouldn't be able to pick and choose *what* you heard either. You might find out stuff about people that you don't want to know. Or what people really think about you. Remember back in middle school when you were in the school bathroom and accidentally overheard your best friend saying something mean about you? *That's* what being telepathic would be like. You'd be stuck listening to people you didn't want to hear—"

Like I'm stuck here with you, she thought. But it couldn't be helped. If Kathleen spotted her, she'd lose even more time explaining what C.B. was doing bringing her home. She'd just have to sit here and listen to him till Kathleen left.

"Good," C.B. said, tuning the radio through more static and then switching it off. "Because there's something I need to tell you."

"About the incident on the *Titanic*?"

"No. And it wasn't on the *Titanic*. It was a World War Two destroyer. But that isn't what I want to talk to you about."

"Because it proves people who aren't emotionally bonded can connect, and you don't want me to hear those incidents."

"No—"

"Then tell me about it."

"Fine," he said. "In 1942 a seventeen-year-old girl in McCook, Nebraska, is sitting listening to the radio with her married sister Betty and the sister's friend Mrs. Rouse, and she suddenly stands up and cries, 'Oh, the ship's going down! Somebody help him!' So Mrs. Rouse thinks the girl's fallen asleep and is dreaming, and she says, 'There's no ship here! You're in McCook, Nebraska,' and the girl says, "I *know*, but I can hear him! He's in the water! We have to help him, Betty! Mrs.

Rouse! Oh, hold on! Don't give up!' And when they finally get her calmed down, she tells them she heard a sailor calling to her, crying, 'Help! We've been torpedoed by a U-boat!'

"They ask her who the man was, and she says she doesn't know, she didn't recognize the voice. And she can't think of anybody it could be. She doesn't even know anybody in the navy. She wrote the whole episode down in her diary, and so did her sister in a letter to her husband, who was in the army. And both of them noted the time."

"Which was exactly the time the sailor's ship went down."

"Yeah, in the North Atlantic, but they didn't have any way to know that because news of naval losses was censored, so the sinking wasn't in the papers."

"So he'd called out as he drowned, and she just happened to hear him. Like you happened to hear me."

"Not quite," C.B. said. "And he didn't drown. He was picked up, badly burned, by a cruiser, after hanging on to a piece of wreckage for fourteen hours, and he told the ship's doctor he'd managed to hold on because he'd heard a strange girl's voice telling him to. A girl from Mc-Cook who mentioned a Betty and a Mrs. Rouse."

"And he didn't know anyone like that in McCook."

"He didn't know *anybody* in McCook. Or in Nebraska. Till the war, he'd never been out of Oregon."

"Which means the communication was between people with no emotional bond at all," Briddey said happily. *And I can tell Trent that.*

"Let me finish," C.B. said. "When the sailor got out of the naval hospital, he went looking for the girl to thank her, and when he found her, they realized they had met after all. At a canteen in North Platte when his train came through on his way to his deployment. She'd been passing out candy and cigarettes to the soldiers, and they'd talked for a couple of minutes."

"That doesn't mean—"

"Yeah, well, they were married three days after he located her. So I'm guessing there was *some* kind of emotional bond there."

And you're implying there has to be a bond between us, too. Trust me, there's not. I'm in love with—

"I'm not implying anything. I'm just saying if you tell Trent and he goes online, this is the kind of thing he's going to find, and it's not exactly going to convince him that our being connected is a case of tangled neurons or crosstalk."

"So what do you suggest I do?"

"Stall. Give me some time to—"

"To what? Come up with more stories about sailors and psychics and people falling down wells?"

"No, to figure out what's going on and what caused it."

"What *caused* it? We know what caused it. The EED—"

"Really? None of those people I told you about—Patience Lovelace or Tobias Marshall or the McCook, Nebraska, girl and her sailor—had an EED or even a head injury, and I didn't have one either. And nobody else who's had an EED has started hearing voices."

"You don't know that. Maybe they did, but they just didn't say anything."

"You really think Jay Z and Beyoncé would keep something like that to themselves? Or Kim Kardashian? She wouldn't just broadcast it, she'd have a reality show about it."

"I thought you said people would have them committed."

"It doesn't apply to celebrities. People already think they're crazy. And you're the only EED patient this has happened to, which means it probably wasn't the EED that caused it. And until we find out what did cause it—"

"There *is* no we."

"Yeah, well, try telling that to your boyfriend," C.B. said. "Look, all I'm asking is that you not say anything to him or Verrick till we figure out what caused this and what else is going to happen—"

"What do you mean, what else is going to happen?"

But he wasn't listening. He was staring up the street.

"What is it?" Briddey asked, afraid he'd seen Kathleen. "Is it my sister?"

He didn't answer.

"C.B.?"

"No," he said abruptly, and started the car.

"What are you doing?"

"Taking you home." He pulled away from the curb and started back to her apartment. "Don't worry, we'll check to make sure your sister's gone first." He drove quickly to Briddey's street and parked just around the corner. "What kind of car does she drive?"

"A white Kia."

He got out. "Stay here," he said, and ran around the corner.

He was back almost instantly. "She's gone," he said, getting back in and starting the car.

"Are you sure?"

"Yeah." He drove around to the front of her building, parked, and opened his door.

"You don't have to get out," Briddey said.

"You can't carry all this stuff by yourself." He handed the violets and the throw-up pan to her and retrieved everything else, including Trent's bouquet of roses, from the back seat, raced up the stairs with them, and came back down to help her.

Once inside her apartment, he set the roses on the coffee table and took everything else into the bedroom. "This was on the bed," he said, returning with a note. He handed it to her.

It was from Kathleen: "Sorry I missed you. What's the favor you need? Call me."

"I wouldn't if I were you," C.B. said. "The nurse said you should rest. Is there anything you need before I go? A cup of tea or something?"

"No, I'm fine," she said, and he immediately went to the door, clearly in a hurry to be gone. Why? Where was he going?

"To do some more research," he said, opening the door. "If anything happens—you connect to Trent or start feeling those 'flickers' Dr. Verrick talked about, or if your head falls off—let me know," and went racketing down the stairs.

Briddey shut the door and looked at the clock. It was a quarter past one. She still had forty-five minutes to connect with Trent before he began wondering why they hadn't. She turned on her phone to see if there were any messages from him and then turned it off again so Kathleen couldn't call and went into the kitchen.

She pulled out a chair and sat down at the table, clasped her hands together, and squeezed her eyes shut. *Trent,* she called. *Come in, Trent—*

I forgot to tell you, C.B. said, *that app we were discussing—*

What app?

The one I was showing you in my lab this afternoon when nobody could reach you. Just in case anybody asks. Rule Number Three of Lying: Have a cover story ready in case people start asking questions.

I thought you said I didn't need—

He ignored her. *It was an app to use with Twitter. For when you send out a tweet you shouldn't have. It automatically holds it for ten minutes so you can decide, "Jesus, what was I thinking? I can't send this!" and delete it before it goes out to everybody and destroys your career. I call it SecondThoughts, which is what you should be having if you're still thinking about telling Trent or Dr.—*

I thought you had research to do, Briddey said, and, just in case he came back, went over to the front door and put the deadbolt on. She wished there was one that would work against his voice.

No, you don't, he said. *What if you need another ride?*

I won't.

You might. You never know. If you do, you know how to get in touch with me.

Very funny. She went back into the kitchen and sat down again. *Can you hear me, Trent?* she called. *Where are—?*

Someone knocked on the door. *If that's you, C.B.,* Briddey thought, *go away.*

"Briddey?" Mary Clare called, knocking again. "Open the door. I have to talk to you! It's an emergency!"

Eight

"Nobody expects the Spanish Inquisition."
—*Monty Python's Flying Circus*

"CAN YOU HEAR ME, BRIDDEY?" MARY CLARE CALLED FROM OUTSIDE THE door. "I've got to talk to you about Maeve. And don't try to pretend you're not in there, because I know you are. You've got the deadbolt on."

Yes, or you'd already be in here, Briddey thought, crossing the room to let her in.

I wouldn't do that, C.B. warned. *Your hospital bracelet, remember?*

"Hang on. I'll be right there, Mary Clare," Briddey called, and sped to the kitchen to get a knife.

And you'd better do something about that bruise from the IV, too.

Briddey grabbed a steak knife, sawed the plastic bracelet off, jammed it far down into the wastebasket, and then ran into the bathroom to find an adhesive bandage for her hand.

None of them were big enough. *Use an Ace bandage,* C.B. told her. *That way you can say you've got a touch of carpal tunnel,* but she didn't have an Ace bandage either. She had to settle for tying some gauze around her hand, with the sinking feeling that that would only draw attention to it.

It did. When Briddey opened the door, Mary Clare said, "What on earth were you doing that took so—oh, my gosh, what happened to your hand?"

"Nothing," Briddey said. "I cut it . . ." And then for the life of her she couldn't think of a single thing she could have cut the back of her hand on.

You don't need anything, C.B. said. *Remember Rule Number Two? No explanations. They only get you into more trouble.*

Go away, Briddey hissed. "I had a flat tire on the way home from my meeting," she said, "and—"

"How on earth did you manage to cut yourself on a tire?"

"I didn't. I cut it on the jack."

"The *jack*? Why on earth were you changing the tire yourself? Why didn't you just call Triple A to come and change it? Or Trent?"

"I didn't have any cellphone coverage—"

"You're kidding! Where were you?"

Told you, C.B. said.

Oh, shut up, Briddey snapped. "You said you needed to talk to me about Maeve. What's happened? Did she lock herself in her room again?"

"Yes. How badly did you cut it? Let me see." Mary Clare reached for her hand.

No wonder Maeve locked herself in her room, Briddey thought, snatching her hand back out of reach. "I'm fine," she said. "Tell me about Maeve."

"She refuses to let me in, and when I tried to get on her Facebook page to see what was going on, she'd unfriended me. I *knew* I shouldn't have let her be on Facebook! You're friends with her, aren't you?"

"Yes—"

"Good. Then you can get me to her page." Mary Clare went over to Briddey's computer. "What's your password?"

Briddey glanced at the clock. After two. She was almost out of time, and if she didn't give the password to her, Mary Clare would be here forever.

You're kidding? C.B. said. *You can't let her invade a little kid's privacy like that!*

Like you're invading mine? Briddey shot back, but he was right.

Maeve would never forgive her. "Mary Clare, I'm not letting you spy on Maeve using my computer. And if she unfriended you, she'll have unfriended me, too."

"True. You don't know how to pick locks, do you?"

"No. I thought you were going to install a nanny cam."

"I did. Maeve did something to it so that it transmits YouTube videos instead," Mary Clare said, and Briddey had to bite her lip to keep from smiling.

"We'll have to call a locksmith," Mary Clare was saying. "Do you know any?"

"No, and even if I did, I am not helping you break into Maeve's room," Briddey said.

"But what if she's arranging to meet a terrorist as we speak?"

"She's *not* meeting terrorists—"

"You don't know that. Just because everything seems fine on the surface, that doesn't mean it is."

That's true, Briddey thought.

"There could be all kinds of things happening that we don't know anything about. You read constantly about children getting into trouble and their parents not knowing. I just read about an eighteen-year-old who was running an international money-laundering operation from the computer in his bedroom, and his parents didn't have the slightest idea."

"Maeve is not running a money-laundering operation. She's nine years old."

"Then what's she doing, and why won't she let me in her room? And why this sudden obsession with reading?"

"I told you, all the third-grade girls are reading *The Darkvoice Chronicles.*"

"No, no, she finished that. Now she's reading something called *The Secret Garden.* Do you know that one? What's it about?"

A nine-year-old girl with lots of freedom and no mother.

"It doesn't have any zombies in it, does it?" Mary Clare was asking.

"No. It's a Victorian children's classic. With a totally unsquelched heroine. Look, Mary Clare, if you're so worried about what she's reading, why don't *you* read the books?" Briddey asked. If she was busy reading, she wouldn't have time to harass poor Maeve.

"That's a good idea," Mary Clare said thoughtfully. "But it still doesn't explain why she's unfriended me. Or why she won't let me in her room."

I have got to get her out of here, Briddey thought. *I'm running out of time.* "Look, how about if I call her and talk to her?"

"Or, better yet, Skype her," Mary Clare said eagerly. "That way we can see if she's hiding something in her room."

What? Stacks of laundered money? "I can't call her while you're here," Briddey said. "She'll know you put me up to it."

"I'll keep out of the frame so she can't see me."

"No. Go home, and I'll call her in a little bit." *After I've safely connected with Trent.* "And in return, you have to promise me you'll stop fussing over her like a psychotic mother hen."

"I am *not* a—you really should get that hand looked at, you know. You might need stitches."

"And stop fussing over *me*," Briddey said, pushed her out the door, and leaned against it, thinking, *Finally. Trent, please make contact before something else hap—*

There was a knock on the door.

I told you you should have come over to my apartment, C.B. said. *There's a lot less traffic.*

Go *away*, Briddey said, and opened the door.

It was Mary Clare. "There's something wrong with your phone," she said. "I just tried to call you and couldn't get through."

"What did you want?" Briddey asked.

"To tell you if you can't get anything out of Maeve when you talk to her, you could suggest taking her to Carnival Pizza and then to a movie."

Though presumably not one with a princess in it, Briddey thought, and tried to shut the door.

"If that jack was rusty, you could get lockjaw. You need to get a tetanus shot—"

"Goodbye, Mary Clare," Briddey said, and shut the door.

"Don't forget to check your phone," Mary Clare called.

"I won't," Briddey called back, and since Mary Clare would come back again if she couldn't get through, she switched her phone on.

It rang instantly.

"I forgot to tell you something," Mary Clare said. "You're not still planning on getting that EED, are you? Because I read this thing about how they can cause terrible side effects."

I should have had C.B. install that app that diverts calls to the Department of Motor Vehicles, she thought. "Goodbye, Mary Clare," she said, ended the call, and sat down on the couch.

Come in, Trent, she called. *Please. Before Mary Clare calls again.*

Her phone rang.

It was Maeve. "Mom said you wanted to talk to me."

"I do. How would you like to go to lunch with me sometime next week?"

"Mom put you up to this, didn't she?" Maeve asked, and Briddey could almost see her eyes narrowing.

"No," Briddey said, and thought, *That makes it official. I am now lying to everyone.*

"She did, too," Maeve said. "She thinks something's going on and I won't tell her, and she thinks I'll tell you."

"*Is* something going on?"

Maeve made a sound of disgust. "You're as bad as her! I bet you think I'm talking to terrorists, too! They cut people's heads off! How can she even *think* I'd talk to somebody like that?"

"She doesn't," Briddey reassured her. "She's just worried because terrorists don't always *tell* kids they're terrorists. Sometimes people seem nice when they aren't."

"I know," Maeve said, "like—"

She stopped short, and Briddey suddenly wished she *was* on Skype so she could see Maeve's face. "Like who?" she asked.

"Umm . . . do you promise you won't tell Mom?"

Oh, my God, Briddey thought. *Maeve is talking to a terrorist online.* "I promise. It's like who?"

"Captain Davidson," Maeve said. "He's this cop in *Zombie Death Force,* and you think he's the good guy and then you find out he's not, that he's the one who created the zombie army in the first place." And then, as if anticipating Briddey's question: "Mom doesn't let me watch zombie movies. She says they give me nightmares."

"And do they?"

"Everybody else in my class watches them."

Which wasn't an answer. But Briddey was hardly in a position to say, "If everyone else in your class jumped off a bridge, does that mean you would, too?"

"Where did you watch *Zombie Death Force*?" she asked instead.

"At Danika's. Her parents have Netflix. Please don't tell Mom. She'd go ballistic."

Actually, she might be relieved to find out Maeve wasn't joining ISIS or running an online money-laundering operation, but Briddey said, "I won't tell her, but *you* have to promise me that if you do get into trouble or have something you're worried about, you'll tell us so we can help."

"But what if you can't?" Maeve asked, and Briddey wished again that she could see Maeve's face.

"Can't what?" she asked cautiously.

"Can't help. I mean, like if you'd been bitten by a zombie, there wouldn't be any *point* in telling anyone because there wouldn't be anything they could do. You're gonna turn into a zombie anyway, and it's *better* if you don't tell them because they'd try to help and probably get bitten, too."

"Has something like that happened, Maeve? Something you think we can't help you with?"

"What? Geez, I can't say *any*thing without you and Mom going all psycho. I was talking about a movie! I'm *fine*!"

But after Briddey hung up, she went and checked Maeve's Facebook page, just in case. There was nothing there except a post saying, "My mom is driving me totally crazy. She keeps asking me what's wrong and I keep telling her nothing, but she won't believe me. Sometimes I wish I was an orphan like Cinderella."

Which Mary Clare would no doubt interpret as Maeve having latent matricidal tendencies. *Although in this case they're perfectly justified.*

She'd wasted half an hour talking to Mary Clare and Maeve, and now she had exactly ten minutes left to connect with Trent before the twenty-four-hour mark. She doubted that was enough time to establish a neural pathway, but she tried anyway.

Nothing. Three o'clock and then four came and went with no sign of Trent in her head and no texts from him. Surely he wasn't still in his meet—

Her phone rang.

It was Mary Clare again, saying, "Well? Did you talk to Maeve? What did you find out?"

"That she's fine. I can't talk to you right—"

"Did she at least tell you why she's locked herself in her room?"

"Yes, she said she had a ton of homework to do, and she locked the door so she wouldn't have any distractions," Briddey said, willing Mary Clare to get the hint.

She didn't. "Oh, dear, I knew it! She can't keep up with her assignments. I read the other day that schools assign far too much homework, and it's causing anxiety attacks and depression—"

"Goodbye, Mary Cla—"

"No, wait. When are you taking her to lunch?"

"We didn't set a date."

"You can take her on Saturday."

"No, that won't work—" Briddey began, but Mary Clare wasn't listening.

"Her Irish dancing lessons are over at eleven," she was saying. "You can pick her up at eleven thirty. Kathleen's here. She wants to talk to you," and put her on before Briddey could hang up.

"I've been trying to reach you all afternoon," Kathleen said. "I think there's something wrong with your phone. You said you needed me to do you a favor?"

Briddey'd forgotten all about that. "No. I thought I did, but I didn't."

"Oh," Kathleen said. "You sounded sort of desperate, and I thought maybe you'd come to your senses and decided not to have the EED, and Trent got mad and dumped you like Chad dumped me, and you needed a ride."

"No," Briddey said.

"Oh. What was the favor?"

"Nothing. It doesn't matter. Have you decided how you're going to keep from going out with Sean O'Reilly?"

"No. That's why I was hoping you'd broken up with Trent, so you could go out with him instead."

"I'm not breaking up with Trent." *Though if we don't connect—or if he finds out about C.B.—he may break up with me.*

"Aunt Oona won't take no for an answer," Kathleen was saying. "You know how she is. I'm going to have to come up with a boyfriend fast. I've been looking at dating sites—you know, Match.com and OKCupid. There's one called Flame. What do you think about that?"

"I think it sounds perfect if you're Joan of Arc."

"Or there's one called RolltheDice. Their philosophy is that all those profiles and compatibility algorithms don't work, that your chances of falling in love aren't any better than if you'd pulled a name out of a hat. Which is true. I mean, remember Ken, the guy I met on eHarmony? We had *tons* in common, and we still broke up."

"So if they don't do profiles, how do they match people?"

"They don't. They just randomly assign you to some guy. What do you think?"

I think it's the worst idea I've ever heard, Briddey thought, and told her so.

"Really? Why? I thought it sounded like fun."

It's not. Trust me, Briddey thought, and said, "What if you get stuck with someone who's a pain in the neck?" *Who keeps telling you you could have connected with somebody worse.* "Or what if Sean O'Reilly signs up?"

"Oh, gosh, I hadn't thought of that. Maybe I'd better go with Tinder instead. Or Hit'n'Ms."

There was no way Briddey was going to ask what that was, but it didn't matter. Kathleen launched into a description anyway. "Listen, I need to go," Briddey said. "Trent—"

"No, wait, Aunt Oona just got here. She wants to talk to you."

Of course she does, Briddey thought. "Hello, Aunt Oona."

"Are you all right, childeen? It's worryin' I've been all day. I had a premonition something dreadful had happened to you."

It has, Briddey thought. *But not the sort of thing you're thinking of.* "Nothing's happened, Aunt Oona. I'm fine."

"You're not still thinking of having that VED thing done, are you? Peggy Boylan—you remember her from the Daughters of Ireland, don't you?—well, she says her neighbor's daughter was after having one and lost all her hearing. Deaf as a post, she is now."

Lucky her, Briddey thought. "Aunt Oona, I have to go," she said. "Trent's here." And hung up. She checked the time—oh, Lord, it was already four forty-five—turned her phone off, and sat down at the kitchen table. She closed her eyes, clasped her hands before her on the table, and began calling: *Trent? Can you hear me? It's Briddey. Come in, Trent.*

She kept it up for the next hour, sending, listening, sending again, but nothing happened, even though it was now well past twenty-four hours since they'd come out of the anesthetic. She was surprised Trent hadn't called to say that.

Your phone's been off, she reminded herself, and when she checked for messages, the only one was from Maeve, wailing, "What did you say to Mom? She's talking about getting me a TUTOR!"—which meant Trent hadn't received any of her transmissions. Or that he was still in his meeting with no way to get a message to her, though surely if he'd felt anything, he'd have found some way to let her know, secure meeting or not.

His secretary phoned at six thirty to say he was still in his meeting and that was why he hadn't returned her call.

"Do you have any idea when it'll be over?" Briddey asked.

"No, but they just had dinner sent in, so I'm assuming it will go to at least eight."

Good, Briddey thought. *That gives me more time,* and went back to sending, but she didn't hear *or* sense Trent, even though she sat there for the next two hours, clasping her hands so hard her knuckles were white.

She didn't hear C.B. either. And now that she thought about it, she hadn't heard him since he'd made that comment about there being less traffic at his apartment, and that had been—what, six hours ago? She couldn't imagine he'd been "researching" all that time. So either she *had* erased the pathway, or the swelling causing the crosstalk had finally gone down—or both.

Encouraged, she began sending to Trent again, but nothing happened. *Maybe I'm going about it wrong,* she thought after an hour, and wished there was someone she could ask. Not Dr. Verrick, obviously, and the only person she knew who'd had an EED was Rahul Deshnev's assistant. If she asked her, it would be all over Commspan by tomorrow. She'd have to see what she could find on the internet.

She typed in, "EED failure to connect," but all that brought up was the *Match Made in Heaven* breakup and two more failed-connection murders.

Very helpful, Briddey thought, and tried "EED connection," and when that didn't work, "EED connection blogs."

That produced a number of entries, but none of the bloggers had had any trouble connecting, or any idea of how they'd done it. "It just happened," one of them said, and another: "I was kind of nervous about it, but it was easy. All of a sudden I felt Jack's love enveloping me, like he'd put his arms around me, and I felt so safe."

All of them reported it happening "quicker than I'd expected," and in none of the blogs was there any mention of talking. Briddey typed in "EED telepathy."

"Did you mean 'OED telepathy'?" the computer asked, and brought up the *Oxford English Dictionary* definition of telepathy: "The communication of impressions of any kind from one mind to another, independently of the recognised channels of sense."

Independent of sense is right, Briddey thought. "No, I didn't mean OED," she said, and retyped "EED telepathy" and then "telepathy."

C.B. was right: There was a lot of junk on the internet. Briddey found the "Lyzandra of Sedona" ad that Kathleen had sent her, which described Lyzandra's "psychic spirit gift" and promised she could open your chakras, change your understanding of the nature of communication, and connect you to the universe.

She also found a number of similar ads and the "hearing voices" study C.B. had talked about. He'd said all the participants had been diagnosed as having schizophrenia. That wasn't true. The two that hadn't been labeled schizophrenic had been diagnosed with acute manic-depressive psychosis.

And C.B. hadn't been exaggerating as far as the "emotional bonding" component went. She couldn't find a single instance of telepathic communication where someone had connected with a stranger, let alone a person they couldn't abide. Every single account involved families, friends, sweethearts, fiancés.

So why can't I connect to Trent? she wondered, and went back to the blogs to look for clues. And after reading several more delirious accounts of improved romantic relationships and improved sex lives, she finally found something helpful: "My friend Adanna and her boyfriend connected right away, but we didn't, and I was scared it meant Paul didn't love me, but the doctor said the problem was that I wasn't concentrating enough. He said I needed to focus on Paul and not think about *anything* else, and once I did that, we connected right away."

"Not think about anything else," Briddey murmured, remembering all the distractions she'd had today: C.B. and the CT scan and Kathleen's online dating and money laundering and psychics and U-boats and zombies. No wonder she hadn't connected with Trent.

She tried again, concentrating on him and only him, determinedly shutting every other thought out, but she still didn't feel anything—except for a growing sense of dread as the evening wore on. Trent's meeting had to be long over by now. What if the reason he hadn't called was that he'd concluded their failure to connect meant she didn't love him?

When he finally phoned at eleven she was so relieved she could hardly speak. "I'm so sorry," he said. "My meeting *just* got out, and I had no way to communicate with you because Management wouldn't allow—"

"I know," Briddey said. "Your secretary phoned when she realized you were going to have to work late."

"She did? Good. Then you didn't have to spend the whole evening wondering why I hadn't gotten in touch with you," he said. "I've been absolutely frantic, worrying about leaving you at the hospital."

Oh, no. Now he's going to ask me how I got home.

But he didn't. He said, "What did the tests show?"

"Nothing. All the results were normal. And just because we haven't connected yet, it doesn't mean—"

"So you haven't felt anything either?"

"No."

"Damn. I was hoping . . . Dr. Verrick said the reception might be one-way at first, and I thought that might be what was happening, that you were receiving but I wasn't. But if you haven't been receiving either . . . We should have connected eight hours ago. We need to call Dr. Verrick."

No! "Twenty-four hours wasn't the deadline for connecting," she said. "It was the soonest we could connect, but it can take a lot longer. When did you come out of the anesthesia?"

"I don't know. Mid-afternoon?"

"Then it's no wonder we haven't felt anything yet. The average for connecting is forty-eight hours, and my nurse said it sometimes takes even longer."

"How *much* longer?"

She debated how long she could get away with. "Seventy-two hours."

"Seventy-two *hours*? That's three days! I can't wait—" He must have realized how impatient that sounded, because he said, "I'm sorry, I just want to be connected to you so much. And Dr. Verrick said our scores on the tests were really high. We should've connected sooner than the average."

"Not necessarily. My nurse said there were all kinds of variables—how long it takes the wound to heal and the brain to develop the neural pathway, how focused both people are—"

"Focused," he said, seizing on the word. "That's the problem. With the meeting and worrying about you, I haven't been able to focus. I'll come over—"

No, Briddey thought. Keeping him from suspecting anything was hard enough over the phone. There was no way she'd be able to manage with him actually here. They wouldn't *need* to be connected for Trent to sense her fear and anxiety. "I don't think that's a good idea," she said. "The nurse told me Dr. Verrick said we'd both need to get lots of rest the first couple of days after the surgery, that it would help us heal faster."

"What'll make me heal faster is seeing you. I want to hold you, to be with—"

No! If by some chance C.B. *wasn't* gone, that would be disastrous. "No, Dr. Verrick said no sex till after we're connected."

"You're kidding! If we connect physically, it's bound to make us connect faster mentally."

"It doesn't work like that. Dr. Verrick told me couples connect faster when they're separated, that being together is a distraction. He said when couples are in the same room, they revert to talking and physical contact as their means of communication, and their neural pathways don't develop. Whereas when they're separated, if they want to communicate, they're forced to connect, and it happens more quickly." *Please, please buy that,* she added silently.

"I suppose that makes sense," Trent said. "And connecting's the top priority. If keeping apart helps speed things up ... all right, I won't come over tonight."

Thank heavens.

"I'll come over in the morning, and we can have breakfast together before work. And speaking of work, did you tell Charla we were having the EED done yesterday?"

"No. I said I was gone for meetings."

"You didn't tell her you were going to the hospital?"

"No."

"Did you tell anyone else?"

"No," she said, afraid his next question was going to be, "What about the person who brought you home? Who did that, by the way?"

But he merely said, "Good," and then, "Listen, this needs to stay our secret for now, so don't say anything about it at work, all right?"

"All right," she said, relieved that it wasn't already all over Commspan and about to go up on Facebook for her family to see.

But he apparently felt he owed her more of an explanation because he said, "Management's really uptight about the iPhone rollout, and they might take our having had the EED now as a sign that I'm not totally committed to the project. You understand, don't you, sweetheart?"

"Yes, of course," Briddey said, "but are you sure we can keep it secret? I mean, they've seen the bandage on the back of your neck, haven't they?"

"Only the people at the meeting, and I told them I got a haircut on the way to work and the barber nicked me, and that I was at a meeting downtown yesterday. The only person who knows I was at the hospital is my secretary, and I've told her not to tell anyone."

She won't have to, Briddey thought. Suki was a genius at putting two and two together, and when she saw the bandage on Briddey's hand ...

"We can tell people later," Trent was saying, "after we've connected. I'll see you in the morning. Seven thirty. If we've connected, we can celebrate. And if we haven't, we'll call Dr. Verrick and find out what's holding things up."

Then I'd better see to it that we connect tonight, Briddey thought, and as soon as Trent hung up, she turned off her phone and began sending as hard as she could, hoping that now that Trent was concentrating, too, she'd get *something.*

Nothing, and she was so tired she couldn't keep her eyes open, let alone concentrate. *Maybe* that's *the problem,* she thought. The nurse had told her she needed rest, that fatigue could delay their connecting. If she could just get a few hours' sleep . . .

But sleeping proved impossible, too. She had far too many things on her mind. Like, how was she going to talk Trent out of calling Dr. Verrick if they still hadn't connected by morning? And what if they *did* make contact, and Trent found out she'd been connected to C.B.? How would she ever convince him it had nothing to do with emotional bonding?

After an endless period of tossing and turning, Briddey got out of bed, made herself a cup of cocoa, and tried to contact Trent mentally again. Still nothing. She went back to bed—and to worrying. Tomorrow Trent was bound to ask her, "If you didn't tell anybody you were in the hospital, how did you get home?"

No, he won't, she told herself firmly. *C.B. was right. Trent will just assume I drove home in my own—*

Oh, no! My car! she thought, sitting bolt upright in bed. *It's still at the Marriott!*

She'd completely forgotten about it. She'd have to pick it up tomorrow morning. No, that wouldn't work. Trent was coming here for breakfast, and when he saw her car wasn't there, he'd ask where it was.

She needed to go get it right now. She looked at the clock. 3:46 A.M. Could she even get a taxi this time of night, and if she did, would the parking garage even be open?

Yep, C.B. said. *I looked it up. It's open all night.*

Nine

"Night Fighter calling Dawn Patrol.
Night Fighter calling Dawn Patrol. "
—*How to Steal a Million*

I TOLD YOU YOU MIGHT NEED ANOTHER RIDE, C.B. SAID.

His voice, coming suddenly out of the darkness like that, startled Briddey just like it had the first time she heard him in the hospital, and she had to stifle the impulse to turn on the light and look around the room. *What are you doing here?* she demanded.

What am I—you called me, he said indignantly. *And don't say you were calling Trent because I heard you say you had to get your car back before he finds out.*

I wasn't calling you or Trent, she said, sitting up and switching on the lamp beside her bed. *I was talking to myself.*

Yeah, well, I'm not sure that's an option anymore. But you're right. We do need to get your car back before Trent starts wondering how you got home from the hospital without it. Only if I take you to get it right now and somebody from Commspan should happen to see us, they're going to wonder what we're doing at a hotel together at three thirty in the morning.

So what do you suggest? she asked, and remembered that every time she talked to him like this, she was reinforcing their neural pathway. She repeated the question aloud.

I suggest we wait till six. At this time of night we're up to no good. At six, we're on our way to an early meeting. So what say you go back to sleep and I'll pick you up at five thirty?

"But—"

You'll be back by six forty-five, tops.

And Trent wasn't coming over till seven thirty. "But what if he and I have connected by then?" she asked.

I assume that means you haven't had any luck so far?

"No."

Not even a flicker?

"No, but we could make contact at any time."

Well, then either he'll be so overjoyed, he won't even notice your car's missing, or the car will be the least of your worries.

"What does that mean?"

It means, if he can hear your thoughts, he'll know you're connected to me, too. And if he can't, if it's just feelings like the EED was supposed to deliver, you've got an even bigger problem, because I have a feeling Trent wouldn't take kindly to having a second-class connection.

But if Trent can only sense my feelings, she thought, *I won't have to tell him I can talk to you.*

You're kidding, right? If he can pick up your emotions, he'll want to know why you're feeling worried and guilty instead of overjoyed. And face it, you're not a very good liar.

"Go away," Briddey said.

Roger, he said. *I'll pick you up at five thirty and take you over to the Marriott. And on the way I'll tell you what I found out. I did some more research.*

"You found out what caused this?"

Possibly. I'll explain when I get there. In the meantime, get some sleep. The nurse told you to rest, remember?

Yes, she thought, and lay back down. But sleep was impossible. She had too much to think about. What if she did only connect with Trent through emotions? How would she explain the anxiety he would definitely pick up from her—and the sense that she was keeping something from him?

But Trent will pick up my love for him, too, she thought, *and the fact that I don't even like C.B.*

If they connected. It had been thirty-eight hours since she'd woken up after surgery, and she still wasn't getting anything from Trent. What had C.B. found out? That it *was* crosstalk? Or something worse? What if he'd found out that once a neural pathway was established, it couldn't be erased? Dr. Verrick had said it was a feedback loop. What if, once in motion, it went on looping and intensifying till it was too strong to stop?

When she couldn't stand going round and round anymore, she turned on her side and looked at the clock: 4:18 A.M. "C.B.?" she called. "What did you find out? From the research you did?"

I thought you were going to get some rest, he said reprovingly.

"I need to know what you found out first."

Oh, I get it. You can't sleep, so you're not going to let me get any sleep either.

Sleep? She'd thought he was in his lab.

Nope. I'm in bed just like you.

She had a sudden vision of him lying there, his tousled dark hair against the pillow, and sat bolt upright, clasping her blankets to her chest.

Oh, for— he said disgustedly. *You don't have to do that.*

She lunged for her robe at the foot of the bed, still clutching the blankets to her.

It's not X-ray vision, it's telepathy.

"I don't care," she said, putting her robe on.

You're acting crazy, you know that, he said, and as she padded barefoot out to the living room: *You don't have to . . . where are you going? Please tell me I'm not going to have to come rescue you from a stairwell again because—*

"I am going to the kitchen," she said with dignity. "To make myself a cup of tea." She took a mug down from the cupboard, filled it with water, stuck it in the microwave, and then stood there waiting for it to heat and wishing it would hurry up. Her bare feet were freezing on the tile floor.

And whose fault is that? If you'd stayed in bed where it was warm instead of . . . what exactly do you think I'm going to do to you? I'm halfway across town, for cripes' sake.

"What did you find out?" she demanded. "From your research."

That acting crazy's a bad idea. It can get you locked up. Or burned at the stake.

"I'm serious."

So am I. I got to thinking about Joan of Arc's hearing voices and decided to see if there were any other saints who did. There were—Saint Augustine and Saint Brendan the Navigator and your very own Saint Brigid and Saint Patrick.

"But they—"

Thought they were talking to God or angels or the Virgin Mary. I know, he said. *But what if they weren't? What if they were talking to an ordinary person and what they were experiencing wasn't a religious vision but telepathy? And they just interpreted it as a holy voice because that was the only way they could make sense of their experience? Or the only way they could keep from getting burned as a witch?*

"But I thought Joan of Arc—"

Yeah, well, the plan didn't always work.

The microwave dinged. Briddey took the mug out, put a teabag in it, and carried it into the living room. "Even if it was telepathy," she said, sitting down in the corner of the couch, "how does knowing that help us?"

Well, for one thing, it tells us telepathy's a real thing, and we're not suffering from some kind of shared delusion. And for another, it tells us it's been going on a long time. Saint Patrick lived in the fifth century. His voice told him to go back to Ireland and plant a tree, by the way, which he interpreted as an order to establish a church, but he could have just been talking to a gardener. And Joan of Arc could have been talking to somebody who really wanted to defeat the English.

"Couldn't you find any telepaths more recent than the Middle Ages?" Briddey asked.

Yeah, Patience Lovelace and Tobias Marshall. And that girl in McCook, Nebraska, and her sailor.

"I meant current ones."

Nope. If there are any real telepaths out there right now, they're keeping their heads down. And no wonder. If people found out telepathy was real, they'd go nuts. The government, Wall Street, the media . . . Just think, no more having to hack phones or follow celebrities around with a telephoto lens. People could read their minds and know *where they're going. And they could read their political opponent's mind, too, and the DA's. And the jury's. Not to mention what the NSA and the military could do with it. Everybody'd want a piece of them. So they're not telling anybody.*

"But what about psychics?" Briddey asked, thinking of that email Kathleen had sent her about Lyzandra of Sedona. "They claim to be telepaths, don't they?"

"Claim" being the operative word. They're either scam artists or they're unconsciously cold reading.

She wished he hadn't mentioned the word "cold." It reminded her how icy her feet were. "Cold reading?" she asked, tucking her feet up under her. "What's that?"

It's skillful guessing combined with reading facial expressions and body language. And asking leading questions. "I'm getting a message from a relative . . . a female? . . . whose name begins with B . . . or M . . . or C," all the time watching your reactions till either they get a hit or you shout, "It's my sister Kathleen!" And marvel that they could read your mind like that.

He regaled her with other tricks professional mind readers and mentalists used while she sipped her tea and then ate a bowl of cereal: secret codes and marked cards and audience shills who gathered information from subjects and communicated it to the mind reader onstage via hidden mikes and earpieces. *Like you accused me of doing last night.*

"But they can't all be scam artists," Briddey said. "What about the ones who work with the police?"

They're fakes, too. But even if they aren't, they're not telepaths. They claim they can find murder victims, who obviously aren't saying anything. Fortune-telling doesn't qualify either. Or claiming to be able to predict what's going to happen in the future.

Like Aunt Oona with her premonitions and her claiming to know who's on the phone before it rings, Briddey thought.

Those fall under the definition of clairvoyance, which is as bogus as all the other paranormal stuff out there, except for telepathy—telekinesis, astral projection, past-life regression. Speaking of which, I found another reason you shouldn't tell Verrick, he said. *Your name.*

"My name? You mean Flannigan?"

No, your first name. Did you ever hear of Bridey Murphy?

"No. Who's that?"

I'll tell you while you get dressed.

"Dressed? Why?"

Because I'm coming to get you, remember? And we're going to the Marriott.

"But I thought we weren't going till five thirty."

We aren't. But it's five fifteen, and I'm about ten blocks from your apartment.

"Oh," she said, hastily setting down her cereal bowl and scrambling off the couch. She'd completely lost track of the time. She hurried into the bedroom, untying her robe as she went, and then stopped short.

Oh, for— C.B. said. *I won't look, all right? Even though I can't see anything. I told you, it's not X-ray vision. You can't see me, can you?*

"No." But he'd known she was lying in bed, and he'd known she was in the stairwell at the hospital. And just now, he'd known she'd started to undress and stopped. Why was that?

Because I can hear what you're thinking.

And why was that? All she could hear was what he said to her, but he seemed able to hear her every thought.

If you don't want me to know you're undressing or taking a shower, just don't think about it, he was saying.

"Fine. I won't," she said, taking off her robe and pulling her nightgown off over her head, thinking determinedly of how glad she was going to be when they were no longer connected. She reached for her bra.

Though I should probably tell you, C.B. said conversationally, *I don't need telepathy to imagine you taking off your clothes.*

She snatched up her clothes, stomped into the bathroom, and slammed the door, even though it wouldn't do any good. Nor would telling him what a loathsome and disgusting individual he was.

I tried to warn you it was a cesspool in there.

"Go *away,*" she said, though that wouldn't do any good either. "Now."

I need to tell you about Bridey Murphy first. She was this housewife back in the 1950s. Her name was Virginia Tighe.

"I thought you said her name was Bridey Murphy," Briddey said, trying to get her bra on without thinking about it, which was easier said than done.

That's what she said her name was. Under hypnosis. She told the therapist she lived in Ireland. In the 1800s.

"The 1800s?" Briddey said, pulling on her sweater and reaching for her jeans.

Yep, and she had all kinds of proof. Details Virginia Tighe was unlikely to have known about life in Ireland back then. She spoke in a thick brogue—

Which doesn't prove anything, Briddey thought. *Look at Aunt Oona.*

And she knew all sorts of Irish tales and folk songs. She sang "Danny Boy" for the therapist and told him all about the house she lived in in Cork and the church she went to, even about her own funeral.

Briddey'd managed to get her jeans and her shoes on while he talked. She tied her hair back with a scrunchie. "Her own funeral?"

Yeah, the therapist believed Virginia had lived a previous life and was the reincarnation of this Bridey Murphy, C.B. said, and went silent.

"Well?" Briddey said after a minute. "What happened? I assume she was a fraud."

No answer.

"C.B.?" Briddey called.

Still nothing.

C.B.? Are you there?

Yep, he said. *Ready to go?*

"Yes," she said, grabbing up her coat and her bag. "Where are you?"

Here.

She opened the door. He was leaning against the doorjamb, wearing a hoodie and a pair of baggy pants, his hair a tangled mess.

Thanks, he said. *You look nice, too.* He held out a flat paper packet. *Here.*

"What's this?"

"An extra-large bandage. To cover your IV bruise."

"I thought you said I should put an Ace bandage on it."

"That was before you told your sister that you'd cut your hand."

"But she won't be at the Marriott or at Commspan—"

He made a face. "Facebook, remember? Plus Instagram and Vine and Snapchat and iChat and youChat and weAllChat and FaceTime and Tumblr and Whisper. Even if your sister hasn't already posted it, somebody else is bound to, and if you tell them it's carpal tunnel . . ." He shrugged. "Fourth Rule of Lying: Keep your stories straight."

"Fine," she said, and started to tear the package open.

He shook his head. "We need to get going. You can do that in the car. Got your ticket for the parking garage?"

"Yes."

"Then let's go."

"Shh," she whispered. "You'll wake up my neighbors."

You're the one who insisted on talking out loud, he said, following her down the stairs and outside.

It was dark, and there was no one on the street, but Briddey still tried to shut the door of C.B.'s Honda quietly when she got in. C.B. turned the key in the ignition, and the radio came on, blaring a song.

Briddey dived to shut it off, got the tuning knob by mistake, and was treated to loud static and a reporter shouting, ". . . rain this weekend," and then ". . . Congress is in recess this week," before she managed to switch it off.

"Don't worry, nobody heard that," C.B. said, pulling away from the curb. "Everybody's asleep. Except people who are lying to their boyfriends. Speaking of which, you might want to work on Rule Number Five: Don't look guilty. If you're going to make a career of lying, you've got to learn to do it with a straight face. Like Bridey Murphy, who completely fooled her therapist."

"She did?"

"Yeah. He was so convinced she was telling the truth, he wrote a book about her past life, did magazine interviews, went on TV with her. He even played the tapes of her hypnosis sessions so people could hear Bridey's voice. They were a sensation. But then reporters started digging, and it turned out there were no records of a Bridey Murphy being born in Cork at that time, no such church, and the words to 'Danny Boy' hadn't been written till 1910. And when they checked into Virginia Tighe's background, they found an Irish aunt and an Irish neighbor who'd told her stories and taught her the songs—and presumably the brogue—when she was a little girl. She was declared a fraud, and the therapist's reputation was ruined, too, just like the reputation of every other doctor or scientist who's ever gotten involved with the paranormal. Even Joseph Rhine."

"Joseph Rhine? Who's that?"

"A respected scientist at Duke University—till he ran a series of telepathy experiments in the 1930s. He put subjects in a room and had them look at Zener cards—you know, the ones with stars or squares or wavy lines on them?—and 'think' the image on the card to a second subject in another room. Laboratory conditions and all very scientific, but Dr. Rhine didn't fare any better than Bridey Murphy's therapist. His research was discredited, he was branded a nutter, and since then, nobody respectable's been willing to touch telepathy with a ten-foot pole."

"And you think Dr. Verrick won't be willing to either, even if I can persuade him I'm telling the truth?"

"I *know* he won't. He's got a cushy practice and a bunch of celebrity patients. He's not going to be willing to risk that, even if it means he has to accuse you of being a fake."

Or mentally ill, she thought despairingly. Everything C.B. had just said was true. If she told them she was telepathic, no one would believe her. And she didn't blame them. If Charla told her *she* was hearing voices, Briddey would assume she was either joking or delusional. Or seriously ill. *So I can't tell Dr. Verrick. And I can't tell Trent because he'll think I'm emotionally bonded to C.B. What am I supposed to do?*

"Stall," C.B. said. "Forty-eight hours aren't up till three this afternoon, and a lot can happen between now and then. In the meantime, I'll look into the crosstalk thing and try to find some telepathic incidents between non-emotionally-bonded people that you can tell Trent about. Hitler was interested in the paranormal. If he was telepathic, we're golden. Everybody hated him."

They were nearly to the Marriott. The sun had come up, but the streets were still largely deserted, and Briddey wondered if 6 A.M. was going to be too early after all for her to pick up the car.

"No, there'll be a bunch of people leaving to catch early flights. You'll be fine," C.B. said, and she wondered again why her mind seemed to be an open book to him but she couldn't hear what he was thinking. When he stopped in mid-sentence, as he seemed to do a lot, she couldn't even hear the tail end of what he was going to say. Why not? And had he just heard her thinking that?

If he had, he gave no indication. He was busy pulling into the drive-thru of a Starbucks. "What do you want?" he asked.

"Nothing. Trent's coming for breakfast, remember?"

"So you told me," he said, and repeated, "What do you want?" And inside her head: *I'm not talking about breakfast. If I were, I'd have taken you to this deli I know that has great lox and bagels. This is for protective coloration. See?*

He pointed across the street at a man heading into an office building carrying a Starbucks cup. *If anybody notices you walking into the hotel, it'll look like you're arriving for a meeting and picked up coffee on the way. So, what'll it be?*

"A tall latte," Briddey said.

C.B. ordered it and then said silently, *I'm going to drop you around the corner from the front entrance so you won't be seen with me, okay?*

No, Briddey thought to herself. *It's not okay at all. It's like we're sneaking around, having an affair.*

No, it's not. I can think of a couple major differences. Would you like me to list them?

She was saved from having to answer that by the barista's saying, "Your tall latte."

C.B. took the cup, handed it across to her, pulled out into the street, and drove toward the hotel. "I looked up the layout of the lobby online, in case you weren't paying attention when you parked your car. You go past the registration desk and turn left, and the elevators are right there. Let me know when you've gotten your car and are started back. And let me know if you connect with Trent or if you experience anything unusual."

"Why?" Briddey asked suspiciously.

"Because it might provide a clue to what's causing this. The more information we have to go on, the likelier we are to figure this out."

He turned right just short of the Marriott. "So I need you to tell me if you sense anything, an emotion or a sound or one of those flickers Dr. Verrick talked about. Anything, even if it seems like nothing."

"All right," Briddey agreed. "But why do I have to tell you? I thought you could read my mind."

"Yeah, well, I don't have time to hang around listening to you all day. I've got things to do, phones to design, people to chauffeur," he said, pulling over to the curb and stopping. Briddey set her latte down so she could grab her bag and reached to open the door.

Hang on, C.B. said.

She stopped, her hand on the door handle. C.B. was looking intently in the rearview mirror. "Did you see someone from Commspan?" she asked nervously.

He took a minute to answer. "Nope, you're good. Don't forget this." He handed her her latte. *And if Trent doesn't show and you change your mind about breakfast—or having an affair—call me.*

"Not a chance," she said, slammed the car door, and walked away. She hurried up to the corner and then hesitated. Starbucks cup or no, she was still walking into and driving out of a hotel at six in the morning. If anyone from Commspan saw her—

They won't, C.B. said.

How do you know that? Don't tell me you can read their *minds, too?*

I don't have to to know nobody'll notice you, he said. *I work at Commspan, remember?*

What's that supposed to mean?

You'll see when you turn the corner.

She did. The Marriott's entrance was lined with people standing waiting for a taxi with their luggage—and staring at their smartphones. Not a single person looked up as she maneuvered her way through them.

Told you, C.B. said.

She went into the lobby. It was full of people, too, all checking out and all just as fixated on their phones. She walked past the registration desk, over to the parking garage elevator, onto the elevator, and down to the level she'd left her car on without being noticed by a soul—including the parking attendant. He took her ticket and her money without once looking up from the videogame on his phone.

She drove out of the garage and headed toward Linden, breathing a sigh of relief. It was only six fifteen. She could get home and still have forty-five minutes before Trent got there in which to concentrate on connecting.

But she hadn't taken the traffic into consideration. Two blocks after she'd turned onto Linden, she ran into bumper-to-bumper morning rush-hour traffic. *Don't panic,* she told herself. *You can concentrate on connecting with Trent while you drive.*

No such luck. She had to focus all her attention on the traffic because every other driver was talking on a phone or slowing down to text, looking up too late to realize the light had changed, and slamming to a halt at the last minute. *C.B.'s right,* Briddey thought. *There is entirely too much communicating going on.*

But not between her and Trent. She didn't hear anything during the long crawl home. He hadn't even texted her, and he usually did the minute he woke up. She glanced at the clock on the dashboard. *It's nearly seven thirty,* she thought. *He has to be awa—oh, no, seven thirty! If he gets there before I do—*

Tell him you were out getting stuff for breakfast, C.B. said.

Which was actually a good idea, though it meant getting home even later, and as she raced through the grocery store, snatching up eggs and juice, she remembered she'd left her computer on. If she'd left up one of those articles about telepathy, and Trent saw it . . .

She sped home, praying his car wouldn't be parked outside, even though it was already seven forty. No sign of his Porsche. Good. She ran up the stairs with the groceries, thrust them into the refrigerator, called up a news feed on her computer, took off her coat, flung it in the bedroom, and went to make an omelet.

Halfway through cracking the eggs, it occurred to her that he always texted her when he was going to be late. *Unless he couldn't. Because I never turned my phone back on.*

And sure enough, once she'd turned it on, there were two texts from Trent: "No connection yet. Don't think being separated is working," and "Cant make it for breakfast. Meeting with Hamilton."

"Thank goodness," she murmured, but she hadn't even finished voicing the thought before he texted her again, telling her to call him when she got to work and he'd come down and walk her to her office.

"Not a good idea if we want to keep our EEDs secret," she texted him back. "The less people see us together, the better. It might remind them we were going to have the EED, and that plus your bandage might make them put two and two together."

Her phone rang the second she was done sending it. It was Mary Clare. "I need to move your lunch with Maeve on Saturday."

Lunch with Maeve on Saturday. She'd forgotten all about it.

"Our mother-daughter book club is meeting from eleven to one," Mary Clare was saying. "I took your advice."

"My—?"

"About reading the books Maeve's reading. I thought, a book club's the perfect way to find out what's going on in Maeve's head. We'll discuss why we liked the books and how they relate to our own problems. We're going to start with *The Darkvoice Chronicles* and then do *The Secret Garden* next week."

Oh, poor Maeve, Briddey thought as Mary Clare prattled on about who she'd invited to join.

"Anyway, you can pick her up at one fifteen," Mary Clare said, and hung up before Briddey could tell her she might be busy. Almost instantly she got Trent's responding text. "You're right. We'd better keep apart."

Thank goodness, Briddey thought, and couldn't believe she was feeling that. The whole idea of having the EED had been to bring her and Trent closer together, and here she was doing everything she could to keep him away from her. Talk about unintended consequences.

C.B. said, *I told you the IED—*

—was a terrible idea. I know. What do you want?

I did some more research.

Did you find out if brain circuits can experience crosstalk?

No, but I found some more stuff on auditory hallucinations. They usually don't start with a voice. They begin with a knocking or the sound of rain falling or someone whispering, and the voices come later.

And how is that supposed to help?

I just thought you might have heard something like that, and didn't realize it was a sign you were starting to connect. Have you?

No. Now go away. I'm trying to connect with Trent.

No, you're not, he said. *You were talking to your sister. I can read your mind, remember?*

Will you stop saying that? she snapped.

So you weren't talking to your sister?

Yes, she admitted, *but I intend to start connecting now. So go away.*

He did, but he was back within five minutes, saying, *Auditory hallucinations also can start with a distinctive odor, like flowers or freshly baked bread. Have you smelled anything funny?*

No, she said. *Go,* and this time he actually went, and she was able (after turning off her phone) to focus on Trent as she took her shower, got ready for work, and drove to Commspan. But it had no appreciable effect. She didn't receive any feelings from Trent on the way, and there weren't any odd smells or rain patterings or scents of roses.

And now she had to face Jill Quincy and Phillip and Charla and tell more lies. And hope Trent was right, and no one had discovered they'd had the EED, though it was almost impossible to keep anything secret from the inquisitive Suki, and Charla had seen her talking to C.B. in the garage. And now here she was with a huge bandage on her hand and a ridiculous story about cutting it while changing a tire, which, thanks to social media, had almost certainly already made the rounds. Getting to her office the morning after Trent asked her to have the EED had been bad. This was going to be much, much worse. And she didn't care what C.B. said—she would have given anything to know where everyone was and what they were thinking.

She parked, braced herself for the onslaught, and went inside. The hallway was empty, but she hadn't gone ten steps before two secretaries emerged from the copy room, talking, and she heard one say to the other, "Have you heard . . . ?"

I knew Suki wouldn't buy that barber story of Trent's, Briddey thought, and turned to retreat, but Art Sampson was bearing down on her from the other direction. "Oh, you're back. Good. Where were you yesterday?"

"Offsite," she said, remembering what C.B. had said about not explaining more than you had to.

"Oh, then you probably haven't heard either. Something's going on, but I haven't been able to find out what."

Oh, here we go.

"You haven't heard anything about them laying people off, have you?"

"Laying people off?" she repeated blankly. "No."

"Oh, good. I was afraid Management had decided the new iPhone was going to do us in and were planning layoffs."

No, I think the gossip's a bit more personal than that, Briddey thought, but when Lorraine came over to join them, she said, "*I* heard they think there's a corporate spy here at Commspan, trying to steal whatever it is the Hermes Project's working on."

"The Hermes Project?" Briddey said. "What's that?"

"It's some new project of Hamilton's. Rahul Deshnev thinks it's something to do with our new phone and that they have something really good, because they're taking all kinds of precautions to make sure there aren't any leaks."

"Or else it's a trick to flush out the spy," Phillip said, coming up to them.

"Or a diversion to keep us from realizing they don't have anything to compete with Apple," Art Sampson said gloomily, "and we're all going to lose our jobs."

And by the time Briddey'd made it to her office a full half hour later, she'd heard that (1) there was definitely a spy at Commspan, but they hadn't caught him yet, (2) that Commspan had gotten hold of the specs for the new iPhone (presumably because *they* had a corporate spy over at Apple) and Apple's new phone was definitely going to do them in, (3) that Commspan was being sold to Apple and/or Motorola, (4) that Commspan was acquiring Motorola and/or Blu, and (5) that whatever the Hermes Project was working on would do Apple in.

At this point, Briddey didn't care which one it was. She was just grateful that everyone was focused on that and not on her and Trent. Not a single person seemed to have noticed her bandage, let alone asked about it. Including Charla, who greeted her before she even got in the door with "Do you know what the Hermes Project is?"

"No," Briddey said, sorting through her messages.

"Oh. I hoped you would, with Trent being at the meeting and all."

"Has he called this morning?"

"No."

Good, Briddey thought.

"They had this big meeting yesterday that lasted all day and didn't break up till after ten," Charla was saying, "and nobody knows what it was about. But whatever it was, it's top secret. Mega-security during the meeting, and nobody who was there is saying anything. Even Suki hasn't been able to find out what it was about."

And that's the first time that's happened, Briddey thought.

"She thinks they've come up with something that'll create a complete paradigm shift and make the smartphone obsolete," Charla said. "Like a smart ring."

"Or a smart tiara," Briddey said sarcastically. "Or a tattoo."

"A tattoo? Really?"

"No," Briddey said. "That was a joke. I need you to tell Art Sampson I need to reschedule our meeting to tomorrow."

"Tomorrow's Saturday."

"To Monday, then. Did I have any other messages?"

"Yes," Charla said, consulting her tablet. "Your sister Mary Clare called and wanted to talk to you about whether she should serve wine at her book club meeting. She said book groups traditionally serve wine, but she read something about alcoholism among elementary school students being a growing problem."

Briddey rolled her eyes. But at least her call meant they hadn't found out about the EED yet.

"Your sister Kathleen wants you to call her," Charla went on. "Something about online dating. And your niece Maeve called. She said she's really mad at you. Now she can't even read in peace, whatever that means."

"What?" Briddey said in mock surprise. "No message from my Aunt Oona?"

"No," Charla said. "She's waiting in your office."

Ten

"If I'm the frying pan, then that out there is the fire."
—Syfy's *Alice*

"AUNT OONA'S IN MY *OFFICE*?" BRIDDEY SAID. "WHAT DOES SHE WANT?"

"I don't know," Charla said. "All she said was she needed to talk to you, and when I told her you weren't in yet, she said she'd wait." Which could only mean one thing. Aunt Oona had somehow found out about her having had the EED.

"I tried to get her to leave you a message," Charla explained, "but she said it was a personal matter."

"It's all right," Briddey said, and went into her office, where Aunt Oona was sitting stolidly with her carpetbag in her lap. "What brings you here?" she asked brightly.

"Maeve." Aunt Oona shook her head sadly. "Poor bairn. 'Tis a worrying feeling I've had about her this last fortnight."

"Oh, for heaven's sake, Aunt Oona, whatever Mary Clare's been telling you, it's not true. Maeve's fine. She can take care of herself."

"Aye, that she can, in most situations. But if she were to find herself in one where she couldn't, I fear she'd not turn to her mother because of how Mary Clare—"

"Completely overreacts to everything she's told?"

"Aye. 'Tis a dreadful thing to be in dire straits and not able to tell a soul, not even your nearest and dearest."

You're right, Briddey thought. *It is.*

"'Tis why I came to see you," Aunt Oona went on. "Mary Clare told me you're after taking Maeve to lunch on Saturday, and I've been thinking it would be a fine time to speak to the poor lamb and let her know she can pour out her heart to you and you'll not tell another living soul."

"I'll try, but—"

"Aye, telling her's one thing. 'Tis another to make her believe it. 'Tis the same with Kathleen." She shook her head. "I've told her this internet foolery's no way to find a good man. Fillin' in questionnaires and looking at photographs! 'Fine airs and fair faces are all very well,' I said, 'but 'tis a good Irish lad you should be wantin'.'"

Like balding, still-lives-with-his-mother Sean O'Reilly? Briddey said silently.

"But seemingly a lad with a kind heart isn't good enough for her. It's 'compatible' he's got to be. Compatible!" Aunt Oona scoffed. "'Kathleen,' I said to her, 'if there aren't times when you're wantin' to break his head in, then 'tis not love you're in, 'tis only a romantic dream.' You lasses shouldn't be wantin' a man who's 'compatible,' but one who'll be there when you need him."

I don't think 'there when you need him' is on the OKCupid questionnaire, Briddey said to herself.

"'Has he a generous heart?' That's what you should be askin' yourselves," Aunt Oona said. "'Would he be willin' to risk life and limb for me? And would I be willin' to do the same for him?'" She shook her finger at Briddey. "And speakin' of riskin' life and limb, you're not still set on having that foolish operation, are you? Never mind, I can see that you are. And all I have to say about that is—"

Here we go, Briddey thought.

"That when a leprechaun is after offering you a pot of gold, sure and there's a trick in it somewhere." She stood up. "I'll be takin' my leave of ye now."

Briddey was so surprised, she blurted, "Really?" and then could have kicked herself.

"Aye," Aunt Oona said, setting her carpetbag on Briddey's desk and rummaging in it. "I'm to be givin' Maeve's science report to the kind lad who helped her with it." She drew out a bright green folder. "C.D., his name is."

What? "You mean C.B.?"

"Aye, that's it. Where would his office be, then?"

Briddey was trying to take this in. "Maeve knows *C.B.*?"

Aunt Oona nodded. "He helped her with a project she was havin' to do for school. On smartphones, it was. Got an A on her report, she did, and she wanted to show it to him."

The *last* thing she needed was for Aunt Oona to talk to C.B. He knew she didn't want her family to know about the EED, but he wouldn't have to tell her. All he had to do was mention the hospital or his driving her home, and she'd figure out the rest. And if he started talking about Saint Patrick hearing voices, or Joan of Arc—

"I'll see that he gets Maeve's report," Briddey said, reaching for the folder.

"No, no, I'll not be botherin' you with it, busy as you are. Just tell me where this C.T. is."

"*C.B.*, Aunt Oona," Briddey said, and in case she was hoping *he* was a fine Irish lad, added: "C.B. *Schwartz.* He's in a meeting right now. I'll give Maeve's report to him when he gets out."

And after some more clucking by Aunt Oona over Kathleen's regrettable taste in dating methods and a suggestion that Briddey talk to Father O'Donnell before she did "something you'll be repenting about this GED," Briddey finally got Maeve's report away from her, and Aunt Oona left.

Briddey checked her email and then took the report out to Charla. "I need you to take this down to Mr. Schwartz. Tell him my aunt brought it, and it's from Maeve."

Charla took it reluctantly.

"He won't bite, if that's what you're worried about."

"I'm not," Charla said. "I was just wondering why she didn't take it down herself."

"My aunt went down to see *C.B.*?"

"Yeah. At least, she asked me where she could find him, and I told her he was down in the lab. She asked if I was sure, if he might not be in a meeting, and I told her he doesn't go to meetings. And then she asked me how to get to the lab, and I told her. Shouldn't I have done that?"

No.

"I warned her about him being kind of . . . you know," Charla said, twirling a finger next to her head to indicate craziness. "Should I have tried to stop her?"

Yes, Briddey thought. "No, of course not. If anyone calls, take a message." She grabbed the folder back from Charla and took off for C.B.'s lab, calling, *C.B., is my aunt down there with you?*

No answer.

Don't talk to her, she said, rounding the corner to the elevators. *Tell her you have a meeting to go to.* And ran straight into Phillip from Logistics.

"Just the person I wanted to see," he said. "What's this about Commspan coming out with a smart tattoo?"

That's got to be some kind of land-speed rumor record, Briddey thought. *It's almost as fast as the news of my EED will travel if Aunt Oona—*

"Please tell me we're not doing tattoos," Phillip was saying. "I'm a phone designer, not a tattoo artist."

"I'm sure we're not," Briddey told him. "Listen, I'm late for a meeting—"

"Well, we'd better not be, or I'll be out of a job," Phillip said, staring fixedly at the bandage on the back of her hand. "Are you *sure* you don't know anything about this smart tattoo?"

"Positive." She resisted the impulse to put her hand behind her back. "Why don't you ask Suki?" she said, and made her escape, calling, *C.B., answer me. Is my aunt down there with you?*

Indeed she is, and we're having a lovely bit of a chat.

C.B.— she said, and heard Art Sampson's voice say, "I'm fifty-nine. If I get laid off, I'll never find another job."

I can't afford to get waylaid by anybody else, Briddey thought, and ducked into the copy room to wait till he'd passed.

She should have looked inside before she did. Jill Quincy was at the copier. "You're just the person I wanted to see," she said. "What are all these rumors about the Hermes Project? What've they come up with?"

"I don't know," Briddey said, keeping an eye on the door so she could see when Art Sampson had gone by.

"But Trent's working on it, isn't he?"

"Yes, but it's all classified."

"I know, but couples tell each other everything, classified or not."

Not always, Briddey thought.

"Suki said they've come up with something that'll change the idea of communication altogether, that'll cause a complete paradigm shift."

Still no sign of Art Sampson. He must have gone the other way. And Briddey couldn't wait any longer. She put her phone to her ear even though it hadn't rung and said, "Phillip, no, I haven't forgotten. I'll be right there."

"Sorry," she said to Jill, and hurried out and down to the elevator. *C.B., answer me,* she called as she reached it. *I don't want you talking to my aunt.*

No answer.

She pushed the DOWN button. *C.B., I mean it.*

The elevator door began to open. Behind her, she heard Art Sampson say, ". . . still six years till I can take my retirement," and turned to see how close he was.

"Briddey!" Trent stepped out of the elevator. "Thank God I found you! We need to talk."

Out of the frying pan, into the fire, Briddey thought, looking longingly at the closing elevator door. "Trent! What are you doing here? I thought we agreed we shouldn't be seen together, and I just heard Art Sampson—"

"We've got bigger problems than Sampson. I still haven't felt anything. Have you?"

Yes, she thought. *Apprehensiveness, frustration, despair, and, right now, panic.* "No," she said.

"That's what I was afraid of. We need to call Dr. Verrick."

"But it hasn't been forty-eight hours yet," Briddey said. *And I've got to get downstairs before C.B. spills the beans to Aunt Oona.*

"I looked up EED connection times online," Trent was saying. "The average was twenty-eight hours. Something's wrong." He pulled out his phone.

"You can't call him here," Briddey said, looking anxiously down the hall. "Someone might overhear you."

"You're right." Trent pushed the button for the elevator. "We'll call him from my office."

"But what about your secretary?"

"She won't say anything. She's the soul of discretion."

"But I have a meeting I've got to—"

"Reschedule it. This is more important."

"And I need to run this report down to Lorraine in Marketing," she said, waving Maeve's science report at him. "It can't wait. I—"

Trent plucked it neatly out of her hands. "I'll have Ethel take it down to her. And I'll have her reschedule your meeting."

And now it was no longer a case of out of the frying pan, into the fire. The frying pan had caught fire, too. "She can't," Briddey said desperately. "Having *your* secretary cancel *my* meeting would cause all sorts of gossip."

"Then she can call *your* assistant and have *her* cancel it," Trent said, punching the button again.

"No, that's an even worse idea. Charla's good friends with Suki. She's bound to tell her. And if we're seen going up to your office together . . . You go, and I'll run this report to Lorraine and then come up."

The elevator door opened. Briddey grabbed the report back and quickly stepped inside. "Wait till I get there to call Dr. Verrick so we can talk to him together," she said, pushing the CLOSE DOOR button.

Trent put his hand on the door to prevent it from shutting. "How long do you think you'll be?"

Just long enough to get Aunt Oona away from C.B., she thought. "Five minutes. Ten at the most. Now go, before someone sees us."

"All right," Trent said, taking his hand from the door. "But—" And the door mercifully closed.

Briddey immediately pushed the button, waited impatiently while the elevator made its descent, and the second the door opened onto the icy sub-basement, shot out of the elevator and down to C.B.'s lab.

It was even colder than before. C.B. was on his knees in a corner, dismantling the heater. *Hi,* he said without looking up.

"Where's my aunt?" Briddey demanded.

Over there, he said, pointing at a metal cabinet. *I chopped her up and stuck her in a drawer. Because I'm*—he made Charla's twirling gesture next to his head—*you know.*

"I'm serious! And stop thinking at me. Talk out loud."

"Oh, right, I forgot. God forbid you'd reinforce our neural pathway. Where do you *think* your aunt is? She left. She had to go to Maeve's school for a counseling session or something." He stood up with a piece of the heater in his hand. "It was too bad. We were having a nice conversation."

Oh, God. "What did you say? You didn't tell her about us, did you?"

"Me?" he said. "You're the one who keeps wanting to tell people. I'm the one who keeps trying to talk you out of it."

"Then what was this 'nice conversation' about?"

"Maeve mostly, and how grateful she was that I helped her."

"Why didn't you tell me you'd been working with Maeve on her science report?"

"I assumed she'd already told you. And if you'll recall, the two of us had other things to talk about. Like why you shouldn't have the EED."

She ignored that. "And Maeve is all you and Aunt Oona talked about?"

"No, we talked about you, too. She thinks you need to dump Trent and find yourself a 'foine Irish lad.'"

Wonderful. "And what did you say?"

"I agreed. She also told me about Kathleen's internet-dating plans. And she had some dating advice for me."

"What did she say?" Briddey asked apprehensively.

"That's between me and Aunt Oona."

"You didn't say anything about taking me to the Marriott or bringing me home from the hospital?"

"Nope, just dating and your family. Who are really nice, by the way. A little overprotective, maybe, but they've got your best interests at heart. You're lucky to have them."

Lucky?

"Yeah. Not everybody has a family who worries about them, you know. Me, for instance."

"Well, you can have mine. You're sure you didn't talk about anything else? My having the EED or—"

"Nope," he said, walking over to the lab table and picking up a screwdriver. "We talked a little about Sean O'Reilly. And about the Daughters of Ireland." He went back over to the heater, squatted down, and began unscrewing a side panel. "Oh, and we discussed premonitions."

"You asked her about her *premonitions*?"

He finished unscrewing the panel before answering. "No, she brought it up. She was talking about my helping Maeve, and she mentioned she'd had a 'premonition' that Maeve needed help, and it had turned out to be true, so I asked her what that was, and she told me all about 'the Sight,' which she described as a kind of clairvoyance, but which I think is probably a combination of cold reading and guessing." He looked up at Briddey. "Don't worry. She didn't suspect anything."

He picked up a screw. "I take it since you're still keeping your EED secret, you haven't connected to Trent yet?"

You know perfectly well I haven't.

"Not even any whispers? Or fragrances, or pattering rain? Saint Deoch always heard 'divers sweet waftings of song' from heaven before she heard her voices. You hear any angelic songs? 'Hark, the Herald Angels Sing'? 'Angels We Have Heard on High'? 'Teen Angel'?"

"No," she said, "but we're not to the forty-eight-hour mark yet. I'm certain we'll connect by then."

"Sure."

"What's that supposed to mean? You don't think we're going to connect at all, do you?" Briddey said accusingly. "Why not? Are you doing something to see that we don't?"

"Like what, for instance?"

"Blocking me somehow," she said. She looked at the dismantled heater. "Interfering with the wiring."

"I told you, brains don't have wiring. And I thought interference was supposed to have caused our connection, not prevented yours and Trent's."

"There are other ways of interfering. Like insisting on talking mind-to-mind. And interrupting me every time I try to connect to Trent so I can't get through to him."

It doesn't work like that, C.B. muttered.

"You see? You're doing it right now. You're trying to reinforce our feedback loop so it's too strong for me to erase!"

"Oh, for . . . I am *not* blocking your boyfriend. I have better things to do with my time," he said, going back over to the heater. "Like fixing this before I freeze to death. And don't you have a meeting with your boyfriend or something?"

She'd completely forgotten about Trent. She raced upstairs, hoping against hope he hadn't gone ahead and called Dr. Verrick.

He had, but hadn't been able to reach him. "I told his receptionist it was urgent," Trent told Briddey, "and she said he wasn't in the office today and had me leave a message. A message! My secretary's looking up the number of his office at the hospital."

"Should she be doing that?" Briddey asked nervously.

"I told you, she's the soul of discretion."

"But if Suki—"

Ethel Godwin knocked and then opened the door. "I have that number for you, Mr. Worth," she said.

"Thank you," Trent said, and called the hospital. "No, next week won't work. We need to see him today. . . . Well, when will he be back? . . . Is there a cellphone number where he can be reached? . . . Yes, it's an emergency!"

He hung up. "Dr. Verrick's not there. He's off somewhere doing an EED—they didn't say where—and he may not be back till next week."

Thank heavens, Briddey thought, trying not to let her relief show in her face.

"They wouldn't give out his cellphone number," Trent said. "He didn't happen to tell you what it was, did he?"

Yes, she thought, and wondered why he hadn't given it to Trent, too. But thank goodness he hadn't. "No."

"Damn. I'll have Ethel see if there's some other way to reach him, through his L.A. office or his nurse—"

His phone pinged. "Sorry. It's Hamilton. He wants to see me right away. I'll text you when I've gotten in touch with him," he promised, and left.

Briddey started back to her office, feeling like the "luck of the Irish" that Aunt Oona was always talking about was actually with her.

Dr. Verrick was safely off in Manhattan or Palm Springs, Trent had raced off without instructing Ethel to locate his nurse's number, and C.B. had apparently been telling the truth when he said Aunt Oona hadn't suspected anything, because there weren't any outraged texts from her. And the ones from Kathleen and Mary Clare (which she read while waiting for the elevator) were, respectively, about whether Kathleen should join Sparks, HookUp.com, Cnnect, or all three, and which internet filter Mary Clare should install on Maeve's computer.

And the elevator arrived just in time for Briddey to avoid a conversation with Art Sampson, whom she heard saying, "Age discrimination's supposedly against the law, but you watch. I'll be the first to be laid off," just as the door closed.

Her luck continued to hold. Trent texted her at two that he was headed into a secure meeting that would probably last the rest of the day, which meant he wouldn't be able to pursue calling Dr. Verrick till after office hours. Or call her in a panic when the forty-eight-hour deadline passed at three o'clock without them connecting. Which it did.

Best of all, at three thirty she got an email saying that, due to "developments regarding the Hermes Project, all personnel are expected to work tomorrow from ten to four."

The email didn't specify what those developments were, and the omission sent Commspan into such a speculative frenzy that no one thought about anything else the rest of the day (except Art Sampson, who promptly rescheduled their meeting for Saturday morning and whom Briddey heard lamenting possible layoffs as she went out to her car) and she was able to make it off the premises without anyone noticing her bandage or asking her about EEDs.

Having to work Saturday also meant she wouldn't have to take Maeve to lunch and face another family interrogation when she picked her up and dropped her off. *I'll call Mary Clare as soon as I get home,* she thought, and then reconsidered. Mary Clare might suggest she come over tonight to talk to Maeve, and she needed to devote the evening to connecting with Trent.

If C.B. would leave her alone. But he must have taken her accusation of interfering to heart, or else he was still busy fixing his broken heater, because he didn't cut in once the entire evening.

Or maybe he wasn't able to get it fixed, she thought, getting ready for bed, *and he's frozen to death.*

For your information, C.B. said, *I've been doing some more research.*

About Bridey Murphy? Or Joan of Arc?

Joan, he said. *She didn't hear just one voice. She started out hearing Saint Catherine and then, later on, picked up Saint Michael and Saint Margaret.*

Or else she couldn't keep her stories straight, Briddey said. *She could have been lying—*

Except she was willing to be burned at the stake rather than say she hadn't heard them. I did some research on Dr. Rhine, too. You said you wanted a telepath who didn't live in the Middle Ages, and I think I found one.

Really? she said, and then thought, *He's just doing this to keep me from connecting with Trent.* "I don't want to hear it. Go away."

He ignored her. *I read the accounts of the Zener tests he did, and his research was discredited for a good reason. He counted almost anything as a correct answer, and the Zener cards were so thin, you could see right through the backs of them . . .*

He's just like my family, she thought, listening to him rattle on, *barging in at all hours, meddling in my affairs, refusing to respect my privacy. No wonder he likes them.*

Which gave her an idea of how to shut him up. She called Kathleen and asked her how her internet dating was going. "So I decided to join Cnnect, OKCupid, *and* Sparks," Kathleen said, "and to pick somebody on Sparks, you just tap their picture. So I tap this guy, and we go out for a drink, and we've only been there five minutes when he starts tapping other women! So I'm going to join something more serious, like JustDinner. Or Lattes'n'Luv."

Lattes'n'Luv? C.B. said. *She's kidding, right?*

Shut up, Briddey snapped. "Lattes'n'Luv?"

"It's for people who think a meal's too big a commitment," Kathleen said, "though if you're not willing to even commit to dinner, are you really good boyfriend material? On the other hand, I'm positive Sean O'Reilly won't be on it. I doubt if he even knows what a latte is. Or maybe I should join It's Only Brunch. It's like JustDinner, but with mimosas."

And you're definitely going to need booze, C.B. commented.

Go away, Briddey said.

"But going out for coffee doesn't last as long," Kathleen mused, and proceeded to compare the merits of brunch versus coffee dates for the next hour, and the only good thing about it was that at some point C.B. gave up and went away.

I wish I could, Briddey thought, yawning.

Kathleen finally hung up at eleven. Briddey checked her phone for messages from Trent, but there was just one, saying he still hadn't been able to reach Dr. Verrick, who was apparently in Morocco doing EEDs on a sheikh and one of his wives.

Even better, Briddey thought, and went to bed. She hadn't realized how tired she was. She fell asleep the minute her head hit the pillow, only to be awakened what seemed like moments later by the phone ringing.

It was Trent. "Get dressed," he said. "I finally got in touch with Dr. Verrick. We've got an appointment with him at midnight."

Eleven

"You really don't understand a word I tell you."
—*French Kiss*

"MIDNIGHT?" BRIDDEY REPEATED, SURE SHE MUST HAVE MISHEARD HIM. "But I thought he was in Morocco."

"He is," Trent said.

"Oh, we're having a conference call," she said, finally understanding.

"Yes, but he also said he might want to run some tests, which is why it needs to be at his office."

Some tests? Or some other kind of scan?

"Here's the address," Trent was saying. "You're going to need to leave right now to get there by midnight." He hung up before she could think of an excuse why she couldn't meet him. But if Trent was going to talk to Dr. Verrick, she needed to be there to keep Verrick from telling Trent that he'd never said they should keep apart and shouldn't have sex. But what if Dr. Verrick wanted to do an fCAT? C.B. had said it mapped brain activity. Could it show that they were connected?

C.B.! she called, getting out of bed and pulling on clothes. *Are you there, C.B.?*

What is it? C.B. said immediately. *What's happened? Did you hear somebody else's voice?*

You mean, did I connect with Trent? No. She explained what had happened.

What? What kind of doctor schedules appointments in the middle of the night?

It's probably daytime in Morocco, she said, putting on her shoes. *I need to know—*

About Dr. Rhine? I was just doing some research on him.

No, not about Dr. Rhine. Trent said Dr. Verrick might want to run some tests. If one of them's an fCAT, could it show that I'm connected to you?

No, he said promptly.

I thought you said it could show brain activity.

It can, but only in very general terms—memory in this part, language in that. It can't tell what you're thinking.

What about the other one you mentioned?

The imCAT? It can produce a more detailed map of synaptic activity, but I think that's all.

Can you find out for sure? Briddey asked, pulling on her coat. *I'd look it up, but I have to leave now if I'm going to make it to the appointment on time—*

And if you try to research it on your phone while you're driving, you're liable to get yourself killed, he said. *All right, I'll see what I can find out.* He went away, only to come back before she made it out to her car to ask, *Where is this appointment? At the hospital?*

Why? Briddey asked anxiously. *Does that mean there is such a scan, and the hospital has one?*

No, I'm just worried you and Trent might run into some nurse who'll say, "Hey, weren't you the patient who we found with her IV pulled out in that staircase the other night?"

She hadn't thought of that. *No, it's at Dr. Verrick's office.*

In the middle of the night. Are you sure he's not going to put you in a coma and steal your organs?

I'm sure, Briddey said, thinking that actually might be preferable. At least she wouldn't have to tell any more lies.

She got in her car and started downtown, wondering if she could make it by midnight, but the streets were nearly empty, and she was almost there before C.B. cut in again, calling, *Dawn Patrol to Night Fighter, come in, Night Fighter.*

What did you find out? Briddey asked.

That you don't have to worry. Dr. Verrick doesn't even have a CT scanner at his office, let alone an fCAT or an imCAT.

But he could make me go over to the hospital and have one done.

Even if he did, it wouldn't tell him you were telepathic. The imCAT can pinpoint synaptic activity more exactly than the fCAT, but it's still pretty primitive. It's not like Google Earth, where every square inch has been mapped. If patients are given math problems to solve, a certain area of the frontal lobe lights up. If they play them a song, the auditory cortex does, but that's as far as it goes. It still can't tell the content of your thoughts.

But wasn't there something in the news recently about a scan that took pictures of your thoughts? They had the person think of an eagle, and the scan showed an image of it—

You're talking about the fMRI, C.B. said, *but the images look more like inkblots than photos. You can see anything you want in them. But let's say there was a scan that snapped perfect pictures of your thoughts. It still wouldn't tell them what you were thinking.*

What does that mean? If—

Take that eagle. You could be remembering one you saw at a zoo or thinking about the Philadelphia Eagles or the Boy Scouts or "The Eagle has landed." And it certainly couldn't tell them I'd told you about one telepathically.

But if the same image showed up in both our brains at the same time, it would, Briddey said. *And even with the imCAT, they could tell someone was talking to me. It would show up in the language and the hearing centers of the brain, and—*

I just won't talk to you while they're doing the scan, C.B. said. *But even if I did, they'd just assume you were remembering a conversation you'd had before. Or were talking to yourself. So unless Verrick is specifically looking for evidence of telepathy—which he won't be—he wouldn't notice anything unusual. The only way he can find out you've been talking to me is if you tell him. You've got nothing to worry about. Except for the fact that he wants you to meet him at a mysterious address in the middle of the night.*

It's not a mysterious address. And Trent will be there, she said, pulling into the parking lot.

But there wasn't a single car in it. Trent obviously hadn't arrived yet. And no lights were on in the building. *I'm telling you, black-market organ transplants,* C.B. said. *If I were you, I'd hightail it before the orderlies with the chloroform show up.*

And she was sorely tempted to do that, to text Trent: "Did what you said, but no one there." But before she could get out her phone, lights sprang on in the reception area, and a nurse unlocked the door and waved to her. "Ms. Flannigan? Come in. The doctor's expecting you."

"Mr. Worth is coming, too," Briddey said.

The nurse nodded and led Briddey through the darkened reception area and into a room with a desk, a paper-covered examining table, and, on one wall, a huge high-resolution screen. The nurse took her vitals and looked at her stitches. "The incision's healing nicely," she said, replacing the bandage at the back of Briddey's neck with a butterfly bandage. "No sign of infection or edema?" She took her through the same questions they'd asked in the hospital: "Pain? Dizziness? Disorientation?"

"No, everything's fine," Briddey said.

"Except you haven't connected yet, is that right? When did you have the EED done?"

"On Wednesday."

The nurse noted it down. "Dr. Verrick's CMT will be in to set up your connection in a minute," she said, and left, and a moment later a young man in scrubs came in.

"Hi," he said. "I'm Dr. Verrick's computer medical technician. If you'll just hop up on the examining table, I'll get you all set up."

"All set up" meant positioning several cameras so Dr. Verrick could see both her face and the back of her head, attaching sensors to her wrist, upper arm, and chest, and using a laptop to bring up an image of an examining room somewhere else. "As soon as we're ready on this end, I'll call Dr. Verrick to come in," the tech explained, connecting the last of the cords.

"Shouldn't we wait for Mr. Worth?" Briddey asked.

"I'll check," he said, and went out. And if this was anything like the hospital, he'd be gone for hours.

Good, C.B. said. *That'll give me a chance to tell you about Dr. Rhine.*

I thought you told me his research had been discredited, Briddey said.

It was, and it deserved to be. He clearly cherry-picked the data. He claimed that his subjects' telepathic ability took time to warm up and then faded when they got tired, which means he only used the periods where they had runs of correct answers.

So his subjects couldn't really read minds?

Probably not. Except for this one subject. He scored amazingly high on the Zener tests.

And you think he was an actual telepath?

It's hard to tell. He had phenomenal scores for several weeks and then suddenly dropped back down to the level of chance and below, and stayed there. Like I said, Rhine messed with the data, so he may not have really been telepathic . . .

Or?

Or he decided he didn't want anybody to know he was and stopped cooperating. My guess is he figured out what would happen if Rhine got hold of the knowledge that he was, and he didn't want to be put in a circus to tell fortunes or be experimented on, or interrogated—

Or burned at the stake, Briddey said sarcastically.

Exactly. And he had the right idea. Telling—

Shh, Briddey said. *The tech's coming back.*

He can't hear me, C.B. said, but he shut up anyway as the tech came into the room.

"Dr. Verrick wants to examine you first," the tech said, hitting several keys in succession, and Dr. Verrick appeared on the screen, sitting at a desk in front of a laptop.

"Can you hear me?" the tech asked Dr. Verrick, and when the doctor said yes, adjusted the audio and the resolution slightly. "It's all yours, Doctor," he said, and went out.

"Ms. Flannigan," Dr. Verrick said, and as always, he seemed genuinely delighted to see her. "How are you feeling?"

"Fine," Briddey said cautiously.

"I understand you and Mr. Worth haven't connected yet. That's not unusual. Many couples take two to five days to connect, or even longer."

Trent should be hearing this, Briddey thought.

"Everything looks good," Dr. Verrick said, staring at the laptop on the desk in front of him. "The surgical site's healing nicely . . . no sign of infection . . . no swelling."

He raised his eyes from the laptop. "Are you certain you haven't connected? As I told you in the hospital, initial contact can be intermittent and faint, a glimmer of a sensation lasting only a second or two. You haven't felt anything like that?"

"No."

"What about other types of sensations? A sudden feeling of warmth or coldness? A tingling or a scent?"

You sound like C.B., she thought. "No."

"What about music? Or a voice?"

"A voice?" Briddey said, her body suddenly tense.

"Yes, several patients of mine have reported that the intensity of the emotional connection was so strong, they thought they heard their partner calling their name." He peered intently at her. "Have you heard something like that?" and Briddey thought, *If other patients have heard voices, he won't think I'm schizophrenic if I tell him.*

Tell him? C.B. said. *You can't—*

If Dr. Verrick's patients have heard voices before, Briddey said, *then maybe he knows what causes it and how to fix it.*

He said people heard their partners' voices, not somebody else's. You want him telling Trent that you—?

He can't tell Trent. Doctor-patient confidentiality, remember?

That's what Bridey Murphy thought, and she ended up on the cover of Life *magazine.*

Will you shut up about Bridey Murphy? she snapped, and said aloud, "Dr. Verrick, I—"

"Doctor?" the nurse's voice called from outside the door. She poked her head in.

"What is it?" Dr. Verrick responded just as if he were there in the room.

You can't seriously be thinking of telling him, C.B. said. *Think about what happened to Joan of Arc—*

Shh, Briddey hissed, trying to hear what the nurse was saying.

"Brad was wondering if he could bring in Mr. Worth now," she said. "He's supposed to be back at the hospital by one."

Dr. Verrick looked annoyed. "Yes, all right."

Why can't the nurse show Trent in? Briddey wondered, and had barely finished the thought when a tech appeared with a metal cart containing a smaller screen and a laptop. He rolled it up next to the examining table and began connecting cords and hitting keys.

You're kidding, C.B. said. *He makes you get out of bed and drive all the way down here, and he phones it in?*

Trent is very busy, she said defensively. *The Hermes Project is extremely important.*

You've got that right, C.B. said.

What does that mean? she demanded.

He ignored the question. *You* do *realize how ridiculous this is, don't you?* he said. *They're not even here.*

Neither are you, she snapped. *And at least Skype has an off switch.*

True, C.B. said. *Good point,* and surprisingly took the hint and left.

"All set," the tech said to Dr. Verrick's image. "They're ready on Mr. Worth's end. Just hit ALT CONTROL and VID2 on your end and then ENTER, and you'll be connected to him."

If only my *connecting to him were that easy,* Briddey thought.

"Thank you, Brad," Dr. Verrick said, and the tech left, but the doctor made no move to bring up Trent's image. Instead, he stood up, came around to the front of his desk, and perched on the corner of it, leaning confidentially toward Briddey, as if he were actually there in the room with her. "Sorry about the interruption. I was asking you if you'd heard Mr. Worth calling your name or speaking to you?"

Once you let the cat out of the bag, there's no getting it back in, you know, C.B. said.

Shh.

"The more empathetically sensitive the patient is," Dr. Verrick was saying, "the more complex the connection and the form the emotions take: tactile sensations, sounds, words—"

There, you see?

See what? C.B. said. *He's talking through his hat. You heard him. "Initial contact is intermittent and faint." Like hell. You and I were completely connected from the moment we started. And he said connecting was impossible for at least twelve hours, which it* obviously *wasn't. He doesn't have the slightest idea how it works.*

Well, he knows more than you, she said, and aloud: "Dr. Verrick, you said emotionally sensitive peop—" and the screen went blue.

Did you do that? Briddey demanded.

Do what?

You know perfectly well what, she said, and the door opened on the tech.

"Sorry," he said, hurrying over to the laptop. "Must be a problem with the feed." He began typing. "I'll have it back up in just a sec."

Moments later Dr. Verrick's image reappeared on the screen, and the tech apparently assumed that Trent had been part of the conversation, too, because he brought up his image on the other screen and said, "Sorry for the delay, Mr. Worth. We had a technical glitch. Can you hear me?"

"Yes," Trent's image said. He was sitting on the couch in his apartment. He looked over at Briddey. "Did you tell Dr. Verrick that we think he needs to run brain scans to see what the holdup in our connecting is?"

No!

Trent turned to look at Dr. Verrick's image. "Did something go wrong with her EED? Is that why we haven't been able to connect?"

"No," Dr. Verrick said, and repeated what he'd told Briddey about there being no sign of a physical problem.

"You're sure?" Trent persisted. "When you decided to keep her in and run more tests—"

Dr. Verrick's going to tell him he did that because of your hospital escapade, C.B. said. *Quick. Ask him if stress could be a factor.*

"We've both been under a lot of stress at work," Briddey said hastily. "Could that be the problem, Dr. Verrick?"

"Definitely. There are any number of factors that could interfere with connecting. Stress, lack of sleep, lack of—"

"If you're going to say lack of emotional bonding, it can't be that," Trent interrupted. "I know that's the main reason couples fail to connect, but I'm a hundred percent emotionally committed to Briddey, and I know she's just as committed as I am. There's no one else in either of our lives, is there, sweetheart?" He and Dr. Verrick both turned to look at her.

A phone rang, and Trent pulled his out of his pocket. "Sorry, Dr. Verrick, but I *have* to take this—"

"Of course," Dr. Verrick said, and reached to hit a key on his laptop. Trent's screen went blank.

"There's a *huge* project going on at work," Briddey explained, "and—"

Dr. Verrick waved her apology aside. "Actually, it's a good thing. I have some questions you may be able to answer more freely without him here. Mr. Worth is right. In ninety-five percent of cases where couples fail to connect, the obstacle is insufficient emotional bonding. Could that be the problem here?"

"Of course not," she said, and then remembered C.B.'s saying that any sentence beginning with "of course" was automatically a lie, and was surprised he didn't cut in with some sarcastic comment.

"There's no romantic involvement in your past you might not be completely over?" Dr. Verrick was asking. "Or another person you might also have romantic feelings for?"

"Absolutely not."

"You're certain? It's not uncommon for people to think they're in love with their EED partner but to actually be harboring feelings for someone else. In some cases the patient isn't even *aware* of those feelings."

So protesting that she wasn't in love with C.B. wouldn't do any good. Dr. Verrick would just think she wasn't "aware" of it. C.B. was right. She couldn't tell him.

"I don't have feelings for anyone but Trent," she said firmly. "And I don't have any doubts. I'm just as committed to our relationship as Trent is."

"In that case, the connection delay is almost certainly just that, a delay." He peered at her. "Didn't you have a question for me before we were interrupted?"

Not anymore, Briddey thought. "You've already answered it," she said.

"And you're certain you haven't received any emotions or sensations at all, in any of the forms I've described?"

"I'm positive."

He nodded and hit a key on his laptop, and Trent's image reappeared on the screen, looking annoyed. "I'm sorry about that," Dr. Verrick said. "There was a problem with the connection."

"Did you tell him the issue couldn't be emotional bonding, Briddey?" Trent asked.

"Yes."

"Well, then, what *is* the problem, Doctor? It's been nearly three days."

"As I was just telling Ms. Flannigan, that's not an unusual length of time," Dr. Verrick said. "It might take four to five days, or even longer."

"Longer?" Trent said, horrified. "How *much* longer?"

"It's impossible to say. There are so many variables." Dr. Verrick looked speculatively at Trent. "But it definitely won't happen if you try to force it. Tension and anxiety alter the brain chemistry and make it impossible for the necessary conduit neurons to form, which results in more stress. It's the same sort of thing which frequently occurs with people attempting to conceive a baby. The harder they try, the more difficult fertilization becomes. It's essential to break that feedback loop."

"How?" Trent asked eagerly.

"You need to relax and let it happen naturally. I'm going to write you a prescription for an anti-anxiety medication, and I want you to stop thinking about connecting and focus on other things. Read, watch television, play a videogame. Go out to dinner, or to a basketball game or a movie, anything that will take your mind off connecting."

"What about sex?" Trent asked, and before she could stop him, "Briddey said you told her we should avoid having sex for the first few days—"

"I said the nurse at the hospital told me that."

"No, you didn't," Trent said. "I distinctly remember. You said Dr. Verrick—"

"I said the nurse said I needed to make sure I'd recovered from the surgery before—"

"Which is good advice," Dr. Verrick said, "but I see no reason why sex isn't fine at this point, as long as it happens naturally and doesn't add stress."

And how could it possibly do that? Briddey thought despairingly. *Us having sex, and C.B. listening in while—*

You don't have to worry about that, C.B. said. *I'm not a complete masochist.*

Oh, she thought, surprised and touched—and oddly flattered. She felt herself coloring.

Please don't let him have picked up any of that, she thought. *He'll think—*

"Ms. Flannigan?" Dr. Verrick said, looking at her curiously.

Was she blushing? *Please don't let me be.* "Yes?" she asked, trying to steady her voice. "I'm sorry. What did you say?"

"The doctor asked if you have any more questions," Trent said impatiently.

"Oh," she said. "No, I think I understand what we're supposed to do."

"And do you have any questions, Mr. Worth?"

"No."

"Good. I've written you both a prescription for Xanax, and I want you to relax. No stress, no anxiety, and no thinking about connecting. Just let it happen naturally. Which it will," he said, and blanked Trent's screen.

"Thank you, Dr. Verrick," Briddey said, getting down off the examining table and reaching for her coat. But he wasn't done with her yet.

"I want you to call me immediately if you experience any sort of contact, no matter how minor or fleeting," he said, and gave her his cellphone number again. "Images, sounds, sensations of any kind, whether you think they're the form contact should take or not. One of my patients experienced a feeling of cold so intense it came through as words, and she heard her fiancé say, 'Shut the door. It's freezing.' Have you experienced anything like that?"

"No."

"A few minutes ago you had to ask me to repeat a question. Were you experiencing some sort of contact then?"

I was blushing, she thought. "No," she said firmly.

Dr. Verrick frowned. "Are you certain? You looked surprised and"—he hesitated, as if searching for the right word—"moved. Softened. As if you'd heard something that—"

The screen went blank.

Thank goodness, Briddey thought. "Dr. Verrick?" she said tentatively. "Can you hear me? I can't hear or see you. I think we've lost contact."

No answer. *Good. Get out of here while you have the chance,* she thought, grabbed her coat and bag, and slipped out of the office. The reception area was deserted, and Briddey hesitated, wondering if she should wait and get the prescription, but she didn't want the nurse checking with Dr. Verrick, realizing they'd been cut off, and calling in the tech again.

And besides, she thought, driving home through the darkened, deserted streets, *anxiety's clearly not the problem. It's all I've felt these last few days, and it hasn't prevented my connection to C.B. at all.*

Dr. Verrick is talking through his hat, she thought. But at least by saying that connecting might take several days, he'd given her some additional time to contact Trent, and she intended to make the most of it. She called to him continually the rest of the way home and late into the night, and again early Saturday morning, with no better luck than she'd had before. Her only contact with Trent was the series of texts he sent her as she was driving to work: "Trying to get tkts to *Dropped Call*" and "No luck. Sold out" and "Meet me for lunch cafeteria?"

Which reminded her that she needed to call Mary Clare as soon as she got to Commspan and tell her she couldn't take Maeve to lunch because she had to work, but before she even made it into the parking garage, Mary Clare called her. "We'll have to reschedule," she said. "Maeve's sick."

"What's wrong?" Briddey asked. "Does she have the flu?"

"No, she doesn't have a fever. She doesn't have any symptoms at all. I'm really worried about her."

Only Mary Clare. "If she doesn't have any symptoms, then how do you know she's sick?"

"Because she told me she was. We were eating breakfast—she was fine when she got up this morning—and we were talking about the mother-daughter book group, and all of a sudden she set her spoon down and said, 'I don't feel good. I think I'd better lie down,' and then went in her room and shut the door. I asked her if her stomach hurt, or if she was in pain, but she said no. I think it's appendicitis."

And I think it's the thought of facing the mother-daughter book group. "It's not appendicitis," Briddey said. "She'd have a fever. And a pain in her right side."

"Not if it had burst. I looked it up online. If she's not better in a couple of hours, I'm calling an ambulance."

Poor Maeve, Briddey thought, pulling into the garage.

C.B.'s car was already there, and so was Trent's. And Suki's. And Briddey was too tired to face any of them right now. Or Art Sampson, whose voice she heard the moment she entered the building. "If I'm laid off," he was saying, "there's no way my savings will last till I'm sixty-five."

Briddey didn't wait to see where he was. She sprinted for the stairs and up to her office. "I need you to call Art Sampson's office and cancel our eleven o'clock meeting," she told Charla. "Reschedule it for next week."

"His assistant already called and rescheduled it for Monday morning," Charla said.

"Oh. Good. Any messages?"

"Yes. A bunch from your sister Kathleen, and Trent's secretary called to say you have reservations at Luminesce tonight at eight, and Trent will pick you up at seven."

"Thank you," Briddey said, and started into her office, hoping there were no members of her family in there. Behind her, she heard, "A decaf latte."

She turned automatically, thinking, *If Charla's going for coffee, I could use some, too,* but Charla was at her computer typing.

It must have been someone out in the corridor, Briddey thought, going back to the door, but there was no one out there.

That sound was in my head, she thought excitedly. *It's finally happened. I've connected with Trent! And not just emotionally—with words!* C.B. had been wrong about them only having a second-class connection. They were going to be able to talk to each other, just like she and C.B. did.

Trent, can you hear me? I can hear you, she called, but he didn't answer.

Maybe it's only working on my end, she thought, and started to text him, pausing at the last second. If it was Trent, why had he said, "Decaf latte"? He hated lattes, and he never drank decaf. And the voice hadn't sounded like him at all.

C.B., are you the one who said that? she called, even though the voice hadn't sounded like him either.

"Is something wrong?" Charla said, and Briddey nearly asked her, "Did you hear somebody talking just then?" and then noticed the glint of curiosity in Charla's eyes. And the fact that she was reaching for her phone, no doubt to text Suki: "Boss acting strange." Or worse: "Boss hearing things."

"No, nothing's wrong. I just thought of something I forgot to do. Hold my calls," Briddey said, walked into her office, and shut the door.

A grande, the voice, still very faint, said. *No, no foam—* It cut off abruptly, and this time there was no question that it was in her head, which meant, in spite of the wrong-sounding voice and unlikely words, it had to be Trent. He was probably sending Ethel Godwin for coffee for the people in the meeting, and his mental voice sounded different from his audible voice.

But C.B.'s doesn't sound different, she thought. And his hadn't been faint, even in the beginning. It had been perfectly clear, and it hadn't cut off in the middle of sentences like they'd been disconnected—

Disconnected. *It was Trent's voice, and the reason it cut off like that was because C.B. was interfering with it.*

C.B.! she called. *Answer me! I know you're there.*

You don't have to shout, C.B. said. *I can hear you. What's up?*

What's up? she thought angrily. *You've been blocking Trent! And don't deny it. I heard him!*

You heard Trent? C.B. said, sounding completely astonished. *What do you mean, you heard him? You sensed his feelings?*

No, I heard his voice, she said. *In spite of what you were doing to keep me from—*

When was this? Never mind. There's something I have to tell you. Now. I need you to come down to my lab.

So you can explain why you've been keeping us from—?

Where are you? In your office? And she must have thought *yes,* because he said, *Stay there. I'll be right up.*

She had no intention of letting him tell her any more lies, here in her office or anywhere else. She grabbed her phone, told Charla she was going down to the cafeteria, and took off for Trent's office, taking the stairs to avoid C.B. *I should have told Trent about the telepathy when this first happened,* she thought, running up the stairs and hurrying down the corridor to his office. *I should never have let C.B. talk me out of—*

A hand shot out from the doorway of the conference room as she passed it and grabbed hold of her wrist. "What do you think you're do—?" she yelped, and saw that it was C.B.

"Shh," he whispered. "First the hospital and now this. Exactly what part of 'Stay there' do you not understand?"

"Let *go* of me," she spat at him, trying to wrench free.

"Not until I've talked to you." He started to pull her into the conference room.

"You can't just kidnap me!" she said, looking wildly around for someone, anyone, to help her.

"Again with the kidnapping," C.B. said. "What *is* it with you?"

"With *me*?" she said furiously, trying to pry his fingers from her wrist. She kicked him in the shins. "You're the one who's acting like the Phantom of the Opera!"

"Hunchback of Notre Dame," he corrected her, and stopped pulling. "Fine," he said loudly. "We'll do it right here, in front of everybody. Is that what you want? I just saw Suki coming this—"

"Shh," Briddey said, and let him usher her into the conference room. As soon as they were inside, C.B. let go of her wrist, took the MEETING IN PROGRESS—DO NOT DISTURB sign off the doorknob, and opened the door just far enough to hang it outside. Then he walked over to the conference table to grab a piece of paper and Scotch tape. Briddey looked at the door, gauging whether she could make it out and to Trent's office before C.B.—

Nope, he said, moving swiftly between her and the door. *I can read your mind, remember?* He taped the piece of paper over the door's window and then pulled out one of the conference chairs. "Sit."

"I'll stand, thank you." She crossed her arms.

"Fine. When exactly did you hear Trent?"

"A few minutes ago."

"That was the first time you'd heard him?"

"Yes."

"And you're sure it was Trent? What did he say?"

"That's none of your—"

"What did he *say*?" C.B. shouted. "I need to know, Briddey."

"So you can block him."

"I'm *not* blocking him!"

"Then why did his voice cut off like that? You were jamming him, that's why. He managed to get through despite it, but that's why his voice was so faint, and why it didn't sound like him—"

C.B. pounced on that. "What do you mean, it didn't sound like him? You didn't think it was Trent's voice when you first heard it?"

"No, thanks to your distorting it or whatever you were doing."

He ignored that. "Tell me what he said."

"Why?" she said belligerently. "I thought you could read my mind."

He ignored that, too. "Tell me. The exact words." And something in his manner made her answer him.

"The first time he said, 'A decaf latte,' and I thought it was someone out in the hallway," she said.

"Are you sure it wasn't?"

"Yes, because a few minutes later I was in my office with the door shut, and I heard him say, 'A grande,' and 'No, no foam.'"

"Like he was ordering at Starbucks," C.B. said, and when she nodded: "Did it sound like he was talking to you?"

"No," she admitted. *And don't you dare try to tell me Trent's emotionally bonded to a Starbucks barista.*

"And that's it? You haven't heard anything else?"

"No, except for you," she said, and he visibly relaxed. *Because he was jamming Trent.*

"No, I'm not! When you said the voice was 'distorted,' what did you mean? How was it different from Trent's voice? Did it sound deeper? More nasal? Did it have an accent?"

"No," she said, frowning, trying to remember, but there'd been nothing identifiable about it at all, nothing to distinguish it from any other—

Shit, C.B. said. *That's what I was afraid of.* "I should have—" He broke off and gestured toward the chair he'd pulled out. "Sit down. Please. I have things I've got to tell you," and he sounded so serious she obeyed.

"What is it?" she asked. "What's wrong?"

He pulled out another chair, sat down opposite her, and leaned forward, his knees spread apart, his hands clenched together between them. "I should have told you all this before, but I thought . . . the thing is, you could only hear me, and I thought maybe it was going to stay that way, especially when so much time went by and nothing had happened. I—"

Why is this taking so long? a voice cut in, sounding annoyed, and Briddey automatically glanced at the covered window in the door, thinking it was someone outside wanting to get in, and then realized

C.B. hadn't looked toward the door. Or given any indication that he'd heard anything.

It's Trent, she thought, even though it still didn't sound like him. But at least this time he'd said something Trent would say.

I'm here, she called. *I can hear you.*

"You can hear who?" C.B. said, reaching forward to grab her hand. "Briddey, did you hear somebody talking just now?"

"Yes. Trent. He asked why our connection was taking so long."

"He did? He used the word 'connection'?"

"No," she admitted, "but that was what he—"

"Tell me exactly what he said. It's important."

"He said, 'Why is this taking so long?'"

"Did his voice sound like the time before?"

It hadn't, though she couldn't say how the two voices were different. She simply had a feeling that they were. "No, because you interfered with—"

She stopped. C.B. was looking at her, but his expression wasn't defensive. It was pitying, as if he had bad news to give her. "What is it?" she asked.

"It wasn't Trent."

"What do you mean, it wasn't Trent? Are you saying I only imagined it?"

"No. Unfortunately."

"What's that supposed to mean? It had to be him. Who else could it have been?"

He looked even more pitying. "Anyone," he said.

"*Anyone?* What do you mean, 'anyone'?"

"I mean it could have been somebody else here at Commspan waiting for his computer to boot up, or an expectant father wondering why his wife's labor is taking so long. Or a guy waiting for the light to change."

"Yet you're certain it wasn't Trent wondering why we hadn't connected yet," she said angrily. "Why not?"

"Because you didn't recognize the voice. That means it's a stranger, and so was the person you heard ordering the latte."

"You're saying I heard *two* strangers?"

"Yes, and they're just the first. Over the next two or three days you're going to hear a lot more—"

"And how exactly do you know all this?" she asked, but she already knew the answer. "You've heard them, too, haven't you? These other voices."

"Yes. And they're not pleasant. I need to teach you—"

"You heard other voices," she said, working this all out in her mind. "You heard complete strangers' voices, and as soon as you heard them, you knew our hearing each other didn't have anything to do with emotional bonding. You knew something else had to be causing it, and yet you didn't say a word."

"Okay, look, I realize I should have told you sooner—"

"*Sooner?* You should have told me *immediately*. When it first happened. Which was when?"

"Briddey—"

"You've obviously been hearing these other voices long enough to have figured out all sorts of things about them, which means you must have been hearing them for a while. How long?"

Since that day he brought me home from the hospital, she thought, answering her own question. *That's how he knew Kathleen didn't see us at my apartment. And how he knew it was safe to go back, because he heard her think about leaving.*

"Or did you hear them before that, when I was still in the hospital?" she asked. "Of course you did. That's how you knew the nurse had gone off duty, and that they were trying to decide whether to tell Dr. Verrick about my running away." He'd said he overheard them talking at the nurses' station, but he hadn't. He'd read their minds. And that was why he'd brought up Joan of Arc's having heard more than one voice—to find out if it was happening to her, too. "You started hearing other voices that first night, right after you heard mine, didn't you?"

He had that pitying look again. "No."

Oh, my God, he'd heard them—and hers—*before* she'd had the EED. That was how he'd caught her as she was leaving for the hospital. And how he'd found out she was having the EED in the first place. "How long have you been hearing voices?" she demanded.

"Briddey—"

"Answer the question. How long?"

He took a deep breath. "Since I was thirteen."

Twelve

"I was in my thirteenth year when I heard a voice from God ...
and the first time I was very much afraid."

—JOAN OF ARC

"THIRTEEN?" BRIDDEY REPEATED, TRYING TO TAKE IT IN.

C.B. nodded. "Three weeks after my birthday. And a couple months after I'd hit puberty, so you can probably figure out what I assumed was causing it—though we were also reading *I Never Promised You a Rose Garden* in school, which is about a schizophrenic teenager, so I figured it might also be that. I didn't know about Joan of Arc then, or all the other saints who'd started hearing voices at the same age."

"You've been hearing voices since you were a teenager," she said. And of course he had. It explained everything: his being such a loner, and Charla's saying she'd heard him talking to himself, and his earbuds not being attached to anything. And it explained why he hadn't been surprised that first night in the hospital, why he'd instantly accepted the idea that they were communicating telepathically. Because he'd been doing it since he was thirteen.

"Wrong. I've been hearing voices since I was thirteen," he corrected her. "Not talking to them. That's a more recent development."

"How recent?"

"Really recent."

"You mean *I* was the first person you were able to talk to? And what do you mean 'voices'? How many voices? Can you hear everybody at Commspan?" Of course he could. He'd probably been eavesdropping on the Hermes Project's meetings and laughing at the security precautions they'd taken to keep Apple from finding out about the new—

"It doesn't work like that," C.B. interrupted. "You don't have any control over who or what you hear. It just happens, like a minute ago when you heard the guy say, 'Why is it taking so long?' The voices just come. And they'll keep coming, which is why I've got to teach you how to block—"

"I *knew* it," she said. "You *were* blocking Trent!"

"Oh, for cripes' sake," C.B. said, dragging his hand through his hair. "For the last time, I am *not* blocking your stupid boyfriend! I'm trying to help *you* block the voices. You've got to erect a bulwark against them, and you've got to do it now, before you start to hear any more of them. You just heard the first one today, so we should have a day or two before it gets bad, but it takes time to get defenses up, and I'm going to need to teach you to—"

"Even if I believed you weren't keeping Trent and me from connecting, which I don't," she said coolly, "you could obviously hear him, which means you knew how much he loves me and how hard he was trying to connect, but you didn't say a word. And you didn't say a word about why I could hear you, even though you knew that, too. You told me it was because we were emotionally bonded—"

"I did not. I said that was what *Trent* would think. And it wasn't like that. I didn't tell you that first night because I was afraid you'd freak out completely. You'd already yanked out your IV and gone running off just from the shock of hearing me. I was afraid if I told you everything, you might throw yourself down an elevator shaft or something."

"And what about since then?"

"I tried to tell you when I took you home from the hospital—"

"That was two days ago."

"I know. I probably should have told you sooner—"

"Probably?"

"Okay, then, I definitely should have, but I was hoping I wouldn't have to. You weren't hearing anyone but me, and I thought maybe the EED had only made you partially telepathic and you wouldn't hear anybody else—"

"And you might be able to convince me we *were* emotionally bonded, and I'd fall into your arms."

"No, of course not—"

"Or at the very least you could use the emotional-bonding thing to keep me from telling Trent. Of course. That's why you told me all those stories about dying loved ones and torpedoed sailors and Mc-Cook, Nebraska. And you told me about Bridey Murphy and the 'hearing voices' study to convince me Dr. Verrick would think I was crazy. You did everything you could to keep me from telling them."

"You're right, I did. Because—"

"Because you didn't want them to find out *you* were telepathic," she said. "That's what all this—the warm blanket and the ride home and taking me to get my car—was about, making sure I kept my mouth shut. You didn't care what it would do to me or my relationship with Trent, whether he thought my not connecting to him meant I didn't love him, and he broke up with me. That didn't matter. All you cared about was keeping your precious secret."

"Precious," he muttered. "That's hardly the word I'd use. Briddey, listen—" He took a step toward her.

She put up her hand to stop him. "No, I *won't* listen." She'd almost *bought* his lies. She'd actually been starting to *like* him. "I can't believe you did that to me. I could *kill* you!" she cried, and flung herself at the door.

"Briddey—" he said, reaching out his hand to stop her.

"Don't you *dare* touch me, you liar, you jerk … y-you … ," she stammered, unable to think of a bad enough name to call him. "You *hunchback!*" She flung the door open. "And *don't* follow me!"

She stormed out of the conference room and down the corridor, fumbling in her pocket for her phone. She had to find Trent, had to tell him—

C.B. said, *Briddey, you can't—* and she whirled around furiously to face him.

The corridor stretched emptily behind her. *Go away,* she said violently.

You can't just walk away from this, Briddey, C.B. said. *I need to teach you how to protect yourself. Once you really start hearing the voices, it'll be much harder to put up defenses.*

I have no intention of letting you teach me anything, she said, though she was fully aware that she had no way to stop him. *I hate being telepathic,* she thought.

Yeah, and you're going to hate it a hell of a lot more in the next couple of days if you don't let me—

Let you what? Tell me more lies?

They weren't lies—

Then what were they? All that stuff about doing research to try to find out what was causing the telepathy—

I did do research. Just . . . earlier. And everything I've just told you about the voices is true—

Why should I believe you? she said furiously. *You've lied to me about everything. I'll bet all this talk about defenses and bulwarks is just crosstalk to jam my line to Trent.*

It doesn't—

Work like that? Briddey said bitterly. *So you keep telling me. And how do I know that's not a lie, too?*

Because—

I don't want to hear it. Now go away, she said, getting out her phone, *or I'll call the police and tell them you're stalking me! I'll get a restraining order!*

I doubt if that would do much good under the circumstances.

I mean it, she said, scrolling through her phone list. *I'm calling the police.*

No, you're not, he said. *I can read your mind, remember? You're calling Trent. Which is a really bad idea.*

No, the bad idea was not telling him in the first place. She called Trent's number.

His phone went straight to voicemail. She called his office. His secretary answered. "Oh, Briddey, I'm afraid he's in a secure meeting," she said.

That's what you think, Briddey thought. *With telepathy, there's no such thing as secure. I've got to tell Trent that.*

"Is there something *I* can help you with?" Ethel was asking.

No. "Can you have him call me as soon as he gets out of his meeting?"

"Of course. Did you get the message about Trent picking you up for dinner at seven?"

"Yes."

You're going out to dinner? C.B. said, horrified. *At a restaurant? You can't. You need to stay away from places like that.*

Away from Trent, you mean. Because if we're together, we might connect, and that would ruin your little plan to keep us apart.

No, because you have no business going anywhere where there are a bunch of people, C.B. said. *Restaurants, movie theaters, churches, football games, parties. A crowd could . . . you need to get your defenses up now, before the voices get any closer together. I need to teach you how to build a barricade.*

I need a barricade, all right—against you! and then was terrified she'd said that out loud.

But Ethel was saying calmly, "I'll tell Mr. Worth to call you the moment he gets out of his meeting."

"Thank you," Briddey said. "You don't know how long the meeting's liable to last, do you?"

"No," Ethel said, and she must have caught the anxiety in Briddey's voice because she asked, "Is everything all right?"

"Yes, of course," Briddey said brightly. "I just wondered."

She hung up and then stood there staring blindly at her phone, debating whether to call Ethel back, ask her where Trent's meeting was, and go bang on the door and demand to speak to him. But all that was likely to accomplish was getting both of them fired. *And I don't have to do that,* she thought. *I have another way of contacting him. And I have no intention of letting C.B. stop me from getting through to him.*

Trent, she called. *Are you there? I need to talk to you.*

That's a bad idea, too, C.B. said. *The last thing you want to be doing right now is opening yourself up to contact of any kind. The voices—*

I want to hear the voices. It'll be better than hearing yours!

You don't mean that. You've only heard a couple of them so far, but you'll start hearing more and more of them, and they'll come more and more often, and in another day or two you'll hear all their thoughts all the time.

Like you've been hearing mine? All those times she'd thought he was gone, he'd actually been lurking there in her mind, spying on her like some common Peeping Tom. *You have been listening to me in the shower,* she said accusingly. *You pervert!*

Fine. Call me whatever names you want. But you have to listen to me—

No, I don't. And whatever it is you're trying to warn me against, it couldn't possibly be worse than you! Go away, and don't ever come near me again!

You can't go to anyplace crowded, and you can't take any relaxants, no alcohol or sedatives—did Verrick prescribe anything for you, Xanax or Valium or something?

That's none of your business, she said, and when would she learn he could read her mind?

Good girl, he said. *Walking out was the smart thing to do. If he faxes you the prescription, don't get it filled.*

Not listening, she said, and began singing, *La la la la—*

That won't work against the voices, and neither will sticking your fingers in your ears. The only thing that will is—shit!

What? she said suspiciously. *Is Trent trying to get through to me again?*

No, he said, but as if he wasn't really listening to her. *Shit. It never rains but it pours,* he muttered. *Listen, promise me you won't do anything till we can talk about this. It's important,* and was gone.

Good, Briddey said, in case he was still listening, which she wouldn't put past him, and started back down to her office, walking in the middle of the corridor in case it was a trick, and he was lying in wait in the copy room or the staff lounge.

He wasn't, and she didn't run into anyone else, thank goodness, though just before she reached her office she heard Art Sampson say, ". . . can't live on what I've got saved."

Poor man, he was apparently roaming the halls nonstop, talking about the layoffs to anyone who'd listen. *It's not going to be me,* Briddey thought, diving into her office. She already had too much to deal with.

Including Charla, who stood up in alarm when she saw her and said, "Are you *okay?*"

"Yes, of course," Briddey said, starting past her.

"You just look so . . . did you have an argument with somebody?"

She must look as furious as she felt. And she'd better say something if she didn't want Charla telling Suki she'd broken up with Trent. "Yes,

I did," she said. "With Art Sampson. He's upset about having to work on a Saturday."

Charla frowned. "Art Sampson? But he's not here."

"Not here?" Briddey repeated blankly.

"No. That's why his assistant called to cancel, because he's sick and couldn't come in today."

But I heard his voice, Briddey thought.

Charla was looking at her worriedly. "Are you okay?"

"Yes. Of course. He must have come in to pick up some files or something."

"But why would he come in if he was sick? And why couldn't his assistant have emailed the files to him?"

"I don't know," Briddey said, belatedly remembering C.B.'s Rules of Lying, and went into her office and shut the door before she could get into any more trouble. She hadn't heard Art Sampson coming down the hall just now. He'd been a voice in her head. Had he been one yesterday, too?

She'd told C.B. she'd only started hearing other people today, but if Art Sampson was one of them, that wasn't true. She'd been hearing them since yesterday morning. And C.B. had said in another day or two she'd be hearing more voices than she could handle, which might be today. If *he was telling the truth. If that wasn't just another lie to keep me from telling Trent.* But she wondered if she should tell C.B.

Not until I know for sure that Art Sampson didn't come in today, she thought, and called his office to find out.

He wasn't here. He'd called in sick this morning. And five minutes later Briddey heard him say, *First layoffs and now the flu. It's not fair!,* and a moment after that: *Where's the damned aspirin? She said it was in the medicine cabinet,* which pretty much confirmed his being at home.

But she didn't hear the decaf latte guy again, or the person who'd said, *Why is this taking so long?* And at least hearing Art Sampson was going to make it easier to tell Trent about C.B. She couldn't possibly be emotionally bonded to him.

Or to Lorraine from Marketing, who popped up to say, *There's definitely a spy here at Commspan. I wonder who it is. Probably my supervisor. I hope it is, and she gets caught and fired. I need to text Jeremiah in Human Resources and see who he thinks it is. He is so cute."*

Now if Trent would just pop up. But he didn't. Happily, C.B. didn't either. *Maybe he finally figured out I wasn't going to listen to any more of his lies,* she thought.

But they hadn't all been lies. She *was* hearing more voices, and they *did* seem to be random. Trying to hear more of what Lorraine thought and *not* to hear Art Sampson had no effect on her ability to pick up what they were saying, which worried her a little. If C.B.'d told the truth about that, could he have been telling the truth about needing to stay away from crowded places?

But he'd obviously told her that because he didn't want her to meet Trent at the restaurant—and Art Sampson and Lorraine hardly needed to be defended against. Hearing them in her head was no worse than what she experienced every day walking to her office. It was better, actually. She didn't have to make excuses to get away from them, and it was sort of fun to know that Lorraine had a crush on someone in Human Resources and that she hated her supervisor.

Charla came in to tell her that Jill Quincy wanted to meet with her and that she had an email from Trent. When Briddey opened it, it was an ad for Tiffany's engagement rings. "To give you something to think about until dinner."

Maybe that means he's out of his meeting, Briddey thought, but when she phoned him there was no answer, and when she looked at the time stamp on his email, she saw it had been sent earlier in the day.

She went up to meet with Jill, wondering if she'd hear Jill's voice, too, and who *she* had a secret crush on. *Careful, you're starting to sound like Suki,* she thought, and pondered how much damage Suki could do if *she* could hear voices.

None of us would be safe, she thought, and had to admit that C.B. had been right about telepathy being dangerous. And unsettling. Except for Art Sampson, who she knew wasn't here, it was impossible to tell whether the voices she heard were real or in her head. When she heard Phillip say, "Briddey Flannigan," she ignored it, only to have him catch up to her and ask, "Didn't you hear me? I wanted to ask you, do you know what the Hermes Project's working on? Somebody told me it's a smart baseball cap."

Which she supposed was better than a smart tattoo. "I don't know," she said. "I've heard all kinds of things. Sorry, I've got a meeting." She started past him.

"Oh, you know, all right. You just don't want to tell," Phillip said, and she had no way to know whether he'd actually said that or not, and, consequently, no idea whether she should answer him.

Maybe schizophrenics don't start out insane, she thought. *Maybe they just end up that way from the strain of not knowing whether the voices they hear are real or not.*

It was a positive relief to reach Jill's office and sit across from the person she was talking to and be able to see whether she was speaking or not, though it turned out not to be necessary. She didn't hear Jill's thoughts at all through the entire meeting—or anyone else's.

"Okay," Jill said as they finished, "so you'll send me the analysis on this?"

"Yes," Briddey said, and got up to go.

"So I suppose you and Trent are doing something exciting tonight?"

I hope not, Briddey thought. "No, he's just taking me out to dinner. To Luminesce."

"Oh, you're so lucky. I've always wanted to go there! I know you'll have a wonderful time!"

A wonderful time, Briddey thought grimly as she headed back to her office. *I rather doubt it, not when I've got to tell Trent I'm hearing voices.* But at least she could finally stop lying and—

"Briddey—" she heard Jill say, and turned around, thinking Jill had forgotten to tell her something, but the hallway was empty.

That was Jill's mental voice I heard, Briddey thought. *That makes five voices. No, six, if Phillip only thought that thing about my knowing what the Hermes Project was doing.* C.B. hadn't been lying about that part. She *was* starting to hear more and more voices.

"No, we're not doing anything exciting tonight," Jill said in a sarcastic, mimicking voice. *"Trent's only taking me to Luminesce, the most exclusive restaurant in town."* Oh, I could just slap her bragging little face!

I wasn't *bragging,* Briddey protested. *You asked me what we were doing.*

I'm so sick of hearing about her stupid perfect boyfriend and her stupid perfect life!

But you brought it up, Briddey thought, mortified. And appalled that Jill felt that way about her. She was grateful when Art Sampson cut back in, fretting about his health insurance again. But when she got back to her office and Charla smiled cheerfully up at her, she wondered, *Do you hate me, too?*

"You have a bunch of messages," Charla said. "Your sister Mary Clare called to say your niece is feeling better but she's still worried about her. And Kathleen called to say she decided to go with Lattes'n'Luv, whatever that is."

"An internet dating site. For people who want to commit to coffee but not lunch."

"I wish I knew if Nate was willing to commit," Charla said ruefully, and Briddey found herself turning to look sharply at her, wondering if Charla'd said that or only thought it.

"Trent Worth's secretary called and said his meeting is running long, so to go on home and he'll pick you up at seven. Oh, and these came for you," she said, pointing to a bouquet of pale pink camellias. The card read simply, "Tonight. Trent."

"Thank you," Briddey said. She picked up the flowers and went into her office, bracing herself for some spiteful unspoken remark.

I hope she goes home early, she heard Charla think. *She looks exhausted,* and Briddey was so grateful she hadn't said something cruel, she came back out and said, "You can go home now, Charla. I'll finish up here."

She didn't hear anything more from Charla or from the others as she finished up her work and went out to the car. She didn't hear anything from C.B. either, which was just as well, because Ethel Godwin phoned as she pulled out of the parking lot to tell her that plans had changed and Trent wasn't picking her up. She was to meet him at the theater.

"Theater?" Briddey said.

"Yes, he was able to get tickets to *Dropped Call* after all, so you're going to the play and having supper afterward." She gave Briddey the name and address of the theater. "The curtain's at eight."

If C.B. didn't want her to go to a restaurant, he definitely wouldn't want her to go to a theater, and she was glad he didn't pop up and start yammering at her again, especially since the traffic on her way home was terrible. She'd never make it home in time to shower and dress. And how was she going to be able to shower anyway, knowing C.B. might be spying on her?

Maybe she should have listened to his instructions for keeping the voices out after all. She could have used them to keep *him* out. What had he said, to put up a barricade? *I'll definitely do that,* she thought. *One made of lead, in case he lied to me about the X-ray vision thing, too.*

The traffic was getting heavier, and up ahead brake lights were beginning to flash on in her lane. She flicked on her turn signal so she could change lanes.

"What the hell do you think you're doing?" a stranger said in her ear.

Panicked, she whipped her head around to see who was in the back seat. Horns blared, and she realized she'd swerved. She pulled back into her own lane, heart thudding, mouthing an automatic "Sorry" to the driver of the car she'd nearly hit. He made a rude gesture and roared ahead of her. *Didn't you ever learn to drive?* the voice bellowed.

There isn't anyone in the back seat, Briddey told herself over her racketing heart. It was just a voice, like the decaf latte guy.

But it took all her willpower to keep her eyes on the road, and she reached for her phone and held it as she maneuvered her way over to the exit lane and down the off-ramp.

Signal, will you? Make up your mind! Are you getting in this lane or what?

He isn't talking to me, Briddey told herself firmly, turning right at the bottom of the ramp onto a surface street.

At the first opportunity, she pulled over to the curb, unlocked her phone, tapped on her contacts list, and scrolled down to 911—finger poised to hit it if someone put a gun to her head—and then turned to look in the back seat.

There was no one there. *It was just someone yelling at some other driver,* she thought, relieved, and got back on the highway, but his anger had left her shaken, even though it hadn't been directed at her.

Jesus, some people! he shouted a mile later. *Look at that! Learn how to drive!* Immediately after, a different voice said, *God, at this rate I'm not going to be done delivering till eight o'clock!*

He must be in the same traffic as I am, Briddey thought, and heard him say, *If I hadn't had to take those camellias to Commspan, I wouldn't be stuck in this . . .* She lost the last part of that, but it was clear who he was—the person who'd delivered the flowers from Trent.

If I get off here, I can deliver the roses and then that funeral spray, he said, and a few seconds later Art Sampson started in again, fretting about getting laid off, a soliloquy he kept up till Briddey got home, with occasional interjections by the angry driver and Jill, all of which convinced Briddey she'd better not drive to the theater.

She called a taxi as soon as she got up to her apartment and stepped into the shower, imagining a barricade around it in case C.B. was eavesdropping. She was surprised he'd been gone this long. She wondered what he was doing, and why he'd said, *Shit. It never rains, but it pours.* Did that mean—?

Will you look at this! a voice said, and Briddey grabbed instinctively for a towel.

"Go *away!*" she shouted, clutching the towel to her and grabbing the shampoo bottle to use as a weapon.

But it was only the florist guy, saying, *Half the stems are broken! I'll have to go all the way back to the shop.*

This is ridiculous, Briddey thought, and was grateful she didn't hear anyone else as she dried her hair and put on her emerald-green taffeta with the short, swingy skirt, and the diamond earrings Trent had gotten her. She twisted her hair into an updo, put on mascara and lipstick, and went in search of her silver evening bag.

Her phone rang. *Please don't let this be any of my family,* she thought. *I've had all I can take.*

It wasn't. It was the taxi. She told the driver she'd be right down, tried one last drawer, where, luckily, she found the evening bag, stuffed her lipstick, comb, credit card, keys, and phone into it, and ran downstairs. She was already in the taxi and halfway down the block when she realized she hadn't eaten anything, and they weren't going to have dinner till after the play. Well, maybe if she got there early, she could grab something at Starbucks.

But it didn't look like that would be the case. They ran into stop-and-go traffic almost as soon as they turned onto Linden. *Of course,* Briddey thought. *It's Saturday night.* She was doubly glad she'd decided not to drive.

"Holy shit!" the driver exclaimed a block later. "Look at this traffic. It's a fucking nightmare!"

"I know," Briddey said, looking ahead at the sea of red brake lights.

"What did you say?" the driver asked, glancing at her in the rear-view mirror.

She leaned forward and put her hands on the back of the front seat. "I said, 'I know.'"

"Know what?"

Oh, God, she thought. *He didn't say that out loud.* "Nothing," she said. "Sorry."

"You okay?" the driver asked, frowning at her in the rearview mirror.

"Yes," she said, and tried to smile. "I was just talking to myself." And, as soon as they were moving again, slid over to the other side so she could see if his mouth was moving the next time she heard someone speak, but it wasn't necessary. She recognized the other voices.

And if Commspan's laying people off, you can bet Motorola is, too, Art Sampson fretted; Lorraine said, *If I have to put up with my supervisor one more day . . . ;* and the florist guy said, *I just hope I don't have to make any more deliveries out there.*

Two blocks later Jill said, *I'm having ramen noodles for dinner, and she's going to Luminesce! It's not fair! Just because she's got that red hair, she thinks she's so wonderful! I'll bet you anything it isn't even natural!*

C.B. wasn't lying about that either, Briddey thought. *It is just like being stuck in the bathroom in middle school.*

I've delivered four arrangements for that Worth guy in one week, the deliveryman said. *He must be cheating on her big-time. Or else she won't put out, and he's trying to sweet-talk her into it!*

."Trent's taking me to Luminesce!" Jill mocked, her voice dripping with contempt. *"Trent's taking me to Iridium!" "Trent and I are getting an EED!"*

"I'm sorry about all this traffic," the taxi driver said. "I'm going to see if I can find something better." He turned onto Lincoln, which was better for several blocks before the traffic came to a complete stop. "What time's this thing you're going to?"

"Eight o'clock." *But it doesn't matter. Trent and I aren't going to the play. I can't with all these voices yammering at me.* And, as if to drive home the point, she suddenly heard Phillip say, *. . . redhead in that car looks like Briddey Flannigan. You can't tell me Worth's getting that EED done to "connect" with her mind. He's doing it for the sex . . . Wouldn't mind nailing her myself . . .*

Telepathy is a terrible *idea,* Briddey thought. *And the sooner I tell Trent about this, the better.* She had to convince him to forget about seeing *Dropped Call* and agree to go someplace where she could explain everything.

And hope he believed her. *I didn't, even after it happened to me,* she thought, remembering how she'd accused C.B. of bugging her hospital room, of playing a cruel trick on her.

And he was, she thought, furious all over again. But would Trent do the same thing she had, accuse her of making up a crazy story to explain why they hadn't connected? Or worse, think she was insane?

No, she thought. *Of course he'll believe you. He loves you. C.B. only told you that story about people who hear voices being automatically diagnosed with schizophrenia to keep you from telling Trent.*

She leaned forward to see how far they were. They were still nowhere near the theater. She glanced at her phone. Seven thirty. "I'm doing the best I can," the driver muttered.

"I know," she said, then thought, *Oh, God, what if he didn't say that either?*

But apparently he had because he said, "Don't worry, I'll get you there on time." He leaned on his horn and roared into the left-hand lane with only millimeters between them and the cars behind and ahead.

Briddey shrank back in her seat. She debated telling him she'd walk from here, but he'd have to pull over to the curb to let her out, which would probably get them both killed, and it might actually be better if she arrived late. If the play'd already started, it'd be easier for her to persuade Trent to forget about seeing it and go somewhere to talk. If the traffic would just cooperate for another half hour . . .

But after another block of gridlock, honking, and near accidents, the traffic suddenly parted like the Red Sea, and her driver swooped up to the door of the theater and deposited her, saying, "I told you I'd get you here on time."

And you did, Briddey thought, looking at the sidewalk full of theatergoers. *Unfortunately.* The people were obviously in no hurry to go inside. They stood there in little knots, smoking, or chatting casually and greeting friends. Briddey glanced at her phone. Only seven forty-five.

She couldn't see Trent anywhere. *Maybe he got caught in traffic, too, and isn't here yet,* she thought hopefully. If *he* was late, that would be even better. She paid the driver and went inside.

And stopped short. The spacious lobby was packed. *C.B. said I shouldn't go anywhere crowded,* she thought, but if he'd meant it would trigger more voices, it didn't. The only voices she heard were from the people around her, chattering about the traffic and the play: "Do you know what it's about?" "No, but it won a Tony." "I *love* your coat!" ". . . absolute nightmare getting here."

She made a circuit of the lobby looking for Trent, slipping between groups of dressed-up women and men in suits, detouring around the lines for the coat check and for souvenir T-shirts and mugs, and looking up the stairway at the people handing their tickets to the ushers and going into the theater, but there was no sign of him. Good.

"Where *is* she?" a woman said close behind her, and Briddey turned to see two middle-aged women in furs. "It's nearly time to go in. If we miss the first act because of her—"

"We won't," her friend said. "I told her if we weren't in the lobby when she got here, that we'd have gone on in, and that we'd leave her ticket at Will Call."

Briddey hadn't thought of the possibility that Trent had left a ticket for her. She worked her way through the crowd to the Will Call window and gave her name. The man behind the window flipped through a box of envelopes and then said, "You said it would be under Flanni-gan?"

"Yes," Briddey said. "Or possibly Worth," and he looked under the *W*'s and then started methodically through the box again while a line formed behind Briddey.

"Oh, my God," a woman said in Briddey's ear. "Could you be more annoying?"

Briddey turned to apologize, but the person behind her was an elderly man, and behind him were two young girls, talking animatedly to each other about seeing *Hamilton* the next week. The only woman anywhere in the vicinity was a pretty blonde, and it couldn't have been her because she was smiling brightly at a stocky young man as he told her about the theater's history. "This is the last time I'm letting Jane fix me up," the same voice said. "The guys always turn out to be complete nerds."

It's another of the voices, Briddey thought, and turned back to the impatient-looking man behind the window, who'd obviously just said something to her. "I'm sorry," she apologized. "What did you say?"

I don't care how old the theater is or who performed here, the blind-date woman said. *I knew I should have insisted on meeting him for coffee first.*

"Miss," the ticket clerk said. *"Miss!"*

"Sorry," Briddey said.

"I *said* I don't have any tickets under either name." He leaned to look past Briddey. "Next person in li—"

If I'd met him for coffee, I wouldn't be stuck with him for a whole evening. Maybe I can sneak out at intermission.

"Come on, already," the elderly man said. "He said he doesn't have your tickets."

Briddey turned to look at him, shocked that he was being so rude, but he was gazing politely at her, and so were the others in line. "Jesus H. Christ, are you gonna stand there all night?"

I'm hearing his thoughts, too.

"*Next,*" the clerk said, annoyed, and Briddey realized she was still standing in front of the Will Call window.

"Sorry," she said, stepping off to the side.

Some people, the man's voice said pointedly. *What the hell was she doing?*

Hearing voices, Briddey thought. C.B. had warned her to stay away from places like this, and now she saw why. And there'd be even more people inside the theater. Which meant she *had* to convince Trent to go somewhere quiet.

I'll never last till intermission, the blind-date woman was saying. *Maybe I should ask Theater Nerd here to buy me a program and sneak out the side door while he's getting it.*

An excellent idea, Briddey thought. *I'll sneak out a side door and wait till after the curtain goes up to come in. I'll tell Trent I was caught in traffic and didn't make it in time.* She started toward the door where the taxi driver had let her out, making her way through the crowd.

Watch where you're going, will you? a woman's voice said, and a voice that was unmistakably Trent's called, *Briddey! Briddey!*

Oh, no, she thought. *Don't make contact now. Not when—*

"Briddey!" he shouted, and he was there in front of her, smiling. "Didn't you hear me? I've been calling your name for the last five minutes."

"No, I . . . th-there's so much noise in here," she stammered. "Can we go somewhere quiet? I need to talk to you about—"

"Listen, there's been a change of plans."

Oh, thank heaven, she thought. *He couldn't get tickets after all.*

"You'll never guess what happened, sweetheart," he said. He steered her through the crowd to the stairs. "During my meeting with Hamilton, I happened to mention we were going out tonight and couldn't get tickets for this, and he said he and his wife were coming and insisted we come with them. Isn't that wonderful?"

Thirteen

"The voices didn't join in this time, as she hadn't spoken, but to her surprise, they all *thought* in chorus."
— LEWIS CARROLL, *Through the Looking-Glass*

"OH, I HOPED YOU'D WEAR YOUR BLACK DRESS," TRENT SAID, FROWNING at Briddey. "It's so much more elegant and understated. Oh, well, it doesn't matter." He took her arm and flashed their tickets at the usher. "The Hamiltons are waiting for us up at the mezzanine bar."

"But I thought it was just going to be the two of us—" Briddey began.

"So did I," he said, propelling her through the inner lobby, "but I could hardly say no to the boss, could I? You know how important the Hermes Project is. And his wife has been wanting to meet you."

"Yes, but we need to—"

"I know, we need to relax so we can connect," he said, leading her over to the stairs on the far side, where arrows pointed up to the mezzanine and balcony and down to the ladies' lounge. "But we can still do that *and* make a good impression on Hamilton. One doesn't preclude the other."

Oh, yes, it does.

"And this is exactly the sort of thing Dr. Verrick told us we were supposed to do. If it was just the two of us, all we'd be able to think about is connecting," Trent argued, leading her up the stairs. "*This* way we'll be forced to think about something else. Between the play and the Hamiltons, we won't have a chance to worry about not connecting."

And I won't have a chance to tell you about the voices. Which might start again any minute. She had to convince him this was a bad idea, that boss or no boss, they needed to go somewhere quiet where they could talk.

But where? The staircase was even more crowded than the lobby had been, with busily chatting couples squeezing past each other and equally talkative women standing against the wall in the line to the ladies' room, which extended all the way up to the landing.

"This is ridiculous," Briddey heard one of them bellow over the general din. "They need more bathrooms!"

I'm going to have to bellow, too, Briddey thought. "Trent!" she shouted.

"Screw this," a voice said practically in Briddey's ear, and she turned to see a flawlessly coiffed white-haired woman leaving the line and starting down the stairs. "I'm seventy years old. I can't stand in a line for twenty minutes."

The woman's lips hadn't moved, but they were pursed in disapproval. *Please,* Briddey thought. *Let somebody else have heard that.*

A second later the voice said just as clearly, "The hell with it. I'm going to go use the men's room," and no one noticed that either.

"Oh, no," Briddey murmured.

"What? Did you say something, sweetheart?" Trent said from in front of her.

"No." *And neither did she.*

"Almost there," Trent said. "Sorry it's such a mob. Just a few more—"

It's sexual discrimination, pure and simple, a different voice said. *Men never have to deal with lines like this.*

The blind-date woman chimed in, *I knew I should have sneaked out the side door.*

The voices are coming faster and faster, just like C.B. said they would,

Briddey thought, and prayed that the mezzanine bar would be less crowded, but it was so crammed with people that Trent had to take her wrist and drag her through the crowd to the Hamiltons, who were mashed against the far wall.

They didn't seem to mind the crush. "Hello!" Graham Hamilton greeted her gaily. "Or should I say, 'Moo'?"

"Absolutely not," his wife said, shouting over the din. "You should say ..." She paused, looking humorously quizzical. "What *do* sardines say?"

"I think they're packed in too tightly to make any sound," Hamilton said. "I'd like you to meet my wife, Traci."

"Hello," Traci said, shouting over the din. "I'm so glad to meet you. I've heard so much about you."

"Get off my foot!" a voice shouted just behind Briddey, and she automatically turned to see who she'd stepped on.

"Is something wrong?" Graham Hamilton asked her.

"No, I ... sorry. I thought I heard someone I knew."

Can't you watch where you're standing? the voice complained, and a different voice said, *It's too crowded in here,* followed by a third saying resentfully, *Eight dollars for a glass of wine!*

I'm starting to hear more and more of them, Briddey thought. *I've got to convince Trent to leave.*

"If you heard someone you knew, you're doing better than I am," Traci was saying. "I can't hear a thing."

"Neither can she," Trent said. "Briddey, Graham asked you if you wanted something to drink."

"Oh, I'm sorry," Briddey said, thinking, *If he and his wife go over to the bar, I can talk to Trent while they're gone.* "I'd love a glass of wine."

"Red or white?" Graham asked.

This white wine tastes like piss, a voice said clearly.

"Red or white, Briddey?" Trent said testily.

"Red, please."

"Red it is," Graham said. "We shall return." He pushed a few steps into the crowd and turned back to say, "If you don't hear from us in a week, send an expedition. Come along, Trent," and they disappeared into the mob.

·   "Oh, good," Traci Hamilton said, moving closer. "They're gone. Now we can talk. I'm dying to know all about your EED."

"My EED?" Briddey said. *But I thought Trent said he was keeping it secret.*

"I know it's all very hush-hush and we're not supposed to talk about it," Traci was saying, "but I'm *so* curious. Did you like Dr. Verrick? I hear he's wonderful."

"Yes," Briddey said absently, wondering what she meant by "all very hush-hush."

"Was it outpatient surgery?" Traci asked, and a voice beside Briddey said, "Charise still isn't here."

Did someone say that out loud, or was that one of the voices? Briddey wondered.

"I need to text Jason and tell him," the voice said.

That's what I can do, Briddey thought. *I can text Trent and tell him we have to leave.* Not the whole thing, of course, but she could at least tell him something had happened and that they had to go *now*, and he could make up some excuse—

"Oh, dear," Traci Hamilton was saying, "you think I'm being rude, asking you all these personal questions."

"No, not at all," Briddey said, though she had no idea what she'd asked. "I'm the one who's being rude. There's a problem with my family, and it's all I can think about."

"Oh, dear! Is someone ill?"

"No, it's my niece, Maeve. She's nine. She's been having emotional problems, and my sister's beside herself with worry," Briddey said, feeling guilty for taking Maeve's name in vain, but it was all she could think of. "I really should call her before the play starts."

"Oh, of course," Traci said. "I understand completely. Go right ahead and text her."

Not here, where you might see what I'm typing, Briddey thought, and said, "I really have to talk to her. I need to get somewhere where I can hear." *Before Trent comes back.*

"Try the stairs," Traci said, and, even though she doubted they'd have cleared off, Briddey immediately started for them, keeping a careful eye out for Trent and Graham Hamilton.

They were still in the crush surrounding the bar. *Good.* Briddey squeezed through the crowd to the door and out to the top landing, which was just as crowded, got her phone out of her evening bag, and unlocked it, wondering what to say. "Urgent. Must talk to you in private"?

He might conclude she'd connected to him. But it couldn't be helped. She began to type the message, though it was nearly impossible—people kept jostling her elbow as they pushed past. And if she did manage to get it sent, would Trent even hear the ping? The noise level seemed to be steadily rising.

"What are you doing out here?" Trent said, suddenly emerging from the crowd. "You're supposed to be talking to Traci."

"I know, but ... listen, I have to talk to you. Something's happened."

"Traci told me," he said. "Maeve's fine. Your sister is always hysterical—"

"It's not about Maeve. It's about the EED. I—"

"My emotions have started to come through?" he asked excitedly, grabbing her by both arms. "That's great! And it couldn't have happened at a better time!" He glanced back toward the bar. "I can't wait to—"

"*No!* That isn't it. It's ... look, I can't tell you here. We need to go—"

"*Go?* We can't go. This is our boss! Leaving would be unbelievably rude."

"I know," Briddey said, "but—"

"*Here* you are," Graham Hamilton said, appearing out of the mob with his wife and two glasses of wine. He offered one to Briddey. "Sorry, they were out of red."

"Did you reach your sister?" Traci Hamilton asked.

"No," Briddey said, slipping the phone into her evening bag so she could take the wine from Graham. "I left her a message. I'll try again at intermission." She glanced at Trent, who was glaring at her. "Or after the play."

She took a sip of the wine. *Whoever that was who said it tasted like piss was right,* she thought, trying not to make a face and bracing herself for the next voice. But they'd stopped for now, and in a few minutes the play would start and she'd no longer be expected to make conversation. If she could just make it till then . . .

The lights dimmed and came back up—the signal that it was time for people to take their seats. Trent plucked the wineglasses out of her hand and Traci Hamilton's and took off to the bar to return them, and Graham Hamilton shepherded Briddey and his wife toward the door and down the stairs with the rest of the crowd.

"Shouldn't we wait for Trent?" Briddey asked.

He shook his head. "He'll catch up."

"I don't suppose Briddey and I have time to run to the ladies' room, do we?" Traci asked her husband.

"No," he said firmly, even though the line on the stairs had dwindled considerably. "The curtain's in five minutes." He led them down to the main floor. "They don't let you in after it's gone up."

"He's right," Traci said. "Remember when we came to *Kinky Boots*, Graham?"

"Yes!"

"He had to go out to the lobby to take a phone call, and they wouldn't let him back in till after Act One," Traci explained as they headed down the aisle. "It was so annoying. He missed half the play."

"Here we are," Mr. Hamilton said. "Sixth row. Ours are those empty seats in the middle." He leaned over the man in the aisle seat. "Excuse me, I believe we're down there." He pointed at their seats.

"Of course," the man said, and stepped out into the aisle, and they made their way to their seats. And if Briddey was going to hear more voices, it would surely be now as they edged past people who were already in their seats and obviously annoyed at having to stand up again.

But the only voice she heard was Traci Hamilton's, exclaiming, "These seats are much nicer than last time! I hate front-row seats! All you can see is the actors' feet!" and then Trent's as he made his way toward them and sat down next to her, talking about how he'd gotten stuck behind some unbelievably slow people.

The voices must have stopped, thank goodness, Briddey thought, and turned to the Hamiltons. "These are wonderful seats," she said. "Thank you so much for inviting us."

"You're welcome," Graham said, and Traci leaned across him to say,

"We should be the ones thanking you, with everything you're doing for the—" She stopped as a man in a tuxedo came onstage. "Oh, good, it's starting," she whispered, and turned to look attentively at him.

The man walked to center stage and raised his hand, and the audience grew quiet. "Welcome to tonight's performance," he said. "Before it begins, we'd like to remind you to turn off your phones or switch them to silent mode, if you haven't already done so."

"Fucking rules!" someone said disgustedly, so loudly and so nearby that Briddey automatically glanced back to see who was being so rude, and realized, too late, that the announcer was continuing his spiel un-interrupted.

She looked over at Trent, afraid he'd noticed her glancing back, but he and the Hamiltons were busy turning off their phones.

"If you must take an emergency call," the emcee said, "we ask that you please go out to the lobby."

Yeah, and miss half the goddamn show!

"No flash cameras or recording devices are allowed in the theater. Thank you for your cooperation."

Cooperation, my eye! The voice cut sharply across the emcee's. *It's a fucking dictatorship!*

"What's the matter?" Trent whispered, looking anxiously at Brid-dey.

"Nothing," she managed, trying to smile even though the voice was shouting, *I didn't pay two hundred dollars so some fag can tell me what I can and can't do!*

How am I going to stand that *for a whole evening?* Briddey thought. And how was she going to hear the play? The announcer was being applauded, which meant he must have said something else, but she hadn't heard it.

I'm not turning it off, the rude man said, and simultaneously, a female voice said, *He's really hot. He looks like that actor . . . what's his name?* and the blind-date woman said, *I don't care* how *old the theater is. I just want this date to be* over! But even though all three were speaking, they didn't mask one another like spoken voices would have. Briddey could hear each one distinctly.

She'd never heard voices speaking at the same time before. She'd assumed when C.B. said she'd hear more voices that he'd meant one after another, but what if he'd meant all at once?

Can you be any more boring? the blind-date woman said. *Come on, please, raise the stupid curtain so he'll stop talking!* and at the same time the first woman was musing, *He was in that Avengers movie. What* was *his name? Alex? Aaron?*

Other voices chimed in: *I should have peed before it started . . . wonder if Marcia Bryant's here . . . hope this is good . . .*

What a fucking waste of money! the rude man bellowed so loudly he should have drowned all the other voices out, but Briddey could still hear them perfectly, one on top of the other. *Two hundred bucks a ticket, and they can't even start the fucking show on time! . . . Is that the Youngs? . . . shouldn't have parked the car there . . . got to get out of this stupid date . . . maybe I could pretend I have an urgent phone call and go out to the lobby . . .*

"Briddey," Trent said, shaking her arm, "I said, you need to turn off your phone."

"What?" she said blankly. "Oh. Sorry. I forgot." She fumbled with the clasp of her evening bag.

"Are you okay?" he asked. "I've already told you twice, and you didn't hear me."

"I'm fine. I'm sorry. My mind was somewhere else."

That was an understatement. The voices had shut out all awareness of Trent, of the Hamiltons, of being here in the theater. She hadn't been conscious of anything but them talking. And threatening her, even though only the rude man had shown any anger, and it hadn't been directed at her. But they were all *there*, pushing at her, forcing their voices on her.

"Don't worry about Maeve," Trent said. "She's probably fine, and your crazy sister is just—" He broke off and began clapping as the conductor appeared and took his bow.

Maeve may be fine, Briddey thought, *but I'm not. I have to get out of here before the voices get any worse. And before the play starts.* Which would be any moment now. The conductor was entering the orchestra pit. In a moment he'd raise his stick and the overture would begin. She had to go *now*. But how?

Her phone. The blind-date woman had talked about saying she had to go take an emergency call out in the lobby. But Briddey'd already turned her phone off.

Trent doesn't know that, she thought. *I could have set it to vibrate.* She put her phone up to her ear. "Oh, my gosh," she said, grabbed her evening bag, and stood up.

"What are you *doing*?" Trent asked, looking horrified.

She flashed the phone at him. "I've got to take this. Something's come up. It's Maeve."

"But you can't just—can't it wait till intermission? You know your family. It'll turn out to be nothing, and you'll have ruined—"

"I'll just be a minute," Briddey said. "No, don't come with me." She motioned him to stay in his seat. "It'll be faster if I go alone."

She pushed past him toward the side aisle before he could get up or stop her. "But the play's about to—" Trent began.

"I know," she whispered, squeezing past the person sitting next to him. "If I don't make it back in time, I'll watch from the back till intermission."

He shot a nervous look at the Hamiltons and then back at her. "Can't you—?"

"No. Stay where you are. I'll text you," and made her way down the row before he could object, squeezing past knees, stepping on toes, murmuring, "Sorry."

"Talk about rude!" someone said, and for a heart-clutching moment she was afraid the voices were starting up again, but it was the middle-aged woman she'd just edged past.

"Sorry," she whispered, squeezing past the woman's equally irate husband, and was finally out in the aisle.

The lights went down, stranding her in darkness, and she gave a startled glance back, as if Trent had done it to stop her, and then realized it must be the play starting. *It needs to start* now, she thought, *because I can't see,* and, thankfully, there was a sliver of light and a wave of applause as the curtains began to part.

She started up the side aisle, her phone in one hand to wave at the ushers and her evening bag in the other, walking as briskly as she could without making people think there was a fire or something and causing a panic, though panic was what she was feeling.

I've got *to make it out of here before the voices start up again,* she thought, and when she heard a man call, from somewhere behind her, "You there, where do you think you're going?" she jerked like a hooked fish.

"Nowhere, Dad," a boy's voice said, and she went limp with relief. *It's only the play,* she thought, and walked faster, ignoring the voices from the stage:

"Miriam, I'm at my wit's end. I simply can't communicate with the boy."

"That's because you don't *listen* to him, Henry."

She was nearly to the back of the theater. Another dozen rows, and then all she had to do was walk to the center and go out through the double doors where two ushers stood with playbills held against their chests.

"This is so exciting!" a voice said, so close she looked over at the row she was passing, even though she knew no one would talk that loudly during the opening scene. It had to be one of the voices. *I love the theater!* it went on, and someone else exclaimed, *I hate these seats!*

Where does she think she's going? the rude man boomed, and a new voice said, *How rude!*

You've got to keep walking, Briddey thought through the barrage of voices. *It's only a few more yards to the back.*

. . . should've used valet parking . . . can't see anything . . . taking us for supper afterward . . . , the voices said, the thoughts coming through in fragments as they multiplied.

The audience was clapping again, but she couldn't hear it at all. *I'll never be able to talk to the ushers,* she thought, looking over at them as they stood guarding the doors. *What if they ask me where I'm going?*

One of them was already looking at her. He bent his head toward the other usher and then pointed. *I have to get out of here,* Briddey thought. She looked wildly around for a route of escape and saw, only a few feet away, a curtained alcove with a green Exit sign above it.

. . . surprised to see them here . . . heard they were getting a divorce . . . leg's asleep . . . hope this doesn't mean something's wrong with . . . maybe they'll take us to Luminesce . . .

One of the ushers was starting toward her. Briddey dived for the alcove and through the heavy curtains. They swung together behind her, and the voices stopped instantly, as if they'd been smothered by the heavy velvet.

Thank goodness. Now all she had to do was find a way out to the lobby. She was on the dimly lit landing of a stairway leading down. *To the ladies' lounge,* she thought, hoping the ushers would conclude that was where she was going and not follow her. *And from there I should be able to get to the lobby.*

She ran down the carpeted steps. *I hope there isn't anyone still in there,* she thought, remembering the line on the stairs, and then: *Oh, no, sometimes there's a restroom attendant.*

But if there was, she'd gone on break when the curtain went up because the marble-walled room—with its row of sinks and long, mirrored makeup counter—reflected nothing but Briddey's image. She looked as if she was about to faint. No wonder the usher had been concerned.

I'd better put on some lipstick before I go out to the lobby, she thought, but her hands shook as she opened her evening bag, and after a minute of fumbling in vain, she gave up, put her hands down flat on the marble counter, and leaned against it, trying to pull herself together.

This is ridiculous, she told herself. They were only voices, and what they were saying—except for the rude man—wasn't even particularly bad. But there were so many of them, and no way she could escape them. It was like being mobbed by paparazzi shouting questions at her and jostling to get close to her to take her picture—bullying her, blinding her with their flashes, crushing her.

I never felt properly sorry for schizophrenics, she thought, *unable to escape the voices in their heads and fighting for their sanity with a maelstrom of noise all around them, making it impossible to think.*

No wonder C.B. had told her not to go anywhere crowded. She wished she'd listened to his warning. She had to get out of the theater before Trent got worried and decided to come looking for her—and before the voices started up again. And she needed to go *now,* while the stairway and lobby were deserted, even though she hated leaving the safe haven of the ladies' room.

She stuck her phone in her pocket and then pulled it out again. If she ran into an usher, she might need it as an excuse. She picked up her evening bag, took a deep breath, and opened the door of the ladies' room a crack. There was no one outside. She hurried down the hall, looking for the stairway leading up to the mezzanine. Here it was. She started up, resisting the impulse to run.

She made it almost to the landing before the voices started in again. . . . *I knew I should have faked a phone call,* she heard the blind-date woman say. *Now it's too late.*

Too late, Briddey thought, grabbing for the stair railing, and the other voices lunged at her: *. . . total rip-off . . . should've escaped while I had the chance . . . if I go out there and find the rear end bashed in . . . could jeopardize the whole project . . . and now I'm stuck with him . . . want to go home . . .*

So do I, Briddey thought. *Please let me go home!* she pleaded, but they yammered on, assaulting her, deafening her, blocking the way up, and she turned and started back down the stairs, stumbling, groping for the handrail she could no longer see, desperate to get away from them. *You were right, C.B.,* she said. *I shouldn't have gone someplace with so many people,* but he didn't answer.

He's not there, she thought, clinging to the handrail. *He's gone for good.*

"I'm sorry I told you to go away and leave me alone," she called aloud. "I didn't mean it." But she *had* meant it, and he knew that. He could read her mind.

The voices grew louder and more insistent. She clapped her hands to her ears, but it didn't help, they were still just as loud. *C.B., please, you have to tell me how to make them stop.*

Just rip the damn thing open, a male voice said, and for a split second, long enough to think, *Oh, thank goodness!,* she thought it was C.B.

There's no time to unbutton it, the man went on. *I've got to be back on that stage in exactly two minutes.*

That's somebody in the play, Briddey thought. *I'm starting to hear even more voices,* and it was as if that thought had opened some sort of floodgate. The voices rained down on her:

. . . who moved these props? . . . get that scrim up . . . not surprised they're splitting up . . . cheating on her since the day they got married . . . should have gone to see The Rainmaker *. . . that's your cue, you moron! . . . bow tie's killing me . . . hate sushi . . . don't put your arms around me! . . . no, no, no, stage right!*

Briddey turned and fled back in the direction she'd come from, no longer trying to find a way out, not thinking consciously at all, only trying instinctively to find a place to hide, like a fox fleeing a pack of baying hounds.

Only it was worse than that. Baying hounds and shouting mobs all blurred together into a dull roar, the individual voices impossible to identify in the general din. But she could hear every single one, even though there were now scores of them, railing at her at once, talking over one another. Their words were all perfectly distinct.

And unbearable. They were like blows, like cudgels, beating on her so that she lost consciousness of everything but trying to ward them off, to get away. But there was nowhere to go. Her back was to a wall, and when she turned to run, she was facing another.

She turned again, terrified, her body backed into the angle of the walls as far as she could go, like a cornered animal.

"Go away!" she shouted, putting her hands up to keep them at bay, but they weren't out there, they were inside her head, calling people names, carping, ranting, howling, and she had no way to shut them out, to fight them off. They poured over her, a torrent of inchoate thoughts and emotions.

I have to get help! Briddey thought, and tried to unlock her phone to call Trent. But he'd turned his off, and she couldn't see to unlock the phone for the voices, she couldn't find his number. . . . *stage right, damn it! . . . she's just as bad . . . slept with her trainer . . . how hard is it to remember six lines, for Chrissake? . . . Get your hand off my knee! . . . thing's crap! . . . total slut . . . loser . . . washed-up has-been!*

Briddey crouched back into the corner, her hands over her head, trying to shield herself against the force of the voices. "C.B.!" she cried, but it was too late, the wave was already crashing over her, dragging her under.

Oh, holy Saint Patrick and all the saints of Ireland, help! she thought, *C.B.!* and floundered in the flood, choking.

Fourteen

"Great were the noise and clamor ... the current which propelled
the crowd ... turned back, agitated and whirling."
—VICTOR HUGO, *The Hunchback of Notre Dame*

BRIDDEY, C.B. SAID, HIS VOICE CUTTING THROUGH THE CACOPHONY OF
voices like the beam of a flashlight through darkness. *What's wrong?
Briddey, talk to me!*

She latched on to his voice as if it were a life preserver, keeping her
head above water. *Where are you?* she called.

Where am I? Where are you? What's happened?

They ... I tried to get out before they ... but I couldn't. The voices ...

They didn't let her get any further. They crashed down over her
again, cutting her off from him, drowning out his voice—and hers. He
wouldn't be able to hear her, to find her. He wouldn't know what had
happened—

Yes, I do, his voice calm and reassuring. *The voices hit big-time, didn't
they? Jesus, I'm sorry. I didn't expect it to go this fast. When it happened to me,
it was almost two weeks before things got this far, and when—* His voice cut
off.

When what? she said, but she couldn't hear his answer for the
roar. *... if he touches me again, I swear I'll kill him ... so much at stake ...*

revolutionize the whole industry . . . fucking money back . . . just say your line, damn it!

C.B.! she sobbed. *Where are you?*

I'm right here, he said. *You didn't take anything, did you? A sedative or Valium or anything?*

No, but I had a few sips of wine.

Shit, he said, and then: *That's okay,* and, just as he had in the hospital, *You need to tell me where you are.*

I don't know*! I tried to make it up the stairs to the lobby of the theater, but—*

You went to a theater*? I told you not to go anyplace crowded.* And she hadn't listened, and now the voices were going to—

No, they're not, C.B. said. *I'm sorry I yelled at you. Are you on the stairs?*

I don't know, she sobbed. *I can't—*

It's okay. Which theater? The Cinemark? The Regal?

She tried to answer, but the voices were beating at her. *No,* she said, cowering from them. *We didn't go to a movie. Trent got us tickets to—*

A play? Where? At the Civic Center? The Broadhurst?

No . . . She waited for him to name another theater, but he didn't. He'd gone away, and the voices were swirling around her like a whirlpool, pulling her in and down toward the center of the vortex. *C.B.!*

I'm still here. I was just checking online for theaters. What play was it? A Sound of Madness? Dames at Sea? Dropped Call?

And she must have thought *Yes,* because he said, *I'll be right there. Just stay put,* which would have been funny if it weren't so terrible. Because she couldn't go anywhere. *Hurry!* she cried, but he didn't answer.

He's already gone, she thought, fighting down the panic. "C.B.!" she cried aloud. "Don't leave me!"

I won't. I'm right here, and I'll be right beside you the whole way. Just focus on me and don't think about the other voices. They're just background noise, like the crowd at one of those fancy cocktail parties Trent's always taking you to. Just shut them out like you would if you were talking to me at the party. I'll be there in a few minutes. I've already left Commspan—

Commspan! If he was at Commspan, it would take him at least twenty minutes to reach the theater, and the voices were already rising, crowding in, and C.B. was wrong, they weren't background noise, and this wasn't a cocktail party. People at cocktail parties didn't say such terrible things: . . . *didn't come here to be pawed . . . sick and tired of covering for you not knowing your lines . . . such a snob . . . my dog could do a better job of acting!* It was like being out in a relentlessly hammering rain, the din deafening.

Not rain, C.B. said, his voice slashing through the downpour. *Niagara Falls.*

Niagara Falls? she said blankly.

Imagine that's what you're hearing. You're at Niagara Falls, and that din is just the roaring of the waterfall. Have you ever been to Niagara Falls?

No—

But you've seen them, right? They've been in lots of movies. Bruce Almighty. Superman II. *The wedding episode of* The Office. *Great place. Big honeymoon destination. Maid of the Mist, Horseshoe Falls . . .* and as he spoke she could almost see them, the water roaring over the cliffs and tumbling to the rocks below, the mist boiling up, and the spray—

They make an ungodly amount of noise, C.B. said, shouting over the sound of the falls. *You can't hear what the tourists are saying, the noise is so loud, but that's all it is: noise. It can't hurt you.*

Yes, it can, she said, and had a sudden image of the voices sweeping her over the edge of the falls and down, submerging her in the smothering water, tumbling her over and over in the foam, in the rocks, and her going under, drowning . . .

Briddey! C.B. said sharply. *You can't go over the edge. There's an iron railing. Can you see it? The railing?*

No . . .

It's chest-high and black, and the bars are too narrow for you to fall through. And the top's just the right size to wrap your hands around and get a good grip, he said. *It's wet from the spray, but it's not slippery. Can you feel it?*

Y-yes, she said, imagining her hand gripping it. *It's cold.* She could almost feel the spray on her knuckles.

Good girl. Just keep holding on to it. The railing'll keep you safe.

What if it gives way?

It won't. It's bolted into the ground.

But what if the ground *gives way?*

It won't. It's solid rock. All you have to do is hang on for a few more minutes, and I'll be there. In the meantime, think about how beautiful the falls are.

They're not beautiful! she said violently. *They're horrible!*

Then think about the great sex we're going to have when I take you there on our honeymoon, he said, and some part of her mind that hadn't been thoroughly traumatized knew he was saying that to distract her, to get her to respond indignantly, "We are not having sex at Niagara Falls or anywhere else. I'm emotionally bonded to Trent." But it wasn't working. The voices were too loud, too fierce.

Okay, then, think about the shredded wheat, C.B. said.

The what? she asked, surprised by the non sequitur into taking her mind off the voices. *What does shredded wheat have to do with Niagara Falls?*

Beats me, he said, *but the shredded-wheat box used to have a picture of Niagara Falls on it. Maybe it was made there. Then again, there's a leprechaun on the Lucky Charms box, and they're not made in Ireland. Though with all the outsourcing these days, you never know. They might be. Froot Loops are manufactured in Finland.*

He chattered on about sugared cereals and the strange ways of outsourcing, and she didn't believe a word of it, but she clung to his talk like she clung to the wet black railing. If he was talking, the voices couldn't sweep her over the edge.

And I have it on very good authority, he was saying, *that Cap'n Crunch is made on the pirate Isle of Tortuga, along with—*

His voice abruptly cut off. *C.B.?* she said, her voice rising in panic.

It's okay. I'm here, he said, but his voice sounded different, both closer and farther away.

Where? I can't hear you!

I'm just outside the theater. I don't suppose there's any chance you could make it outside under your own steam, is there?

No! She clutched the icy railing. *Why?*

I'm not sure they'll let me in. I'm not exactly dressed for the theater. If you could just make it out to the lobby—

He could rescue me from the voices, she thought, but at the idea of letting go, of going up the stairs, the voices surged toward her.

I can't, she said, and it was more a whimper than an answer.

That's okay, he reassured her. *I'll think of something. But listen, I need you to tell me where you are.*

At Niagara Falls, she said, bewildered. *You said—*

No, where in the theater? Are you still on the stairs?

No.

Where did you go after the stairs? Try to remember.

I can't—

Okay, then open your eyes, just for a second. The voices won't sweep you over, I promise. I've got hold of you. But I can't come get you if I don't know where you are. Open your eyes.

I can't, she said, holding desperately to the railing, but the thought of being left alone with the voices was even more terrifying than the possibility of going over the falls. She opened her eyes.

She had only a momentary impression of metal pipes and black-and-white tiles, had just long enough to think, surprised, *I'm sitting on the floor,* before the voices poured through and she had to squeeze her eyes shut again.

But it must have been enough because C.B. said, *The bathroom. Good, I'll be right there. And until then, don't think about Niagara Falls. Think about Lucky Charms. Remember, they have little marshmallows in them of different shapes and colors? What are they? There are pink hearts and what else?*

I don't know—

Come on, he coaxed. *Maeve eats them, right? And you're Irish. They're your national cereal. You've got to know what the marshmallows are. Pink hearts and . . .*

Yellow moons?

Good girl. That's two. What were the others? Think.

She did, squeezing her eyes shut against the spray and the roaring water, gripping the wet iron railing so hard, the rectangular edges cut into her hands. "Pink hearts," she murmured, "yellow moons, green shamrocks," and what else? Stars. But what color were they? Blue? Purple? She strained to see the box, the cereal.

But it wasn't enough. The voices were breaking through, they were splashing up over the railing, dousing her, numbing her like icy water. And C.B. had lied to her. They weren't just a harmless waterfall or a tourist sight for honeymooners, they were dangerous, raging with anger and spite and resentment: *How hard is it to remember six lines, you moron? . . . see how they like being snubbed . . . garbage . . . pervert . . . drunken . . . hate her!*

They crashed over her, washing her off the rock into the current. She grabbed for the railing, but she couldn't find it. *C.B.!* she called, listening for his voice in among the others, but she couldn't find it either. The voices were too numerous, and the current was carrying her away. She couldn't breathe.

C.B.! she thought, and reached out a desperate hand to him.

And he was there. Not in her head—but really *there,* squatting beside her on the tile floor in a denim jacket and flannel shirt over a *Star Wars* T-shirt, his hand on her arm, murmuring, "It's okay, I'm here now," over and over.

"You lied to me," she said shakily. "The railing gave way. I almost went over the falls."

I know. I'm sorry. I had trouble convincing the usher I wasn't trying to sneak into the play for free. And then we had to find the right bathroom.

"I'm sorry I didn't believe you, and I'm sorry I—"

Shh, not out loud, he cautioned. He was afraid someone outside the bathroom would hear them.

I'm sorry I said I never wanted to speak to you agai—

And I'm sorry I didn't get here sooner. Do you know how many bathrooms they've got in this place? There's one on every level. They must be expecting a lot of business during intermission. Which is when?

I don't know, she said, but he must not have heard her because he asked, "When's intermission?" out loud.

"After Act Two, about forty-five minutes from now," a woman's voice said, and Briddey realized with a shock that there was someone else in the bathroom with them.

It's one of the ushers, C.B. explained. *So go along with whatever I say, okay?*

Okay.

"Is she all right?" the usher was asking. "Should I see if there's a doctor in the house?"

No! Briddey thought.

"No," C.B. was saying calmly to the usher. "It's just an anxiety attack. She gets them when she's in crowded places." He turned back to Briddey. "I told you you had no business coming to the theater by yourself, Lucy."

By myself? Briddey thought, confused. *Lucy?*

"I was afraid this would happen," he said. *Now you say, "I know, Charlie. I'm sorry."*

I don't under—

If Trent starts asking questions, you don't want the usher to know your name, do you? And to tell him she found you in here in this state?

Oh, God, Trent! *We have to get out of here before—*

Exactly. So say, "I know, Charlie."

"I know, Charlie," she said. "I'm sorry," and to C.B.: *I forgot all about Trent.*

Did you tell him about the voices?

No! He'd—

What about when the voices overtook you? Did you call to him for help?

"Overtook," that was the right word. They'd overtaken her, like wolves pursuing her or a mob of bloodthirsty—

Briddey! C.B. said sharply. *Did you call to him?*

Yes, but he couldn't hear me.

What about your phone? Did you try to call him on your phone?

No, I took it out, she said, remembering, *but then I remembered his phone was turned off. They make you turn it off when the play starts.*

Did you call anyone else? Your sisters or somebody at Commspan?

She shook her head. *The voices—*

I know, he said. *And you didn't text him or try his number, so that it'll show a missed call?*

No.

Good. That means we've got till intermission to get out of here. But we need to go now.

Okay.

Which means you need to let go of the pipe.

Pipe? she thought. *What's he talking about?* It wasn't a pipe, it was a railing, and she couldn't let go of it, or she'd be swept over the falls.

No, you won't, he said. *I've got you. Can you come out?*

Out? she said blankly, and realized she was underneath the counter that held the sinks. She was wedged into the back corner and hanging on to the curved chrome drainage pipe with both hands. *Like a cornered animal,* she thought, ashamed.

Don't worry about it, C.B. said. *The voices would have that effect on anybody.* He reached under the counter and extended his hand to her. *Can you come out?*

She nodded. *I think so,* but when it came down to it, she found she couldn't. Her hands were frozen to the pipe.

It's okay, C.B. said, and crawled in after her, hitting his head on the underside of the sink. "Ow," he said.

"What happened?" the usher asked. "Did she hit you?"

"No, I cracked my head, that's all."

The usher didn't sound convinced. "Are you sure you don't want me to call 911? Or an ambulance?"

"I'm sure," he said. "I've already called her therapist. She'll be fine once I get her home." He extended his hand to Briddey. *I won't let you go over the falls, I promise. But we've gotta go, darlin', or she's gonna call the cops.*

And Trent will find out everything, Briddey thought, and let go of the pipe.

There wasn't even a nanosecond between her letting go and C.B.'s snatching her hands up in his. "I've got her," he said to the usher, and to Briddey: *I knew you could do it. That's it, darlin'. Come on. Almost there.*

He backed out, pulling her slowly toward him with both hands, then using one hand to push her head down, saying, *Don't crack your head,* as they emerged from under the counter. He put his arm around her waist and helped her awkwardly to her feet. "Do you think you can walk?"

She turned to him to say yes and caught sight of herself in the mirror above the sinks. She looked terrible, her updo half fallen and her beautiful green dress wrinkled beyond recognition. Her white face stared back at her, haggard and frightened. *I look completely deranged,* she thought. *No wonder the usher wanted to call 911.*

And she still might, C.B. said, *which is why you need to say, "Yes, I can walk, Charlie. I just want to go home."*

"Yes, I can walk, Charlie," she said, even though she wasn't at all sure she could. "I just want to go home."

"She's fine," C.B. said to the usher, who still looked skeptical. "Ready?" he asked Briddey aloud, and she nodded.

He picked up her evening bag from the floor and stuck it in the pocket of his jeans. *Have you got your phone?* he asked.

Yes, she said, reaching into the pocket of her skirt for it, but it wasn't there. *I must have dropped it.*

But you had it with you when you left the theater. You said you tried to call Trent. Were you in here when you did that?

I don't know, she said, trying to remember if she'd been in here or on the stairs.

It's okay, he said to her, and to the usher: "Could you go check and make sure there's nobody around? I need to get her out to the lobby, and the sight of other people might set her off again."

The usher nodded and went out. The moment the door closed behind her, C.B. let go of Briddey's waist and darted over to the counter.

No! Don't leave! she cried, unable to stop herself from lurching after him, hands out.

I'm not leaving, he said, peering under the counter. *I just need to find your phone. It'll only take a second.*

He was just looking for her phone, she told herself. He wasn't leaving her. He was only a few feet away, and he had to find it before the usher came back. If she grabbed on to his arm, it would only slow him down. She needed to let him look and not panic, but that was impossible, because behind her, in the mirror, the roar of the falls was already splintering into individual voices, hundreds of them, thousands of them, into a million shrieking pieces flying at her, slashing her—

Aren't some of them pirates? C.B. asked her, looking under the doors to the stalls.

Some of what? The voices?

No, some of the Lucky Charms marshmallows. Aren't some of them shaped like pirates? He opened the door of the first stall. *Or am I thinking of Cap'n Crunch?*

Cap'n Crunch doesn't have marshmallows.

Oh. He opened the door to the next stall. *What's the one with the toucan on the box?*

Froot Loops, she said, *but it doesn't have marshmallows either.*

Well, one of them does, he said, going on to the next. *Count Chocula or FrankenBerry or Zombie—aha!* He lunged inside the second-to-the-last stall, snatched up her phone, dropped it into his pocket, and had his arm back around her waist when the usher opened the door.

"All clear," she told C.B.

"Good," C.B. said to her. "Can you hold that door for Lucy and me? Thanks." *Okay,* he said to Briddey, *let's blow this pop stand,* and they started over to the door.

"Are you sure you're all right?" the usher asked Briddey anxiously.

"Yes, I'm fine," she said, managing a smile, and let C.B. lead her out the door.

Speaking of getting out of here, how'd you get here tonight? he asked, helping her up the steps.

I took a taxi. The voices were starting to break through—

Good. That gives us one less thing to worry about. You're doing great, darlin', he encouraged her. *We're almost to the landing—*

I can't, Briddey said, pulling back against his grip. *That's where the voices—*

I know, he said, tightening his hold on her. *We're not going anywhere near the falls. We're going to focus on those marshmallows, and before you know it, we'll be out of here and someplace quiet.*

Someplace quiet, she thought. It sounded heavenly. But to get there, they had to get past the landing—

Don't think about that, C.B. ordered, continuing to walk her up the stairs. *Think about someplace quiet. And dry. Arizona. Or Death Valley. How would you feel about going to Death Valley for our honeymoon?*

She didn't answer. She was looking at the landing. The voices were just beyond it, they were already pouring down the steps—

And speaking of moons, honey and otherwise, I seem to remember the yellow marshmallows were stars, which means the moons must have been blue, as in "once in a blue moon." What did you say green was?

Shamrocks.

Ah, yes. Shamrocks. The symbol of Ireland. That's singularly appropriate, considering our situation.

What situa—?

I'll tell you later. What are the other colors? Orange? Orange pumpkins?

Pumpkins aren't Irish.

You're right. Okay, what is? Whiskey? IRA sympathizers?

No, it's got to be something like rainbows. Or a pot of gold.

Also singularly appropriate, since here we are, he said, and she looked up to see that they were nearly all the way across the empty lobby, and the usher was outside on the sidewalk, holding the door open for them.

"You're sure Lucy will be okay?" the usher asked.

"Positive," C.B. said, walking Briddey to the door.

"I'll be glad to give you a refund. Or to exchange your ticket for another night."

She's afraid you're going to sue them and she'll get in trouble, C.B. said. *Tell her you're not, or she's likely to call 911 just so she's covered.*

"A refund's not necessary," Briddey told her. "This was all my fault. I should have known better."

The usher looked relieved. *Good girl,* C.B. said, and walked her through the open door and outside.

Away from the voices, Briddey thought, limp with relief. But they were still there on the sidewalk, in the dark street. "Do you need help getting her out to your car?" the usher was asking anxiously.

"No, I'm fine," Briddey managed to say. "Really."

The usher looked doubtful, but she went back inside. *Very good girl,* C.B. said. *Now, let's hope they didn't tow my car. Oh, good, they didn't.*

He indicated his battered Honda, which was parked at the curb where the taxi had let her out, between two large No Parking signs. "This is my lucky day," he said aloud, walking her around to the passenger side of the car and opening the door. "It must be those green shamrocks. Here you go." He eased her inside.

"Okay, now," he said, trying to extricate himself from the arm she still had around his neck. "You've got to let go so I can get in the driver's side."

"No—"

"It'll only take a second, I promise," he said gently. "And then I'll get you out of here and away from the voices. Okay?"

She shook her head. As soon as he let go of her, the voices would come back.

"Look, we can't stay here," he said. "If Trent shows up, it could seriously interfere with our honeymoon plans."

He was trying to get a rise out of her so she'd let go of him, but she couldn't. The voices would swamp her, they'd wash over her—

"No, they won't," C.B. said. "Look, I'll open the driver's door right now so I won't have to stop and do it when I go around." He reached across her, pushed down on the door handle, and shoved the door slightly open. "And I'll be really fast, I promise. You just concentrate on that last marshmallow. Okay?"

No, she murmured, but he was already starting for the front of the car. "C.B.!"

I'm right here, he said, dashing across the front of the car, talking as he went. *The fifth kind of marshmallow, wasn't it a top hat? No, wait, I'm thinking of the Monopoly game. An iron? No, that's Monopoly, too, and anyway, didn't I read they got rid of the iron?*

He was opening the door on the driver's side, sliding in. She grabbed for him the instant he was inside, clinging tightly to his arm. *Like some idiotic Victorian heroine,* she thought, but she couldn't help herself.

And he didn't seem to notice. He just kept on talking. "What did they replace the iron with? It was something more modern. Like a Kindle. Or a drone."

"No," she said, "it was a cat."

"That's right, it was," he said, shutting his door. "*Very* modern," and when she smiled: "I'm afraid I need you to let go of me again for a sec."

"Why?" she asked, her grip tightening.

"Because I've got to start the car. So you either need to let go or else you have to get my keys out of my jeans for me."

"Oh!" she said, letting go as if she'd been bitten, and her mortification should have been enough to make her pull herself together, but the moment he had the keys out and the key in the ignition, she grabbed for his arm again. "I'm sorry. I know I'm acting like a baby. They're just so—"

"I know," he said. "I wrapped myself around my bedpost the first time it happened to me and had to be pried loose."

"You did?"

"Yup," he said, putting the car in gear with difficulty and pulling out into the street. "Though putting your hand on my leg instead of my arm might be a better idea till we get out of all this traffic."

She nodded and grasped his thigh just above the knee, and it took every bit of willpower she had not to wrap both arms around his leg like a demented fan at a rock concert.

"You're doing great," C.B. said. "I'll have you away from here in just a sec."

Out of the city, she thought, glancing fearfully out her window at the passing streetlamps and buildings. *Out of reach of the voices.* "Please hurry," she murmured. "They're catching up."

He nodded, glanced at his watch, and stepped on the gas. *Good,* she thought, straining to see ahead to the on-ramp sign. *In another minute, we'll be on the highway.*

But even as she thought it, C.B. was slowing down. He turned right onto a dark side street, stopped the car, and shut off the ignition.

Fifteen

"Thankfully the rest of the world assumed that the Irish were
crazy, a theory that the Irish themselves did nothing
to debunk."
—EOIN COLFER, *Artemis Fowl*

"WHAT ARE YOU DOING?" BRIDDEY SAID, LOOKING NERVOUSLY AROUND
at the dark street. "Why did you stop the car?"

"I'm buying us some time," C.B. said, sliding forward in his seat and
fishing her phone out of his jeans pocket. "What's your password? And
don't think it. Say it out loud."

"You don't have to do that. I'm not worried about reinforcing our
neural pathway anymore. The more reinforced, the better." She laughed
shakily. "I'm just so grateful we had one."

"Me, too. But that's not why I told you to talk out loud. Speaking
helps to screen out the voices. So what's your password?"

She told him. "But shouldn't you do that after we get away from
the voices?"

C.B. shook his head. "We need to do this before intermission."

At which point Trent would come looking for her, and when he
couldn't find her, he'd ask the usher, "Have you seen a redhead in a

green dress?" and it wouldn't matter that C.B. had called her Lucy and told the usher she'd come to the theater alone.

"Exactly," C.B. said. "What reason did you give Trent for leaving?"

"Maeve."

"Maeve?" he said, looking up, horrified, from the phone. "Why did you do that?"

"Because before in the bar, when the voices started, I'd told Traci Hamilton I was worried about Maeve, that she'd been having problems and I needed to go call Mary Clare. It was the only thing I could think of to get away and—"

"Deal with the voices," he finished for her. "Did you tell her—or Trent—what those problems were?"

"No. Trent wasn't there. And all I said to Traci Hamilton was that my sister was worried about my niece. So then in the theater I pretended Mary Clare had just called me, and I told Trent something had happened and I had to go find out what."

"Then we should be okay," he said, and began rapidly typing a text message.

"What are you telling him?" she asked.

"That Maeve ran away."

"Ran *away*! She wouldn't do that!"

"And *you* wouldn't have gone tearing out of the theater and over to your sister's because Maeve got a B on her report card. It has to be something serious enough to justify abandoning him and the Hamiltons, which means either Maeve ran away or broke a body part, and running away's easier to fake. There's no cast."

"But if Trent calls my family—"

"He won't. I'm sending a follow-up that you found her at your Aunt Oona's, and she's fine."

"But if you tell him that, he'll want me to come back to the theater," she said, her hand involuntarily tightening on his leg.

"Don't worry. I'm telling him Mary Clare's having a meltdown, and you've got to stay and try to calm her down."

"But what if Trent calls me during intermission and tells me to forget Mary Clare, that the Hamiltons are more important?"

"He won't be able to. I'm turning off your phone."

"What if he calls Aunt Oona's house?"

"I've got that covered," he said, continuing to type.

"What do you mean? You didn't text Maeve, did you?" If he'd asked Maeve to provide an alibi, she'd insist on knowing why, and—

"I didn't text Maeve," he said, pocketing her phone and starting the car. "And anyway, Trent won't call. He'll be too busy convincing the Hamiltons that your sudden departure wasn't a reflection on them. After intermission I'll send another text saying it looks like calming your family down's going to take longer than you thought, and you'll talk to him tomorrow."

Trent will be so upset, she thought.

"Too bad," C.B. said.

He glanced in the rearview mirror and pulled out onto the street, and she felt a wave of relief that they were moving again and getting away from the voices.

"You didn't hear Trent back there, did you?" C.B. was saying. "His wasn't one of the voices, was it?"

"*No,* of course not," she said. "The voices I heard were *horrible!*"

"Actually, they were just your average theatergoers. And your average everything else—friends, relatives, co-workers—"

"But they were so—"

"Vulgar? Vindictive? Spiteful? Scheming? I'm afraid that's what people sound like in the privacy of their own heads." He gave her a wry grin. "I told you it's a cesspool in there."

He stopped at a red light. "It's not entirely their fault. They can say out loud the nice stuff they think—'Wow, you look great!' or 'What a pretty day!' or 'I'm filled with the milk of human kindness!'—but not 'Go to hell!' or 'Man, what great tits!' Inside their heads is the only place the bad stuff can come out, which tends to make their thoughts disproportionately unpleasant. But also, people are brutish, hateful, greedy, mean, manipulative, and cruel."

"But everyone can't be awful."

"You haven't listened to them for as long as I have."

"Are you telling me there's nobody nice?"

"I didn't say that. But that just makes it worse. Nice guys really do finish last. And nice girls. They get lied to and betrayed and stuck on somebody who's in love with somebody else and get their hearts broken. And listening to that's even worse than listening to the creeps and the monsters. Speaking of which, you still haven't answered my question. Did you hear Trent?"

"I told you, Trent couldn't have—"

"Been one of the voices. Yes, he could have. But like I told you this morning, if you'd heard him, you'd have recognized his voice, like you recognized mine."

And Jill's and Art Sampson's, she thought.

"Exactly. If you've heard the person before, your brain automatically assigns their speaking voice to the thoughts. If not, sometimes it'll assign gender or age based on the things the voice says, but otherwise it's completely characterless. That's why you couldn't describe the decaf latte's voice."

And why the blind-date woman's voice had sounded female the second time she'd heard it. "Can they hear me, too?" she asked.

"No."

"Are you sure?" she asked, her hand tightening convulsively on his leg. If they could hear, they'd know where she was. They'd come after her.

"I'm positive," C.B. said. "I've been listening to them for fifteen years, remember? They have no idea you can hear them."

"But it felt like they were shouting at me and—"

"Attacking you? Trying to kill you? Yeah, I know. But they're not. They don't even know you exist. You're just overhearing their thoughts. It's like being in a restaurant and accidentally hearing a stranger talking at the next table."

No, it's not, she thought. It was possible to shut out people you overheard but not these—

"That's because the mind's hardwired to make sense of whatever it hears," C.B. said. "It tries to do that with the voices, but there are too many of them and they're all speaking at the same time. And unlike the voices of the people you hear with your ears, they don't mask one another or merge together into background noise. They remain distinct. So the mind ends up panicking from sensory overload."

Sensory overload? Is that what you call it? she thought, feeling again the ominous voices beating relentlessly on her.

"But if they can't hear me, then why does it matter whether I heard Trent?"

"Because of the EED. If you could hear him, it might have suggested he was beginning to be able to sense your emotions, and the last thing we need right now is for him to be picking up a feeling that you're in trouble and deciding he needs to come find out what's going on. We've got too much work to do. But you didn't hear him, so we're good."

And in a few minutes they'd be safely on the freeway and out of reach of the theater and the voices. She wondered how far they had to go.

Please don't let it be far, she thought, looking out at the passing darkness and willing C.B. to drive faster. *If he doesn't, they'll catch up, they'll wash over the car . . .*

Stop, she ordered herself. *Don't think about the voices.*

"Nope, bad idea," C.B. said. "Trying not to only makes you think about them, like when somebody says, 'Whatever you do, don't think about an elephant,' and then that's all you can think about. No, you want to think about something else altogether. Like elephants. Or Lucky Charms. Or where we should go on our honeymoon. Anything to create some white noise."

"You mean like those CDs that are supposed to help you sleep? The ones with the sound of rippling streams and soothing waves?" She was immediately sorry she'd said that. It reminded her of the roaring waterfalls.

"Which is why you can't use those," C.B. said. "Plus they don't work. And neither does blasting loud music or listening to audiobooks. Or wearing noise-canceling headphones. The voices don't have anything to do with sound. They come from inside the brain."

"But I thought you said I needed to create white noise—"

"Mental white noise. Inhibiting one set of signals by focusing on another, like when you're working on a report and don't hear your phone ringing. By focusing on the report, your brain automatically boosts the signals you want and turns the volume down on all the others."

"So by trying to list the Lucky Charms marshmallows, I can do the same thing to the voices—"

He nodded. "Or listing Monopoly tokens or movie stars or brands of designer shoes. Or you can recite Monty Python routines or sing songs, especially songs with lots of verses, like the theme from *Gilligan's Island*. You know the theme from *Gilligan's Island*, don't you?"

"Everyone knows the theme from *Gilligan's Island*."

"Good, then you can sing that. Or the Pokemon theme. Or 'When Irish Eyes are Smiling.'"

"And singing those songs will stop the voices?"

"No, nothing can stop them. But singing—"

She gasped. "What do you mean, nothing can stop them?"

"Sorry, I didn't mean to scare you. There are ways to keep them at bay—"

"At *bay*?" she cried, thinking of them always there, coiled and snarling, waiting to pounce.

"Sorry, bad metaphor. I should have said there are ways to control them. It's a lot like tinnitus—you know, that continuous ringing in the ears some people have? There's no way to eliminate it—"

No way to eliminate it? "But Mary Clare said the EED's effects can wear off."

"Yeah, well, I've had the voices for fifteen years, and they haven't shown any sign of going away yet. I'm afraid they're permanent. But there are ways to control them. I'll teach you—"

She'd stopped listening at the word "permanent." The voices would always be there, poised to attack, every time she went to a play or a meeting—

That's why C.B. refuses to go to them, she thought. *Because the voices are there, waiting. And have been since he was thirteen. They'll never go away, and I can't sing or recite poetry forever—*

"No, no, you won't have to," C.B. said. "Those things are just interim measures till we can get your permanent defenses up."

"Permanent defenses?"

"Yeah. I'm going to teach you how to build barricades that'll keep the voices out, but I can't do that till I get you someplace safe, and the sooner I do that, the better."

Someplace safe. That meant that even though there was no way to stop the voices, there were places they couldn't reach. The knowledge that she could get out of range was immediately calming, and with the calmness came the awareness that she had a death grip on C.B.'s leg.

"Sorry," she said, and loosened her hold.

"That's okay. I still have a little circulation left." He grinned at her and went on with what he'd been saying about reciting lyrics. "Or poetry. Narrative poems work the best. What do you know? 'The Harp That Once Through Tara's Halls'? 'The Lake Isle of Innisfree'?"

"No," she said, thinking, *I should have gone to those Daughters of Ireland meetings Aunt Oona kept pestering me about.* "I know 'The Highwayman,' sort of. I had to memorize it in high school, but I'm not sure I remember all the words."

"Then how about Christmas carols? Or show tunes? Show tunes are great. Stephen Sondheim. Rodgers and Hammerstein. *Wicked.* *Rent. The Music Man.* Almost any musical will do. Except *Cats.*"

"Why? Doesn't it shut out the voices?"

"No, it shuts them out fine. But it's a *terrible* musical. And that reminds me, you need to be careful which songs you sing. Getting an annoying song stuck in your head can make you wish you were hearing the voices instead."

"*Nothing* could make me wish I was hearing the voices instead," she said fervently.

"That's what you think. You've obviously never had 'I Got You Babe' wedged in your neurons for weeks. Or 'Tie Me Kangaroo Down, Sport.' Or 'Feelings.'" He shuddered. "I made the mistake of thinking that would be a good song for fending off the voices, and at the end of two weeks I wanted to kill myself *and* Engelbert Humperdinck. And it's worse if it's *their* song."

"Their song?"

"One they've gotten stuck in *their* heads. The voices aren't always kvetching and ranting and swearing and screaming. Sometimes they're singing—and they're just as nasal and off-key inside their heads as they are out loud. Plus, they've got terrible taste. They never sing something by Bob Dylan or Cole Porter or Stevie Wonder. It's always 'Achy Breaky Heart' or 'Shake Ya Ass' or that godawful Celine Dion *Titanic* thing. And half the time they get the words wrong. Especially when it comes to Christmas carols—'Rudolph the Red-Nosed Stranger' and 'dashing through the snow in a one-horse soap and hay.' And no matter how much you shout at them, 'It's "Joy to the world, the Lord is come," not "the Lord has gum," ' it doesn't do any good."

He's trying to distract me again, she thought. *All this talk about songs is just white noise to keep me from hearing the voices till we get to wherever it is we're going.*

Which was where? They'd been driving for fifteen minutes, and they didn't seem to be getting any closer to being out of the city. Or to a highway.

"You know the song 'Molly Malone'?" C.B. was saying. "Of course you do, you're Irish. Well, you know the part where she wheels her wheelbarrow through streets broad and narrow, crying cockles and mussels? Well, one of my voices was convinced she was crying 'cocker spaniels,' which not only is wrong, but doesn't even scan! Nearly drove me insane." He turned to look at her. "Speaking of which, just how Irish are you?"

"What do you mean?"

"I mean, how much Irish blood have you got? With a last name like Flannigan and that red hair, I'm guessing at least three-fourths of your ancestors are from Ireland. Is that right?"

"No. All of them are. My family is pure Irish. I'm surprised Aunt Oona didn't tell you that. It's usually the first thing out of her mouth."

"We had other things to talk about," C.B. said. "Pure Irish, hmm? And your people are from—what? County Kerry? County Cork?"

"County Clare. Why? You think my hearing the voices has something to do with my ancestry?"

"No. It has *everything* to do with it—or more particularly, with the haploidgroup gene R1b-L21 the Irish carry."

"That's why you tried to stop me from having the EED done," she said. "Because you knew I was Irish and you were afraid this would happen."

"Well, that, and the fact that elective brain surgery is a spectacularly bad idea. As you have discovered."

"But if it's a gene the Irish carry, then wouldn't everyone Irish be telepathic? I know *dozens* of Irish people, and none of them can read minds."

"That you know of. They could be keeping it quiet, like me. Or that subject of Dr. Rhine's I told you about. Bad things have been known to happen to people who hear voices, like—"

"Being diagnosed as schizophrenic or burned at the stake. I know," she said. "So you're saying all these people are secretly telepaths?"

"No. I think it's more likely they're only part Irish. Most of the 'Irish,'" he said, taking his hands off the steering wheel for a split second to make air quotes, "actually have a good chunk of Viking or Germanic or Anglo-Saxon genes in them. And if they've been in the United States for a generation or two, they've got all kinds of other genes, too."

"And only people who are a hundred percent Irish carry this gene?" she asked, thinking, *Aunt Oona wouldn't be so determined for me to marry a "foine Irish lad" if she knew about this.* "But if that's the case, why aren't my sisters telepathic? And don't try to tell me they are. If they were, Mary Clare wouldn't spend all her time worrying about what's going on with Maeve, and Kathleen definitely wouldn't date the guys she does. And you yourself said Aunt Oona's premonitions weren't real. Or were you lying about that?"

"No, there's no such thing as clairvoyance. Or telekinesis. Just telepathy."

"And if they were telepathic, they'd have known I had the EED," Briddey said, "which they didn't. If your theory's right, why aren't they? And why was Joan of Arc telepathic? She wasn't Irish. And neither are you. Your name's not Murphy or O'Connell. It's—"

"Schwartz," he said.

"So your theory is what? That this haploidgroup R1b gene is carried by the Irish *and* the French *and* the Jews?"

"Nope, just the Irish, though there's a small possibility the Romany carry it, too, and that that's where the tradition of Gypsy fortune-telling comes from."

"And you have Gypsy blood?"

He shook his head. "Nary a drop."

"Well, then, why can you hear the voices? You're obviously not Irish."

"Um ... about that," he said. "Actually, I am."

Sixteen

"The library, and step on it."
—DAVID FOSTER WALLACE, *Infinite Jest*

"YOU'RE *IRISH*?" BRIDDEY SAID.

"Yep. All the way back on both sides, just like you."

"But—"

"Schwartz is my stepfather's name. My *father* was an O'Hanlon. And my mother was a Gallagher."

"But you . . . ," she began, frowning at his dark hair, nearly black in the light from the passing streetlights.

"Don't look Irish? Actually, I do. Dark hair's common in Ireland, especially in County Clare, where my mother's people are from," and the moment he said it, she thought, *I should have seen it.* He had the classic dark hair and black-lashed gray eyes "put in with a sooty finger" of the Black Irish.

"But you said my red hair—"

He shook his head. "If you have the gene for red hair—which is a mutation of a different gene, MC1R—and you're Irish, you're also likely to have the telepathy gene, but one's not dependent on the other."

"But you . . . ," she said, still unable to take this in. "I mean, every-one at Commspan thinks you're Jewish."

"I am, for all intents and purposes. My dad died when I was two, and my mom remarried when I was four. Then she died, and my step-dad raised me till *he* died," he said. "But the name also serves as protective coloration."

"But if you're Irish, why isn't your *first* name Irish?" she asked, and realized she had no idea what his first name was. C.B. could stand for anything—Christian Bale, Charlotte Brontë—or be a nickname for computer bandwidth or CB radio or something.

"As in 'Breaker, Breaker, good buddy, this is Big Trucker,' you mean?" he said, turning his attention from his driving to grin at her for a moment. "That'd be appropriate, considering. But actually, C.B. stands for Conlan Brenagh. Conlan Brenagh Patrick Michael O'Hanlon Schwartz."

"And so because we're both Irish, you think this haploidgroup gene is what's causing the telepathy?"

"Afraid so."

"But two people is hardly proof. Or *is* it just two? Were your mother and father telepathic, too?"

"I don't know. They both died before it happened to me, and it's not the kind of thing you'd tell anybody, even your own kid, unless it was absolutely necessary."

"Then how can you be so sure that's the cause? Why couldn't it be the EED?"

"Because I didn't have one. Remember?"

"But that still doesn't explain why you think being Irish caused it unless you've found another telepath with the gene. Have you?"

He turned his head sharply to look at her. "What?"

"That's it, isn't it? You've found someone else who's telepathic, and they're Irish, too. Who is it? One of those professional psychics you were talking about?"

"Of course not. I told you, they're fakes."

"You said most of them were fakes. I thought maybe you'd found one that wasn't, and he—or she—was Irish."

"No. I told you, so-called mind reading is all just tricks."

"Then why—?"

"Because nearly every documented historical incident of telepathic communication involves someone who's Irish, including Dr. Rhine's

ESP subjects *and* the messages from the *Titanic,* whose steerage decks were full of immigrants from County Clare—plus the incident I told you about the Nebraska girl who heard the torpedoed sailor. She was a Donohue and he was a Sullivan. And Ireland has a long-standing history of its inhabitants hearing voices, from Saint Patrick and Saint Cieran to—"

"Bridey Murphy, who's *completely* reliable," Briddey said sarcastically. "To say nothing of all those Irishmen who claim to have seen leprechauns."

"Don't knock leprechauns. If you look closely at those stories, you'll see the vast majority are about talking to someone no one else can see."

He can't be serious, she thought. *This is just more white noise—or maybe "blarney" is a better word under the circumstances—to keep the voices at bay till we get safely out of the city.* Which they were still nowhere close to doing. The darkened streets they were driving along were lined with businesses and office buildings that showed no sign of thinning out.

"We're almost there," C.B. reassured her. "And my theory's not blarney. I've spent a lot of time researching this."

"And this research said the early Irish developed some sort of gene that gave them—and *only* them—telepathic ability?"

"No, just the opposite. Everybody—or at least a sizeable chunk of our ancestors—once had it, but now the Irish are the only ones left with it. Did you ever hear of Julian Jaynes's theory of the bicameral mind?"

"No."

"It's a theory that for most of human history, hearing voices was a common occurrence. People attributed the voices to the gods, but it was actually the two halves of the brain talking to each other. And when the brain evolved into a single entity, the voices stopped. Or, rather, people stopped thinking of them as voices and realized they were just hearing their own thoughts."

"So you're not really talking to me—I'm just talking to myself?"

"Obviously not. Jaynes's conclusion about why the voices went away was totally wrong, but he was right about hearing voices being a common phenomenon that then disappeared. I think back then everybody was telepathic, but over time the ability largely died out through natural selection. My guess is that some people had a gene—or genes—which inhibited the uptake receptors that made it possible to hear the voices—probably the neural equivalent of either a perimeter or the words to 'Teen Angel.'"

"A perimeter? What's that?"

"A kind of defense. I'm going to teach you to build one when we get where we're going. Anyway," he continued, "that inhibitor gene gave them an evolutionary advantage. Telepathy's not exactly a survival trait, you know. Hearing howling voices in your head when you should be concentrating on the battle you're in is likely to get you killed before you can pass on your genes, and so is being believed to be possessed by demons. And I wouldn't be surprised if a bunch of the voice-hearers threw themselves off a cliff to escape the voices. Or off a bridge. Like Billie Joe McAllister."

"Who?"

"The guy in 'Ode to Billie Joe.' Great song. Lots of verses and nice, distracting white-noise-type words—Tupelo and black-eyed peas and Tallahatchie Bridge."

"Which he jumped off of?"

"Yeah, but not because he was telepathic. Though I guess he might have been. In that part of the South, a lot of people are descended from the Irish, and his name *was* McAllister. Anyway, my *point* is, over time the inhibitors won out over the no-inhibitors, and telepathy died out."

"But why wouldn't the same thing have happened among the Irish?"

"Because during those centuries when the rest of Europe was invading and being invaded and hooking up with other peoples who had inhibitor genes, the Irish weren't. Ireland was way off the beaten path, especially the western reaches, which meant the inhabitants' original genes, even the recessive ones, like red hair and telepathy, were able to survive."

"But the Irish didn't *stay* isolated," Briddey said. "England invaded in the 1500s, and during the Famine hundreds of thousands of them emigrated to America—"

"Right, and they married people with one or more inhibitor genes, which is why most Irish today are only partially telepathic, if that."

"Partially telepathic?"

"Yeah, they can only hear someone calling to them in circumstances of heightened emotion, or they have a vague sense when something's wrong. Just a few Irish still have the genetic makeup to be fully telepathic."

"And you and I are two of them."

"Yeah. Lucky us, huh?"

"But if your theory's right, I inherited the gene from my parents, so why aren't Kathleen and Mary Clare—?"

"Because it's the kind of gene that has to be activated, either by an alteration in brain chemistry or a change in the circuitry."

"Like the EED," Briddey said grimly.

"Exactly. Though it could just as easily have been the anesthetic. Anything that lowers the brain's natural defenses or causes an increase in receptivity to the telepathic signals can trigger it—drugs, hypnosis, sleep deprivation, physical trauma, emotional stress. Any heightened emotional state, really. Fear, longing, adolescent angst."

"Which is what triggered yours."

"And Joan of Arc's. Thirteen's when she first heard the voices, too."

"But she wasn't Irish."

"No, but she lived long enough ago that the genes could still have been found in other parts of Europe. And Domrémy's not that far from Dublin. She was also trying to connect, which seems to be a trigger, too."

"Connect?" Briddey said blankly. "Who was Joan of Arc trying to—?"

"Connect to? God. When she heard Saint Michael the first time, she was praying, which is definitely a kind of reaching out." He leaned forward and peered through the windshield. "Can you make out the name of that street up ahead? I want to see how much farther we've got left to go."

"My phone has GPS on it," she said, and then remembered that they couldn't turn her phone on. She squinted at the sign, which was barely visible in the darkness, trying to make it out. "Palmer Boulevard," she said finally.

"Good."

"Are we almost out of the city, then?" she asked, looking ahead for signs that they were nearing the outskirts.

"No," he said, stopping at a red light. "We're not going out of it."

"What do you mean? Why not?"

"Because it wouldn't do any good. The voices aren't affected by distance. Well, they are, but not enough that driving out in the country would put you out of range. And if you did go far enough to get away from the ones you heard in the theater, you'd just be within range of a bunch of others."

There was no way to get beyond the reach of the voices, and no way she could get them to stop. Which meant they'd catch up, they'd wash over the car, they'd swamp her, and—

"Briddey!" C.B. was saying. "Briddey! Listen to me!"

"They'll drown me!" she cried hysterically. "They'll—"

"No, they won't. I won't let them. I'm taking you someplace safe."

"There's no such place. You just said—"

"No, I didn't. There is, and I'm taking you there right now, but you've got to let me drive so we can get there," and she realized she'd grabbed hold of his arm with both hands, and that the light had turned green and someone was honking at them.

"I'm sorry," she said, and let go of his arm, only to be deluged all over again.

"You're okay, you're okay," he said, snatching her hand up in his and holding it tightly.

The car behind them honked again.

"Oh, shut up," C.B. said amicably, and held her captured hand against his chest for a minute before putting it on his knee. "Just hang on to me and sing 'When Irish Eyes Are Smiling,' or some other foine Irish song, and I'll have you there in two shakes of a lamb's tail. Though the truth is, 'When Irish Eyes Are Smiling' isn't an Irish song at all, at all. It was written in Tin Pan Alley by someone who'd never set foot on the auld sod, and so were 'Too Ra Loo Ra Loo Ra' and 'Christmas in Killarney.' And 'Danny Boy,' the ultimate in Irishness. *It* was written by a lying brute of an Englishman."

This is just more blarney to keep me from falling apart till we get there, she thought, and tried to pull herself together, to ignore the frightening knell that had begun ringing inside her when she realized that there was no place beyond the reach of the voices.

"Speaking of getting there," C.B. said, "you might want to freshen up before we do. Not for me, you understand. I like messy hair." He grinned at her. "But we're going to be out in public—"

"We are? Where are we going?" she asked, looking out the window to see where they were.

C.B. had turned south, toward the tech center. *He's taking me to his lab at Commspan,* she thought. *Of course. That's why he works down there in the sub-basement, because he can't hear the voices down there.*

"No, afraid not," he said. "Unfortunately, concrete and insulation don't have any effect on the voices, and neither do sub-zero temperatures. Besides, some of the Hermes Project team are at Commspan, working late, and we can't run the risk of them seeing you. You're supposed to be at your Aunt Oona's with Maeve, remember?"

"So where *are* you taking me?"

Instead of answering, he reached into his jacket pocket, pulled out her evening bag, and handed it across to her. She opened it and took out her makeup mirror. Oh, God, she looked even worse than she had in the ladies' lounge, if that were possible, her mascara streaked and her hair a tangled mess. "You wouldn't have a Kleenex, would you?" she asked.

C.B. obligingly fished a wadded-up tissue out of his pocket and handed it to her. She spat on it, propped the makeup mirror on the dashboard, and tried to repair the damage, wiping at the mascara and applying lipstick—all with one hand so she could keep the other on his knee. She ran a comb through her hair, wishing she had something to tie it back with.

"How's this?" C.B. said, reaching across her to the glove compartment and producing a short length of computer wire.

"Perfect," she said, and then bit her lip, wondering how she was going to pull her hair back and wrap the wire around it without letting go of C.B.'s knee.

"Easy," he said without turning to look at her. "I'm going to sing 'Ode to Billie Joe.'" He launched into the song, which seemed to be about a family having dinner and casually mentioning that Billie Joe McAllister had jumped off the Tallahatchie Bridge, not noticing that the girl narrating the song was devastated by the news.

Briddey didn't really listen. She was too busy trying to get the wire twisted around her hair and her hand back on his knee before he finished the song.

She made it, barely. "And nobody ever knew she was in love with Billie Joe," C.B. said as she did, "since apparently they weren't Irish *or* telepathic. And here we are," he concluded, pulling over to the curb and stopping.

"Where?" she asked. They were parked on a street lined with dorms, and above the roofs she could see the buildings of the university. "Where are you taking me? A frat party?"

"Nope," he said, taking the key out of the ignition and unbuckling his seatbelt. "If you think the thoughts of theatergoers were bad, you should hear a bunch of drunk college guys." He glanced at his watch again and then reached across her to open her door a couple of inches. "Okay, now I need to break contact while I come around to get you."

She nodded and then realized that he was waiting for her to let go of his knee. She took a breath, exhaled, pulled her hand away, and clasped her hands together in her lap.

"Unless of course you *want* to go to a frat party," he said, getting out of the car and starting around the front of it, still talking. *Actually, listening to their thoughts isn't much different from being at the party.*

And he was there, leaning in her door, grabbing her hand and helping her out of the car, saying aloud, without missing a beat, "And you get a lot less beer and vomit spilled on you."

It was cold on the street. She shivered in the sleeveless green dress, and before she realized that C.B. had let go of her hand, he'd taken off his denim jacket and draped it over her shoulders.

"I can't take your jacket—" she began.

"It's protective coloration," he said, "so we don't look quite so mismatched."

"You mean like an escaped mental patient and her keeper?" she asked, glancing down at her hopelessly wrinkled dress.

"No, like the prom queen and the Hunchback of Notre Dame. Put it on," he ordered, and while she did, he opened the back door and began rummaging in the car. He straightened up and looked at her appraisingly. "Nope," he said, shaking his head. "Still too gorgeous for the likes of me. Come on, my Irish colleen."

They started up the street. As they walked, he handed her what he'd gotten out of the back seat. It was a stack of books.

"You're taking me to the library?" she asked.

"No, I had some overdue books," he said sarcastically, "and I thought we might as well return them since we were out running around. Yes, I'm taking you to the library."

Good, she thought, thinking of silence and light and card files— and rows and rows of books between her and the voices. If they could just get there before the voices caught up with them . . .

"I'm sorry we had to park so far away," C.B. said, walking her quickly up the street, "but they check the campus parking lots every hour."

"It's okay," she said, clutching the books to her as tightly as she'd clutched his knee. But it wasn't. They were *blocks* away from the library, and it was so dark out here. The streetlight up ahead was out, so the next block would be even darker, and she didn't see how a song about a boy who'd killed himself was going to stop the voices from breaking through, and—

C.B. took the books from her, shifted them to his outside arm, and grabbed her hand.

"*Thank* you," she breathed.

"Anytime. It doesn't have to be 'Ode to Billie Joe,' by the way. It can be any song you want so long as it has plenty of words—country-and-western, folk, rap, or, like I said, show tunes. *Hamilton. Kinky Boots. Guys and Dolls.* That's got tons of good songs—'Luck Be a Lady' and 'Adelaide's Lament' and 'Fugue for Tin Horns.' No, on second thought, forget 'Fugue for Tin Horns.' It sounds too much like the voices. You'd better stick with 'Adelaide's Lament.' Eight verses, and it's got all kinds of nice white-noise-ish words like 'psychosomatic syndrome' and 'streptococci' and 'postnasal drip.'"

"Postnasal *drip*?"

"It's a song about having a cold. Or if you don't like that, how about something from *Finian's Rainbow*? Musical about an Irish lass and a scruffy guy—*and* a leprechaun. Which reminds me, I've been thinking about those marshmallows. Could one of the shapes have been a pot of gold?"

He nattered on, talking about the marshmallows and "How Are

Things in Glocca Morra?" and non-Irish Irish songs, and she knew he was only doing it to get her through the dark streets, but she didn't care. He was keeping the voices at bay till they reached the library.

C.B. stopped just outside the door. "Don't panic," he said, "but when we go inside, I'm going to let go of your hand."

"Why?"

"Because I want the librarian to think we're here to study and not to go up to the stacks. This time of night they're full of oversexed undergrads canoodling."

"Canoodling?"

"Old Irish term for necking, making out, hooking up. I don't want the librarian deciding she needs to come check on us, though I doubt if anyone would believe someone as gorgeous as you would actually go out on a date with a guy like me. But don't worry about my not holding your hand. It doesn't mean I'm letting go of you. Ready?"

She nodded, and he took his hand from hers and put it firmly on her back. He opened the door with his other hand and stopped. "Hang on." He bent to peer at the Library Hours sign posted on it. It read, SATURDAY 10 A.M.—10:30 P.M.

Shit, he said. *Their budget must have gotten cut. They've shortened their hours again.*

"Does that mean we can't stay here?" The thought of having to walk back those four dark blocks to the car—

"No," C.B. said. "Shh." He cocked his head, staring past the door.

He's not reading the sign, she thought. *He's listening to hear how many people are inside,* and there must have been only a handful because after a minute he handed her back the stack of books, said, "Say what I tell you to, and try not to attract attention," and opened the door.

"Yeah, Iverson's exams are a real bear," he said aloud, and ushered her inside, his hand still on her elbow. *Now* you say, *"I've got to get at least a B on it."*

She clutched the books to her chest, trying hard to look like a student. "I've got to get at least a B on it."

"I can help you with that," C.B. said.

The young woman at the circulation desk looked up from her terminal and fastened her gaze on them. *I should never have worn this dress,* Briddey thought. *Trent was right. It's too conspicuous. I should have worn my black—*

Trent's a moron, C.B. said. *You look beautiful. Say, "It's the thing about nonvocal communication I don't get." And look at me, not her.*

She obediently turned to look at him. "It's the thing about non-vocal communication I don't get," she said, and the librarian's attention dropped back to her terminal.

"Yes, well, you came to the right guy," C.B. said. "I happen to be a whiz in the nonvocal communications department," and they were past the circulation desk and into the large study area beyond it.

But it wasn't deserted. There were scores of people here—studying, staring at laptops, whispering to one another. And thinking. Briddey looked fearfully at C.B. *I thought you said I was supposed to avoid crowded places,* she whispered.

You are, he said, hustling her through the room. *You don't have to whisper, you know. I'm the only one who can hear you.* He hurried her past the stairs marked TO THE STACKS and down to a second stairway.

I thought we were going to the stacks, she said.

Nope, too distracting, he said, leading her up the stairs. *Unless you want to hook up. Which wouldn't be a bad idea, voices-wise. Sex is a great defense. It pretty much shuts everything out. I was going to teach you a different kind of defense, but if you'd rather—*

I do not *want to hook up, and if that's why you brought me here—* she said, snatching her hand away from his. And was immediately sorry. The voices seemed to surge forward.

You're okay, I'm right here, C.B. said, and took her hand.

Thank you, she breathed.

Anytime, he said, and started up the stairs again. He stopped on the landing. "Hang on a sec. I need to text Trent again." He turned her phone on, swiped to a screen, and scrolled down.

"Did he leave any messages?"

"Afraid so." He handed the phone to her, and she saw that there were five texts and three voice messages from him. "I promised the Hamiltons we'd go out with them to Iridium afterward. I told them you'd meet us there. Can't you tell your family they need to handle this on their own?" plus several variations on "Why aren't you answering

your phone?" and, worst of all, "Any progress in the connecting department yet?"

Not the kind you're *thinking of,* Briddey thought, wondering how
on earth she was supposed to respond to that.

"Like this," C.B. said, taking the phone from her. He typed a rapid
message and hit SEND. "I told him you can't meet him, that it's taking
longer to calm everybody down than you thought, and you'll call him
in the morning." He switched her phone off and pocketed it.

"See? No problem. Come on," he said, and led her up to the next
floor and down a hall to a door marked READING ROOM. He paused
outside it, listening, and then said, *We're in luck.*

He opened the door onto a large open space like the one downstairs, except that there was no one at the reference desk and the study
tables were longer and wider. Racks of newspapers lined the sides, and
there were fewer people up here than downstairs, but it was still far
from deserted. There were at least two dozen people seated at the tables, hunched over laptops or books or reading newspapers. Two dozen
people. All thinking. And that wasn't even the worst part.

The worst part was the room itself. When C.B. had told her he was
taking her to a library, she'd imagined the walls lined with books, which
would offer some kind of fortification against the voices, but there
were no books anywhere here except for the few the people at the
tables were reading, and two of the walls were all window, black from
the darkness beyond and no protection at all from the voices.

What do we do now? she asked C.B., hoping he'd say he had a backup
plan, and they could go to the archives or even back to the staircase,
anywhere so long as it didn't have people and windows. But instead he
said, *This is good,* and gave her a push toward the nearest table. *Go all
the way to the end.*

She turned to look beseechingly at him. *The voices—*

*It'll be fine. Go. And try not to look like I'm kidnapping you. We're sup-
posed to be here to study, remember?*

Briddey went, keeping her eyes down so she wouldn't see the windows and the darkness beyond them, and, clutching her books, took
the chair C.B. indicated. He pushed it in for her, said, *Put the books on
the table, and open the top one to page six,* and went around to the chair
opposite her.

Page six, she thought, concentrating fiercely on finding the page, trying not to think about the fact that C.B. had let go of her and that they were less than a foot from the windows and the table was too wide. If he sat across from her, he wouldn't be able to hold her hand, and the voices would—

I'm not going to sit across from you, he said, pulling his chair around so he was at the end, sitting catty-corner from her, and reaching across the table not for her hand but for the next book on the stack. He opened it and looked down at it. *I'm right here. And you're perfectly safe. The voices can't get in here. Listen,* he said, and it was an order.

She looked longingly at his hand resting casually next to his book. *You don't need it,* he said, and when she still hesitated: *Trust me. Just listen.*

She did, gripping the edge of the table with both hands, bracing herself against the crashing wave of voices she was afraid would follow.

It didn't. The voices weren't gone, but they no longer roared over her, deluging her. They were calmer, quieter, like a harmless, murmuring stream. She looked over at C.B., amazed. *How did you do that?*

I didn't, he said, nodding in the direction of the other people seated at the long tables. They *did.*

But how—?

He grinned. *Never underestimate the power of a good book.*

Seventeen

"Ahem!" said the Mouse with an important air. "Are you all ready?
This is the driest thing I know. 'William the Conqueror, whose
cause was favoured by the pope, was soon submitted to by the
English, who wanted leaders, and had been of late much
accustomed to usurpation and conquest. Edwin and
Morcar, the earls of Mercia and Northumbria—'"
—LEWIS CARROLL, *Alice's Adventures in Wonderland*

I DON'T UNDERSTAND, BRIDDEY SAID, LOOKING AROUND AT THE READING
Room in wonder. She'd been wrong about the drone of the reading
voices sounding like a murmuring stream. It was warmer and more
pleasant, like the drone of bees in a garden. *How do the books—?*

It's not the books, C.B. said, *though I thought that, too, the first time I
encountered it. It's the thoughts of the people reading them. Reading's an entirely different process from ordinary thinking. It's more rhythmic and focused,
and it screens out all extraneous thoughts. And—if there are enough people
reading—everybody else's, too.*

But how—?

*I discovered it by accident. I'd come here to do some research to try to find
out what was causing the voices in my head.* He smiled at her. *People always
say books can be a refuge, and they're definitely right.*

"Refuge" was the right word. Her heart had stopped thudding for the first time since the voices started in the theater.

Which is why I brought you here, C.B. said. *The readers'll screen them while we get your defenses up.*

But I thought that the readers were the defenses.

They're one of them, and, luckily, one that's almost always available. There's hardly any time of day or night when people aren't reading, so if the voices start to overwhelm you, you can come here or go to the public library or a bookstore or Starbucks. And if that's out, you can do the reading yourself.

But I thought you said audiobooks didn't work.

They don't. What's screening the voices is the synaptic patterns of the readers. So you need to either read yourself or listen to an actual person reading. Preferably something Victorian, with nice, long, droning sentences. Like this, he said, and began reading from the book in front of him: *"But a case more trying by far to the nerves is to discover some mysterious companionship when intuition, sensation, memory, analogy, testimony, probability, induction—every kind of evidence in the logician's list—have united to persuade consciousness that it is quite in isolation."*

That's Hardy, he said, *who works great, and so does Dickens—and Anthony Trollope and Wilkie Collins. Nothing too boring, though. If your mind starts to wander, it won't work, so no Henry James. Or Silas Marner. What you need is Barchester Towers or Our Mutual Friend. Download them to your phone so you'll have them with you all the time. And brush up on "The Highwayman."*

And the songs you told me about.

Exactly. But all those are just stopgap measures. What you really need are permanent defenses. He glanced at his watch.

Briddey reached automatically for her phone to see what time it was and then remembered that C.B. still had it. She glanced over at the clock behind the reference desk: nine forty-five. And the library closed at ten thirty. That gave them less than an hour.

So we need to get busy, C.B. said. *The first step is to put up your perimeter. It'll do on a permanent basis what the readers' voices are doing right now. You know those baffles you see along highways? The ones that keep the traffic noise down to a dull roar for the people who were dumb enough to build houses next to a major road? You're going to erect the same kind of thing, only inside your head.* He glanced across the room at the various readers. *You need to look like you're reading, by the way. We're supposed to be studying.*

Sorry, Briddey said, and hastily bent her head over her book.

It's okay. Nobody's looking at us right now. But the librarian will be back soon, and we don't want her getting suspicious. He propped his chin on his hand and bent his head over his own book, looking for all the world like he was reading intently. *The first thing you need to do is envision a fence,* he said.

Like a highway baffle.

Not necessarily. It can be any kind of fence: a computer firewall or one of those invisible electronic dog barriers or the Great Wall of China—anything at all so long as you believe it will keep the voices out.

As long as I believe? she said, looking up at C.B. *The voices are real, not something I imagined! They're—*

The fence is real, too, C.B. said, his eyes never moving from his book. *And so was the railing you were hanging onto back at the theater. And the woodland path you envisioned when Verrick was talking about establishing a neural pathway.*

But—

The voices are telepathic signals to the brain. They cause synapses to be fired, just like auditory signals. Well, the fence is signals causing synapses to fire, too, only in this case they inhibit the signal uptake receptors.

I thought you said we didn't have the inhibitor gene.

We don't. We have to manufacture our own inhibitors. They don't work as well as the real thing, and they take more energy and more concentration to sustain, but they can still protect you.

So you're saying I have to visualize inhibiting the uptake receptors?

Yes, but you have to visualize it in images that make sense to you. Concrete, everyday images, like the railing you visualized at the theater.

She thought of the wet, black iron railing she had clung to. *But it wasn't strong enough,* she thought. If C.B. hadn't come and rescued her, the water would have come pouring through it and over the top—

So you need to put up something that is strong enough, C.B. said. *How about a levee? Or a dike?*

A dike, Briddey thought eagerly. *Like the ones in Holland.* But dikes got holes in them. That little Dutch boy had had to stick his finger in the dike to keep the water from squirting through—

Sorry, C.B. said. *I should have told you it needs to be something you don't associate with collapsing or being breached. I made that mistake myself the first time. I envisioned a castle wall—*

A castle—?

I know, he said, embarrassed. *I was thirteen, okay? Anyway, it had ramparts and a drawbridge and boiling oil. Perfectly safe—except for all those movies I'd watched that had battering rams and catapults. And mobs of peasants carrying torches.*

So what did you switch to?

A white picket fence. You never see one of those being smashed with a battering ram.

No, seriously, she said. *What's your barrier now?*

He didn't answer.

C.B?

Still no answer, and when she stole a glance at him, he'd looked up from his book and was staring blindly at the window behind her.

C.B.? she called again, and he seemed to come to himself.

Sorry, he said. *I got distracted by the book. What did you ask?*

What your barrier is now.

Oh. After the castle, I decided the maximum-security prison route was the best way to go, so long as I avoided watching prison-break movies. You know, chain-link fences, razor wire, searchlights, dogs.

But chain-link fences won't keep out water either.

True. Maybe you should—

He stopped again, and when Briddey sneaked a glance at him, he was looking over at the double doors. Was the librarian coming back?

No, I don't think so, he said. *Hang on. I need to check something. Read your book.*

She obediently dropped her eyes to the page. "It might reasonably have been supposed that she was listening to the wind," she read. And what was he listening to? The voices, obviously. But how could he stand to? They were so drowningly loud and clamoring. It would be like voluntarily walking into a howling storm. Unless this perimeter he wanted her to build somehow tamed them, because he didn't look frightened or even braced to face the blast. He was gazing blindly ahead of him, like he had before.

And what was it he needed to check? *C.B.?* she said, but he didn't answer—or even seem to be aware of her having said anything.

He's somewhere else altogether, she thought. *Or else he's concentrating on keeping the voices from overwhelming him.* And she certainly didn't want to distract him from that. She needed to keep quiet and read her book.

"The wind, indeed, seemed made for the scene as the scene seemed made for the hour . . ." she read. "What was heard there could be heard nowhere else."

Which is why she should be in a library instead of out on the moors, C.B. said. He looked up from his book to grin at her. *Sorry about that. For a minute I thought I heard the librarian coming, but she's not.*

And he knew that because he could hear her individual thoughts, just as he'd heard Kathleen's. And the nurse's. But how? The voices were a maelstrom of words and emotions. How had he been able to pick a single voice out from the rest?

It's an acquired skill, C.B. said.

Can you teach me how to do it? Briddey asked.

Yes, but not till after we've gotten your basic defenses in place. We don't have much time.

She glanced at the clock. Ten o'clock. Only half an hour till closing.

Exactly, he said. *So okay, you need a barrier that water can't get through. How about Hoover Dam?*

I don't know what it looks like, she said. *I mean, I know it's big and made of concrete, but that's all.*

That won't work, then. You need to be able to visualize it in detail. How about a seawall?

I don't know what that looks like either. Would a brick wall do?

Like the one in Tennyson's "Flower in the Crannied Wall" or the one the bad guy builds in Poe's "Cask of Amontillado"? he asked, then grinned ruefully. *Sorry, I spend a lot of time in libraries. A brick wall it is.* And proceeded to take her through every detail of how it looked, from the exact color of the bricks to the thickness of the mortar between them.

The more details, the more real it is to you, he said, *and the better it can withstand the voi—* He stopped in mid-word and listened again for a second. *The librarian's coming.*

Briddey fought the impulse to look up. She heard the door open. *Okay,* C.B. said, *look up casually at the door and then go back to reading.*

Briddey did, trying to think how she'd act if she really *was* studying and wondering if they were fooling the librarian.

Yep, C.B. said, *though she's thinking you must really be in danger of flunking out to be here with a nerd like me on a Saturday night. Let's give it a minute. Keep reading.*

Okay, Briddey said, and concentrated on the page. "So low was an individual sound from these," she read, "that a combination of hundreds only just emerged from silence——"

And let's hope that the voices are that quiet after I get the wall built, she thought, though she didn't see how an imaginary wall could keep anything out, let alone the voices.

Where's your faith in me, darlin'? C.B. said in a brogue nearly as broad as Aunt Oona's, and Briddey glanced up at him and then abruptly down again.

Sorry, she said. *I keep forgetting I'm not supposed to look at you.*

It's okay. The librarian's forgotten about us. It's one of the other librarians' birthday, and she's busy thinking about the party after work. She's worried she didn't buy a big enough sheet cake. He turned the page of his book. *Describe your brick wall to me.*

Briddey did, trying to focus on exactly how it looked, to make it as real as the room they were in, the table they were sitting at, but C.B. kept glancing worriedly at his watch.

The library was going to close at ten thirty. When it did, they'd have to go back out into the darkness, and it was four blocks to his car. If she didn't have her perimeter up by then, or if it didn't work . . . Visualizing a brick wall here, in the safety of the Reading Room, was one thing. But droning and safe as the readers' voices were, she could hear the other voices waiting beyond them, like falls ahead on a river. She glanced involuntarily over at the windows and the darkness beyond them.

Put your left hand under the table, C.B. said, and when she did, he took it and held it tightly, resting it on his knee. *Better?*

Yes, she said gratefully. *But I can't hang on to you forever.*

Sure you can. Now tell me again what your wall looks like.

She described it to him, imagining it there in front of her, standing impenetrable between her and the voices, comfortingly solid and watertight.

I think I've got it down now, she said when she'd finished, but he shook his head.

It's not just a question of getting it down. You've got to be able to visualize it without thinking. It's like when you're learning to type or drive a car. It's got to become automatic.

He took her through her wall's appearance three more times, and then said, *Okay, I'm going to let go of your hand, and you're going to hear the voices. As soon as you do, I want you to think of your wall. Ready?*

No, she thought.

It's okay. You've got the readers, and I'm right here. And you've got your brick wall. Nothing can get through it. Ready? And don't nod. You're supposed to be reading. Keep your eyes on your book. And think about your wall.

I'm ready, she said, clenching her hand into a fist under the table to keep from grabbing for him as he pulled his hand away.

Don't look over at the windows, she told herself. *Look at your book,* and heard the droning buzz of the voices begin to swell into a noisy clamor: *. . . got to study . . . the antebellum South was governed by the idea . . . if I flunk out, my father . . . as X approaches plus or minus infinity . . . subjunctive tense . . .*

They can't get past the wall, she told herself firmly, staring at the book, at the bricks, red and rough-cast and standing solidly between her and the voices—

Good, C.B. said, taking her hand. *Okay, try it again. And this time I'm not going to tell you when I'm letting go.*

Okay, she said, taking a deep breath, and began reading. "Suddenly, on the barrow, there mingled with all this wild rhetoric of night a sound."

I'm not sure this is what I should be reading, she thought, and C.B. let go of her hand.

The voices roared in: *. . . Carolinian dynasty . . . reduction of sulfuric acid . . . never remember all this crap . . . basis of tort reform . . . fucking stupid class!*

Think of the wall, she told herself, gritting her teeth, and immediately saw it standing there, keeping the voices out.

The next time was even easier, and by the third try she wasn't even giving the voices a chance to speak before the wall was in place, stopping them.

Very good, C.B. said. He glanced at the clock and shut his book. *Okay, we've gotta go.*

Go? she said, looking over at the clock: 10:10. *I thought you said the library was open till ten thirty.*

It is, he said, reaching over to close her book.

But I'm not ready. Envisioning the voices safely behind the brick wall was one thing here in the brightly lit Reading Room, but outside, in the darkness with them . . . *Can't we stay till they close?* she pleaded.

Yes, but not here. Pick up your book and push back your chair. He gathered up the other books. "You want to go get some sushi or something?" he said aloud.

The librarian looked up and over at them. "Sorry," he mouthed at the librarian and repeated the question to Briddey in a whisper, adding silently, *Say you can't, that you're meeting your boyfriend.*

"I can't," she whispered, standing up and pushing her chair in. "I'm sorry, I promised my boyfriend—"

C.B. steered her toward the door past the librarian, saying disappointedly, "Yeah, that's what I figured," as he opened one of the double doors for her. "I just thought—"

"I'm really sorry," she said as she went through.

"Where are you meeting him?" C.B. asked as the door swung shut behind them. "Do you need a ride?"

Do I? Briddey asked.

No, he said, leading her in the opposite direction from which they'd come.

Where are we going? she asked.

For starters, the bathroom, he said, stopping in front of a door marked Women and taking her book from her. *We may not get another chance for awhile. I'll meet you out here.*

Briddey stared at the door, paralyzed, thinking of the ladies' room at the theater, of the mirror and the sinks and herself, crouching back under the counter to get away from the voices. *You want me to go in there by myself?*

You're not by yourself, C.B. said. *You've got a nice, solid brick wall to protect you. And Gilligan. And Billie Joe.*

I know, but—

And we're still within range of the Reading Room. Listen, he ordered, and he was right. She could still hear the beelike hum of the students' reading. But that could cease any time now, as they stopped reading and prepared to go home.

Do you want me to come in with you? C.B. asked. *Mentally, I mean? It wouldn't be the first ladies' room I've been in. Or bedroom. Or back seat. You would be amazed at some of the things I've had to listen to. Bathrooms are nothing. I've—*

No, thanks, I can do this on my own, she said hastily.

Good, he said. *You'll be fine. I'll meet you back here in a sec.* He disappeared into the men's room.

I can do this, Briddey told herself, pushing the door open. She had to. The only alternative was the humiliation of having him accompany her in here. If he wasn't doing that anyway.

He's right, she thought. *Telepathy's a terrible idea.* She fixed her mind firmly on her brick wall, reciting for good measure, "Yellow moons, green clovers, Tallahatchie Bridge . . . ," till she was safely back outside the bathroom.

C.B. was waiting for her, looking at his watch. He immediately handed her the stack of books, put his hand on her elbow, and walked her rapidly back toward the stairs down to the main floor.

I thought you said we were staying here at the library, she said, the panic beginning to beat against her rib cage again as she thought of the darkness outside and the endless blocks to the car.

We are, he said, opening the door to the stairway and ushering her inside.

Then where are we going?

The stacks, he said, and turned to grin at her.

Eighteen

"But, gentle friend, for love and courtesy, lie further off."
—WILLIAM SHAKESPEARE, *A Midsummer Night's Dream*

THE STACKS? BRIDDEY REPEATED.

Yeah. After I make sure nobody sees us going up. C.B. cocked his head and listened. "Okay," he said aloud after several seconds. "The coast is clear. Come on, hurry." And he hustled her out of the stairway and back to the door marked TO THE STACKS.

Inside was a metal staircase very much like the one she'd fled to in the hospital. *Fond memories, huh?* C.B. said, trotting up the stairs. *You didn't know how well off you were with only one voice to contend with, did you?*

"Attention," a voice said out of nowhere. Briddey gasped and looked sharply around.

PA system, C.B. explained, and the voice continued.

"The library will be closing at ten thirty. If you have books or materials to check out, please take them to the circulation desk now."

Sorry. I should've warned you about that, C.B. said.

"It's okay," Briddey said, and hurried up the stairs after him, her heels making an incredible amount of noise on the metal steps. "Should I take them off?" she asked.

Yeah, C.B. said, looking up at the stairs above them.

She unstrapped them, leaning against him for support. He scooped them up, handed them to her, and they started up the stairs again, past landings with doors marked A–C and D–EM.

"The library will be closing in fifteen minutes," the PA announced.

And the students in the Reading Room will stop reading, Briddey thought, a shudder running through her, and C.B. must have sensed her fear because he took her hand and hustled her up the next flight to EN–G.

He listened, his hand on the door for a moment, and then said, *Too crowded,* and started up the stairs with her again, going through the same routine for H–K and L–N.

Outside the O–R door, he listened intently for what seemed like an aeon and then said, *There's one couple on this level. Down at the end. In Macrobiology, appropriately enough. Come on.* He moved to open the door.

Shouldn't we try to find a level that's empty? Briddey asked in a whisper, and this time C.B. didn't tell her it wasn't necessary.

He whispered back, *No,* listened for another moment, and then opened the door onto a large, shadowy space filled with aisle after aisle of floor-to-ceiling bookshelves. The only lights were dim ones at the head of each narrow aisle, and a brighter one in the farthest aisle. The other aisles lay in shadow, the shelves and the books disappearing into darkness.

No wonder students come up here to make out, she thought. *It's like the Black Hole of Calcutta.* She wondered how they'd be able to see if they *did* come up here to find a book.

She'd assumed, since the couple was at the far end, that C.B. would lead her down the first aisle at this end, but he didn't. He pulled her over a half dozen aisles. *Where are we going?* she whispered.

Communications. Where else? he said, and led her into the aisle labeled P148–160. As they made their way down the aisle, small lights clicked on above them, illuminating each section of the shelves as they passed.

Energy-saving device, C.B. said. *They click off after fifteen minutes, but the librarian'll be up here before then.*

And the lights being on would tell the librarian there were people on this level. Which was why they needed the other couple—to justify the lights.

You got it, C.B. said.

But won't the other couple notice?

He shook his head. *They're not noticing much of anything right now.* He led her to a break in the shelves, an aisle at right angles to theirs.

But if they're at the other end, Briddey persisted, *won't the librarian think it's odd that there are lights on at this—*

The PA cut in: "The library will be closing in ten minutes."

Come on, C.B. said. *We don't have much time.* He rushed her across the gap and down the aisle to the next cross-aisle.

He stopped just short of it, took the books from Briddey, squatted down, and stuck them on the bottom shelf between *Basic Communication* and *Interpreting Body Language.*

I thought those were your books, Briddey said.

They are. But if we should get caught, I don't want to be escorted down to check them out. He straightened up, listened a moment, and then leaned out to look up and down the cross-aisle. *All clear. Come on.*

She followed him quickly across the gap and down the next section of bookshelves and the next, trying to stay to one side to avoid triggering the lights, but to no avail. They winked on one after the other.

The lights will tell them exactly where we've gone, she said. *And how do you know they don't have surveillance cameras, too?*

They used to, but not anymore, he said, motioning her to follow him to the next cross-aisle. *Budget cuts.*

How do you know that?

I can read minds, remember? he said, continuing down the aisle toward the back wall.

Where we'll be trapped like rats, Briddey thought. *With a spotlight on us.*

Have ye no faith in me, mavourneen? C.B. said, plowing ahead, and as she neared the end of the shelves, she saw there was a narrow space between it and the wall, running the full length of the room. C.B. repeated his routine of listening and looking, then led her sideways into the narrow space and back along it.

It was scarcely wide enough to walk in, but at least no lights clicked on as they went along it. C.B. stopped at the end of a darkened aisle two rows from the door they'd come in. And nowhere near the lighted aisles. But even though they were in darkness, C.B. flattened himself against the wall and motioned her to stand against the end of the bookcase, facing him.

See? Nothing to worry about, he said. *We're invisible from the front of the stacks.* He glanced down. *Except for that dress of yours.*

He was right. The flared skirt of her green dress stuck out beyond the sides of the bookcase. She gathered it in, bunching its fullness together with one hand and holding her shoes to her chest with the other.

Good, C.B. said. *The librarian'll never see us now.*

But won't she check back here, too?

No. She's checking for people who might not have heard the announcement or are dawdling, not for people trying to get themselves locked in.

You don't know that, she said, and then realized he probably did.

"The library will be closing in five minutes," the PA announced.

When it stopped, Briddey said, *But what's to keep the other couple from ducking back into this space, too, when they hear her coming?*

Because they've got to get back into their clothes first. If they hear her, he said, tilting his head to one side and listening. *Which I'm not sure they will.*

You're listening to them having sex?

He made a face. *I wish I were. That might be kind of entertaining. No, I'm listening to what they're* thinking *while they're hooking up, which is a completely different thing.*

I thought you said sex shut everything down. W-well, not everything, obviously, she stammered, *but you said it shut down the voices.*

I was talking about having *sex, not having to listen to somebody else have it. And I was talking about having sex with somebody you're absolutely crazy about,* he said, and she was suddenly aware of just how close they were to each other in this narrow space. At some point he'd put his hands flat against the end of the bookcase on either side of her head so that he was leaning over her, his face only inches from hers. *And he can hear everything I think.*

So those two over in Macrobiology aren't crazy about each other? she said hastily.

Not by a long shot, C.B. said. *He's thinking about what he's going to tell his buddies, and she's wondering whether she should change her Facebook status or not. And both of them are thinking how uncomfortable the floor is and wishing they were doing it with somebody thinner and better-looking.*

That's terrible.

Actually, it's not that. At least she's not wondering what she's going to have to do to get him to give her his econ notes and he's not wondering if his spy cam is working. And neither one's wondering what to do with the murdered body.

But surely some people—

Are madly in love? You bet, but a bunch of those people are also thinking about how to wrap things up so they can make it home before their spouse gets suspicious. I told you, it's a cesspool in there.

That's still no excuse to listen to them having sex like some disgusting voyeur, she said reprovingly.

He shook his head. *A voyeur wants to listen. We're talking involuntary here. I would love not to have to hear the voices at all.*

I would, too, Briddey said fervently.

Well, as soon as everybody leaves, we'll get to work on that.

On what? she wondered, her pulse beginning to race in spite of herself. *And he knows it.*

Don't worry, I'm talking about teaching you to protect yourself, he said. *Your perimeter's just the first line of defense. There are other ones.*

One of them had better be a wall that keeps me from being such an open book, she thought. *Telepathy really is a terrible idea.*

I tried to tell you that, he said, and then seriously, *How are you doing in the meantime?*

She'd been so busy hurrying and hiding and trying not to make any noise that she hadn't thought about the voices since they'd started up here. They were still present, but as background noise, the way they'd been in the Reading Room. Her perimeter must be working. Or else she was acclimating to the voices. Or C.B.'s proximity, combined with the tens of thousands of books above and below and around them, formed some sort of protective shield, and that was why he'd picked the stacks for them to spend the night in.

We're not spending the night here. For one thing, as our amorous friends pointed out, the floor's uncomfortable. And with the budget cuts, they've been turning the heat way down. It's worse than my lab. We'd freeze.

She was already freezing. The tile floor was icy against her bare feet. If they stayed here much longer, her teeth would start chattering.

Sorry, C.B. said, *but we can't leave yet. The whole place is crawling with staff locking up and getting ready to go home. We'll have to wait till—* He raised his head, alert. *Shh, someone's coming.*

He put his finger to his lips, even though neither of them had made a sound, and took a half-step toward her to get out of sight. She bunched her skirt more closely in front of her and listened intently for the sound of a door opening.

Is it the librarian?

Nope, a TA. A guy.

The door clanged open, and Briddey held her breath, waiting for lights to begin clicking on, but nothing happened.

The TA's standing in the doorway, C.B. said. *He's listening for noises.*

After a silence, a male voice called out, "The library is now closing."

"Oh, shit!" a female voice said at the far end, followed by frantic whispering, scrambling noises, a stifled giggle, and the sound of the TA striding purposefully in the direction of the noises, calling out, "If you have materials to check out, please proceed immediately downstairs to the circulation desk."

She's trying to button her blouse, C.B. said, providing a running commentary, *and he's looking for his shoes and hoping this won't get him in trouble with his coach.*

And the TA?

He's thinking this is the fourth time this week, and they'd better not be doing anything he has to report because . . . oh, good, the TA's got a hot date after work. Which hopefully means he'll be in a hurry to get out of here.

There was more scrambling and whispering, and then a silence of several seconds. "Hi," Briddey heard the girl say, and could imagine her trying to make her hair look more presentable. "We didn't realize what time—"

The TA cut her off. "The stacks are closing. You two need to get downstairs."

"We were just getting ready to," the guy said.

"Anybody else up here?" the TA asked, and C.B. laid his hand on Briddey's shoulder, ready to yank her around the corner into the aisle if necessary.

"No," the guy said. "Listen, I'm on the basketball team, and I'd really appreciate it if you didn't report this."

"That depends on how fast you two get out of here," the TA said, and there was the sound of two pairs of footsteps heading quickly for the door. "And go straight downstairs," he called after them.

"Okay," the girl said.

"Thanks," the guy muttered, and the door banged open and then shut.

Did the TA go with them? Briddey whispered.

No.

A light blinked on at the far end and then several aisles closer. *He's coming this way,* Briddey whispered.

I know, C.B. said. *Come on, buddy, it's obvious there's nobody here. And I thought you had a hot date,* and, as if the TA had heard him, he called, "Anybody else here? The library's closing."

Footsteps as he walked back to the front. "Last call," and then the sound of the door opening and shutting again.

Is he gone? Briddey whispered.

C.B. nodded.

"The library is now closing," a voice said practically in Briddey's ear. She jumped.

The PA again, C.B. reassured her.

"Please proceed to the ground floor," the voice said. "The library will reopen at eleven A.M. tomorrow."

The voice fell silent, but C.B. made no move to go, which didn't surprise Briddey. They obviously couldn't leave the stacks till after the staff had finished up their work, made their rounds, and left the building. But he made no move to step away from her either. He stood where he was, leaning over her. Her pulse began to race again.

C.B., I— she began, and realized he hadn't heard her.

He was listening to someone else, his head up. Who? The TA? Or one of the other librarians on their way up here for a last look around? She had no idea. Close as he was, she wasn't picking up so much as an inkling of a thought from him.

He must have some kind of defense that keeps me from reading his mind, she thought, and he didn't hear that either.

Who was he listening to? His gaze, fixed blindly on the end of the bookcase, seemed almost too distant and too intent for it to be a mere librarian. Could it be Trent? The play would be out by now. Could Trent be thinking about calling her to see what was going on? She needed to text Maeve—

Don't worry, C.B. said, coming back from wherever he'd been. *I already took care of it. While you were in the bathroom. I texted Maeve and explained the situation, and told her that if Trent called, she was to tell him you were there and that you'd call him back.*

But what if he called Mary Clare or Aunt Oona? God knew what they'd tell him.

I told Maeve to be sure she was the one who answered the phone. And she said she'd see to it everybody else's was turned off.

But how would she be able to do that? Aunt Oona—

C.B. gave her a look as if to say, "You're kidding, right?" *In case you haven't noticed, your niece is a very smart kid—and a whiz with computers,* he said. *When she was down in my lab, she showed me how she'd disabled the V-chips and spyware her mom had installed on her laptop, and I was impressed. Remotely switching off Oona's phone would be child's play for her—literally. Don't worry. I'm sure she's got the situation under control.*

That was easy for him to say, but even if Maeve did manage to keep Trent from reaching Mary Clare and Oona, there was still the problem of explaining to Maeve why they needed her to lie. Maeve would have dozens of questions, and—

We've gotta go, C.B. said abruptly. He grabbed her hand and hurried her back along the wall to the still-lighted aisle they'd come down originally.

But what about the TA? she asked, following him up the aisle to the door.

He's up on w–z, C.B. said, opening the door and starting down the steps. *It's amazing how fast you can check ten levels of stacks when you've got a hot date.*

What about your books?

I'll get them later. He went swiftly down the steps from landing to landing, stopping at the last one. He turned to face her. *You need to put your shoes back on before we go out.*

But what about—? Briddey began, looking nervously back up the stairs.

It's okay. He's got five separate couples up there he's got to dislodge. But it was obvious that C.B. wanted her to hurry. When she had trouble fastening her shoes' straps, he knelt down and did it for her.

But wouldn't it be safer to wait up in the stacks till after the staff's left? she asked.

He shook his head. *They turn all the lights off up here, including the motion-controlled ones, which means we'd have to use a flashlight to find our way, and we'd run the risk of somebody outside seeing it. It's okay. They're all at the birthday party right now.*

But what about the custodians?

They don't work Saturday nights. He hurried her down the last of the stairs to the third floor. He took hold of the door handle, and then stood there a long minute, listening. Satisfied, he put his finger to his lips, said silently, *Tiptoe,* and opened the door.

It was clearly a staff-only area. The corridor looked just like the ones at Commspan, lined with offices, one of which she supposed they were going to hide in. But C.B. said, *Nope, they're locked,* and strode quickly down to a door marked COPY ROOM.

Of course, Briddey thought, remembering how he'd waylaid her in the one at Commspan. But after a quick look inside, C.B. shook his head, shut the door, and started down the corridor again.

Why can't we stay in there? Briddey asked, scurrying after him.

There was a smartphone on the table, which means somebody'll either come back for it or borrow somebody else's phone to call it so they can hear it. Not good for us either way. He walked quickly down to where the corridor made a ninety-degree turn, and stopped to listen again.

I thought you said everybody was at the birthday party, Briddey said.

I think they are, but thoughts don't have GPS. Unless they're actively thinking, "Here I am walking down Broadway toward Forty-second Street," it's impossible to tell where they are or what they're up to. When this first happened to me, I thought maybe the telepathy was a superpower, and I could fight crime with it. You know, be Spider-Man and solve mysteries, catch bad guys. But unfortunately—

It doesn't work like that, she said, thinking of the anonymity—and the violent flooding force—of the voices.

Yeah, C.B. said. *That, and the fact that it's impossible to tell from their thoughts where they are and whether they're actually stabbing somebody*

*to death or just stuck in line behind somebody really slow at the grocery
store.*

He listened for another minute and then said, *They're all still down
at the birthday party, except for the TA, who's texting his hot date that he's on
his way.*

Which might mean he was coming down here.

Exactly, C.B. said, turned the corner onto another empty corridor,
and hurried her down it to a door labeled STORAGE CLOSET. He opened
the door and pushed her in ahead of him.

Into a solid wall of stacked chairs and boxes—and file cabinets
topped with old computer monitors and daisy-wheel printers. *I don't
think there's room . . .* Briddey began, but C.B. had already stepped inside
and pulled the door three quarters of the way shut, colliding with her
as he did.

Can't you move any farther back? he asked.

No, she said, banging into something that wobbled. *There's nowhere
to go. I thought you said we were going someplace more comfortable.*

We are. As soon as . . . shit. There's no lock on this door.

Does that mean we need to find someplace else?

Maybe, he said, looking over her shoulder at the jumble of furniture dimly visible in the light from the hall. *On the other hand, this may
be perfect. It doesn't look like anybody's been in here in years. If we can just . . .*
He stretched his neck, trying to see what lay beyond the file cabinets
and boxes.

Change places with me, he ordered her. *I want to see what's behind this
stuff.* He squeezed awkwardly past her and began shifting chairs.

What's back there? Briddey asked.

"More stuff," C.B. said aloud. "Jeez, this place could be on one of
those shows about hoarders. I doubt if they'll bother to check in here.
It's too crowded to hide in."

Should you be talking out loud? she asked nervously, looking at the
still partly open door.

"It's okay. The TA's still in the stacks, and Marian's singing 'Happy
Birthday.'"

"Marian?"

"The Librarian. From *The Music Man.* Marian the Librarian's what
I call the librarian I've been listening to. She's the one who's been des-

ignated to lock up tonight. It's also a good song, by the way. Lots of verses. I think there might be some room in the back." He paused, and then said, "Go ahead and shut the door."

She did, and thought, *Oh, no, I'm alone in the dark, and the voices—*

"No, you're not," C.B. said. "I'm right here, and you've got your brick wall. *And* I brought a flashlight."

He switched it on, but even if he hadn't, there was a line of light under the door from the hallway, which kept the closet from being totally dark. And her perimeter must be working, because the voices remained at a murmur.

C.B. was shining the flashlight around at the stacked furniture, looking for a way behind it. He handed the flashlight to Briddey so he could use both hands to shove the file cabinet back and then push the stacked chairs aside, and the chairs made an ungodly scraping sound as he moved them. She hoped he was right about the staff still being out of earshot.

Me, too, he said, flattening himself to slide between two stacks of boxes. He took the flashlight back from her and motioned her to follow him. "Come on. There's loads of room back here."

I wouldn't call it loads, Briddey thought, squeezing between discarded tables and chairs and head-high stacks of computers, their dangling cords looking like vines in the beam of the flashlight.

C.B. threaded his way through them to the back wall. There an old-fashioned card file stood, surrounded by more boxes and a library table topped with an ancient mimeograph machine and a pile of black encyclopedias. The table, boxes, and card file formed a small enclosed space from which Briddey couldn't see the door. Which meant someone opening the door wouldn't be able to see them either.

Exactly, C.B. said, shining the flashlight around at a globe, a tattered READING IS GOOD FOR YOU poster, a plastic potted palm, and a portrait of a glaring George Washington. *Why do they always hang Washington's picture in libraries?* he asked. *Lincoln was the one who read all the time.*

He stood the flashlight on end on top of the card file, opened one of the drawers, and riffled through the cards. *Just as I thought. They've got the Lost Ark of the Covenant in here.*

He cocked his head, listened for a minute, and then said aloud, "They just cut the cake, which means we may be here awhile. Make yourself comfortable."

"I don't think that's possible," Briddey said. "There's hardly room for both of us to stand in here."

And we're still much too close. He was standing even nearer than he had been in the stacks, and when she backed away from him, the brass handles of the card file pressed into her back. Their faces were mere inches apart.

"Here we go," C.B. said, pushing the encyclopedias to the end of the table. He put his hands on Briddey's waist and lifted her up to sit on the oak table. "Better?"

No, she thought, still feeling the sensation of his hands on her waist. "Yes," she said. "Where's the TA?"

"Still up in the stacks," C.B. said. "Sexting his girlfriend." He listened a moment. "Nope, I was wrong. Sexting his *other* girlfriend. I told you, it's—"

"A cesspool in there," she said. "I know. What about the lost phone?"

"Whoever lost it hasn't noticed it yet, so we're good—" He raised his head suddenly, listening.

"What is it?" Briddey whispered. "Is the birthday party over?"

He didn't answer.

"C.B.?"

"What?" he asked, coming back from wherever he'd been. "Sorry, what did you say?"

"I said, 'Is the party over?'"

"You could say that, yeah," he muttered. He reached for the flashlight. "They're still down there, but the librarians are starting to have 'I really should be getting home'–type thoughts," and he must have heard her thinking of the possible telltale light from the flashlight because he said, "I need to go lay something up against the door."

"Okay," she said, and got down off the table.

"No, you stay here. One person's less likely to knock something over than two."

"Do you need your jacket back?"

"No, I can take this off," he said, pointing to the plaid flannel shirt he wore over his T-shirt. "I'll be right back." *And I'll be right here with you,* he added silently.

Thank you, she said. And it wasn't as if he'd left her in the dark. She could still see the wavering flashlight beam as he made his way to the door, and make out stacked chairs and cartons and the disapproving glare of George Washington.

And if you can see it, so can the librarian, he said, and she could hear the muffled sounds of him taking off his flannel shirt and jamming it into the space under the door.

Can you tell if the party's breaking up? she asked.

He didn't answer for a long minute, and then said, *Yeah. Some of them are coming back up here to get their coats and purses.*

What about Marian?

No, she's cleaning up after everybody—and not very happy about it.

Good, Briddey thought. That meant C.B. could finish covering the space under the door with his shirt and come back here. But he didn't, and Briddey didn't dare call to him again for fear the librarian had finished cleaning up, and he was trying to determine her whereabouts now.

He was right. People didn't necessarily think about where they were or where they were going, especially if they were on familiar ground. Their movements were automatic, like C.B. had said erecting her perimeter needed to be, and he probably had to really listen to catch a clue that might tell him where the librarian was.

But several minutes went by, and C.B. still hadn't said anything, nor had the beam of the flashlight moved. *C.B.?* Briddey called. *Can you hear where the librarian is?*

What? C.B. said blankly, as if he had no idea what she was talking about. *Oh. No, she's—oh, shit. She's coming right this way,* and the light went out.

The darkness was instantaneous and total—cave dark, coal-mine dark—and it caught her completely by surprise. She gasped, and grabbed automatically for C.B., but in the smothering darkness she couldn't even tell which direction he—and the door—lay in.

And her mind hadn't acclimated to the voices. Her perimeter and the library's books and C.B.'s distracting chatter about Victorian novels and the Ark of the Covenant and sex hadn't been protecting her from them. They'd merely been biding their time, waiting for her to let her guard down, to let go of C.B., to be alone again. In the dark.

Nineteen

"They often came without my calling, but sometimes they did
not come. I would pray to God to send them."
—JOAN OF ARC

IT WAS THE THEATER ALL OVER AGAIN, ONLY MUCH, MUCH WORSE BE-
cause she couldn't see anything. And C.B. couldn't come to rescue her
because it was too dark. He would bump into something, trying to
work his way back here, and the librarian would hear him and catch
them. And she mustn't move either, mustn't make a sound, even though
the voices were crashing all around her in deafening waves of frustration and fear and fury.

She clapped her hand over her mouth to keep from crying aloud
and called, *C.B.!,* but there was no way he'd be able to hear her over
the voices. They were too loud, too violent.

Your perimeter, she thought. C.B. said if the voices came back, she
should imagine her brick wall, and she tried, visualizing the red bricks,
the thick gray mortar, but it was too late. The voices were already inside.

C.B.! It didn't work! What do I do now? she called, but even if by
some miracle he heard her, she wouldn't be able to hear him through
the roar of the voices plunging around her, inundating her—

Don't think about them, she told herself sternly. *Think about the marshmallows—green shamrocks, yellow stars. And songs.* But she couldn't remember the words to the theme from *Gilligan's Island,* and C.B.'s Victorian novels were up in the stacks.

She was all alone with the voices, and they were dragging her under, into the drowning darkness. She was going down. *C.B.!* she gasped, choking, swallowing water.

And he was suddenly there, reaching for her, saying, *Jesus, I am so sorry!,* ordering her to give him her hand. But she had already flung herself at him, wrapping her arms around his neck like a shipwreck victim grabbing for a spar floating past.

Where were *you?* she sobbed. *I couldn't hear you, and the light went out and the voices—*

I know. I am so sorry. Marian the Librarian was right outside, almost to the door, and I was afraid she'd see the light under it—

Don't leave me again! she cried, tightening her arms around his neck.

I won't, I promise. And his arms went around her, enfolding her, shutting out the voices, the darkness, shutting out everything but his lips against her hair, his voice in her head saying, *I'm here, I'm here. Shh, it's all right.*

She was holding onto him so tightly, she was practically choking him, and she knew she should let go, but she couldn't. The voices would come back, they'd—

Hang on as long as you need to, C.B. said. *We can't leave for a little while anyway. Marian's still making the rounds. She's checking the bathrooms. I'll spare you her thoughts on the subject of the men's room. Now she's checking the Reading Room. She's really mad about having to lock up again. It's the third time this week. Why is she always the one? Because she's a pushover, that's why . . .*

Briddey knew full well C.B. was doing the running commentary to distract her, just like he'd done in the theater with the Lucky Charms, but she didn't care, so long as his arms were around her and his voice was in her head.

She's getting her coat and purse out of her office, C.B. said. *Now she's going downstairs . . . she's locking the front door . . .* A long pause, and then he said aloud, "I think she's in her car. I just heard, 'big pileup on the south-bound interstate,' which means she's listening to her car radio. And now she's wondering why she has to sit at a red light for hours when there's no traffic coming either way. Definitely out of here and on her way home. We can go." Which meant she needed to let go of him.

"Not if you don't feel ready," he said gently, and she was suddenly very conscious of her body, pressed against his.

"I'm fine," she said, taking her arms from around his neck and stepping back. "Thank you."

"You're sure you're okay?"

"Yes," she said. *No.* The voices—

He grabbed her hand. "Now?"

She nodded.

"Good, then let's go." He made his way through the darkness and the maze of furniture to the front, bent to get his flannel shirt, grabbed the flashlight, and opened the door.

The corridor was dark, lit only by the red exit sign at the end, and it had an echoing, empty quality that was reassuring, but Briddey hung back. *Are you sure there's not a security guard?* she asked.

"Positive," he said aloud. "Those budget cuts, remember? And besides, I can read minds. Everyone's gone," but he must have been worried, too, because he shut the door soundlessly behind them and didn't turn on the flashlight.

The lost phone, Briddey thought as he hurried her back down the corridor. *He's afraid somebody will remember where they left it and come back for it.*

They can't, he said, *unless it's Marian's. She's the only one here tonight with keys to the building.* But he didn't slacken his pace.

Where are we going? she wondered as he led her soundlessly into a staircase and down a floor, but he didn't answer. *The staff lounge,* she thought, and sure enough, he stopped at a door marked WORKROOM, opened it, and switched on the light.

The lounge wasn't much larger than the storage closet and about as crowded. They'd crammed a half dozen plastic chairs, a sagging bile-green couch, a counter with a sink and cupboards, a refrigerator, and a microwave into it. And a large table with a half-eaten pink-and-white sheet cake on it, which must be from the birthday party earlier. The librarian needn't have worried. There was tons of it left.

C.B. walked to the counter, set down the flashlight, and shrugged on his flannel shirt. Then he opened the cupboard, lifted up a can of coffee, took a key from under it, shut the cupboard, picked up the flashlight, and came back over to Briddey. "Come on," he said, switching off the lights, and they set off again.

So not the staff lounge. *The Reading Room?* she thought, but they were going the wrong direction. And C.B. had said the stacks were too cold. Then where?

C.B. still didn't answer. He led her down yet another hallway, stopping finally in front of a door marked AUTHORIZED PERSONNEL ONLY. It opened onto a flight of stairs leading up, this one much narrower than the others. He shut the door quietly behind them, switched on the flashlight, and led her up the stairs.

At the top was a metal door marked NO ADMITTANCE. C.B. handed Briddey the flashlight. *Shine this on the lock,* he said, unlocked the door with the key he'd taken from under the coffee can, and opened the door.

Inside was another staircase, and at the top of it, another door. *What will this one say?* Briddey wondered. *"Keep Out. This Means You. I Mean It"?*

But it was unmarked and unlocked. And pitch-black inside when he opened the door. He pulled her in and shut the door behind them. "I just need to find the light switch," he said. "Will you be okay if I let go of your hand for a second?"

"Yes."

He dropped her hand, and she heard him pat around as if for a wall switch, then stumble against something. *Shit,* he said, followed by a whack as he bumped into something else.

I hope it's not another storage closet, she thought.

"It's not," he said, sounding amused, and he must have found the switch because the room sprang into brightness.

Briddey's mouth fell open. She was standing in an elegant, book-lined room with a polished wooden floor and a ceramic-tiled fireplace at the far end, and, drawn up cozily to it, a sofa and two red leather wing chairs. At this end was a many-drawered wooden card file like the one in the storage closet with a bust of Shakespeare on it and an old-fashioned oak library table and chairs; and, against the far wall, a chest-high wooden desk piled with books.

"Wh-what . . . how . . . ?" she stammered, looking around in amazement at the rows of books and the Tiffany stained-glass lamps. "Where *are* we?"

"The library," C.B. said, lighting the lamps next to the sofa and on the table between the wing chairs.

"But I thought you said there were budget cuts," she said, taking in the ornate fireplace, the Persian rugs, and the rich-looking cashmere throw on the back of the sofa.

"There were," C.B. said, going over to the counter and reaching behind it for an old-fashioned brass key. He went back to the door, inserted the key in the old-fashioned doorplate, and locked it, and then switched off the overhead light, so the room was lit only by the Tiffany lamps. "But not in 1928, which is when the library looked like this, and when Arthur Tellman Ross was a freshman."

"Who's Arthur Tellman Ross?"

"Him." He pointed at a portrait of an elderly, stern-looking man. "And this is the Arthur Tellman Ross Memorial Room, though the librarians all call it the Inner Sanctum. *I* call it the Carnegie Room because that's what it looks like—those great old Carnegie libraries. Or the library in *The Music Man.*"

"But what's it doing here?"

"Long story, which I'll tell you later." He went over to the table and switched on the green-shaded brass reading lamp that stood in its center. It cast a pool of light over the table and on the books on the shelves behind it, turning their blue and green and red bindings to jewel tones.

"It's beautiful," Briddey said.

"And invasion-proof. There aren't any windows; the door locks from the inside; it's solid oak, so nobody can hear us in here; and they don't have any idea I even know about this place—and anyway, they've all gone home."

And we're safe from the voices, Briddey thought, looking around at the book-lined walls. Even though she knew it was the readers' thoughts and not the books that screened them, she felt even safer here than she had in the Reading Room.

Which was ridiculous. They had no business being here. They could be arrested at any moment, and even if they weren't caught, there'd be hell to pay tomorrow with Trent over her having left him at the theater. She had no idea what she was going to tell him—or Maeve—but it didn't matter. So long as she was here in this lovely, lighted space, she was safe from everything, even the voices.

"But we can't stay here forever, unfortunately," C.B. said. "Which is why we need to build you a panic room." He pulled a chair out from the library table. "Sit down."

She did, and C.B. went around to the other side, pulled out the chair across from her, and sat down. "The process is pretty much like the one we used to put up your perimeter," he said. "Only this time we're not building a wall, we're building a room. You know what a panic room is, don't you?"

"One of those lead-lined rooms where you hide if intruders break into your house, like in that Jodie Foster movie a few years ago."

"Yes, only safer than that," C.B. said, "and better acted. And it doesn't have to look like the inside of a bomb shelter. In fact, it shouldn't. I can't imagine anybody feeling particularly safe inside a bomb shelter, since the only reason you'd be in there is that nuclear war was about to break out. And the only reason you'd be in a panic room is that somebody was breaking into your apartment—hardly conditions for feeling safe. So 'panic room' probably isn't the right term. Think 'safe room' instead, or 'sanctuary.' A place where you can feel warm and protected."

Like I do here with C.B., she thought.

"Yeah, well, I may not always be around," he said. "As you found out in the storage closet."

"That wasn't your fault! You said yourself you couldn't always tell where people are from their voices, and if I'd been visualizing my perimeter the way I was supposed to be, it wouldn't have happened."

"And if I'd . . . never mind. The important thing is that it not happen again, and that's what the safe room is for. It'll provide a sanctuary where the voices can't get to you, and it'll also keep your thoughts from getting out and being overheard."

Is that why I can't read C.B.'s mind the way he reads mine, Briddey thought, *because he's in his safe room?*

"Yes, but before you get on your high horse again and start accusing me of blocking Trent," C.B. was saying, "a safe room only makes it possible to block your own thoughts from being overheard, not somebody else's."

"I wasn't going to accuse you. When you told me about the Irish gene, I realized the reason Trent and I haven't connected is that his ancestors are English, and they probably have the inhibitor gene."

"That's one reason," C.B. muttered.

"What do you mean?"

"Nothing. You're right. The English got every invasion the Irish missed out on and did a fair amount of invading of their own; there's almost *no* history of telepathic occurrences, even with English saints. You, on the other hand, have more communication than you know what to do with, so let's get this safe room built." He leaned forward. "I need you to think of a place you feel safe and protected from the outside world."

The storage room, she thought, with C.B.'s arms around her, but obviously that wasn't what he meant, and even if it was, she couldn't tell him that. Where else had she felt protected? Her imagined apartment with Trent, with a doorman to keep her family at bay, but she didn't think that was what C.B. meant either, and besides, all she felt now at the thought of being there was dread at all the questions Trent would ask. Safe and protected. "You mean like a fortress?" she asked.

"No, we're not going for a battles-and-sieges kind of safe here; that's for your perimeter. We need a place you associate with quiet and serenity. Not a park or a forest, though—someplace inside. Like your apartment, maybe, or your bedroom when you were a kid. Someplace no one else can get into unless you allow them in."

Then definitely not her apartment or her childhood bedroom, which she'd shared with Mary Clare and Kathleen. And not her office. No place at Commspan was safe from people popping in, except possibly the sub-basement, and even there Kathleen had tracked her down. Besides, it was too cold.

She shivered at the memory of it, and C.B. said, "Are you feeling chilly?"

"No, I—"

"Well, you will be," he said, walking over to the desk again. "Remember, they turn the heat down after the library closes."

He disappeared behind the desk and came up holding a remote. He pointed it at the fireplace, and flames leaped up, casting a warm orange-red glow on the Persian carpet and the leather chairs, on the rich wood.

"What about *this* room?" Briddey asked. "Could I use it for my safe room?"

"Maybe, but it'll work better if it's something more familiar to you. Did you have a favorite hiding place when you were little? A closet you liked to play in? Or a tree house?"

"No. What do you use for your safe room?"

"I've had a bunch of them over the years: a western cavalry fort, a submarine, the Tardis," and when she looked blank: "Doctor Who's blue police-box time-travel machine."

"I thought you said it needed to be someplace real."

"It *was* real. I'd watched about a million episodes of *Doctor Who*. Do you have something like that you could use, from your childhood? Rapunzel's tower or something?"

"No, that's Maeve's territory."

"What about in college? Did you live by yourself?"

"No," she said, and thought suddenly of a trip she'd taken during spring break to Santa Fe with one of her roommates. Allison's parents had had a sprawling adobe hacienda with a walled courtyard in the middle. She'd gotten up early every morning and gone out to sit in it.

"Alone?"

"Yes. Allison slept in, and her parents were in Europe."

"Now you're talking. What kind of walls did this courtyard have?"

"Adobe. But it didn't have a roof. Doesn't that disqualify it as a safe room?"

"No, we're dealing in metaphor here, remember? If you think of it as a place nobody can get into, it will be. How tall were the adobe walls?"

"Tall. Above my head."

"Did the courtyard have a gate?"

"No, a door, a blue door," she said, remembering the heavy, brightly painted wood.

"Heavy is good. Did it have a lock on it?"

"No-o," she said, trying to remember, "but it had an iron latch, and there was a wooden bar you could lower across it to keep people out."

"Even better. You said the door was heavy. It wasn't too heavy for you to open, was it?"

"No. Why?"

"Because the instant the voices start to become too much for you, you're going to lift that latch and get yourself inside that door, so it needs to be something you can open fast."

"But if I can open it, can't the voices open it, too?"

"No, because the moment you get inside, you're going to put that bar across the door."

"But what if the voices have a battering ram?"

"They don't have a battering ram. This isn't a castle, it's a Santa Fe courtyard. There are no battering rams in New Mexico. And your voices are a flood, remember? Not an army. And the water can't get in because your adobe walls are too high and thick. So all you have to do to escape the flood is to run into the courtyard and slam the door shut. Which is what we are going to practice in a minute." He looked at her. "You felt safe there? And happy?"

"Yes. I loved being by myself, and it was beautiful, all green and shady. There was a big cottonwood tree with a wooden bench under it that I loved to sit on."

"Tell me what the rest of the courtyard looked like," C.B. ordered, and for the next half hour took her methodically through every detail she could remember—the flagstone floor, the old gardener's cupboard that stood against one wall, the pink and red hollyhocks growing by the door.

"Okay," he said when she'd finished. "I want you to close your eyes and visualize yourself standing in the courtyard."

"Wait," Briddey said. "If I'm in the safe room, how will I talk to you? And hear you talking to me?"

"It doesn't block talking, just thoughts, and you can let in—or keep out—whoever you want, so you'll still be able to hear my voice. Unless you don't want to."

"Why would I not—?" she began, and then remembered the countless times she'd told him to go away. "I won't shut you out, I promise."

"I'm glad to hear that," he said. "Now visualize yourself standing in your courtyard."

She did, imagining the flagstones under her feet, the high, leaf-shadowed adobe walls, the weathered cupboard with its stack of terra-cotta flowerpots on top.

"Okay, now I want you to open the door and go out."

"Open the door? Why can't I just stay in here all the time?"

"Because it takes too much focus and energy to visualize it continuously. This is only for when you're in a crowd or the voices get too ugly or threatening."

Or when I don't want you to hear what I'm thinking, she added silently, remembering her reaction when he'd said, "I'm not a masochist."

"You use it just like you'd use an actual panic room," C.B. was saying. "For emergencies. The rest of the time you rely on your perimeter. Which is what you're going to do now. Think of your brick wall, and then open the door and go out."

Reluctantly, she raised the wooden bar, lifted the iron latch, opened the heavy door, and went outside. "Now what?"

"Tell me what you see."

"My perimeter," she said, looking at the brick wall in the distance. She turned around to look at the adobe walls of the courtyard and the blue door. "It's got carved panels, and there's a *ristra* of dried chiles hanging on it." She heard a low rumble behind her. The voices were coming.

"C.B.—" she said, and yanked the heavy door open. She flung herself inside, slamming it shut and pushing the bar across it and then leaning against it, out of breath.

"Excellent. Are you okay?" C.B. asked, and when she said yes, had her do it again—and again—trying to shave seconds off each time.

"You're doing great," he said after the sixth run-through. "Let's take a break." He walked over to one of the wing chairs and flopped down in it. "Gorgeous place, huh? A lot better than the stacks."

No, it isn't, she thought, and flung herself through the blue, *ristra*-hung door and into the courtyard to keep him from hearing the thought that had come to her, unbidden, of standing there in the stacks, her back pressed against the bookcase and him leaning over her, their faces only inches apart. *Thank goodness I've got a safe room to keep him from hearing that. If it's working.*

It apparently was. C.B. wasn't looking at her. He was staring into the fire. She looked around the cozy room at the walls of dusty-smelling books. An old-fashioned library ladder stood against the shelves, there was a painting of George Washington—this one of him crossing the Delaware—above the checkout desk, and a large, leather-bound dictionary stood open on a stand.

"What's this place *doing* here?" she asked, walking over to look up at the portrait C.B. had pointed out before. "And who's Arthur Whatever-His-Name-Is?"

"Arthur Tellman Ross," C.B. said. "He's the guy who donated eighty-six million dollars to the building of this library, provided they retained the old card file. And the bust of Shakespeare, the dictionary stand, the checkout desk"—he held up an old-fashioned wooden-and-metal date stamp—"and, of course, the books." He waved his arm expansively at the ceiling-high shelves.

"Including *Ivanhoe*," he said, bending his head sideways to read the titles, "*The Adventures of Robin Hood, Robinson Crusoe*,"—he straightened—"and every other book Mr. Ross remembered from his college days, including a lovely selection of Victorian novels."

"But you still haven't explained what this room is doing here," Briddey said.

"It's here because the library had no intention of keeping card files *or* date stamps in this era of automated checkout, catalog terminals, and Kindle. So they came up with this," C.B. said, walking over to the sofa. "It meets the letter of the agreement, and it's a perfect place for the university president to entertain other potential millionaire donors. And canoodle. If *he* wants to have sex, he doesn't have to deal with that uncomfortable floor in the stacks. It's also a perfect place for us to work."

Except that we're trespassing, Briddey thought. *If we get caught—*

"We won't," C.B. said confidently. "The campus police are busy answering a call to the Sig Ep house, where some guy passed out on the front lawn, and Marian's at home in bed, worrying about budget cuts. And even if we did get caught, we have a perfect right to be here. Arthur Tellman Ross apparently didn't trust the university to carry out his wishes—with good reason—so he put it in his will that anything he donated had to be available to the public at all times, which is why the door to this room isn't locked, even though the approach to it is. And why they keep its existence a deep, dark secret from the students."

"How did you find out about it?"

"I was looking for *The History of Telepathic Experience,* which was in the library's online catalog but wasn't in the stacks and wasn't checked out, and one of the TAs said, 'Maybe it's up in the Inner Sanctum.'"

"And he brought you up here?"

"She," C.B. said. "No, she clammed up as soon as she said it, but, as you know, I can read minds."

"Yes," Briddey said. "Speaking of which, why can you hear the campus police and the librarian, and I can't?"

"You can," he said. "The problem is you can't separate their voices out from all the others."

"And you can?"

"If it's someone whose voice I've heard before or I can figure out who it is from what they're saying—"

"Like the campus police."

"No, actually, the Sig Ep who called 911. He gave the address of the Sig Ep house, and I heard him think, *The dispatcher said they're sending an officer right over.* That doesn't happen very often."

"The police sending an officer right over, or a Sig Ep passing out on the lawn?"

"Somebody thinking an address," he said. "Or their name. People hardly ever muse, *It is I, Jason P. Smythe, wishing I had a girlfriend,* so unless you know them—in which case you recognize their voice—it's very difficult to separate them out from the crowd. It's like trying to find a needle in an audio haystack."

He'd obviously heard Marian the Librarian's voice and the TA's before, but what about the couple in the stacks?

"Proximity. With practice, it's also possible to determine who's nearby by changes in the timbre of their voices."

That was how he'd known when there was someone in her hospital room—and what he'd been listening for when he dropped her off at the Marriott. He was making sure no one from Commspan was in the vicinity. "Are you going to teach me how to do that?" she asked.

"Yes, when you're ready. But you're a long way from that. It requires searching through the voices, which means—"

"Wading right into the middle of them," she said, panicked all over again at the thought. C.B. was right. She wasn't ready for that, if she ever would be. There was no way she'd be able to locate a specific voice, even C.B.'s, in that raging torrent of sound.

How does he do it? she thought wonderingly.

"I didn't when it first happened," he said. "All I wanted was to get away from the voices, just like you. Speaking of which, we need to get back to work. Before we leave, I want getting to your safe room to be something you can do without even thinking, so we need to practice."

She nodded and started back to the table. "No, no, sit down," C.B. said. "We can do it here, where it's closer to the fire. And warmer."

She sat down on the sofa, and C.B. pulled one of the wing chairs over closer and sat down in it, knees apart, hands clasped together. "Okay," he said. "We're going to do the same thing we did with the perimeter."

"Do I need to get a book to read?" Briddey asked, looking over at the bookcases.

"No, we can just talk like we've been doing, and then I'll say, 'The voices,' and you get inside your courtyard as fast as you can. Okay?"

"Okay," she said, and gripped the arm of the sofa, her eyes on the blue *ristra*-hung door, poised to take off for it.

"No, I don't want you ready to run. I want you relaxed and focused on other things. Did you ever decide where we should go for our honeymoon?"

"No," she said, and thought, *We need a less dangerous topic.*

"So, if you can hear people who are nearby or whose voices you've heard," she said, "that must mean you're able to hear everyone at Commspan." *And you know what the Hermes Project is working on.*

"Just because I'm able to hear them doesn't mean I listen to them," C.B. said, "particularly since all they think about is how to get promoted, whether they're going to get laid off, and what they're going to have for lunch. I only listen to find out where they are, so I can avoid— The voices are coming."

Briddey leaped for the door.

"Not fast enough," C.B. said. "We need to try it again. What were we talking about?"

"How boring everyone at Commspan's thoughts are."

"Oh, it's not just Commspan. It's everybody. Listening to cows grazing would be less stupefying."

"You can listen to *cows*?"

"No, just people, more's the pity. Think how nice it would be to hear your dog telling you about his unconditional adoration," he said, but she was secretly relieved. She didn't have to worry about hearing lions or tigers—

"Or bears," C.B. said. "Or flatworms, though sometimes with people it's hard to tell the difference. Do you know what people spend the majority of time thinking about?"

"I suppose you're going to tell me it's canoodling."

"Nope, except for the under-twenty-five set. For everybody else, it's the weather. Is it going to rain? Is it going to stop raining? Is it going to snow? Is it going to warm up? They think about it constantly. That, and money and how much they hate their jobs. And thank-you notes."

"Thank-you notes?"

"Yep. Or rather, the lack thereof: 'Why didn't I get one from my nephew? What kind of manners is his mother teaching him? I'm not sending him another present till I get a thank-you from him—and not an email or a phone call either—a proper handwritten note!'" C.B. clutched his head. "On and on and on for hours. It's worse than the sex and the rest of the griping. And the bodily functions. That's another thing people spend an inordinate amount of time thinking about. Belching and fa—"

"I get the picture. So you're telling me there's no one fun to listen to?"

"No, kids are great. I'm crazy about—" He stopped.

"Crazy about what?" she asked.

"Three and four-year-olds. The way they think is amazing. It probably goes for babies, too, but their thoughts aren't verba— The voices are coming."

She was faster that time, though still not fast enough to suit him. He took her through the drill again and again.

"How many times do I have to do this?" she asked. It felt like they'd been at it for hours.

"Till it's completely automatic," he said.

"Okay," she said, stifling a yawn. "Sorry. I—"

"Had a roaring dose of fear-produced adrenaline—no, make that two doses, counting the storage room—and now they've worn off, so you're crashing. Besides which, it's"—he glanced over at the clock—"three A.M. No wonder you're yawning." He pointed at the sofa. "Why don't you lie down?"

"That sounds wonderful," she said, looking longingly at it. "But I'm afraid I'll fall asleep, and you said we needed to practice—"

"We do, but we've got loads of time. The library doesn't open till eleven on Sundays. And a nap might actually be a good idea. It'll give your brain a chance to process the stuff it's learned and put it into long-term memory. Go ahead, lie down." He walked over to the table and turned off the lamp.

"*Thank* you," she said, suddenly so tired that she could hardly keep her eyes open. She lay down—and immediately sat up again. She'd forgotten about the voices. Her barricades worked because she was visualizing them, and if she fell asleep—

"You don't hear them when you're sleeping," C.B. reassured her.

"Why not?"

"I don't know. Maybe because people's brain chemistry alters during sleep. Or maybe REM sleep involves a fundamentally different kind of thought. Whichever it is, you can't send or receive messages while you're asleep."

Thank goodness, she thought. "But what about while I'm falling asleep? And when I first wake up?"

"Those *are* the times you're most vulnerable," he admitted, "but only till your defenses become fully automatic. When they do, they'll kick in the second you wake up."

"And how long will it take for them to become fully automatic?"

"A few days," he said, switching off the Tiffany lamps at either end of the sofa, leaving on only the one between the wing chairs. "But don't worry. I'll stand guard till then."

"How?"

"With my trusty Victorian sword," he said. He went over to the bookcase and pulled out a thick volume. "How does *The Decline and Fall of the Roman Empire* sound?"

"Boring."

"Agreed. But the fall part should keep it from being too boring." He put the book on the table next to the wing chair and came over to the sofa. "Now lie down," he ordered, and covered her up with the cashmere throw. "Close your eyes and forget about everything else but your nice, adobe-walled, impenetrable safe room."

"I will," she said. "But if it's going to take a couple of days for my pre- and post-sleep defenses to automatically kick in, when will *you* sleep?"

"While you're awake. So the sooner you get to sleep, the sooner you'll wake up and I can take *my* nap. Okay?"

"Okay," she said doubtfully.

"It'll be fine. I'll be right here. Well, not *right* here. A nice, safe distance away," he said, walking over to the wing chair on the far side of the fire and plopping down in it. "So you don't have to worry about me attacking you."

"I'm not—"

"Yeah, well, just in case. Besides, I can concentrate better on *The Decline and Fall* from over here." He grinned at her. "I won't let anything get in, I promise." He opened the book. "Now go to sleep."

That was easier said than done. She kept thinking about what would happen if C.B.—

"I won't nod off," he said. "This chair is too uncomfortable. And this idiot girl keeps talking."

"Sorry," she murmured. She curled up under the soft cashmere throw, closed her eyes, and concentrated on going into her courtyard, pulling the door closed behind her, lowering the heavy wooden bar across it, fastening the latch. Shutting the voices out.

But they weren't the only thing she had to worry about. There was also how they were going to get out of here in the morning without getting caught. And what she was going to tell Trent. And Maeve—

"Want me to tell you a bedtime story?" C.B. asked.

"Yes, please," she said, tucking her hand under her cheek.

"'The Pannonian army was at this time commanded by Septimius Severus,'" he read aloud, "'who had concealed his daring ambition, which was never diverted from its steady course by the allurements of pleasure, the apprehension of danger, or the feelings of humanity.'"

My feelings are that this cashmere throw is really warm, Briddey thought, *almost as warm as the blanket C.B. brought me in the hospital,* and fell asleep.

She woke to darkness. She wondered drowsily where she was, and then remembered, and felt a rush of sheer panic. *The fire went out!*

No, that's not possible, some rational part of her brain insisted. *It's a gas fire.* And she could feel its heat. In a moment her eyes would adjust to the darkness, and she'd be able to see the reddish orange glow from the flames.

Unless C.B. turned it off, she thought. *If he did, I'm in the dark. With the voices. And they'll . . . C.B.!*—and then reassurance as she felt him lying beside her, her hand clasped in both of his and held tightly, safely, against his chest.

She knew she should be angry with him for not keeping his distance, but she was too relieved. And too filled with gratitude that he was there like he'd promised, shielding her, keeping the voices at bay. And she could hardly accuse him of putting the moves on her. He was sound asleep. She could hear his even breathing, feel the rise and fall of his chest beneath her captured hand, hear his heartbeat.

C.B., she thought tenderly, and heard a murmur from across the room that made her sit up in the darkness. She'd been right about the fire, because she could see C.B., lit by its ruddy glow, sprawled in the wing chair, his head resting against the back, his hands dangling over the arms as he slept.

She looked down in surprise at her own hand, not clutched in his after all, and must have made some sort of sound because his head came up, and he murmured sleepily, "What is it?"

"Nothing, it's okay. I must have been dreaming," she whispered, lying back down and putting her hand under her cheek again to show him everything was all right. "Go back to sleep." Though telling him that wasn't necessary. He hadn't ever been awake. He leaned his head back against his wadded-up flannel shirt, where it had obviously been all this time, and immediately began to snore.

He looked utterly exhausted. She shouldn't be surprised. He'd had to rescue her twice tonight, and before that once—no, twice—in the hospital, and in between he'd raced around taking her home, and to the Marriott to get her car, and finding them places to hide. And, she suspected, listening to her every moment in between, watching for signs that she was starting to hear the voices, guarding her, protecting her. And he was still doing it, even in his sleep.

She smiled at how vulnerable he looked, lying sprawled there in the wing chair, his face flushed from the firelight—and how young. He'd said the voices had started when he was thirteen, only four years older than Maeve. What must that have been like for him?

He'd spoken lightly of his attempts to stop them, to discover what was going on, to devise barricades, but it must have been terrible. School would have been a nightmare, and college out of the question. And most jobs. He'd been lucky to find Commspan, with its no-coverage sub-basement.

Movies would have been out of the question, too, and going to graduation and weddings and funerals and football games and the mall. Which probably went a long way toward explaining his clothes. And his ancient car. Virtually every aspect of normal life would have been a struggle.

And that was *after* he'd erected barricades and a safe room. Before that, when the voices first appeared, it must have been beyond terrifying. How horrible to have had that tidal wave of thoughts and emotions crash in on him without any idea of what was causing it—and without anyone to rescue him or reassure him he wasn't going crazy, or teach him how to build defenses! Or to hold his hand safely to their heart while he slept.

What if this had happened, and I hadn't had C.B.? she thought, and knew the answer. She wouldn't have survived. She'd have gone insane. Or committed suicide.

It was amazing that C.B. hadn't, flung as he had been into a world of wrath and lasciviousness and malice before he was ready for it, exposed to the full vileness and viciousness of the world without any filter at all, a helpless victim of, and witness to, how many things he had no way of dealing with?

And with no one to help him, or explain what was happening, not even anyone he could tell—and everyone around him thinking he was a freak. *Just like the Hunchback of Notre Dame.* It was a wonder he hadn't become a rapist or a serial killer.

But not only hadn't he become a monster, he'd figured out how to defend himself against the voices' unending onslaught—and reached out to help her when the same thing happened to her. He could have simply stayed silent. He'd had plenty of reasons to do that, not the least of which was her own kicking-and-screaming response when he tried to tell her, accusing him of everything from bugging her room to blocking Trent.

But he'd helped her in spite of that, and risked having his secret exposed in the process. And that was probably the most remarkable thing he'd done, because everything he'd said about what could happen if people found out he was telepathic was true. Suki would tweet the news instantly, the press would descend, and Commspan would probably fire him for making them a laughingstock. Or worse, they'd co-opt him as a corporate spy and demand he tell them what Apple's new phone had on it, and it would be no good trying to explain that it didn't work like that, that the voices couldn't be searched like a database for information. They wouldn't believe him. They'd be convinced telepathy would give them a business advantage, and they'd invade his lab and interrogate him.

No, the smart thing for him to have done was definitely to have kept quiet and let her deal with the voices on her own. She was infinitely grateful that he hadn't.

She watched him a while longer and then shut her eyes again. And even though she knew her hand was tucked beneath her cheek and he was on the far side of the room, the instant she closed her eyes he was there beside her again, his hands crossed on his chest and her hand held tightly under them, pressed safely against his heart.

Who says you can't communicate when you're sleeping? she thought, smiling, and went back to sleep.

Twenty

"The course of true love never did run smooth."
—WILLIAM SHAKESPEARE, *A Midsummer Night's Dream*

WHEN BRIDDEY WOKE AGAIN, THE LAMPS WERE BACK ON, AND THE chair—and the room—were empty. *C.B.?* she called. *Where are you?*

Out rustling us up a midnight feast, he said, and she automatically glanced over at the clock behind the checkout desk. Five thirty.

Okay, an early breakfast, he said. *Don't worry. I'll be back in two shakes.*

I'm not worried, she thought wonderingly, and went into her courtyard so he wouldn't be able to hear what she was thinking. Because he wasn't gone. Even with the room full of lamplight and her eyes open, even with her having pushed off the throw and stretched her arms up in a luxurious yawn, he was still holding her hand close to his chest.

Hurry up, she called to him. *I'm starving!*

Be right there, he said, and a minute later burst through the door. He had a large, bulging plastic grocery bag in one hand, a paper plate full of cake in the other, and a bag of chips under his arm. *I found all sorts of goodies.*

He put them on the table and emptied out the bag, naming his finds as he did. "Birthday cake, Doritos, salsa, grapes, half a pepperoni pizza, a package of peanut butter crackers, a partially eaten Snickers, olives—"

"Did you steal all this from the staff lounge?" Briddey asked.

"Just the salsa, the olives, and the cake—I heard Marian wondering how she was going to get rid of all of it. The rest is contraband I found in the stacks. Except for these," he said, bringing out two cans of soda, "which I got from the vending machine. They didn't have lattes. You'll have to settle for Pepsi or Sierra Mist."

"Pepsi," she said, and reached for the pizza. C.B. produced paper napkins from his flannel shirt pocket and handed her one. It was obviously from the party, too. It had bluebirds on it and the words A LITTLE BIRD TOLD ME YOU WERE HAVING A BIRTHDAY.

Everything tasted wonderful, even the Doritos, which must have been up in the stacks for weeks. They were very stale. "But good, huh?" C.B. said. "Oh, and you won't believe what else I found. While I was out foraging, I did a little research to see what the other marshmallow was—"

"Research? You mean you found someone who happened to be thinking about Lucky Charms?"

"No, I googled it on Marian's computer."

But I thought the offices were locked. And wouldn't a computer have needed a password?

"We were right about the pink hearts, blue moons, and green clovers—*not* shamrocks," C.B. was saying, "but they're *shooting* stars, not stars. There are also horseshoes, rainbows, balloons, and for some unknown reason, hourglasses. And then what do you think I found up on the top level of the stacks? A box of . . . ta-da!"

He reached in the food bag and pulled out a cereal box with a flourish. "Lucky Charms!" He poured out a handful of cereal onto the table. "So we can confirm my findings."

"Or not," Briddey said, looking down at the multicolored blobs. She picked up a pale green one with a lump of bright green in the middle. "This does not look like a shamrock."

"Clover," he corrected her.

"It doesn't look like a clover either. It looks like a hat with a bow on it."

"What kind of Irishman would have a bow on his hat?" C.B. said, taking it from her, turning it upside down, and squinting at it. "Maybe it's a pot of gold."

"Then why is it green? And look at this one," she said, picking up a purple U-shaped marshmallow. "What's this? The rainbow?"

"No, *this* is the rainbow." He showed her a multicolored half circle.

"Or a slice of watermelon."

"They're all supposed to be Irish. What's Irish about a slice of watermelon?"

"Or a dog bone?" she said, picking up a brownish yellow marshmallow.

"At least this pink thing is definitely a heart," he said. "And this blue blob is a moon."

"But what on earth is this?" she said, fishing a white marshmallow out of the pile. It was oblong and had an orange line down its middle and an irregular splotch at one end.

"I have no idea," C.B. said, taking it from her and turning it one way and another. "An albino eggplant?"

"An albino *eggplant*?" she said, laughing. "Why would they put an albino eggplant in a children's cereal?"

"Beats me," he said, popping it into his mouth. He made a face. "The real question is, why would they put pieces of chalk in a children's cereal and call them marshmallows? Speaking of which, unless you want to be stuck reciting, 'Albino eggplant, dog bone, purple U-shaped thingy,' the next time the voices hit, we need to get back to work. Your safe room needs to be—"

"Totally automatic. I know."

"And after we've done that, I want to teach you some auxiliary defenses. It's a good idea to have ramparts, and an inner sanctum for backup."

And even with all those defenses, he still has to wear earbuds and hide from the voices down in the sub-basement, she thought, feeling afraid all over again.

"I don't actually have to stay in the basement," C.B. said. "I partly stay down there because when you're talking to people, it's easy to make mistakes and let slip that you know stuff they haven't told anyone—"

"And they'll find out you're telepathic."

"Exactly. I'd much rather have them think I'm crazy. I also stay down there by choice. Years of listening to the innermost secrets of your fellow human beings gives you such a low opinion of them, you don't *want* to associate with them. It doesn't have anything to do with the effectiveness of my defenses. Don't worry, your courtyard will keep you perfectly safe. Provided we get it finished," he said, and for the next solid hour he had her practice talking to him while remaining safely inside her courtyard. And not looking like that was what she was doing.

It was hard to master, but she was eventually able to see both the adobe walls and blue door *and* the book-lined walls of the Carnegie Room, to stand simultaneously under the cottonwood tree and in front of the fire, carrying on a conversation about "Ode to Billie Joe."

"The song was a huge hit," C.B. told her, "and people came up with all kinds of theories as to why he jumped."

"Why do *you* think he did it?" Briddey asked, trying to keep both C.B. and the courtyard in focus. "I mean if he and the girl were in love, why would he commit suicide?"

"Maybe he didn't. Maybe he was just trying to get away from the voices."

"Did you ever do that?" Briddey asked.

"Do what? Jump off a bridge or try to kill myself?"

"Either. Both. Did you?"

"Yeah, once, when things were going pretty bad. My stepdad had pretty much written me off—I don't blame him. I couldn't exactly explain *why* I was refusing to have a bar mitzvah or go to college. And the voices were . . ." He shook his head in disgust. "So, anyway, I thought taking a bunch of tranquilizers would be a good way out. But it just made the voices worse. That's why I told you no alcohol or Xanax. Relaxants just make you more receptive to the voices—and less able to keep them out."

Briddey thought of what that must have been like, the voices out of control and roaring over him, and him nearly unconscious and helpless to fend them off.

"Yeah, well, but it had its advantages," he said lightly. "One, I learned that there are things even worse than the voices, stomach pumps being one. And two, it's kept me from turning into a drug addict or an alco-

holic, which just goes to show you that not all unintended consequences are bad."

He grinned at her, but she didn't smile back. She was busy following a different train of thought. "If relaxants make the voices worse,
then wouldn't stimulants—?"

"Nope, no effect. And every other kind of drug makes them worse,
too. Defenses are the only thing that work for the long term."

"But if you can visualize defenses that keep the voices out, why
can't you visualize something that shuts them off altogether?" she asked,
and waited for him to tell her it didn't work like that.

"You can," he said.

"You *can*? Then why—?"

"Because you can only do it for brief periods, and it takes an enormous physical and mental toll. You can't sustain it, and the minute your
attention wavers, the voices come roaring back."

"But there must be some way to . . . surgery or—"

He shook his head. "Surgery's out. In the first place, it's not like a
blood vessel you can tie off. It's a network of neural pathways, and
there's no guarantee that messing with it wouldn't make it permanently worse. And in the second place, to get a doctor to do the surgery, you'd have to tell him about the telepathy—"

"And that's out. I know. But couldn't you make some kind of device—?"

"I've tried. That's another reason I spend most of my time in the
basement, because I've been trying to come up with a jammer."

"And have you made any progress?"

"No. I thought interference—and crosstalk—might cancel the
voices out, but they didn't, and creating the voice equivalent of a spam
filter didn't work either. Or an electronic version of the safe room."

"So you haven't found anything that *does* work?"

"Yeah, Victorian novels. And frequency hopping."

"Hedy Lamarr's invention," Briddey said, thinking, *That's why he's
got her picture hanging up in his lab.*

He nodded. "The idea was to keep the voices from finding me
instead of blocking them directly, and it works pretty well in the short
term. But in the long term it requires an enormous amount of energy—
far more than any device could ever generate." He smiled apologeti-

cally at her. "Sorry, Briddey. If I had a way to shut the voices off for good for you, I would," and she realized how ungrateful she'd sounded—as if his rescuing her and teaching her and protecting her weren't enough.

"C.B., listen," she began, but he was listening to something else, his head raised and a faraway look on his face, which quickly turned to a frown.

"What is it?" Briddey asked.

"It's time to get out of here," he said, pushing back his chair. He stood up and began clearing the table.

"But I thought the library didn't open till eleven."

"It doesn't," he said, scooping the Lucky Charms off the end of the table into one of the "a little bird told me" napkins and putting them both in the bag. "But the later it gets, the more people will be around. I don't want anyone seeing us leave."

He was lying. He'd heard something and he didn't want to tell her. "There's someone in the building, isn't there?"

"No," he said, and then, as if he realized lying wasn't going to work, "not yet. But the person who left the phone here just realized she doesn't remember having it when she got home, and unfortunately it's Marian the Librarian."

Who had the keys to the building. Briddey glanced nervously at the door. "Is she on her way back?"

"Nothing as dire as that," he said, screwing the lid on the salsa jar. "In fact, she's still home in bed. She hasn't even figured out where she left it, but she's mentally retracing her steps, so it's just a matter of time before she figures out where it is. Besides," he added, closing the top of the cereal box, "I'm guessing you don't want to be seen coming home on a Sunday morning dressed like that." He gestured at her green dress. "Especially since one of your neighbors is bound to be on Facebook."

He's right, she thought, gathering up the candy-bar and peanut-butter-cracker wrappers. And the neighbors weren't the only ones to worry about. Her family had a habit of dropping by unannounced on their way to early Mass, and Maeve would be dying of curiosity after those mysterious texts from C.B.

"You said you explained the situation to Maeve when you texted her," Briddey said. "What exactly did you say?"

C.B. licked the last of the frosting from the paper plate, folded the plate over on itself, and stuck it in the pizza box. "I just told her you and I were in the middle of an emergency."

"You didn't tell her anything else?"

"Only that it was a matter of life and death," C.B. said, cramming the laden pizza box into the bag, "and she was the only one I could trust to keep our secret safe. She said I could count on her."

Of course she did, Briddey thought, crumpling up the wrappers and putting them in the bag. *She's obviously got a huge crush on you.*

"Yeah, well, I think she's pretty great, too," he said. "Listen, Briddey, about Maeve, there's something I—" He stopped.

Briddey looked up at him. He was listening again. "What is it?" she asked. "Is Marian on her way?"

"No," he said after a long minute. "But she just remembered she left her phone in the copy room. We need to go. Hand me the olives."

"Wait, you were going to tell me something about Maeve."

"It can wait," he said, taking the jar of olives from her and screwing on the lid. "Turn off the fire." He handed her the remote and began wiping down the table.

Briddey switched off the fire and the lamps, put the remote back behind the checkout desk, and then folded the cashmere throw, draping it over the back of the sofa like it had been when they first came in. The book C.B. had been reading was on the floor beside the wing chair. "What about the books you left in the stacks?" she asked, picking it up and putting it back on the shelf. "Do we need to go back and get them?"

"I already did," he said, pointing toward the door, where they sat on top of the card file. "Before I went out foraging for food. Oh, and before I forget, here's your phone." He handed it to her.

She stuck it in her pocket and picked up the box of Lucky Charms. C.B. handed her the bag of Doritos and the salsa, then jammed the rest of the trash and the empty soda cans into the grocery bag. "Have we got everything?" he asked.

"I think so," she said, taking a last look around at the darkened room, at the no-longer-cozy hearth and the now shadowed bookshelves—and the wing chair where C.B. had sprawled, asleep. She felt suddenly bereft at the thought of leaving. *I wish we could stay here forever.*

"Yeah, me, too," C.B. said, and she looked over at him, but he was turned away from her, picking up the bag and the olives. "This is the only warm room in the building. It's going to be like a deep freeze out there." He picked up the flashlight and opened the door. "And now I'll never find out how *The Decline and Fall of the Roman Empire* ends. Does it? Decline and fall?"

"I'm sure Marian knows," Briddey said, trying to match his light tone. "And if we don't hurry, you'll be able to ask her." But as she followed him out the door and down the stairs, she wished more than ever that he'd taught her how to audit individual voices so she could tell what he was thinking.

They reached the foot of the stairs. C.B. stopped to listen before opening the door, and he was right, it was cold out here. She shivered, and C.B. must have interpreted it as a sign of fear because he said, "If it's the voices you're worried about, you'll be fine. It'll be light by the time we get out of here, and you've got your defenses now."

"Has Marian left home yet?" she asked.

"Nope, she's still fretting over whether it's worth it to get up and come all the way back here," he said, opening the door to the corridor. He held out the books and flashlight to her, and she shifted the Lucky Charms and salsa into her other arm so she could take them.

"Shine the flashlight on the door so I can see to lock it," he said, and as he inserted the key into the lock, "Having to listen to squirrel caging's another charming aspect of telepathy."

"Squirrel caging?" Briddey asked, watching him lock the door.

"Yeah." He took the flashlight back from her, and they started down the hall toward the staff lounge. "You know, going around and around in circles wondering whether you should drive back to the library to get your phone or wait till morning, or worrying . . . hang on," he said, stopping to dump the grocery bag into a trash can. "Or worrying about how you're going to pay the bills or whether that funny pain in your side is cancer."

Or whether Commspan's going to lay people off, Briddey thought, remembering Art Sampson, and then thinking about her own fretting over why she hadn't connected to Trent and what he'd do if he found out she was talking to someone else. Which poor C.B. had had to listen to.

"They should probably call it gerbil caging," C.B. said, opening the door to the staff lounge. "Or hamster caging. I mean, how many squirrels have you ever seen on an exercise wheel?"

He switched on the light, and she was relieved to see that, in spite of the pieces they'd eaten, the cake looked exactly the same. C.B. stuck the key back under the coffee can and put the salsa and olives in the refrigerator.

"Won't they notice the jar's nearly empty?" she whispered.

"Nope," he said, taking the box of Lucky Charms and the Doritos from her and sticking them in the cupboard. "They'll assume one of the TAs ate them."

"We should at least put some money in the donations jar," she said, pointing at the can marked COFFEE FUND.

"We can't. Then they'd *know* somebody was here. When's the last time anybody at Commspan chipped in for coffee? And the best defense against our being caught is them not even suspecting we were here. Besides, the Doritos aren't theirs. I found them up on s–v."

"But won't they wonder—?"

"No. Do you want another piece of cake? They'll never miss it."

"No," Briddey said, making a face.

"Neither do I. We need something more substantial. Man cannot live by Lucky Charms alone." He looked tentatively at her. "Remember that deli I told you about with the great lox and bagels? It's only a few blocks from here. We could get some breakfast, and I could teach you those auxiliary defenses."

"That sounds wonderful."

"Yeah," he said. "It does."

He motioned her out of the room and turned off the light, and she followed him down the hall, refusing to analyze why her heart felt suddenly so much lighter. *You're hungrier than you realized, that's all,* she told herself, going past the storage closet they'd hidden in to the end of the hall and into a stairwell.

"This isn't the way we came," she whispered.

"That's because the front door's got an alarm on it, and so does the staff entrance. And all the emergency exits."

"Then how are we going to get out?"

This way, he said, pointing down the stairs.

He'd reverted to speaking silently. *Does that mean Marian's here?* Briddey asked.

No, she's still trying to make her mind up about coming to get her phone, but there's no point in making more noise than we have to, and this way we'll be sure to hear anybody in the building before they hear us. That's one of the advantages of being telepathic. You can talk to your cohort in crime and still hear the cops coming.

I thought you said there weren't any advantages to telepathy, Briddey said, tiptoeing after him down the steps.

Oh, no, there are lots. I never once got caught by the jocks and stuffed into my locker in high school, and there was no such thing as a pop quiz.

But you also heard every taunting and cruel thing people thought about you.

And some nice things, C.B. said. *Nothing's all bad.*

Except that horrible deluge of voices.

True, C.B. admitted. *Though who knows? Even it might come in handy for something. Last step.*

He waited for her to come down it and then switched off the flashlight. She heard him open the door and look out, then the flashlight came on again, and he led the way down another hallway, this one with bare concrete walls, which had to be in the library's basement. It was almost as cold as his lab.

C.B. stopped in front of an unmarked door and switched off the flashlight. *There are windows,* he explained, opening the door, motioning her through, then shutting it behind them.

There might be windows, but they must have curtains over them because the room was nearly as dark as the storage closet had been. C.B. put his hand on her arm and said, *Are you okay?*

Yes, except that I can't see anything. She took a cautious step forward.

Wait, he said, pulling her back. *This place is an obstacle course. We need to let our eyes adjust first,* and held her there by the door while they waited.

Shapes became visible, but only dimly. The rectangles high up on the walls, which had to be the windows, were only a fractionally lighter shade of charcoal. *I thought you said it was supposed to be light by now,* she whispered.

It should be. What time is it?

She turned on her phone to see and then was sorry. The light from the screen undid all the adjusting their eyes had done. *Sorry,* she said. *It's six forty-five.*

Hmm, he said, and she could sense his puzzlement. He was silent a moment and then said, *Oh, that explains it.*

What? Are we in the wrong place?

No. Come on, this way, and led her deeper into the room.

Her eyes had finally adjusted, and she could see long rows of book-cases in the gray dimness. He was right, it *was* an obstacle course. There were plastic bins everywhere and rolling carts filled with books and papers. C.B. led her through them toward the back of the room, oc-casionally glancing up at the high windows.

I hope you don't expect me to climb out one of those, she said.

Only if we can't get to the door. He led her to the very back, where the bookcases were filled with a jumble of boxes, ledgers, folders held together with rubber bands.

If there was a door here, she had no idea where it could be. The bookcases went nearly all the way to the wall, and more boxes and shopping bags full of papers were piled halfway to the ceiling at their ends, but C.B. said, *Good. This isn't bad at all,* and began pulling out boxes and bags.

Arthur Tellman Ross's archives, he explained, reaching for a shopping bag crammed with papers. *The library had to promise to preserve them, too—all of them, including his grocery lists. And some very bad love poems. Can you put this over there?* he asked, pointing.

Yes, Briddey said, setting down C.B.'s books, putting the shopping bag next to a stack of metal file boxes, and taking another bag from him.

He pulled out another box. *What were we talking about before?*

You were telling me the many joys of being telepathic.

Oh, yeah, he said, setting it down on top of the first. *It's great. You can avoid traffic jams and bores and being stuck in line at the grocery store be-hind somebody who's got six hundred coupons and can't remember the PIN number of her debit card.* He lifted out another box. *And you don't have to find out the hard way that someone's a jerk and/or a liar.*

He set the box down next to the others and dragged out the last one. *Or have brain surgery to find out whether somebody loves you. You already know.*

So no hopeless crushes, Briddey said lightly.

I didn't say that. Hand me the flashlight.

She did, and he switched it on. And there was the door, painted the same color as the wall and set in from the edge of the bookcase, which was why she hadn't been able to see it.

Is it locked? she asked.

No, unless somebody's been here since the last time I came out this way. Which, he said, opening it outward a crack, *apparently they haven't.* He peered out. *Good, the coast is clear. Come on.*

Briddey retrieved C.B.'s books, and he helped her over the boxes. Then he reached past her for the shopping bags, set them on the boxes again, and opened the door, and she saw why it had been so dark in the room: it was raining. The sky was a leaden, lowering gray, and the steps outside the door, leading up to the parking lot, were wet. The parking lot was even wetter.

I thought you said people thought about the weather, she said.

They do, but apparently nobody's up yet. You didn't happen to bring an umbrella, did you? Or a boat?

No, she laughed. *It might not be as bad as it looks,* and as if in response, it began raining harder, the drops bouncing up from the already inundated parking lot.

Maybe we'd better wait for it to let up, C.B. said, frowning.

I don't think it's going to. And the longer they stayed, the greater the risk that Marian would pull into the parking lot. *We'd better go.*

Yeah, he said reluctantly. *Are you sure you'll be okay?* And she realized he was worried not about the rain but that the sight of the water might trigger the deluge of voices for her again. She also realized that she hadn't once thought about them on the way down here, even though it had been dark most of the way and she could hear the faint murmuring of them beyond her perimeter. As long as C.B. was with her, she could face even Niagara Falls.

Really? he said.

Yes, really. I'll be fine. Let's go, she said, and to herself: *Before you read any more of my thoughts.*

Niagara Falls it is, he said. *Here, hand me the books.* He tucked them inside his flannel shirt, pulled the door shut behind them, grabbed her hand, and they took off running across the parking lot.

They were instantly soaked. "Bus shelter," C.B. shouted, pointing at a blurred shape halfway down the street on the other side. She nodded, and they ran toward it down the wet sidewalk.

The water in the street was running like a river. "This is ridiculous," C.B. said.

"I know," she agreed, and they raced across it, totally soaking their shoes, and down to the shelter, laughing.

It didn't provide much shelter. Rain dripped from the roof's edge, and the green-painted metal bench was beaded with drops of water. They huddled together in the middle of the shelter, trying to keep away from the rain blowing in from three sides. C.B. pushed his wet hair back from his forehead and wrung out his sleeves, and Briddey shook out her dress. "Your dress'll get ruined," C.B. said.

Briddey looked down at the blotchy water stains on the bodice and skirt. "I'm afraid it already is."

"Yeah, well, no reason to make it worse. Or for both of us to get soaked. You stay here, and I'll go get the car."

"But—"

"You'll be fine," he said reassuringly. "I'll only be a couple of minutes, and if the voices start to break through, you've got your perimeter and your safe room."

And his hand, clasping hers, held close against his heart.

"I won't really be gone," he said. "We can keep talking."

"I know. Here." She shrugged out of his wet denim jacket and handed it to him. "You'll need this more than I do."

"Thanks." He handed her the books. "If the voices start again, or you have trouble keeping them out—"

"I won't," she said. "Go."

He nodded. "Here goes nothin'," he said, put the jacket over his head, and took off running. She stood there clutching the books and watching him as he ran down the street and rounded the corner and breathing in the sweet smells of grass and wet earth.

You still okay? he called.

Yes.

Well, I'm not. It's like an Old Testament flood out here. I could drown before I make it to . . . shit.

What is it? she asked, alarmed.

Nothing. Sorry, I didn't mean to bring up drowning. Or deluges.

It's okay, really. I'm fine. But hurry! I'm freezing!

You're freezing? I'm about to succumb to hypothermia out here!

Nonsense, you just need to think about something else. Like Lucky Charms. Blue lips, red noses, albino snowflakes—

Very funny.

Or songs, she said. *Ones with lots of verses. Like "Raindrops Keep Falling on My Head." Or "A Little Fall of Rain" from Les Miz.*

And this is the thanks I get for rescuing you? he said. *Next time I'll leave you in the ladies' room.*

"Singin' in the Rain" would be good, she mused. *It's got lots of verses, plus you could do a tap-dance, like Gene Kelly.*

My Nikes are too waterlogged, he told her, and he sounded as giddy as she felt. *And don't tell me to think about "Let a Smile Be Your Umbrella" or "Rainy Days and Mon—" Damn it!*

What happened? Did you step in a gutter?

No, a tree just dumped a gallon and a half of water down the back of my neck. Stop laughing!

Sorry, she said contritely. *Are you to the car yet?*

No, I'm still two blocks away, but I should be able to see it in another minute or two. If it hasn't floated away. I hope it starts. It doesn't like cold, rainy weather any more than I do.

And it was getting colder and rainier by the minute. The drops blowing in on her were as icy as sleet. She retreated to the back of the shelter, feeling guilty that she was in out of the rain and C.B. wasn't, and praying he wouldn't have trouble starting the car.

Briddey? C.B.'s voice cut in. *Are you okay? The voices aren't—*

No, I'm fine. Are you to the car yet?

No, I've still got a block to go. So keep talking. Only make it about something warm. No more rain songs.

Think about breakfast, she said. *It'll be nice and warm in the deli. You can take your jacket off and hang it over the radiator to dry, and the waitress'll bring you a hot mug of coffee—*

Tea, he said. *'Tis a foine Irish lad I am, remember?*

That's right, you are, she thought happily. *The waitress will bring you a hot mug of tea, then, and you'll wrap your hands around it to warm them. And the windows will be all steamy—*

I'm at the car, C.B. interrupted. *Now, if my fingers aren't too frozen to get the key in the lock . . .*

There was a pause. Briddey leaned forward, focused as intently as if she could see his numb fingers fumbling with the door lock, fumbling to get the key in the ignition. *Did it start?* she called. *C.B.?*

Yeah. Don't worry, I'm still here, he said.

I know, she thought, and smiled.

All right! he shouted.

It started?

I don't know yet. I just got the door open. But I'm in out of the rain at least. Another, briefer pause, and then, *Come on, darlin'. You can do this,* he said, sounding just like he had with her in the theater bathroom. *Come on.* Another pause. *It started!* he crowed. *Sit tight. I'll be there in two minutes, and we'll go find that deli and steam up the windows like you said. Okay?*

Okay, she said, more grateful than ever that he was blocks away so he couldn't see her suddenly reddened cheeks.

But he'd be here in a matter of minutes. *And then we'll go have break-fast,* she thought, envisioning them sitting across from each other like they had in the Reading Room, holding hands under the table.

Minutes passed with no sign of him. Where was he? She went to the edge of the bus shelter to see if he was turning the corner, but the street was deserted. *Where are you?* she called. *I'm freezing here.*

He didn't answer, which probably meant the windshield had fogged up when he got in and he was busy trying to swipe at it, turn on the defroster, and drive at the same time. *And the last thing he needs is you yammering in his ear,* she thought, hugging his books to her to keep warm. She waited another minute so as not to distract him and then said, *Hurry up, C.B. You're not the only one getting hypothermia, you know.*

Still no answer, and no sign of his car, and the rain was blowing in harder by the second. Where *was* he? *Maybe the car stalled at an intersection,* she thought, remembering how deep the water had been. *Or he hydroplaned and hit a tree.*

Are you okay? she called worriedly. *Talk to me. Can you hear me?*

Yes! Trent said. *Oh, my God, Briddey, is that you?*

Twenty-One

"It cannot rain but it pours."
—JONATHAN SWIFT

OH, NO, BRIDDEY THOUGHT. *IT CAN'T BE!*

But it was. *I don't believe this, Briddey!* the voice said, and this time there was no mistaking it. It was definitely Trent.

Not now, she thought.

Oh, my God! I can actually hear you! Trent crowed. *Not your feelings, your voice! We're reading each other's minds! Do you realize what this means?*

"Yes," Briddey said, clutching C.B.'s books to her chest. *It will change everything.*

I've got to warn C.B., she thought. But what if Trent heard her talking to him? He'd said, "I can actually hear you." What exactly had he heard? Her calling to C.B.? Her thoughts?

But how could he have? He was English. He had the inhibitor genes. So perhaps this was a fluke, and they'd only connected for a moment, like those people who heard a loved one calling—

I can't believe this! Trent broke in. *I can read your mind!*

And there went that theory.

What did you say? Trent said. *I'm having trouble hearing you.*

Thank goodness for that, Briddey thought. *Maybe if I don't answer, he'll decide this is all a hallucination, like I did that first night in the hospital, and—*

Hospital? Trent said, alarmed. *What happened?*

Too late, Briddey remembered to run for her courtyard. She flung the blue door open, slammed it behind her, and leaned, panting, against it.

Did something go wrong with your EED? Trent was asking worriedly. *Is that why you're in the hospital?*

I'm going to have to tell him I'm not in the hospital, Briddey thought, staring blindly at her courtyard and the rain, *or he'll call Dr. Verrick.*

But if she answered him, it would prove that the contact was real and not just something he'd imagined. *C.B.,* she called. *What should I do?*

No answer.

He's busy trying to drive in this rain, she told herself.

Trent broke in again. *Briddey, answer me!* he shouted. *Did something go wrong with your EED? Speak to me! You need to tell me where you are.*

No, that's the last thing I need to do. C.B.! Come in! I need you.

Still no answer. What if he wasn't preoccupied with the car and the pouring rain? What if he couldn't hear her anymore? What if it *had* been crossed synapses, and now they were uncrossed, and she was connected to Trent instead? *But I don't want—*

What do you want? Trent asked. *I can't hear you. Do you want me to call Dr. Verrick, is that it? I'll call him right now—*

There was nothing else for it. She had to answer him and convince him she was all right, that there was no need to call Dr. Verrick. *Trent?* she said. *Is that you?*

Briddey? Oh, thank God! I was afraid . . . where are you?

I'm in my safe room, she told herself. *He can't hear anything I don't want him to from in here.* But even so, she'd better not think about the bus shelter or the rainy street. Or C.B. *And you can't call him by name. Call him Conlan. Trent doesn't know that's his real name.*

Talk to me, Briddey, Trent was saying. *What happened?*

Happened? she said groggily, as if she'd just woken up. *Nothing. What do you mean?*

Are you at the hospital? I heard you say—

Hospital? No, I didn't . . . what are you talking about? I'm at my apartment. I was asleep, and I thought I heard you calling my name. I thought I was dreaming. Where are you?

Trent didn't answer.

It was a momentary connection, she thought, relieved. *And I'll be able to convince him he was just imagining—*

. . . beyond anything I'd hoped for! Trent said. There was a pause of several seconds, and then she heard, *. . . can't wait to tell . . . ,* his voice less clear, as if he were on a phone going out of range, becoming muffled and skipping syllables. *. . . this will—* he said, and his voice cut off.

Trent? she called tentatively.

No answer.

Good. *Conlan?* she called. *Night Fighter calling Dawn Patrol. Come in, Dawn Patrol.*

Silence.

He's gone, she thought.

No, I'm not, Trent said. *I'm not going anywhere now that we've finally connected! I was beginning to think it was never going to happen—and now this!*

I should have listened to C.—to Conlan, Briddey thought bleakly. *He warned me there'd be terrible side effects.*

What did you say? Trent asked. *I can't hear you. Your voice keeps breaking up. I heard you say, "listen" and then noth—*

His voice cut out again, and this time it didn't come back, though Briddey waited for several minutes. She waited another thirty seconds to make certain he was gone and then called, *Dawn Patrol . . . Conlan? . . . C.B.?*

Nothing, except for the hammering of rain on the curved roof of the shelter.

What if I've lost him for good? she thought sickly. If she had, if their connection had been rerouted so she was connected with Trent, did that mean C.B. was calling to her, too, and getting no answer? Or was he too focused on his car and the rain to have noticed her absence?

No, because here was his car, rounding the corner and roaring down the street in front of her. She stepped out of the bus shelter into the rain, trying to protect the books from getting wet, and over to the curb, trying to see his face through the windshield, to tell from his expression whether he'd realized what had happened yet, but the rain was coming down too hard, the wipers whipping back and forth too fast.

He pulled over to the curb, sending up a spray of water that made her step back to avoid getting splashed. "Sorry I took so long," he said, leaning over to open the door for her. "I got the car started, but then one of the stupid windshield wipers wouldn't work, and I had to get out and mess with it and got wet all over again."

Not wet, drenched. His T-shirt and jeans were stuck to his skin, and his hair was plastered to his forehead. "And then, when I finally got it fixed," he said, "the car died, and it took forever to get it started again."

He doesn't know yet, she thought, her heart sinking. *I'm going to have to tell him.*

Tell me what? he asked, and a radiant feeling of relief swept over her. "You can still hear me," she said happily. "Conlan, listen, I have to tell you something—"

"Get in the car first," he said gruffly. "You're letting all the warm air out."

She nodded and got in. It didn't seem any warmer in the car than outside, in spite of the warm air blowing from the heater. C.B. looked frozen. His hands on the steering wheel were bright pink with the cold.

"C.B . . . ," she began, but he'd already roared away from the curb and up to the main thoroughfare, intent on the road. And on the rain, which was coming down with hurricane force. It pounded deafeningly on the car roof, and the windshield wipers weren't even beginning to keep up with it.

But noise or not, difficulty in driving or not, she had to tell him now. She pushed her wet hair back from her forehead, took a deep breath, and said, "Listen, something happened while you were getting the car."

"The whole, 'my boyfriend's back' thing? Yeah, I know. I heard him while I was tightening the windshield wiper," he said as if it were the most ordinary thing in the world.

"But I thought you said he had inhibitors."

"Apparently I was wrong about that. He must have had an Irish ancestor in there somewhere, a seduced Irish scullery maid from Dublin or something."

"Or you were wrong about what causes the telepathy. Maybe it doesn't have anything to do with being Irish."

"I wasn't wrong," he said.

"How do you know?"

"Because . . . I just know, okay? And how it happened is beside the point. What matters is that it did."

He was right. "So what do I do now?"

"Well, hopefully, you'll stop accusing me of blocking your boyfriend—"

"This isn't funny."

"You're right," he said grimly, "it's not," and leaned forward to swipe at the steam on the inside of the windshield with his hand.

"So what should I—?"

"Turn on the defroster. I can't see where I'm going."

She peered at the dashboard, trying to figure out which knob was the defroster. She turned the likeliest one, and the radio came on. "It's a really bad morning out there, folks," an announcer was saying.

"Sorry," she said. She switched the radio off, found the defroster, kicked it to high, and looked over at C.B., waiting for him to answer her question, but he didn't say anything.

"C.B.? What should I do?"

"I don't know," he said. He turned to look at her. "If it was just a matter of his hearing your voice, we might have been able to convince him it was one of those exceptionally strong emotions Dr. Verrick talked about, the kind that are so strong they come through as words, but with you answering him—"

"I *had* to. He was about to call Dr. Verrick. But I didn't think he'd react like he did. I thought he wouldn't be able to believe it, that he'd—"

"Think it had to be some kind of trick, like you did?"

"Yes, and I'd be able to persuade him afterward that it hadn't really happened, that he'd imagined it. But he was immediately convinced it was telepathy, and he was thrilled."

"I can imagine," C.B. muttered.

What did that mean? Could C.B. think she was thrilled, too? Well, why wouldn't he? Connecting with Trent was all she'd talked about since this had started. "C.B.—" she said, and her phone rang.

It can't be ringing, she thought. *It's turned off,* and remembered C.B.'s asking her what time it was when they were down in the library basement. She'd turned it on to look and must have forgotten to turn it back off afterward.

Please let this be Kathleen, she thought, staring at Trent's name on the screen. *Or even Mary Clare.* But the only way to find out was to answer it, and if it was actually Trent . . .

"You'd better answer it," C.B. said, "in case he wants to come see you."

She hadn't thought of that. He might be on his way over to her apartment already. But what was she going to say to him? *Maybe I can deny it ever happened and say I don't know what he's talking about.* She hit TALK.

"Hullo?" she said, making her voice sound blurred with sleep. "Who is this?"

"Trent!" he said.

"Oh." She yawned loudly. "Good morning, Trent. What are you doing up so early?" But that didn't even register. He was shouting, "My God, Briddey! I can't believe what just happened!"

"What? What do you mean, what just hap—?"

"We were actually *talking* to each other!" he shouted so loudly that C.B. didn't need to be able to read minds to hear him. His voice filled the car. "I never dreamed . . . I expected the EED would let us communicate feelings, but *this*!"

"Trent, wait. What are you talking about?"

"I mean, it's amazing! A whole new kind of communication—no filters, no barriers! And to think I doubted you! When we didn't connect, I imagined all sorts of things—that you weren't emotionally bonded to me, even that you were in love with someone else, but now I realize how ridiculous that was! Of *course* you love me!"

This cannot get any worse, Briddey thought.

"This has all worked out better than I could have imagined! Telepathy! I can't wait to see you. I'm coming over!"

"No, I don't think that's a good idea," Briddey said. "Not till you've told me what's happened. You're not making any sense, Trent. You need to sit down and tell me what—"

"I can tell you when I get there. I'll be there in a few minutes."

It was only fifteen minutes from his condo to her apartment, and they were at least half an hour away. She had to stall him somehow. "No!" she said. "I mean, I'm not even up yet, and I need to take a shower and . . ." She looked over at C.B. for help, but he was staring straight ahead at the road. "Listen, how about if I meet you at Piazza Venetia at ten? They have that champagne brunch—"

"Are you *kidding*? I want to see you *now*! And someplace where it's just the two of us."

Oh, God, she'd forgotten about him saying they'd get engaged as soon as they connected. What if he—?

"This isn't something we can discuss at the Piazza Venetia," Trent was saying. "I don't think you realize what this development means!"

Yes, I do, Briddey thought miserably. "But couldn't we meet for brunch first and then go back to my—"

"No, we need to talk about this, and we can't do that in public."

"Why don't I come over to your place instead? You know how my family's always barging in unannounced—"

"Not this early, and in this rain. You get dressed. Or better yet, you just stay right there in bed—"

I was wrong, Briddey thought. *It can get worse.*

". . . all warm and sexy, and when I get there, I'll—"

"Trent, stop!" Briddey cut in desperately. "You're acting insane! Telepathy? What are you talking about? The EED doesn't make people telepathic—"

He wasn't listening. "I'll be there as soon as I can," he said.

"No, wait, I don't have a thing in the house. Why don't you stop and pick up breakfast on your way over?"

"How can you even think of food at a time like this? All right. See you in a few minutes," he said, and hung up.

"He's coming over to my apartment," she said unnecessarily.

"Which means I've got to get you home so you can get out of that dress before he gets there," C.B. said, and stepped on the gas.

"I'm sorry I won't be able to go to the deli with you."

"It doesn't matter. I've taught you the basic defenses."

That isn't what I meant, she thought.

But he wasn't listening either. "All you really need to keep the voices out is a perimeter and a safe room," he said, "and you've got those."

"Plus the lyrics to 'Teen Angel.'"

"Yeah, though 'Get Me to the Church on Time' might be more appropriate under the circumstances," he said, and sped up.

"Do you think you can get me there before Trent arrives?"

"Yeah, with a little luck," he said, which meant he was listening to Trent and knew exactly where he was. And he must already be on his way because C.B. kept going faster—and tapping his fingers impatiently on the steering wheel at every red light. Which meant he didn't think they'd make it, and she'd better come up with an explanation for what she was doing with C.B. and why they'd been out all night.

My car broke down on the way home from Aunt Oona's, and he had to come pick me up. No, because why wouldn't she have called Trent instead? Or Mary Clare or Kathleen? And it wouldn't explain how both of them had gotten so wet. Or why her car was parked out in front of her apartment building.

She looked over at C.B., wishing he'd suggest an excuse, or at least say something about the Rules of Lying, but he was staring straight ahead, the muscles in his jaw clenched tight. *Because we're cutting it so close?* Or because he knows this changes everything, too?

She wished fervently that this hadn't happened now, that C.B. had taken her to the deli and taught her how to audit individual voices so she could read his mind.

Or maybe it's just as well I can't. What if she heard him think she'd been nothing but trouble and that he couldn't wait to dump her at her apartment and be rid of her?

He's right. Telepathy's a terrible idea, she thought, shivering in spite of the turned-up heater. She stared blindly out her fogged-up window at the rain-soaked streets. All the promise and sweetness the morning had held was gone, the smell of wet earth turned to mud and the gray sky depressing. The radio announcer was right. It was a really bad morning out there.

And in here. I wouldn't blame C.B. if he does want to get rid of me. He'd spent the last few days having to race to her rescue and cope with her hysterics and fend off her accusations that he was blocking Trent, which he obviously hadn't been doing.

I wish he had been, she thought wistfully. But he hadn't, so she was going to have to come up with some lie that would convince Trent they weren't telepathic, though she couldn't imagine what that would be, no matter how many Rules of Lying she employed.

She was going to have to tell him the truth. No matter what happened, it would be better than this constant lying—

"No, it wouldn't," C.B. said. "It'd be worse. Much worse. Which is why we're not going to let it happen." He put his foot all the way down on the accelerator, plowing through the water, throwing up wings of spray on either side, and cursing every time he had to stop.

We're hitting every light red, Briddey thought, looking over at him. His hands were clenched on the steering wheel, and he looked even grimmer. Did that mean he was afraid they wouldn't make it to her apartment in time? Or that Trent was already there?

"He's not," C.B. said, clicking on his turn signal, and she saw the next corner was the turn for her street. "He's not to Broward yet."

That meant he *had* stopped to pick up breakfast. Thank goodness. But it still didn't give her much time.

"I know," C.B. said, turning down her street. "I think I'd better just drop you outside your building."

Like a guy who can't wait to ditch his date, she thought, and the moment he stopped the car, she had her door open, thanking God she had a safe room so he couldn't witness the full spectacle of her humiliation.

"Wait," C.B. said, grabbing her arm to hold her in the car. "Before you go, I need to tell you"—she stopped, her hand on the door, waiting to hear what he was going to say, hoping—"don't tell Trent any more than you absolutely have to about the whole telepathy thing, especially not about your being able to hear other voices. The only one he can hear right now is yours, and he thinks that's because you're emotionally bonded, so it won't even occur to him that you've been connected to anyone else. The only way he can find out is if you tell him. And you mustn't. It's important. And you can't tell him what causes the telepathy either, not about the Irish connection or the R1b genes—"

Because if he finds out about the other voices, he might find out about you, she thought. *And that's what really matters, isn't it? That he doesn't find out about you.*

But she owed that to him. He'd saved her life, and he'd taught her how to defend herself against the voices. And told her he'd take her to

Niagara Falls on their honeymoon. "You don't have to worry," she said. "I won't give you away."

She got out of the car. "Thank you for everything," she said, shut the car door, and ran up the walk to her building, anxious to be inside before he could say anything.

And when would she learn that it didn't work like that, that there was no way to get away from C.B.'s voice?

That isn't it, he said. *Briddey, listen, there's more at stake here than you realize! It's not my secret I'm worried about, it's—shit, he must have hit every light green. Get inside.* And she turned, startled, to see C.B. roaring off down the street. And Trent's Porsche rounding the corner two blocks up.

Twenty-Two

"Hey, where are you goin' with that elephant?"
"What elephant?"
—*Billy Rose's Jumbo*

BRIDDEY RACED THROUGH THE FRONT DOOR AND UP TO HER APARTMENT, fumbling for her keys as she ran. She managed to drop them and then put the wrong key in the lock. *Panicking won't help,* she told herself, searching for the right one.

She unlocked the door, ducked in, slammed it behind her, and ran to the bedroom, yanking off her earrings as she went. She thrust them into a drawer and hurried over to the bed to take off her shoes.

No, she'd better not sit down on it. She'd get it wet. She leaned against it instead and unstrapped her shoes, struggling with the sodden buckles, and then took them off, pushed them under the bed, and started to do the same with her evening bag.

Her phone rang. *Maybe it's C.B. wanting to warn me about something,* she thought, and answered it.

It was Kathleen. "I can't talk right now," Briddey said, hung up, and hurried into the bathroom—and then back to the living room to put the deadbolt on so Trent would have to knock. That would give her an extra couple of minutes, though probably not enough to take a shower.

But she didn't need to. Her hair was already wet enough to fool him. She turned the shower on to make the bathroom look convincingly steamy, wishing she *did* have time. She was *so* cold.

Her phone rang again. "Look, Kathleen," she said. "This is a really bad time—"

"I know," Kathleen said. "Trent's there, right?"

No, but he will be any minute, and—

"I'll make this quick. I've got this really big problem, and I don't have anybody else I can talk to about it. I'm at Mary Clare's. They're getting ready to go to Mass, and all Mary Clare can think about is how Maeve is still shutting her out—"

"Kathlee—"

"And Aunt Oona will just tell me I need to stop trying to meet guys and go out with Sean O'Reilly, and I have to talk to *somebody*. I signed up for the Lattes'n'Luv thing, and I was supposed to go to coffee with this guy Landis. He's a hedge fund manager, and he's really handsome—"

Waiting for Kathleen to pause for breath was *not* going to work. She wasn't ever going to breathe. "Ka—"

"I mean he's exactly what I want in a guy, but when I went to Starbucks to meet him—"

"I really can't talk. I'll call you back as soon as I can, okay?" Briddey said over her, hung up, turned her phone off, and started back into the bathroom, unzipping her dress as she went.

Too late. Trent was already knocking on the door. "Coming!" she called, shut off the shower, and grabbed her robe, wishing she had one that buttoned all the way up to her neck. She bundled the robe tightly around her, making sure the neckline of her dress didn't show, wrapped a towel around her wet hair, and hurried out of the bathroom.

"Briddey!" Trent was calling from the hall, and she could hear him trying the lock. She padded barefoot to the door—darting back at the last minute to shut the bedroom door—took a deep, collecting-herself breath, and opened it.

Trent had his hand raised to knock again.

The rain must have let up, Briddey thought. His dress shirt and khakis weren't even damp, and his neatly combed hair had only a few drops of rain on it.

"Why did you have the deadbolt on?" he asked.

"Shh," she said, vaguely resentful of how neat and dry he looked. "You'll wake the neighbors." She opened the door wider with one hand, holding her robe closed at the neck with the other.

He came in. "You obviously didn't hear me calling."

"I was in the shower."

"I meant, calling you mentally. You didn't hear me at all?"

"No."

"You need to concentrate harder. I kept calling you the whole time I was standing there. I still can't believe this! Telepathy!"

He reached for her, but she neatly evaded his grasp. "I really need to dry my hair and get dressed," she said, starting for the bedroom. "You stay here and set out breakfast—" She stopped, frowning at his empty hands. "I thought you were going to stop and pick up something."

"I was, but I decided I had to get over here and see you!"

But if you didn't stop, then how did we beat you here?

"I don't think you understand just how momentous this thing is, sweetheart," he said. "The most I was counting on was being able to communicate feelings. I never dreamed I'd be able to read your mind!"

And hopefully you still can't, or you'd know I'm desperately wondering how to get back into that bedroom and out of this dress before you find out I'm still wearing it.

"I mean, telepathy!" Trent said jubilantly. "No wonder it took us so long to make contact! I was so worried about our not being able to connect, and then when you ran off in the middle of the play like that—and in front of the Hamiltons. And then this morning, there you were, *speaking* to me! This is so amazing! I'm still having trouble believing it's real!"

Good, Briddey thought. "Maybe it's not," she said. "Dr. Verrick said sometimes emotions come through so strongly, the person receiving them thinks he's hearing words—"

"This wasn't emotions. You *talked* to me. I heard you, and you heard me. We were telepathically linked."

"But how can we have been? There's no such thing as telepathy. So how can we be hearing each other's thoughts?"

"Hearing each other's thoughts?" Trent said sharply. "Not just communicating with each other? What did you hear?"

"I . . . um . . ."

"Tell me exactly what you heard. Word for word."

That was the last thing she wanted to do. "I thought I heard you calling my name . . . ," she said uncertainly. "And then I sensed you were saying you could hear me."

"And that's all?"

"Yes," she said, and he looked distinctly relieved. But why? He'd been so thrilled that they could hear each other's voices, she'd have expected . . . "What did *you* hear?"

"You calling, 'Where are you?' and that you thought I couldn't hear you, and then that you were afraid you'd lost me."

I was talking about C.B., she thought, and hoped Trent hadn't heard her say his name. "Did you hear anything else?"

"Just fragments."

Good—this wasn't as bad as she'd been afraid it might be. At least she hadn't given away anything about C.B. or where she was—

"I heard you say you were cold," Trent said. "And something about windshield wipers. You didn't go out this morning, did you?"

She resisted the impulse to grab the neck of her robe and pull it more securely around her neck. "No, I just got up. I remember thinking the floor was cold, but not anything about windshield wipers. Are you sure you didn't just imagine—?"

"No, I definitely heard you say it. Maybe you heard the rain and were thinking about me having to drive over in it. I didn't hear the rest. You faded out, and then I didn't hear anything while I was driving over. But I think that's because I was calling to you, and I'm not able to send and receive at the same time."

If only that were true, Briddey said silently. But she needed to encourage him to think that. It might keep him from listening at least part of the time. "That sounds logical," she said. "Or maybe it was just a fluke, something that only happened because we were half awake."

"No, because when I turned onto your street, I started hearing you again. You said 'hurry' and 'listen' and then a word I couldn't make out."

Not "C.B." Please.

"'Bag' or 'bad'? You said it a couple of times."

Bag. My evening bag, she thought, relieved, and then remembered she'd been about to hide it under the bed when Kathleen had called.

"So what were you trying to say to me?" Trent asked.

"That I felt bad about you having to come out in the rain," she improvised, trying to remember if she'd put the bag under the bed. She'd picked up the phone—

"Oh," Trent was saying. "I didn't get any of that, the words *or* the emotion. In fact, I haven't picked up any emotions from you at all."

Thank goodness. If he'd picked up how unhappy she was that they'd connected, or how bereft she'd felt when she thought she'd lost the ability to hear C.B.—

"Maybe it's only possible to hear words *or* feelings, but not both," he said. "We'll have to ask Dr. Verrick." He pulled out his phone.

No. "You're not going to call him now, are you? We don't know what's going on yet, and he's not even here. And who knows what time it is in Morocco."

"It doesn't matter. He said to call him if we made contact or if anything unusual happened, and this is both. I already called before I came over."

Oh, God. "Did you tell him what happened?"

"No, just that we needed to talk to him," he said, scrolling through his messages. "I haven't gotten anything from him yet. I left messages with his office and his answering service. I don't know why they haven't gotten back to me yet."

Because it's Sunday morning. How was she going to stop him from telling Dr. Verrick when he *did* reach him?

"Don't you think we should wait to try and contact him again till we find out more about what this is and what's causing it?" she asked. "Or if it's going to last? Especially since it's telepathy we're talking about. He's liable to think we're crazy," and surprisingly, Trent said, "You're right. We need something definitive to show him."

"Definitive?"

"Yes, like those ESP tests where one person thinks of an object and the other person tells them what it is. Here, I'll go in the bedroom and—"

No! she thought, forcing herself not to fling her body in front of the door to stop him. "We can do that after breakfast. I'll make us an omelet—"

"We can eat later," he said, walking over to the bedroom door. "I want to do this now in case Dr. Verrick calls back. Think of an object"—he reached for the doorknob—"and then concentrate on that image for thirty seconds."

"But if it's hard evidence we're looking for, won't we need to document it?" she asked, and clearly he wasn't sensing her emotions, or he'd be picking up her panic. "There are pens and notepads in the left-hand drawer of my desk," she said to get him away from the bedroom door, and while he rummaged in the desk, she positioned herself firmly in front of the door.

"I'll go in the bedroom," she said when he came back, "and you can go in the kitchen and fix breakfast, since you didn't bring any."

"We need to be concentrating," he objected.

"I know, but I'm starving."

"All right, though how you can think of food at a time like this . . ." He handed her a pen and paper. "I'll think of ten different things, each for a full minute."

"And then I'll send you ten," she said. *And that should give me long enough to get out of this incriminating dress.* "Okay?" she said, and before he could object, opened the door, squeezed through it, and closed it again.

Which was a good thing, because there on the bed in plain sight was her evening bag. She looked down at the door's lock, wishing she could use it, but she was afraid Trent would hear the snick.

She put her ear to the door, trying to hear if he'd gone into the kitchen. "Write down any words or images you get," Trent called, obviously just outside. "Or emotions."

"Okay," she said, and waited, her ear to the door again till she heard him move away, and then darted over to the bed, snatched up the wet evening bag, and slung it under the bed. It had left a damp patch on the coverlet. She unwound the towel from her hair, dumped it in a heap over the dampness, and dashed back to the door.

"Ready to start?" Trent shouted through the door.

"Wait, I need to get my phone so I can time it exactly," she called, and darted over to the dresser to grab it. She hurried back and turned on the phone, leaning her body against the door so Trent couldn't suddenly open it.

Kathleen had left her four messages. She switched the ringer to vibrate, set the timer, and stuck it in the pocket of her robe. "Okay, ready."

I'm thinking of the coffeemaker, he said. *Coffeemaker.*

He's right, she thought. *The connection's getting stronger.* But at least if he was focused on sending messages, he wasn't listening to her. And the fact that he'd sent "coffeemaker" meant he was in the kitchen, and it was safe to get out of her wet dress.

She locked the bedroom door, untied her robe, shrugged it off, unzipped her dress, and stepped out of it.

"The *Mona Lisa,*" Trent said.

She opened the closet door and took a hanger from the rack, being careful not to let it clink against the bar.

Bacon.

She hung up the dress and draped a raincoat over it, thinking, *I should have worn this last night.* She stuck the hanger at the back of the closet and shut the door quietly.

Jasmine, Trent said.

Jasmine? He must be looking at the teas in the cupboard, she thought. *Which means he's still in the kitchen, and I can get dressed.* But she was supposed to be concentrating on the words he was sending. She'd better just put her robe back on. She changed into dry underwear and combed her wet hair and then sat down on the bed and tried to decide what to put down on her list.

He was now on number seven, and she'd heard every one of them. She obviously couldn't let him know that, but just writing down wrong answers wouldn't persuade him the telepathy hadn't happened. It might convince him something was wrong and he needed to get in touch with Dr. Verrick right away. But if she wrote down correct answers . . .

She wished she could ask C.B. what to do. *But he's not here.* He'd gone off and left her, and if she wanted to keep all this secret, she shouldn't even be thinking about him.

"And that's ten," Trent said. "Did you get them?"

"Not all of them," she said, hastily numbering the page and writing down "clock" for "coffeemaker," "jackal" for "jasmine," "bear" for "bacon," random words—"kitten" and "pillow" and "building"—for three others, and question marks for the rest of them.

"Let me see," Trent called.

"Not till after I send mine. Go back in the kitchen."

She put the list on the dresser and went into her safe room so she could make a list of the words she was supposedly sending without Trent hearing her. *And then I won't send anything,* she thought, *and I'll tell him—*

"Are you sending?" Trent called through the door. "I'm not getting anything."

Good—at least that means my safe room works, she thought. "Yes," she shouted.

"Well, it's not coming through. Maybe we should just forget this and see if we can reach Dr. Verrick at the hospital—"

No. "No, I'm probably just not concentrating enough," she said. "Let me try again. Go back in the kitchen, and I'll start over." She was going to have to send him something. But what? Obviously not the words she'd just listed.

She hastily composed a second list, making the words as different as possible from those on the first list—and words he couldn't possibly guess on his own, like "tear gas" and "petunias" and "Angkor Wat."

But would the words be the only thing she sent? C.B. had said her thoughts couldn't be heard when she was inside the safe room, but she'd only had it up and running for a few hours. She'd better screen her thoughts, just in case.

"Briddey!" Trent called. "I'm still not getting anything."

"I'm just starting now," she called back, said, *Petunias. Repeat, petunias,* and began singing the theme from *Gilligan's Island,* but her mind kept straying to the problem of how she was going to keep Trent from talking to Dr. Verrick when the test was over—and how she was going to keep him at bay. He'd said when they connected, he'd propose, and now—

Don't think about that, she told herself, and started reciting "The Highwayman," but she couldn't remember the words, and she found herself thinking about what C.B. had said. "It's not my secret I'm worried about." What had he meant by that? Did he—?

Her phone vibrated. *Kathleen,* she muttered. *That's all I need,* and then thought, *I can use* her *to screen my thoughts. What she says won't be related to any of this,* Briddey thought, *and it won't matter if Trent hears it.* She answered.

"Kathleen? Hang on a sec," she whispered. She padded into the bathroom and shut the door so Trent couldn't hear her talking, and then sat down on the edge of the tub, set her phone's alarm to warn her when ten minutes was up, and said, "Okay, shoot. You were on a date with the Lattes'n'Luv guy, and he's perfect—"

"Yes," Kathleen said unhappily, "but he was late, and while I was waiting, I got to talking with the barista—his name is Rich—and he's really nice."

"Umm," Briddey said, listening to her rattle on and periodically sending Trent a word from the second list: "tear gas," "endive," "NASCAR."

"Anyway," Kathleen said at the end of her story, "now I think I like him and not the other guy."

I shouldn't have done this, Briddey thought. *Talking to Kathleen was a mistake.*

"I don't know what to do," Kathleen said. "It's all such a mess. I mean, I don't even know if Rich likes me. He might just have been being friendly."

Or taking pity on a poor hysterical girl and trying to calm her down. And that bit about hopeless crushes was his way of trying to let me down easy—

"What if it didn't mean anything to him?" Kathleen was saying. "It isn't like he asked for my number."

Or stayed here to help me.

And if Trent heard her thinking any of this . . . "I need to go," Briddey said.

"But you have to tell me what to do!" Kathleen wailed.

I don't know what to do, Briddey thought, and her phone's alarm went off. "Look, I've got another call coming in that I've *got* to take. I'll call you back," she said, hung up, tore the list of words she'd sent into tiny pieces, and washed them down the sink. She took the other list out to the bedroom, unlocked the door, and sat down on the bed to wait for Trent, trying to think what to do if he did propose.

I can't let him, she thought. *I've got to think of some way to stall him—*

Wonderful, she heard Trent say disgustedly.

Briddey froze. *Oh, no, he heard me think that.*

I can't believe I have to listen to him, too.

He can hear someone else, Briddey thought. But how was that possible? He'd only started hearing her this morning, and it had been well over forty-eight hours after hearing C.B. before she'd begun hearing other people. And it was obvious from what he was saying that this wasn't the first time he'd heard it. Was that why he hadn't been all that shocked when he first heard her voice, because it hadn't been the first one?

But then why had he said all that about their connection proving they were emotionally bonded? If he could hear other voices, he knew that wasn't how it worked—

No, I can't meet you, Trent said. *It'll just have to wait till tomorrow.*

He's not just hearing other people, Briddey thought with a shock. *He's talking to them. But how?*

I can't believe I have to waste my time on this when I should be communicating with Briddey. How did he get this number anyway?

He's not connected to someone else. He's talking on the phone, and I'm picking up his thoughts while he does, Briddey thought, and put her ear to the door to make sure.

Yes, she could hear him talking, though she couldn't make out what he said. And who would he be calling this early?

Oh, God, I hope it's not Dr. Verrick, she thought, but Trent *wanted* to talk to him. Could it be someone from the hospital who was refusing to give him Dr. Verrick's number?

Whatever it is, Trent said, *I don't need it anymore, now that I've got . . .* His thoughts faded out and then came back. *Suppose I have to see him . . . make an appointment with my secretary . . .*

It was just someone calling about business. Briddey sank down on the bed with relief, and her foot hit something. One of her shoes, not pushed far enough under. She got down on her hands and knees, retrieved it, and was reaching for the other one when she heard Trent say, *I need to tell Briddey I didn't hear those last two words.*

It gave her only a few seconds of warning, but it was enough. When he opened the door, the shoes were back under the bed, the closet door was shut, her phone was in her pocket, and she was sitting on the edge of the bed, pretending to add "measles" to the list of words she'd supposedly sent.

She stood up and handed the lists to Trent. "Is breakfast ready? I'm starving," she said, and walked past him out of the bedroom to the kitchen.

The kitchen table was empty, and there were no pans on the stove. "I thought you were going to make breakfast," she said.

"I didn't have time," Trent muttered, comparing her list with his own. "I got six of the ones you sent right."

Six? she thought. *How did he get six? There is no way he could have come up with "measles." Or "Angkor Wat." And I thought he said he didn't hear the last two.*

"See?" he said, showing her his list. "Number two was 'diapers' and I put down 'person,' so I was obviously receiving an image of a baby, and for 'measles' I wrote 'tomato,' and they're both red."

His interpretation of correct answers was as loose as Dr. Rhine's. "What other images did you get?" she asked, taking the list from him. He'd written down "petunias" and "NASCAR," which meant he'd heard at least two of the words she'd sent. He'd also written "hedge," "star? Starbucks?" and "drove off." Which meant he'd also overheard parts of her conversation with Kathleen.

"You're sure you didn't send any of those words?" Trent was asking, pointing at "cigarette" and "hedge" on his list.

"No," she said firmly.

"You might have been thinking of them in connection with the image you were sending. Like the baby might have been sitting next to a hedge?"

"No."

"Oh," he said, disappointed. "Let's see the list of what you received from me."

She watched him, thinking, *Thank goodness I just put down question marks for some of them, or by his standards I'd have gotten a ten, even with random words.*

As it was, he gave her credit for "building." "I was sending 'the *Mona Lisa*,'" he said, "and you clearly received an image of the Louvre." He frowned. "You didn't get 'spaghetti' at all?"

"No."

"What about feelings? I tried to send emotions along with the images."

"No, I didn't pick up any feelings, though when I was sending, I heard a phone ringing. Was that something you were thinking about, or did someone call you?"

"Someone called me," he said disgustedly. "That moron C.B. Schwartz. He wanted me to come see some stupid new app of his."

No, he didn't, she thought. *He was trying to rescue me.* Her spirits soared. *I thought he'd abandoned me, but he hadn't. He's been here the whole time, listening to us.*

Trent was gaping at her. Oh, no, had he heard that?

"I take back what I said before about not getting any emotions from you," he said. "I just got this . . . I don't even know what to call it . . . this unbelievably powerful feeling of love from you." He enfolded her in his arms. "Do you realize what this means, sweetheart?"

Yes, she thought. *It means I'm in even more trouble than I thought I was,* and fled to her safe room. But it was too late. If Trent had been able to feel it, so had C.B.—

"It means the EED's even better than I thought it was!" Trent was saying. "Thoughts *and* emotions!"

"Trent—"

"This is going to change everything! We'll be able to—" He caught himself. "I mean, knowing you love me will change our relationship! We—"

He stopped again. "What is it, darling?" he asked, and before she could open her mouth, said, "You don't have to answer. I can sense what you're feeling. You're concerned that you aren't getting emotions from me yet, and that I can hear you better than you can hear me, but don't worry. You heard Dr. Verrick. Some people are just more sensitive than others. I'm sure you'll catch up."

He pulled her close. "And in the meantime, there are other ways of communicating." He nuzzled her neck. "I'll bet you can tell what I'm thinking right now. Because I definitely know what *you're* thinking."

No, you don't, she thought, *because I'm thinking now would be a really good time for C.B. to phone again.*

"You're thinking," Trent said, "'let's go to bed and—'"

There was a knock on the door.

Thank you, Briddey thought, and moved to answer it.

"Ignore them, whoever it is," Trent murmured, pulling her back into his arms.

"I can't," she said. "It might be my family."

"Shouldn't they be in church?"

"They sometimes stop by on the way home from Mass," she said, prying his hand off her sleeve. "And they've got a key, remember?"

"Oh, for God's sake," he said, and let go of her.

"Be there in a sec!" she called cheerfully, tied her robe more tightly around her, and ran over to the door, wondering how exactly C.B. was going to explain his presence.

He'll think of something, she thought confidently, and opened the door.

"Hi," Maeve said. "Why aren't you dressed?"

Twenty-Three

"Do it on the radio."
—*Educating Rita*

SAVED IN THE NICK OF TIME, BRIDDEY THOUGHT, LOOKING GRATEFULLY AT
Maeve standing there in the doorway with her pink umbrella and
heart-covered rain boots.

"You forgot you were supposed to take me to brunch this morning, didn't you, Aunt Briddey?" Maeve said, glaring at Trent. "I told
Mom you'd forget."

"Of course I didn't forget," Briddey lied, wondering when she'd
promised that. It didn't matter. This was a way to get away from Trent.

"I forgot that I promised Mary Clare I'd take her," she told him,
pulling him into the kitchen, "and try to find out what prompted her
to run away last night. And I've been thinking, our being apart might
help me hear you better. Remember what the nurse said about it keeping us from falling back on other, easier methods of communication?"

"You're right," Trent said. "And it'll give me a chance to see if I can
find another number for Dr. Verrick, too. What restaurant are you taking her to?"

Oh, God, she hadn't even thought about that. She wasn't sure her
defenses were sturdy enough yet to protect her in crowded places, and

Carnival Pizza was at the mall, which would be jammed. She'd have to try to talk Maeve into somewhere less crowded, if there was such a restaurant on a Sunday morning.

"I'm not sure," Briddey said. "I'll text you."

Trent laughed. "Don't you understand, sweetheart? You won't have to. We can communicate directly now. Send me words and feelings like you've been doing, and I'll do the same. And keep a log of all the things you hear me say." He pecked her on the cheek.

"'Bye, honey," he said to Maeve. "You have a fun time with your auntie."

He left, and Briddey had to hightail it to her courtyard to make sure he didn't sense the gust of relief she felt at his being gone.

Maeve was looking malevolently at the door. "How old does he think I am? Three? He doesn't have very good communication skills, does he, Aunt Briddey?"

Not yet, Briddey thought. *And let's hope he doesn't get better ones anytime soon.* "No," she said, and tried to think of how to address the subject of not going to the mall.

"Mom said you were going to take me to Carnival Pizza, but can we not go there?" Maeve asked. "It's so *childish.*"

You blessed girl.

"There's a restaurant in the park. By the lake. Can we go there instead?"

"The park? But it's raining." *And freezing,* she added silently, remembering the bus shelter.

"It's almost stopped. And anyway, you can eat inside."

And it would be deserted in this weather. "Are you sure it will be open?" Briddey asked.

"Yes, because Danika went there one time when it was *pouring,* and it was. They have really good food. And you can feed the ducks."

Which apparently wasn't childish, but Briddey wasn't going to quibble. The park was much better than the mall, and if Trent somehow managed to get hold of Dr. Verrick, it was the last place he'd look for her. Plus, if Maeve went off to feed the ducks, it would give Briddey a chance to figure out what to do.

C.B. had said it was essential that Trent not find out about their connection, but Briddey wasn't at all sure it was possible to keep it from him. He was already able to hear some of her thoughts, and now, with him starting to pick up her feelings, too, he was bound to sense that she was withholding something and start asking questions. And she didn't know whether a safe room worked for emotions, too.

I need to ask C.B., she thought, and wondered if Maeve would agree to their swinging by his lab to see him on their way to the park so she could find out.

"The park it is," she said. "You go find something to feed the ducks, and I'll get dressed." As Maeve started for the kitchen, Briddey asked, "Can you wait till I've taken a shower?"

"Sure," Maeve said. "Do ducks like ice cream?"

"No," Briddey said, "they like breadcrumbs," and went into her bedroom. She dug her wet shoes and evening bag out from under the bed, wiped them off with the wet towel, wrapped them up in it, stuck the bundle in the bottom drawer of her dresser, and turned around.

Maeve was standing in the doorway with a mesh bag of onions in one hand and a jar of capers in the other. "Do ducks like either of *these*?" she asked.

"*No.* They like breadcrumbs."

"You don't have any breadcrumbs."

"Then bread. They like bread. Or crackers."

"Okay," Maeve said, but she didn't budge.

Briddey braced herself for Maeve to ask, "Why are you hiding your shoes?" but she didn't. She said, "You don't have any crackers either."

"Then cereal," Briddey said, and Maeve went off to the kitchen, but she was back again immediately.

"You don't have any *good* cereal."

By which Maeve presumably meant Trix or Cap'n Crunch. Or Lucky Charms. *I'll bet she knows what the marshmallows are,* Briddey thought, and asked her, "Can you name the marshmallows in Lucky Charms?"

"Why are you asking that?" Maeve said, so defensively that Briddey wondered if Mary Clare had put a ban on Lucky Charms as well as Disney movies.

"I just wondered," Briddey said. "A friend and I were talking about them the other day, and we couldn't remember if there were five or six different marshmallows."

"Eight," Maeve said promptly. "Pink hearts, purple horseshoes, green clovers, blue moons, yellow hourglasses—"

That's what the yellow dog-bone thing was, Briddey thought. *An hourglass.*

"—red balloons, orange shooting stars, and rainbow-colored rainbows. But there are lots of ways to find that out. It's on the internet and everything. Do bagels count as bread?"

"Yes," Briddey said, frowning at the abrupt change of subject.

"Even chocolate chip bagels?"

"Where did you find chocolate chip bagels?"

"I didn't. I just wondered. Are ducks supposed to eat chocolate? Dogs aren't. It's *poison* to them. This one time Danika left her Twix bar on her bed, and Tootsie—that's her dog—ate it, and they had to take him to the vet and everything."

"Then chocolate's probably bad for ducks, too," Briddey said. "And sugar. Go get them some Wheat Chex." She pushed Maeve out of the room and went, *finally,* to take her shower and concoct an excuse for what she'd been doing with the shoes and bag, which, knowing Maeve, she would definitely ask her about.

Though she hadn't said a word about C.B.'s phoning her last night and asking her to cover for them. Why not? She was usually as nosy as Suki.

Maybe she's waiting to interrogate me till we get to the park, Briddey thought. In which case, she'd better think of a plausible story. Or change the subject, like Maeve just had. And hope Trent hadn't heard her thinking about going to the park.

He apparently hadn't, because as she was shampooing her hair, he asked, *Are you still in the car on your way to brunch?* And a moment later: *Where did you decide to take Maeve?*

Carnival Pizza, she said. He'd never consider eating at a place like that.

I still haven't heard from Dr. Verrick, he said. *I'm on my way out to Commspan to see if I can get IT to find me his nurse's number.*

Which meant that swinging by to talk to C.B. was out. She'd have to think of something else. She finished showering, dried her hair, and put on a warm sweater, jeans, wool socks, and her rain boots. "Did you find something to feed the ducks?" she called to Maeve.

"Yeah," Maeve said, appearing in the kitchen doorway with the Wheat Chex, a bag of bagels, a box of Special K, a box of Raisin Bran, a package of rice crackers, and an entire loaf of French bread. "I've got some popcorn in the microwave, too. Do you think this'll be enough?"

"Probably," Briddey said dryly, and as soon as the popcorn was done, they set off for the park.

The rain had *not* let up. There were only a few hardy souls out walking their dogs, and while Maeve had been right about the restaurant being open, her claim that they could eat "inside" was a stretch. It consisted of metal tables on a patio covered with a sagging canopy from which rain dripped.

But there were no other customers, and after seating them at a table next to a heater, the waiter handed them very damp menus, disappeared into the kitchen, and left them alone, except for a gaggle of sparrows hopping frozenly around on the patio looking for crumbs.

Briddey had convinced Maeve to leave the duck provisions in the car till after they ate, but Maeve begged, "Can't I just go get the popcorn? They're starving!"

"So am I. You can after we've ordered," Briddey said, and looked at the menu. The "really good food" consisted of hot dogs, corn dogs, chili dogs, and a wide array of ice cream treats. Briddey ordered a hot dog and a large hot tea. "In a mug." *Which I can wrap my frozen hands around.*

Maeve ordered a mango raspberry shake with whipped cream and sprinkles, and Briddey wondered again how Mary Clare could be worried about her. She seemed so utterly normal.

"And a hot dog," Maeve told the waiter. "*Now* can I go get the popcorn, Aunt Briddey?"

Briddey nodded and gave her the keys, and she was off like a shot. *Good,* Briddey thought. *While she's gone I can figure out some way to contact C.B.*

Or not. There was no coverage down in his lab, so she couldn't call him there, and she didn't know his home phone number. If he even had one. Or had a home, for that matter. For all she knew, he might simply alternate between the lab, the library, and that kosher deli he'd talked about. Which she didn't know how to find either.

Her phone pinged with a text from Trent. "No luck with nurse.

Found number but she wasn't home. Left message for her to call me. Calling hospital next."

He didn't mention having gotten any messages from her, which might mean he was so busy trying to find Dr. Verrick that he'd forgotten about their connecting. And even when he'd been receiving, he'd only heard fragments, so she might be able to talk to C.B. mentally after all, provided she didn't say his name and did it right now, before Trent found Dr. Verrick.

Her phone pinged again. "Just got mental message from you," his text said. "Heard you say 'Call . . . say his name . . . right now.' Couldn't hear rest."

Thank goodness for that, at least, she thought, and her phone pinged with yet another text: "Also heard something about 'park.' Thought you were going to Carnival Pizza."

Oh, no. She hastily texted him back, "We are. It's jammed. Having terrible time finding place to park. Must have been what you heard," and turned her phone off.

But I can't turn Trent off, she thought, so calling to C.B. was out. She'd just have to hope he was aware of the situation and would get in touch with her—and that Trent wouldn't get any better at hearing her. Or succeed in finding Dr. Verrick. Or her.

The waiter was bringing their order. The mango raspberry shake came in a glass the size of a flower vase.

Maeve'll never get through that, Briddey thought, and turned in her chair to see what was keeping her.

She was trudging back across the grass with her arms full. "I brought the Wheat Chex, too, and the bagels," she said, "in case sparrows don't like popcorn."

"I'm pretty sure they like anything. You can feed them after you eat," Briddey said, but Maeve was already squatting down and holding out a piece of popcorn to a sparrow.

Briddey let her, still trying to think of a way to get in touch with C.B. If he *did* have a home phone, it might be listed in directory assistance. She turned her phone back on to look up the number, and it immediately rang.

Kathleen. "You never called me back," she said.

"I'm sorry," Briddey apologized. "Things got a little crazy."

Maeve looked up from trying to coax the sparrow. "Who is it?"

"Your Aunt Kathleen."

"Oh," she said uninterestedly, and went back to feeding the sparrow.

"Did you decide what you were going to do?" Briddey asked Kathleen.

"No. I don't want to make a fool of myself by saying something if Rich was just being nice. He'll think I'm some kind of lunatic stalker. On the other hand, he might not be saying anything because he saw me with Landis and thinks I like *him*. And that's another thing. I think Landis really likes me, and I'd feel like a jerk falling for somebody else while I was dating him, you know?"

Yes, Briddey thought. *I do.*

"I just wish I knew what he was thinking. It would make it all so much easier. Maybe you were right, and the smart thing to do is get an EED."

No. It's definitely not. But Kathleen was right about one thing: It would help to know what Trent was thinking, or more specifically, exactly how much he could hear of her thoughts. If he was only picking her up periodically, and it was limited to intermittent words and phrases, it would be safe for her to call to C.B. But if not—

"I think I'll look Rich up on the internet and see what I can find out," Kathleen was saying. "Maybe that'll tell me something. I need more information."

So do I, Briddey thought, and after Kathleen hung up and Briddey shut off her phone, she sat there watching Maeve feeding the sparrows, thinking, *I wish C.B. had had time to teach me to audit individual voices.* But he hadn't, and he obviously couldn't do it now with Trent listening. She was going to have to learn how to do it on her own.

Maeve tossed out a handful of popcorn, and the birds converged from all over like tiny vultures to pounce on it. *And that's what'll happen if you open the door of the courtyard,* Briddey thought, her heart quailing at the thought of the voices roaring in like a tsunami.

But she had to know how much Trent could hear. She hurried Maeve through her meal, and when Maeve asked if she could have dessert, said, "It looks like the rain's stopped. How about if we go feed the ducks now and then come back for dessert?"

"Great," Maeve said, and took off for the car again while Briddey paid the bill, asked when the restaurant closed—"We're always open," the waiter said forlornly—and gathered up what was left of the pop-corn, the bagels, and Maeve's forgotten umbrella.

"You can use it," Maeve said when she came back laden with food. "I can't hold it and feed the ducks at the same time."

"Thank you," Briddey said. "Do you mind feeding them on your own? I need to call Trent," and then was sorry. Maeve didn't like Trent.

But Maeve said cheerfully, "Sure. I won't fall in, I promise," and ran down to the edge of the pond.

"Watch out for the geese," Briddey called after her. "They can be mean."

"I *know*," Maeve shouted back disgustedly. "You sound just like Mom."

"Sorry," Briddey said, and sat down on a bench. The bench was very wet, and she was grateful for Maeve's umbrella. Rain dripped in great wet blops from the trees.

It doesn't matter, she told herself. *You're in a sunny courtyard in Santa Fe.* She took out her turned-off phone and put it to her ear so it would look to Maeve like she was talking to someone, and then walked across the courtyard's flagstones to the bench under the cottonwood. She took a long look at the solid blue door, wondering if she might be able to open it after all, just for long enough to distinguish Trent's voice among the thousands of others, but at the mere thought, the voices outside seemed to rise like a huge wave, ready to crash through, and she dived for the door, slamming the bar more securely against its brackets.

I can't do it, she thought, gripping the wet arm of the metal park bench. *I can't.*

She looked enviously down at the lake's edge. Maeve was com-pletely surrounded by ducks, a couple of large geese, and a swan angrily flapping its wings, but she didn't look frightened or even worried. She was happily scattering Wheat Chex.

If she can do it, you should be able to, Briddey thought, but even her shame at having less courage than a nine-year-old couldn't persuade her to lift the latch and open the door.

There had to be some other way to audit the voices, something more controllable. C.B. had said that it was a matter of visualizing, and that it didn't make any difference what you visualized. All right, then, what would stand for sorting through huge numbers of something, looking for a single item?

The card file in the storage closet, with its alphabetically ordered drawers. Maybe she could riffle through the cards like C.B. had done that night, and find Trent's ... but the voices weren't written words; they were sounds. She needed something that would let her hear individual voices and tune out the ones she didn't want.

A radio, she thought, remembering C.B. tuning through the stations on his car radio, looking for a song to screen the voices. *I can visualize the voices as stations and the roar of the voices as the static in between.*

It couldn't be a car radio, though. It had to be something that could fit in the courtyard, like the portable radio C.B. had in his lab.

There's one in the gardener's cupboard, she told herself, opening the weathered doors and hoping she could do this without C.B. here to coach her. What did Aunt Oona have in her potting shed? Gardening tools and packets of seeds and flowerpots.

There was a stack of cobwebbed flowerpots on the top shelf. Briddey reached behind it and pulled out the radio. She blew the dust off the pink plastic, took the radio over to the bench, and sat down, holding it on her lap. She wiped the face of the horizontal dial clear of dust, looked at the red needle and the black lines and numbers—550, 710, 850—and switched the radio on.

The dial lit up and voices rushed out, barking, bawling, screeching. Briddey reared back in fright and nearly dropped the radio onto the flagstones. The sound was earsplitting. She fumbled wildly to turn it off.

The voices stopped instantly. *It's only noise,* Briddey told herself, heart thudding. *You had the volume too high, that's all.* But she wasn't sure she had the courage to turn it on again.

She looked down at the lake. Maeve was still happily feeding the ducks and geese. But for how long?

Briddey took a deep breath and switched the radio on again, turning the volume all the way down first. The voices emerged from the speaker as a faint whisper, like the sound of the ones beyond her perimeter.

They're not voices, they're static, she told herself firmly, and began moving the needle, searching for Trent's voice: *. . . traffic is terrible. I should have taken . . . so cranky . . . must be cutting a new tooth . . . leak in the basement . . . worst hangover ever! I need a beer . . . Jesus, who drank all the Budweiser? . . .*

At this rate it could take forever. She needed to do this scientifically, so she could eliminate frequencies and narrow it down. She turned the knob all the way to the low end of the dial and began inching it slowly up, noting the station numbers as she went and hesitating only long enough to make sure it wasn't Trent before she moved on. At 550: *. . . marble sculpture . . . ;* 575: *. . . sniveling sycophant! I hope he . . . ;* 610: *. . . no business going off without leaving a contact number for his patients . . . ;* 650 . . .

Wait, that was Trent, she thought, belatedly recognizing his voice. *He's talking about Dr. Verrick.* But it was too late, she'd already gone on to the next station. *. . . think I'm coming down with the flu,* a voice was saying.

She dialed back to 610. *I won't. You can't make me,* a child's voice said angrily.

She must have overshot. She inched the knob forward. *. . . scratchy feeling in my throat . . . ,* the person coming down with the flu said. No, that was too far.

He has to be here somewhere, she thought, inching the knob back: *Oh, why do I have to get up? It's Sunday,* and then, faintly, *. . . tell Briddey . . .*

Definitely Trent, but even as she heard her name, it blurred into static, like a station going in and out of range. She moved the knob gingerly back and forth, trying to get a fix on it, but she couldn't find him *or* the flu woman, and she was about to give up when she heard, *. . . my head aches . . . ,* and before she could go a notch back, Trent's voice.

It was faint and static-y, and other voices kept breaking in, but she didn't dare adjust—or even touch—the tuning knob for fear of losing him altogether.

Trent was apparently thinking about the Hermes Project because she caught, *. . . adapting . . . wireless signal . . . Apple won't know what hit . . . what'll I tell . . . ?* and then, perfectly clearly, *Where the hell is Dr. Verrick?* followed by more static, and then, patchily, *. . . can't afford to let . . . if Briddey finds out, she won't . . .* And she lost the station completely.

Twenty-Four

"Grown-ups never understand anything by themselves,
and it is tiresome for children to be always and forever
explaining things to them."
—Antoine de Saint Exupéry, *The Little Prince*

IF I FIND OUT, I WON'T WHAT? BRIDDEY THOUGHT, TRYING TO GET THE station with Trent's voice on it back, but there was only static.

What is he afraid I might find out? she wondered, turning the knob slowly, trying to get him back or at least find a voice she recognized, but they all had that flat, anonymous quality: . . . *never going to that church again . . . why do I always have to let the damned dog out? . . . still raining . . .*

That's why he was so alarmed at the idea that I could hear his thoughts and why he demanded to know exactly what I'd heard, she thought, inching the tuning knob along. *Because he was hiding something.*

. . . *weatherman said . . . need to get gas . . . I'm not standing here all day!* And then a little girl's voice saying weakly, . . . *know he said to . . . but I'm . . .*

That voice had sounded like Maeve. Briddey nudged the dial, trying to bring it in more clearly, and lost it altogether.

This is hopeless, Briddey thought, and Maeve's voice cut in clearly. "Freezing," she said.

That's not on the radio, Briddey thought, and looked up to see Maeve standing in front of her.

"What is it?" Briddey asked, thinking, *And now she's going to ask what I'm doing,* but she didn't.

"I *said,* can we go now?" Maeve pleaded.

"I thought you wanted to feed the ducks."

"I ran out of food. You've been on the phone a really long time." And when Briddey glanced at the time, she was shocked to see it was almost one o'clock. She'd been sitting here for hours.

"And besides," Maeve said, "it's raining again."

It was, as witness Maeve's draggling wet hair and her pinched-with-cold face. *Oh, God, she'll get pneumonia, and Mary Clare will never forgive me,* Briddey thought. She hastily handed Maeve back her umbrella. "We'll get you a nice hot chocolate," she said, hurrying her back to the restaurant, "and that'll warm you up."

"You said I could have dessert later. And this is later, right?"

"Yes," Briddey said because she was mortified she'd kept Maeve out in the cold so long, and Maeve proceeded to order an enormous ice cream sundae.

"Won't that make you cold again?"

"No, because I'll eat it first and *then* drink my hot chocolate. Don't you want anything, Aunt Briddey?"

Yes, Briddey thought. *I want to know why Trent said, If Briddey finds out, she won't . . . , and I can't do that with you here, so I need you to hurry up and eat your sundae so I can take you home,* and amazingly, Maeve did, wolfing down her ice cream and gulping her hot chocolate in record time.

I can tell Mary Clare she's definitely not anorexic, Briddey thought, and remembered the purpose of the outing had been to pump Maeve for information. *I'll do it on the way home,* she thought, hustling Maeve back to the car and turning on the heater full blast.

But she didn't have to. When her phone pinged with a text from Trent saying he'd still had no luck locating Dr. Verrick, Maeve said disgustedly, "I bet I know who that's from. My mom. And I bet she wants to know what you found out."

"About what?" Briddey said, careful to keep her eyes on the road so as not to seem too interested.

"*I* don't know. She's always worrying about me. It's so stupid."

"She just wants to protect you."

"I know, but I'm fine. Or I would be if everybody'd just stop asking me questions."

I know exactly how you feel, Briddey thought. *But that's because I'm keeping secrets.* Was Maeve keeping secrets, too?

She glanced over at her niece, wondering how to approach the subject without making her instantly defensive, and while she was pondering strategies, Maeve dumped it in her lap: "If I tell you something, Aunt Briddey, will you promise not to tell Mom? There's . . . I like this guy—"

"A boy in your class at school?" Briddey asked casually.

"*No,*" Maeve said in a how-could-you-possibly-think-that? tone. "He was in *The Zombie Princess Diaries,* and he's really cute. I want to use his picture as my screensaver, but if I do, I'm afraid Mom will find out—"

"That you've been watching zombie movies. Is he one of the zombies?"

"*No.* Do you want to see his picture?" She pulled out her phone and began busily swiping, and at the next stoplight, held it over for Briddey to see. "His name's Xander."

He had gray eyes and even messier hair than C.B.'s. Maeve was gazing dreamily at his image. "So what do you think I should do?"

"Has he been in any other movies? Maybe you could tell her you saw him in something else."

"You don't get it," Maeve said. "It doesn't matter what he's in. If she finds out I think he's cute, she'll start worrying that I'm starting to like boys, and she'll give me 'the talk' and make me watch sex-ed videos and stuff."

Maeve was right. Knowing Mary Clare, she might even try to get a restraining order against poor, unwitting Xander. But she could hardly tell Maeve that lying was all right—even though she herself had been doing it more or less continuously for the last few days. "You really shouldn't be keeping secrets from your mother," she said.

"But it's not like it's a *bad* secret. And everybody has secrets, right? I mean, *you've* got stuff you don't want anybody to know about."

Here it comes, Briddey thought. *She's going to ask about my stuffing my wet shoes in the drawer.* Or worse, about C.B.'s phoning her and asking her to cover for them last night. "What do you mean?"

"The EED. I saw the bandage when you were drying your hair. You didn't tell Mom or Aunt Oona or Kathleen you had it. But don't worry. I won't tell anybody. If you promise not to tell Mom about Xander."

A spy and *a blackmailer,* Briddey thought. *It isn't your daughter you should be worried about, Mary Clare, it's the rest of the populace.* And she shouldn't let her get away with it, but she didn't have time to deal with this right now, so she settled for saying sternly as she let Maeve out in front of her house, "I'll keep your secret for now because I have to be somewhere, but we are *not* done talking."

"I know," Maeve said, her eyes dancing with merriment.

"What's so funny?"

Maeve sobered instantly. "Nothing. I was thinking about this funny thing Danika said the other day."

Which was obviously a lie, but Briddey didn't have time to deal with that either, so she said goodbye, watched to see that Maeve got into the house safely, and left to find someplace where she could try to get Trent on the radio again.

A library would be ideal—the screening voices of people reading would cut a lot of the static out and make him easier to find—but this was Sunday. The public libraries were closed, and the university library where she and C.B. had been last night was clear on the other side of town. He'd said Starbucks was a good place, but Kathleen might be there with her pair of suitors, so Briddey drove to the nearest Peaberry's, ordered a latte, and sat down next to a middle-aged woman reading *How Do You Tell If It's Truly Love?* Not exactly *David Copperfield,* but all the other customers were staring at their phones or watching cat videos on their laptops.

Briddey went into her courtyard, switched on the radio, put the needle on 650, and began nudging it back in tiny increments, afraid she'd miss Trent if she went too fast, even if it meant she had to go through scores of voices.

It took forever. In spite of her care, she overshot twice to the woman with the flu and had to start all over again, and by three o'clock she'd gone through two lattes and hundreds of stations and was beginning to think she'd never find him. . . . *why does it always have to rain on the weekend? . . . worst job I've ever . . .* , and faintly, . . . *never thought it existed . . .*

Trent. She leaned forward to catch his words. . . . *always thought . . . fake . . . can't believe . . . actually real . . .*

She adjusted the tuning knob a micrometer.

. . . *sound insane . . . when I called Hamilton this morning . . .*

Which was why C.B. and I were able to beat him to my apartment, Briddey thought. But he'd just found out he was telepathic. Why had his first reaction been to call his boss?

. . . *Dr. Ver . . .* , Trent said. . . . *need . . . get him back here now . . . think they'd have some way to reach . . . if it were an emergency? . . . try . . .* Then nothing but static. She was losing the station.

She turned the dial back a smidgen, and Trent's voice suddenly came through crystal clear. But he was talking about Apple and Commspan's new phone. . . . *will need to analyze the circuitry,* she heard him say, and . . . *write code . . .*

No, tell me what you don't want me to find out, she thought, and remembered C.B.'s telling her that people mistakenly thought telepathy meant being able to listen to the people and thoughts you wanted to hear. He was right. She could sit here and listen to Trent all afternoon and never hear what it was.

Or how to tell if it's truly love, she thought, and heard Trent say, *How am I going to tell her? . . . have to find a way to convince . . .* She strained to hear the end of that, but couldn't pick it up. . . . *revolutionary . . . can't wait . . . Apple might come up with . . .*

No, forget Apple. Tell me what you're afraid I'll find out. And why you called Hamilton.

. . . *thought I could just have the tests and get the data, and she'd never have to know about it . . .*

What?

. . . *thinks we had it done to make us communicate better . . . but that was when it was just emotions . . . now that it's telepathy . . . have to tell her . . . but when she finds out I needed us to have the EED so we . . . phone . . . she'll be furious . . .*

You've got that right, Briddey thought. He'd asked her to have the EED so he could get data to use with the new phone?

Of course he had. Hamilton had said, "Instantaneous communication is no longer enough. We need to be able to offer something more." And that "something more" was emotionally enhanced communication. What had they planned to do? Design an app that identified a person's emotions and added them to their texts as emojis?

Whatever it had been, Trent had been only too happy to volunteer as a guinea pig. *And to volunteer me, too. Because it takes two people to have an EED. You snake!*

He'd never loved her, in spite of all those flowers he'd sent her, all those dinners at Luminesce and emails and endearments. All he'd cared about was talking her into having the EED with him so he could get data for designing an emotionally enhanced phone.

That's why he was so frantic when we didn't connect right away, she thought, *and so upset when Dr. Verrick wanted to keep me in the hospital and run more tests.* He hadn't been worried about her. He'd just been afraid something had gone wrong with his plan. And that was why he'd insisted on her seeing Dr. Verrick, even though he was out of the country and it was the middle of the night. Trent had promised his boss results, and she wasn't delivering. She thought of Traci Hamilton saying, "I know it's all very hush-hush and we're not supposed to talk about it," and, "We should be thanking you, what with everything you're doing—"

Trent was still talking. *. . . figure out something . . . get engaged if I have to . . .*

I don't want to hear any more, Briddey thought, and reached for the tuning knob.

. . . sure I can convince her how crucial . . . once she's on board . . . can focus on finding out how the telepathy works . . . translating the circuitry into software.

Oh, my God. He wasn't talking about emojis. He was going to try to turn the telepathy into code and put it into the new phone! I've got to tell C.B., she thought, standing up so abruptly she knocked her latte over. The woman reading the *How to Tell If It's Truly Love* book looked up, annoyed.

"Sorry," Briddey said. She mopped it up, grabbed her phone, dumped the sodden napkins and her latte cup in the trash, and ran out to her car, trying to think of how to get in touch with C.B. She couldn't speak to him telepathically with Trent listening in, and after the night he'd had, he might be asleep, in which case calling to him wouldn't do any good. And with Trent at Commspan, she couldn't risk going to see him. She'd have to phone him. But she couldn't use her own phone, for fear of leaving a trail to C.B. She had to find another phone she could use.

Whose? Not Charla's. Now more than ever, it was critical that no one at Commspan know of a connection between them. And Kathleen would ask too many questions.

Maeve, she thought, and drove back to Mary Clare's. She could take Maeve aside, tell her she'd lost her phone, and ask her if she remembered her having it in the car after they left the park. And when Maeve said no, she'd ask her if she could borrow her phone to make a couple of calls and then try the lab, or use Maeve's phone to look up his home number.

If she could get past Mary Clare, who took one look at her and said, "Oh, my God, you found out something when you took Maeve to brunch! Something so bad you couldn't tell me over the phone!"

True, Briddey thought. *Or in person either.*

"Maeve's in some kind of trouble. I *knew* it!"

"She's not in any trouble. I just can't find my phone, and I thought Maeve might remember what I did with it."

"Oh," Mary Clare said. "She's over at Danika's doing homework. I'll phone her and ask her, and then we can sit down and have a nice cup of tea."

And you can pump me about Maeve, Briddey thought, but Mary Clare had barely gotten her phone out when Maeve burst in, shouting, "I forgot my math book." She was red-cheeked and out of breath. "I ran the whole way," she said, taking in the kettle on the stove and the teacups in her mother's hand.

She's going to think I came back to rat her out, and there's no way she'll help me, Briddey thought, but Maeve said cheerfully, "Hi, Aunt Briddey. What are you doing here?"

"She's lost her phone," Mary Clare said. "Do you remember seeing it at the restaurant?"

Of course she does, Briddey thought, *and now she's going to say, "She talked on it the whole time I was feeding the ducks," and Mary Clare will launch into the dangers of avian flu.*

"I can't remember," Maeve said, furrowing her brow in concentration. "I think so. You put it on the table, and then the waiter came and brought our pizza." She turned to her mother. "We went to Carnival Pizza at the mall, and it was so fun!" She turned back to Briddey. "I bet he laid the pizza pan on top of it, and that's why we didn't see it."

"I bet you're right," Briddey said, and since there was no hope now of getting access to Maeve's phone, she stood up and put on her coat. "I'd better go see if they've got it."

"Can't you just call and find out and then ask them to hold it for you?" Maeve said. "You can use my phone. It's in my room. Come on." She grabbed Briddey's hand and dragged her off.

Bless you, childeen, Briddey thought as she followed Maeve into her room, which now had crime-scene tape across the door in addition to the sign saying, KEEP OUT—THIS MEANS YOU, MOM.

Maeve took down the tape, ushered Briddey in, put the tape back up, shut the door, and locked it. "So Mom can't come in," she said unnecessarily.

Briddey looked around at her room. A large poster of *Tangled* was pinned to the wall above her bed next to several photos of male teen stars, which had apparently been cut out from *Tiger Beat* magazine, though Briddey didn't see any of the messy-haired Xander. There was a stuffed Olaf the Snowman from *Frozen* on her pillow, and a screensaver of *The Twelve Dancing Princesses* on her computer. Not exactly the meth lab or international money-laundering operation Mary Clare was imagining.

"You really should let your mother in here," Briddey said. "She'd feel a lot better."

"No, she wouldn't," Maeve said, sitting on her bed and picking up Olaf. "The squelched-girl thing, remember? Plus, I don't want her to fix the nanny cam." She pointed to it, and Briddey remembered Mary Clare saying Maeve had disabled it. "Or my computer."

"What's on your computer?"

"*Nothing,* but she'd just say I must've deleted it, you know?" Which was true.

Maeve pulled her smartphone out of her pocket and handed it to Briddey. "You didn't really lose your phone, did you?"

"No. I said that because I need to call somebody, and I can't use my own phone."

Maeve nodded wisely. "Like in *Zombienado*. The zombies bugged the hero's phone—"

That sounds highly unlikely, Briddey thought.

"—and he had to use this dead guy's, only it was still stuck to his hand because the zombies had eaten everything except his arm—"

"As soon as you two are done in there," Mary Clare called through the door, "come to the kitchen. I'm making a nice loaf of Irish soda bread."

"Okay," Maeve shouted, and turned back to Briddey. "You're not going to tell Mom I saw *Zombienado,* are you?"

I'm not exactly in a position to, am I? Briddey thought. "No," she said, reaching for the phone.

Maeve yanked it away. "You have to tell me who you're going to call first, because if you're committing a crime or something, I'd be an accessory, like in *Zombie Cop*. This zombie—"

"I'm not committing a crime."

"How do I know that if you don't tell me who it is?"

"Fine. It's somebody I work with at Commspan, C.B. Schwartz. I need to get him a message—"

"C.B.?" Maeve said, frowning. "But if it's him you need to get a message to, you don't—" She stopped short.

"I don't what?"

"Have to look up his number. I've got it on my phone. Which one do you want, the lab or at home? I've got both. He gave them to me that time he helped me with my science project in case I needed to ask him anything else. Hang on. I'll find them."

She turned her back to Briddey and hunched over her phone, clearly not wanting Briddey to see what she was doing, though it didn't look like she was doing anything. She was just standing there staring at the phone as if it were a crystal ball. Briddey wondered if she'd forgotten her password.

After a long minute, she began alternately swiping through screens and typing busily, which meant the numbers must not be on her list of contacts. *She's probably hidden it from her mother,* Briddey thought, not blaming her.

Or else she didn't really have the numbers and was trying to look them up. Briddey was about to say something when Maeve put the phone up to her ear and said, "It's ringing."

Briddey reached for the phone, but Maeve shook her head. "Hi, C.B. This is Maeve. Remember? You helped me with my science project?"

"Maeve," Briddey whispered, motioning to her to hand her the phone.

"I'm fine," Maeve said. "No, none at all."

"Give me the phone," Briddey said, reaching for it.

"Okay," Maeve mouthed, and said into the phone, "My Aunt Briddey wants to talk to you." She handed the phone over.

"C.B.? This is Briddey Flannigan. From work. I'm calling about a matter I need to discuss with you," she said, trying to sound impersonal and businesslike with Maeve listening—and possibly Trent. And she must have succeeded because Maeve sat down at her computer, put in earbuds, and began playing Cinderella's Castle Adventure.

"I assume that Maeve's still in the room?" C.B. said.

"Yes, and I don't have a solution for that problem."

"You're right about that," C.B. said, amusement in his voice.

"This isn't funny—"

"Sorry. What is it you phoned about?"

She lowered her voice to a whisper. "Trent is—"

"Yeah, I know," he said, and she could tell from his tone that he did know, and not just what Trent had said this afternoon but all of it— why he'd suggested the EED and what he was planning to do with the results.

He's known all along, Briddey thought. *That's why he kept trying to talk me out of having the EED. And out of telling Trent after we connected. Because he knew what Trent would do with the telepathy if he got hold of it.*

Why didn't you tell me? she said, but she already knew the answer. She wouldn't have believed him. *You must think I'm a complete idiot.*

"No, I think Trent is, for not appreciating what he had. And I'm so sorry you—"

"It doesn't matter. What matters is that he's trying to get in touch with"—Briddey glanced anxiously over at Maeve, but she was completely engrossed in her videogame—"in touch with Dr. Verrick," she whispered, "to tell him about the . . . project. And if he runs tests or scans—"

"He won't run tests if he doesn't believe Trent, and it's not like Trent has anything tangible to show him."

"Yes, he does. This morning, he—"

"I know. Don't worry about those tests he had you take. You did great, by the way. I especially liked the whole Angkor Wat petunias thing. But even if you'd written down what you actually sent him, it still wouldn't prove anything. Look, we shouldn't be talking about this right now."

"Because of—" She glanced over at Maeve, who was busily chasing Cinderella's mice.

"Little Miss Curiosity? No, because of your boyfriend."

"He's *not* my—"

"Well, we can't let him know that. It's imperative that he not find out you're onto him. Right now he's only able to hear you sporadically, but you were only able to hear *him* sporadically, and look what you found out. So you can't think about *any* of this—about me or the telepathy or what a low-down, rotten, dirty piece of pond scum he is. You've got to think things he can hear—you're madly in love with him and you're thrilled to be connected and you can't wait to see Dr. Verrick and tell him what's happened."

"But—"

"I know. We need to come up with a plan of action. And we will. But not till we can be sure he can't hear us."

Did that mean she shouldn't have called him? That they weren't safe talking?

"No, we're fine. Trent's on the phone with Verrick's nurse right now, trying to get her to divulge his whereabouts, and talking out loud like this helps screen your thoughts. And anyway, I've got defenses up. But I don't want to take any chances. So I want you to go home and read a nice, boring book. *The Decline and Fall of the Roman Empire.* You can tell me how it turns out."

But what if Trent decided to come over again? "I'm at my sister's right now, and I'm sure they'd let me stay for supper." Or she could go to the Daughters of Ireland meeting with Aunt Oona. They were bound to be having one, and Trent would *never* think of looking for her there.

"*No,*" C.B. said. "The last thing we want to give Trent is any hint of the Irish connection, including overhearing your family talking about 'foine Irish lads.'"

Or bad boyfriends, Briddey said, thinking of Kathleen.

"You don't have to worry about Trent coming over to your apartment. He's too busy trying to reach Verrick. And if he should decide to head your way, I'll give you a heads-up so you can get out of there. Go read. Or better yet, take a nap. If you're asleep, Trent won't be able to pick up anything at all."

"But if I"—she glanced over at Maeve, who was still seemingly engrossed in her videogame—"do what you say, how will you get in touch with—?"

"Don't worry about that. And don't worry about Trent or Dr. Verrick. It'll be fine. Get some sleep," he said, and hung up.

"You'll email me the report, then?" Briddey said into the dead phone. "Good. I'll contact you when I've gone over the figures. Goodbye." She gave Maeve her phone back, expecting a barrage of questions, but Maeve scarcely looked up from her game, even when Briddey stood there a minute, memorizing his phone number in case she needed to call him again. "Thank you," she told Maeve.

"What are you two doing in there?" Mary Clare called anxiously through the door.

"*Nothing!*" Maeve shouted back, and rolled her eyes at Briddey. "Jeez, Mom."

"Well, come have some tea, then," Mary Clare said. "Aunt Oona's here."

Of course she is, Briddey thought, *and now how am I going to get out of here? Aunt Oona will insist on going over all the reasons I shouldn't get an EED and then try to convince me to talk Kathleen into going out with Sean O'Reilly.*

"I need to go," Briddey said, without much hope of getting away. "The restaurant had my phone, and I need to go get it before they close."

"Oh, surely you can stay a few minutes," Mary Clare began.

"No, she can't," Maeve said. "Carnival Pizza closes at five."

"Aunt Oona, convince her there's no reason she has to leave this second," Mary Clare said, and Briddey braced herself for the onslaught, but Aunt Oona said, "You don't want to get there after they've closed. It's hurryin' off you'd better be. Maeve, fetch your aunt's coat, won't you?"

Maeve hurried to get it, and Briddey, still shocked that Aunt Oona hadn't tried to force her to stay, put it on.

"Go on, then," Aunt Oona said, "and may Saint Patrick and all the holy saints of Ireland protect you on your journey."

"Thank you," Briddey said, and gave Aunt Oona a grateful kiss on the cheek. She hugged Maeve, whispered, "*Thank* you" to her, told Mary Clare, No, she didn't have time to wait for her to wrap up some soda bread to take with her, and was out the door before Mary Clare could hunt up the aluminum foil.

She would have made a clean getaway if Kathleen hadn't pulled up and blocked her car, giving Mary Clare time to catch up to her and ask her what she and Maeve had been doing in Maeve's room all that time.

"She wanted to show me something on her computer after I made my call," Briddey said. "And no, Mary Clare, not porn. It was a You-Tube video about kittens."

"She didn't have any YouTube videos on her browsing history when I checked it this morning. It was completely empty."

I just got an image of a cat from you, Trent said suddenly. *Are you still at the mall?*

"I've been trying to call you, Briddey," Kathleen said, coming over. "I have to tell you what I found out about Rich—"

Are you there, Briddey? Trent said. *If you can hear me, turn your phone on.*

I couldn't even if I wanted to. It's supposed to be at Carnival Pizza, Briddey thought, and tried to go into her courtyard, but Kathleen was saying, "I looked him up like I told you, and you'll never guess what I found out—"

"You need to move your car first," Briddey said, and Kathleen trotted off obligingly to do it. *Now if I could only get rid of Trent and Mary Clare as easily.*

I can't hear you, Trent said.

"Why wouldn't there be anything on her browsing history?" Mary Clare asked. "It doesn't show her being online at all."

"A few days ago, you were complaining that she spent too much time online," Briddey said.

"I know, but she obviously has been on. And why would she delete a kitten video?"

"I don't have time to talk about this now," Briddey said.

"You can't leave yet," Kathleen said, returning. "I have to tell you about Rich first. And Landis. Remember how I told you he was a hedge fund manager? Well, he isn't. He works for a hedge-trimming company, the big liar—"

This is exactly the kind of conversation C.B. said you shouldn't have, Briddey thought. *If Trent hears your thoughts—*

What did you say? Trent said. *I heard you say "thoughts" and then lost you.*

"And that's nothing compared to what I found out about Rich," Kathleen said. "He's an even bigger liar than Landis."

"Why don't you call me later? I really need to go," Briddey said desperately, and tried to get into her car, but Mary Clare was blocking the door.

I've been trying to call you all afternoon, Trent said.

"There's been nothing on Maeve's browsing history for the last two weeks," Mary Clare said.

"Rich is *engaged!*" Kathleen said. "And he seemed so nice!"

"What's Maeve hiding?" Mary Clare demanded.

This is as bad as Zombienado, Briddey thought.

You need to concentrate, Trent said.

No, what I need is to get out of here.

"Mom! Telephone!" Maeve called from the house.

"Who is it?" Mary Clare said, stepping away from the car, and Briddey was in it—and into her safe room—like a shot.

"Call me," she said, shutting the door and starting the car. "Both of you."

"But I thought you lost your phone—"

Exactly, Briddey thought, *and I intend for it to stay lost.* "Which is why I've got to go," she said. "To get it. 'Bye."

She drove off, blessing Maeve for coming to her rescue again. As soon as she was out of sight, she pulled over to enter C.B.'s number into her phone before she forgot it, and then decided she'd better not, scrawled it on the torn-off lid of the empty Wheat Chex box, and stuck it in her pocket.

I need to tell her to delete his number from her phone, she thought, driving on, although it probably wasn't necessary. She was obviously already hiding the movies she watched and the books she read—and the computer sites she visited—from her mother, and that was why she'd turned her back when she was looking up the number, because she didn't want Briddey to see how she'd encrypted it.

But Maeve hadn't been typing during that interval. She'd just been standing there motionless, as if she were . . .

That's impossible, Briddey thought. But what if Maeve's computer log was empty not because she'd deleted the files but because she hadn't been on her computer at all? Or reading? What if she'd been using the books and the movies as a cover for what she was really doing?

She got in trouble at school for not paying attention, Briddey remembered suddenly, *and when Mary Clare asked her why, she said, "I was thinking about something else."*

You're being ridiculous, Briddey told herself. *She was probably only thinking about Xander.* But his picture hadn't been anywhere on the walls of her bedroom, and Maeve had volunteered the information about her crush on him right after Briddey had wondered if she was keeping secrets. *And I wondered it to myself, not aloud.*

And Maeve had wanted to go to the park instead of the crowded mall. And had shown up immediately after Briddey'd arrived at the house—out of breath, as if she'd run all the way home from Danika's. And shown up on Briddey's doorstep just in time to save her from Trent.

But she can't be. She's only nine. She remembered C.B.'s saying what a precocious kid she was—and Mary Clare's conviction that Maeve was keeping something from her.

What if she is? Briddey wondered, thinking of Maeve standing there looking defensive when Briddey'd asked her about the marshmallows in Lucky Charms. Why? Because she was who C.B. had gotten the list of marshmallow shapes from? He'd said he'd looked them up on a library computer, but the offices had been locked. *He didn't text her to tell her to cover for us,* she thought. *He didn't have to.*

An angry honk behind her jerked Briddey back to the present. She was sitting at a light that had been green for who knew how long. She drove through the intersection and down the block, parked, and then went back into her courtyard so Trent couldn't hear her. And C.B. couldn't either.

C.B., who'd said, "Listen, Briddey, about Maeve, there's something I—" and who'd been certain something bad would happen to Briddey if she had the EED done. And who'd been utterly convinced that telepathy was inherited, but who'd instantly dismissed Aunt Oona's "Sight" as bogus—because he hadn't wanted Briddey thinking about the possibility that someone else in her family might be telepathic.

C.B., who'd gone periodically silent, as if he were listening to someone else, and had been off somewhere when the voices attacked her at the theater and in the storage closet. Who'd said, "I'm so sorry. I was—" and then bitten off his words mid-sentence.

Like Maeve had when Briddey had told her she needed to contact C.B. "Oh, if it's him you need to get a message to, you don't—" she'd said, and stopped without finishing her sentence.

"You don't have to call because I can ask him myself," Briddey said, finishing it for her. She had to talk to Maeve. She started the car and headed back to Mary Clare's.

You don't have to do that, Maeve said. *We can talk anyplace.*

Twenty-Five

"Then look for me by moonlight."
—ALFRED NOYES, "The Highwayman"

THAT'S THE GREAT THING ABOUT TELEPATHY, MAEVE SAID. YOU CAN TALK *to people anywhere. And any time.*

Not while they're driving in traffic, Briddey said.

You can so, Maeve said. *I'm talking to you and doing my math homework.*

That is not *the same thing,* Briddey said. *Don't talk to me till I've had a chance to pull over.* And to think what to do. C.B. had told Briddey not to talk to him telepathically when Trent might be listening in, and she obviously had no business talking to Maeve either.

It's okay, Maeve said. *Trent can't hear us. I know because I'm listening to him. He's wondering why he can't hear you. He thinks you're not trying hard enough. What a creep!*

I agree, Briddey thought, turning off Linden onto a side street, *but just because he can't hear me right now doesn't mean he won't be able to a second from now.*

Yes, it does, Maeve said confidently, *because—*

Shh, Briddey said firmly, pulling over to the curb and parking. She turned the ignition off, went into her courtyard, and said, *C.B. says I'm not supposed to be talking about you-know-what—*

C.B. can't hear us either. He's busy listening to Trent, and now Trent's busy yelling at somebody about why can't they find Dr. Verrick, so it's okay. And I have to talk to you. It's important!

I don't care. If you want to talk, you need to call me on the phone.

I can't call you. I'm over at Danika's, and her mom's almost as bad as Mom. That's why I have to talk to you right now, to tell you you have to promise not *to tell Mom about this!*

Maeve— Briddey began, wishing fervently there was a way to hang up on her. In another minute Maeve would say the word "telepathy," and Trent—

No, I told you, he can't hear us. This is a secure channel. My zombie gates are shut. He can't get in. I've got the moat up and everything.

A moat and zombie gates? What on earth did Maeve's safe room look like?

The moat and zombie gates aren't in my safe room, Maeve said, as if that were obvious. *They're in my castle, and that's in my secret garden, which nobody can get into without the key. I've got the key on a chain around my neck. And inside the castle is Rapunzel's tower, and inside* that *is my safe room, but we don't need to go in there. We're safe here. And anyway, Trent can't hear hardly anything, even when he's trying to.*

Which was good news, but—

So do you promise not to tell Mom? You have to. If she finds out I can do it, she'll figure out a way to do it, too. I bet she'd even get an EED just so she could listen to me all the time.

She won't have to, Briddey thought. *If Trent manages to do what he's planning, Mary Clare will be able to do it on her phone.* And she would jump at the chance to know exactly what Maeve was thinking—and all the moats and zombie gates and towers in the world wouldn't be enough to keep her out. Maeve was right. She wouldn't have any privacy at all.

I know, Maeve said. *Parents would be even worse than zombies. That's why we have to keep it a secret from everybody.*

Zombies? Briddey'd assumed from what C.B. had said that the voices always took the form of a flood.

A flood? Maeve said. *That doesn't sound very scary. Mine are zombies. The really fast, really scary kind, like in* World War Z.

Where did you see World War Z? Briddey started to ask, but the answer was obvious. Maybe it *would* be a good idea for Mary Clare to be able to read her mind.

No, it wouldn't! Maeve said. *I'm fine. C.B. rescued me from the zombies and taught me how to build my castle and my safe room and stuff. They won't get in again.*

She sounded utterly confident. The voices didn't seem to have traumatized her at all. Or if they had, she'd recovered. *How long has . . . you-know-what . . . been going on?* Briddey asked her.

About a month. I thought maybe it was premonitions, like Aunt Oona has, but she could tell stuff that hadn't happened yet and I couldn't, it was just voices, so I looked up a bunch of stuff online—

Which explains why she changed her computer password and deleted her browsing history, Briddey thought. *She didn't want Mary Clare to see what she'd been looking up.*

Yeah, Mom would have totally freaked, Maeve said, *and I couldn't ask Aunt Oona 'cause she'd tell Mom, and I couldn't find anything online except about crazy people, and I didn't know what to do. But then C.B. started talking to me, and telling me what was going to happen, how scary the voices were going to be and what to do to keep them out and stuff, and when they got really bad he rescued me.*

Like he rescued me, Briddey thought, and was infinitely grateful he'd been there for Maeve, too.

He promised he wouldn't tell Mom, and you have to promise, too. Please! Hang on . . . oops, Trent's thinking about calling you. 'Bye, she said, and was gone.

Calling me or calling to me? Briddey wondered, and a moment later got her answer.

Briddey? she heard Trent call. *Can you hear me?*

Yes, she thought. *Unfortunately.*

I'm not getting anything from you. If you can hear what I'm saying, call me on your phone.

Not a chance, Briddey thought, starting her car and pulling away from the curb. She drove back to Linden and toward home.

I'm going to send you a series of images like I did this morning, he told her. *If you can hear any of them, write them down.* And for the next fifteen blocks, she had to listen to him droning, *I'm thinking of a Porsche Cay-*

man GT4—repeat, Porsche Cayman GT4, followed by a smartwatch, a smart bracelet, Bali, a cucumber serrano martini, and an IPO.

When she was six blocks from her apartment, Trent said, *Forbes Magazine. Repeat, Forbes—* and cut off, which hopefully meant he'd given up, and not that he'd reached Dr. Verrick. Or that he was on his way to her apartment.

No, Maeve said. *He's at Commspan. He can't leave in case Dr. Verrick calls his office instead of his smartphone.*

Good, Briddey thought. *I thought I told you to only talk to me on the phone, Maeve.*

I can't. I'm still at Danika's. I was just trying to help, she said, sounding wounded, and went away.

Briddey reached her building, started to park in front of it, and then thought better of it and parked around the corner so Trent wouldn't see her car if he found Dr. Verrick and decided to come see her. But if C.B. came over, he might think she wasn't there—

No, he won't, Maeve said. *He can read your mind, remember?*

Maeve! I thought I told you—

And anyway, he's way smarter than Trent. He's really nice, too, isn't he?

Yes. She got out of the car. *Now go. I mean it, Maeve!* she said, slamming the car door for emphasis.

Do you like him?

Maeve . . .

You don't still like Trent, do you? Maeve asked. *He's a creep. All he cares about is his stupid job, not you. Not like C.B. He really likes you, but you can't let him know I told you that. He said I wasn't supposed to tell you.*

Maeve, go away, or I'm calling your mother and telling her everything you just told me.

Maeve seemed to have gone away. But for how long? Briddey wondered, going up to her apartment. And what might she say about C.B. or telepathy next time?

Her phone rang. Trent. "Do you have C.B.'s home number?" he asked.

Oh, my God, he heard me thinking about C.B. "C.B.?" she repeated, as if she couldn't quite place the name.

"Yes, you know. *C.B.,*" Trent said impatiently. "The guy who called me this morning. The crazy one who works down in the icebox and came up with the TalkPlus app."

"Oh, C.B. Schwartz. No. Why?"

"I still haven't been able to get in touch with Dr. Verrick. Wherever he is, he's got his phone turned off, and I thought maybe C.B. could rig up some way of getting through, an emergency override or something, but I can't get through to *him* either, and he's not down in his lab. You don't know any way to contact him, do you?"

"No," she said. "I'm sure Dr. Verrick will be in tomorrow morning, and if he isn't, one of his office staff will surely know how to reach him."

"We can't wait that long. I don't think you realize just what this whole thing is going to mean to us, sweetheart."

Sweetheart, she thought disgustedly and then frowned. If Trent didn't care anything about her—and it was painfully obvious he didn't—then why had he thought the EED would work? As far as he knew, only couples who were emotionally bonded could connect. So why had he had it done with her? Had he thought he could fool it the way he'd fooled her?

"Did you get any of the words I sent you?" he asked.

"Words?"

"Yes. I sent you another list of words. You mean you didn't get *any* of them? I've been getting lots of words from you."

"You have?" she said, her heart beginning to thud. "What were they?"

"I heard you say 'ice cream' and 'duck,' which I assume were both from the restaurant menu, and then something about a snake. And zombies."

"Zombies? Why on earth would I be talking about zombies? Or snakes? You must have heard me wrong."

"Well, at least I'm hearing you. You need to stop messing with your niece and concentrate on listening," Trent said. "You don't have any idea where Schwartz hangs out when he's not at work, do you?"

Yes, she thought. *Ladies' rooms, libraries, storage closets.* "No."

"Damn," Trent said. "Listen, I've got to go. My secretary's calling me. I hope that means she's found C.B.'s home number. Concentrate on connecting," he said, and hung up.

I need to warn C.B. that Trent's looking for him, she thought, but there was no telling what Trent might hear if she did, and all he had to hear was C.B.'s name. She was just going to have to wait till Trent was asleep and C.B. contacted her, and hope Trent couldn't find him in the meantime.

And do what till then? C.B. had told her to get some sleep, which was a good idea. If she were sleeping, Trent wouldn't be able to hear anything. But she was afraid her mind might wander as she dozed off, and she'd start thinking about him—or Maeve. Like she was doing now.

You need to think about something else, she told herself, and downloaded "Ode to Billie Joe."

Bad idea. C.B. was just like the girl in the song—forced to keep secrets, unable to share what was happening to him with anyone, not even his family. And as she pored over the lyrics, she found herself thinking about what he'd said about Billie Joe jumping off the bridge to get away from the voices, and wondered if that had really been why, or if Billie Joe had done it to protect somebody else, like C.B. had been protecting Maeve? It was obvious now why he'd said it wasn't his secret he was worried about—

Stop it, she told herself. *Trent'll hear you.* She switched to "Teen Angel," wondering why lovers always came to such bad ends in songs. And in poems. In "The Highwayman" the king's soldiers had tied up Bess, the landlord's daughter, with a booby-trapped musket pointed at her heart, and she'd had to shoot herself to warn the highwayman. If they'd been telepathic, Bess wouldn't have had to sacrifice herself to warn him, and the girl in "Ode to Billie Joe" would have known he was going to jump and come to stop him.

And both songs would have been a lot shorter, Briddey thought. But she didn't need short. She needed something long that wouldn't make her think about C.B. or telepathy. Which let out *The Hunchback of Notre Dame.* And *Far from the Madding Crowd.* She downloaded *The Secret Garden* and settled herself into a corner of the couch to read it.

Mistake. Mary Lennox's uncle heard a "far clear voice" calling to him, talked about thoughts being "as powerful as electric batteries," and wondered if he was "losing his reason and thinking he heard things which were not for human ears." *No wonder Maeve was so wrapped up in it,* Briddey thought, and went back to memorizing song lyrics.

At midnight Trent called again. "Did you find C.B. Schwartz?" she asked him.

"No, but I found Dr. Verrick. Or at least I found out what city he's in. It turns out he wasn't in Morocco. He's in Hong Kong."

Which meant it would take him a couple of days to get back here. She was so relieved that she dozed off almost immediately after the call and didn't wake up till the phone rang again. She groped for it, knocking her tablet off the couch in the process, and heard C.B. say, *Dawn Patrol to Night Fighter, come in, Night Fighter.*

Shh, she ordered him. *Trent might hear you. I think he's calling me on the phone right now.*

No, he isn't, C.B. said. *I am. Or I was,* and the ringing promptly stopped. *And don't worry, Trent can't hear us. He's asleep.*

He was looking for you, she said.

I know. He didn't find me.

Good, she said drowsily. *What time is it?*

A little before three.

In the morning?

Afraid so. I kept hoping Trent would give up and go to sleep, but he was still talking to IT till half an hour ago, trying to locate Dr. Verrick.

He's in Hong Kong.

I know. IT's calling hotels, so it's just a matter of time till they find him, and when they do, they'll call Trent, which'll wake him up. So we need to take advantage of the time we've got.

Of course. *I'm sorry,* she said, sitting up. *I'm awake now.*

It'll be better if we talk out loud in case Trent happens to wake up. So if you'll get dressed—

I'm already dressed, she said, slipping on her shoes. *Where do you want me to meet you?*

Downstairs.

You mean you're here? Do you want to come up?

No. You come down. I've got something I want to show you.

I'll be right there, she said, pulling on her sweater. She debated getting her coat, too, but she wouldn't need it for the short dash to C.B.'s car. She grabbed her keys, turned off the lights, and ran silently downstairs and outside into the dark.

She couldn't see C.B.'s car anywhere. She walked out to the sidewalk and looked up the street in both directions, wondering if Trent had woken up and C.B. had decided it wasn't safe to meet after all.

"Nope, he's still asleep," C.B. said, stepping out of the shadows. "And Hong Kong has a *lot* of hotels, so I figure we're good for at least an hour or two. Come on."

They set off up the dark street. "Listen," he said as they walked. "About Trent and the telepathy-phone thing. I'm really sorry. I should have told you about it before, but I didn't want—"

"—me to fly off the handle again and accuse you of trying to keep us apart, like I did when you tried to warn me about the telepathy?"

"No, that isn't—"

"It's okay. I don't blame you. I probably wouldn't have believed you if I hadn't heard it from his own mouth—I mean, mind."

"It was still a lousy way to find out." He stopped and turned to face her. "Are you okay?"

"I thought you could read my mind."

"I can."

"Then you know I'm furious that he lied to me—and used me. And furious with myself for not seeing through him. But there's something I don't understand. Why did he think the EED would work?"

"You don't actually need to be emotionally bonded to—"

"*I* know that, and *you* know that, but Trent didn't. He thought you had to be, and he knew he wasn't—"

"I'm not so sure about that," C.B. said. "From what I've picked up of his thoughts, he thinks he is."

"He wouldn't know love if it smacked him in the face."

"True, but he'd hardly be the first person to mistake the trappings of romance for love."

Like me, you mean, Briddey thought.

"Plus, he needed the EED to work for his phone, and he needed to be 'emotionally committed' for the EED to work, so he had every reason to convince himself he was. I told you, people are masters of self-deception."

"You're right, you did," she said, and realized all that talk about people not knowing what they felt and thinking Hitler was a nice guy hadn't just been to talk her out of having the EED. He'd been trying to warn her about Trent, and she'd been too stupid to understand. And too stupid to see through Trent and his camellias and combed hair and candlelit dinners.

"Don't beat yourself up," C.B. said. "Joan of Arc believed in the Dauphin, who was a lying, spineless, traitorous little creep, too. But how was she supposed to have known? And saving France was a good idea," he said, looking down at her. "She just put her faith in the wrong person," and she was suddenly aware of how close C.B. was standing and how dark it was.

Time to change the subject, she thought, and said, "I still don't understand how he could connect with me without being Irish. I know you said there was a servant girl in his family tree—"

"Or more than one, plus a couple of stableboys."

"But isn't it more likely that your theory about genes causing telepathy is wrong?"

"No."

She waited for him to elaborate, but he didn't. He started walking again.

Now look who's changing the subject, she thought, and decided not to allow him to. "But you said the English had inhibitors," she said, keeping pace with him, "so how—?"

"Maybe something made Trent more receptive. Do you know if he's been taking that antianxiety med that Verrick prescribed?"

"No. You think that—?"

"Combined with a heightened emotional state, which the pressure of needing to come up with the EED data for his boss would certainly produce, yeah, that could have triggered it."

"Plus, my calling out, 'Where are you?'" Briddey said glumly, remembering standing in the bus shelter and calling to C.B. "If I'd called you by name—"

"He'd know we were connected, which means we'd be in even more trouble than we are now."

He stopped walking again, and she looked around, surprised at how far they'd come. They were three blocks from her apartment building, and there was still no sign of C.B.'s Honda. "Where did you park?"

"Next to your car," he said, pointing back the way they'd come.

"Then where are we going? I thought you said you had something to show me."

"I do," he said. "This." He waved his arm to indicate the empty street and darkened buildings. "Listen to how quiet it is."

It *was* quiet. No breeze ruffled his tangled hair as she looked at him, and there was no sound of traffic, not even a car passing on the main thoroughfare two blocks up.

"That's not what I'm talking about," C.B. said. "I'm talking about the voices. Listen."

He was right. The distant roar beyond the brick wall of her perimeter had faded to the merest whisper. "Is everyone asleep?" she asked wonderingly.

"No. Unfortunately, that never happens. There are always long-distance truckers up, and insomniacs and people working the graveyard shift, but three A.M.'s as good as it gets. The bars have been closed for an hour, the mothers have gotten their babies back to sleep, the wife beaters have passed out, and the delivery people and paper-route kids and nurses who go on duty at five aren't up yet."

"But aren't there people lying awake squirrel caging?" Briddey asked, thinking about her own 3 A.M.s since this whole thing had started.

"Yeah, they're worrying about the mortgage and that mole on their back and all the things they wish they hadn't said and done. Three o'clock's when every doubt and regret and guilty thought bubbles up out of your subconscious to plague you. 'The dark night of the soul,' F. Scott Fitzgerald called it."

But that wasn't what she was hearing. The voices were a peaceful, placid murmur.

"That's because it's also the time when those same insomniacs read or count sheep or watch old movies on TV to put themselves back to sleep, which turns the whole world into a library reading room. I love this time of night."

She could imagine. C.B. had to spend all day every day trying to shut the voices out. This was the only time when he didn't have to, when he could be almost like other people.

"Exactly," he said, looking happily around. "It's my time of day, as Sky Masterson would say."

"Sky Masterson?"

"From *Guys and Dolls*. Remember the movie I told you about

with all the good screening songs in it? 'Luck Be a Lady' and 'Adelaide's Lament'—"

"The song about catching cold?" Briddey asked, thinking, *She probably caught cold because she didn't wear her coat.* She wished she'd worn hers. It was freezing out here.

"Umm-hmm, that's the one," C.B. said, taking off his jacket and draping it over her shoulders.

"You're always loaning me your jacket," she said. "*Thank* you."

"It's my pleasure. So, anyway, Sky Masterson's this gambler. He's bringing Sister Sarah back—"

"Sister Sarah?"

"Yeah, she's a Salvation Army missionary. Another case of a girl who's hooked up with a guy she's way too good for. Anyway, Sky and Sister Sarah are coming back from Havana just before dawn, and he tells her it's his favorite time of day, with the traffic stopped and nobody else around, and—" He stopped walking and stood still, listening.

"What is it?" she asked anxiously. "Is Trent awake?"

"No, it's Darrell in IT. They got a line on Verrick. They think he's in Hong Kong to do EEDs on a high-up Chinese official and his mistress, which is great news. His location'll be classified, and Trent'll have a hard time reaching him. And even if he succeeds, Verrick'll have a perfect excuse for not coming back."

"But why wouldn't he want to come back?"

"Because Trent's going to tell him his EED has made the two of you start hearing voices. Like I told you, Verrick can't afford to get mixed up with anything crazy-sounding and have his career go down the drain like Bridey Murphy's hypnotherapist or Dr. Rhine."

"But what if he's already mixed up with telepathy? What if he and Trent are in it together?"

"They aren't. I haven't picked up anything at all that indicates Trent's told Verrick about his phone idea. He was waiting till you two connected to broach the idea of doing scans, and he was genuinely surprised that Verrick moved your appointment up."

"Oh, good. I've been worried about that. But if Dr. Verrick had proof telepathy existed—"

"He won't. All Trent's got is you, and if Verrick asks you to demonstrate your telepathic ability, you can do what you did this morning and write down different words from the ones he sends, and Verrick will decide it was just a case of over-active imagination."

"But what about Trent? He talked to me. He heard my voice. He'll tell Dr. Verrick that."

"And you can tell Verrick you have no idea what he's talking about. It'll be your word against his."

I wish I could believe it was that simple, Briddey thought, clutching C.B.'s jacket to her against the late-night chill. "But what if Trent improves to where he can read my mind like you can, and knows that I *did* hear it and I'm lying?"

"It'd still be his word against yours. Anyway, he won't get to that point, though I'm a little disturbed that you were able to overhear him thinking about the phone—"

"But I didn't overhear him," Briddey said. "I was intentionally auditing him."

He stopped and looked down at her. "But I didn't teach you—"

"I know. I taught myself."

"But the voices . . . how did you keep from being overwhelmed when you—?"

"Opened the door? I didn't. I was too afraid to. I figured out a way to listen to them in the courtyard. On the radio."

"The *radio?*"

"Yes, like the one in your lab." She told him what she'd done.

"Wow," he said. "Very impressive! You're almost—" He stopped short.

Trent must be awake, she thought, and felt a pang that they'd have to put an end to this. It was so nice being out here together. She pulled C.B.'s jacket closer around her. "Did they find Dr. Verrick?"

"Dr. Verrick?" C.B. said. "Oh. No. I was just checking. Trent's still asleep."

Good, she thought. *Then we don't have to go back yet.* She looked happily around at the darkened buildings, the empty street. The air smelled of wet earth and lilacs, and in the spaces between streetlights, the black sky was spangled with stars.

But C.B. was oblivious to their surroundings. "The IT guys are onto something regarding Verrick's whereabouts, which means they could be calling Trent any minute now, and before they do, there are some things I need to tell you." He took a deep breath. "The first thing is, you wouldn't be in this mess if it weren't for me."

"What? It's not your fault that Trent—"

"Yeah, it is. A couple of months ago he came down and asked me to do some research into how EEDs worked, and after I did, he asked me if I thought it would be possible to map the electronic circuitry of the neural pathways the EED produced. I told him no, not without brain scans of patients who'd had the EED done."

He looked apologetically at her. "I only said that because I knew there was no way he could get access to them, what with doctor-patient confidentiality. I obviously didn't want Commspan to start messing around with the idea of mind-to-mind communication, even if it was only emotions," he said. "And the next thing I know, he's dating you and the two of you are getting an EED. I thought you probably had the gene, given your red hair and your Irish name, and that's why I tried to warn you. I was afraid if you had the EED, it might trigger the voices, and you'd tell Trent, and I didn't want him finding out telepathy was real."

"You're lying," she said. "My name and my red hair isn't why you thought I might become telepathic. You thought I might because Maeve was."

C.B. was staring at her in astonishment. "You know about *Maeve*?"

She nodded.

"How? And don't tell me she told you. She's been absolutely terrified you'd find out and tell her mother. She swore me to secrecy." He looked consideringly at Briddey. "I suppose you heard her on this radio thing of yours."

"No, and no. She didn't tell me. I figured it out."

"It was the Lucky Charms, wasn't it?"

"Partly. You used thinking about the marshmallows to distract her from the voices, too, didn't you?"

"Yeah."

"I wondered why you were talking about a kids' cereal," Briddey said. "I also figured out she was who you were talking to those times I couldn't contact you, like when I first started hearing the other voices at Commspan and when you suddenly went off in the middle of our fight."

He nodded. "I thought I'd taught her how to keep the voices out, but I'd never had to do it for anyone else before, so it wasn't perfect, and I kept having to go rescue her and shore up her defenses. And always at the worst possible moment. The last time it took me forever to get her calmed down to where she could get her defenses back up, especially since I was doing it long-distance, and by the time I did, you were already in trouble at the theater. And then, when we were in the storage room, she managed to get herself in trouble again. That's why I went back over to the door, so I could concentrate on talking her down, and why I didn't hear the librarian till she was almost to the door. All I had time to do was switch off the light, and when I did—"

"I fell apart," Briddey said. "I figured that out, too. And that you didn't text her to tell her what to say if Trent called. You just talked to her telepathically."

"Wow! You're almost as good a detective as your niece. Does she know you know about her?"

Briddey nodded. "She was eavesdropping on me when I figured it out."

"And she's probably eavesdropping on us right now," C.B. said, "although if she were, you can bet she'd be putting in her two cents' worth." He cocked his head to one side for a moment. "That's what I thought. She's sound asleep."

Thank heavens, Briddey thought. There was no telling what Maeve would say if she were here. "You said she panicked when the voices hit. Is she all right?" The voices were so vicious and so nasty ...

"I was able to block a lot of the bad stuff temporarily till she got her defenses up," C.B. said. "And her voices didn't come on nearly as fast as they did with you. For the first couple of weeks she only heard one or two at a time."

Which was why she was reading The Darkvoice Chronicles, Briddey thought. *She was afraid she was schizophrenic, too.*

"Yeah," C.B. said. "I heard her worrying about it. I'd seen her at Commspan a couple of times when she came to see you, so I recognized her voice, and I was afraid her concern about schizophrenia might be because she was starting to hear voices, even though she was awfully young."

"So you reached out to her, and the two of you cooked up the story about the science project to cover the fact that you were teaching her how to protect herself against the voices."

"Pretty much."

"*Thank* you for doing that. I hate to think what would have happened to her if you hadn't been there to help."

"Yeah, well, I didn't want her to have to go through what I did, though actually she might have been okay even without me. She has a tendency to overestimate her abilities and underestimate the voices, but she's also got a real talent for keeping intruders out."

"That's because she's had tons of practice with her own family."

He grinned. "Yeah, she told me all about Oona and her mother. The Stasi agent, Maeve calls her, but if you want my opinion, she's no match for Maeve or her computer skills. Maeve's a prodigy when it comes to writing security code, and now that she's learned how to audit Mary Clare's thoughts, your poor sister doesn't stand a chance. And you don't have to worry about Maeve's voices now. She's got a perimeter and a safe room *and* an encrypted firewall."

"And a castle with a moat and a tower. And zombie gates."

He laughed. "See? She can take care of herself."

"Unless Trent finds out about her."

"Yeah," he said, suddenly serious. "That's why we've got to make sure he doesn't."

"And that he doesn't find out about you."

C.B. nodded. "So far we're okay. He hasn't heard you mention my name or what happened last night. He still thinks you left the theater to go to your aunt's house. Nobody from Commspan saw us on our way to pick up your car from the hotel, and there's nothing else to connect us."

"Except that call you made to the hospital, telling them I'd left my room and was in the staircase."

"But I didn't give my name, so unless the hospital traces the call, we're fine. And they won't have any reason to, because Dr. Verrick's not going to believe Trent."

She prayed that was true. If they ever found out about C.B., with all he knew, they'd hound him to death. And once they discovered he was actually Irish—

"Trent hasn't made the Irish connection either. He hasn't even realized *you've* got anything to do with the telepathy. He thinks this is just a lucky accident that'll make an even better phone than an empathic connection would have. He's totally focused on that, so much so that he hasn't even considered how nuts this is all going to sound to Dr. Verrick."

"Just the same, I'd better make it clear to Maeve that she can only talk to me over the phone."

"Good idea," C.B. said. "And it wouldn't be a bad idea for us to use a code name when we talk about her. We definitely don't want Trent to realize she's a part of this."

"How about Rapunzel? Or Cinderella?"

"No, he'd spot that as code. Make it Cindy. And make sure you *think* Cindy, not just say it, so her real name doesn't come through underneath."

"I'll be careful." She thought of something. "When you were talking about Dr. Verrick, why did you say you had no indication he was in on it with Trent? Don't you know?"

"You mean, can't I read his mind? No, unfortunately. I've never heard his voice. That night I came to see you in the hospital, he'd gone home. I was planning to go talk to him at his office that night you had the midnight appointment, but he turned out not to be there, and Hong Kong's out of range. But I can hear Trent, and if Verrick was in this with him, I'd definitely have picked it up, and I haven't. He—" He stopped, and his chin went up in that alert attitude again.

She watched him as he listened. He looked worn out. *Of course he is*, she thought. *He's had even less sleep than I have*. She felt guilty that she'd fallen asleep tonight while he'd stood guard, waiting for Trent to doze off. He'd been standing guard for days on end, keeping Maeve—and her—safe.

He came back from whatever he'd been listening to, and she asked, "Was that Trent?"

"No, Darrell in IT again. It seems the good doctor's not in Hong Kong after all. He's in Arizona."

"Oh, no. That means he could be back here by tomorrow—I mean, by today. By this afternoon."

He shook his head. "They haven't found him yet. He flew into Phoenix, but he's not booked into any of the hotels there, and he rented a car, which probably means he was headed somewhere else— Palm Springs or the Grand Canyon or Mexico. Plus, he's in an area with some of the worst coverage in the country. If he's out in the middle of the desert, it could be days before they find him. Which means *I've* got time to tell you—"

"About Sky Masterson and Sister Sarah."

There was a pause, and then he said, "Yeah, about Sarah and Sky," and she had the feeling he'd intended to say something else. "Where was I?"

You were standing here with me in the middle of the night, she thought. *In the lovely lilac-scented dark.* "You said they were coming back from Havana."

"Yeah," he said, looking down at her. "He took her to Cuba to—"

"Keep her boyfriend from finding out she was telepathic?"

"No, to win a bet. And to get her into bed. He wined and dined her and got her drunk, but then—"

He fell in love with her.

"Yeah," C.B. said huskily, "and took her back to New York, and told her the bit about his time of day and was about to say he had some things he needed to tell *her,* just like I have some things I need to tell you, when—shit."

"What's wrong?" she asked, but she already knew. Trent was awake.

"No," C.B. said disgustedly, "but I just heard Darrell say—think— that he's going to call Trent and ask him if he's got any idea where in Arizona the doctor could be. Sorry. I didn't think they'd call till they found him. Come on, we need to get you back home," he said, walking her rapidly down the street. "Trent may call you, and I don't want him picking up anything about your being awake and outside at this hour."

"But I thought you said he was only picking things up sporadically."

"He is, but I didn't think he'd be able to connect with you either, and we can't afford to take any risks, not with Maeve involved. You and I are one thing, but she's just a little kid. A moat and a tower wouldn't be any match for the kinds of things the press and the military would throw at her. Speaking of which," he said, hurrying her along the sidewalk, "from here on out, we need to stick to ordinary lines of communication. And not ones connected to Commspan. Come down to my lab as soon as you get to work, and I'll fix you up with a burner phone so you can call me if something develops."

"And what if something develops before then?"

"It won't," he said. "It's"—he glanced at his wristwatch—"nearly four A.M. already, which means we've only got five hours till I see you at Commspan. I doubt if Trent'll find Verrick by then, and even if he does, the good doctor's phone is probably in sleep mode, so he won't get the call till morning. Or else he'll be annoyed at being awakened, especially if Trent tells him he wants to install ESP into a smartphone."

"Can he?" Briddey asked, practically running to keep up with him. "Actually devise a way to translate the telepathy into a technology you could put into a phone?"

"Not if he assigns *me* to do it."

"I'm serious. Is it possible?"

"Not till they know how it works and what causes it, which is why it's important for Trent to go on thinking the EED did it and that you're the only two people it's happened to."

"And that we were only able to connect because he and I are emotionally bonded."

"Yeah," C.B. said. "Sorry." They'd reached her apartment building. He cocked his head, listening for a few seconds, and then said, "Darrell's looking for Trent's number. You'd better go in."

"But you said you had something else you needed to tell me."

"Yeah," he said. "It'll have to wait."

"Are you sure there isn't some way you could block Trent for just a few minutes? You could come up and tell me whatever it is and then finish telling me about Sky Masterson and Sister Sarah—"

He shook his head. "It doesn't work like that. Look, you need to get inside, and I need to get to bed. We're both going to need to have our wits about us tomorrow. G'night," he said, and loped down the street before she could even give him his jacket back.

C.B.! Wait! she called, and ran after him. She handed him his jacket. "Thank you for lending it to me," she said.

"Anytime," he said gravely, and for a long, still, breath-held moment she thought he was going to kiss her, but he didn't. He shook his head regretfully, said, "I'll see you in the morning," and took off toward his car.

Briddey stood and watched him go and then hurried inside and up to her apartment and her phone.

Trent hadn't called, and in spite of what C.B.'d said, she doubted he

Briddey another five minutes to end the conversation, after which she switched off the light and then lay there in the dark, thinking about C.B.'s voices.

She'd thought a flood was terrifying, but fire was infinitely worse. Even Joan of Arc hadn't been brave enough to face it on her own. They'd had to bind her to the stake. But C.B. had voluntarily plunged into the flames to rescue her—and Maeve. And done it not once, but over and over. *And he'd do it again if I got into trouble,* she thought wonderingly.

You have no business thinking about this, she reminded herself. *Trent could wake up any minute,* and as if voicing the thought had made it happen, her phone rang.

"I've been trying to get through to you mentally for ten minutes," Trent said. "Didn't you hear me calling to you?"

"No. I was asleep. What time is it?"

"Ten till four," he said. "Good news. I got in touch with Dr. Verrick, and he's coming back right away."

"Coming back?"

"Yes. I could feel your anxiety and sensed you'd want to know I found him. He's coming straight back to meet with us. I don't know when he'll get in, but I'll let you know as soon as I find out. Come to my office as soon as you get to work, and we'll practice sending and receiving. I've been practicing all evening, and I've gotten much better at picking you up. I'm sure you can do it, too. You just need to focus."

No, what I need *is to get in touch with C.B.,* Briddey thought after Trent hung up. But how? He'd said he was going home to bed, and if he was asleep, he wouldn't be able to hear her calling. And Trent might. Which meant she couldn't call to Maeve and have her phone him either.

She'd have to call him herself. But he'd told her not to use her own phone, and waking up the neighbors to use theirs at four A.M. was out.

This is ridiculous, she thought. The EED was supposed to have opened up new avenues of communication, and instead all it had done was cut her off from every single one she'd previously had. *It's a paradigm shift, all right. In the wrong direction.*

She was either going to have to locate a carrier pigeon, go out and

find a payphone, or wait till Trent went back to sleep and then call out
to C.B. But it had sounded like Trent intended to stay up the rest of the
night "practicing," and she needed to tell C.B. about Dr. Verrick *now*.

That meant a payphone. If she could find one. Kathleen had said
there were still some at gas stations and convenience stores, but she'd
also said something about not having any change when she'd been
stranded at the 7-Eleven. Did that mean they only took coins?

Briddey had exactly one dime and three pennies in her wallet, and
she had no idea how much a phone call even cost nowadays. A quarter?
Fifty cents? No, better have a dollar's worth, just in case.

She spent the next ten minutes upending handbags and ransacking
coat pockets and kitchen drawers to come up with enough change. She
pulled on jeans and a top, stuffed the coins in her pocket, grabbed her
keys, the box lid with C.B.'s number on it, and the jacket she hadn't
taken before, and tiptoed downstairs and outside.

Three o'clock in the morning might be romantic, but four fifteen
definitely wasn't. It was dark and cold, and when she finally found a
7-Eleven, it was closed. Of course. That was why it was called 7-Eleven.
And its phone was inside. She could see it through the window.

The Exxon station two blocks down was closed, too, but there was
a phone kiosk outside it. But no phone. The Conoco station (also
closed) had a phone but no handset. She was ready to turn around and
go home when she spotted a convenience store ahead—BizziMart.

There was no phone kiosk outside, but a sign in the window said
ATM, PHONE, AMMO, and it was open. The parking out front was full of
motorcycles.

She circled the block, parked on the side, and went in. And was
immediately sorry. BizziMart made the 7-Eleven look like the Luminesce of convenience stores. The clerk looked interestedly at her when
she came in, and so did a homeless man over by the coffee machine and
the two tough-looking guys loitering in the chips aisle, who obviously
belonged to the motorcycles outside. She wished briefly that she knew
what they were thinking so she'd know just how much danger she was
in, and then decided she was better off not knowing.

There was a guy on the phone who looked even tougher than the
other two. From the way he was draped over the phone box, he'd been
on it for some time, and she was about to go somewhere else when he

suddenly shouted, "Fuck this and fuck you!" slammed down the phone, and started straight toward her, followed by his friends.

She backed hastily into the candy aisle as they passed, and then hurried over to the phone, digging coins and C.B.'s number out of her pocket as she went.

She needn't have wasted all that time searching for change. The phone only took credit cards. She slid hers through, trying to ignore the sticky smear of dried Coca-Cola (or blood) on the receiver, and punched in C.B.'s number.

It rang—and went on ringing. *Wake up!* she shouted, even though she knew he couldn't hear her if he was sleeping, and then listened with bated breath, terrified Trent had heard that instead.

He apparently hadn't, and the phone's ringing must not have woken C.B. up either, or else he wasn't answering because the screen on his phone said "unknown number." Or would his phone even have caller ID? Knowing him, he—

"Briddey?" C.B.'s voice said on the other end.

"Yes," she said in a rush of relief. "Did I wake you?"

"No, I was working on something. What's going on? You're not calling from your smartphone, are you?"

"No," she said, glancing at the homeless man, who was now in the candy aisle, openly ogling her, and at the clerk, who was leaning on the counter, alternately eyeing her and the motorcycle guys. They were still outside, talking angrily and looking like they might come back in at any moment and wrench the phone away from her. "I'm calling from a payphone at a convenience store on Linden," she said, lowering her voice. "I have to talk to you."

"I take it somebody's listening," C.B. said.

"That's right."

And he must have been listening in on her thoughts because he asked, "Exactly how bad is this place you're calling from?"

"Pretty bad," she whispered.

"Do you need me to come get you?"

"No," she said, glancing over at the clerk, who was all ears. "Can you talk, or is this a bad time?" she said for the clerk's benefit.

"I'll check," C.B. said, and there was a brief silence. "We can talk. Trent's gone back to sleep."

Oh, good, I don't have to stay here, Briddey thought, and was about to hang up when she heard, "Yeah, well, fuck you, too!" from outside. Two of the motorcycle guys had faced off angrily, and a dozen more had appeared out of nowhere. *On second thought,* she decided, *I think I'd better stay where I am.* But she couldn't just stand there without saying anything, or the clerk would get suspicious.

"No problem," C.B. said. "Repeat after me, 'So I said, "I never want to see you again," and I got out of the car,' after which I'll tell you your boyfriend's a creep—"

Which he certainly is, Briddey thought.

"—and you should never have gone out with him in the first place, et cetera, and all you'll have to do is say, 'I know' and 'You're right' every few minutes, and in between we can talk."

"So I said," Briddey said, raising her voice so the clerk could hear, "'I never want to see you again,' and I got out of the car," and added silently, *Trent phoned. He got in touch with Dr. Verrick, and he's coming back right away.*

"Did he say where Verrick was?"

No. You're missing the point. If he's coming back, that means he believes Trent!

"No, it doesn't," C.B. said calmly. "If he was in Scottsdale meeting with some rich client about having the EED, he may have been coming back anyway."

But Trent made it sound like he was changing his plans. And you said before that you didn't think he'd come back at all, that he wouldn't want to get involved with something like this.

"Yeah, well, maybe he's decided he already is and needs to come back to do damage control."

But Trent doesn't want anyone else to find out about it. He needs to keep it secret so Apple won't—

"Yes, but Verrick may not know that. He may have assumed that Trent's planning to take it public, and he's coming back to try to talk him out of it. Like I did with you over having the EED. Hang on a sec while I get my laptop."

Briddey took advantage of the pause to glance out at the motorcycle guys, who had stopped shouting but were still glaring menacingly at each other. *I don't want to hear what they're thinking,* she thought.

The clerk was looking at her. "You tried to warn me about him," she said clearly into the phone. "I should have listened to you."

"You certainly should have," C.B. said. "Okay, I'm looking at flights for that part of the Southwest, and no matter where Verrick was, he's pretty much got to fly out of Phoenix or Tucson, and even if he took the earliest flight tomorrow morning—I mean, *this* morning—it wouldn't put him in here till ten fifteen, and the first flight out of Tucson gets in forty minutes later. So that puts him at his office at eleven thirty at the earliest, if he's on that first flight. Which he's not. It's full, and the next three flights show first-class and business as having been sold out for a week. Verrick doesn't strike me as a squashed-in-coach kind of guy—"

You're still missing the point, Briddey said. *What if he's coming back because Trent told him we're telepathic, and he believes him?*

"Verrick doesn't strike me as the type for that either. He didn't mention ESP or psychic powers or remote viewing to you at the hospital or his office, did he?"

No, she said, frowning, though a memory of something had flickered through her mind as C.B. said "psychic powers." That hadn't been the phrase, but it had been psychic something—psychic ability? psychic gift?

"What did he say about a psychic gift?" C.B. asked alertly.

Nothing, she said, certain the more she thought about it that the memory hadn't involved Dr. Verrick. It had been something Kathleen had said, or texted her . . . no, whatever it was, it had gone.

"How about clairvoyance or telekinesis?" C.B. was asking. "Did he ever mention those?"

No.

"Then I think it's a lot more likely he's returning because he's afraid Trent's having auditory hallucinations and is going to sue him for malpractice."

But whatever the reason, he's coming back, Briddey said, *and he's going to ask me questions and want to run tests—*

"Which won't tell him anything. I told you, the scans can't tell what you're thinking unless you cooperate."

You also told me Dr. Verrick wouldn't be looking for signs of telepathy because he doesn't know it exists. But if Trent tells him, he will know. And if Trent sends me a word, and the same area lights up in both our brains—

"It won't. Even if it was the only message you were getting at that moment, which it's not—your brain's constantly bombarded with sights, sounds, emotions, nerve impulses, and unrelated thoughts—that wouldn't happen. Your brain's not a library. The place you store a particular thought isn't the same place Trent does—or I do. We all have our own personal filing system, and it's more like the Cloud than a card file. Thoughts are stored in dozens of places, with hundreds of links and cross-references. Take Lucky Charms. You've got the way it's spelled in one place, how it's pronounced in another, what the box looks like in the third, plus its taste and your memories of eating it and buying it and running out of it—"

And of you asking me in the theater what the marshmallows were—

"Yeah," he said, "and it's in a bunch of other places, too—breakfast-related things, Irish things, things that taste like chalk. And that's not counting all the thousands of cross-connections your mind makes with the words 'lucky' and 'charms'—a charm bracelet, a lucky rabbit's foot, 'Luck Be a Lady,' some guy you overheard saying, 'Maybe I'll get lucky tonight!'—all of them in different places with different neural connections. And *those* thoughts are connected to others in a giant web—like *the* Web—where every thought's linked to every other, and the only one who can negotiate the web, to translate it for other people, is you. Trust me, Verrick won't have any more idea of what you're thinking than the clerk there at your convenience store does. Speaking of which, to keep it that way, you probably need to stick in another 'You're right' here."

No, I don't have to, she said, looking over at the clerk, who was now reading a magazine. The homeless guy had moved to the far aisle and was sticking something in his coat, and the motorcycle guys had apparently settled their argument. They were on their bikes, revving them up and roaring off, one by one.

"Better say it anyway, just in case."

"You're right," she said, and silently, *You're wrong. You said the only way they can find out what I'm thinking is if I tell them, but what about Trent? He could tell them—*

"It's still your word against his," C.B. said. "Trent can only tell them what he thinks he heard you say. There's no way to prove you actually did."

Unless Trent heard more than he's told me—like C.B.'s name—and they haul him in for questioning, Briddey thought, and remembered C.B.'s telling her about Joan of Arc being captured by the British and interrogated, tortured.

"Trent hasn't heard my name. He doesn't have any idea I'm telepathic, let alone that I'm talking to you. I can read minds, remember?"

"Not Dr. Verrick's."

"True," he said. "And the first thing I need to do when he gets back is get a fix on his voice so I can."

You're not thinking of going to see him, are you?

"No," C.B. said. "I want to stay off his radar just as much as you want me to. And there's no reason for me to see him in person. We'll have you call him from the lab after he lands and put him on speakerphone so I can hear his voice and we can know what he's thinking during your appointment."

Or I could come up with some sort of excuse why I can't make it—

"No, that might make Trent think you've found out what he's up to. We want him to believe you're still convinced the only reason he wanted to have the EED done was to make you more emotionally bonded, and that you didn't hear anything till . . . Jesus, was it just yesterday morning? It seems like years."

I know, she thought, remembering the rain and the bus shelter. And the Carnegie Room and hiding in the stacks and the Reading Room and sitting in his car . . .

"Yeah," C.B. said, "and hiding under the sink from the voices, only to have me leave you stranded in the dark with them in that storage closet. Talk about a romantic weekend."

It was, she thought.

"But as far as Trent and Dr. Verrick are concerned, none of that happened. You left the theater to go help with a family crisis, and when you finally got home, you fell into bed. And in the morning you called to Trent, hoping to connect emotionally, and when he answered you in words, you were totally shocked. You had no idea such a thing was possible, and now you want answers as much as Trent does."

C.B. was right. She'd be demanding to know why this was happening to her, not trying to avoid seeing Dr. Verrick. But that didn't mean she wanted to go.

"Don't worry," C.B. said. "We've got plenty of time to get you ready. You can come to my lab like we planned, and we can go over everything. And in the meantime—"

I know, don't think about you or Mae— I mean, Cindy.

"Right. Remember in the library, when I said the best defense against being caught was that they didn't know we'd been there. *Our* best defense is that they don't have any idea you've talked to anybody but Trent. They can't figure out who Cindy and I are if they don't even know we exist. Speaking of which, maybe I'd better have a code name, too."

I could call you Conlan. He doesn't know that's your—

"No, nothing even remotely Irish. We don't want to give him any clues to what's causing this."

I could call you Ishmael.

"Too Jewish."

Highwayman?

"No, too obviously code, just like Cinderella. It needs to be something that doesn't stand out, that could just be an ordinary word, like—"

Sky, she said.

There was a silence on the line.

You know, from Guys and Dolls. *Sky Masterson.*

"Are you sure you want to do that, Sister Sarah? As you recall, she ended up in Havana with him."

I'll take my chances, she answered, turning her head so the clerk couldn't see her expression. She was, after all, supposed to be sobbing to a friend about being stranded. Smiling clearly wasn't appropriate.

"Great," C.B. said. "You don't happen to like *dulce de leches,* do you?"

No alcohol, remember? she reminded him. *The voices aside, I don't want to accidentally let anything slip to Trent. Speaking of which, we need to tell Cindy she mustn't talk to me. If Trent finds out she's telepathic . . .*

"Don't worry. I'll tell her to go inside her castle and raise her drawbridge and close her zombie gates. And meanwhile, Sister Sarah, you go home and send your secretary an email moving your appointments to the afternoon so your morning'll be free, and then try to keep from thinking thoughts you don't want Trent to overhear."

"Is he awake?" Briddey asked nervously.

"No, not yet, but from this point on, you're going to behave as if he is, and as if he can hear anything you say or think. Which means we'd better maintain radio silence, too." He hesitated. "I suppose it's pointless to tell you to try and get some sleep."

Yes.

"Okay, well then, memorize 'Marian the Librarian.' When you come to the lab I'll teach you some other screening techniques. And when you're not reading, think about what you're going to have for breakfast or what you're going to wear to work. Or how the castaways are going to get off Gilligan's Island. Anything except Maeve, me, telepathy, or Ireland. I'll check out Verrick's history to make sure there are no paranormal skeletons in it—which I'm pretty sure there aren't—and see if I can find out what celebrity client he went to see. It's all going to be fine, I promise. Now say, 'Thanks for giving me a ride. I'll see you in a couple of minutes,' and hang up so I can talk to Maeve."

"Thanks for giving me a ride," she said. "I'll see you in a couple of minutes."

"Good girl," he said. "I'll see you in the morning," and hung up.

And she should hang up too, particularly since the clerk had resumed leering at her from the counter. But instead she said, even though C.B. was no longer there, "I really appreciate your doing this for me. I was an idiot to have ever thought I was in love with him. I didn't even know what love was."

The clerk gave a derisive snort.

"I'll be waiting outside," she said to the dial tone. "I love you," and hung up the phone.

She hurried out of the store to a position on the curb where she could both look up the street and keep an eye on the clerk, and as soon as he turned his back, sprinted to her car and drove back home, wondering if she might be able to find Dr. Verrick on the radio so she could confirm he wasn't working with Trent and find out why he was coming back. And why he'd told his nurse he was in Hong Kong when he was actually in Arizona.

She tried as soon as she reached home, but the doctor was apparently asleep—or out of range. She couldn't find his voice on any frequency.

I'll try again later, she thought, called up "The Highwayman" on her laptop, and spent the next hour committing the lines to memory—and wishing she'd chosen a cheerier poem, especially when she got to the part where the highwayman found out Bess was dead and came racing back for revenge, only to be shot down by the soldiers lying in wait.

She had to force herself to learn the last stanza, where he lay drenched in blood on the highway, "with a bunch of lace at his throat." *I need something with a better ending,* she thought, and ordered up "Adelaide's Lament" from iTunes.

She should have known by the title that it wouldn't be upbeat either, but at least nobody got killed. And it had lots of verses. *Good,* she thought, *it'll take me till morning to memorize it,* but when she looked at the clock afterward, it was barely five.

I'll just have to memorize the rest of Guys and Dolls. *And* The Music Man, she thought, downloaded their scores, and started in. C.B. was right, "Fugue for Tin Horns" *did* sound too much like the voices, and she didn't think "The Sadder but Wiser Girl" was a good idea—the title was a little too close for comfort. But Professor Harold Hill's spiel about trouble right there in River City was perfect. She memorized it, and then tried to find Dr. Verrick's station again.

Nothing, which was good. He was still out of range. She took her shower, recalling ironically that a couple of days ago her biggest worry had been being spied on by C.B. *What time is it now?* she wondered, getting out and drying off. *Surely it's close to seven.*

It was five forty-five. She wondered how early she could go into work without it looking suspicious. Eight? A quarter till? The sooner Sky taught her those "other screening techniques," the better she'd feel.

She sang "Luck Be a Lady" to herself as she dried her hair and dressed and then tackled *Decline and Fall*, and immediately regretted it. Its pace made the actual centuries-long collapse of the Roman Empire look like the hundred-yard dash by comparison.

At quarter to seven, she decided she didn't care about the fate of Rome *or* looking suspicious and went to get her purse and keys.

There was a knock on the door. It couldn't be Sky. He'd specifically said they shouldn't be seen together, so that meant it was Kathleen. Or Mary Clare.

But it was Trent. "Oh, good," he said, looking approvingly at her. "You got my message."

"Message?"

"Yes. I've been mentally telling you I was coming to pick you up for the last half hour. Didn't you hear me?"

She shook her head.

"Then why are you ready to go?"

"I was going to go into work early. I'm so far behind—"

"Or you were subconsciously receiving my message and knew you needed to be ready."

"Ready for what?" she asked, afraid she already knew.

"Dr. Verrick's back, and he wants to see us right away."

Twenty-Seven

"There's nothing so bad that it couldn't be worse."
—IRISH PROVERB

"D–DR. VERRICK'S BACK?" BRIDDEY STAMMERED. "BUT, TRENT—"

"He flew back on his Lear jet right after he got off the phone with me."

Of course. She and C.B.—correction, Sky—should have thought of the possibility that he had a private plane.

"I told you about him flying back in the mental message I sent you," Trent said. "I can't believe you didn't hear me! I'm hearing you more and more. Are you sure you're concentrating?"

She fastened the bar more firmly across the door of her safe room. "Yes," she said. "What did you hear?"

"Oh, all sorts of things. I heard you say you need me, and 'I wonder if Trent's asleep,' and a bunch of stuff about needing to make a phone call, which you don't seem to understand we don't need to do now."

"Is that all you heard?"

"No. There were other things, but they didn't make any sense, something about a dog on the highway and needing change and the sky. What were you thinking about?"

"I have no idea," she said. "I must have been dreaming."

"That's what I thought. We'll have to ask Dr. Verrick why I can hear you so much better than you can hear me. So, are you ready to go see him?"

"No. I mean, I need to run by Commspan first, so why don't you go on ahead, and I'll meet you there? I have a meeting with Art Sampson this morning. I'll have to reschedule—"

"You can do it from the car. Where's your phone?"

"I'll get it," Briddey said, walking swiftly into the bedroom for it. She wished she'd given C.—Sky a key to her apartment so she could at least scrawl "Help!" on her mirror with lipstick for him to find when she didn't show up at work.

She grabbed her phone, checked the call log to make sure Sky's name wasn't on it, deleted Cindy's calls and messages, and then stopped, staring blindly into the mirror she couldn't write on, trying to think of some way to convince Trent to let her take her own car so she could at least lose him in traffic and stop at BizziMart to tell Sky what had happened.

"What's taking so long?" Trent said, appearing in the doorway. "I told him we'd be there by eight, and we don't want to keep him waiting after he's flown all this way. Not that he'll mind once he hears what we've got to tell him." He hustled her out of her apartment, down the stairs, and over to his Porsche.

"I really think I should meet you there," she said again as he opened the car door for her. "I've already rescheduled my meeting with Art Sampson twice, and he's going to be furious at my canceling again unless I explain—"

"Text him," Trent said, and there was nothing for it but to get in the car.

While he pulled out of the parking place, she looked at the dashboard, with its elaborate computerized streaming/CD/satellite radio system, wondering how hard it would be to find "Ode to Billie Joe." She reached for the MENU button.

"No music," Trent said, reaching past her to turn it off. "If we're going to convince Dr. Verrick we can communicate telepathically, we need to be totally focused on sending and receiving." He headed downtown.

"But I don't understand *why* we need to convince him, or why he has to be involved at all."

"Because this isn't just about us anymore. The fact that telepathy exists means it affects everyone. Don't you understand? People won't have to use smartphones or email or social media to communicate anymore. They'll be able to do it directly. It'll be a whole new form of instant messaging. Mental IM."

"But how?" she asked, turning wide, innocent eyes on him. "Wouldn't they have to be emotionally committed to each other?"

"No. If we can find out what's causing this and how it works, we can make it work for everyone. That's where Dr. Verrick comes in. He can run tests that'll show us the brain circuitry involved, and we'll be able to use that to design a device that lets anyone communicate telepathically with anyone else."

"Have you told Dr. Verrick this?"

"Not yet. All I told him was that something extraordinary had happened, that you and I were able to hear more than each other's emotions. I didn't call it telepathy. I didn't want to scare him off. I just told him he needed to get back here."

So Sky was right, Dr. Verrick wasn't part of this. "But if you haven't told him, how do you know he'll agree to running tests?" Briddey asked, and Trent took his eyes off the road long enough to look incredulously at her.

"How could he not? This is the scientific discovery of the century! Think what it'll mean. People will be able to truly understand each other. There'll be no more secrets or misunderstandings or conflicts."

It doesn't work like that, Briddey thought.

"Think of all the problems it'll solve, and not just personal problems. Important problems. Take terrorists. We'll be able to stop them *before* they kill innocent victims, and we'll know exactly where our enemies are and what they're planning to do. Telepathy will give us an enormous advantage in foreign affairs. And in business. And on Wall Street. The possibilities are endless."

You're right, Briddey thought. *Corporate spying, insider trading, police states. And for telepaths like Sky and Mae—Cindy, testing, experiments, torture, burnings at the stake, and horrible, horrible voices, torrents of them, raging wildfires of them, roaring out of control.*

"You'll see," Trent said confidently. "Dr. Verrick will be as excited about the possibilities as we are," and turned into the hospital's parking garage.

"I thought we were going to his office."

"No, he asked us to meet him here." Where they could run into one of the staff who'd found her in the staircase. Or the nurse who'd taken her out to Sky's car.

But the office that the volunteer at the information desk directed them to was on a different floor and at the opposite end of the hospital, and Briddey didn't recognize any of the staff they met on the way there.

Dr. Verrick himself came out to meet them. "Good morning, Ms. Flannigan, Mr. Worth. We'll be meeting just down here," he said, gesturing toward the end of the hall.

He didn't look at all put out by having had to fly back from Arizona in the middle of the night, even when a doctor stopped him halfway there to say, "I thought you were in Sedona."

"I was," he said cheerfully.

Sedona. Why did that name ring a bell? She'd heard it somewhere . . .

"We really appreciate your cutting your trip short to see us," Trent was saying.

"Not a problem," Dr. Verrick said. "Here we are." He showed them into a consulting room with a desk and two upholstered chairs pulled up in front of it. "Sit down. I'll be right with you. I just need to speak to my nurse."

He went through the door behind the desk, and Briddey could hear him say, ". . . should be coming in shortly . . . want to know the moment she arrives," and then, ". . . airport . . ." Did that mean he was going back as soon as he'd dealt with them and this patient who was flying in?

I hope so, Briddey thought.

Dr. Verrick came back in and sat down. He leaned across the desk. "Now tell me exactly what's going on. You've connected, I take it?"

"We've more than just connected," Trent said eagerly. "We're not just sensing each other's emotions, we're talking!"

"Talking?" Dr. Verrick looked from one to the other. "You mean that now that you're more empathetic to each other's feelings, you're communicating better?"

"No, I mean we can talk to each other like you and I are talking right now, only in our heads."

Briddey hadn't realized just how crazy it would sound until Trent said it. *Sky was right. If he'd told me before it happened to me, I never would have believed him.*

"There!" Trent said, pointing at her. "Just now I heard Briddey say, 'He's never going to believe us!' That's what you were thinking, wasn't it, Briddey? Tell him!"

"Yes, but—"

"But that would be easy to guess from her expression," Dr. Verrick said. "And her body language. Are you certain that's not what you're doing? Using her emotions and nonverbal cues to—?"

"No," Trent said. "I can hear her when we're miles apart. And she can hear what I'm thinking, too."

"Is that true, Ms. Flannigan?" Dr. Verrick asked, turning to her.

"No."

"No?" Trent said. "How can you say that? We were talking! I can prove it. Look." He pulled out the lists of words they'd written and slapped them down side by side on Dr. Verrick's desk. "We went into separate rooms and each thought of ten things, and the other one wrote them down. I got nearly three-fourths of the ones she sent right, and she got almost as many of the ones *I* sent. And we'd do a lot better now. My ability to communicate keeps improving. Run a brain scan on us, and you'll see we can hear each other—"

"First things first," Dr. Verrick said, looking at the lists.

I hope he's as unimpressed by Trent's notion of a correct response as I was, Briddey thought, trying to gauge the doctor's reaction as he went over the lists, but his face remained completely impassive. Finally, he laid them back down, clasped his hands together, and leaned forward. "I think you'd better begin at the beginning, Mr. Worth."

Trent nodded. "The night before last, we took your advice about taking our minds off connecting and went to a play."

"And this was where you first had this ... mental communication?"

"No, Briddey had to leave for a family problem, and we were apart for the rest of the night. But the next morning I heard her calling, 'Where *are* you?' and I said, 'Briddey, is that you?'"

"And you heard him say that?" Dr. Verrick asked, turning to Briddey.

"Ye-es," she said, putting as much uncertainty in her voice as she dared. "At least, I thought I heard it."

"You *did* hear it," Trent said, "because you said, 'Yes,' and then I said, 'I can't believe we connected,' and I asked her where she was, and she told me she was in her apartment in bed."

Briddey watched Dr. Verrick closely as Trent told him what had happened. His expression remained skeptical, and he asked all the right questions for someone who'd just heard a patient make a ridiculous—and possibly disturbing—claim.

And yet there was something not quite right about his responses. He didn't seem surprised enough, nor angry enough that they'd dragged him all the way back from Arizona to tell him some insane story. But it wasn't just that. His responses were off in some other way that she couldn't put her finger on.

He is *in on it with Trent, and this is all a charade put on for my benefit,* she thought, but, as Dr. Verrick asked more questions and Trent grew more and more frustrated attempting to explain, she decided that wasn't it. *So what is it?* she wondered, watching him. *Why do his reactions seem wrong?*

It hit her with a shock: *He's not just not surprised; he's not interested.* He was distracted, like a person holding one conversation while worrying about something else, and she wondered momentarily if he was thinking about the patient he'd talked to the nurse about, the one he'd wanted to be told about "the moment she arrived."

But unless that patient's brains had started leaking out through her EED incision, her problem couldn't possibly be as bad as what Trent was telling him, especially considering the dangers it held for his reputation if word leaked out. And she knew that was a concern, because at one point he asked sharply, "Who have you told about this?"

"No one," Trent said. "That was why we were so anxious to have you return, so we could speak to you first."

"I'm glad," Dr. Verrick said, and there was no mistaking his relief. But that didn't tally with his being indifferent, or whatever it was he was: Bored? Detached? On hold?

That's it, she thought. *On hold. He's just marking time talking to us while he waits for something.* But for what? An orderly from the psych ward with a pair of straitjackets? Or some new brain scan Sky didn't know about that could tell exactly what someone was thinking?

I need to find out, Briddey thought, and went into her courtyard. She hadn't been able to find Dr. Verrick's voice on the radio before, but hopefully that was because he'd been out of range. He was here now, and—

A nurse stuck her head in the door. "Doctor? I'm sorry to interrupt, but you asked me to let you know when Ms. Walenski arrived."

"Yes," Dr. Verrick said, and went over to the door. He and the nurse conferred in undertones for a moment and then she withdrew, and Dr. Verrick came back over to them. "I'm terribly sorry. There's a patient issue I need to deal with. It should only take a few minutes. Please, have some coffee." He gestured toward the coffeemaker and went out.

Trent immediately took out his phone, looked at his messages, and called his secretary. *Good,* Briddey thought, and went cautiously over to the cottonwood tree, sat down on the bench, and picked up the radio to see if she could find Dr. Verrick's station.

"When did he call?" Trent was saying. "I said, when did he call? . . . What? I can't hear you. Let me get someplace with better reception." He put the phone to his chest. "Tell Dr. Verrick I'll be right back."

Briddey nodded and went back to the radio, and then thought, *Forget Dr. Verrick. Now's your chance to talk to Sky, while Trent's focused on his call,* and the moment the door snicked shut behind him, said, *Sky?*

I'm here. What's up? Where are you?

With Trent and Dr. Verrick.

He's back? Are they in the room with you?

No, Dr. Verrick went to deal with a patient, and Trent left to make a phone call—

It's still not safe, C.B. said. *Go to Santa Fe.*

I'm already there, she said, but Sky had gone. *He must think Trent can hear me even when he's talking to someone else,* she thought, replacing the radio on top of the gardener's cupboard and then pacing the flagstones, wondering what Sky intended to do. Was he going to go into *his* safe room and talk to her from there?

"Nope, we'll use yours," C.B. said, and she looked up to see him coming over the top of the adobe wall, one jeans-clad leg flung over it. "You didn't have to make these walls so damned high. You wouldn't happen to have a ladder, would you? Or a rope?"

"If you give me a minute, I can visualize one," she said, running back over to the cupboard.

"Never mind," C.B. said. He jumped lightly down onto the flagstones and came over to her. "Nice place," he said, looking around at the flowers and the cottonwood tree.

"How did you do that?" she asked him.

"It's one of those auxiliary defenses I told you I'd teach you," he said, walking over to the cottonwood tree and sitting down on the bench. "So what did you need to tell me? And how'd the good doctor get here so fast?"

"He has his own private jet."

"Sorry. I should have thought of that. Where was he? Did you find out?"

"Yes," Briddey said, sitting down next to him. "Sedona. Does that mean anything to you?"

"No. I know it's a haven for the rich, like Aspen or the Hamptons, which means he was probably there to set up an EED, though if that's the case, why would he have told people he was in Hong Kong?" He frowned. "I'll see what I can find out. Did Verrick buy Trent's story?"

"No. At least I ... I don't think so, but there's something funny about his reactions. You said he'd reject the idea of telepathy out of hand, but he didn't. He—"

"And you're sure he's not just humoring Trent? Doctors are awfully good at saying 'Hmm' and thinking, 'Somebody get me the psych ward.'"

She shook her head. "It was more as if his mind was on something else, as if he was waiting for something."

"And you don't have any idea what?"

"No. Are you *sure* there's not some revolutionary new scan that can detect if you're reading someone else's mind?"

"Not without you cooperating. All the same, I think I'd better get down there and listen to Verrick's voice so we'll know exactly what he's thinking and whether we have anything to worry about. Are you at his office?"

"No, the hospital, but coming here's a bad idea. So far they have no way of connecting us—"

"We'll make up some excuse for why I'm there. We can say I needed to talk to you about some app or something. Where in the hospital are you?"

"The east wing, first floor," she told him, "but I still think ... can't I listen to his voice and relay it to you?"

"No. In the first place, I don't want you listening to Verrick. Trent's right, his connection's getting better. He might overhear you. In the second place, relaying Verrick's voice wouldn't work. I'd be hearing him in your voice, not his."

"Not if you listened to it on the radio," she said, going over to the cupboard.

He shook his head. "That'd be relayed through you, too. No matter how convincing a visualization all this is, I'm not actually here. We're just exchanging thoughts."

"What about the internet? Maybe there's video of him giving a speech or something."

"That's an idea. I'll check out YouTube and his website," he said, and he was obviously still reading her mind, because he said, "Don't worry. I won't come to the hospital unless I absolutely have to."

"Good," she said. "And what about Cindy? Did you convince her she's got to lie low and not talk to me?"

"Yes, I told her to raise the drawbridge over her moat and then go lock herself in her secret garden. Show me your radio."

"I thought you said that wouldn't work."

"It won't," he said. "But show me anyway."

She did, turning it on and tuning it to Trent's station. "Hamilton, this is Trent Worth," his voice said from the radio. "Yes, I'm meeting with the doctor who did our EEDs right now." A pause. "No, sir, we haven't gotten that far."

C.B. listened for a moment and then moved the dial through several stations, listening to the static and the voices.

"You think it might work for your hearing Dr. Verrick after all?" Briddey asked.

He shook his head. "No, but you gave me an idea for—"

"I've got a *way* better way to listen to them," Maeve said.

Both Briddey and C.B. looked over at the barred door and then up at the adobe wall, expecting to see her clambering over it, but it was apparently just her voice, saying, *You don't have to turn a knob or anything.*

"I thought I told you to stay inside your safe room and not talk to your aunt Briddey!" C.B. said angrily.

I am inside it, Maeve protested, *and I wasn't talking to Briddey. I was talking to you. You didn't say anything about not talking to you.*

"Well, I'm saying it now."

Nobody can hear us, Maeve said. *I've got a whole bunch of defenses up, and besides, Trent's talking to Mr. Hamilton and Dr. Verrick—*

"I don't care," C.B. said. "I don't want you talking to anybody *or* listening to them."

You never let me do anything, Maeve said sulkily, but she left.

"Oh, my God," Briddey said. "If she'd said something like that while Trent was listening—"

"I know," C.B. said grimly. "I need to go talk to her and make sure this doesn't happen again."

"... and don't schedule any other appointments for this afternoon ...," Dr. Verrick said. Briddey looked automatically at the radio, wondering how it had gotten tuned to his station, then realized his voice had come from outside her safe room.

"I have to go," she said. "Dr. Verrick's coming back."

"Right," C.B. said. "I'll go see if I can find his voice on the internet, and if it's there, I'll listen to him and let you know what he's thinking. And I'll see if I can find out what he was doing in Sedona."

"Okay."

"And if you get in trouble in the meantime, come in here and holler for me. Don't worry, you're doing great." He kissed her on the cheek and disappeared over the wall.

"I'm sorry that took so long," Dr. Verrick said to Briddey, coming into the office and looking questioningly at the empty chair beside her.

"Trent had to make a phone call," she told him. "He'll be right back."

"Actually, you're the one I wanted to talk to," he said, sitting down and smiling at her. "Mr. Worth has told me what he experienced. I want to know what *you've* experienced. Have you heard messages like he described?"

"Ye-es," she said doubtfully. "At least I think so. When we connected, I definitely could sense his presence and his excitement . . ."

"But it didn't take the form of his voice?"

"No . . . I mean, a couple of times when Trent was sending me messages, I thought I heard him speaking, but . . ." She frowned, as if trying to think how to describe exactly what she'd experienced. "You know how you said that sometimes emotions could be so intense they came through as someone talking? That was how it felt."

"But you weren't actually hearing words, like Mr. Worth?"

"No. I mean, how could I have been? People can't hear each other's thoughts. That's crazy!" She leaned toward him. "I'm not losing my mind, am I, Doctor?"

"Absolutely not," he said, and as Trent returned: "Ah, Mr. Worth, we were just discussing your 'unusual' experience. You said the two of you had done a test sending messages back and forth—"

"Yes," Trent said eagerly. "We can do it for you again right now. Just make a list of the words you want us to send to each other, and we'll—"

Dr. Verrick was shaking his head. "That sort of test wouldn't prove anything, I'm afraid. It'd be entirely too subjective. To prove actual communication, you'd have to be tested under controlled laboratory conditions."

"We'd be willing to do that, wouldn't we, Briddey?" He looked eagerly at her. "We'll both be happy to do any kind of test you want."

"Good," Dr. Verrick said. "You must understand, Mr. Worth, you've made some extraordinary claims, and extraordinary claims demand extraordinary evidence. What you perceived as thought transference could simply have been nonverbal communication reinforced by the emotional closeness of connecting."

He doesn't believe us, Briddey thought, limp with relief, as Dr. Verrick went into an explanation of unconscious information exchange, tonal cues, and confirmation bias. *Sky was right. He was just humoring us. I misread what I thought was his distraction and his lack of surprise.*

"The test I want to run will determine whether what you experienced was actual mind-to-mind communication or something else. You'll be in separate, soundproof rooms, and the information sent will be codified and randomized so we can compare the results with statistical chance."

Which I will try to make it look like, Briddey thought, *and Dr. Verrick will tell us we were victims of our emotions and wishful thinking and send us home.*

"We'll also be able to compare it to previous research in this area," Dr. Verrick said.

"Research?" Briddey said, alert.

"Yes, Dr. Rhine at Duke University did extensive research on mental communication. Are you familiar with Zener cards?"

Twenty-Eight

"Are you making something up in your head, miss?"
—FRANCES HODGSON BURNETT, *A Little Princess*

ZENER CARDS? BRIDDEY THOUGHT. OH, NO, SKY WAS WRONG. DR. VERrick *is a True Believer. Which will make it that much harder to convince him that there's nothing to see.*

Or maybe not. "Zener cards were used in the Duke University experiments of the 1930s," Dr. Verrick said, "and used properly, they're an excellent way to objectively determine whether communication is occurring or whether the subjects merely think it is. There are five different symbols." He listed them, explained how the test worked, and then led them through the inner door and down a short hall to a small room with soundproofing tiles on the walls and ceiling. It contained a chair and a table. "You'll be in here, Ms. Flannigan. A nurse will be in in a moment to set you up."

Set me up is right, Briddey thought as he shut the door behind her. She went over to the table. On it were a pair of headphones, a microphone, a pencil, and a sheet of paper with numbers down the side.

And let's hope this nurse isn't one of the ones from my hospital stay, she thought.

It wasn't. It was a young blonde with a ponytail who introduced herself as Dr. Verrick's assistant. She wore a lab coat and carried a clip-board and a plastic bag like the one the nurse had had Briddey put her clothes in before her surgery.

"No handbags, phones, or jewelry are allowed in the testing area," she said apologetically, handing Briddey the bag. "Put them in here, and we'll hold them for you."

Briddey surrendered her smartphone and wallet and took off her earrings, and the assistant zipped the bag shut, wrote Briddey's name on it in marker, and had Briddey sit down at the table while she took her through the testing procedure.

She opened a deck of Zener cards and placed it face-down in front of Briddey. "When the buzzer sounds, pick up the first card," she said, demonstrating, "look at it, and concentrate on the image. Don't say it out loud or shape it into words. Just focus on the image and try to send it to Mr. Worth. Do you understand?"

Yes, Briddey thought, nodding. *It means you don't know we can simply tell each other what's on the card,* which was reassuring.

"When the buzzer sounds again, lay the card face-down on the table, pick up the next card, and do the same thing until you've gone through the entire deck. When you're receiving, the buzzer will sound, and you'll focus on receiving the image Mr. Worth is sending, then write it down on this paper. If you don't receive anything, put *NI.* If you're uncertain, write *U* and then what you think the image was. Don't guess." She showed Briddey the headphones. "These are noise-canceling, to shut out distracting sounds and help you concentrate."

And to keep Trent from signaling the right answers from the next room, she thought, remembering Sky's stories of cheating in the Duke experiments.

"They're also connected to Dr. Verrick so he can give you addi-tional instructions," his assistant went on. "And you'll be able to talk to him through this." She clipped a microphone to Briddey's collar. "It'll be off during the testing, of course."

"What if I have a question?"

"You'll signal him with this"—she showed her what looked like a TV remote—"and he'll activate your mike. But please try not to use it. There'll be breaks between the test rounds, and you can ask questions then."

"So you won't be in here during the testing?"

"No," the assistant said, glancing up at the ceiling in front of the table.

There must be a concealed camera, Briddey thought.

"Any other questions?"

Yes. How do I get out of this? "I don't think so," she said.

"We'll start in a few minutes." The assistant scooped up the Zener cards, put them in her lab-coat pocket, and pulled an unopened deck from the other pocket. "You'll be sending first. Dr. Verrick will tell you when to open the deck," she said, set the cards on the table, put the headphones on Briddey, and went out.

Don't panic, Briddey told herself. *They can't find out anything unless you cooperate.* All she had to do was write down different symbols from the ones Trent sent her and send him wrong answers when she was transmitting.

But that wouldn't work. A score that was radically lower than random guesses would be just as suspicious as a high score. And that went for the answers she wrote down, too. She'd need to give some right answers. How many?

Logic dictated that it should be one out of five, which meant it probably wasn't, but contacting Sky to ask him about it would be even more dangerous than giving Dr. Verrick an encouraging score. She couldn't let them find out about him.

Which meant she needed to figure it out on her own. And fast. They'd be starting any minute. The hidden camera meant flipping a coin was out, and mentally rolling dice wouldn't work. *So what are you going to do?*

What people who aren't telepathic do when they take the Zener test, she thought. *They guess.* She'd guess a symbol before she turned the card over, and then stick with it whether it matched what was on the card or not. And when it was Trent's turn, she'd guess before he had a chance to send an image.

And hopefully after the first round of testing, Dr. Verrick would decide Trent was suffering from an over-active imagination and send them home.

In the meantime, all she had to do was sit still, stay in her courtyard, and look like she was concentrating. And not give any sign of what she was actually thinking. *Poker face,* she thought. *You can do this.*

"Ms. Flannigan, can you hear me?" Dr. Verrick's voice said through the headphones, and he must have turned her microphone on because when she said yes, he responded, "Good. You understood the testing procedure?"

"Yes."

"Then break the seal on the deck, place it face-down on the table in front of you, and begin when the buzzer sounds. You'll have thirty seconds for each card."

Which gave her plenty of time in between telling Trent, "Square, circle, circle, wavy lines," to try to remember why the name Sedona had rung a bell. Had Mary Clare mentioned it in regard to one of the hundreds of things she was worried about? The online money-laundering syndicate, maybe? Or hantavirus? Or maybe someone at work had talked about someone going there on vacation?

No, because she hadn't known it was in Arizona till Dr. Verrick said that was where he'd been, and besides, she had a feeling she'd read it somewhere, not heard it. Where? Online? In an email?

Briddey frowned, trying to place it, and then remembered she needed to maintain a poker face. Hopefully Dr. Verrick would think she was frowning in concentration.

If he was even watching her. When he'd given her the instructions, he'd still sounded both distracted and bored. And impatient. *Like he's waiting for something to happen, and this test is just to pass the time till it does.* But then why do the test?

Maybe what he's waiting for is some sign that we're actually telepathic, and if that's the case, it's doubly important that he doesn't get it, she thought, and focused on looking at a sequence of stars, wavy lines, and squares, and telling Trent, "Cross, circle, circle, cross."

When the buzzer sounded on the last card, the assistant with the ponytail reappeared to take the deck. As soon as she left, Dr. Verrick's voice came through the headphones, saying, "This time you're going to receive images from Mr. Worth. Do you know what to do?"

"Yes," Briddey said, picking up her pencil.

"Good. When the red light comes on, Mr. Worth will begin send-ing."

The light blinked on. *Square,* she thought. *Star,* Trent sent. She started to write down "square," then hesitated. If she was going to get most of these wrong, she needed to look like she was having trouble getting the image. She began to count instead.

Twenty seconds should be about right, she thought, counting them off, and then: *Thirty seconds is far too long for sending these images.* Especially with the headphones cutting out all exterior sounds. With them gone, all that was left was Trent's thoughts: *As soon as this round's over, I'll tell him he needs to do simultaneous fCAT scans while Briddey and I are sending and receiving so they can pinpoint the location of the telepathic activity. Star. It's a star, Briddey. Let me know if you're getting this. Is it coming through? Star.*

"Wavy lines," Briddey wrote firmly, and waited for the next one, wishing it *was* possible to block him like she'd accused Sky of doing.

She could at least tune him out. As soon as he sent her the next word, "circle," she went into her courtyard, got the radio, brought it over to the bench, and tuned it to static.

Mistake. With his thoughts not there to act as a screen, she could hear the voices. Her perimeter should be keeping them to a murmur, but it wasn't, they were too angry and frightened, crying out, *It hurts . . . can't afford . . . no insurance . . . overdose . . . are you trying to stab me, you goddamned bitch? . . . considerable damage . . . so scared . . . what if it's cancer? . . . afraid it's malignant . . . on duty since midnight . . . blood clot . . . can't be happening to me!* Words of anxiety and terror and despair.

This is the real reason Sky hates hospitals, she said to herself, and thought of him braving the voices to come to the hospital to get her. Twice. Through flames and suffocating smoke. And she'd been rude to him; she'd told him to go away—

Stop, she told herself. *You aren't supposed to be thinking about him. And you've got more pressing concerns—like writing down answers every thirty seconds—"cross"—and keeping the voices out. And your own thoughts in.*

This would be an excellent time to have those auxiliary defenses, but since Sky hadn't had time to teach them to her, she'd have to see what she could do about shoring up the ones she already had. *Maybe I could add more barricades,* she thought, remembering Cindy's walled gardens and drawbridges and moats.

No, not a moat. Adding more water to the flood of voices outside the door would weaken her defenses, and a walled garden was out. She would have to venture outside the courtyard to erect it, and the voices were already washing up against the adobe walls: *. . . inoperable . . . so* *exhausted . . . been on my feet forever . . . six months to live . . . no!* They were growing louder and the waves higher by the minute. Why?

It isn't just the hospital, Briddey thought. *It's because I'm focusing all my energy on keeping Trent and Dr. Verrick from hearing what I'm thinking and not on my perimeter.*

She needed to strengthen it, but that meant going outside, too, and the voices sounded like they might crash through any minute. Whatever she did, she'd have to do it from in here. But there wasn't room for a castle, and she wasn't sure what zombie gates looked like—or how effective they were against water. What *was* effective against water?

Sandbags? That was a possibility. She could pile them against the door . . .

But not now. There wasn't time. Two more answers, and she was going to have to start sending again. Or perhaps Dr. Verrick would conclude there was nothing to see here and send them home.

He didn't. His assistant—a different one this time, a middle-aged woman with chestnut hair, in a lab coat and Prada heels and clutching a clipboard to her chest—came in to get Briddey's answer sheet, saying something Briddey couldn't hear because of the headphones.

She took them off. "Excuse me?"

"I said, 'Dr. Verrick wants to do another round.' I'm Liz, by the way. And you're Ms. Flannigan, right?"

Briddey nodded.

"Can I get you anything? Water? Coffee? Juice?"

"No, thank you. I'm fine." Did she dare ask for a bathroom break so she could try to find out if Sky had located a recording of Dr. Verrick's voice? No, better not, at least not till she knew how much Trent was able to hear.

"You understand the procedure for sending?"

Briddey nodded again.

"Can you repeat it back to me, just to make sure?"

"Of course," Briddey said, and did.

"Yes, that's it exactly," Liz said, and gave her a new, unopened deck of cards. She told her to wait to open the deck till she'd left the room, and went out.

Briddey put her headphones back on and then pulled at the cellophane tab. "Are you ready to begin, Ms. Flannigan?" Dr. Verrick asked.

Briddey put her hands up to her headphones. His voice was different. She could hear excitement in it, and the sense that he was waiting distractedly for something was gone. *The scan that can spot telepathy without the subject's help has arrived,* she thought.

But Sky had assured her there was no such technology, and the only other thing that could have excited Dr. Verrick was their test results. Could Trent have somehow, in spite of her defenses, in spite of her sending false answers, heard what was really on the cards, and Dr. Verrick had decided they *were* telepathic?

"Ms. Flannigan?" Dr. Verrick called. "Can you hear me?"

"Yes," she said. "Sorry. I'm having trouble opening the deck." She plucked, she hoped convincingly, at the corners of the cellophane wrap, pulled an end free, opened the deck, and set it down in front of her. "Now I'm ready."

"Good. Begin when you hear the buzzer."

She did, thinking of a symbol, turning over the card and then sending the symbol she'd thought of to Trent while she thought furiously about what to do. C.B. had told her not to audit Dr. Verrick, but she *had* to know what he was thinking.

First, though, she needed to barricade the door to make sure Trent couldn't hear her. *I'll visualize a pile of sandbags against the door,* she thought, then remembered C.B. telling her the more detailed the visualization, the stronger it was, and imagined them next to the gardener's cupboard instead.

She took hold of one and dragged it over in front of the door and then went back for the next, saying loudly with each trip, *Trent, I'm sending you an image of a circle (or star or wavy line). Can you see it?*

When she had a solid layer piled against the door and the wall on either side, she said, *I'm sending . . . image . . . Trent,* and went over to the radio to locate Trent's station.

He said from the radio: *I didn't catch that last one.*

I said, it's a star. Repeat, square, she said, and began looking for Dr. Verrick's station.

Did you say square or star? Trent asked.

I said "stare," she said to throw him off while she inched the needle up the dial. *Repeat, s . . .* She let her voice trail off and began humming tunelessly.

What? I can't hear you, Trent said. *You need to concentrate.*

I am, she thought, leaning closer to the radio to try to catch the doctor's voice over Trent's talking and turning the knob again.

"Are you able to hear the images she's sending?" Dr. Verrick asked, his voice emerging from the radio, and in spite of what she'd just heard Trent thinking, he must have said yes, because Dr. Verrick said, "Excellent. Did you write them down?"

Well, of course he wrote them down, Briddey thought. *Isn't that the point?*

"And her responses to the images sent to her?" Dr. Verrick asked, and Trent must have answered in the affirmative again because Dr. Verrick said, "Circle, star, wavy lines, star," apparently comparing the lists. "Just as I thought. A hundred percent accuracy."

What? Briddey thought. Trent had just said he couldn't hear her.

She tuned quickly back to Trent's frequency to hear his response to that, but she was too late. Trent was saying, ". . . buzzer sounded. Send the next one."

She flipped back to Dr. Verrick. ". . . obviously trying to keep the extent of her telepathic ability from us. Have you been able to pick up anything else?"

She flipped back to Trent, too quickly, overshot the frequency, then had to fiddle with the knob to bring it in again—too late.

I need to be able to listen to both of them at the same time, Briddey thought. Maybe if she visualized two radios—

"You don't have to do *that,*" Maeve said, appearing at her elbow in a Rapunzel dress and tiara. "All you need to do is—"

"What are *you* doing here?" Briddey said. "Sky told you to stay in your safe room. Trent will *hear* you!"

"No, he won't. I told you, I've got tons of defenses. If you want to hear who the person's talking to, you just turn the tuning knob to the person's frequency and then tap this." "This" was the volume knob. "Then you can hear both of them. I don't know why you did a radio, though. It would have been way easier to do a phone and just click on group chat and then—"

"Go *home!*" Briddey said desperately. "If they find out about you—"

"They won't. I've got like sixteen layers of defenses. Not like this place." She looked doubtfully around at the courtyard. "I could help you imagine a forest of brambles or something."

"No. Go. Now, before Trent hears you talking."

"I could help. I know lots of stuff. C.B. taught me——"

"I don't care. I need you to go inside your castle and stay there, no matter what happens."

"Even if——"

"No exceptions. Now go, or I'll tell Sky."

"Who's Sky? Is that like a code name for——?"

"Yes," Briddey said. "Go."

"What's *my* code name? I think it should be——"

"Now!"

"Okay, fine," Maeve said disgustedly. "I was just trying to help." She disappeared, only to pop back in a moment later. "I forgot to tell you, it only works if you've heard the person's voice before," and vanished again.

Please, please, please don't let Trent have heard any of that, Briddey thought, and dialed the tuning knob back to Trent.

"What's wrong?" his voice issued from the radio. "Why isn't she sending? I haven't gotten anything the last two times."

Briddey hastily turned over a card. It had a cross on it. *Wavy lines,* she thought at him.

"Wavy lines," Trent said, "finally!" He began fussing over whether it was the tenth or eleventh word. Cindy must have been right about him not being able to hear her, thank goodness. But just in case, Briddey tuned to Dr. Verrick.

"What else did you hear?" he asked.

There was a pause, during which Briddey cursed herself for not tapping on the volume knob like Maeve had said. "And you didn't hear anyone else?" he asked.

Briddey tapped frantically at the knob, afraid she'd miss the crucial part of Trent's answer, and then thought she must have done it wrong because there was silence. "Curse you, Cin——" she began, reaching for the tuning knob. And heard a female voice say, "No, but she's definitely sending him incorrect answers."

The assistant, Liz. But how could——?

She has auburn hair, Briddey thought. *That's why she made me go through all the steps of the Zener test again for her, because she needed to hear my voice so she could separate it from the others.*

She must be one of Dr. Verrick's patients who'd become telepathic, too, when she had the EED. That explained why Dr. Verrick had had the testing rooms and the Zener cards all ready, and why he'd come back when Trent phoned him and then seemed so uninterested in what he had to say and in the tests. He hadn't needed them. Liz could tell him whether they were telepathic or not. He must have been waiting for her to get to the hospital.

Trent had thought he'd been using Dr. Verrick to get his phone, but the reverse was true. Dr. Verrick had been using Trent to get to her. *That's why he suggested the possibility of hearing voices to me that day at his office,* she thought, *and why he moved our surgery up. Because I was a redhead, and he thinks that's what's causing this.* And Liz's being one of his patients hopefully meant he thought the EED was the trigger for the telepathy.

"Do you think she's sending the incorrect answers consciously?" Dr. Verrick said from the radio. "Or could it be a problem with her connection?"

"I'll need to hear more of her responses to be certain," Liz said, "but I sense she's doing it deliberately."

"But why?" Dr. Verrick asked. "She and Mr. Worth contacted me to tell me they were communicating."

"Perhaps her psychic gift frightens her," Liz said, "or perhaps ... could she have made psychic contact with someone else, too?"

"It's possible, I suppose," Dr. Verrick said, "but—"

"If the person she's communing with is a man, she might be afraid Mr. Worth would be jealous. Don't you tell your patients they have to be emotionally bonded to connect?"

Your patients? That meant Liz wasn't one. *Then who is she?*

"I'm sensing a feeling of spiritual strife from her," Liz said. "Her chakras are closed, and her aura is emanating emotional conflict."

Aura? Briddey thought. *Chakras? Who* is *this?* And knew, the memory that had been just out of reach before, slotting neatly into place. The ad Kathleen had emailed her, for the psychic who claimed she could put couples in touch with each other's souls. Lyzandra. At the Spa of the Spirit. In Sedona, Arizona.

Twenty-Nine

"Those who have courage to love
should have courage to suffer."
—ANTHONY TROLLOPE, *The Bertrams*

BUT C.B. SAID PSYCHICS WEREN'T TELEPATHIC, BRIDDEY THOUGHT. *HE
said they were fakes who used mentalist's tricks and cold reading to make it look
like they could read minds.*

Yet Lyzandra was saying, her voice coming confidently from the
radio, "I haven't heard anyone else's voice yet, but a short while ago I
lost the connection for nearly five minutes, and at the end of the disruption, I heard her think, 'Please don't let Trent have heard that.'"

Briddey leaned close to the radio, listening. "And when I was in the
testing room with her," Lyzandra was saying, "I caught something
about her wondering if she dared call someone."

Oh, my God, Briddey thought, trying not to panic. *My safe room's
not strong enough to keep her out. I've got to tell Sky.*

But that was the worst thing she could possibly do. If Lyzandra
heard her talking to him—

Briddey, C.B. called. *I've got to talk to you. It's ur—*

No! Briddey flung herself at the courtyard's blue door, pushing with all her might against it. *Night Fighter to Dawn Patrol! Maintain radio silence!* she called urgently, but he wasn't listening.

I did some research on Sedona, C.B. said. *It's a big mecca for—*

We are under attack, Dawn Patrol! Repeat, we are under attack! she cried, trying to think of a way to warn him that Lyzandra was listening without giving his presence away.

"The Highwayman," she thought, and began reciting the part of the poem where Bess, the landlord's daughter, had shot herself to warn her lover of the soldiers, praying C.B. would get the message.

And either he did or he gave up trying to get her to answer, because he retreated. Briddey jammed the bar more firmly into its brackets, made sure the latch was in place, and still reciting "The Highwayman," ran across to the sandbags. She had to make the courtyard stronger to keep Lyzandra out. She started dragging the sandbags over to the door one by one and piling them in front of it.

"She's stopped sending the symbols and seems to be reciting something," Lyzandra said from the radio, and Briddey remembered that she was supposed to be transmitting the pictures on the Zener cards.

Circle, she thought, heaving a sandbag into place. *Square. Wavy lines. Cross.*

The bags were impossibly heavy and hard to get a grip on. *I should have let Maeve imagine that forest of brambles for me,* she began, and then stomped firmly on both the name and the thought. If only Sky had had time to teach her those other screening techniques.

But he taught me some, she thought, and launched into "Ode to Billie Joe" and then the theme from *Gilligan's Island*, interspersing the verses with *star, wavy lines, blue moons, pink rainbows. Night Fighter calling Dawn Patrol. Zeroes at twelve o'clock. Maintain radio silence. Repeat, maintain radio silence.*

"Are you getting anything?" Dr. Verrick asked.

"No. Her chakras aren't open, so what I'm hearing from her spirit-mind voice is very cloudy."

"Can you make out anything at all?"

"Yes. Something about the sky and stars and fighter pilots and a bridge. Nothing that makes sense."

Good, it's working, Briddey thought, dragging another sandbag over and casting about for something else to recite. Not "My Time of Day," which made her think of that late-night walk with Sky, and not "Molly Malone." Or *Finian's Rainbow*, which meant she shouldn't be thinking about Lucky Charms either.

Monopoly playing pieces. *Cat, wheelbarrow, top hat, iron . . .* But there were only eight of them, even counting the discontinued shoe, and "Teen Angel" only had a measly four verses. She needed longer songs, longer lists.

Victorian novels, she thought. *The Master of Ballantrae, The Moonstone, The Old Curiosity Shop, Far from the Madding Crowd . . .*

"Her spirit-mind voice is still very clouded," Lyzandra said from the radio, "and I'm getting negative vibrations. I think she may be intentionally concealing her thoughts. You need to ask her about the telepathy directly."

"But if she's intentionally giving us wrong answers," Dr. Verrick said, "what makes you think she'll tell us the truth?"

"She won't. But when you ask someone a question, their spirit thinks of the truth, no matter what they may say, and it's sometimes possible to read that thought."

She's right, Briddey thought. *It's the "don't think about an elephant" problem.* And it was equally impossible to try to make her mind a blank.

I could run away, she thought, remembering that first night in the hospital. But that would only convince them she was hiding something. Her strongest defense right now was that they didn't know she'd overheard them and knew what they were up to, and she had to keep it that way. Which meant staying here and looking innocent and thinking about things completely unrelated to telepathy, like movie stars and flowers and designer shoes.

"Ms. Flannigan?" Dr. Verrick's voice came over the headphones. "We need to ask you some questions."

"About the Zener test?" she asked, thinking, *Gucci, Manolo Blahnik, Ferragamo, Christian Louboutin, Christian Bale,* at them. "Was I doing something wrong?"

"No, no, not at all, but Mr. Worth picked up some interesting things in your responses, and we need to ask you about them. He said he heard you mentally communicating with someone else."

You're lying, she blurted out and immediately squelched the thought. *Sandra Bullock, Brad Pitt, Johnny Depp, Emily Blunt—*

"Whose voice did you hear? Was it someone you knew?"

Yes, she thought at them. *The highwayman and Professor Harold Hill and F. Scott Fitzgerald.* "I don't know what Trent can be referring to," she said. "The only voice I've heard is his."

"Ask her again," Lyzandra said, and Dr. Verrick promptly asked, "Are you certain? The voice of one person can sometimes be mistaken for another."

"How could I have heard someone else?" Briddey asked, making her voice register bewilderment. *Anthony Trollope, Thurston Howell III, Jimmy Choo.* "I'm emotionally bonded to Trent."

"Ask her something more general," Lyzandra ordered.

"Have you ever had a feeling that someone was in trouble?" Dr. Verrick asked.

Besides me, you mean? she thought, and hastily changed her answer to, *The castaways are in trouble. And so's the innkeeper's black-eyed daughter. And Adelaide. She's got a terrible cold.*

"Have you ever had a premonition of death?" Dr. Verrick asked. "Have you ever had a vivid feeling of déjà vu? Have you ever been forewarned of danger? Have you ever had an out-of-body experience?"

Briddey answered the barrage of questions as best she could, singing snatches of "Luck Be a Lady" and "I Wish I Were an Oscar Mayer Weiner," and listing as many flowers as she could remember—*camellias, violets, petunias*—but it was hard to stay focused and not let anything else through.

When Dr. Verrick asked, "Have you ever had a feeling you knew what was going to happen before it did?" she had a sudden image of Aunt Oona saying, "'Tis Mary Clare on the phone, I can feel it," and had to stomp the thought out forcibly, as if it were a brushfire, and loudly recite other types of fires: *forest fires, wildfires, campfires, Chariots of Fire.*

But that wasn't safe either. When she thought *bonfires,* she had a sudden memory of Sky sitting in the car with her, telling her about Joan of Arc. She veered instantly away to junk food, but that reminded her of the stale Doritos of their midnight feast—and the popcorn

Cindy had fed the ducks. Shoes made her think of her sodden sandals thrust unceremoniously under the bed; movie stars of Hedy Lamarr.

Sky was right. Every thought *was* connected to every other in a tangled maze of memories and cognitive links and associations, so that no matter what she thought about or what neural pathway she took, it circled treacherously back to the elephant in the room.

So, fine, think of elephants, she thought, and spent the next five minutes naming every one she could think of, African and Asian and circus elephants, Babar and Jumbo and Dumbo—no, that was a Disney movie and too close to the Disney princesses. Think about their tusks and their trunks and their fear of mice. And of snakes, which Saint Patrick threw out of—

No, you can't think about Ireland. It will lead them straight to Cindy. Think about someplace else. Angkor Wat, Mount Fuji, Mount Rushmore, Niagara Falls—no, not that either. Sky had said he'd take her there on their honey—

"Her spirit is in contact with another spirit," Lyzandra said from the radio. "A man's. Someone much more accomplished in mind-spirit contact. A seer, perhaps, who instructed her in resistance."

"Do you know who he is?"

"No. I'm getting an image of his name, but it's obscured. It begins with *S.*"

I shouldn't have chosen Sky as a code name, Briddey thought sickly. *It's too close to*— and slapped the thought of C.B.'s name away. *Saint,* she thought. *You heard me think "saint." Saint Margaret, Saint Michael, Saint Catherine,* and wondered if that was whose voices Joan of Arc had really heard, or if she'd only told her interrogators that to keep them from finding out who she was really talking to.

"Mr. Worth, is there anyone at Commspan whose name begins with an *S?*" Dr. Verrick was asking.

"There's Suki Parker," Trent said. "And Art Sampson. Briddey said she had a meeting with him this morning. She was very upset that she had to cancel."

"Could the name be Sampson?" Dr. Verrick asked Lyzandra.

It will be now, Briddey thought. Instead of just throwing up a screen of random thoughts, she should have been sending red herrings to throw them off the scent. *Whatever happens, I can't let them find out I've been talking to Art Sampson,* she thought at them.

"The name *might* be Sampson," Lyzandra said doubtfully. "I'm not sure."

If they find out Art Sampson's telepathic . . . , Briddey said, and imagined herself going up to his office. But as she thought about getting out of the elevator and walking along the corridor, the image came to her unbidden of Sky grabbing her and pulling her into the copy room.

This was like walking in a minefield. Everywhere you put your foot was dangerous. And the questions kept coming through the headphones: "Can you hear any other voice besides Mr. Worth's? Do you recognize it? Is it a stranger or someone you know? How often have you heard it? When did you first hear it?"

This was just like the voices—a relentless barrage of words coming too fast, too continuously, for her to do more than put her arms over her head and try to protect herself. The effort of coming up with answers and white noise, of preventing Dr. Verrick and the psychic from reading her thoughts and keeping Sky and Cindy out of them, was exhausting. She felt like she had that night in the hospital stairway, as if she'd used up every bit of her strength—

No, you can't think about the hospital either, she thought. *Think about songs you wouldn't want to get stuck in your head—"Itsy Bitsy Teenie-Weenie Yellow Polkadot Bikini," "The Little Drummer Boy," "Tell Laura I Love Her," Laura Linney, Laura Bush, Laura Ingalls Wilder . . .*

Ten minutes in, she knew she wasn't going to be able to hold them off. Try as she might to shut the questions out, to shield her answers with Froot Loops and *Bleak House* and songs, some part of her mind was registering the questions and automatically answering them, and as time went on, she'd make more and more mistakes, it would take her longer and longer to recognize the potential danger in a line of thought.

She thought suddenly of Sky telling her about the ESP subjects at Duke whose scores had fallen as they tired. Maybe he had it backwards. Maybe those low scores had happened when they were hiding their ability, and more and more correct answers had seeped through as their energy flagged.

Like mine's flagging right now. It was only a matter of time before she let slip the clue they needed, before she gave up from exhaustion and told them what they wanted to know. *You can't,* she thought. *You have to protect Sky and Cindy, no matter what toll it takes.* Like Joan of Arc. She had gone to the stake rather than betray her voices.

But I'm not Joan of Arc. I'll break under torture. Was already breaking. When she looked over at the door, water was seeping in in spite of the sandbags she'd piled against it, and flowing along the spaces between the flagstones, along the base of the adobe wall. And behind it she could hear the dull, watery roar of the voices.

They're going to get in! she thought, and saw them flooding the ladies' lounge, saw herself huddled under the sink, clinging to the pipe, sitting hunched in the stairwell in her bloodstained hospital gown, and C.B. coming to—

Stop! Don't. Think of something, anything else: Charles Dickens, Cap'n Crunch, Monty Python, McCook, Nebraska, Oliver Twist, orphans, organ transplants . . .

But it was too late. Lyzandra was saying, "It's definitely someone she knows and is emotionally bonded to."

"Did you get his name yet?" Trent asked.

"No, but I got an image of a hospital. Did someone come to see her that first night after she had the EED?"

"I can ask the staff," Dr. Verrick said.

No one saw him, Briddey told herself desperately.

"Did someone come to see you after you had your EED?" Dr. Verrick asked Briddey through the headphones. "Or call you?"

Oh, God, the phone call, Briddey thought. *They'll . . . no! Think of Trix! And tulips and Choctaw Ridge, the Black Hole of Calcutta and psychosomatic symptoms and albino eggplants and soldiers shooting the highwayman down in cold blood . . .*

"I couldn't hear her answer," Lyzandra said. "She's definitely resisting. It was all an incoherent babble about pirates and lace and vegetables. Can't you do something to make her less resistant? Hypnotize her or give her some kind of relaxant? Valium or Xanax or something?"

No! A relaxant would lower her defenses. It would let the voices in.

"You're certain a relaxant won't disrupt her telepathic ability?" Dr. Verrick asked. "Or damage it in some way?"

"I'm sure," Lyzandra said. "I've taken Valium a number of times to open my chakras and make me more receptive."

More receptive? Briddey thought, trying not to panic. *More receptive?*

"And you're sure there won't be any negative side effects?" Dr. Verrick was asking.

You're not seriously going to take medical advice from a psychic, are you? Briddey thought, but apparently he was, because he said, "There's still the problem of gaining her consent. She'll have to sign a form."

"I'm sure I can get her to sign it," Trent said. "We're practically engaged. And if I can't persuade her to cooperate," she heard him add, and knew she was hearing his unspoken thoughts, "I'll tell her her job depends on it."

You really are *a snake,* Briddey thought.

Lyzandra said, "I'm worried that asking for her consent will put her on her guard and make her even more resistant. *I* could take the relaxant instead. It will enhance my ability to hear her—"

And I won't be able to stop her, Briddey thought, because she had the voices to hold off, too. And they were slamming with more and more force against the door, determined to find a way in. And while she was trying to keep them out, Dr. Verrick would hit her with question after question till she accidentally told them Sky's name—and Cindy's. And delivered them both into Trent's hands.

And there's nothing at all I can do to keep that from happening. She thought of Bess, the landlord's daughter, helplessly bound and gagged with a revolver pointed at her breast. And of Billie Joe McAllister. What if he'd jumped off the Tallahatchie Bridge to keep someone from finding out something—and to protect somebody? And hadn't been able to tell the girl because if he had, she'd have come to stop him? *I can't let that happen.*

"I'm administering the drug now," Dr. Verrick said.

"How long before she begins to feel its effects?" Trent asked.

"Just a few minutes."

Long enough, Briddey thought, and moved the radio from the bench to the top of the cupboard and then went over to the door and began dragging the sandbags away from it, singing "Teen Angel" to keep C.B. from hearing what she was doing.

The sandbags were wet and very heavy. It took all her strength to pull them off to the side, and as soon as she did, water welled up and began to flow across the flagstones.

"You should be beginning to feel the drug's effects," Dr. Verrick said, and Briddey heard Trent ask, his voice full of excitement, "Are you getting anything yet?"

"Yes," Lyzandra said dreamily. "Something about water and a door. And something she intends to do that she doesn't want us to find out about."

We can't have that, Briddey thought, and threw everything she could think of at them—and at C.B.—poems and shoes and song lyrics and the kitchen sink—and just for Trent, water moccasins, rattlesnakes, cobras, pit vipers.

Square, cross, wavy lines, she thought, dragging the sandbags. *Crosstalk, Cap'n Crunch, corporate spies, calling Dr. Black, please report to the nurses' station, please turn off your cellphones, closing in ten minutes, all personnel will be required to work Saturday due to the paradigm shift and the decline and fall of the Roman Empire, it's a crummy morning out there, folks. Roger that. Rainbows, roses, Rice Krispies . . .*

But it didn't do any good. "I've almost got it," Lyzandra said. "Ask her again who she's talking to."

The rivulets were spreading out across the flagstones in a widening sheet. After Briddey dragged the last sandbag away, she had to splash through the water to get to the door.

"There are definitely two people. Ask her directly what their names are."

Saint Catherine, Briddey said. *Saint Margaret, Saint Michael, Thomas Hardy, Tobias Marshall, Patience Lovelace, Ethel Godwin, Bridey Murphy, Adelaide . . .*

She put her hands on the bar to let it out of its brackets, and then stopped, looking past the door at the wall of roaring voices rising beyond it, waiting to drown the courtyard and Dr. Verrick's questions—and her answers. And her.

I can't, she thought, remembering the ladies' room and the storage closet. *They'll wash me over the edge, they'll dash me against the rocks.*

"Can you tell who they are?" Dr. Verrick was asking.

"A male and a female," Lyzandra said. "She calls the female Cindy, but that's not her real name. It begins with an M. Mary, I think, or Ma—"

"McAllister," Briddey said, lifting the bar. "Billie Joe McAllister," and opened the door.

Thirty

"Christl! the sluice gates are going!"
— DOROTHY L. SAYERS, *The Nine Tailors*

FOR AN ENDLESS MOMENT NOTHING HAPPENED, AND BRIDDEY THOUGHT, *It's not going to get here in time. They'll hear Maeve's name before it*— And then the voices hit her head on, not like water at all but like a battering ram, so fierce it had to be every single person, every single thought in the hospital: *It hurts, oh, it hurts! . . . what do you mean there's nothing you can do? . . . my fault . . . should never have let him drive . . . multiple lacerations . . . stroke . . . bad news . . . metastasized . . .*

The force of them flung her violently up against the cottonwood tree, and she wrapped her arms around its wide trunk and clung there, gasping. The voices had been bad before, but these were far worse, throwing up a deafening spray of panic and fury and pain. *I'll never be able to hold out against them,* she thought.

And there was no railing to cling to, no C.B., only the cottonwood's trunk, and it was too big around to get a decent hold. Her hands scrabbled against the rough bark, trying to gain a purchase as the voices crashed against her: *. . . no chance of recovery . . . hemorrhage . . . tumor . . . inoperable . . . but she's only six . . . third-degree burns over eighty percent of his . . . where the hell is that crash cart?*

And above them she heard Lyzandra say clearly, "I can hear other voices," and then cry out, "Oh God, what's happening?"

Briddey glanced over at the radio. It was still on the top of the cupboard, and the water had nearly reached it. "What's wrong, Lyzandra?" she heard Dr. Verrick say anxiously. "Talk to me."

"... thousands of them!" Lyzandra shrieked, and Briddey heard Trent shout, his voice rising, "Get them off me!"

Oh, no, Briddey thought. *They're being deluged by the voices, too.* She glanced over at the door as if she might be able to reach it and shut it, but water was pouring through it in a raging torrent and rising by the minute.

"Nurse!" Dr. Verrick called, and then the radio was swept off the cupboard and into the water as it surged against the inside walls of the courtyard, carrying radio and cupboard with it.

"She's having a seizure!" a man shouted as the radio bobbed past her. "Get a nurse in here! Stat!" and she couldn't tell if it was Dr. Verrick or one of the voices because they were all calling for help: *Nurse!* and *Get them off me!* and *Don't let me die* . . .

Briddey needed to call for help, too, or the voices would carry her over the edge, they'd dash her on the rocks. *But you mustn't,* she thought, clinging desperately to the cottonwood's trunk. *If you do, you'll give him away, and they'll burn him at the stake.*

The voices and the water were rising faster now— *. . . never regained consciousness . . . terminal . . . couldn't save . . . nothing we could do . . . save . . .* —and her fingers were slipping. She was losing her hold. She was going to call for help in spite of herself, to betray C.B., and there was nothing she could do . . .

Yes, there is, she thought, and shut her eyes and let go of the tree. And she was in the roiling water—flailing, floundering—and under it, and her mouth was full of water.

Thank heavens, she thought as she gulped and choked. *Now I can't betray him.* Her lungs filled, and she began to gag, to cough.

But not from the water she'd swallowed. From the smoke.

No, she thought frantically. *It can't be smoke,* but she could smell the acrid tang of burning, and when she opened her eyes, it was everywhere, so thick she couldn't see the walls or the door, and C.B. had his arm around her, he was holding her head above water.

"No!" she sobbed, fighting against him. "Go away! If you stay, they'll hear you."

"Not over this din, they won't," he said, plowing chest-deep through the water toward the smoke-filled courtyard.

"You don't understand! Dr. Verrick's got a psychic, Lyzandra, who can hear everything I think, even in my safe room! They'll find out about you!" She hit wildly at him. "You've got to go!"

"What are you—? Ow! Geez, Briddey, that was my nose!" He grabbed her wrists, pinioning them against his chest so she couldn't hit him again. "What the hell are you trying to do, kill me?"

"No, I'm trying to get you to leave!" she cried, struggling to free herself from his grasp, to dive away from him.

He hauled her back to the surface. "Well, then stop fighting me," he said, and half pushed, half dragged her out of the water and onto a dry patch of flagstones. It was covered with burning embers, and smoke obscured the adobe wall behind it. She collapsed against the wall, coughing.

C.B. was coughing, too, bent over, his hands on his knees. He was drenched, and his face was streaked with soot. Water dripped from his clothes and down the back of his neck onto the flagstones. "Are you okay?" he asked Briddey between bouts of coughing.

"No," she said. "Why did you come?"

"You're kidding, right? When have I not come when you were in trouble?"

Never, she thought. *But this time you weren't supposed to.* "I'm so sorry. I didn't mean to call to you."

"You didn't. I was already here. As soon as I realized Sedona was famous for its psychics and that one of its most famous ones had red hair, Verrick's going there and wanting to keep it secret suddenly all made sense, and I tried to call to *you.* And when you shut me out, I figured something must be wrong, so I came straight to the hospital to find out what."

"You came to the *hospital*?" she said, horrified, looking past the courtyard to the reality of the testing room, hoping against hope that he wasn't *here,* that he was somewhere else in the building—on the floor where she'd been that first night, or in the stairwell she'd fled to— and was doing this remotely.

But he wasn't. He was kneeling next to her as she sat huddled on the floor against the soundproofed wall. The headphones lay on the floor beside her, and she was surprised to see that they and the floor were both dry, and so were C.B.'s clothes and hair. She looked down at her own sopping clothes. They were dry, too.

The chair she'd sat in was overturned, and Zener cards were scattered everywhere. The door was ajar, as if it had been kicked open, and in a minute Dr. Verrick would catch sight of C.B. on the camera and come in—

"No, he won't," C.B. said, "but I'd better shut the door anyway. Correction, doors."

He stood up with an effort. "Stay here," he ordered Briddey, and she watched as he walked through the scattered cards over to the testing room door to shut it and then waded back into the water, now only knee-deep and receding rapidly, and over to the open door of the courtyard.

He pushed it closed. That shut out the worst of the voices, though Briddey could still hear their angry murmur behind it. He retrieved the bar, which was floating nearby, and jammed it into its brackets. He slid the iron bolt across and then sloshed back across the flagstones to sit down beside her. He looked exhausted, his face drawn and white under the streaks of soot. His hands were covered with soot, too, and beginning to blister. From the fire. The fire he'd come through for her.

Tears stung her eyes. *C.B., I am so sorry.*

"It wasn't your fault," he said tiredly, and leaned his head back against the wall. He closed his eyes.

"No, you can't do that," she said, getting to her knees. "You've got to leave. There's a camera—"

"It's okay. I disabled it."

"But you still have to go. Before Dr. Verrick finds out you're here, before she tells him—"

"She's not telling him anything right now. Neither's your boyfriend, and Dr. Verrick's got his hands too full to worry about us."

"You don't know that."

"Yes, I do. I was in the hall outside Verrick's office when you let loose that deluge and heard both him and the psychic shouting, so I can read all three of their scheming little minds. And, trust me, eavesdropping is the last thing they're doing. You didn't just unleash those voices on yourself, you know. The psychic and Trent were both listening to you, and the voices roared straight through you and into them at full blast. They're too traumatized to tell anybody anything right now. Especially Lyzandra. Was Verrick giving her something?"

"Yes, a relaxant of some kind, Valium or Xanax. To enhance her receptivity."

"Well, from all the medical personnel in Verrick's office right now, I'd say it enhanced her, all right. A relaxant," he said, shaking his head. "Jesus."

"Will she be okay? I didn't mean to hurt her. I was just trying to keep her from hearing me. They were asking me all these questions, and I was afraid I'd give you and Maeve away, and I thought if I let the voices in . . ."

"I know," he said. "You couldn't have known what would happen."

"But they're going to be all right, aren't they?"

"Yeah," C.B. said. "Trent's okay—he's only partially telepathic. And I think I got the door shut before Lyzandra suffered any permanent damage. But if Verrick had given her something stronger . . ." He shook his head angrily. "The man should be shot."

"I agree, but right now our priority's got to be getting you out of here while she's still traumatized and won't notice."

"You're right," he said, but he made no move to get up.

"If you're worried about me, you don't have to be. I'll be fine. It's you they can't find out about."

He leaned his head back wearily against the wall and said, "I haven't told you everything."

And whatever it was, it was bad. "They heard me say your name?" Briddey asked fearfully. "Or, oh, God, Maeve's?"

"No," he said.

"Then why can't you leave?"

"Because they're still hearing the voices."

"But I thought you—" She looked automatically over at the blue courtyard door. It was shut and holding, the bar and bolts still in place, and no water was coming in.

"I stopped your voices by using the defenses you already had in place," C.B. said, "but neither Trent nor Lyzandra has any. If we don't teach them how to erect some—"

They'll keep on hearing the voices, and it will drive them mad, she thought. *Or kill them.* "But if you tell them how to keep the voices out, they'll know you're telepathic. Can't you put up a barricade *for* them, like you did with Maeve? And like you did with me in the Carnegie Room?"

"No," he said. "I wasn't blocking nearly as many voices, and that was only for a short period of time—"

"But you'd only have to do it till the relaxant wears off."

He shook his head. "We can't count on the voices stopping then. The deluge obviously did more than trigger their receptivity. It overwhelmed their inhibitors."

"So they'll go on hearing the voices forever, like us."

He nodded. "I'd have to block them indefinitely. And not just take them down to a murmur, but shut them out completely, which takes a *lot* more energy and focus."

Briddey thought of the toll just trying to keep them from hearing C.B.'s and Maeve's names had taken on her. It had exhausted her completely. And C.B. would have to block them from hearing his thoughts, too—and hers—or they'd know what he was up to.

"Two people are exponentially harder to block than one," he said. And he was already completely worn out from saving her from the flood.

And the fire, she thought. And from rescuing her before in the hospital and the theater and the storage room, and getting almost no sleep because he'd had to take her home from the hospital and take her to get her car and rescue Maeve.

And stand guard over me, she thought, gazing at him as he sat slumped against the wall, looking defeated and bone-weary. He was right. There was no way he had the strength or endurance to block Trent and Lyzandra for long enough to do any good.

"We can't just leave them to the mercy of the voices," C.B. said. "Even though I'd like to. You'll notice they didn't send a nurse in here to make sure *you* were okay. You could be in here having seizures, for all they know. Or care."

And if Lyzandra hadn't volunteered to take the relaxant, they wouldn't have hesitated to give it to me. But—

"Exactly," C.B. said. "We can't just stand by and watch them have a psychotic break when we're the ones who caused it."

You mean I am, Briddey thought sickly. *This was my bright idea.* And it had totally backfired. Not only had she nearly killed Trent and Lyzandra, but instead of protecting C.B., she'd delivered him right into their hands. "I am so sorry I got you into this," she said.

"You couldn't have known opening the door would—"

"No, I mean all of this. If I'd listened to you when you tried to warn me about having the EED, none of this would ever have happened. Your secret would be safe—"

"Yeah, well, and if I'd told you what Trent was up to in the first place, it wouldn't have happened either. But it did, and we need to go try to get those voices under control. Come on, get up," he said, even though he was the one sitting on the ground.

"But couldn't *I* go in there instead? I know how to erect a perimeter and a safe room. I could teach them—"

He was shaking his head. "A perimeter and a safe room won't be enough to protect Lyzandra. She needs—"

"You could give me directions. You could stay in here and tell me what to say, and I could—"

"It would take too long. And they already know you were talking to somebody. They'll be determined to find out who, and I'm not sending you in there alone to face an inquisition."

"But—"

"Besides, this is going to take both of us. Come on," he said, extending his hands to her so she could help him up.

She reached for him, and the two of them were instantly back in the testing room, and she was the one sitting on the floor, and he was standing over her with *his* hands extended. There wasn't a mark on them—no soot, no burns.

Thank God, she thought, clasping them tightly.

He pulled her up.

But if they find out he's a telepath, they won't think twice about sending him back into the fire, she thought. *They'll interrogate him, they'll give him drugs to enhance his receptivity, and he won't be able to hold back the voices. He'll be burned alive—*

"Ready?" C.B. was saying.

"No. There has to be something else we can do. In the library, you said you'd been working on a jammer. Could you—?"

"Invent something in the next five minutes to block the voices? Afraid not." He smiled at her gently. "Maybe it won't be as bad as we think. Maybe after what's happened, they'll decide they don't want to have anything more to do with telepathy. From what I'm getting from Trent, his voices take the form of bugs crawling all over him, and the psychic's reaction has to have scared the hell out of Verrick. They may already have figured out telepathy's a terrible idea—"

You're crazy! Maeve's voice said out of nowhere. *They won't ever think that. Aunt Briddey, tell him he can't let them find out who he is!*

"What are you doing here?" C.B. demanded. "I thought I told you to stay in your safe room."

I was listening, Maeve said defiantly, *and it's a good thing. Helping them's an awful idea!*

"So is them finding out about you. Get inside," C.B. ordered her, and they were all abruptly back in the courtyard, Maeve standing there on the blackened flagstones in her Rapunzel dress and tiara, arms akimbo.

"You *can't* tell them about the telepathy," she said. "Once they know about it, they'll never leave you alone. They'll keep pestering you till you tell them everything."

"She's right," Briddey said. "Once they smell blood in the water—"

"—they'll *make* you tell them," Maeve said. "And Trent'll put it in his phone, and all the moms will buy it, and they'll know all the things their kids do that they aren't supposed to, and nobody'll be able to do anything or go anywhere! Danika's mom is really strict. If she finds out about Danika watching zombie movies, she'll ground her *forever*, and some of the kids have parents who are really *mean*! It'll be worse than hearing the voices even! You *can't* let them find out!"

"I know," C.B. said. "And that's why you've got to go home. They don't know about you, and we've got to keep it that way. You need to go—"

"Not till you promise me you won't tell them! Remember when Mom went to that Helicopter Mom rehab seminar?" she said, appealing to Briddey. "And she promised she was going to stop reading my Facebook page and my texts and hovering over me every second, but she *didn't*! You can't *trust* them."

"We don't," C.B. said. "It'll be okay."

"No, it *won't*!" Maeve was practically crying. "They're like *zombies*. It's not good enough to just shoot them. You have to blow them up, or they'll just keep coming. And why do you have to save them anyway? They're creeps!"

"Because we're not," C.B. said.

"But that doesn't mean you have to let them find out about you! I know you said you couldn't block the voices for them, but if we do it together, we could. I could help, and we—"

"No," C.B. said.

"We can't risk them finding out about you," Briddey explained.

"They won't," Maeve said confidently. "I've got *tons* of barricades, and C.B. taught me frequency hopping. They'll never find me. And I know lots of tricks for getting inside people's defenses—"

Obviously, Briddey thought.

"—and ways to block them. We could take turns, and—"

C.B. was shaking his head. "We couldn't keep it up forever. Teaching them to build defenses is the only thing that'll work. Come on, Briddey." He extended his hand to her.

"But it *can't* be the only thing!" Maeve wailed. "There has to be something else. Maybe we could trick them like in *Zombiegeddon*. They made the zombies think they were hiding in this mall and the zombies all went there and they locked them in and gave them this drug that made them forget all about them—"

"There's no drug that will make them forget about us," C.B. said.

"*No!*" Maeve said in frustration. "I meant we could *trick* them. You said people don't believe telepathy's real and that there are all these people out there just pretending to read minds. So you guys could go help them build their defenses, and I could tell Mom I'm sick and get her to bring me to the hospital and—"

"No. Absolutely not."

"Just *listen*. I could bring the nanny cam with me and hide it in here, and after you're done, you could say to Aunt Briddey, 'Do you think we fooled them?' and Aunt Briddey could say, 'Yeah, they really think it's telepathy. I hope they don't look in the testing room,' and then they will and they'll find the nanny cam and think the telepathy was all a big trick and you guys were bugging them like Aunt Briddey thought you were bugging her hospital room."

"No," C.B. said. "In the first place, they're not going to be fooled by a nanny cam—"

"But I could—"

"And in the *second* place, you're not coming anywhere near the hospital. You're going to go home and into your castle and pull up the drawbridge and stay there till I tell you you can come out."

And I know exactly how well forbidding her to do something will work, Briddey thought. The minute they took their eyes off her, she'd be over the wall and undertaking some even more dangerous scheme she'd gotten from *Zombiegeddon* or *Beauty and the Beast.* The only way to stop her was to make her understand how disastrous it would be for them to discover her ability.

"Come here, Maeve," she said, going over to the cottonwood tree and righting the overturned bench. She sat down on one end and patted the space beside her. "Sit down."

"No." Maeve folded her arms and jutted out her chin.

"C.B. isn't doing this to protect you—he knows you're really smart and that you're not afraid. He's doing it because it's *crucial* they not find out what causes the telepathy."

"I wouldn't tell them—"

"I know you wouldn't. But just letting Dr. Verrick and Lyzandra find out you exist would give it away."

"But C.B.'s letting them find out about *him*. That's the same thing."

"No, it's not. Right now they think the EED caused my telepathy, not my being Irish. And they don't know C.B.'s Irish, they think he's Jewish. But if they find out about you, that will give them the clue they need—"

"Like when the witch sees the horse," Maeve said.

"The witch?" Briddey said, lost. "In *Zombiegeddon?*"

"*No.* In *Tangled.* She sees the horse and figures out it must have had a rider and then she thinks, 'Maybe he found the tower,' and she goes back and finds out Rapunzel's gone—"

"Exactly. Each clue will lead them to the next one, and we won't be able to stop it. It'll be like a—" She started to say "a snowball" and then changed her mind. They didn't have time to listen to the entire plot of *Frozen,* too. "Like a feedback loop," she said instead. "You know what that is, don't you?"

"Of course I know what a feedback loop is," Maeve said.

"A feedback loop," C.B. murmured.

"What?" Briddey said.

"Nothing," he said, and waved her to continue.

"So, Maeve, you know that once a feedback loop is in motion, it keeps getting stronger and stronger, till there's no way to stop it. Right, C.B.?" she asked, but he didn't answer.

"Like dominoes," Maeve said. "Where you knock one over, and it knocks the next one over, and the next."

"Till they all fall down. Yes," Briddey said. "If they find out you're telepathic, they'll realize it's inherited, and they'll find the R1b gene cluster, and it'll tell them how the telepathy works—"

"And *that* will show them how to replicate it electronically," C.B. said, coming out of his reverie. "And once they know that, there won't be any way we can stop them."

"So it's *really* important they don't find out about you," Briddey said.

Maeve nodded. "Like in *Silence of the Zombies.* They're hiding from the zombies, and they have to be totally quiet—"

"Exactly," C.B. said. "Your Aunt Briddey and I will take care of this part. I need *you* to go inside your castle and pull up the drawbridge and then go into the safest part of the castle—"

"My tower," Maeve said. "It's really safe. Nobody can get in."

"Good," C.B. said. "I want you to lock yourself in and stay there till I tell you it's safe to come out. And not talk to anybody *or* listen to anybody, not even Briddey and me."

"How can I hear you telling me it's safe to come out if I'm not supposed to listen to you?" Maeve asked practically.

"I'll text you," C.B. said.

"How can you? You don't have a smartphone."

"I'll borrow your Aunt Briddey's. And don't worry. Everything's going to be fine. I have a plan."

"What is it?" Maeve asked eagerly. "Tell me."

"I can't. They might be listening. But I can tell you this much. It won't work unless you do your part."

"Okay," Maeve said grudgingly. "But it better be a good plan." And she disappeared.

"Is it?" Briddey asked after she was gone. "A good plan?"

He ignored her question. "When Dr. Verrick talked to you about connecting, he told you the neural pathway operated as a feedback loop, right? And that each signal between you intensified it exponentially?"

"Yes, and you told me it didn't work like that."

"It doesn't."

"So how does that help your plan?" she asked, and when he didn't answer: "You don't have a plan, do you?"

"No, not yet. But don't worry. I'll come up with something. And if all else fails, we'll throw miscellaneous arms and legs and hands at them while we escape, like they do in *Zombienado*." He grinned at her. "Seriously, we'll cross that bridge when we come to it. And hope it isn't the Tallahatchie. In the meantime, we need to go help your boyfriend and Lyzandra get their defenses up."

"He's *not* my boyfriend," Briddey said.

"We'll cross that bridge when we come to it, too."

C.B. held out his hand again and led her out of the courtyard into the testing room. "Right now we need to get in there before they come looking for us. If they aren't already." And when she hesitated he said, "I got you out of the theater, didn't I? And out of the library? I'll get us out of this."

I hope so, she thought fervently.

"Come on," he said, and smiled at her. "Let's go save France."

Thirty-One

"Do you trust me?"
"Completely."
"Good. Follow me. I'm getting us out of here."
—SYFY's *Alice*

C.B. HAD BEEN WORRIED THAT THEY MIGHT BE LOOKING FOR THEM, BUT they were all in the other testing room, along with a nurse, who knelt next to Lyzandra as she sat huddled on a chair with a blanket around her shoulders, breathing raggedly into an oxygen mask. The nurse was taking her blood pressure, and at every touch Lyzandra flinched. Trent sat across from them, brushing compulsively at his arms and pant legs.

Dr. Verrick looked up, saw C.B. and Briddey, and said brusquely, "Why aren't you in the testing room?"

At the same time, Trent said, "What are you doing here, Schwartz? Did Commspan send you down?" And Lyzandra backed against the wall, pointed an accusing finger at Briddey, and shrieked, "Don't let her near me! She'll do it again!"

Nobody's going to do anything to you, Briddey heard C.B. say to her. *I'm here to help,* and it was obvious Lyzandra had heard him because she turned, her finger still pointed at Briddey, to look at him in surprise. It was equally obvious that Trent hadn't heard, because he said anxiously, "I'd rather you didn't say anything about this at Commspan, Schwartz."

Dr. Verrick strode toward C.B. "You can't be in here. Ms. Flannigan, who is this?" he demanded. "And what's he doing here?"

"He's C.B. Schwartz," Trent answered for her. "He works at Commspan. I'm assuming he's here on business." He turned to C.B. "Aren't you?"

"No," C.B. said.

"He's—" Lyzandra began.

C.B. cut her off. *Tell Dr. Verrick the nurse has to leave,* he ordered her. *You want to avoid publicity about this, right?*

Lyzandra nodded and ordered the nurse out.

"She needs to be admitted," the nurse protested, looking at Dr. Verrick. "She's obviously distraught, and her heart rate—"

"I want her to leave *now,*" Lyzandra said, but Briddey was scarcely listening. She was wondering why she could hear C.B.'s thoughts but not Lyzandra's or Dr. Verrick's.

The radio, Briddey thought. *It got turned off in the flood.* And while the nurse was objecting to being sent out, she went back into the courtyard to find it. It was lying on its side in a puddle of water, and the tuning dial was half melted, but she managed to get it switched on. She couldn't find Dr. Verrick's station or Lyzandra's. She had to settle for Trent's.

Mistake. His thoughts were a nearly incoherent tangle of fear, loathing, and insects crawling all over him, mixed with concern about what C.B. was doing there and what he was going to tell Commspan. She tapped on the knob, and Lyzandra's thoughts poured out, more hysterically incoherent than Trent's.

The nurse was still arguing with Dr. Verrick. "Either she leaves or I leave," Lyzandra said, and, still wrapped in the blanket, tried to get up out of the chair.

"No, don't," Dr. Verrick said hastily. "Nurse, that will be all." He motioned her out.

"But—"

"Your presence is upsetting my patient. I'll call you if I need you." The nurse went out, and the moment the door shut behind her, Dr.

Verrick said to Briddey, "Now suppose you tell me exactly what's going on and what this man is doing here?"

"He's the mind reader she was talking to," Lyzandra said, "the person she was trying to keep secret."

C.B.? Briddey heard Trent think disbelievingly.

"Is that true, Ms. Flannigan?" Dr. Verrick asked Briddey.

It's okay, Briddey, C.B. said. *Tell him.*

"Yes," she said reluctantly.

"Why wouldn't you tell us you were talking to him?" Dr. Verrick asked.

Because I knew what would happen, Briddey thought bitterly. *Exactly what's happening right now. An interrogation.* "You said two people had to be emotionally bonded to connect," she said. "And I was afraid Trent would—"

"Think that you were emotionally bonded to C.B. Schwartz?" Trent said. "You're joking, right?" and Briddey winced.

Dr. Verrick turned to C.B. "How long have you two been able to communicate?"

"Since right after Ms. Flannigan's surgery."

"Right after—?" Trent said.

Dr. Verrick silenced him with a look. "That was why you left your hospital room that night," he said to Briddey as if it confirmed what he'd suspected all along. "Because you heard his voice, and it frightened you."

"Yes," C.B. answered for her.

"Are you the one who did this to my patients?"

"No," Briddey said. "I did."

"*You* did?" Trent burst out.

"It doesn't matter who did it," C.B. said. "What matters is making sure it can't happen again." He started toward Lyzandra. "I need to talk to them. I need to—"

Dr. Verrick moved to stop him. "You're not going anywhere near my patients, not until you've told me how you came to be connected to Ms. Flannigan. Who did your EED?"

"We don't have time for this," C.B. said. "You heard the nurse. Lyzandra's heart rate is dangerously high. Let me—"

"Not till you answer my questions. Who did your EED?"

"Nobody."

Oh, don't tell him that, Briddey thought.

"I tripped over some cables in my lab a few days ago and cracked my head," C.B. said, pointing at a place on the back of his neck in the same location as Briddey's stitches. "Knocked myself out, and when I came to, I could hear voices. Including Ms. Flannigan's. And that mob of strangers these two just heard." He gestured at Trent and Lyzandra. "And that they'll hear again if I don't show them how to defend themselves."

"Defend themselves?" Dr. Verrick said. "What does that mean? And how do I know you won't do them further harm? Or that you're even telepathic? You haven't given me any proof."

"I was the one who called the hospital that night," C.B. said, "to report that Ms. Flannigan had left her room and was in the stairwell. You can check the hospital call log and Commspan's. I made the call from there."

"That's hardly proof."

"Look, I'll give you any proof you want after I've—"

"I'm not letting you do anything until—"

"Fine," C.B. said, and snatched up the Zener cards from the table. "Briddey, go to Dr. Verrick's office and write down what I send you." He handed the cards to Dr. Verrick. "Shuffle them."

Are you sure you want to do this? Briddey asked.

Yes, he said. *Go.*

She nodded and went down the inner hall to the office where they'd been before, hoping she wouldn't have to contend with the banished nurse, but the office was empty. She grabbed a pen off the desk and began opening drawers, looking for something to write on. The bottom one held the plastic bag of her belongings that the nurse had taken from her.

Ready? C.B. asked.

Almost, she said, taking her phone out of the bag and pocketing it. *Okay. Am I supposed to—?*

Just write what I tell you, he said, and rattled off a series of symbols— star, star, cross, wavy lines, circle—which she transcribed.

Okay, come back in, he said, and the moment she did, he grabbed the list from her and thrust it into Dr. Verrick's hands. "There's your proof. Now let us help them."

Dr. Verrick wasn't listening. He was looking from the list to the upturned cards. "This is a perfect score," he said, sounding astonished.

You gave me all right answers? Briddey said, horrified. To let Dr. Verrick know the full extent of his telepathy was suicide. He'd—

I didn't have time for anything else, C.B. said. *It was the only way to convince him.*

Only it hadn't. "This is impossible," Dr. Verrick was saying. "Is this some kind of trick?"

"No," Lyzandra said shakily. "It's real. I heard them sending. Please, let them help us."

Dr. Verrick glared at her. "This is completely against medical—"

"Look," C.B. said, "I'll agree to whatever tests or scans you want—"

No! Briddey thought.

"—but you've got to let us help them now."

"Please!" Lyzandra begged, shivering convulsively. "Let him. Before the voices come back!"

"All right," Dr. Verrick said. "But then I want answers."

"It's a deal," C.B. said, and went immediately to Lyzandra. "You help Trent," he told Briddey. *And keep Verrick out of my way.* He squatted down in front of Lyzandra and said, *You're okay. I'm right here. I've got you.*

"What are you going to do?" Dr. Verrick asked, looking at them.

"Repair the damage you did when you gave her a relaxant," Briddey said. "If he can. Did you give her anything else?"

"Information regarding a patient's treatment is protected by physician-patient confidentiality," Dr. Verrick said stiffly. "It can't be shared—"

"It already has been, whether you like it or not. Now, did you give her anything else? Or hypnotize her?"

Dr. Verrick looked over at Lyzandra, who was still shaking, though not quite as violently now that C.B. was talking to her.

"No, just the relaxant," Dr. Verrick said, "and she assured me she'd taken it before without any adverse effects." He told Briddey the name and dosage, his eyes fixed on Lyzandra, who was watching C.B. intently as he said over and over, *You're okay. They can't get you.*

They were everywhere! Lyzandra sobbed. *Everywhere!*

I know, C.B. said comfortingly, *but it's okay now. They—*

"Where did you go?" Lyzandra cried, grabbing wildly for him. "I can't hear you."

Briddey looked inquiringly over at C.B., who was still saying, *They can't get you.*

"I can't *hear* you," Lyzandra wailed, and then, as C.B. repeated, *I'm right here,* she suddenly relaxed.

Oh, thank goodness, she said. *For a moment there—*

"What just happened?" Dr. Verrick asked Briddey.

What did *happen?* Briddey asked C.B. *Why couldn't she hear you?*

I don't know, C.B. said, frowning. *The other voices must have drowned mine out for a few seconds.*

No, they didn't, Lyzandra said. *I couldn't hear anything!*

"Why did Lyzandra say she couldn't hear you?" Dr. Verrick was asking.

"Because you distracted her," Briddey said. "You need to sit down and keep very quiet so you don't break their concentration. If you do, she could go into shock. Or worse."

"Worse?"

"The relaxant you gave her increased her sensitivity to the tele-pathic signals, causing a sensory overload that could produce a psy-chotic break. Which would hardly look good on your record."

Dr. Verrick nodded, looking suddenly pale, and sat down.

Good job, C.B. said. *You've got him worried about malpractice suits, which should keep him busy awhile. Now go help your boyfriend before he gets the heebie-jeebies again.*

Briddey looked at Trent. He had started swiping nervously at his pant legs. *What do I do first?* she asked C.B.

What I did with you in the library, C.B. said. *No, scratch that. Just tell him how to build a perimeter.*

Roger, Dawn Patrol, just the perimeter, she said, and sat down facing Trent.

"What are you smiling about?" Trent said. "You have no idea what

I've been through. There must have been at least a dozen voices, and they were swarming all over me!"

A dozen, she thought, thinking of the thousands that had swamped her and of C.B.'s poor burned hands.

Trent shuddered. "They were crawling up my clothes and into my ears. It was horrible!"

"I know," she said sympathetically, noticing that Dr. Verrick had reached for a notebook. So much for having scared him. "I can make sure it doesn't happen again." *But we have to talk mentally, not aloud,* she added, trying to keep what Dr. Verrick found out to a minimum.

All right, Trent said, digging at his neck. *You should have warned me. Just think if we'd gone ahead with the phone and then something like this had happened!*

At least he recognizes how dangerous telepathy is, she thought, and started to explain how to put up a perimeter. *You need to imagine a wall or a—*

Imagine? Trent said scornfully. *You're going to teach me to* imagine *these things away?*

No, your brain will be creating electrochemical defenses, but the way you make it do that is by visualizing a wall or—

Did Schwartz tell you that? Trent said, looking over at C.B. Lyzandra had a death grip on his knee just like Briddey'd had that night in his car.

It was more fun when you did it, C.B. told her, and she started to smile again and then decided she'd better not let Trent see that.

But he wasn't looking at her. He was still watching C.B. *I can't believe you thought I'd be jealous of him! I mean, I know Dr. Verrick told us an emotional bond was necessary for people to connect, but come on! The Hunchback of Notre Dame?*

You have no idea how close you are to me opening that door and letting you be devoured by bugs, Briddey thought, but C.B. had said to help him, so she took Trent through the steps of putting up his perimeter and then said, *If you hear the voices, you focus on it and think, "They can't get through it."*

Trent nodded. *I focus on—* His voice cut off.

Briddey frowned. *Trent, can you hear me?*

Nothing. She couldn't hear him at all. And his wasn't the only voice to have cut out. C.B.'s voice and Lyzandra's, which she'd heard continuously in the background as she coached Trent, had gone silent, too, and so had the always-present murmur of the voices beyond her perimeter.

She glanced over at C.B., but he and Lyzandra were obviously still able to hear each other. He was still focused intently on her, and she still had that death grip on his knee. So what was happening?

C.B.'s decided to try to block the voices after all, in spite of the difficulty, Briddey thought. *He concluded it was the only way to keep the telepathy out of their hands, so he blocked Lyzandra, and now he's blocking me.*

But if that was what he was doing, he'd have blocked Trent, not her. Maybe since she was talking to him, he'd had to block both of them. *C.B., did you do that?* she called.

Nothing, and not only didn't he respond, *Yes*, or, *Doing what?*, but his attention never wavered from Lyzandra's face.

He can't hear me, she thought. And she couldn't hear anything at all.

Then Trent was back, saying accusingly, *Why didn't you answer me? I asked you whether you wanted me to focus on the wall, and you didn't answer me.* He stopped to swipe reflexively at his shirt front. *And the bugs—*

Which meant she was the only one who'd been blocked. *I'm sorry,* Briddey said. *Yes, focus on your wall and think, "It's impregnable." Say it over and over.* And as soon as he'd started, she returned to pondering the shutdown. It must have been some reaction to the deluge. All those voices had been too much for her mind to process, and she'd done the neural equivalent of fainting or something.

She wondered if she should tell C.B., but he already had enough to worry about. Plus, he'd said they didn't have much time to get the others' defenses up, and she hadn't even started on Trent's safe room.

Trent was still repeating, *It's impregnable.*

All right, Briddey said. *Now you're going to build a safe room inside your perimeter,* and explained what it had to be like, listening warily for another abrupt loss of sound, but it didn't happen again.

Which was good, because they didn't need anything else to worry about. Neither Lyzandra's collapse and Trent's twitching nor C.B.'s dire warnings of how dangerous telepathy was had had any effect on Dr. Verrick. He was earnestly taking notes, and Briddey heard him think,

If Lyzandra's too traumatized to continue monitoring their tests, I'll need to bring in Michael Jacobsen and the Dowds.

Oh, no, Briddey thought. *He's got other telepaths.* Which meant even if they could convince Trent and Lyzandra that telepathy was a terrible idea, Dr. Verrick would still have a way to continue doing research. She needed to tell C.B.

I don't understand what you mean by pleasant associations, Trent was saying.

It needs to be somewhere you'd feel both safe and happy, Briddey said absently, *like—*

An executive suite like Hamilton's.

Of course, Briddey thought. *I might have known,* and was glad C.B. was too busy with Lyzandra to be listening to this.

Perfect, she told Trent. She set him to imagining the executive suite's walls and furnishings and then said to C.B., *I need to tell you something. Can you meet me in Santa Fe?*

You bet, he said, and, after telling Lyzandra to focus on her perimeter, came into the courtyard.

But when Briddey told him, he already knew about the other telepaths. "They're Verrick's patients. I heard him thinking about them earlier. Michael Jacobsen was the first one to report hearing his fiancée's voice after they had the EED. She couldn't hear him, though, and both Dowds are only partially telepathic. He thought you were a more promising prospect."

"Because of my red hair."

"Yeah. Jacobsen's a strawberry blond, and both Dowds have chestnut hair."

"At least he hasn't tumbled to the Irish connection."

"No, but it's just a matter of time before he does. Because red hair's an inherited trait, he's already leaning toward a genetic explanation, and the name Dowd's Irish."

"But Schwartz isn't, and Jacobsen's Scandinavian. And Lyzandra's last name is Walenski."

"Yeah, but we need to give him another reason quick—he's already wondering why I don't have red hair, and if Lyzandra recovers enough to answer questions, he'll find out that her mother's side of the family came from County Mayo."

"What kind of reason?" Briddey asked.

"Preferably something that leads him away from inherited traits, like brain damage or drugs. Find out if Trent took that relaxant Verrick prescribed, and if he ever had a concussion—played soccer or wrapped his Porsche around a tree or something. I mean, it's obvious from his treatment of you that he was dropped on his head as a baby, but see what else you can find out that we might use. Finish getting his safe room up first, though. I don't know how much longer I can shield them from the brunt of the voices," he said, and left before she could tell him about her fainting spell.

She went back to helping Trent visualize his executive suite, which he'd apparently been coveting for months—or years. He knew exactly what he wanted in it, right down to the paintings on the walls. *Hamilton has a Modigliani, but I'm thinking maybe an Andreas Gursky or an Orozco.*

Briddey wondered if Lyzandra's safe room was as elaborate as Trent's. No, listening to C.B. coaching her, she seemed to be more focused on making it as strong as possible. *What if they break through the door?* she was asking C.B. anxiously.

They won't, C.B. said. *But you can add another lock, if that'll make you feel safer.*

Can it be a deadbo—? she said, and her voice cut off.

Lyzandra? C.B. said.

"Where did you go?" Lyzandra said. "Why can't I hear you?" and Briddey couldn't hear her thoughts, only the words she spoke aloud. She could still hear C.B.'s thoughts, though.

I'm right here, Lyzandra, he was saying. *Don't panic. The voices can't get in.*

"I can't *hear* you," Lyzandra said, her voice rising.

"What's going on?" Dr. Verrick demanded. He stood up.

Talk to me, Lyzandra, C.B. said. *Tell me what's happening.*

She stared at him with wide, frightened eyes.

"Lyzandra." He gave her a little shake. "Lyzandra."

"I can't hear your voice," she said. "Your mind-voice, I mean. I can still hear when you talk aloud."

C.B. frowned. "What about the other voices? Can you hear them?"

"No."

Briddey, say something to her, C.B. said.

Lyzandra, can you hear me? Briddey asked.

"Did you hear that?" C.B. asked Lyzandra.

"Hear what? I can't—oh, now it's back."

"I said, what is going on?" Dr. Verrick demanded, advancing on them.

"Shh," C.B. said. *Lyzandra, tell me what happened.*

Everything suddenly went silent, like it did before, and I couldn't hear you. I couldn't hear anything.

Did it fade out? Briddey asked. *Or cut off suddenly?*

Suddenly. Like somebody flipped a switch.

And it came back the same way?

Lyzandra nodded, and C.B. asked, *Briddey, why—?*

She looked at him, and this time he didn't need to be told to meet her in the courtyard. He was instantly there, saying, "Why'd you ask her that?"

"Because the same thing happened to me."

"When?"

"Just a few minutes ago."

"Was it like when you started hearing Trent, and you could only hear him intermittently?"

"No," Briddey said. "This was much more abrupt, like someone hanging up a phone, and I couldn't hear anything, including the voices beyond my perimeter. I don't think Trent could hear me either. He asked where I'd gone."

"Lyzandra said the same thing to me," C.B. mused, "and when she was talking just now, I couldn't hear her underlying thoughts. When it happened to Lyzandra before, I thought it was because she was too hysterical to listen to me, but if you experienced the same thing ... how long did it last?"

"Maybe a minute. Do you know what's causing it?"

"Your guess is as good as mine," he said. "Look, tell me if it happens to you again, okay?"

"How? You won't be able to hear me. I called to you last time, but I couldn't receive *or* send."

"Okay, then tell me out loud. And get Trent's safe room up as fast as you can. If this is some after-effect of the deluge, who knows what other ones there might be," he said, and went immediately back to instructing Lyzandra.

Briddey turned her attention to Trent. *I need you to tell me exactly what your executive suite looks like,* she said.

I don't have it done yet, Trent said. *I'm trying to decide on what kind of desk I should have. Hamilton's is mahogany, but I think teak gives a more professional—*

It doesn't matter, Briddey said. *What's important is—*

But you said to visualize every detail. How can I do that if—? He cut out.

Trent? Briddey said. "Trent?"

"What?" he said aloud. "I thought you told me we had to talk mentally."

I did, Briddey said. *Can you hear me?*

He didn't answer her.

"Did you hear what I just said?" she asked aloud. "When we were talking mentally?"

"No," he said, and she could see from Trent's expression that he was saying something to her and waiting for an answer that didn't come.

C.B., she said, but he was already asking her, *What's going on? Is it happening to Trent now, too?*

I think it must be. His voice stopped in mid-word.

"What's happening?" Dr. Verrick asked.

Neither Briddey nor C.B. paid any attention to him. *Trent?* C.B. asked, *can you hear me?*

I'm the only one he can hear, Briddey reminded him.

Then you call him, C.B. said, and watched Trent carefully as Briddey began repeating, *Briddey to Trent, come in, Trent.*

He still didn't answer, but a suspicious look came over his face. "If you're doing this . . . ," he said to C.B.

"Doing what?" C.B. said. "Tell us what's happening."

"Is Mr. Worth having a disruption now?" Dr. Verrick asked.

"Shh," C.B. said. "Trent, can you hear Briddey's voice?"

"No," Trent said, glaring at her accusingly. "I was asking her about the desk for my executive suite—"

"Executive suite?" Dr. Verrick interrupted. "What are you talking about? Mr. Schwartz, you said—"

"Shh," C.B. said. "Then what happened, Trent?"

"She broke in asking me out loud if I could hear her. And I said yes, but she didn't hear me, and if she's talking mentally to me, I can't hear her either. I can't hear anything."

"Including the voices?"

"Yes, there's no sound at all. One second I could hear"—Briddey suddenly heard him think—*and then I couldn't.*

I can hear him again, she told C.B.

So can I, C.B. said. "Trent, can you hear Briddey?"

"Yes."

"I demand to know what's going on here," Dr. Verrick said.

"We don't know," C.B. said.

Liar, Trent thought. *Schwartz is probably the one behind this. How do we know building these so-called defenses didn't cause . . . oh, no, they're back!* And he began brushing madly at his legs.

Good, Briddey thought, *the voices will keep him from telling Dr. Verrick that,* and said, *Trent, this is why you need your safe room. Forget about the paintings and finish visualizing your walls.*

"What do you mean, you don't know?" Dr. Verrick was asking.

"We don't know," C.B. said. "We lost telepathic contact with Trent for a short time, but we got it back."

Which meant he wanted to downplay what had happened. *And I should help,* Briddey thought.

"It's not an uncommon occurrence," she said. "Trent and I have experienced gaps in our communication before. The first few hours after we connected, we only caught occasional words and phrases, didn't we, Trent?"

"Yes, but—" Trent began.

Briddey cut him off. "You said stress could interfere with connecting," she told Dr. Verrick, "and Trent and Lyzandra have just undergone a tremendously stressful experience." *And stress can also cause the voices to break through again,* she told Trent, *so you need to get a lock on your safe-room door now.*

I will, Trent said, and hastily began envisioning a deadbolt while Briddey retreated to the courtyard to consider what Trent had said about C.B.'s being behind this.

Was he? The blackout had felt like someone had put a soundproof barrier between her and the voices—like her perimeter, only much more effective—but C.B. had said he didn't have the strength to block the voices, and he hadn't been lying about how exhausted he was. Looking at him now, coaching Lyzandra, she could see the lines of weariness in his face and the shadows under his eyes. There was no faking those.

She believed what he'd said about not being able to block the voices completely for more than a few minutes, but that was all this was. He could have done it. Only what good would blocking them for a few moments do? It would hardly convince Dr. Verrick that the telepathy had stopped working. And if C.B. was behind the disruptions, he wouldn't have downplayed them.

Unless he's trying to make them think he had nothing to do with them, that they're a natural occurrence, so he can pretend to be blanked out when Dr. Verrick wants to do a scan. That would explain why she'd been blanked out, too. He'd had to block her once to make it look like the disruptions were affecting all of them. It also explained why he'd agreed so readily to the scans. He'd never intended to undergo them.

How are you coming with Trent's safe room? C.B. asked. *Can it stand up to the voices yet?*

I think so.

Good, he replied, *because I can't—*

His voice cut off, slicing through the "t" in "can't," and Briddey thought, *He's blocking me again.* But why? He only needed to block her once to convince the others.

So what do I do now that I've got this executive suite? she heard Trent say.

Meaning I'm not the one who's blocked, Briddey thought, glancing over at C.B.

His head was raised in a listening attitude, and the look on his face was one of shocked bewilderment. *C.B.,* she called to him. *What's wrong?* but he didn't answer.

Because he's the one who's blanked out. That's why I couldn't hear him, because his voice couldn't get through to me. Or at least that was what he wanted them to believe. Nobody would suspect him of causing the disruptions if he was a victim of them, too.

But if he was faking it, why didn't he say aloud, "I just got cut off,"

and tell Dr. Verrick he thought something was happening to the telepathy, that it seemed to be disappearing? He didn't say anything. He
just stood there, looking stunned.

He isn't faking this, she thought. And a minute later, when it ended
and he said, *Briddey, I think the thing that happened to you just happened to
me, too,* and she asked him what was causing it, and he said, *I have no
idea,* she believed him.

When yours started, he asked, *did it—?*

She was abruptly surrounded by silence. *Did he get blanked out again?*
she wondered, but it was obvious this time she was the one being
blanked out. She couldn't hear Trent either—or the voices.

C.B.? she called, even though it was clear she couldn't send messages in this state, and then said aloud, "It just happened to me again."

"It did?" C.B. said, and there was no way he could be faking the
confusion and anxiety in his voice or on his face.

He isn't causing it, she thought. *I'm convinced of that.* But then what
was? Or who?

Maeve, she thought, and was glad she was blanked out so neither
Trent nor Lyzandra could hear that. *Maeve's doing it.*

Maeve had promised she'd stay in her castle. She'd also been certain
her defenses could protect her. And a mere promise wouldn't stop her.
She'd promised her mother she wouldn't do any number of things and
then promptly gone and done them.

I need to talk to her, Briddey thought. But she couldn't while she was
blanked out, and when the disruption ended, Trent and Lyzandra would
be able to hear her. And her top priority had to be keeping Maeve off
their radar.

I'll have to wait till they're blanked out at the same time, she thought. *If
that happens.* So far the disruptions had only lasted a minute or two,
though this one seemed to be going a little longer.

Perhaps if they get longer, they'll start to overlap, and I'll be able to— she
thought, and could abruptly hear again.

Lyzandra was telling C.B., *I don't think my door's strong enough to hold
them,* so she obviously wasn't blanked out.

Trent? Briddey called.

He's incommunicado, C.B. said. *I take it you were, too?*

Till just now. Were we out at the same time?

I'm not sure. I think they're getting longer.

I need a stronger lock, Lyzandra said. *And not just a deadbolt. I need—*

"It just happened again!"

"It's happening to me, too," Trent put in.

"What—?" Dr. Verrick said, advancing on C.B.

I should stay and help him, Briddey thought, but this was more important. And it might be her only chance to talk to Maeve while no one was listening. She dived for her courtyard, shut herself in, and called to Maeve, *I want to talk to you right now.*

No answer.

Of course not, Briddey thought. *Because she knows what I'm going to ask her. Cindy!* she called again. *Rapunzel! Maeve! Answer me this instant!*

Still no answer, and Briddey was rapidly running out of time. Lyzandra or Trent could come out of the disruption any second, or C.B. would notice she'd gone into her safe room and—

I can't believe you guys did that! Maeve said. *I stayed in my castle just like C.B. told me to, and I didn't talk to anybody. So how come you blocked me like that?*

Thirty-Two

"This time it vanished quite slowly, beginning with
the end of the tail."
—LEWIS CARROLL, *Alice in Wonderland*

SHH, MAEVE, BRIDDEY SAID AUTOMATICALLY, LOOKING AT LYZANDRA AND
Trent and Dr. Verrick. *Not so loud. They'll hear you.*

No, they won't, Maeve said. *I've got like fifteen firewalls and encryption
walls up around me. You didn't have to block me, too! I can't believe you did
that!*

Tell me exactly what happened.

Oh, like you don't know!

I don't, Briddey said. *I swear. Tell me.*

I was listening to C.B.—*he didn't say I couldn't listen, just that I couldn't
talk*—*and all of a sudden I couldn't hear anything. It was like when your laptop crashes and the screen goes blue, you know? I couldn't hear anything, not
even the zombies.*

And then what?

*Then I yelled at you and C.B. that I couldn't believe you guys did that.
It's so not fair!*

What did you do after you couldn't hear anything? Briddey asked.

I tried to reboot it, but I couldn't. I hit every key I could think of—

Every key?

Yeah, you know, like on a keyboard. They're not really keys, it's just visualizing, like the safe rooms and your radio. Anyway, I visualized my laptop, and did everything you're supposed to do when it crashes, like turn it off and back on again, and I reset the default codes, in case it was a V-chip or something. But nothing worked. And then the sound came back on, just like that.

How long did it last? The not being able to hear?

A really long time. Like fifteen minutes. You guys didn't have to do that. I did just what C.B. said to. I pulled up the drawbridge and lowered the portcullis and then went in my tower and stayed there. All I wanted to do was find out what was going on.

And you didn't do anything but listen?

No! Maeve said vehemently. *I told you, I—* Her voice bit off in mid-syllable.

Oh, no, now I've been cut off, Briddey thought, which would make Maeve furious—she'd think they were blocking her again—and then heard Lyzandra saying, *It happened again. Why does it keep happening?* and realized Maeve *was* the one who'd been cut off.

That'll make her even more furious, Briddey thought, and then, *I've got to tell C.B.*

But how? She couldn't risk them being overheard, which meant she needed to wait till both Lyzandra and Trent were blanked out, and from the sound of things, neither one was. They were both clamoring to know why the disruptions were happening.

"I don't know," C.B. told them.

"A likely story," Trent said. "How do we know you're not doing it?" He turned to Dr. Verrick. "He could be disrupting the telepathy to keep us from getting the data we need. This whole 'helping' thing could have just been a ruse so he could sabotage—there, you see? He just cut me off again."

Good, that's one down, Briddey thought.

"If you're interfering with my patients' telepathy, Mr. Schwartz—" Dr. Verrick said, moving forward menacingly.

"He isn't," Briddey said, inserting herself between them. "It's happening to us, too. We don't know what's causing it."

"Is that true?" Dr. Verrick demanded.

"Yes," C.B. said, "although . . . I've been thinking, Lyzandra was the first to experience it. Right, Briddey?"

"Yes," she said, hoping that was what he wanted her to say.

"Okay, it happened to Lyzandra first and then to Briddey," C.B. said, pointing at them in turn, "and then to Lyzandra again, and then to Trent—"

"What difference does it make what order it happened in?" Dr. Verrick asked impatiently.

"Because I think Lyzandra may have caused it."

"Me?" Lyzandra said, outraged. "My psychic spirit gift is everything to me. Why would I—?"

"Not intentionally," C.B. said. "Dr. Verrick, when you were attempting to get information from Ms. Flannigan, you gave Lyzandra a relaxant. It diminished her ability to limit the number of voices she heard, and she began to hear more of them, hundreds—"

"Thousands," Lyzandra said. "Millions."

"Exactly," C.B. said. "She suddenly heard many more voices than her mind could handle, and her mind shut down, like when an electrical system becomes overloaded and blows a fuse."

So Maeve was right, Briddey thought. *The system did crash.*

"But *I* wasn't given a relaxant, and neither were they," Trent said, pointing at her and C.B., "so why did the shutdown happen to us?"

"Because all three of us were telepathically linked to Lyzandra," C.B. said, "so both the voices and her reaction to them would have cascaded from her to us in turn. And when her mind shut down, ours did, too, like when a breaker trips, and that trips the next, and the next."

I thought it was a fuse, not a breaker, Briddey said to herself. *And if it was a response to the deluge, why didn't it happen right then, instead of half an hour later?*

But Dr. Verrick didn't seem to have a problem with that—or with the rest of C.B.'s explanation. "So as the effect of the relaxant wears off, these shutdowns should get shorter in duration and then stop," he said.

C.B. nodded.

"I want to know exactly when each one begins." And while C.B. and Briddey worked with Trent and Lyzandra on getting into their safe rooms the second they heard the voices, Dr. Verrick charted the pattern and duration of the disruptions.

They didn't grow appreciably longer, but they didn't grow shorter either, and Trent's and Lyzandra's didn't overlap, so Briddey had no chance to tell C.B. that Maeve was having them, too.

If she was. *Just because she told you that, it doesn't mean it's true,* Briddey thought. Maeve was perfectly capable of lying. And very good at it. She had to be, with Mary Clare for a mother. Her entire story could have been concocted to keep Briddey from suspecting her.

Because she knows I'd tell her to stop, that it's too risky. And impossible, no matter how much of a whiz she was. To do any good, she'd have to block both Trent and Lyzandra for long enough to convince Dr. Verrick and Trent that the telepathy had permanently vanished, which might take days or even weeks, and she could only keep it going for as long as she could stay awake.

And even if she could somehow manage that, it wouldn't convince Dr. Verrick. He had other patients who were telepathic, and Maeve couldn't block them. She didn't know they existed. And even if she'd been listening when Briddey and C.B. had discussed them, she hadn't heard their voices, so she'd have no way of finding them in amongst the thousands of clamoring voices. And she was already having trouble just blocking Trent and Lyzandra for more than a couple of minutes at a time.

Or not. When Briddey came out of the disruption, Dr. Verrick told her it had lasted nearly six minutes, and that the frequency of the breaks was steadily increasing. "I want to run an fCAT on all of you to see exactly what's happening."

Briddey automatically looked at C.B., expecting him to tell Dr. Verrick that wasn't a good idea, but he said, "Okay. Maybe it'll tell us something."

Now see what you've done, Maeve, Briddey thought, and tried to think of some way to signal C.B. that he shouldn't agree to it, but Dr. Verrick was already saying, "Mr. Schwartz, I'll take you and Lyzandra first. This way," and leading them down the hall.

Please, please go into your safe room, C.B., Briddey thought.

Okay, I'm in it, he said.

You can't do this.

I've got to. I need to find out what's going on.

You don't understand, Briddey said. *I think*— And the voices vanished again.

Maeve, she thought furiously, *if you did this* ... But Maeve couldn't hear her. Nobody could. She was locked in a dome of silence.

She did this to keep me from telling C.B., Briddey thought, and hopefully that meant she would see to it that nothing would show up on his scan. But what if the signs of her interference could somehow be seen? Briddey had to talk to her. But she couldn't, not trapped in here.

You can call her on the phone, she thought. If she could get out of here and away from Trent without him getting suspicious.

He had picked up his phone the moment the others left the room. Briddey waited till he started texting someone and then said, "Tell Dr. Verrick I need to use the ladies' room."

Trent nodded vaguely, and she slipped out of the testing room, along the inner hall, through Dr. Verrick's office, and out into the hallway. She darted along the hall to a stairwell like the one she'd fled to that first night here in the hospital, and ducked into it. She took out her phone, listened a moment to make sure she was still blanked out, and called Maeve.

Mary Clare answered. "I'm sorry, Briddey," she said briskly, "but you can't talk to Maeve. She's lost her telephone privileges. She's grounded."

"Grounded?"

"Yes. I caught her watching *Brains, Brains, Brains!* She *knows* she's not allowed to watch zombie movies, and she expressly disobeyed me. Did *you* know she was watching them?"

"No," Briddey lied. "How did you catch her?"

"I went in to ask her to take some soup over to Aunt Oona. I'm worried her rheumatism's acting up again. She didn't want to talk when I called her this morning, and now she isn't answering her phone, so I thought somebody'd better check on her, but Kathleen's not answering *her* phone either. So anyway, when I went into Maeve's room to ask her to run over, there she was, watching this awful zombie movie on her laptop. She tried to blank the screen, but she wasn't quick enough. Thank goodness she'd only watched the first few minutes. If she'd watched the whole movie, she'd have nightmares for weeks. Why did you need to talk to her?"

"It wasn't important," Briddey said, thinking, *It's not her*. Because if Maeve had been blocking the voices and just pretending to be blocked herself, she'd never have let her mother catch her watching *Brains, Brains, Brains*.

Which meant it *was* some sort of blown fuse or tripped breaker, like C.B. had said.

But he'd also agreed with Dr. Verrick that the disruptions would grow shorter as the drug wore off, and that wasn't happening. Briddey was still blanked out when she got back to the testing room, and Trent, who was now on the phone with Ethel Godwin, stopped talking long enough to tell her he'd blanked out again, too. And when Dr. Verrick returned with C.B. and Lyzandra, she learned that disruptions, first in C.B. and then Lyzandra, had kept him from getting conclusive results.

Worse, C.B.'s blackout had lasted twelve minutes, and Lyzandra had been blanked out for nearly eighteen and still showed no signs of coming out of it. "They're not diminishing," Dr. Verrick said. "They're lengthening! What's your explanation for that, Mr. Schwartz?"

"I don't have one," C.B. said, "except"—he grabbed a sheet of paper and began drawing a diagram. "Look, it happened to Lyzandra and then to Ms. Flannigan and then Lyzandra again—"

"We've been through all that," Dr. Verrick said.

"And then Mr. Worth and me," C.B. went on, adding connecting lines to the diagram, "and Ms. Flannigan again and then Lyzandra."

"Yes, yes, we know," Dr. Verrick said impatiently.

"Right, but look at this pattern." C.B. showed them the diagram. "It starts with Lyzandra and keeps bouncing back to her. That could mean it wasn't just a cascade, that it's a feedback loop—"

A feedback loop? Briddey thought.

"—which would mean that each time it travels from one person to another, it intensifies the effect."

"The effect of what? The overload?"

"Or Lyzandra's reaction to it," C.B. said. "What if the incoming flow of telepathic signals didn't trip a breaker but triggered a signal inhibitor of some kind? Because everyone is linked, that action would be communicated to all the others, triggering their signal inhibitors, too."

"But if it were a signal inhibitor, it would inhibit the voices completely. It wouldn't cause intermittent disruptions."

"It would if it takes more than one inhibitor to cancel out the signals," C.B. said, "or if the inhibitor mechanism was too weak to sustain that cancellation. With a feedback loop"—he drew a continuous loop on the diagram, circling to each of their names in turn and back again to Lyzandra—"not only does Lyzandra's information cascade to the three of us, but our reactions to it do, too. So with each circuit, the cascade's amplified, and the number of inhibitors increases, or the inhibitor response is strengthened, or both."

And the disruptions would grow longer and more frequent. Which was exactly what was happening.

"But it wouldn't affect anyone else?" Dr. Verrick asked.

He's worrying about his other patients, Briddey thought.

"They'd have to have been telepathically linked to you for it to affect them, wouldn't they?" Dr. Verrick persisted.

"Or listening in," C.B. said. That was why Maeve had been affected. She'd been listening in, so she'd become part of the feedback loop.

Maeve experienced a blackout, too? C.B. said, and when Briddey automatically shushed him, he told her, *It's okay. Lyzandra and Trent are both blanked out right now. How long was this disruption, and how long ago did Maeve have it?*

Briddey told him and informed him of Mary Clare's catching Maeve watching *Brains, Brains, Brains.*

Then she must be telling the truth, he said, and she realized he'd suspected Maeve of being behind the blocking, too.

Yeah, it did cross my mind, he said, *though I didn't really think she was capable of it, her moats and brambles and firewalls notwithstanding.*

But you're capable of it, Briddey said.

Not this, I'm not. I don't know anybody who is.

What about Lyzandra? We don't know anything about her. Maybe she's more telepathic than you thought, and she doesn't want any competition, so she's shutting us down—

No, I can read her mind, remember? She's completely bewildered by all this, and terrified at the prospect of losing her "psychic spirit gift," as she calls it. And if she had even rudimentary skill at blocking the voices, she'd never have let herself be hit that hard by them. Trust me, it's not her.

So it wasn't Lyzandra, and it obviously wasn't Trent. He didn't even have the ability to *hear* C.B. and Lyzandra, let alone block them. And besides, this was the last thing he wanted to see happen. Which only left C.B.'s feedback-loop theory.

But C.B. and I don't have— she thought, and hastily shoved the rest of the thought away till C.B. blanked out again.

As soon as he did, she checked on Lyzandra's and Trent's status— she was blanked out, and Trent was worrying about how he was going to break the bad news to Hamilton—and then went into her safe room and barred the door. Only then did she allow herself to finish the thought and consider its implications.

C.B. had said the cascade had triggered the inhibitors, but she and C.B. didn't *have* inhibitors. They lacked the genes. Plus, he had asked her all those questions in the testing room about what Dr. Verrick had said regarding the neural pathway being a feedback loop. Those questions and now this explanation couldn't be a coincidence, and there was only one reason for him to have lied about their inhibitors being the cause of the disruptions: *He* was causing them.

And the reason the disruptions were intermittent was because that was all he could manage for now. He was too exhausted to do all three of them continuously, so he'd come up with this intensifying-feedback-loop story, and tomorrow, after he'd had some sleep, he'd block everyone. Except Dr. Verrick's other patients. He hadn't heard their voices either.

And just shutting down Trent and Lyzandra wouldn't solve anything. And if he could block people, why hadn't he blocked Trent yesterday morning before Trent ever heard her? Then they wouldn't be in this mess.

And if he was doing it, why had he looked the way he did the first time he'd been blanked out? *He couldn't have faked that expression,* she thought, remembering how bewildered—and frightened—he had looked. *I don't care how expert a liar he is.*

But if he wasn't doing it, why had he lied about the inhibitors? And why did the timing of their disruptions correspond so perfectly with the scans? When Dr. Verrick took her and Trent for their fCATs, she blanked out before they even got her into the room, and Dr. Verrick wasn't able to get anything.

C.B. has to be doing it, she thought. *Maybe he has some plan for getting Dr. Verrick to bring the other telepaths here to the hospital so he can hear their voices,* and hoped he had enough energy to carry it off. When he came back from a second unsuccessful fCAT, he looked utterly worn out, and she half expected the disruptions to grow shorter in duration because he lacked the energy to sustain them.

But they didn't. As the day progressed, they became longer and closer together, and by late afternoon they'd begun happening to all four of them at once.

"This is terrible," Trent said. "Can't Schwartz do something to stop this? Start a second feedback loop to inhibit the inhibitors or something?"

Briddey stared at him in disbelief. "You honestly want the voices back?"

"No, of course not, but what about the project? What am I going to tell Hamilton?" He waved his phone at her. "He just texted me asking how today went."

Briddey looked at C.B., who was going over his scan with Dr. Verrick, looking strained and exhausted. "Tell him it didn't go very well," she said.

"Wonderful," Trent said sarcastically. "We have barely two months till Apple rolls out their new phone, I've already told Hamilton we were on the verge of a breakthrough that would blow them out of the water, and now I have nothing to show for it. Everything—my future, my career, my *job*—is riding on this, and *you* think I should tell Hamilton it didn't go very well? How do you suppose he'll respond?"

"Better than he would if you'd gone ahead with your phone and then this had happened," Briddey said. "Just think of the ads Apple and Samsung would air: 'At least our smartphones won't drive you mad. Or kill you.'"

"Oh, my God, you're right! I hadn't thought of that." He looked down at his phone again. "But that still doesn't help me with Hamilton. I've got to tell him *something*."

"Tell him the truth, that the telepathy turned out to be too dangerous to use, that there were unintended consequences that made putting it in a phone non-viable."

"I can't tell him that! I assured him it *was* viable—and perfectly safe. And 'unintended consequences' makes it sound like I didn't think it through."

Which you didn't, Briddey thought. "Then tell him there have been complicating factors."

He grimaced. "Everyone knows 'complicating factors' is code for 'unmitigated disaster.'"

Then that sounds perfect for this situation, she thought.

"Can't you think of something less negative-sounding?" Trent said.

"How about 'interesting developments which need to be looked into further'?"

"Oh, that's good. Interesting developments. Tell Dr. Verrick I had to make some calls. I'll be back in a minute." He went out.

C.B. was still talking to Dr. Verrick. He looked like he was on his last legs, his face drawn, his whole body slumping with fatigue.

There was a knock on the door, and a nurse leaned in. "I'm sorry to interrupt, Doctor," she said, "but one of your patients is on the phone. He says it's urgent."

Dr. Verrick nodded. "This will just take a moment," he said, went out, and shut the door behind him, presumably so he could speak to her in private.

Which either means he thinks we're all blanked out, or he still doesn't fully grasp the concept of telepathy, Briddey thought. She might not be able to hear the person on the other end of the conversation, but she could hear Dr. Verrick's voice. And his nurse's.

She went into her courtyard and located Dr. Verrick's frequency on the radio, and then tapped the volume knob. "It's Michael Jacobsen," she heard his nurse say. "He says he's lost all mental contact with his fiancée. Her voice suddenly went dead half an hour ago, and he hasn't heard anything from her since."

Thirty-Three

"To be Irish is to know that in the end the world
will break your heart."
—Daniel Patrick Moynihan

Dr. Verrick immediately phoned his two other telepathic patients, the Dowds, and asked them if they'd noticed any difference in their ability to communicate. They hadn't, but half an hour later the nurse interrupted again to report that someone named Paul Northrup had just experienced a "momentary disruption."

At that point Trent and Lyzandra were both blanked out and had been for the last half hour, and Briddey'd just come out of a twenty-four-minute silence she'd begun to think was never going to end. *Did you hear that, C.B.?* she asked.

Yeah, he said grimly. *And in case you're still thinking I'm the one behind this, I didn't even know this Paul Northrup existed.*

Then how—?

I don't know. Maybe they were listening when the deluge happened, too, or . . .

Or it *was* a cascade effect, and the disruptions were looping from telepath to telepath, triggering shutdown after shutdown. And circling back with ever-increasing strength.

By the time they left the hospital, Briddey's blanked-out periods far outnumbered the ones during which she could hear, and she didn't have to worry about the fCAT scans Dr. Verrick ordered, or lie to get terrible scores on the Zener tests he made them take.

Just like that guy in the Duke experiments, C.B. said after the second test. *Remember the subject I told you about, the one Dr. Rhine was convinced was telepathic? And how he got such high scores and then, all of a sudden, they fell off sharply?*

You told me you thought he'd stopped cooperating, Briddey said.

Yeah, but what if I was wrong? What if the same thing that's happening to us happened to him? What if Rhine gave him a relaxant to "enhance receptivity," and it caused a deluge that shut down the telepathy?

Is there any way to find out? she asked, but if he answered her, she couldn't hear him. Everything had cut out again.

And it apparently had for C.B., too, because he said to Dr. Verrick, "Look, I just lost it again, and both of us are shot. Maybe if we go home and get some rest, we'll be able to communicate again."

"*No,*" Trent said. "By tomorrow this could be gone, and we need to get as much data as we can before that happens."

"Forget data," Lyzandra said. "You need to figure out a way to stop this," so Dr. Verrick ordered an imCAT for each of them.

But Trent was still blanked out, Briddey and C.B. both experienced disruptions less than a minute into the scan, and Lyzandra blanked out before the tech even got her onto the table, so Dr. Verrick ended up sending them home after all.

"Come in at nine tomorrow," he said, "and in the meantime I want you to keep track of the times and duration of the periods during which you can send and receive. And phone me if those periods increase."

"What about me?" Lyzandra said. "Am I supposed to go home, too? You brought me here, you destroyed my psychic spirit gift, and now you expect me to just go back to Sedona? What if it doesn't come back? What am I supposed to do? I'll be ruined!"

Dr. Verrick turned to deal with her, and Trent said, already putting his phone to his ear, "I've got to get back to Commspan. Hamilton wants to see me," and left.

Good, Briddey thought. *This'll give me a chance to talk to C.B. alone.*

But when the two of them had successfully escaped Dr. Verrick's office, C.B. said, "I really need to get back to the lab and see if I can figure out what's going on. Would you mind—?"

"Getting home on my own?" she said. "Of course not. Do you think it *is* a feedback loop, like you told Dr. Verrick?"

"Maybe. I guess. I don't know."

"But you said neural pathways didn't work like that."

"Ordinarily, they don't, but . . ."

"But even with a deluge and a cascade or a feedback loop or whatever it is, how could it trigger inhibitors we don't have?"

"I don't *know*," he said testily. "Maybe I was wrong, and we do have them, and they just hadn't been activated before. Or maybe the cascade's transmitting not only the order to trigger the inhibitors but the instructions for constructing them." He rubbed his hand tiredly across his forehead. "Or maybe it's something else entirely," and left her standing there in the hospital lobby.

She called Kathleen for a ride—it no longer seemed to matter whether her family found out about the EED or not—but Kathleen didn't answer. She debated calling Aunt Oona, but if she was laid up with rheumatism, Briddey shouldn't bother her, and she was in no shape to deal with Mary Clare, especially after a look at her messages, which demanded to know whether Briddey had let Maeve watch *Brains, Brains, Brains* on her phone when they'd gone to the park.

She called a taxi and tried not to think about the last time she'd left the hospital, with C.B. waiting for her, smiling and saying, "My lady, your chariot awaits."

She was half afraid Mary Clare might be waiting at her apartment when she got home, but she wasn't, and there were no new messages from her. Or from Maeve. Not even mental ones. *The disruptions are getting longer for her, too,* Briddey thought, staring blindly at the phone.

She checked the rest of her messages, almost hoping there was one from Kathleen so she could call her back and hear a friendly voice, but all Briddey had was a text from Trent, telling her not to say anything about what had happened to anyone at work, and when she decided to try Kathleen anyway, she still didn't answer.

Briddey supposed she should try and get some rest, but she doubted if she could—she felt too wrung out. And too empty. She hadn't eaten anything all day.

Maybe that's part of the problem, she thought. *C.B. said heightened emotional states could affect the telepathy. Maybe hunger can, too,* and went into the kitchen to see what was in the refrigerator.

Nothing edible, and the cupboard wasn't much better. All that was left after Maeve's raid for the ducks was a can of beets and a nearly empty box of organic MultiGrain Squares.

At least it isn't Lucky Charms, Briddey thought, pouring a bowlful and taking it to the couch to eat, but the squares were just as tasteless as the marshmallows had been, and their shapes just as indeterminate. She thought of C.B. sitting across the table from her in the Carnegie Room, trying to guess what the marshmallows were: green hats, yellow dog bones, albino octopi.

Are you there? she called to him, but either he was experiencing a disruption or he was too absorbed in trying to find out what was causing them to hear her.

Or he doesn't want to talk to me, she thought, no longer hungry, *because I'm the one responsible for this. Lyzandra and her inhibitors may have triggered the cascade, but I opened the floodgates. I let the voices in.*

She took the uneaten cereal back to the kitchen, dumped it down the sink, and went back into the living room.

You need to go to bed, she told herself, but she went on sitting there, hoping that C.B.—or Maeve—would break in to tell her that the blanked-out intervals were lessening. But the only voice she heard was Trent's. *What in the hell am I going to tell Hamilton?* she heard him say, an edge of desperation in his voice. *Maybe I won't have to tell him anything. Maybe this is just temporary, and I can stall him until—*

His voice cut out, but Briddey didn't notice. When everyone had been trying to talk her out of having the EED, Kathleen had sent her something about its effects being temporary. Could that be it? Could her EED have worn off, and since they were all linked together, it had affected the others? If that were the case, it might be possible to redo the EED . . .

"I thought of that," C.B. said when she saw him the next morning at the hospital, "but that would have taken months, not days. And you would have had the first disruption, not Lyzandra." He dragged his fingers wearily through his hair.

He looked even more exhausted than he had the night before. "Did you get any sleep at all?" Briddey asked.

"Not much," he admitted, "but enough to know I'm not blocking the voices subconsciously, which I was secretly hoping might be the case. How about you? Did you get any sleep?"

"Some."

"Are you still blanked out?"

"No, but the disruptions are getting steadily longer." She showed him the time chart she'd made. "They're sixty percent longer now than the intervals when I can hear."

"Yeah, mine, too."

"C.B., I am *so* sorry. When I opened that door, I didn't realize—"

"I know. Don't blame yourself. That may not even be what did it. We won't know for sure what the underlying cause is till Dr. Verrick runs more tests. He wants to try to do another pair of imCAT scans while both subjects are still able to send and receive, though I don't know if he can find a window."

He couldn't. Trent and Lyzandra were blanked out almost continuously now, and although Dr. Verrick waited till Briddey had just come out of a disruption to start their scan, she blanked out again almost immediately, and C.B. followed three minutes later. Dr. Verrick told them he'd wait to do further tests "until the situation improves," and told them they could go.

C.B. stayed behind to go over the scan results with Dr. Verrick. "I'll call you as soon as I find out what they showed," he told Briddey, "but it's looking more and more like the deluge is the culprit. I did some research on the saints and found a couple who heard voices several times and then had some kind of overpowering religious experience, after which they 'fell down as one dead'—and after that didn't hear the voices anymore. Which sounds a lot like a deluge followed by shutting down."

"What about Joan of Arc?" Briddey asked. "Did that happen to her?"

"I don't know. Look, I'll talk to you later," he said, and went back into the testing room.

As soon as Briddey got out to her car, she looked up Joan of Arc on her phone and found to her relief that Joan had continued to hear her voices till the very end. But she was the exception. C.B. had played down the number of saints who'd abruptly lost their voices after a "vision" and never gotten them back. There were at least a dozen of them. Saint Brigid had "heard nothing more from that time hence," and neither had Saint Bega of Turann, though she'd "begged most fervently for its return with penance, prayers, and much weeping," convinced she had lost the ability to hear the voice because of a sin she'd committed.

Like me, Briddey thought.

She drove back to Commspan, shut herself in her office, and tried to work on the still-unfinished interdepartmental communications report and not think about the fact that Maeve still hadn't contacted her.

Maybe she's continuously blanked out, like Trent and Lyzandra, Briddey thought. But Maeve could still call her on the phone. Mary Clare's taking away her phone privileges wouldn't stop her, and at school she could easily borrow Danika's.

Briddey called Mary Clare. "Oh, good, I was just going to call you," Mary Clare said. "Have you heard from Kathleen today?"

"No."

"I haven't either, and I've been trying to reach her since Sunday night. She doesn't answer."

Because she knows you want to interrogate her about letting Maeve watch zombie movies, Briddey thought. "She probably forgot to turn her phone on," she said. "How's Maeve?"

"Sulking because I called Danika's mother and told her Maeve was *not* to use Danika's phone or computer," Mary Clare said.

Which explains why she hasn't called. Maybe.

"Have you heard from Aunt Oona?" Mary Clare was saying. "I can't get her to answer either."

"Are you still worried about her rheumatism?"

"No, she said on Facebook she had some Daughters of Ireland thing, but that doesn't explain why she won't answer her phone."

Maybe she doesn't want to talk to you either.

"You don't think Kathleen would do something stupid like elope with that Starbucks guy, do you?" Mary Clare asked.

"Where did you get that idea?"

"Late Sunday night she posted something about finding happiness where you'd least expect it, and you know how she's always falling in love with someone she just met, even though I've told her it's ridiculous, that she couldn't possibly get to know someone well enough in only a few days to be in love with him. Right?"

"I have to go," Briddey said. "I've got a call on the other line."

She hung up and checked to see if C.B. had called while she was talking to Mary Clare. But he hadn't, and even though Dr. Verrick said C.B. had left the hospital at one, she didn't hear from him all afternoon.

By four thirty she couldn't stand it any longer. She gathered up her things, told Charla she had a headache and was going home, and started down to C.B.'s lab.

But he was standing in the corridor talking to Suki, who hurried toward Briddey as soon as she saw her. "*What's* gotten into C.B.?" Suki whispered, looking back at him. "He looks almost presentable."

He did. He was wearing a buttoned-down collared shirt and no earbuds. He'd also shaved, and he looked more rested and less despairing than he had that morning. *He found out what's causing the disruptions,* Briddey thought, hope springing up.

"He was positively friendly," Suki was saying. "Did he have a brain transplant or something?" She looked speculatively at him. "He's actually kind of cute, in a geeky sort of way, don't you think? Or he would be if he'd comb his hair. Not as cute as Trent, of course. Speaking of which, what's up with *him*? I saw him earlier and he looked awful! Has something gone wrong with the Hermes Project?"

Careful, Briddey thought. *Remember this is Gossip Central you're talking to.* "No, everything's going great. Trent says they're making real progress. He's probably just stressed because there's so much to do. Speaking of which, I need to catch C.B. I have to talk to him about an app," she said, and hurried after him.

"C.B.!" she called, *C.B.!* But he didn't even slacken his pace.

She caught up to him outside the copy room and pulled him inside. She shut the door. "Did you find out what's causing this?" she asked.

"Yes and no," he said.

Which means no, she thought, and looking at him, she realized she'd been wrong about his looking better. What she'd mistaken for rested was merely resignation.

"I found a study on tinnitus patients who'd spontaneously recovered," he told her. "And the pattern's the same—emotional shock followed by the tinnitus disappearing for progressively longer periods, and, after a certain period, total silence."

"And the ringing sound never comes back?"

"No. Also, Verrick called a few minutes ago to say the Dowds have both been blanked out since last night. And when I graphed the durations of everybody's disruptions, they were consistent with the multiplying intensity of a feedback loop, so it's definitely the cascade that caused it."

"And it somehow transmitted the directions for constructing inhibitors?"

"Yeah, or else our brains came up with a work-around on their own."

"A work-around?"

He nodded. "Damaged brains come up with work-arounds all the time—new pathways and connections to replace the ones that were destroyed. Maybe to survive, our brains rigged up something to double for the missing inhibitors."

"You said the tinnitus stopped 'after a certain period.' How long?"

"A few days."

A few days. "C.B., I am so sorry I—"

"Sorry? Are you kidding? You did me a favor. With the voices gone, I'll be able to go to baseball games and movies and restaurants. And interdepartmental meetings," he said, and smiled at her.

"I didn't mean I was sorry the voices are gone. I meant I was sorry I made you lose your telepathic ability."

"The important thing is that you kept Verrick and your boyfriend from getting their filthy paws on it—and on Maeve. And being telepathy-less isn't all bad. It's let me out of that dungeon." He spread his arms to indicate the copy room. "I can eat in the cafeteria and everything. I may even get a haircut now that I can go out in public like a normal person."

No, don't, she thought. *I like your hair.*

But he couldn't hear her. "And I'll finally be able to buy some decent clothes," he said. "I'll need them if I'm going to go on job interviews."

Her heart caught painfully. "You're leaving Commspan?"

"Maybe. I don't know yet. But I've been thinking it'd be nice to work someplace where I could concentrate on limiting communication, not trying to drown people in it—sorry, unfortunate metaphor. I've also been thinking it'd be nice to work someplace warm. Right?"

She nodded unhappily.

"Hey, don't look so glum. You said you wanted things back the way they were, didn't you?"

I said a lot of things, she thought. *I said I never wanted to speak to you again. I said we weren't emotionally bonded. I said I wanted you to go away and leave me alone. And none of that was true. None of it.*

"I mean, think of it," C.B. said lightly, "you won't have to worry about being spied on in the shower anymore or barged in on in the middle of the night, and I won't have to listen to psychopaths and perverts and people who don't know the words to 'The Age of Aquarius,' and spend the rest of my life screaming, 'It's Aquarius, not asparagus!' at them."

"But you won't know what people are thinking—"

"I can always ask Suki," he said, and turned suddenly serious. "The main thing is, Maeve won't have to grow up like I did, constantly afraid somebody'll discover her secret and use it to destroy her. Or the world. She'll be able to live a normal life," he said. "Or as normal as possible with your sister Mary Clare for a mother." He grinned.

Briddey nodded. "She's conducting an investigation to find out who corrupted Maeve into watching zombie movies."

"I know," he said. "Maeve told me. She called me last night."

But not me, Briddey thought.

"I explained to her what was happening," C.B. said.

"Was she upset?"

"Yeah, you might say that." He winced. "But I managed to convince her it was all for the best."

For the best.

"Lyzandra, on the other hand, is threatening to sue Verrick for everything he's got if he doesn't give her her psychic spirit gift back.

Speaking of which, I promised I'd call Verrick and tell him what I found out about the tinnitus."

He opened the door a crack and looked out—an action that convinced her more than anything thus far that he could no longer hear the voices. "The coast is clear," he said, and headed for the elevator, calling back over his shoulder, "I'll talk to you tomorrow."

No, you won't, she thought sadly, going out to her car and driving home. *You won't ever talk to me again.*

And he was wrong about them having a few days. At the rate things were going, the intervals when she could hear would be completely gone by the time she got home.

Or not. On her way up the stairs to her apartment, she heard a male voice too faint to identify say, ". . . can't get through."

C.B.? she called hopefully.

"I've tried to make her understand," the voice said, and it wasn't C.B. after all. It wasn't even one of the voices. It was just someone coming down the stairs. "But she can't accept that it's over. I just can't forgive her for what she did, you know?" There was a pause, and then he said, "I don't know what to do."

Neither do I, Briddey said, wondering how she was going to get through the evening. *You can't spend it just sitting here wondering when you're going to be blanked out for the last time.* Right now she could still hear the voices when she listened closely, a faint murmur like the one that had been beyond her perimeter—the perimeter she no longer needed.

C.B.? she called. *Maeve?* But no one answered.

It was too early to go to bed, so she went into the kitchen, poured the last of the tasteless multigrain cereal and some milk into a bowl, and took it back to the computer.

There was an email from Mary Clare. Kathleen hadn't eloped after all. She'd been with Aunt Oona at the Daughters of Ireland meeting. "Apparently they're getting ready for some big Hibernian Heritage thing, and that's why I haven't been able to reach them. They were there all day yesterday and last night, and they've been there all day today."

I thought Aunt Oona was laid up with rheumatism, Briddey thought, wishing they were home so she could go talk to them.

It was still too early to go to bed. She went online and looked up "tinnitus," hoping to find an example C.B. might have missed of a patient whose symptoms had come back, but she didn't, and after an hour she gave up and decided to go get ready for bed.

The phone rang. "I've been trying to reach you," Trent said impatiently. "Have you gotten any mental messages from me since you got home?"

"No. Why?" she asked eagerly. If he'd started hearing her again, maybe C.B. was wrong about the cascade's effects being permanent. "Have you?"

"No," he said. "Damn. I was hoping you might still be hearing enough that Dr. Verrick could do another imCAT—the ones he did didn't get enough data to identify the telepathic synapses—and I could show it to Hamilton. Without something that definitively proves the telepathy existed, he won't be willing to commit the resources we need to move forward on this thing."

Move forward? "Trent, you can't still be thinking of designing a direct-communication phone! You saw what happened when the voices—"

"I know." She could hear the shudder of disgust in his voice at the memory. "But now that we know there's a way to stop them, we know there must also be a way to control them—"

Maeve was right, Briddey thought bitterly, seeing the smoke-ravaged walls of the courtyard and the blistered paint on the door. *Once they got hold of it, there was no way we could have convinced them to stop.*

"But we can't do anything till we find a way to reactivate the telepathy," Trent went on. "And we can't do that without a scan that shows what's going on in the brain during the communication. Is Schwartz still in contact with you?"

"No."

"Damn. He didn't happen to mention knowing of anyone else who might be telepathic, did he?"

"No. And even if he did, their connections would have been shut down by the cascade, like Dr. Verrick's patients' were."

"Well, there must be *someone* out there we can test."

Like Maeve? Briddey thought. Thank goodness the cascade had wiped out her telepathic ability, too, or Trent would have had no qualms about using her, even if she *was* nine years old.

"We need to find somebody fast," Trent was saying. "I don't know how much longer I'll be able to stall Hamilton. Call Schwartz and tell him how critical this is, that we've *got* to have a telepath. Damn, I can't believe this happened! We were so close to getting the proof we needed."

So close. Thank goodness it happened when it did, she thought. *And that it affected everyone.* Otherwise, they'd be busily administering relaxants to Verrick's other patients, not caring whether they killed them or not. And Trent would be busily designing the circuitry for his phone.

We were so lucky, she thought, and had a sudden memory of Maeve showing up at her door Sunday morning just in time to rescue her from Trent. She'd thought that was a lucky coincidence, too.

"Did you hear me?" Trent said. "I said to text me the minute you find out anything from C.B. This is your future hanging in the balance as well as mine, you know."

"I know," she said. She hung up and then stood there, thinking, *It can't have been a coincidence. Or luck. The timing was too perfect.* And illogical. If the shutdown had really been caused by Lyzandra's reaction to the voices, it would have started the moment they overwhelmed her, not half an hour later.

And why had it affected C.B.? He'd been hit with the full force of the voices at age thirteen, with no defenses at all, and *that* hadn't triggered the creation of inhibitors or work-arounds. So why had this?

It didn't, she thought. *He lied to you. He's blocking the voices, even though he said it wasn't possible.* Maybe Maeve was helping him, the two of them taking turns blocking while the other slept. Or maybe C.B. had lied about its being impossible, and he could block anybody and everybody whenever he wanted.

But if that were the case, why hadn't he kept Lyzandra from hearing her thoughts during the Zener tests? Or better yet, kept Trent from hearing her when she called out, *Where are you?* to C.B.? Or kept her and Maeve from hearing the voices in the first place?

Believing C.B. could block the voices at will meant she also had to believe he'd intentionally let her nearly drown and let Maeve be terrorized by zombies, and she couldn't. *He isn't like that,* she thought stubbornly.

Plus, there was how he'd looked the first time he'd been blanked out, so shocked and so . . . stricken. She'd been certain then—and she was certain now—that he'd had no idea what was happening.

Which left Maeve. *But if she's doing it, and she thought I suspected her, she'd pop up with a story to throw me off the trail.*

She didn't. The only one who did was Trent, texting her at eleven to ask if she'd gotten in touch with C.B. yet, and when she told him no, Trent texted back, "Probably in lab. No coverage down there."

Or anywhere, she thought, listening to the silence. It seemed to her as the night progressed that it was deepening, taking with it the final vestiges of the voices beyond the perimeter. And any hope that Maeve—or C.B.—was doing the blocking.

At eleven thirty the phone rang. *It's Trent again,* she thought, and then, when she saw the number, *It's Mary Clare.* But it wasn't either of them. It was Maeve. "I have to talk to you," she said.

"I thought your mother took your phone privileges away."

"She did."

"So how are you calling me now?"

"On the stupid landline. I had to wait till she was, like, snoring, and then call you. I *hate* it that I can't just talk to you whenever I want to anymore! I can't do *anything.*"

"You're still grounded?" Briddey asked.

"Yes," Maeve said disgustedly, "and it's all your fault. If you hadn't let the voices out, none of this would have happened. There wouldn't have been that stupid cascade, and I wouldn't have been blanked out, and I'd have heard Mom coming into my room, and she wouldn't have caught me. And now I can't watch *anything* on my laptop. She put a block on everything, even Hulu and YouTube, so I can't watch videos at all. You ruined everything!"

I know, Briddey thought, and knew it wouldn't do any good to tell Maeve—or C.B.—that she hadn't meant to. The fact remained that she'd done it. C.B. had tried to warn her about unintended consequences, but she hadn't listened.

"This so sucks!" Maeve wailed. "I mean, the zombies were really scary, and I'm glad I don't have to hear them anymore and hide all the time and worry about what'll happen if I go to the mall and school and stuff. But some of it was fun. I *loved* having a castle and being able to talk to you guys—"

"You can still talk to us—"

"It's not the *same!*" Maeve wailed. "I could talk to you anywhere! I *hate* not having that anymore."

So does C.B., Briddey thought, *in spite of what he told me.*

He'd hated the hiding and the roaring voices and having to constantly witness humanity's nastier side, hated being an outcast and having people think he was crazy. But it was still his life, and the only one he'd ever known. And his gift—and it *was* a gift, in spite of everything bad that went along with it—had molded him and made him who and what he was: kind and funny and selfless and unbelievably brave.

And there had been parts of it he'd loved—the late-night silences and the Carnegie Room and the crosstalk they'd shared.

"And now *not* having it is like way worse than before I got it," Maeve was saying, "because before, I didn't know what it was like, but now I do, and I know how neat it was, and I really miss it, you know?"

"Yes," Briddey said, thinking of C.B. sitting next to her in the car, leaning over her in the stacks, talking to her about *Guys and Dolls* and Bridey Murphy and where they were going to go on their honeymoon.

"You don't think there's a chance it'll come back, do you?" Maeve asked wistfully.

"C.B. doesn't think so."

"That's what I thought." Maeve sighed. "I really liked him. You're not going to marry Trent now, are you?"

"No."

"Well, that's good, anyway. Are you *sure* it won't come back? I was watching *Tangled* before I called you, and the witch kills Rapunzel's boyfriend, and it's *awful.* You don't think there's *any* way they can fix it, but then Rapunzel starts to cry and one of her tears falls on his cheek and it grows into this big gold fireworks thing and he comes back to life and they live happily ever after."

I don't think tears are going to bring the telepathy back to life, Briddey thought. And because she was afraid *she* might start to cry, she asked, "How were you watching *Tangled*? I thought your mother blocked your laptop."

"She did, but I figured out a way around it. You can't tell her. If she finds out, I'll be grounded *forever!*"

Which you probably deserve, Briddey thought, but she said, "I won't, I promise."

"You have to promise you won't tell her about my watching *Zombiegeddon* either, or—" Her voice dropped to a whisper. "I've gotta go. I think Mom's awake. I *hate* this!" Her voice cut off.

I hate it, too, Briddey thought. *And I hate that I'm the one who did it to you.*

And if she'd needed any more proof that her theory had been wishful thinking, that phone call should have been it. There was no way Maeve could have faked the frustration and disappointment and sorrow in her voice.

Although Maeve was an even better actor than C.B., and she'd been able to get around all of Mary Clare's restrictions and blocks and V-chips to watch the movie she wanted. A movie in which something dead had come to life again. Could Maeve, sworn to secrecy by C.B. and unable to communicate any other way, have been sending her a message that all was not lost?

I hope so, Briddey thought fervently. *Because otherwise I have to face the fact that I've destroyed C.B.'s gift. And his life.*

He would never be able to get into the Carnegie Room again. Without the telepathy, the librarians would almost certainly catch him. And three A.M. would no longer be a star-scattered, enchanted time of night. It would be just like it was for F. Scott Fitzgerald and everybody else—a time for lying awake in the darkness squirrel caging about the terrible things that might happen. And the terrible things you've done.

"Unless there's some other piece to the puzzle that explains everything," she murmured, and finally fell asleep at a little after one.

She woke abruptly to even deeper darkness, convinced she'd heard something, though the room was completely silent. *Middle-of-the-night silent,* she thought, and reached for the clock. Three A.M. C.B.'s time of day.

C.B.? she called hopefully into the darkness. *Are you there?*

Nothing.

And it wasn't a voice, she thought, staring into the darkness, trying to reconstruct the sound in her head. *Or a noise.* It had been a sudden cessation of sound, like the stopping of a refrigerator's hum. Or a car outside switching off its engine.

Only this wasn't outside, she thought, and knew with sickening certainty what had stopped: the feeling of C.B. clasping her hand in both of his and holding it close to his heart.

She'd first felt it in the Carnegie Room when she'd woken and found him asleep, and it had been there ever since, though she hadn't been consciously aware of it. It had even been there when she was blanked out. That was why she'd believed—in spite of all the evidence to the contrary—that the telepathy hadn't shut down, that he and Maeve were somehow blocking it. She'd known that wasn't possible, but she'd believed it because he'd still been there, holding tightly to her hand, pressing it hard against his chest. Until now.

The thought that it had been the very last thing to go comforted her a little. It meant he must not totally hate her for ruining everything, though she didn't see how that was possible. He had rescued her, protected her, waded through floods and fire for her, like Joan of Arc. Or the Hunchback of Notre Dame. And she'd repaid him by burning down the cathedral. And the library.

You were wrong about the whole three A.M. thing, C.B., she said, though she was certain he couldn't hear her. And would never hear her again. *Fitzgerald had it right. It isn't the best time of day. It's the worst. Definitely the dark night of the soul.*

Thirty-Four

"So what happens after he climbs up and rescues her?"
"She rescues him right back."
—*Pretty Woman*

THE GOOD THING ABOUT HITTING BOTTOM IS THAT THINGS CAN'T GET *any worse,* Briddey thought, lying there in the dark listening to the silence, but she was wrong. She didn't even make it out of the parking garage the next morning before she ran into Suki. "You look awful," Suki said. "Did you and Trent break up?"

At least she hadn't asked her if it was true the Hermes Project had gone smash, which meant Trent must have thought of something to tell Hamilton, and they all still had jobs. For the moment.

"You did, didn't you?" Suki was saying, her eyes glittering with curiosity.

"Of course we didn't break up. I was just up really late dealing with a family problem. Why? Were you hoping we had?"

"No," Suki said, "although I love his car. And those flowers he sends. But right now I've got my eye on somebody else. Do you know if C.B. Schwartz is involved with anyone?"

Not anymore, Briddey thought. *Not since I ruined his life.* "I don't know," she said.

"He's not gay, is he? The cute ones are always gay."

Briddey thought of him in the stacks, leaning over her, so close she could hear his heart beating. "No," she said.

"Oh, good," Suki squealed. "He's Jewish, isn't he? Do you know if he's Reform?"

"Why don't you just ask him?"

"I was going to google him, but I lost my phone yesterday. I can't find it anywhere," Suki said, and launched into the saga of all the places she'd looked. "I borrowed a phone and tried to call it, but there wasn't any answer—"

"Which reminds me, I've got some calls I need to return," Briddey said, and started toward her office.

"Let me know if you find it!" Suki called after her. "Do you think I should try to get him to ask me out, or should I just ask *him*?"

And as if that wasn't bad enough, when Briddey reached her office, Charla told her, "Trent Worth just called. He wants to see you right away. It must be about your EED."

"M-my EED?" Briddey stammered.

"Yes. He sounded really excited. I'll bet he was able to get the date of your surgeries moved up."

Or he's located a telepath who hasn't been affected by the cascade, Briddey thought, and hurried up to his office. But when she got there, the first thing he asked, after sending Ethel Godwin to make copies of a report, was, "So, did Schwartz know of any other telepaths?"

"No," Briddey said.

"And I'm assuming you didn't hear anything last night after we talked, or you'd have called me?"

"No, it's completely gone. Did you?"

"No. And neither did Lyzandra or Dr. Verrick's other patients. I just talked to him. He said none of them have heard a thing since yesterday. So it looks like Schwartz's theory was right, and the trauma of the voices caused a reaction that shut down the telepathy permanently."

So why aren't you upset? Briddey wondered. Yesterday he'd been practically suicidal over the prospect of having to tell Hamilton the telepathy was gone. But now, not only wasn't he upset, but he was excited, just like Charla'd said. Why? Had Dr. Verrick somehow gotten enough telepathy data from the scans they'd done to make the electronic circuitry after all?

"I'm going to need your help," Trent was saying. "I need you to get the word out that we had the EED done."

The word out? "But you said you wanted it kept secret—"

"That was before it shut down. Now we *need* to tell people."

"Why?"

"Tell them we had it done last week," he said, ignoring her question, "but we didn't want to tell anyone till after we'd connected. And hint that the connection is even better than you'd imagined."

"But I don't understand. Why would you want anyone to know—?"

"It's all part of the plan I've come up with. We say we secretly had the EED, and we hint that the reason we had it done has something to do with the Hermes Project and we can't say what, but it'll revolutionize the communications industry. And *then* we hint that the something we found is telepathy."

Oh, God, they *had* been able to get enough data. *I have to warn C.B.,* she thought.

"We drop all these hints about how we can communicate telepathically and how we've found a way to duplicate that communication in a phone."

"But none of that's true," she said. *I hope.*

"No, but they won't know that. Or that we've gone to Management and told them the whole thing's a ruse."

"A ruse?" Briddey said, completely lost.

"Yes, we tell Management it was all a trick, that we came up with it because we were convinced Apple had planted a spy here at Commspan to find out what our new phone has, and that the entire thing—having the EEDs, the telepathy, the scans—was a diversion we came up with to catch the spy. And to keep Apple from finding out what we were really working on," he finished triumphantly. "Clever, huh?"

Yes, Briddey thought. The story would no doubt save his job. And if there was a spy, and the spy reported the telepathy back to Apple and they fell for it, Commspan would have proof of their corporate spying, and Trent would be a company hero and probably end up getting that executive suite he wanted.

If his plan worked. But for the EEDs and the telepathy to have been a diversion, there had to be some other project it was diverting attention from. Which they didn't have. She pointed that out.

"Yes, we do," Trent said. He showed her a schematic. "Behold, Commspan's new phone, the Refuge. Designed to protect you from the daily bombardment of unwelcome phone calls and messages. It screens out people you don't want to talk to by putting them on a permanent 'call on hold' list. Or, if you just don't want to talk to them right then, by sending a 'call cannot be completed at this time' message. And if you've already connected with the person and you want out of the call, you hit a key, and it'll automatically cause the sound of your voice to break up."

Those are C.B.'s ideas, Briddey thought. *That's his Sanctuary phone.*

"I got the idea when that swarm of voices hit me," Trent was saying. "We need to be protected from unwanted intrusions. We need a refuge from all the people and information bombarding us. What do you think?"

I think you stole it from C.B. and you don't even intend to give him credit, you snake. "But if you just thought of it, how will it be ready in time to beat Apple's rollout?" she asked.

"We don't have to have it ready. Don't you see? We *want* Apple's phone to come out first. That way they announce that their phone offers enhanced communication, and we say, 'But don't worry. We're going to protect you from it.'"

And who's here to protect us from you? she thought bitterly. It was bad enough that she'd destroyed C.B.'s telepathic ability. Now Trent intended to steal his phone design and, worse, possibly put Apple on the trail of the telepathy. And even though the deluge had destroyed it, they might be able to find someone somewhere who hadn't been affected—or there might be enough data on the scans Dr. Verrick had done to re-create it electronically. And Apple had unlimited resources . . .

I have to warn C.B., she thought. *Now.*

But Trent had no intention of letting her go till he'd told her all the details. "My phone can also fake an incoming call, so you can say, 'I've got to take this.' I call the function 'TrapDoor.' What do you think?"

I think it's C.B.'s SOS app, and you stole that, too. "It's an intriguing idea. Look, Trent, I need to go—"

"No, you can't go yet," he said. "I haven't told you the rest." He caught up her hands. "To make all this work, we're going to need to tell Management our seeing each other was part of the plan. That because the EED only works with emotionally bonded couples, you volunteered to date me to lend credibility to the ruse."

"Credibility?" she asked absently, trying to think of an excuse that could get her out of here so she could go tell C.B. what Trent was up to. A TrapDoor app would be nice. Or an actual trapdoor to drop Trent down.

"Of course *we* know the emotional-bonding thing has nothing to do with it, or you'd never have connected with Schwartz," Trent said, "but they don't know that. And if people think we were involved, they may not believe the EED was just a cover story."

He's dumping me, she realized belatedly, and supposed she should try to act a little upset. "Does this mean we have to stop seeing each other?" she asked.

"I'm afraid so, honey. They've got to believe it was nothing but a setup, or they might start checking hospital records and asking Dr. Verrick questions, and our whole plan could fall apart. So you can see why it's vital that everyone believe—"

"That it was all for the sake of the project, and you weren't really in love with me. Yes, I see that very clearly."

"Oh, good," Trent said. "It kills me that we have to do this, sweetheart, but there's too much at stake here for us to be worried about our personal feelings."

You're right, there is, Briddey thought. *Which is why I've got to get out of here and go find C.B.*

"Of course, for the next couple of days it'll still have to look like we're a couple," Trent said. "You need to start dropping a few subtle hints about the EED, maybe some comment about 'when I was in the hospital,' or something, and tomorrow morning I'll send you flowers and call your office. Will Charla be there?"

"Yes," Briddey said, thinking, *If the telepathy still existed, I could tell Maeve to call me right now and give me an excuse to leave.*

"I'll text you asking you if you've felt any connection yet, and—"

Her phone rang. *Thank goodness,* Briddey thought, pulling it out of her pocket.

"—you can make sure your assistant sees it, and—"

"Sorry, I need to take this. It's Art Sampson," Briddey said at random, and put the phone up to her ear.

Trent nodded. "Drop some hints to him, too," he said. "The sooner the news gets around Commspan, the better."

"I will," Briddey said, walking rapidly out of his office and down the hall, ending the call as she walked. She hurried to the elevator and was halfway down to the sub-basement before it occurred to her that C.B. might not be there. He could be anywhere—in the copy room photocopying his résumé or off flirting with Suki.

But thankfully he was in the lab, squatting next to the portable heater, which was apparently still broken, if the temperature in the lab was any indication, though C.B. wasn't wearing a parka, just a flannel shirt over his Doctor Who T-shirt. He had the back of the heater off again and was doing something to the wiring. "What are you doing here?" he asked, looking up briefly.

"I have to talk to you."

"Can you hand me those pliers?" He pointed over at the littered lab table.

"Yes. No. This is important."

"So's this," he said. "We could both freeze to death if I don't get this fixed."

He was right. It was even colder down here than usual. "Which ones?" she asked, looking through the mess of tools, circuit boards, meters, and wires on the lab table.

"The needle-nose pliers on the end there."

She handed them to him, and he gave something inside the heater a twist and then stood up, wiping his hands on the tail of his shirt. "So what's so urgent? What's this all about?"

Before, when you could read my mind, you wouldn't have had to ask, she thought. "Trent's planning to co-opt your Deadzone and SOS ideas and tell Management they're *his*."

"Well, technically they *are* his ideas," C.B. said calmly. He knelt and began fitting the plate back onto the heater. "Or at least Commspan's. Everybody who works for the company has to sign an intellectual-property assignment agreement for ideas they come up with while they're working here."

"But you should at least get *credit* for them! And that's not the worst of it. He's going to tell everyone at Commspan we had the EED and about the telepathy and the scans."

"I know," C.B. said without looking up. "It was my idea."

"*Your* idea? But . . . I don't understand. If there *is* a corporate spy—"

"There is," he said, fitting the back on the heater.

"There *is*? Who?"

He didn't answer. He was busy trying to make the back panel fit.

"The spy will tell Apple," Briddey said, "and if Apple starts research-ing it and word gets out that they're working on something to do with telepathy, then it won't matter that it doesn't exist. Everyone will—"

"No, they won't," C.B. said, finally succeeding in getting the panel on. "Because we're only going to give Apple a week or so to take the bait, and then we're going to put the story out on Twitter that it was all a Commspan ruse, and that Apple fell for it and actually *believed* that telepathy—and who knows what other nonsense? ghosts? channeling? alien abduction?—was real."

Which will humiliate Apple and cause them—and every smartphone com-pany—to avoid telepathy research like the plague, Briddey thought, *just like the scientists did after the Bridey Murphy and Dr. Rhine debacles, and send telepathy back to the status of pseudoscience for another fifty years.*

"We tell them," C.B. was saying, "that it was all—"

"A diversion to keep Apple from finding out what they were really working on," Briddey said. "I know. And what they're working on is *your* Sanctuary phone."

"Yep," he said, threading screws into the back of the heater. "I fig-ured after his attack of the creepy-crawlies at the hospital, Trent would think shutting out anything, even unwanted calls, was a good idea, and he did."

"But to give him your ideas—"

"I had to give him *something* he could put up against Apple's new phone. Apple's rollout is less than two months away, and all he's got is some ridiculous story about hearing voices, only he can't hear them anymore. Which meant he was going to lose his job, and if he did, his only hope for vindication would be proving telepathy was real. Which meant he'd keep digging, and I didn't want him to find out about Maeve. Can you hand me that screwdriver?" he asked, pointing.

She gave it to him. "Thanks," he said. "Giving him the Sanctuary stuff means he keeps his job and is too busy for the next few months to worry about anything but the phone, and after that he'll be too busy giving interviews to *Wired* and *The Wall Street Journal* about 'How Commspan Changed the Communications Conversation from More, More, More to Protecting the Consumer' and fielding offers to work for Samsung and Motorola. He won't have a moment to think about telepathy. Believe me, giving him the Sanctuary was a small price to pay for getting the spotlight off us."

"But if that's what you're trying to accomplish, then leaking the EED story's the last thing you should do. So why did—?"

"I had to. Trent had already told Hamilton, and I wasn't sure Hamilton would be willing to give up on the telepathy otherwise. He thought he had a game changer in his grasp. The only thing that would convince him to settle for the Sanctuary phone instead was the threat of looking like an idiot."

He was right. If Trent told them he'd experienced telepathy first-hand and then it had disappeared, Hamilton would refuse to accept it. He'd insist on pursuing the research. But if he was told it had never existed, that it was part of a trick to fool the competition, he wouldn't dare admit he'd been gullible enough to fall for it, too.

"But what if Apple has something really big that the Sanctuary phone isn't revolutionary enough to counter?"

"They don't."

"How do you know?"

"I can—that is, I *could*—read minds. And all the new iPhone's got is a set of defenses to protect the Cloud from hackers. Ironic, huh? Plus it's got a longer-lasting battery, and a slightly bigger screen."

"But then Apple will need to find something to counter the Sanctuary phone. And to get back at Commspan for making them look like idiots. What if they start digging and find out Trent and I really did have the EED? Lyzandra's threatening to sue Dr. Verrick. If she—"

"She won't," C.B. said confidently. "A lawsuit would mean publicly admitting she'd lost her 'psychic spirit gift.' She can't afford to let her clients know that. They'd desert her in droves."

"But won't they desert her anyway when they realize she can't read their minds?"

"They won't find out. She did almost all her stuff by cold reading anyway—and telling people what they wanted to hear. And as for Dr. Verrick, I was just about to take care of that problem," he said, flipping a switch on the front of the heater.

His repairs must not have worked. No operating hum came on, and the coils didn't turn orange, but C.B. didn't seem to notice. He was too busy pulling a smartphone from his back pocket and typing in a number. He put it to his ear. "Hello, this is C.B. Schwartz calling Dr. Verrick. You can reach me at this number." He rattled it off, hung up, and began typing a message, his head bent over the screen.

Briddey frowned at him. "Are you sending a text?"

"Nope, a tweet," he said, continuing to type. "And I'll bet you were going to ask, since when am I on Twitter?"

"No, I was going to ask, since when do you carry a smartphone?"

"I don't. I borrowed this from Suki. Stole it, actually."

Or Suki left it down here on purpose so she'd have an excuse to talk to him again, Briddey thought. *And she knew when she called that there wouldn't be an answer because it didn't work down here, so she'd have to come down here to get it. But then, how—?*

"How are you going to send a tweet?" Briddey asked. "There's no coverage down here."

C.B. hit SEND and then looked up at her. "Oh, yeah, about that," he said. "That lack of coverage isn't entirely a natural phenomenon."

She looked over at the heater. "You've been interfering with the reception," she said. No wonder it had never given out any heat.

"Yeah, I have been," C.B. admitted, "and I just switched it off, so if you were counting on not being able to get calls down here, you might want to turn your phone off," and Suki's phone rang. "Sorry, I need to take this," he said.

Briddey nodded, turning off her phone before it rang, too.

"Dr. Verrick," C.B. said. "What? . . . Slow down, I can't . . . Slow down . . . Sorry, I didn't get that last part. Can you say that again?" He took the phone from his ear, hit the speakerphone icon, and set the phone on the lab table.

"I *said*," Dr. Verrick's agitated voice said, "it's gotten out!"

Gotten out?

Briddey glanced up at C.B. in alarm, but he was looking calmly down at the phone. "How do you know?" he asked.

"I just got a tweet. It says, 'Breaking: EEDs make patients able to read minds,' and there's a link to my website."

Oh, no, Briddey thought. *Is this Trent's idea of "a few subtle hints"?*

"Do you *know* the damage this could do to my practice?" Dr. Verrick shouted. "*Mind reading?* I have clients who are members of the royal family. If word of this gets out—"

"Do you know who sent the tweet?" C.B. asked.

"It says it's from Gossip Gal, but I know it's from Lyzandra. This is her way of getting revenge for losing her psychic powers."

"What's the hashtag?" C.B. asked.

"EED equals ESP question mark."

"When did you—?"

"Wait, I'm putting you on hold," Dr. Verrick said. There was a brief silence, and he came back on, even more agitated. "I just got two more tweets. Same sender, same hashtag. The first one says, 'Rumor going around a certain celeb EED doc is doing ESP experiments on his patients à la Duke University,' and it has a link to Dr. Rhine's Wikipedia page." Dr. Verrick sounded completely beside himself. "And the second one says, 'Could Briddey Flannigan be the new Bridey Murphy?'"

Briddey gasped.

"Do you *know* who Bridey Murphy was?" Dr. Verrick shouted.

"Yeah," C.B. said. "You're right, this is really serious. If your name got linked to a fraud like that, it could ruin your reputation. I remember what happened to Dr. Rhine. And to Shirley MacLaine when she—"

"That's why you have to *do* something!" Dr. Verrick shouted. "You have to stop those tweets from getting out!"

But he can't, Briddey thought. *They've probably already produced a storm of retweeting.* There were probably already reporters calling her, wanting to know if she'd lived past lives. She was glad she'd turned off her phone. But the moment she went upstairs, she'd be hit by a new kind of deluge, and, with the reference to Bridey Murphy, the press was bound to see the Irish connection and insist on interviewing her family. Including Maeve. *I shouldn't be down here with C.B.*, she thought. *If they find us here together . . .*

She started for the door. C.B. grabbed her arm to stop her. "Don't go," he mouthed, and asked aloud, "When did you get the tweets, Dr. Verrick?"

"Just now, right before I called you."

"Good. It's sometimes possible to delete tweets after they've been sent."

Briddey said, "No, it isn't—"

"Shh," C.B. mouthed at her, taking the phone off speakerphone and putting it back up to his ear. "I think I can stop this, Dr. Verrick, but we'll have to move fast. In case I can't, who else knows about the telepathy thing?" A pause. "Good. And who has access to the records of the Zener tests and scans you did?"

Briddey watched him, frowning, as he talked. There was something she didn't understand here, something wrong with this whole conversation. Why hadn't he panicked about the tweets? He should have, unless . . .

Of course, she thought. *Gossip Gal didn't send those tweets. He did.*

"What about your other patients?" C.B. was saying. "The ones who showed signs of being telepathic? How much did you tell them?" A pause. "Good. I'll see what I can do. No, don't send me the tweets. I don't need them. Just delete them. I'll call you as soon as I know whether I've been able to fix this or not. In the meantime, don't call or tweet or text anyone else."

He hung up. "Good news. He didn't tell anyone about the telepathy—he wanted to wait till he had definitive test results. So he told everyone—including his nurse—that he was testing mirror-neuron enhancement. And physician-patient confidentiality will prevent anyone from getting hold of the scans or the Zener test results, though I think there's an excellent chance he's shredding them as we speak."

"Thanks to your scaring him to death by sending those tweets."

"I thought you'd figure that out," he said. "I was afraid he might have told the other EED patients he'd tested what he was up to, or talked to some other psychics, but he hadn't—apparently Lyzandra was the only redheaded one he'd been able to find. And he told the other patients what he told you, that the emotions they felt were so strong, they seemed to take the form of words. Not a peep to them about its being telepathy, which means they won't say anything. And we should be okay."

"Except for those tweets being out there and being retweeted as we speak."

"No, they're not," he said, bending over his phone again. "I only sent them to Verrick, and I just deleted them from his phone." He tapped the phone. "And from Suki's, both within the ten-minute fail-safe interval, which keeps them from going out to anyone else. I told you the SecondThoughts app was a good idea."

He showed her his phone's screen, which said "tweets deleted," and then began swiping again. "All that's left to do now is to call Verrick back and tell him I was successful. Hang on," he said, and put the phone to his ear. "Dr. Verrick? I've got good news. I think I managed to get them all deleted before they went out."

Briddey watched him as he talked, thinking about how cleverly he'd handled not only Dr. Verrick but Trent. But to what end? Why were all these elaborate ruses necessary? She understood his wanting to keep his connection to this whole thing quiet and to protect Maeve, but Trent had no idea that Maeve had been telepathic, and Dr. Verrick didn't even know she existed. So no matter how much Trent investigated, he was no threat. And the telepathy was gone, which meant it wasn't necessary for Dr. Verrick to destroy the records of the scans and the Zener tests.

So why had C.B. made sure he did? And why had he given Trent his design for the Sanctuary phone *and* an excuse that would not only get Trent out of trouble, but make him a hero in Commspan's eyes?

He isn't just trying to cover his and Maeve's tracks, she thought, watching him talk to Dr. Verrick. *There's something else going on.* And even though C.B. could no longer read her mind, she thought, *I need to be in my safe room,* and went through the blue door into her courtyard.

The walls were still streaked with soot, and pools of water stood here and there on the flagstone pavement, but she didn't see them. She barred the door and then stood there staring blindly at its blistered paint, trying to figure out what C.B. was up to and what it was his conversation with Dr. Verrick reminded her of.

That night in the theater, she thought, *when he was talking to me about*

Niagara Falls and Lucky Charms and going to Death Valley on our honeymoon, trying to distract me from the voices. He was trying to take Trent's and Dr. Verrick's minds off the telepathy. That's what this was all about—the Sanctuary phone and the spreading of rumors and the corporate spies and the tweets, and it was no wonder it didn't make sense. It was all just chatter, designed to keep them from thinking about something else. But what?

"I'm ninety percent sure I got all the tweets deleted," C.B. was saying, "but just in case I didn't, it might be a good idea to steer clear of reporters for a few days. You do surgeries all over the world, don't you? Oh, good, you're way ahead of me. Great minds think alike, huh?"

I was wrong, Briddey thought, listening to him. *He isn't just distracting them—he wants Dr. Verrick out of the country and Trent busy designing phones and spreading rumors. And it isn't the theater this reminds me of.* She squinted at the barred door, trying to capture the relevant memory, as if the blistered paint could tell her the answer. *It was somewhere else.*

In the car. After he'd rescued her from the theater, when he was driving her to the library. He'd talked to her about reciting poetry and singing the theme from *Gilligan's Island* and "Ode to Billy Joe" to keep the voices under control.

"But I can't do that forever," she'd protested, and he'd said, "These are just interim measures till we can get your permanent defenses up."

Interim measures. Distracting Trent, getting Dr. Verrick out of the country, giving Commspan and Apple a shiny new phone to focus on, they were all interim measures, designed to keep them at bay just like he'd done with the voices. *Till he gets the permanent defenses up.* And there was only one thing he could need defenses for.

The telepathy isn't gone, she thought. *He's blocking the voices. He lied to me when he said he couldn't. He's been doing it this whole time.*

But if he could block the voices, he'd have done it before Dr. Verrick ran the tests and did the scans, and Dr. Verrick wouldn't have had to shred them. And he could have done it from the testing room, and they'd never have known about him at all. And if he could block the voices, then why would he need permanent defenses? It didn't make any sense. He couldn't be blocking them.

But he is, she thought. *And the reason he's so certain the telepathy isn't coming back is because it didn't go away in the first place. And I'm not leaving here till he admits it and tells me what's going on.*

But if he hadn't admitted it to her before, he wouldn't now just because she confronted him. She had to think of some other way to get the truth out of him.

"You can count on us, Doctor," C.B. was saying into the phone. "We want to put this whole thing behind us as much as you do. Good-bye. Have a good trip."

He hung up. "The good doctor's going to perform EED surgery on the king of Tupanga and his favorite wife in the Lesser Sunda Islands," he said to Briddey, "an area that I understand has very limited coverage." He began typing something into the phone. "And it looks like Lyzandra's back at work in Sedona." He held the phone up so Briddey could see. "Look."

The image on the screen was an ad for a summer Seminar of the Spirit, featuring Lyzandra, "newly returned from a cleansing retreat in the Himalayas, where she studied ancient techniques of seeing into the innermost recesses of the mind."

Cleansing retreat, Briddey thought. *I guess that's one name for it.*

"See?" C.B. said. "I told you we don't have to worry about her."

"So that just leaves Trent," Briddey said, and went over to the door of the lab. "He asked me to start spreading rumors about us having had the EED, so I guess I'd better go do that."

"Good idea," C.B. said, walking over to his laptop. "And I'd better email Suki and tell her I found her phone."

"Yeah." Briddey reached the door. "Commspan's grapevine can't function without it."

C.B. began typing the email, his eyes on the screen. Briddey opened the lab door a few inches and said, *If you want, I could take Suki's phone up to her and save you a trip.*

"No, that's okay. I kind of like going upstairs now that—" He stopped.

Their eyes met.

Briddey smiled grimly at him. "Now that what? You don't hear voices anymore?" she said.

Thirty-Five

"Things are indeed hopeless—hopeless—but they're not serious."
—*Finian's Rainbow*

THEY STOOD THERE FOR A LONG MINUTE, FACING EACH OTHER ACROSS THE heater, and then C.B. said, "I was afraid you'd figure it out." Not "I was going to tell you." Or even "Listen, I can explain." And definitely not "I'm glad you did. I've hated having to lie to you." Just "I was afraid you'd figure it out."

You lied to me, she thought numbly. *Just like Trent.*

But it wasn't the same thing at all. Betrayal by Trent was one thing. This was so much worse. This was C.B., who she'd trusted, who she—

"I didn't figure it out," she said, glad her hand was still on the door. It gave her something to hang onto. "Not till just this second. The deluge isn't what shut the voices down, is it? You were. You've been block—"

"Shh," he whispered, diving past her to shut the door and lock it. *Did you tell anybody you were coming down here?*

She shook her head.

Did anybody see you?

"I don't think—"

Shh, keep your voice down, he said fiercely, and put his ear to the door. He listened for a long moment and then said, *We're okay. Nobody followed you,* but he opened the door and looked out anyway, checking in both directions. Then he grabbed a KEEP OUT sign from the wall and stuck it on the outside of the door.

He shut the door again, locked it, taped up a second sign saying DANGER—NO ADMITTANCE—EXPERIMENT IN PROGRESS in its window, and walked over to the heater that wasn't a heater. He flipped the switch, strode over to the radio, turned it on full blast, and then came back and motioned her over to the middle of the room. "You cannot say a word about this to anybody," he said, his voice lowered. "Especially Trent."

"You think I'd tell *him*?" Briddey said incredulously. "I can't believe you'd—"

"No, of course I don't, but you don't understand. You can't even *think* about it. That's why I—"

"Why you didn't tell me," she said angrily. "Because you thought I'd give it away if I knew. So you let me think *I* was the one who was responsible for destroying the telepathy. You let me think I'd ruined your life!"

"Look, I'm sorry," C.B. said, "but it couldn't be helped. There was just too much at stake. I couldn't risk him finding out about Maeve or—" He stopped himself and began again. "You saw what he's like. That onslaught of bugs didn't even slow him down. He's still convinced telepathy is something he can control, and if he had even the slightest hint it still existed, he wouldn't rest till he'd stuck it in his stupid phone and inflicted it on the whole world. It was essential to convince him it had stopped, and you were our best bet. If you thought it was true, you couldn't accidentally—"

"Give away the secret."

"Yes, and it's still critical you don't, now that you know. You're going to have to keep completely away from Trent."

"How? Thanks to this little diversion plan of yours, he and I are supposed to be convincing everyone we're a happy, EED-connected couple. And I can't avoid him indefinitely."

"You won't have to. Just a couple more days."

"What happens then?"

He hesitated, looking torn.

"You've already told me this much. You might as well tell me the rest. What happens in a couple more days?"

"I finish programming the jamming equipment," he said.

She looked automatically over at the heater. No wonder it was always so cold down here. It wasn't a heater. It was a signal jammer.

"Nope," C.B. said. "That just prevents cellphone coverage. *This*"—he plucked a smartphone out of the clutter on the lab table— "is what jams the voices."

"A *smartphone*?"

"No, it just looks like one. It's actually a jammer. It sends out a signal that'll block the voices. Or it will as soon as I finish writing the code."

"So you lied when you said the jammer didn't work."

"No. There really wasn't a way to generate enough power to block the telepathy permanently for all those people."

"But now you've discovered one?"

"No," he said. "You did."

"I did—?"

"Yep. One of the many unintended consequences of your EED, only this turned out to be a good one."

"I don't understand. How—?"

"After you had it done, you told me we had to talk out loud because the neural pathway acted as a feedback loop."

"And you said it didn't."

"And it still doesn't. But after the flood, when you were telling Maeve why she needed to stay in her castle, you mentioned a feedback loop again, and I realized I'd been thinking about the problem all wrong."

I knew all those questions he asked me about the feedback loop and then his saying the deluge had caused one couldn't be just a coincidence, Briddey thought.

"You were right, they weren't. A feedback loop was the perfect explanation for the disruptions, except for the part about it triggering inhibitors we didn't have—which you spotted. But I'm talking about blocking the voices. I realized that if I could create a feedback loop, I wouldn't *have* to come up with all that power. All I'd have to do was set it in motion, and the feedback loop would do the rest."

And that's why he can do it with something the size of a smartphone, Briddey thought, looking at it on the lab table. "So it works using Hedy Lamarr's frequency-hopping thing?"

"Partly. It also partly uses Maeve's zombie-gate and forest-of-brambles and moat defenses and the synaptic patterns produced by reading *Little Dorrit* and *The Mill on the Floss*—combined with a mechanism for feeding the defenses back on themselves that will work like the one I told Verrick was shutting down the telepathy. Only this one actually will." He held up the jammer. "A *real* Sanctuary phone."

The effects of the jamming would intensify with each listener who received it, with each circuit of the loop, till the voices were completely shut down. And the effect would be exactly the same as if C.B.'s story about the deluge creating a cascade had been true. The telepathy would be gone for good.

"You're right, it will," C.B. said. "But if it keeps Verrick and Trent and all the other potential exploiters from getting their mitts on it and on Maeve, it'll be worth it."

"But—"

"And if it's us you're worried about, we'll still be able to communicate. We'll just have to do it by joining Canoodle.com and swiping each other's photographs, like normal people."

But I'll still have deprived C.B. of his gift, Briddey thought to herself.

"Yeah, but we'll get to go to Carnival Pizza. And plays."

But not the library.

"Well, maybe not the Carnegie Room, but we can still go to the Reading Room. And the stacks." He grinned at her. "And there won't be any more floods. Or zombies."

Or fires, she thought, looking at C.B.'s hands.

"Or fires. Which will be great. And anyway, it's probably just as well that telepathy won't be around anymore. There are some things about it I didn't tell you—some of those unintended consequences. Trust me, we'll be better off without it."

He set down the jammer and went over to his laptop. "But that means I need to get the jammer up and running, so I'd better get back to work, and you'd better go start spreading the rumor that you and Trent had the EED. I'd suggest starting with Jill Quincy," he said, and began typing. "Tell her, 'This is supposed to be a secret, but I *had* to tell somebody,' and swear her to secrecy."

"But I thought you wanted everyone to find out—"

"I do, and there's no better way to guarantee it than to tell people not to tell. Especially malicious people. Make sure no one sees you on your way back upstairs. Oh, and when you leave, can you stick a DANGER: RADIATION sign up opposite the elevator so I won't be interrupted?" He turned back to his laptop.

It was a clear dismissal. And he was right: The sooner he completed the jammer, the safer they'd all be. But it was more than that. He seemed anxious to get rid of her, as if he was afraid *he* might give something away if she stayed.

And now that she thought about it, he hadn't explained how he was blocking the voices right now. Or what those "unintended consequences" were that made it "just as well" that they were doing away with it. Or how he was blocking everyone while he worked on this jammer.

He's still keeping something from me, and I'm not leaving here till I find out what it is.

She went back over to where he was working on the laptop. "How are you doing it?" she asked.

C.B. glanced up from the screen. "Doing what?"

"The blocking. If you haven't finished the jammer, how—?" and Suki's phone rang.

"Sorry," C.B. said, and answered it. "Hi, Suki. Yeah, I found your phone in the copy room. I was just going to call you. I'll bring it right up." He hung up. "Apparently she can't survive longer than five minutes without it."

He held it out to Briddey. "You wouldn't mind taking it up to her, would you, since you're going upstairs? You can tell her about the EED while you're at it. But you'll have to be quick. She said she needs it right away."

"No, she didn't. That was your SOS app. You showed me how it worked before, remember? And how useful it was for getting out of conversations you don't want to have. Like this one," she said grimly. "Besides, you turned the cellphone jammer back on. There's no coverage down here."

She slammed Suki's phone down onto the lab table between them. "You have to sleep sometimes. So how are you blocking us then? And how are you blocking so many people? You said each person you blocked made it exponentially harder. And how can you be blocking them *and* working on the jammer at the same time?"

He isn't, she thought, suddenly certain of it. *Someone else is, and that's what he's been avoiding telling me.* "It's Maeve, isn't it?" she asked. "I can't believe you let her do this!"

"I didn't. Are you kidding? She's nine years old! I'd never put her in jeopardy. Besides, you heard her in the lab after the fire. I knew if I let her help, she'd go off half-cocked and do something that would tip off Verrick to the Irish connection." He shook his head. "Besides, she had school."

"So you expect me to believe you did this all by yourself?"

He didn't answer. He just stood there looking at Briddey for a long, measuring moment. *While he decides whether I'll buy the lie he's about to tell me,* she thought.

No, she said to him, *I won't. You taught me the Rules of Lying, remember?* "You had to have a partner," she said aloud. "If it isn't Maeve, who is it?"

"I can't tell you," he said, and she realized with a sinking heart that he didn't have to. She already knew. And no wonder C.B. had been avoiding her. And telling her she wouldn't have to put up with him anymore. He'd connected to someone else, someone who hadn't nearly exposed his secret, who didn't need to be constantly rescued and coached and calmed down—someone who was a natural telepath like he was. And there was only one person that could be.

I should have seen it, Briddey thought. *That's how she knows everything that goes on at Commspan, because she can read everybody's mind.* He hadn't stolen her phone. She'd given it to him. "It's Suki, isn't it?" she said.

C.B. stared at her incredulously. "Suki? Grapevine girl? You're kidding, right?"

"That's not an answer," she said.

"You're right. No, it's not Suki. She's not a telepath, natural or otherwise. She's just incredibly nosy. And no, she's not Apple's spy either. You'll never guess who that is."

"Who?"

"Ethel Godwin."

"Ethel *Godwin*? Trent's *secretary*?"

"The very same."

"But Trent said she was the soul of discretion. And completely loyal."

"She is. To Apple. And she's already told them all about your EEDs and the Hermes Project and Trent's telling Hamilton there'd been a revolutionary breakthrough, so it'll be easy to convince them the direct communication phone's real."

"But how—?" she began, and then realized C.B. was simply creating another diversion to keep from telling her who'd helped him. "If it's not Suki, then who is it?" she demanded. "And don't say you can't tell me, because I'm not leaving this lab until you do."

"Fine," he said, throwing up his hands in surrender. "But not here."

"What do you mean, not here? The door's locked, there's no coverage, nobody can hear us—"

"That's what you think," he said. "Go into your safe room. She won't be able to hear us in there."

"If this is another one of your diversions—"

"It's not. Go."

Briddey went, shutting and barring the door behind her and then stopping to stare at the courtyard. It had been miraculously restored to its before-the-flood state, the water and the streaks of soot gone, the blue door shining with fresh paint and the flowers blooming again.

She hurried over to the adobe wall C.B.'d scaled before. She looked up at the top of it, waiting in dread for him to clamber over and tell her who was helping him block the voices. "She," he'd said.

It is *Suki,* she thought, or some other girlfriend who he didn't want to have find out he'd been talking to Briddey—

"True," C.B. said from behind her. "In fact, she'll kill me if she finds out I told you."

Briddey turned. C.B. was standing by the bench. "She swore me to silence," he said. "On the holy blood of Saint Patrick and all the saints of Ireland."

"All the . . . ?" Briddey said, and sat down hard on the bench. "Are you telling me it's Aunt *Oona*?"

"Yep," he said, and Briddey knew she should be feeling shock at the news that her great-aunt was telepathic and dismay that she'd been eavesdropping on everything for who knew how long. And fury at C.B. for keeping that from her and, worse, putting her through the hell of thinking she'd destroyed the telepathy and ruined his life. But all she felt was relief that he didn't have a girlfriend.

"Of course I don't have a girlfriend. How could you even think that?" He frowned. "Maybe Maeve was right and I should have—" He stopped himself.

"Should have what?" Briddey asked.

"Nothing. Yes, it's Oona. And she made me swear I wouldn't tell you, so you can't say a word about this. Or even think about it."

"But I don't understand. How—?"

"What do you mean, how? Telepathy obviously runs in the family."

"But then why aren't Mary Clare and Kathleen telepathic, too?"

"Mary Clare is. Since the day she gave birth to Maeve. Oona's been blocking her to protect Maeve, or as she says, 'to keep the poor wee bairn from being smothered in her cradle.'"

"And Kathleen?"

"Is apparently a late bloomer like you and your great-aunt. Oona didn't start hearing voices till she was forty, and your mother didn't till—"

"My *mother*?"

"Yep. Her telepathy wasn't triggered till she was thirty, and neither were any of your ancestors' 'psychic spirit gifts,' which is why Oona didn't recognize the signs that it was happening to Maeve. And by the time she figured it out, I'd already intervened."

"But . . . ," Briddey said, still trying to take this all in. "Why didn't they tell—?"

"For the same reason I didn't."

It can get you burned at the stake, Briddey thought.

"Exactly," C.B. said. "And remember, Oona was forty when hers started, by which time she'd had a lot of years to observe the human race in action. She's got an even lower opinion of humanity than I do." He grinned at Briddey. "She was also old enough to remember Bridey Murphy, so she knew exactly what would happen if people found out she was a telepath."

"So she kept it a secret like you did," Briddey said, and then realized that wasn't quite true. "Does this mean her premonitions are *real*?"

"No. I told you, clairvoyance doesn't exist. But 'the Sight' is a lot safer to talk about than hearing voices, especially if you're, as Oona puts it, 'an auld, lone spinster' who's just the sort of person everyone's inclined to think is a wee bit touched in the head anyway. *And* if you're from Ireland, where people have a reputation for believing in second sight and presentiments."

"So you're saying it was all a cover for her telepathy—the shawls and the crubeens and that awful Maureen O'Hara accent?"

"Aye, lass. 'Tis all a diversionary tactic. And it works great. It had me fooled. I'd never have pegged her for a telepath if she hadn't told me. And I couldn't tell you because—"

"She swore you to secrecy."

"Yes, and because Trent and Lyzandra could both hear your thoughts, and we couldn't be sure we could block them a hundred percent, so you *had* to think the cascade was destroying the telepathy."

Which Briddey could understand. Any inkling that they were being blocked, or that the telepathy still existed, would have sabotaged the entire plan.

"Oona wouldn't have told me she was a telepath either if she hadn't had to. She'd overheard me talking to Maeve and knew I was helping her understand what was happening to her, but she wasn't sure I knew how to build defenses."

That day at Commspan, Briddey thought, when Aunt Oona had supposedly gone down to the lab to thank him for helping Maeve with her project.

"She had to find out whether she could trust me to protect Maeve from the voices," C.B. said, "or if she was going to have to pitch in."

Which would have meant Maeve finding out that Aunt Oona was telepathic.

"Yeah, and Oona wasn't sure how she'd take it—you know how Maeve feels about being spied on. She was afraid Maeve might reject her help, and the voices would overwhelm her. So we agreed I'd do it, and she'd provide backup if I needed it."

"And she did," Briddey said. "You enlisted her help with blocking Lyzandra and Trent."

"Wrong. I didn't want to risk Verrick and Trent finding out about her either. And besides, I didn't see how one additional person blocking the voices was going to help. I wasn't lying about how much energy it takes to block that many people nonstop, and Oona already had her hands full blocking Mary Clare."

"But if you didn't enlist her help, then how—?"

"She took it upon herself to start blocking. Without telling me."

"And that's why you looked so stunned," Briddey said, suddenly understanding. "Why you looked like you had no idea what was happening."

"Right," C.B. said. "I didn't. Which turned out to be an advantage. My reaction not only convinced you, it convinced Lyzandra. And Verrick."

"And you've been ... what? Doing alternating shifts with Aunt Oona?"

"Along with the rest of the Daughters of Ireland."

"The Daughters—?"

C.B. nodded. "Which she didn't see fit to fill me in on either—another reason I thought the deluge was what was shutting the telepathy down. It was the only explanation I could think of. But it turns out the Daughters is an undercover organization/support group/outreach society for telepaths like Oona—"

"And all that Irish poetry reading and step-dancing and matchmaking is just a *diversionary* tactic?"

"Some of it is. And some of it's recruitment. If my mother hadn't taken my stepdad's name, I've no doubt they'd have found me and invited me to a meeting long ago. And some of it—the most important part—is the Irish version of the Reading Room, with them reciting 'The Harp that Once Through Tara's Halls' and 'The Lake Isle of Innisfree' and reading *Finnegan's Wake,* which may well be the best screening device ever written."

"And that's who's been blocking the voices? The Daughters of Ireland?"

"And *their* daughters. And sons. Including my chief competition, Sean O'Reilly, who, in addition to having very little hair and living with his mother, can block up to six people at once."

"And all of them are on board with this? They're willing to give up being telepathic, too?"

He nodded. "They know it's the only answer. They've all been blocking twenty-four/seven, and they're really good, but even with them calling in the reserves, they're fully aware that they can't block the voices forever. And they know what'll happen if they don't."

"But for now they're doing alternating shifts with you?" Briddey asked, trying to understand how all this worked.

"Yeah, though actually they've been doing the lion's share of the blocking so I could work on the jammer. And Oona's been blocking you and Maeve. She told me she didn't trust me not to break down and tell you everything, especially on the three A.M. shift." He smiled ruefully at her. "She was probably right."

So he hadn't been there listening to her pour her heart out about him, thank goodness. On the other hand—oh, God!—Aunt Oona had been.

"That's the other reason she swore me to secrecy," C.B. said. "She knows how you feel about the family constantly barging in and not respecting your privacy, so she didn't want you knowing that she could read your mind."

And that she's been doing it for years. That was why she'd been so against her dating Trent. She'd been listening to him just like C.B. had, and knew what he was up to. She'd just been trying to protect her.

"She doesn't want the rest of the family knowing about her telepathy either," C.B. was saying. "She doesn't want them to think she's been meddling."

"You mean, she doesn't want us to *know* she has been."

"True," C.B. said. "But you still can't tell them. And you *really* can't tell Maeve."

Tell me what? Maeve's voice cut in. *That you guys lied about the telepathy being gone?* she said, outraged, and Briddey could almost see her standing there with her hands on her hips, looking daggers at them. *You were blocking me the whole time, weren't you? I* knew *it!*

"How long have you been listening to us?" C.B. demanded.

Oh, don't ask that, Briddey thought. *That'll just make her determined to find out what we were talking about.* "What I want to know," she said aloud, "is what you're doing here, Maeve. This is my safe room, and we are having a private conversation."

I didn't know it was private, okay? You should have put a sign on the door or something. And besides, I didn't even know you could have *conversations. You told me that big mob of voices destroyed the telepathy. But it didn't, did it? You guys just put up a really good barricade.*

"Yes," C.B. said. "How did you get through it?"

Maeve ignored that. *I want to know why you blocked me.*

"Because C.B. had to convince Dr. Verrick and Trent that the telepathy had shut down completely," Briddey said.

But if you wanted to do that, how come you didn't ask me? Maeve asked. *I'm way better than Aunt Briddey at blocking. I know all kinds of things we—*

"No," C.B. said. "Absolutely not. I told you, we can't risk anyone finding out about you. You aren't to say or do *anything*. Including talking to us like this. If what we're saying should happen to leak—"

It won't, Maeve said confidently. *We're in Aunt Briddey's safe room, and I've got the drawbridge up and like fifteen firewalls. And a zombie horde. You know, like the one in* Zombiegeddon.

"I don't care," C.B. said. "I don't want you eavesdropping *or* talking. You've got to act like you think the voices are gone till I get *my* zombie horde done."

What zombie horde? she asked. *Oh, you mean the jammer? I know all about that.*

"How?" C.B. and Briddey said in unison.

I can read your minds, remember?

Briddey thought, *And the first thing that's going to pop into C.B.'s is "Oh, my God, she'll find out about Aunt Oona."* "I'm glad you know about the jammer," she said, to keep Maeve from hearing C.B. "Then he doesn't have to explain it to you."

Yes, he does. Why are you going to shut down all the telepathy? Nobody'll be able to talk to each other.

"It was the only way we could keep people from doing bad things with it," C.B. said.

No, it isn't.

And now we'll be subjected to what someone in Guys and Zombies *or* Beauty and the Beast *did to save the day,* Briddey thought. "We will discuss this later," she said. "Now go."

Why? Maeve said suspiciously. *So you guys can talk about* more *secret stuff?*

"Yes," C.B. said.

Like what?

"None of your business," he said. "This is just between me and your Aunt Briddey."

Oh, I get it. Sex.

"No, not—" Briddey said.

I'll bet. You think I don't know about sex, but me and Danika watched Zombie Girls Gone Wild *last night.*

"I thought you were grounded," Briddey said.

I am. But I told you, I overrode the block Mom put on my laptop. And on Danika's mom's Netflix account. Which explained the movie, but not how she'd smuggled Danika into her room.

She wasn't here, Maeve said. *We were on FaceTime together. If it isn't sex, why can't I listen?*

"Because I said so," C.B. said.

That isn't going to work, Briddey thought.

"I know," he said, and grabbed Briddey's hand. "But this is. Come on," he whispered.

Whispering doesn't do any good with telepathy, Maeve said.

"True," he said, and to Briddey, as he hustled her across the courtyard to the weathered wooden cupboard: "That's why we need to get out of here." He opened the cupboard doors, pulled out the clay pots, stacked them on top next to the radio, and then yanked out the shelves and dumped them onto the flagstones.

What are you doing? Maeve asked.

C.B. didn't answer. He stepped inside the cabinet and then reached back out to take Briddey's hand.

Hey, Maeve said. *Where are you going?*

"Narnia," C.B. said. "Duck," he told Briddey, and pulled her into the cabinet.

Thirty-Six

"There's someone at the door."
—*Walk, Don't Run*

THERE SHOULD HAVE BEEN A WOODEN BACK TO THE CUPBOARD AND, BE-hind it, the adobe wall of the courtyard, but there wasn't. There was a white plastic wall with a control panel at waist height. C.B. pressed a button, and a door irised open.

"Blast door," C.B. said, standing back so Briddey could precede him. "Sorry. Relic from my *Star Wars* phase." He stepped through after her, and the door whooshed shut, leaving them in a torchlit stone passage with an arched wooden door at the end. "And my Hunchback of Notre Dame phase."

"I thought you told me it was a maximum-security prison," Briddey said as they started down the passage.

"My perimeter is."

It's no use running away, Maeve said. *I'll just find you.*

"You were right. Telepathy *is* a terrible idea," Briddey said.

C.B. grinned, unlocked the wooden door with a huge iron key, hustled her through it, relocked the door from the other side, and led her down a corridor with a tile floor. And a wheelchair and an IV-stand. "We're in the hospital?" Briddey said.

"Yep."

"But you hate hospitals."

"We won't be here long," he said, hurrying her along the corridor past her room.

Come on, where are you guys going? Maeve called.

"Death Valley," C.B. said.

"Where *are* we going?" Briddey whispered.

"*My* safe room," he said, pushing the door open onto the stairwell she'd taken refuge in that first night.

"This is your safe room?" Briddey asked as they clattered down the stairs.

"No," he said, hurrying across the landing where she'd sat and on down the steps to a door marked SECOND FLOOR, which opened not onto another hospital corridor, but into a different stairway.

"You built all these layers of defenses to keep the voices out?" Briddey said, following him down it.

"No. Remember, I was figuring it out as I went, so some parts of this were just early attempts. And a lot of it," he said, indicating the stairwell they were in, which she now saw was the one that led down to his lab at Commspan, "is here for frequency hopping, to keep the voices from finding out where you are. I intended to teach you how to do this at the deli while we had breakfast, but then we were rudely interrupted."

He hustled her down the last few steps, through the door to the sub-basement, and over to the elevator. "Right now," he said, pushing the UP button, "we're using it to keep a certain small child from finding us." And it must have been working because there was no outraged *I am* not *a small child!* from Maeve.

The elevator dinged, and they stepped through the opening door into the hallway they'd sneaked along after the library closed. Halfway down it, he said, "Hang on," and darted into the staff lounge. The half-eaten birthday cake and the donations jar were still on the table. C.B. began opening drawers and rummaging through them.

"What are you looking for?" Briddey whispered.

"These," he said, holding up a roll of Scotch tape and a flashlight. He stuck them in his pocket, grabbed a sheet of paper off the counter, scrawled something on it with a marker, dropped the iron key in the donations jar, grabbed the key to the Carnegie Room and Briddey's hand, switched off the light, and hurried her along the darkened hallway to the stairway that should have led up to the Carnegie Room. But it didn't. It led to Commspan's parking garage. And no wonder she hadn't been able to read his mind. Nobody could find their way through this maze of defenses.

"Yeah, well, that's not the only reason," C.B. said, racing her along the rows of cars, their steps echoing, toward the door.

"What's the other one?"

"I'll tell you when we get there."

"Get where?" she asked as he pushed through the doorway. Into the stacks. And apparently she'd been wrong about nobody being able to follow them through the maze, because before they were halfway along the row of books, Maeve called, *Come on, you guys! Tell me where you're going.*

"Havana," C.B. said, opening the door to the stairs, pulling Briddey through, and shutting it behind them.

They were in the lobby of the theater.

This is no fair! Maeve wailed as C.B. raced Briddey across the lobby, and it seemed to Briddey that Maeve's voice was growing fainter as they went.

They ran up the carpeted stairs to the theater doors and through them—to the stairway that led to the Carnegie Room. He bent to unlock the door.

His safe room's the Carnegie Room, she thought, touched. *If this* is *the Carnegie Room.*

It was. As they ran up the narrow stairs and through the oak doorway, she could see the fireplace and the bookshelves and the table, on it a box of Lucky Char—

You might as well give up, Maeve said. *You can't get away from me.*

"Oh, for the love of Mike!" C.B. said, pushing Briddey into the room and dropping to his knees in front of the card file. "I don't believe this. Nobody's *ever* been able to find my safe room, not even your intrepid aunt. 'Poor wee bairn,' my foot."

He pushed the Persian carpet back from the floorboards. "Come on." He pulled up a square section of the polished wood floor, dropped down into the dark hole it exposed, and extended a hand to Briddey.

She clambered down to him, he pulled the trapdoor shut, and they hurried along what might have been the street in front of her apartment, though it was too dark to tell. "Where are we going?" she asked.

"Inner sanctum," he whispered. "Where even Maeve won't be able to find us. I hope."

He rushed her around the corner and up another dark street to the library's front door. "We need to hurry. Here," he said, handing her the flashlight and taping up the sheet of paper he'd brought from the staff lounge. It read, KEEP OUT! THIS MEANS YOU, MAEVE! I MEAN IT!

He took the flashlight back from Briddey and opened the door. Onto pitch darkness. "In. Hurry," he whispered, stepping inside after her and pulling the door shut. "Come on." He fumbled for her hand and led her into the impenetrable darkness.

"Where are we?" she asked. "The Black Hole of Calcutta?"

"No," he said, finally stopping.

"What happened to the flashlight?"

"It's right here. But before I turn it on, there's some stuff I need to tell you."

"You *do* have X-ray vision," she said.

"No. I'm serious, Briddey. The reason I've been able to read your mind and you couldn't read mine wasn't just my safe room. I've been intentionally blocking you because—"

"Because you were afraid I'd hear you thinking about Trent and find out what a creep he was being, and you didn't want me to be hurt. I know."

"That was part of it—"

"Plus, I was hearing the voices, and you didn't think I could handle the idea of hearing any more thoughts than I was already. And then Trent showed up, and you didn't dare send any thoughts because he might hear them."

"True, but that's not the only reason I blocked you. You know how I said it was just as well that the telepathy wouldn't be around anymore? Well, I meant it. It—" He stopped, took a deep breath, and started again. "Remember what I said about things having unintended consequences? Well, it turns out telepathy's no exception. You know how that first night in the hospital you—"

Here you are, Maeve's voice said from the darkness beside them. *I told you I'd find you! I can't believe you guys tried to ditch me.*

"'Tried' being the operative word," C.B. said. "How did you get in here?"

Are you kidding? It was easy.

"Yes, well, then it should be easy to get out," C.B. said. "I told you I needed to talk to your Aunt Briddey alone."

You mean you guys still didn't have sex? Did you at least kiss her?

"That is none of your business," Briddey said. "Kissing is a private—"

No it's not, Maeve said. *It's not even PG. They kiss in* The Twelve Dancing Princesses *and* Frozen *and* Enchant—

"I don't care!" C.B. shouted. "*Go* away!"

"Let me handle this," Briddey interjected. "Go away," she said quietly, "or I'll tell your mother you watched *Zombie Girls Gone Wild.*"

You wouldn't dare!

"And *Zombie Terror* and *World War Z,*" Briddey went on ruthlessly. "And *Saw Reborn: Revenge of the Zombie Torturers.*"

I did not! Maeve said indignantly.

"*I* know that," Briddey said, "and you know that, but your mother doesn't, and who do you think she's going to believe? Now, are you going?"

Yes, Maeve said grudgingly. *I hate grown-ups!* and they heard the door slam.

"Is she gon—?" Briddey began, and heard the door open.

Not that you care, but I fixed your stupid jammer! Maeve said, and slammed the door again.

"What do you mean, you fixed it?" C.B. shouted. "Maeve, come back here!"

I thought you told me to go away. Make up your minds.

"What do you mean you fixed the jammer?"

I mean, I fixed it. I made it so we could still talk to each other.

"You did *what?*" C.B. said, sounding like he wanted to throttle her. "Maeve, I swear, if you've jeopardized—"

I didn't. The feedback loop will still shut down Trent and Lyzandra and all the other people so they'll think it's gone and they won't be able to do anything bad with it. It just won't shut down us.

"Us?" C.B. said. "You mean full telepaths?" and Briddey remembered that Maeve didn't know about Aunt Oona and the Daughters of Ireland, and then hastily quashed that thought so Maeve wouldn't hear it.

Apparently she didn't, because she said, *Yeah. You and me and Briddey. Don't worry. I got rid of the bad parts and just kept the nice stuff.*

"What do you mean the bad parts?" C.B. demanded.

You know, the scary voices. I shut them down and made it so they can't ever come back, but I kept everything else. It's okay. Nobody else'll know about it. They won't even know it exists.

"And how exactly did you do this?"

I took the stuff you did and put it behind a firewall and then disabled . . . I'm not sure I can explain it to you. It's kind of complicated. But don't worry, it works really good, she said, and was gone.

C.B. didn't try to call her back. "Oh, my God," he said. "If she's been fooling around with the program and messed it up . . . come on!" He grabbed Briddey's hand and started back through the blackness toward the door.

"We don't have to go back through the whole maze, do we?" she asked, trying to keep up with him.

"No, of course not. You *do* know we've been in my lab the entire time, right?"

"Yes," she said, though that wasn't strictly true—the illusion had been so complete. And still was. When they reached the door and C.B. opened it onto his lab, she blinked against the sudden light, and it took her a minute to adjust to the idea that she was actually standing by the lab table, looking down at the smartphone/jammer, not walking through the doorway from his inner sanctum.

It was a minute that cost her. During it, C.B. had shut the door behind them, and it had returned to being the wall with the pinup of Hedy Lamarr on it, which meant she'd missed her chance to see what his inner sanctum had been.

C.B. had already dived for his laptop and was typing madly, his face intent on the screen. Lines of code scrolled by, and he checked them with his finger as they did, frowning, and then began typing again.

"Did she mess it up?" Briddey asked anxiously.

"I don't know," C.B. said, drawing his finger along a string of numbers. "I can't figure out what she's done here. She's altered the code—" And beside Briddey on the lab table, the phone he'd stolen from Suki rang. "Can you get that?" he asked, his eyes still on the laptop screen.

Briddey nodded and picked it up, thinking, *I thought he turned the cellphone jammer back on.*

"He did," Maeve's voice said from the phone. "I figured out a way to bypass it."

And apparently a way to get Suki's number. "Maeve," Briddey said warningly, "I told you—"

"You said to go away. You didn't say I couldn't call you on the phone," Maeve said with maddening logic. "I need to talk to C.B. and tell him I didn't mess up his stupid code. I *fixed* it. The way he was doing it, it would have taken forever, and we wouldn't have been able to talk to each other anymore, so I—"

C.B. grabbed the phone from Briddey. "Tell me exactly what you did to the program," he said, cradling the phone against his shoulder and typing again. "Um-hmm . . . um-hmm . . . how did you . . . ? Wow! I never thought of that. What about . . . ? Um-hmm . . . okay." He ended the call, stared intently at the screen for several more minutes, and then straightened.

"Well?" Briddey asked C.B. "Did she fix the code?"

"No, she wrote a whole new program," he said, looking bemused, "which is, as far as I can tell, a vast improvement on mine. And, as near as I can tell, it does exactly what she said it does. It eliminates the voices but lets full telepaths go on talking to one another and shuts down the signals completely for everybody else." He frowned.

"But that's good, isn't it?" Briddey asked. "It means you won't have to give up being telepathic?" *And I won't have ruined your life.*

"Yeah, it's good. It's great," he said, though he didn't look like it was.

"What's wrong?" Briddey asked. "Do her changes mean it'll take you longer than two days to finish the jammer?"

"No. She's already started it. It's been running since five minutes after we took off for my safe room."

"But how could . . . she wasn't even here."

"She did it on her laptop and sent it to my computer. At least that's what she said—and let's hope she's telling the truth, because otherwise I was wrong and telekinesis does exist."

Which was a *very* scary thought, especially in Maeve's hands, but it was impossible to feel worried about that, or about anything. The jammer was up and running, and telepathy had officially vanished off the world's radar. Neither she nor Maeve nor Commspan's customers would ever be in danger from the voices again. Telepathy would return to the realm of crackpot internet theories and sci-fi movies, and telepaths would find themselves free from the voices and able to go to movies and malls and kosher delis even when they were full of people. And Aunt Oona and the rest of the Daughters of Ireland could stop blocking and go back to matchmaking and forcing their nieces' daughters to take Irish dancing lessons.

And C.B. won't have to face being interrogated and tested and forced to provide information to anyone, Briddey thought happily. *Or be burned at the stake. He's safe, and our problems are over.*

"I wish," he said. "There's still Maeve. And—"

"Sooner or later she'll figure out how you did the blocking, and once she does, it's just a matter of time till she realizes Aunt Oona's telepathic—or worse, that Mary Clare is—and she'll completely freak out."

"Yeah, well, she's not the only one who may be freaking out," C.B. muttered. He looked seriously at Briddey. "Remember in the hospital when you were trying to figure out why we'd hooked up, and you said the connection might be due to crosstalk?"

"You told me it wasn't."

"It wasn't," he said, "but—"

Suki's phone rang, and Briddey snatched it up. "Maeve, I thought I told you not to call again."

"I know, but I have something to tell you."

"What?" Briddey said tightly. "And make it snappy."

"Okay, don't get *mad.* I thought you'd be done kissing by *now.*"

We haven't even gotten started, Briddey thought, *thanks to you.* "What is it you needed to tell me?"

"It's about Aunt Oona."

Oh, no. Don't tell me Maeve's found out about her.

"She wants to know if you can come to dinner tomorrow night. To celebrate Kathleen's engagement."

"Engagement?" Briddey said bewilderedly. "She got engaged to the Lattes'n'Luv guy? I thought he was already engaged."

"Not to *him*," Maeve said. "To Sean O'Reilly."

"Sean O'Reilly?" Briddey repeated, and turned to look in astonishment at C.B. "The fine Irish lad Aunt Oona was trying to hook me up with?"

"Yeah, only he's not really a lad. He's kind of old. And bald. Aunt Oona and Kathleen went to this Hibernian Heritage thing they were working on, and he was there, and I don't know what happened—"

I'll bet I do, C.B. said. *And I'll bet you and Maeve aren't the only Flannigans whose telepathic abilities have been triggered recently.*

And if Kathleen's *had* been, and Sean O'Reilly had had to rescue her and teach her how to put up defenses . . .

"Anyway, they're engaged," Maeve was saying. "Mom's having a fit. She says nobody can fall in love that fast, but I think they can."

So do I, Briddey thought, smiling at C.B.

"I mean, Rapunzel and Flynn Rider fell in love in two days, and in *The Zombie Princess Diaries,* Xander fell in love with Allison in like five minutes, but that's because there's not much time when there are zombies chasing you."

No, there isn't.

"So anyway, Aunt Oona's having everybody over," Maeve said. "She's making corned beef and cabbage, and she said to ask you. She said you don't have to come if you don't want to."

"Of course I want to come," Briddey said. "Tell her I'll bring a loaf of soda bread. And crubeens."

"You can bring C.B., too, if you want," Maeve said. "I already asked Aunt Oona."

"I don't know," Briddey said, looking doubtfully at him.

"I'd love to come," he said.

Are you sure? You've already been through one interrogation—

"No, I already made it so it won't be," Maeve said. "When Aunt Oona told me to ask you, I said, 'Can I invite C.B. because he helped with my science project?' and she said yes, so she thinks that's why he's coming, and that way nobody'll ask you since when are you dating and what happened to Trent and are you getting married."

"And what do you want in return for doing that for me?"

"To get out of being grounded."

"Fine," Briddey said. "I'll talk to your mother tonight. Goodbye. And no more calls."

She ended the call. "Are you *sure* you want to go to dinner with my family?" she asked C.B.

"Positive. That is, if you still want me to come after you hear what I have to say." He took a deep breath. "Maeve said she got rid of the bad parts and just kept the nice stuff, but that isn't entirely true. There are things that are intrinsic to the telepathy that can't be eliminated without eliminating the telepathy, too."

"So we won't be able to talk to each other, after all?"

"No, we'll be able to talk. But when telepathic signals get too closely aligned, it causes interference, particularly crosstalk."

"I don't understand," Briddey said, and felt a thrill of fear. "Are you saying the voices aren't shut down? That they'll come back if we—?"

"No," C.B. hastened to reassure her. "No, the jammer shut them down for good. But . . . you said one of the reasons I blocked you was that I didn't think you could handle hearing any more thoughts than you were already. You're right. I didn't think you could. But it wasn't ordinary, everyday thoughts I was worried about. It was . . ."

"It was what?" Briddey prompted.

"The crosstalk. And the problem is, it's not like electronic crosstalk. You can correct that or filter it out. But this is part and parcel of the telepathy. And even if both partners are crazy about each other, there's a limit to how much honesty and openness the human race is equipped to handle. Maybe that's why they developed inhibitors, because they *couldn't* handle it, and they realized getting rid of it was the only way to survive. I wasn't kidding when I said telepathy isn't a survival characteristic."

"C.B.," Briddey interrupted. "I have no idea what you're talking about, or what all this has to do with crosstalk."

"I know. I'm sorry. What I'm trying to tell you is . . . you know how I called having sex 'hooking up'? Well—"

The phone rang.

Briddey answered it. "Maeve, I told you—"

"I *know,* but I forgot to tell C.B. something."

"What is it?"

"I have to tell it to C.B."

Briddey handed him the phone. "It's for you."

He listened a minute and then said, "You really think I should? But what if she . . . ?" There was a pause, and then he said, "Yeah, I think you're probably right."

He handed the phone back to Briddey. Maeve said, "It'd be way easier if you'd just let me talk to you in your heads instead of using the phone."

"No," Briddey said firmly. "Now go away. And no more phone calls. Or eavesdropping. I mean it." She ended the call.

C.B. was squinting at her, as if trying to make up his mind about something. "What exactly did Maeve tell you to do just now?" Briddey asked.

"This," he said, and kissed her.

The world came apart—and it wasn't just the kiss, which Briddey realized now she'd been wanting ever since she saw him standing there at the hospital, waiting to take her home. It was what was happening inside her head. She was sensing C.B.'s feelings, hearing his thoughts. She was doing what she'd thought she was never going to be able to do. She was reading his mind. And he was reading hers.

Wanted to do this ever since . . . , he was saying; *. . . didn't dare . . . afraid you didn't . . . I mean, how could you? . . . too beautiful and smart to even* look *at someone like me, let alone . . .*

And she was saying, *. . . thought I'd lost you . . . thought we'd never be able to talk to each other again . . .*

And they were both talking at once, their thoughts and feelings tangling together till it was impossible to tell which were whose: *. . . thought I'd ruined everything and you didn't love me anymore . . . how could you think that? . . . thought that was why you were blocking me, because you couldn't forgive me . . . blocking you because I was afraid if you knew how I felt . . . in the stacks . . . so close . . . so beautiful . . . so were you . . . yeah, yeah, I know what you think of my messy hair . . . I love your hair!*

Their thoughts flowed together in an incoherent torrent of relief and joy and delight, colliding, crashing, looping in a cascade of longing and explanations and desire as overwhelming, as drenching as the deluge of voices had been, but wonderful, wonderful, wonderful, and she was going under, she was going to drown—

She broke out of the kiss like a swimmer breaking the surface and staggered back against the lab table, groping for support. "What was *that*?" she said shakily.

"I told you, when the signals get too closely aligned, it causes crosstalk—"

"Crosstalk?" she said breathlessly. "I thought you were talking about a few words or phrases getting through, but that was—"

"A deluge. I know. I'm so sorry. I shouldn't have—"

"Is that going to happen all the time?" Briddey asked, still having trouble getting her breath. Because if it was—

"No, just when there's sexual contact. You know, kissing or canoodling or—"

"But I thought in the library you told me sex shut down the voices."

"The *other* voices," he said. "Not the ones of the people involved. It has sort of the opposite effect on them."

That's the understatement of the year, Briddey thought.

C.B. was looking at her anxiously. "Are you all right?"

"I don't know," she said honestly. "I've never . . ." She put her hand unsteadily to her chest. "It was so . . ."

"Yeah, I know. It's pretty . . . overwhelming. Even more so than I thought it would be, and I totally understand if you don't want to have anything to do with this. Or with me. After all you've been through, being deluged with even *more* thoughts and feelings is probably the last thing you want, and I'll totally understand if you decide you want to forget the whole thing."

"Forget the whole . . . ? C.B.—"

"No, it's totally okay. I don't blame you. If I were in your shoes, I'd probably feel exactly the same way. Look, we can forget about Havana. I can take you back to New York, like Sky did Sister Sarah, and not . . . we can keep things completely platonic."

"*Platonic?*"

"Or if you'd rather, I can have the jammer block you altogether, and things'll be just like they were before you had the EED."

"What?" Briddey said. "I can't believe this. You've been lying to me this entire time!"

"Lying?" he said, taken aback. "No, I haven't. I just didn't tell you the whole—"

"I don't mean about the crosstalk. I'm talking about you constantly telling me you could read my mind."

"What do you mean?" he said, bewildered. "I—"

"Because if you could, you wouldn't have made that ridiculous speech just now."

"Ridiculous? You mean you still want—?" he said, and she didn't need to be able to read his mind to know how he felt. It was all right there in his face.

"Yes," she said. "I do."

He reached for her again.

"Not so fast," she said, putting up a hand to hold him off. "We need to set a few ground rules first."

"Like what?"

"Like no more blocking. If you're going to read my mind, I get to read yours, so I'll at least have a fighting chance."

"Okay, but I have to warn you, it's a cesspool in there. Like right now, for instance. All I can think about is—"

"I know," she murmured. "Me, too."

He reached for her again.

"Second," she said, holding him firmly at arm's length, "you have to promise to teach me how to build those auxiliary defenses."

"To keep me out?"

"Maybe. Sometimes. Like you said, there can be such a thing as being too connected. But mostly I'm going to need them to keep Maeve out so we can have *some* privacy."

"I don't know if that's possible. She seems to be able to break through every firewall and barricade ever erected, and she's a whiz at decryption. And she's only nine. What'll she be capable of at thirteen?"

"Saving France," Briddey said.

"You're right. She's a great kid. Maybe she'll even be able to figure out some way for everybody to experience telepathy—the nice parts, not the bad ones—without destroying the planet in the process. But in the meantime . . ." He shook his head.

"Don't worry," Briddey said. "There are other kinds of auxiliary defenses."

"Like what?"

"Like," she said, raising her voice slightly so Maeve could hear her, though that probably wasn't necessary, "threatening to tell her mother Maeve's telepathic. And telling her if she doesn't leave us alone when we tell her we need some privacy, I'll tell Mary Clare she's not only been secretly watching zombie movies but *Cinderella*. And *Tangled*. And wants a Rapunzel tiara more than life itself," and heard a disgusted *Fine!* and a very final-sounding slam of a door.

"See?" Briddey said. "Problem solved."

"Good," C.B. said, and reached for her.

She pushed him away. "I'm not done yet. There seem to have been a *number* of things regarding telepathy that you failed to tell me the whole truth about. So what else have you neglected to mention?"

"Nothing at all," he said, and grinned. "My mind's an open book."

"I'll bet. You probably *do* have X-ray vision."

"No, but if I asked Maeve to put her devious little mind to it, I'm pretty sure she could come up with an app."

"Don't even think about it," Briddey said. "Besides . . ." She took hold of the front of his flannel shirt with both her hands and pulled him down onto the couch. "You won't need it."

"Hang on." He disentangled himself. "Not here. Come on," he said, and they were in her courtyard again.

"Why can't we stay in the lab?" Briddey asked. "If you're afraid Maeve will interrupt us, she won't. *Tangled*'s her favorite movie in the entire world."

"Exactly," he said. "She's temporarily cowed, Oona doesn't know the jammer's up and running yet, which means she's still busy blocking the voices, your sister Kathleen's busy quitting her dating sites, and Suki's too busy looking for her phone to be spreading any gossip. This may be the last chance we ever have to be completely alone, and I intend to make the most of it."

He grabbed her hand and started for the blue courtyard door, which was no longer latched. Nor barred. It didn't have to be. There were no longer any roaring voices outside, not even a murmur. "So where are we going?" Briddey asked. "Niagara Falls?"

"There isn't time," he said, opening the door onto the pitch-blackness of his inner sanctum. "I'll take you there on our honeymoon."

He pulled her through the door, shut it, and let go of her hand. She heard him taking off his flannel shirt and stooping to lay it against the door so the light from under it couldn't be seen, and her heart gave a queer jerk. *I know where we are,* she thought.

"Yep," C.B. said, and switched on the light. They were in the storage closet. C.B. was standing there in front of her in his Doctor Who T-shirt and jeans, and behind her stood the wooden card file and the oak table, piled high with the *Encyclopedia Britannica.* And behind C.B., propped against the stacks of chairs, George Washington still glared disapprovingly at them.

"Go away," C.B. said cordially to him, and clambered up the chairs. He turned the painting around and jumped back down to stand in front of her.

"I expected the stacks would be your inner sanctum," she said lightly to keep him from hearing her thudding heart, her flushed and skyrocketing thoughts. "Since that's where all the hooking up takes place."

"Not all," he said. "Plus, your arms weren't around my neck in the stacks," and took her hand in both of his and clasped it to his chest.

"Oh," she breathed, and put her free hand to the back of his neck and pulled his face down to hers. *I should have done this the first time we were in here,* Briddey thought.

You're right, C.B. said, *you should have,* and kissed her.

It was even more dizzying, more drenching than the first time, but now there was a deep current of happiness running through it, and splashes of amusement: *. . . thought you said connecting didn't have anything to do with emotional bonding . . . never said that, said it didn't have to . . . you were the one who kept saying we weren't . . . I know . . . such an idiot . . .*

I should have known the minute you put your arms around me, Briddey said. *I felt so safe.*

If you'd heard what I was thinking, you wouldn't have, C.B. said, and they were suddenly surrounded not by water but by golden fireworks and then, abruptly, fire. Flames sparked and flared around them, through them, so hot they couldn't even form their thoughts into coherent sentences: . . . *no idea how much . . . me, too . . . want . . . love . . . oh, me, too, me, too . . .*

This time it was C.B. who broke off the kiss. He backed away from her, crashing into the stacked chairs. "What's wrong?" Briddey asked.

"What's *wrong?*" he said. "We practically spontaneously *combusted*. If that's what kissing you does, sex is liable to—"

"Kill us?" she said. She shook her head. "It doesn't work like that."

"But what if—?"

"We'll cross that bridge when we come to it," she said, and put her arms around his neck.

Someone banged on the door.

Aunt Briddey! Maeve said. *C.B.! Let me in. I know you're in there. I can't believe you guys didn't tell me about Aunt Oona!*

THE END

About the Author

Constance Elaine Trimmer Willis was born in Denver, Colorado, in 1945. Having earned a BA in English and elementary education from the University of North Colorado, she spent a brief stint in the late 1960s working as a teacher, until she left to raise her first child. During this period she began writing SF, with her first publication, 'The Secret of Santa Titicaca', appearing in *Worlds of Fantasy* in 1971. Willis is a highly decorated author and has won, among other accolades, ten Hugo Awards and six Nebula Awards for work of all lengths: short stories, novellas, novelettes and novels alike. She was recently named an SFWA Grand Master. Willis currently lives in Greeley, Colorado with her family.

ABOUT GOLLANCZ

Gollancz is the oldest SF publishing imprint in the world. Since being founded in 1927 Gollancz has continued to publish a focused selection of bestselling and award-winning authors. The front-list includes **Ben Aaronovitch**, **Joe Abercrombie**, **Charlaine Harris**, **Joanne Harris**, **Joe Hill**, **Alastair Reynolds**, **Patrick Rothfuss**, **Nalini Singh** and **Brandon Sanderson**.

As one of the largest Science Fiction and Fantasy imprints in the UK it is no surprise we have one of the most extensive backlists in the world. Find high-quality SF on Gateway written by such authors as **Philip K. Dick**, **Ursula Le Guin**, **Connie Willis**, **Sir Arthur C. Clarke**, **Pat Cadigan**, **Michael Moorcock** and **George R.R. Martin**.

We also have a strand of publishing in translation, which includes French, Polish and Russian authors. Gollancz is home to more award-winning authors than any other imprint, with names including **Aliette de Bodard**, **M. John Harrison**, **Paul McAuley**, **Sarah Pinborough**, **Pierre Pevel**, **Justina Robson** and many more.

The SF Gateway
More than 3,000 classic, rare and previously out-of-print SF novels at your fingertips.
www.sfgateway.com

The Gollancz Blog
Bringing you news from our worlds to yours. Stories, interviews, articles and exclusive extracts just for you!
www.gollancz.co.uk

GOLLANCZ
LONDON